MW00444907

GOD
IN THE IMAGE OF WOMAN

GOD
IN THE IMAGE OF WOMAN

A NOVEL

D.V. BERNARD

A

SBI
PUBLICATION

A STREBOR BOOKS INTERNATIONAL LLC PUBLICATION
DISTRIBUTED BY SIMON & SCHUSTER, INC.

Published by

Strebor Books International LLC
P.O. Box 1370
Bowie, MD 20718
http://www.streborbooks.com

God In the Image of Woman © 2004 by David Bernard. All rights reserved. No part of this
book may be reproduced in any form or by any means including electronic, mechanical or
photocopying or stored in a retrieval system without permission in writing from the
publisher except by a reviewer who may quote brief passages to be included in a review.

ISBN 1-59309-019-6
LCCN 2003112281

This book is a work of fiction. Names, characters, places and incidents are products of the
author's imagination or are used fictitiously. Any resemblance to actual events or locales or
persons, living or dead, is entirely coincidental.

Distributed by Simon & Schuster, Inc.
1230 Avenue of the Americas
New York, NY 10020
1-800-223-2336

Cover Design: www.mariondesigns.com

First Printing August 2004
Manufactured and Printed in the United States

10 9 8 7 6 5 4 3 2 1

ACKNOWLEDGMENTS

For Zane, Charmaine, Pamela and Destiny and Tiffany—
The goddesses of Strebor Books, whose good intentions
I have always appreciated

*Some day there will be girls and women whose name will no longer signify
merely an opposite of the masculine, but something in itself, something that
makes one think, not of any complement and limit, but only of life and existence...*
—RANIER MARIA RILKE, *Letters to a Young Poet*

BOOK I
LIFE BEFORE DEATH

I

In the beginning there was nothing, but then men began to dream.
VERSE 1:1 OF *The Teachings*

D r. Vincent Mansmann blinked drowsily and transferred his gaze to the dark, smog-cloaked streets outside his car. After hours of sitting idle in traffic, he had the peculiar feeling that his body was melting into the seat. Because of the heat of the summer night, he had turned up the air conditioner so high that he was shivering. His eyes were red and bulging; his hair was long and untamed; and as he had neither bathed nor changed his clothes in days, a musty stench hovered in a low, ominous cloud around him. Presently, as the chill of the air conditioner reached a new threshold, he shuddered and squinted out of the windshield to see what was about him. The smog was now so thick that the only clue that there were thousands of stalled cars ahead of him was the eerie glow of their taillights. He was in Times Square now, but with the smog, all the bright lights and neon signs of the surrounding buildings and billboards registered only as blurred etchings in the darkness. Even the throng of pedestrians on the sidewalk seemed to be nothing but ghosts drifting aimlessly through the world. There was something dreamy about it all—especially with the calming hum of his car's engine—but he felt somehow beyond sleep and the simple blessings of normal men. There was a strange energy around him—the quiet panic of someone who was still in shock. He felt both as though something in him had died, and that some new thing were gestating within him—sucking nutrients and *life* from his already frail body....

It had been three days since he had slept. He had spent those restless days and nights at his laboratory, crouched over microscopes and computer printouts and calculations that had left him numb and staring blankly into space. With the exception of some stale, caustic coffee, which had eaten away at his stomach lining, he had consumed nothing during that time. The horror of what he had discovered had nourished him and kept him awake—

And just then, as he once again blinked drowsily and transferred his gaze to the outside world, he saw a figure approaching through the smog. The figure's features were of course obscured by the smog, but the voluptuous proportions immediately identified it as a woman. Its swaying, stylized stroll was somehow mesmerizing. Some of the other male drivers were honking their horns wildly now; some were leaning out of windows, yelling propositions and declarations of their sexual prowess. Mansmann stared on as the figure continued to walk up the middle of the clogged street. A flimsy miniskirt was stretched taut over the figure's shapely body. Its hips were wide, rocking in a daunting manner that seemed to threaten the structural integrity of its spine. Its breasts seemed incredibly huge and firm; and as the figure drew near, Mansmann leaned forward in his seat eagerly. His mouth gaped; his eyes bulged as he stared hungrily into the smog. It was only when the figure was about two car lengths away that a feeling in Mansmann's gut told him that something was amiss. He noticed that some of the other drivers had stopped honking their horns—and yes, those breasts were impossibly huge. Now that the figure was close enough, he saw that its nipples, which stood out prominently, even in the smog, were more like spiked battlements than objects of desire. The figure's face, finally coming into focus, had the telltale signs of excessive plastic surgery. Its cheekbones were accentuated to the point where the effect was macabre—especially with those huge, vapid eyes—

Mansmann shuddered: it was one of those women of dubious sex, as he referred to them—a transsexual prostitute in search of its next john. Mansmann looked away, feeling suddenly queasy; but the transsexual, no doubt attracted by his Ferrari, came up to the side of his car and started dancing. When Mansmann looked over, the transsexual was gyrating its voluptuous hips, its tongue hanging out of its mouth in a manner that was supposed to be erotic, but which was only grotesque. As he watched the freak show, Mansmann found his mind returning to a thought that had been building to a frenzy over the last three days: *Women were objects of worship, sent down to the earth as conduits of hope and magic, and their desecration by the hand of man had thrown the universe out of balance....*

After a while, the transsexual left, returning to the smog like a woebegone wanderer. Mansmann looked around warily, as though checking for other smog-borne horrors. All seemed clear, but he was more on-edge now—maybe just more awake. His thought about women being desecrated by the hand of man came back again. Feeling suddenly restless, and remembering the small TV mounted on his dashboard, he gave the voice command for the screen to turn on. He stared at the show—an emergency news report—for about 30 seconds before it made sense to him. He had been so dazed from the events of his laboratory that in the four hours he had been waiting in traffic he had never wondered why traffic was stalled. After watching the news for about three minutes, Mansmann gleaned that there were two reasons.

First of all, this was the President's final night in town; and as the woman had shepherded the country out of its deepest depression, huge crowds of worshippers were gathering to get a final glimpse of her. Actually, now that America was being drawn into the Asian war, the woman rose up like some kind of god of war and vengeance to the millions of people whose only goal in life seemed to be to defer to her will. With all the fanfare, and the restrictive security measures that had been put in place, perhaps one-third of the city was now inaccessible to vehicular traffic. The other two-thirds was choked with cars that would still have been moving at a snail's pace if they had had access to the entire city. That was the first reason for the traffic jam.

The second reason for the traffic jam was perhaps more difficult to explain in logical, objective terms. Now, as Mansmann stared at the screen, what he saw could only be described as mass insanity. Just a few blocks away from where he was trapped in traffic, a huge protest had gotten out of control. On Mansmann's TV, there were images of hundreds of thousands—if not *millions*—of protesters and anarchists. As he watched it all, he felt himself being pulled in two directions. On the one hand, given what his experiments had revealed about the world and its future prospects, all the information of the emergency report was irrelevant; but on the other hand, after driving himself mad with those same revelations, he was desperate for some respite—some distraction....It was strange how the sight of anarchy could be a calming influence on him now. On the TV, there were images of angry mobs...scenes of groups of youths throwing Molotov cocktails at armed columns of policemen—images of fear and paranoia and people striving to destroy the social fabric...And yet, there was something inherently ridiculous about it all. There was a story about a notorious doomsday cult, whose leader was a 10-year-old black girl from the South Bronx. Supposedly, her cult had blown up several water mains throughout the city, killing two-dozen people in the process. Elsewhere, a group dedicated to the rights of homosexuals in Papua-New Guinea was shown running through the streets naked. All this was on top of more bewildering stories, like the one on armed insurrectionists who had thrown a grenade at the mayor's motorcade earlier that evening. As Mansmann watched these events, he genuinely wished that he could be swept up in the panic—perhaps in the same way that an adult often wished that he could view Christmas with the innocence (and, indeed, the naiveté) of a child. However, in the end, he merely shrugged his shoulders.

In actuality, for *months* now, New York City had been the Mecca for every fringe group that claimed to have a grievance against the powerful. In a sense, tonight was only the natural culmination of what had been put in motion 10 months ago, when a corporation known simply as The Company announced a technological breakthrough: a telecommunications complex that would allow information to be beamed directly into people's minds. Mansmann had thought little of it at the time, but the protests that arose to stop the construction had grown into a kind of religion over the months. Protesters had come not only from all over the country, but the *world*. In its effort to neutralize the protests, The Company had even enlisted the services of the President. For the last few months, the woman had been appearing in The Company's commercials, smiling in her grandmotherly way as she attested to the safety and unobtrusiveness of the complex. Yet, even her godlike powers had not been enough to keep the protest from growing. Soon, thousands had been protesting at Company Square—the site of the complex and The Company's other buildings. The movement was like a newly formed moon, changing tides and gravitational fields. It was up there in the heavens: a constant reminder of the insignificance of man; and with the complex ready to go online in the morning, millions of protesters were taking to the streets worldwide, as though this were their last chance to save their souls.

As Mansmann watched the screen, and his mind went over the series of events that had brought them to this place, he could not deny that there seemed to be a kind of precision behind it all. Something about the way the movement had escalated reminded him of the frenzied last days of salmon, when millions of the fish fought their way upstream, struggling against natural and man-made barriers, in their genetically programmed determination to spawn and die; and just then, as this thought passed through his mind, the emergency news report returned to the events of Company Square. The crowd of protesters stretched across the square like a sea of bitterness and desperation—like a reservoir for all the rage and madness that had been built up in society over the eons. The camera zoomed in as a few of the protesters broke free of the barricade. The entire sea seemed to surge forward then, but the guards quickly fired their stun guns; and after the lightning of the guns crackled in the air, frying the clothes and flesh of some, and incapacitating hundreds of others, the fried and the unconscious were heaved back behind the battle line by the guards, and the barricade was returned to its former position, as though nothing had happened.

Mansmann sat back in the seat and closed his eyes—not in horror of what he had just seen (or even in some lamentation to the state of the world) but with the renewed assurance that all of it was just a showy prelude to the thing that perhaps only he, as the scientist responsible for its development, had knowledge of. As his gaze returned to the TV, and his mind went to the calculations he had completed just hours ago, he felt like a god looking down on all the irrelevant actions of men. He could not really think of himself as a human being anymore—he had gone too far for that. He looked back on his former life—his former existence as a man—with wonder and disbelief. Only four years ago, he had been Norman Needlebaum: a frail, bald, fifty-seven-year-old, five-foot-five-inch genetics professor from Queens. Then, after his scientific breakthrough, and the rise of his pharmaceutical empire, Needlebaum had faded from existence and Mansmann had risen like a phoenix, soaring to that place of gods that America set aside for the rich and famous.

In fact, just three days ago, right before he went to his laboratory, he had been on stage—the focal point of a bizarre burlesque show. Around him had been a dozen semi-nude, Las Vegas-style cabaret dancers. The lights had been bright and colorful; the audience, lost somewhere in the glare, had been boisterous; and the weird music of youth (which got louder and less melodic with each generation) had been ear splitting. Mansmann had been the center of it all. The dancers had been performing pirouettes around him, while he performed a stiff, uncoordinated maneuver that had been a bad imitation of a dance kids were doing that year. On the corners of the stage, four other geezers had pranced around as well, aping horribly— if not *bastardizing*—the energetic dances of youth. Yet, none of that had mattered, because Mansmann was a *star*—a mogul and guru and drug dealer combined into one. His scientific breakthrough, Luxuriant Hair, had the almost supernatural power to make hair sprout on bald heads overnight; but more than that, it was like a combination of Viagra and crack, which empowered the hairless and impotent, gave courage to the slight of heart and shy…*it had even been proven to increase penis size*! As such, every man on the planet had been a potential customer.

Even the depression had not been able to stop him. The world had needed him: his blithe spirit and the aura of sexual adventurousness that he exuded like cheap cologne. His long, flowing tresses of bleach blond hair had become one of the icons of their generation. His trademark arrayment of platform shoes and gaudy, sequined outfits from the disco era had had a strangely aphrodisiacal effect on society; and as his power over the masses became complete, the maddeningly addictive slogan of all his ads, "I'm a

Mansmann's Man!" became stuck in everyone's head, like one of those jungle parasites that bored under your skin and laid eggs in your brain.

...But three nights ago, after the burlesque concluded in a pyrotechnic extravaganza, all of that had come to an end. As he walked offstage, Mansmann had waved and bowed and blown kisses for minutes on end; when he finally shuffled behind the curtains, he had been grinning and panting as he heard the audience (which had of course been composed mostly of geezers) clapping and asking for an encore. It had been then that two of his lab assistants confronted him. Looking as though they were in shock, they had informed him that something was very wrong. Somehow, the Luxuriant Hair formula had gone airborne, and was in everyone's bloodstream—even in people who had not bought the product! Mansmann had looked on dubiously, telling the men to go home and rest, because they had obviously been mistaken; but later that night, he had gone to his uptown lab to investigate and do some calculations. After an hour bent over a microscope, he had known that it was far worse than his formula having gone airborne. The formula had been acting in new ways, operating on a genetic level that he had never thought possible. Going on a horrible hunch, he had eked a sperm sample out of himself and done a DNA analysis of it. When the first set of results came back, a chill had traveled up his spine, and he had stared ahead numbly. Still, holding out hope that the results could be wrong, he had run the test again. When the second set of results came back, and they also showed the mutation, the realization of what had happened, had seemed to drain years from his life. It was the sperm that decided the sex of a child; as such, Mansmann's sperm sample should have had the genetic material to produce both boys and girls...but that had not been the case. The results had seemed impossible, yet there had been no denying the cold facts of science. According to the results churned out by his computer, his genetic material had been corrupted by a series of molecules found only in his Luxuriant Hair formula. That led to only one conclusion: his formula had caused some kind of genetic mutation, and now it was impossible for daughters—for *females*—to be born.

All societies are built on brutality. Those societies that survive for extended periods—great societies—manage to codify and bureaucratize that brutality, so that it takes on the veneer of justice.
VERSE 194:9 OF *The Teachings*

F our months ago, when the protests at Company Square began to show the telltale signs of impending anarchy, the FBI had been called in to set up a command center at The Company. Five hundred and eighty-seven agents had been assigned the task of investigating all the groups that had gathered to protest; every protester in Company Square had unwittingly had his or her picture taken—and matched against an FBI database of known terrorists. One hundred and thirty-seven cameras were now trained on Company Square and the surrounding blocks, documenting the steady dissolution of society, and accumulating evidence for the thousands of cases that were going to be prosecuted when this was all over.

In order to guard against the very real possibility of a terrorist bombing, the FBI had located the command center on a secure sublevel of The Company's main building—a 150-story skyscraper. The command center was a gigantic cube whose sides were all about 100 meters. Within the cube, the FBI agents sat in rows, at consoles arrayed with the latest computing and telecommunications devices. There were 50 consoles to a row and 10 rows in the room; and as all the rows faced a huge screen (which took up an entire wall) the command center was reminiscent of Mission Control at NASA. The noise of the place was mind numbing, with phones constantly ringing and people yelling across the room. Just to have a simple conversation with one's neighbor, one had to yell above the din. Furthermore, with scenes of chaos flashing on the gigantic screen before them, and the cacophony blaring all around them, it was as though they were being systematically driven insane. The musty odor of anxious sweat pervaded the place—especially as the air conditioner was broken. It had actually been broken for days now, but nobody knew whom to call to get it fixed; and in that way peculiar to huge bureaucracies, the small, simple tasks that would make everyone's life easier were tantamount to moving heaven and earth....

Special Agent Mark Respoli was a tall, swarthy man who had the kind of delicate facial features that women found handsome, and other men thought to be a sure sign of homosexuality. His entire life had probably been spent overcompensating for this by engaging in overtly manly pursuits—like sports, the military and now the FBI. He had excelled in all three; and until he had been assigned the task of tracking down the 10-year-old girl/Messiah from the South Bronx, he had probably never been in doubt about who he was and what was to be expected from life. He had been a naval intelligence officer before joining the FBI; and all his life, he had been single-minded and uncompromising—especially, as the cliché goes, in defense of God and country.

However, the 10-year-old seemed to be the harbinger of a storm that was still gathering strength on the horizon. After months of searching for the girl, he felt more as though he had been tracking down a myth, rather than an actual human being. The girl left no clues behind: no fibers, no residues...nothing that could be used to find her hideout. Her followers' attacks seemed so precise that Respoli had often found himself thinking that they had somehow managed to metamorphose into one monstrous creature, which had the girl as its soul, and her followers as the vast tentacles. In the city alone, 8,496 people (including the girl's mother and the other people blown up in her tenement) were now dead because of her; 17 buildings, including the girl's elementary school and her *church*, had been blown up. Thousands of people had been wounded and maimed in these attacks, and yet each new terrorist act only seemed to attract more followers. He called them *followers*, not believers, because he was seriously beginning to doubt that the girl's worshippers—that is, *the vast majority of them*—believed that she was God. It was more that they did not believe in anything anymore and that the girl was somehow the embodiment of that. The senselessness of their attacks attested to this. They had no grand philosophy; they presented no manifesto—no demands...All they did was destroy and kill. Even anarchists believed in something—or were at least *against* something—but the girl's will negated all beliefs and all motives.

Now, as Respoli daydreamed at his post, he sat leaning forward, so that his elbows rested on the console, and his outstretched head rested on the vertex of his clasped hands. He had been sitting in that pose for about 15 minutes now, staring up at the gigantic screen before them all. His eyes were glazed; he had two days' worth of beard on his face; and as he stared up at the huge screen, and saw the chaotic, hive-like events of the city, he was overcome by the feeling that the forces of evil had been underestimated.

Shaking his head at it all, he finally began to come out of his reverie. Looking around, he realized that the agent to his left (a gray-haired man on the verge of retirement) was snoring loudly with his head resting on the console. The agent to Respoli's right was talking on the phone, trying to sweet talk his fiancée—whose loud cries of heartache and anguish Respoli could hear reverberating through the telephone headset.

Respoli yawned and sat up straighter, then groaned as his tired muscles protested against his sudden movement. With all the work to be done, he had not been home in about a week. That morning, he had washed himself in the bathroom sink, using a wad of toilet paper as a washcloth. Half a dozen other agents had been there doing the same thing. One of the men had had a stick of deodorant, and they had passed it around. In actuality, few of them had gone home in days—nor *slept* in days. With the Image Broadcast Complex going online tomorrow, and the chaos of the city rising to a climax, it was as though they were all hostages of current events.

Now making a conscious effort to return to work, Respoli pressed a button on the console. Instantaneously, a picture of the 10-year-old appeared on his monitor. It was the picture from the girl's yearbook. After all these months of staring at it, the waif-like image of the girl had been seared into his mind. Yet, the girl had one of those faces that seemed different every time one saw it—which always seemed to present new possibilities for those willing to open their minds and hearts. He frowned, disturbed by his thoughts, and yet unable to keep them from unfolding to their natural conclusion. He had thought before that people flocked to her because she was a conduit for their lack of belief, but the more he looked at her picture, the more he found himself thinking that maybe that was not such a bad thing. Maybe the time had come for all their beliefs to be cleansed by the storm that always hovered on the periphery of civilization.

The ability to kill is man's only tangible weapon against death.
VERSE 2137:1 OF *The Teachings*

G.W. Wang stamped on the accelerator, and the tires of the huge, tank-like SUV pealed in the dark emptiness of the parking garage. He could not believe that he had gotten this far—and that he was still alive. Just then, a drop of blood trickled down his temple: a reminder of all that had passed. He wiped it away nervously, then grimaced as he felt the damp, matted region on top of his head—where one of the guards' bullets had left a groove. He still held a handgun in his right hand, and had another in his lap; and as the SUV lurched forward in the darkness, he gripped the steering wheel tighter, only to realize that his left hand was broken. He had fractured it when he broke the jaw of one of The Company's security guards. He had thrown the man down a flight of stairs, breaking his neck, and had gunned down three other guards. The imperatives of survival had demanded that brutality; but in the back of his mind—in that place of circumspection and *conscience*—there was a voice screaming that he had damned himself tonight. Some dark force had called to him; mesmerized by that siren song, he had taken a step that seemed like madness itself. He could not even begin to explain it, but somehow *he had just murdered the President of the United States*! One moment, he had been going about his life; then, out of nowhere, he had found himself overcome by terrible instincts…and then the President had been lying at his feet in a bloody heap….All the forces of heaven and earth would be unleashed on him now: there was no crevice that would hide him from that impending wrath. Even as he held the guns, he knew that there was no weapon on earth that could protect him from what was coming—

He was only a 37-year-old, but he was a wreck. He had lost weight over the past few weeks, but he had lost it the way a starving man lost it. There was something sickly and attenuated about his face now—as there was about all of him. His corporate attire was soaked through with nervous sweat and stained with blood; and with all that had happened, his mind was a kaleidoscope of madness, pulsing with images of the President's bloody, unmoving form lying at his feet—with her bodyguards heaped to the side... all of them dead...and the smoking gun still in his trembling hand—

He had killed the President of the United States...! He kept repeating it to himself, but he could not even conceptualize it. *The President of the United States!* He *could not* have killed her—it did not even seem possible. A side of him wanted to go back and check—

But just then, the SUV swerved precariously as it went up on the ramp: only one more level before he reached the surface. With all that had happened, and his loss of blood, he was barely managing to hold onto consciousness. Everything around him was like a dream placed within a dream; and as these thoughts passed through his mind, there were gunshots behind him, which caused the rear window to shatter in a loud explosion. In his desperation to escape, he had not noticed the two guards getting out of the elevator. Everything was passing him by so quickly...and now, another guard appeared before him on the ramp: old Ernie—a 20-year veteran, with whom G.W. had joked for *years*. Some savage cry blared in G.W.'s mind, and he pressed the accelerator: stamped down on it mercilessly, so that the huge vehicle lurched forward like a rampaging beast; and in the blink of an eye, old Ernie, who had stood there with his gun drawn, but in total shock, disappeared as if he had been nothing but a flimsy scarecrow stuck in loose soil.

G.W.'s mind went blank. He could practically feel the life draining from his body. He mumbled a Chinese epithet under his breath and blasted through the final barrier of the parking garage—which old Ernie had been manning. As he sped up the incline, G.W.'s eyes focused first on the dark, smoggy abyss of the nighttime sky and the upper stories of Manhattan skyscrapers; and then, as he reached the surface and looked at what was happening to the world, a primal, irrational fear was triggered within him. He stamped on the brake; after the vehicle came to a screeching, jarring halt, he sat on the edge of his seat, gasping for air. He had been seeing this scene for months now; and yet, every time he saw it, the same creepy feeling came over him. He was now on the perimeter of Company Square; before him, in a region which measured perhaps six football fields placed side-by-side, there had to be at least 500,000 people, all of whom were screaming and waving their hands in the air. He could literally feel their chants reverberating in his chest—as if they were planting a seed in his soul. Two huge searchlights kept sweeping across the multitudes; and as G.W. watched the briefly illuminated sections of the crowd, and saw their enraged, almost *disfigured*, expressions, it was as if the light were torturing them. The huge pyramid-shaped building across the square was what they were all there to protest. There was a gigantic digital clock over it, counting down the time until it went online and was able to beam information directly into their minds. Nine hours, forty-seven minutes, twenty-two seconds and counting...G.W. stared at it for a while, mesmerized by the flashing numbers—and the inescapable precision of time. He forced himself to look away—from the clock, from the pyramid-shaped building, from the hundreds of thousands of people ready to rush in and tear it down with their bare hands...And it occurred to him that if they only knew what he had done, then they would turn that rage on him. All the hatred they had for The Company would be supplanted by the hatred they would feel for him when they rose up to rip him to shreds. For a moment, the weight of the thing left him numb and indecisive and fatalistic. Where could he really go at this point—and what could he *do*? He was so overcome by a feeling of inevitability that he found himself considering giving up. He had killed the President of the United States, and there was nowhere to go— nowhere to *hide*—

But just then, he glanced in his rearview mirror, seeing half a dozen guards running up the incline; and as the first shot rang out, G.W. stamped on the accelerator and entered the night. The SUV again rocked precariously as he swerved to the left and started down the driveway. With all the protesters, The Company had posted thousands of guards in the driveway surrounding the square. The latter were fully armed and armored. When G.W. started down the driveway, the first few guards managed to jump out of the way—but others disappeared beneath his tank, and still others began firing their guns at him. As he passed the entrance of The Company's main building—the 150-story skyscraper—his stomach churned with the realization of all that was lost to him... But he was cruising on automatic pilot, now barely aware of the outside world. Shots splintered his front windshield, so that he was forced to duck down as he drove. Everywhere, people were screaming and running for cover. The screams, not to mention the thuds and bumps as the vehicle rolled over people, were sickening—*maddening*... but it made no difference.

And then, to exit the square, he had to go down another ramp. Due to lack of space in the city, the huge square was actually on top of 20 ten-story buildings. The world of The Company was like another city in the sky: another reality, just slightly out of phase with everything else. G.W. sped down the ramp, curling down and around, so that he felt giddy and sick. And then, at last, he was on the street, in what was supposedly the real world. There were brightly colored billboards all along this block, which lit up the smog in perverse colors. The entire thing again conjured the feeling that he was trapped in a fanciful dream world. As he looked around, a huge billboard of The Company's spokesperson caught his attention. He had always thought it strange how that computer-generated character looked so much like the 10-year-old girl/terrorist from the South Bronx...but he did not have time to think about that now. He did not have time for anything....He zoomed down the avenue like a madman; the streets were of course clogged with traffic, but he went down the lane reserved for emergency vehicles....The traffic signal at the upcoming intersection changed to red, and the cars before him ground to a halt; still, with the smog, he saw neither the cars nor the light; and even if he had, he was so desperate to get away from everything—even his own thoughts—that it would not have made a difference. With his foot firmly on the accelerator, he plowed into a waiting cab, obliterating it; and then, running over a few dozen screaming, darting protesters in the crosswalk, he zoomed through the intersection, narrowly avoiding a truck.

…What difference could any of it mean to him now? He was as good as dead anyway. A horrible feeling of inevitability again came over him, so that even his frenetic flight seemed pointless. He realized, all at once, that one of the guards' bullets had penetrated his shoulder, and that he was bleeding profusely. The sensation was a dull ache, which quickly faded into the numbness that was rising about him. He was supposedly fleeing to his home in the suburbs, where his pregnant wife would be waiting, but even she did not seem to exist for him anymore. Behind him, were his career, his life and his sanity—all the things that would be useless in the world that was coming. He had gotten a glimpse of that world today; and like a child corrupted by filth, there was no going back to innocence—

But he had lost so much blood that the world was getting blurry. He did not see the policeman trying to wave him away from one of the areas where a water main had been sabotaged by the 10-year-old Goddess' followers— nor did he notice when the man disappeared beneath the SUV. About a block later, he came upon a parked tractor; and at the speed he was going, when his SUV hit the tractor's huge shovel (which had been left in the down position), it flipped in the air three times before landing in the window of a pizzeria. By then, G.W. had already passed out.

Science is the systematic pursuit of myth and superstition.
Verse 1083:12 of *The Teachings*

Even now, as Mansmann sat in his car, staring blankly into the smog, he could hardly grasp the immensity of what he had put in motion. If his formula had the same effect on other men—*and really was in everyone's bloodstream*—then soon millions of hospitals worldwide were going to experience statistical flukes in their maternity wards. Maybe the first day or so everyone would laugh at the fact that only boys had been born. Maybe they would see it as good fortune, in the way that our patriarchal society saw boys as good fortune. However, it was only a matter of time before one doctor mentioned it to another, and they called around to all their colleagues, and good-natured, humorous banter turned to worldwide panic. He looked to the sidewalk then, to the restless procession of pedestrians and beggars, thinking of what was going to happen when they finally found out. In a flash, he saw it all: society turning on itself, without patience—without the civility that the hope of passing on genes had somehow engendered. The revelation of what had happened would be a kind of Pandora's Box. Society, reeling from the shock, would wake up from its trance and see its illusions gone. News like this could not be suppressed for long. In fact, it would not be the "news" that was spread at all, but fear and madness....A few nights ago, there had been a report on the news about a right wing group that refused to drink milk because they believed that the government was treating it with enzymes to shrink white men's balls and keep them from having children. Mansmann had laughed out loud at the time. However, when *this* got out, there would be no laughter. If a cure was not found within the next few months—maybe even weeks, or *days*—then it would all be over—

And yet, as he stared at the vague outlines of the throng on the sidewalk, he all at once found himself thinking that maybe the world's population could stand to be thinned out a little. He looked at all the traffic, all the pollution, all the shabbily dressed, half-starved people on the sidewalk, again finding himself thinking that maybe what he had done was the will of God. Maybe he was to be like Abraham, or Noah. Maybe the world, bloated and filthy, needed to be cleansed, and he was to be the agent of that purge. For a moment, his mind, gripped by the possibilities, was not so much horrified as thrilled by the place that he would have. After all, billions of people were already dying from the effects of wars and starvation and disease and environmental degradation; entire countries were already paralyzed by terrorists and drug gangs: maybe what he had done was only hastening the inevitable—perhaps putting them all out of their misery. Indeed, the end of the world was passé. With the war between India and China raging out of control—and America being pulled into the fray—the world had been hovering on the precipice of nuclear annihilation for months now. This was an age when mob violence and internecine warfare were every year responsible for the slaughter of millions of innocents. Billions of people were out there starving at this very moment, subsisting in poverty that was at the same time heart-rending and repulsive; and in the face of all that…no, Mansmann could not really be horrified by what he had done. The coming apocalypse would not be some grand cataclysmic event, but the natural culmination of human existence. Moreover, as Mansmann glanced at the TV and saw more images of the protest at Company Square, he knew that any blood that was spilled because of what he had done, would be spilled onto land that was already blood-splattered. Thus, the only real concern he had left was if he should kill himself now, or wait until he got home. His handgun was in the glove compartment, promising a sudden, eternal silence—

He groaned and settled himself uneasily in his seat. When he looked up, one of The Company's commercials was playing on the TV. With all that weighed on his mind, he did not have time for such nonsense, but he nonetheless found himself being drawn into the world of the commercial. Every image flickering across the screen seemed somehow perfect; every sound seemed to satisfy a deep psychological yearning that he had been unaware of before this very moment....In the commercial, The Company's computer-generated spokesperson—an incredibly beautiful, raven-haired woman—was floating in the heavens. She was dressed in a billowing white gown, and below her was the dark world of men and filth and chaos. She gestured majestically with her hand and the light came: the filth was cleansed; the men were healed and civilized; the crude mechanics of society were made more efficacious and efficient. And then that computer-generated vision of beauty and majesty bowed her head and there was sorrow there— but also forbearance and hope, as though she had taken all that filth and crudeness within herself as to save us—

Mansmann forced himself to look away—to block it all out. It was all propaganda of course—no doubt with hypnotic undertones....He suddenly thought about having sex—about spending these last hours or days, or whatever the case may be, in some kind of orgasmic daze. There were women to go to—he definitely had the money to buy this momentary bliss— but it suddenly occurred to him that he was bored with sex...perhaps as they were all bored with it. In fact, since becoming a star, so many women had spread their legs for him that he had begun to think of himself more as a gynecologist than as a lover. His lust, surfeited by the mercenary sexuality of countless whores and groupies, was now just a mechanical shell of its former self. He was bored with listening to fake screams of ecstasy from women that dispensed their sexuality with the efficiency of an automaton. The mystery and allure of women—all the things that made a mistress exciting—had long been replaced by the sterility of a business transaction. He was tired of the entire sexual industrial complex, as he had come to think of it....

He sighed....For the first time in years, he thought about praying: he suc- cumbed to that momentary weakness of cynics and nonbelievers throughout the ages; and, in his desperation, he found himself on the verge of beseeching God for mercy—for some loophole out of what was coming. However, as his tired eyes again wandered over to the TV, there was another report about the 10-year-old girl whom some thought to be the Second Coming of Jesus. It was ridiculous of course—another part of the cosmic farce; and with all that weighed on his mind, the idea of a murderous 10-year-old Messiah from the ghetto was suddenly amusing to him. He could still remember how he had laughed a few months ago, when he first heard about the bloodthirsty exploits of the girl's cult. It all seemed fake—perhaps like all the news reports had become. Moreover, what made Mansmann more suspicious, was that the girl literally seemed to be a 10-year-old version of the beautiful, computer-generated angel that appeared in The Company's ads. It was a little too convenient: while her grownup version was telling people that technology would solve their problems—would bring peace and tranquility, nourish the hungry, salve the wounds and diseases of the sick and infirm—her prepubescent version was blowing up schools and factories, leaving death and destruction in her wake. Mansmann wanted to laugh at the contradictions, but in light of all that was happening in the world, he suddenly found himself thinking that maybe they had outlived a Jesus preaching peace and love and happiness. In fact, it occurred to him that if Jesus were to come back again, He would need an *army* (lest He wanted to end up the way He had the first time). Just to survive and have time to spread His message, He would have to find a way to outwit and overpower the terrible brutality and ruthlessness of men; and now, as Mansmann stared at the TV screen, allowing his mind to drift on the possibilities, all the scenes from his fears and the news headlines blurred into one; and as he sat there in awe and horror, all these terrible things congealed into the serene face of a 10-year-old black girl.

If one's intention is solely to pursue pleasure, then seek out the basest and most convenient means of doing so. If one desires sex, for instance, then seek out the most repulsive of partners. That way, when the objective of one's pleasure seeking has been achieved, one will not be deceived into embarking on further adventures—and therefore losing sight of one's original intentions. In all things, never allow a tryst to become a preoccupation.

VERSE 528:5 OF *The Teachings*

Just a few blocks away from where Mansmann sat in traffic was The Erotic Palace: an establishment whose name was a euphemism for a dilapidated theater that showcased pornographic movies from decades past, which it referred to as "classics." Business was relatively good, but as the proprietor, Anthony Dimitri, knew well, it was not the type of business that would ever make a man a success—especially in an age where technology allowed people to fully interact with their fantasies. The real money was in holographic chambers called Dimensional Portals, which were a communion of virtual reality and the Internet. They allowed anyone worldwide to interact within the same realistic, three-dimensional scenes, called "Dimensions." Like most great technological achievements as of late, Dimensional Portals were products of The Company. That also meant that they were everywhere, and that their usage grew in a kind of frenzy that was as all encompassing as teenage lust.

Of course, being a connoisseur and pornographic purist, Anthony Dimitri hated Dimensional Portals with a passion that verged on religion. He was a portly gentleman of middle age who wore a beard to cover up his badly pockmarked skin; and as he lumbered out of the lobby of the Palace, there was a sense of self-satisfaction about him. Just then, he nodded almost regally to the ticket girl—a silver-haired matron that squinted at him through the smog then grinned and waved demonstrably when she recognized him. He was about to smile in response, when he realized that she had forgotten her dentures again, and that her "grin" was a gaping black hole fenced in by three unusually long, yellowish teeth. He moved on with haste....

Every man had one deep regret in his life, and Dimitri's was that he had missed out on his chance to become a porn star. At the moment of truth, he had been unable to perform before all those lights and cameras. The bored-looking porn queen, known as The Ghoul (purportedly for her ability to suck the meat off of men's bones), had only chewed a huge wad of gum and looked on disdainfully while Dimitri attempted to bring his flaccid equipment to life manually. After that fiasco, it had taken him a year of therapy before he could even have sex again; and after that, his affairs with women had been more of the celluloid and digital variety, than flesh and blood—hence The Erotic Palace.

Dimitri now made his way to the corner of the block, where there was a huge, noisy arcade filled with video games and the aforementioned Dimensional Portals. When he first started going to the arcade two years ago, his only intention had been to get a beer and ogle the teenage girls; but as he was the kind of man that made a pastime out of complaining about his woes (and he had found a ready ear in the bartender at the arcade), he had quickly built up a kind of therapist/patient relationship with the bartender.

Indeed, it was probably this strange dynamic, along with the prospect of a cold beer, which explained Dimitri's high spirits. As he entered the arcade, he was reassured by the noisy crowd, the flashing lights and the huge video screens on the walls—which currently showcased the frenzied events of Company Square. As the arcade was a haven of the young, coming here made Dimitri think that he was hip. Accordingly, when some teenage girls passed by, Dimitri gave them a sickly grin that years of practice before his bathroom mirror had deluded him into believing was sexy. When the girls shivered in disgust and went on their way, Dimitri was unfazed. He was like a puppy that chased after a speeding truck, barking and frothing at the mouth: not only would he be unable to do anything if he actually caught the truck, but the poor fool would probably be run over.

Still self-satisfied, he surveyed the arcade with a smile. The Dimensional Portals were the dozens of doorways lined up to the wall on his left. About 200 holographic video game machines were situated in the middle of the room, then the concession and payment areas were on the right. Dimitri spotted the bartender in his usual spot, and nodded to himself. The latter was also a short man with a dangling paunch, but he did not have a beard. He instead had a ruddy, affable face that made him look more like one of those gnome lawn ornaments than an actual human being. He seemed to be mulling something over as he rubbed a glass with a rag—

"Hey, Charlie!" Dimitri said when he was close enough.

Charlie looked up at him absentmindedly, still lost in his thoughts. And then, with a helpless expression: "Tony, do chickens got pussies?"

"Huh...?"

"I mean, where the hell do eggs come out of? I *know* they come out the chicken's asshole. There has to be something else, right?"

Dimitri flashed back to having the same thought about women and babies when he was six, and shuddered at being drawn back into that intellectual and emotional rigmarole. "Geez, I don't know, Charlie," was all he said at last, looking sorrowful. "Give me a beer, will ya?"

"Sure thing," Charlie said with a sigh. As he went to get the beer, Dimitri looked at one of the huge screens that showcased the events of the city. He looked at it for a few seconds, then grunted noncommittally. On another screen, there was an emergency report on what had happened to the President; but as there was no audio for the screens, nobody realized what had happened. Dimitri sighed, then sought out Charlie—and his beer. It was then that the girl came in. Charlie noticed her first as she entered the arcade and stood just beyond the door. Dimitri followed his friend's eyes and was equally enchanted by the blonde girl who was no more than 18—and quite possibly much younger than that. It was not that she was extraordinarily beautiful, but that there was an appealing quality about her: a freshness that men like Dimitri and his colleague translated into gullibility—i.e., susceptibility to their charms. She had long blonde hair and a thin sundress that was practically see through—especially in this humidity. Furthermore, she had a huge bag that seemed about half her size and weight—a telltale sign of either a runaway or a young girl chasing big dreams in the big city. It was almost too good to be true. Dimitri and Charlie both seemed to gasp when they realized that she was naked under the dress—or at least was not wearing a bra. Their eyes seemed to zoom in on the supple breasts; when they looked at one another again, they were practically salivating.

Dimitri forgot about his beer and lumbered through the crowd, towards the girl. Charlie, who had to remain behind the bar, hated him then. The girl was looking around wide-eyed, seemingly impressed.

"First time in New York?" Dimitri said when he reached her.

She looked down at him (she was actually taller than he was) as though she had been expecting him. There was a slight smile on her face, but it was not the sneering expression he was used to seeing from women. It was calm and confident, and this left him a little unsure as she said, "Yes, I just got here from Kansas." There was something in her eyes and timbre of her voice—some hidden ease and single-mindedness that he could not account for. Having answered his question, she went back to watching the huge screen, where there was a scene of protesters throwing something at guards at Company Square. Dimitri followed her eyes in that awkward moment, then turned to her again, saying:

"You here to protest like the rest of them?" There was a slightly mocking tone to his voice, and this pleased him. He went on: "Think The Company is going to take over your soul when that Image Broadcast Complex thing comes online tomorrow?"

"No," she said, looking him in the eyes again, "—I'm here to have sex."

"...Pardon me?" he said, thinking that he was in a dream—or at least one of his plot-less pornos.

"Sex," she said with the same calm confidence, "—it's the reason I came all the way here."

"They don't got dicks in Kansas?" he joked, then groaned nervously when she did not laugh. She just stared at him for a while before saying:

"Would you like to have sex with me?"

He looked her over greedily; he could feel his heart beating in his chest.

"*Me?*" he said anxiously, "—hell yeah! …You ain't no prostitute, is you?" he said, cautiously—not that he would have rejected her on those grounds or *any* for that matter.

"No," she said with a smile, "I'm not going to charge you any money, if that's what you mean—I just like sex. In fact, I think of sex as an act of worship. All that pleasure lurking within our bodies [she placed her hand on his chest then, and began massaging his B-cup]…all that pleasure and so many people are afraid to seize it. You're not afraid, are you?"

"Me?" he said with drool in his mouth, "of course not!"

"Do you like my body?" she asked, still massaging his breast.

"Yes!" he said, trembling with excitement.

"Do you think it could give you pleasure?"

"Oh, I *know* it can!" he said, looking her over greedily, "—without a doubt!"

"Then go and rent a Dimensional Portal," she ventured.

He set off quickly, but then turned back uncertainly, "How long should I rent it for?"

"How long do you think it's going to take?"

"Fifteen minutes?"

"*Fifteen* minutes?" she said with a frown and a smirk.

"—Half an hour—an *hour*," he corrected himself quickly, flustered and ashamed. "Just hold on," he said, gesturing for her to stay there. "I'll go rent it now," he said breathlessly. Then, looking around uneasily for any threats to his prize, he ran off. In his haste, he bumped into a scrawny kid with a tray full of tortillas and salsa, so that the entire tray fell noisily to the ground. Dimitri was in too much of a hurry to stop. He pushed past some more kids, then grinned proudly at Charlie as he passed him and went to the attendant in charge of renting the Dimensional Portals.

In the interim, the girl smiled and took a mobile phone from one of the side pockets of her bag. With one press of a button, a number was automatically dialed. After two rings, the man on the other end answered with:

"FBI, Agent Respoli speaking." He had had to scream. Now that news of the President's assassination had gotten out, all agents had been reassigned to the manhunt for the murderer—the *assassin*. His old feelings of patriotism left him almost wanting to cry—a few of the agents around him actually were crying. Respoli felt as though this were the thing he had sensed approaching on the horizon—

"You're the man in charge of finding the Goddess," the girl said then. It was a statement, not a question.

"...Who is this?" Respoli said with a frown.

"I'm someone who wants what you want—to find the Goddess."

There was something about her voice that Respoli could not quite place; something about it called to him on a deep, primal level, and this both disturbed him and intrigued him. He forgot all about the President. "...What makes you think you can help me?"

"I'll answer all your questions when you come and get me. I'll leave the line open, so you'll be able to trace my location. Come alone," she said at last. Having said that, she placed the phone back in the side pocket. As she looked around, her attention again went to the screens, where the emerging report on the President's assassination had gained supremacy. She smiled. As she waited for Dimitri to return, other men ogled her. She ignored them. Besides, Dimitri was back in a flash, panting and sweating as he wore a silly nervous grin on his face. He grabbed her bag for her, surprised by its weight.

"What's in here?" he said as he picked it up with a grunt.

"All the teachings of the universe," she said enigmatically.

He looked at her uneasily, but he was so eager for the sex she had promised that that uneasiness was soon lost. When they got to the Dimensional Portal that he had rented for an hour and a half, he was panting horribly, his face streaming with sweat. "Okay," he said through gasps of air, "which Dimension do you want to go to?"

"I have the perfect one all picked out," she said with a smile as she entered the code. She then held the elevator-like doors open for him as he lugged the bag in. They entered a tropical beach at sunset. There were neither people nor edifices around them, and the majestic sun hovered just over the horizon. Groaning from his effort by now, Dimitri dropped the bag into the sand, huffing and puffing. He turned to her then, and she pushed him playfully, so that he toppled into the sand. For some reason, he was disturbed by her strength. He had wanted to be the one to push her to the sand and hold her there while he ripped off her dress. But she was undressing now. With a simple tug of a band, the dress was open and he gasped at her perfect body.

"Tell me something," she said as she stood above him, "do you believe in the Goddess?"

"That 10-year-old bitch blowing up half the city?" he said without thought, his eyes devouring her body.

"Yes," she said, stepping up to his torso now, so that to look at her, he had to look past the arch of her legs...His eyes did not get past the mass of pubic hair; his trembling hands, as if of their own volition, began moving up her smooth, soft thighs.

"Do you believe in her?" she asked him again as he lay there mesmerized.

"What?" he said absentmindedly; and then, "—of course not."

"—But you believe in sex, don't you: in the pleasure of the body."

"Believe in it?" he said, chuckling as his trembling hand cupped her pubic area, "—I guess you could call it that."

"Would you sell your soul to me for sex?"

"My soul?" he mumbled, still preoccupied with her pubic mound.

"Yes, would you freely give your soul to me in the name of the Goddess?"

He looked up at her sharply, unsure again.

"Don't tell me you're afraid?" she said with a smile.

"I ain't afraid," he said defensively. "I ain't afraid of nothing."

"Don't you like my body?"

At that, his eyes again went to her pubic mound, "Yeah, but...be *quiet* won't you," he pleaded.

"I'll be anything you want—all you have to do is offer your soul to the Goddess."

"All right!" he said in frustration, "—*anything*."

She smiled then and lowered herself onto his paunch, straddling him. As she smiled, he thought about how incredibly beautiful she was. In that strange way of men, his lust now transformed her into the most beautiful woman he had ever seen. Now, as she brought his trembling, clammy hands to her breasts, she closed her eyes and smiled again. Then, all of a sudden, the wind began to pick up, blowing her hair wildly and erotically. It had been sunset before; but all at once, it was the darkest night. No stars shone in the heavens; everything was as dark as pitch; and except for the howling of the wind, there was nothing. Then, from nowhere, lights began to flash, giving a strobe light effect to everything. His head began to swim; nothing seemed clear anymore. He could not even see the woman anymore. It was at that moment that he felt a jolt of energy go through him. It literally made his hair stand on end. He wanted to cry out, but it seemed suddenly pointless. All about him, there was now a bizarre sensation. He felt as though he could feel every pore in his body; and that through each of these millions of pores, he could feel his energy—his *soul*—leaving him. He panicked at first, remembering what the woman had said about the Goddess; he tried to push the woman off and flee from this place, but he could not even move his arm! He lay there shuddering, suddenly realizing that he had reached orgasm….A millisecond or so later, everything went black, and his blank eyes stared into space, seeing nothing. Technically, he was still breathing and alive, but there was no consciousness—no *soul*.

When the woman finally stood up, the wind died down and the scene returned to the idyllic beach at sunset. "Goddess be praised," she whispered as she looked down at Dimitri. A terrified expression was frozen on his face, and this amused her for some reason. She felt refreshed and at peace. She went to the huge bag and unzipped it, revealing a portable Dimensional Portal. All the consciousnesses of her victims were stored within it, working together to bring about the sum of all human thought and emotion: a living oracle of human existence, which she and her followers referred to only as *The Teachings*. She checked the phone in the side pocket then—to make sure that the connection to Agent Respoli was still open—then she went for a swim in the ocean.

The danger of madness is that it seems so reasonable at the time.
VERSE 322:3 OF *The Teachings*

When the report of the President's assassination came on the air, Mansmann stared at it with the renewed belief that it all had to be the will of God. Suddenly restless, he got out of his car. It felt good to stretch, but the hot, smoggy air was putrid, with its usual burnt garbage smell. Their cars all burned Syntheline now that oil stocks had become unreliable. It was cheap and easy to make, but it was filthy. After breathing it for a few seconds, Mansmann gagged and spit out the thick, discolored phlegm before looking about the world in bewilderment.

Somewhere, lost in the smog, someone was cursing—several people were arguing in fact. He tried to get the threads of the arguments, but they were as incomprehensible as the staccato horns and sirens littering the air. He had a sudden urge to tell them all to shut up, but the only thing he did was walk away from his car. He did not even bother to lock the door. He had been waiting four hours already, and the car would probably be there if he came back in another four…But he would not come back of course. He had the handgun in his vest pocket….

His gait was stiff and timid—as if he actually were an old man. *It's a perfect night for the apocalypse,* Mansmann thought to himself as he reached the sidewalk and began walking towards lower Manhattan. He had a condominium on 35th Street; when he reached the corner and squinted up at the sign, the realization that he was on 41st Street opened for him the heretofore-untapped possibility that he could have walked home hours ago. He groaned and walked on....Someone bumped into him in the smog and ran off without bothering to apologize or acknowledge him. Numb, Mansmann grunted and walked on.

He probably walked another block before he came to one of the places where the Goddess' followers had burst a water main. He was only aware of the fact that he was walking in water by the splashes his feet made. The area was of course barricaded and blocked off by emergency vehicles, so he was forced to walk down a cross street. This street was somewhat deserted, and the businesses that lined it were mostly closed. He probably walked another two blocks before the sound of a speeding vehicle broke his reverie. He looked up just in time to hear the loud crash—and then to see the huge vehicle flying towards him. He stood there frozen as the careening black blur passed no more than five meters in front of him and crashed into a pizzeria. The force of the blast knocked Mansmann to the ground, where he lay cringing. It was perhaps another ten seconds before he picked himself off the ground and looked around. The vehicle—the huge SUV— had totally obliterated the front of the shop. The SUV had actually landed sideways—and on its top. The neon lights around the pizzeria flickered on and off eerily as Mansmann stepped up. The dust from the crash joined the smog, so that everything remained dark and inarticulate. Somewhere in the pizzeria, a man was screaming hysterically. However, with the heavy smog, it was as though they were the last people left on earth—

Mansmann stumbled over some debris and fell to the ground, cutting his hands on some shards of glass. The driver of the vehicle had gone through the windshield. His torso was actually lying outside of the SUV. The man was a mess—Mansmann saw this at once. Blood was dripping from the man's matted hair as he lay supine on the ground. As Mansmann walked over, he expected to find a corpse; but when he bent down to discern the man's vital signs, the man mumbled something that took a few seconds for Mansmann's stunned mind to decipher: "...*I killed the President of the United States!*"

The man was in fact mumbling it over and over again. He was delirious of course, but the realization that this man was the President's assassin set

Mansmann's mind off in strange directions. Before, the realization of what he had done—and of the hatred and madness that would descend on him when the world found out what he had done—had stunned and incapacitated him. But now, looking down at this man—this *killer*—Mansmann saw not a wanted criminal, but a *brother*. Death was a solitary thing, and those who took their own lives (as Mansmann had been on the verge of doing) more often than not did so because of the loneliness: the perception that no one else understood or cared. However, finding this strange man here, confessing his crime from the depths of his stupor, changed the vital dynamic that had guided Mansmann's thoughts. The man below him was literally something that had been tossed from the heavens—an aegis perhaps against the loneliness. This reasoning was seriously flawed of course, but Mansmann gripped onto it nonetheless. He felt himself imbued with new energy and resolve; and now that his mind was on this new track, he found himself thinking that he had to do something to help—that he could not let this man die. Yes, in the long run, they were all as good as dead, but Mansmann would do what he could to help the man. And even though he only had a Ph.D. in genetics—and not a medical degree—two years of medical school had taught him how to stabilize a wound until it could be properly dressed. Examining the man in the darkness, he tried to assess what had to be done—

It was then that the owner of the pizzeria emerged from the wreckage. The man had no doubt been trying to close up the shop when the accident happened. He was a middle-aged Italian of sallow complexion and pendulous gut. He squeezed past the SUV and came out looking like he was in shock.

"You hurt?" Mansmann asked from the ground, where he squatted, tending to G.W.; but once the Italian was outside, he squealed:

"Look at my goddamn business! Look at what that dickhead did to my shop!" the man cursed again; and then, looking towards the curb, he squealed out and ran up to a car parked there: "Look at my car!" he said, pointing to a classic Cadillac that now had a missing roof. "Look at what he's done!" the man screamed, his voice now taking on a shrill edge; then, turning back towards his business, he squealed out again as he got a full view of the damage.

As the man continued to squeal an incomprehensible mix of Italian and

English, Mansmann, who was applying pressure to G.W.'s head wound, glanced over and cursed: "Calm down, goddamnit!"

"*Calm down!*" the man cried, outraged, "—Look at what he's done!"

Mansmann was not a combative man—in fact, he was probably about a quarter the size of the Italian; but preoccupied as he was, he again yelled out, "Would you shut the hell up already!"

"*Shut up?*" the Italian yelled, as if that were the final straw. "I've got your 'shut up' right here!" the man said then, picking up a brick from the ground.

Mansmann saw the man out of the corner of his eye; and before he knew it, he grabbed his handgun from his vest pocket and pointed it at the man. The latter, finally discerning the gun through the smog, stopped short. In fact, the man was so stunned that the brick fell from his hand.

"All right!" Mansmann said, getting up, "give me your keys!"

"What!"

"Your car keys—give them to me!"

The Italian's face configured itself into a horrified scowl!

"Give them to me!" Mansmann demanded, brandishing the gun again.

The Italian got out his keys from his pocket, then tossed them to Mansmann as he began to sob and enumerate his sorrows and grievances against the universe.

"Pick him up!" Mansmann said, pointing to G.W.

"*What!*"

"Pick him up and put him in the back seat!" Then, as he brandished the gun again, the Italian blanched, picked up G.W. by the shoulders, and dragged him over to the car. Mansmann opened the back door while keeping the gun pointed at the Italian. When that was completed, Mansmann got in the car and drove off.

This is how the two great devils formed their alliance.

II

Trust is an act of war.
Always be willing and able to kill those you trust.
VERSE 321:4 OF *The Teachings*

It was one week earlier. G.W. was in the midst of a dream when the world finally began to reveal itself to him. The dream, itself, faded away, and he was left trapped in a formless netherworld. However, as he emerged slowly and fitfully into the waking world, he was overcome by the feeling that something horrible had happened. The feeling was so powerful and *devastating* that his awakening was more like losing consciousness. Shapes were all blurred; noises were all garbled in a high-pitched manner reminiscent of speeded up recordings. Fanciful, barely recognizable images flashed in his mind, further eroding his connection to reality. Then, as his strange awakening continued, he remembered that he had a family: a wife and an unborn son. The thought, itself, calmed him; the idea of them provided something concrete that he could focus on, but then his mind conjured images of them mangled somewhere—butchered by some monster. An insane impulse to kill and take revenge seemed to explode within him then. The impulse felt like the jolt of electricity from a defibrillator: his body convulsed; his heart and chest felt like someone had dropped a trunk on them; and as the jolt coursed through him, a disconcerting, tingly feeling spread over his skin—as though he were on fire—

Suddenly, the universe regained its substance, and he was gripped by the feeling of falling—of careening through space. Then, as his journey drew to an abrupt close, there was the feeling that his body was crushed and splattered against the ground. Whether real or imagined, he now felt as though his body were a sack of broken bones and ruptured organs. The pain was impossible to describe; but beyond the pain, the feeling that a hidden monster was stalking him, made more inroads into his psyche; and finally, when some unsustainable level of terror was reached, his body and soul rebelled, and he sprang upright. His eyes had been closed: they now burst open. He went to search the landscape frantically (as if to check for the hidden monster), but no sooner did he look out on the waking world than he was forced to clamp his eyes shut! A hot, blinding light was on him. The light was so brilliant that his eyes felt as though they were melting in their sockets. In fact, the pain was so intense that his skull felt like it had been cracked open with a sledgehammer. On top of that, the air reverberated with a sound that brought to mind the cries of a million madmen. The chaotic screams rose all around him, *deafening* him, so that he brought his trembling hands to his ears and clamped them there so as to block out the noise—

It occurred to him that he was in the sitting position—and that he was restrained in some kind of chair…but his thoughts went off in crazy directions, trying to piece together how he could have possible gotten into this position. With the hot, blinding light and the chaotic screams, it was impossible to discern what was around him. The sudden fear that the monster was using this confusion to sneak up on him, left him quaking inside; and even when his eyes began to adjust to the light—and to *focus*—there remained huge blind spots for things too painful to be perceived. The noises in the air were too powerful; the light was too bright; he, himself was too overwhelmed and confused to believe that he was a real man in the real world. He was about to grasp his head in frustration when he miraculously realized that he was in a cab—and that the restraint he had felt earlier was a seatbelt.

Still, as he had absolutely no idea *how* he had come to be there, this bit of information only confused him further. Desperate to get his bearings, he began looking around and realized that the cabbie—who was looking back at him through the bulletproof glass—was yelling that they had arrived. It was an old woman with a huge nose that made her seem like a fairy tale witch. G.W.

looked at her hopefully for a moment, thinking that she might be the source of all the noise and confusion; but then, as he saw what lay over the woman's shoulder, he turned his head to the left (towards the brilliant light and out of the window) cringing against the seat.

…And at first, the tens of thousands of screaming protesters did not seem real. They were simply a sea of forms: tens of thousands of people drowning in blinding light. For a moment, he thought that he was in hell—and that they were all suffering in lakes of fire. However, as he looked up, he realized that the brilliant light was the blazing sun; and in the distance, there were skyscrapers and other tangible proofs of the world of men. All at once, he realized that he was on the perimeter of Company Square—up in that strange super-world. Then, as he forged more links to reality (and the facts that explained his current circumstances) he realized that he had just come from the airport, and that he had fallen asleep in the cab during the ride. His suitcases were on the floor beside him, and he instinctively touched them with his foot to prove to himself that they were real.

His spirits brightened: he was a human being—a businessman returning from a trip; but as he considered the trip, and his life, new anxieties began to grow within him. With the war between India and China escalating into madness and genocide, The Company's CEO had sent him to make a report on The Company's Asian holdings. In that endeavor, G.W. had spent the last two weeks in India and China, talking to businesspersons and ambassadors and military attachés…but his mind had never been able to get over the bewilderment of being in countries where every possible nook and cranny of the landscape had seemed to be crammed with people and their edifices. India was a behemoth that was just past the threshold of two billion people; China was conservatively placed at 1.9 billion; and crammed into that pressure cooker of human activity and *filth*, the people had not seemed like human beings anymore, but as maggots consuming a corpse.

The two weeks of his trip had felt like lifetimes, in which the horrors of poverty and overcrowding—*and the human drive towards self-destruction*—had left him with the conclusion that they were all doomed. This was a world of *billions*—11.5, or whatever it was now—where everyone was clambering for space, willing to kill one another over the most elementary of resources. In fact, the strange war between India and China had supposedly started out as a dispute over water rights. Now, at least seven million people were dead. There was absolutely no sense to be made of it. The reasons and rationales for the war were too convoluted to be explained by any but a few of the true believers. To everyone else, it was all like a story that had been passed from person to person, evolving as it went.

Worse still, India and China were not isolated examples of degradation. In Africa, there were the so-called AIDS Wars, where overlords had managed to unify the horrible invulnerability of those who had AIDS (and therefore had nothing to hinder their brutality but death) and those who simply had nothing (and therefore had nothing to lose but their lives); so that now, the continent was pockmarked with vast fiefdoms and/or expanses of anarchy. In Latin America, and all over the globe, there were similar developments: similar desperation, leading to similar self-destructive capacity. Even in the United States and Europe, martial law had to be instituted every few weeks in order to combat the ubiquitous terrorist attacks and ethnic strife.

Yet, even the age-old struggle over finite resources could not fully explain what he had seen on his trip—and what he now felt. It was almost as though they had all been enchanted—possessed by some dark, malicious entity that drew strength from their sufferings. Their lives were like G.W.'s awakening—full of indefinite horrors and stimuli so overpowering that they warped and short-circuited the senses. Nightly news reports seemed like imaginative ghost stories—the kind of things made up by adults to scare children into behaving—

G.W. blinked deeply to further clear his vision, and his mind. However, as he imbedded himself in the surrounding reality, a kind of lassitude came over him. He sat back in the seat, staring up thoughtfully at the blank ceiling, while the cabbie continued to yell and the protesters outside continued their chaotic mix of chants and execrations. G.W. nodded to himself then: his trip to Asia had not simply been an event that took place over two weeks, but one of those points of no return in his life. He was not the same man he had been two weeks ago. Indeed, China, the home of his ancestors, had once been a kind of moral and spiritual ideal to him. As a boy, growing up in New York City's Chinatown, his father would take him on his knee at night, telling him wondrous stories about China, while his doting mother looked on from the couch. China's history, its breathtaking scenery, its people…everything had unfolded in those vivid stories, so that G.W. had felt himself being transported into that wondrous place. His father had told these stories in Chinese; but every once in a while, the man had interjected an English word: Beautiful, Peaceful, Nice; and in this way, G.W. had grown up with an unusually nostalgic view of China, based not on his own recollections, but another man's homesickness. Indeed, all the people he loved most dearly in the world—including his wife—had been born in that distant, fairy tale place. As he, himself, had never actually been there, he had embarked on his trip expecting to see all of his loved ones' stories come to life. Instead, he had been confronted by filthy, packed cities, a ravaged landscape…polluted skies and rivers…and death hanging over everything like a shroud—

The cabbie was still yelling for him to leave. G.W. looked up at the woman sharply, but he was so dazed from his strange awakening that he continued to look around confusedly. Despite the reality of his trip—and the surrounding world—he could not free himself of the feeling that reality itself had been corrupted somehow. Worse still, he did not merely feel as though he had fallen asleep during a 45-minute cab ride from the airport: he felt as though he had been in a coma for weeks, recovering from broken bones and head trauma. Actually, his sleeping patterns had been weird over the last few weeks. A couple of times, he had seemed to fall asleep at his desk at work and awaken at home—and vice versa. Just a few days ago, he had gone to bed at one hotel and awakened at another. In fact, he could not even remember traveling from China to India—he had just seemed to awaken there one morning. Everything seemed disjointed, so that even now his old thoughts about being trapped within a dream began to gnaw at him again. Considering all the blind spots that plagued his life, it was as though he had stumbled upon God while He was in the process of rewriting the universe; and in order to blind him and shield him from that sacred knowledge, God had glossed over his mind with a blurry sketch, which, while it kept his mind from conceptualizing the Master's grand design, was devastating, in that it would forever damn him and separate him from other men....

G.W. looked up from these vague thoughts and noticed the small TV screen in front of him. It was placed within the back of the cab's front seats; and as his eyes focused, he saw the face of a young Latino with long black hair and incredibly delicate features. The man was saying, "Sex Cult Goddess" in that contrived voice that reporters used when they were trying to be dramatic. Actually, with the noise from the mob outside, G.W. was barely able to hear the man's voice: he actually gleaned what was going on by reading the man's lips and looking at the images. The man was standing in front of the smoldering wreckage of a building that the 10-year-old black girl's cult had just bombed, talking about death and madness; and for whatever reason, G.W. stared down at the screen as if it held some key to his own existence—

But the next report was on the President and her visit to New York City. At the mention of politics, G.W., who was totally apathetic in that regard, was about to look elsewhere. However, when the President's picture came on the screen, his heart seemed to leap in his chest; new feelings of rage and hatred rose to a frenzy within him; images again seemed blurred; noises again took on that warped, speeded-up aspect. On the TV, the President was smiling and shaking hands in a crowd, but he found his mind going to things he could not fathom, like the placement of the Secret Service body-guards. The impulse to kill and take bloody revenge again seized him; and yet, these things seemed so strange to him that he found himself thinking that something alien and toxic had been rammed down his throat while he was unconscious. Some poison seemed to have been introduced into his body—and his *soul*. As he sat there gagging on his rage and vengefulness, this seemed to be the moment of truth, when he would either expel the poisons from his body or succumb to them. His skin was crawling now. The rancid odor of his sweat only seemed to heighten his panic and rage and horror—as though he were reacting to his own pheromones. And then, as he sat there shuddering, one realization broke free from the swirling mess that was his mind: his sole reason for being—indeed, the only thing that made sense to him—was to kill the President of the United States....

More seconds flew past. The cabbie was still cursing him, exhorting him to get the hell out of her cab; the protesters outside the cab continued their chants...Still, all he could do was stare at the President's image. Mercifully, the news story on her visit came to an end; and as a segue to the next story, the theme music of the show—several staccato notes played on a synthesizer—boomed in the air, so that G.W. jumped in the seat. Released from his trance, he once again looked around confusedly. He felt drained beyond reason now. His queasy stomach now seemed like an ocean churning in a storm....He shook his head...he looked at the TV warily, but the report on the latest sports scores did nothing to him. It was not the TV—it was the President's image that had seized and provoked him. He nibbled at his fingernails, asking himself why he would want to kill the President. It did not even seem like the kind of thing he would have thought. He was a family man. He lived in the suburbs with a loving wife and a son on the way. He was not a maniac...! In fact, what had just happened was so inexplicable that he found himself wondering if it had even happened. Returning to the last thing he knew was real, he reminded himself that he had just come back from Asia; like a criminal trying to get his alibi straight, he went over everything in his mind once more. Again, he tapped his suitcases with his foot so as to validate all that had passed—and his own existence in reality.

Stupidity is nature's way of covering its ass and leaving the way open for those revelations that are so profound that they can only be reached through bungling.
VERSE 5232:7 OF *The Teachings*

The cabbie was still yelling at him; the guards surrounding the perimeter began to get suspicious of the lingering cab, and looked into the window. One of the men came over to the cabbie and demanded that she pop the trunk; but as all vehicles—and *people*—were automatically scanned when they entered the super-world, the cabbie assailed the guard with a shrill tirade on the conspiracy to waste her time....G.W. watched these events disinterestedly—as though they were events in someone else's life. Desperate for something of his own, he again returned to thoughts of his family—his wife and the son that was to come. He felt a hunger for his wife that was stronger than anything he had ever felt. He remembered the way her skin smelled after she took a shower...the smooth elasticity of her skin...and that place on the nape of her neck that always made her giggle when he kissed it. Unfortunately, with all his traveling, he had not been able to talk to his wife in days—almost a week! As a consequence, even his wife now seemed like a distant fantasy. Similarly, at that moment, his unborn son only had a theoretical place in his life. In his desperation for something concrete—and *indissoluble*—his mind suddenly conjured the image of his huge, tank-like SUV. He had left it in The Company's parking garage before embarking on his trip....

He shook his head and noticed (beyond the agitated crowd, and the guard trying to get his attention by banging on the window) the huge pyramid on the opposite side of the square. It was the soon-to-be-completed Image Broadcast Complex; and despite all his anxieties and preoccupations, he could not help thinking that there was something magical about it. The dark, lustrous alloy that it was composed of was engrossing; the way it glistened in the sunlight gave one the impression that it was *exuding* power. However, there was something unnerving about the huge digital clock above the complex, which counted down the time (now seven days) until the next epoch of human history. Something about it reminded him of one of those time bombs in movies, so that his mind went off on another tangent, with wild conjectures about what was going to happen in seven days' time. There had already been riots and bomb threats: what would happen when they were all pulled along by a technological leap that would change the nature of communications—*and everything else for that matter*—forever? …Billions of minds, able to exchange information instantaneously and *perfectly*: the world was bound to change. The Company was already the standard bearer of world technology. Eighty-five percent of the computers in the world were either made by The Company or used so many of The Company's components that they may as well have been. What would happen when The Company had everything: was defining the very nature of possibility, if not *thought*! As an employee of The Company, G.W.'s reaction to all those screaming protesters was instinctively that of a true believer to sinners—to *infidels*. The Company was changing the world—pushing it into the future—

But glancing at his watch, he suddenly realized that he was supposed to attend a board meeting in a couple of minutes! He was to give a report on Asia before the CEO and all the board members! The imminence of the meeting made his stomach churn; his first impulse was to rush into the 150-story building, in front of which the cab was parked. However, for some reason, he could not bring himself to step outside the cab. He was like a child that was terrified that the monsters would get him if he got out of bed—

The guards were still arguing with the cabbie. A second guard was now trying to get G.W.'s attention by banging on the window to the right. Yet, despite the commotion, and the fact that it was imperative that he rush in order to make the board meeting, G.W.'s mind unwittingly returned to thoughts of an unknown monster stalking him—peering at him from the shadows. More troublingly, his mind unwittingly drifted back to the image of the President; and as it did so, those old feelings of rage and madness began to build within him—but stronger than before, so that he suspected that they were taking over his mind with each successive assault. He gnashed his teeth—

But it was at that moment that a beautiful aria issued from the TV. The aria accompanied another of The Company's commercials; and despite everything that was going on around him—and *within* him—G.W. felt himself being drawn into that universe of ease and security. In the commercial, The Company's founder and CEO—a 51-year-old black man who went by the single name, Shaka—was standing heroically on a mountaintop, his eyes glistening as he watched the sunrise. The camera retreated, so that Shaka was seen holding the hands of two awe-stricken kids—an Asian boy and a cherubic European girl; a further enlargement of the scene showed that the man was surrounded by dozens of other kids, all of whom were of different races and creeds and nationalities. They were all looking at the spectacular sunrise with hope, and one felt one's self being drawn into it—mesmerized as the kids were mesmerized. Then, the angle changed, so that the viewer realized that everyone was staring up at The Company's computer-generated spokesperson. She was up there in the sky, in a sheer, billowy dress that gave her a regal appearance. The sun behind her acted like a kind of halo—but she was brighter than the sun, seeming not only able to illuminate the universe, but to *purify* it. And there was something almost hypnotic about the way the aria came to a crescendo in the background, and the way that Shaka's deep baritone declared, "We are making the future *now!*"

G.W. sat back in the seat and took a few deep breaths to calm himself. That small reminder of what The Company was (the scale and *perfection* of everything it did) was as unsettling as it was reassuring. G.W. had a bad habit of scratching the nape of his neck when agitated, and he did this now. He felt so very weak—and indecisive; and, on a level that seemed out of proportion with everything, *terrified*. He had lost something over the last few weeks, which may have been as inconsequential as his train of thought, or as all encompassing as his conceptualization of himself as a human being. So much had happened…He felt older—like a boy suddenly realizing that he was a man, and that he would either succeed in the world, or break under its weight. That moment, sitting there in the cab, was strangely poignant: he wanted to hold onto it for as long as possible—even though he knew that he should be rushing in order to make his appointment with the board. It was one of those rare moments when one could see just how one had changed—and that there was no going back. For a moment, he was overwhelmed by the changes—and the weight of the world. He was afraid, like a child was afraid of the dark. The huge, angry crowd, and his strange urge to kill the President, and the waiting board members, and his pregnant wife sitting at home…all of these things combined into a wall of darkness, and his only respite again seemed to be in hiding inside the cab like a frightened child. However, just then, the cab driver's screams reached a pitch that literally made G.W.'s skin crawl; and coming to his senses, he looked up at the screaming woman—who was now red in the face—and nodded contritely….

When G.W. alighted from the cab, he was almost immediately overcome by the heat—and the pollution. The cabbie took off in a huff, leaving a huge exhaust cloud in her wake. The burned garbage smell of Syntheline sickened him. He could actually taste the air and see it wafting by. Confused, he realized that the cab had had those holographic windows, which projected bright, clear skies on an otherwise smoggy world. In reality, the day was overcast and brooding—as it usually was—and there was no sun in sight. He wondered how the tens of thousands of screaming protesters kept up their energy in this place, but then he considered that maybe they had simply been driven mad by the filth in the air—and the heat. He, himself, was already drenched in sweat; and he realized, after he had taken a few steps, that his left buttock had fallen asleep. As a consequence, he was forced to waddle up to the guards surrounding the perimeter. Several of the men gathered around to scrutinize his ID and himself. He was a disheveled mess: from his hair to his sweat-drenched, rumpled suit. On top of that, he had the tendency of tall, overweight men to appear clumsy. He needed a shave—and a shower; and as he looked around, his eyes were red and puffy, and his face wore an expression that was at once harried and forlorn. The guards patted him down several times and looked through his suitcases; and then, when they seemed to be finished, the head guard, who had been rifling through his suitcase, stood up and said:

"Here is your gun, sir."

"…What?"

"Your gun, sir," he said, proffering the .45.

"I don't have a gun," he said in bewilderment.

"It was in your bag, sir. No problem—your permit seems to be in order," he said, handing over a laminated card that had supposedly been in G.W.'s wallet.

G.W. looked at the card in disbelief. "I don't have a gun!" he said hysterically.

"Relax," the guard said with a smile, seeming unusually cordial, "I said you're all right. Here," he said, putting the gun in G.W.'s trembling hand, "just take it." G.W. shook his head feebly; the weight of the weapon in his hand seemed unbearable. "Take it," the guard coaxed him. And then: "Maybe you should put it in your holster."

"I don't have…" But looking down, G.W. saw that he wore a holster. His mind was like a car sputtering down an isolated desert highway. Did he have a gun? He could not remember having had one—he had never even *held* one before. He was G.W. Wang—family man….The guard nodded encouragingly, and G.W. put the gun in the holster….

Suitcases in hand, and his buttock slowly coming back to life, he waddled up the building's walkway as if he were somnambulating. The walkway was only about 50 meters; but with his mind pulverized by all that had happened, he felt as though he were setting off on an epic journey….Did he have a gun? Of course not! He *could not* have one. He could not have come from the airport with a gun. No airline would have allowed him on board with a gun—especially during these times, when the fear of terrorism made passengers and the authorities paranoid. He would not have even made it through the scanners on the street below, which the cab had to go through to get up to Company Square. And he did not have a holster either! He had never put the thing on. Yes, he was dazed from the trip and the jetlag, but he did not have a gun! That was not the kind of thing a man forgot! This all had to be some trick! Someone was doing something to him—that *had* to be it. Either this was all a trick or he was having some kind of nervous breakdown....He returned to the same thought he had had when he woke up in the cab: someone had trapped him somewhere—was forcing him to see and feel things....He was now trembling to the point where he was losing his grip on the suitcases. He touched the gun with his elbow to prove to himself that it was real—and that what had just happened had actually happened. He wanted to stop and make sense of things, but he felt too vulnerable out in the open. He wanted to go somewhere and hide again....Thoughts of the imminent board meeting made him sick and lightheaded—he was in no shape for any of that! He was so desperate to reconcile all the incomprehensible things around him that he scoured his mind like a starving child scraped a bowl for the last speck of food. Like he had been doing for the last few weeks, he asked himself when was the last time he had been sure of who he was and what he wanted from life; and like all the previous times, he acknowledged that everything had changed a month ago—the day he had met Shaka....

As incredible as it seemed to him now, just four weeks ago, G.W. had lived another life. Back then, he had manned a cubicle in a forgettable nook of The Company's International Finance Department. As had typically been the case over his eight years of employment with The Company, he had been working late to translate the continuous stream of data into charts and figures and projections. Exhausted by the tedium of the work, but happy to be going home, G.W. had been waiting by the elevator, his mind inevitably going to thoughts of his wife and the family that was to come. It had been then that Shaka seemed to emerge out of the nothingness, like a stray thought impinging on G.W.'s daydreams. The man had walked up in his trademark white suit, with his entourage of attendants and bodyguards, and G.W. had stood there frozen—the way a punctilious peasant stopped in his tracks at the sight of the king, or the *Pope*. G.W. had been staring in awe when Shaka, who stopped before the door of the elevator in deep thought, looked over and said:

"Pardon me, sir, do you happen to speak Chinese?"

"...Yes, sir," G.W. had responded after the shock of being spoken to.
"What is your name?"

"G.W. Wang, sir—from International Finance."

"Come up to my office," Shaka had ordered, just as the elevator opened.
And then, in that vast penthouse suite, with its daunting array of flickering
TV monitors and computer consoles, G.W. had been given the mission to go
to Asia and make a report on the escalating strife. On the surface, it had
seemed like the chance of a lifetime—an opportunity to impress the CEO
and finally make some headway in his career. But deep down, G.W. had
always been honest enough with himself to know that it did not entirely
make sense. Certainly Shaka already had people to make such reports for
him. Besides, to get a report like that nowadays, Shaka needed only to open
a Dimensional Portal to his Asian offices—or to look at television. It had
been like sending a man on a Pony Express delivery when Internet and satellite links between the farthest reaches of the globe made communication
instantaneous. Ultimately, it all came down to the question of why Shaka had
picked *him* of all people. Obviously he had not distinguished himself—

G.W. groaned. As he waddled up to the entrance, he felt as though his
soul had been sucked dry. He had not really slept in weeks. He had closed
his eyes and retreated from what was ostensibly the waking world, but
the complexities of his dreams—and the truths shown only to his subconscious—had only drained him further. Now, as he walked along, all the
uncertainties again flared up in his mind, so that he had the sensation that
he was being swept along by a raging river. So many things were happening
in his life—and in the world. The good (like his career advancement and
unborn son) seemed inconceivably good; and the bad (or *potentially* bad),
seemed so horrific that it did not seem possible either. It was as if he had lost
the ability to put things in perspective. Simple realities, like the fact that he
was, for all intents and purposes, Shaka's herald, did not, in the face of what
his life had been, seem possible. It seemed like a passing daydream, from
which he would soon awaken—either relieved that the horror had been
dreamed, or devastated because his place of importance in the world (as Shaka's
herald) had been imagined. His life and dreams and accomplishments—not to
mention his fears—seemed like delusions that were escalating wildly out of

control; and several times a day, he would find himself thinking that he was imagining it all, and that he was lying around somewhere, in a world where the dark pyramid had been online for *years*, living a fantasy in which he, the all-American, pure-of-heart, every-man protagonist, was destined to rise above all the powers of heaven and earth.

G.W. sighed again. How much of that actually registered in his mind it was impossible to say. Everything was passing him by so quickly now; and with the heat, and the undulating cries of the crowd, he felt more and more unreal by the second. He needed rest badly—rest on a *spiritual* level, not just physical. For a moment, he stopped and craned his neck, looking up at the 150-story building. As he was so close to it, the building seemed to go on forever, like some stairway to the heavens. He could actually see it swaying in the wind, and the motion made him feel slightly sick, so that he closed his eyes and took a deep breath before continuing on.

The uneasiness waxed in him as he entered the revolving door: this seemed to be the point of no return. However, once within the air-conditioned confines of the building, he felt relieved for some reason. The heat was gone, and the screams of the thousands seemed distant. Furthermore, with the expansiveness of the lobby, the relative silence and emptiness were solemn—and peaceful. The lobby was enclosed by rose-tinted glass; and just then, as a few faint rays of the afternoon sun penetrated the huge chamber, the effect was spectacular. It was almost like a cathedral: he had the urge to bow and whisper a supplication to God. However, the sun soon disappeared behind a smog bank, and the supernatural solemnity of the lobby disappeared, leaving only glass and brick and stone.

He groaned again as he headed for the security console. With his appointment with Shaka and the board imminent, he desperately needed to focus; but the more he tried to channel his thoughts, the more diffuse and convoluted they became. It was then that it occurred to him that the lobby, which was usually bustling with hundreds of people, 24 hours a day, was empty. The only other people were the two guards at the security console, who were watching a monitor and chuckling between themselves.

G.W. was happy for the familiar face: "Hey, Ernie," he addressed the old guard when he was close enough, "what's so funny?"

"Hey!" Ernie said with a laugh—more at the screen than G.W. He then glanced up from the screen, which still had his partner totally engrossed, saying: "Haven't seen you in a while."

"I was out of the country," he said with a certain amount of pride, "—went to India and China for Shaka."

Ernie nodded his head, seemingly impressed; but as something on the screen caught his attention, he and his partner again began to laugh.

"What's going on?" G.W. demanded, like a child left out of a secret. He leaned over the console to get a look, and saw the same TV show that had been in the cab. Now, a reporter was interviewing a homeless man that was convinced that the 10-year-old black girl was God. The man was sweaty and fidgety—he looked insane in fact.

The guards continued to laugh, but all G.W. could think about was how unreal it was. Still anxious, he glanced about the lobby again. "…Where's everyone else?" he asked then, more to hear himself speak than anything else.

"What?" Ernie said, barely glancing up from the screen as he chuckled again.

"Everyone else—all the other workers. I've never seen the lobby this empty before."

"*Oh*," he said, finally understanding. "Shaka sent them home—especially with all the protests and bomb threats."

"Things gotten that bad?"

"You don't know the half of it," he said, still staring down at the screen. "I'm surprised you made it through. Some of our workers have been *killed*. Anyone connected with The Company is a likely target."

"Maybe Shaka should hold off on the complex."

At first, Ernie only grunted equivocally; but when a commercial came on a few seconds later, he sighed and looked up, as if refreshed. Then: "*What*?" he said, as if he had just heard what G.W. had said. "Hold off on the complex?" he said as if outraged. "Trust me, those people outside are just a tiny band of paranoid nuts—a small, vocal minority. They think The Company is going to take over their minds or something—turn them into zombies. Ninety-five percent of people—the *world* over—are excited by the Image Broadcast Complex."

"I guess," G.W. said vaguely, still looking at the screen. The commercial was for Luxuriant Hair. Mansmann was shown besieged by half a dozen bikini-clad women whom, along with Mansmann, were all chanting, "I'm a Mansmann's man!" over and over again. Something about it—and the weirdness of everything else—was maddening, and G.W. again felt the urge to get away. He quickly placed his palm on the security sensor, which scanned both his identity and his body; then, when the green light came on, he nodded to Ernie and continued on to the elevators. Behind him, the two guards again began to chuckle between themselves as the reporter said, "Sex Cult Goddess," and more of the girl's victims and converts gave their testimonials. As he stepped away from the security console, G.W. remembered his gun; and as he did so, it occurred to him that he should *never* have been able to make it through the scanner! The queasy feeling intensified in him again, but he walked on, still with his waddling gait.

The elevator was a technological breakthrough, designed specifically for the 150-story building. It not only went up and down: it moved laterally as well, switching shafts, so that one could get anywhere one needed in the huge building. When the doors closed behind him, the airy, formless music playing within the elevator seemed to encompass him. In fact, he felt as though the music were emanating from within him. He stared blankly at the digital display, watching the floors pass by: 15, 16…35, 36….He closed his eyes and leaned against the back wall of the elevator, trying to clear his mind; and then, when his mind was as formless as the music, there was a loud ding, and the elevator opened onto the 150th floor. G.W. seemed to have to rouse himself back into consciousness. Once again taking his suitcases in hand, he rushed out, onto the marble floor. Right across from the elevator, there were huge windows; rather, the entire wall was a window. The top of the building was above the smog banks, and the sky here was blue and bright. For a moment, he stared in awe and wonderment, but then he found himself wondering if even that was real. There was always the possibility that it was another holographic window—

"Can we help you?" demanded a gruff voice to G.W.'s left, in a tone that actually meant: *What the hell are you doing here*! About 20 meters away, four burly guards, all of whom were wearing the same dark suits, were sitting behind a security console. The console was right before the huge mahogany double door that led to Shaka's office chamber. The entire floor was in fact Shaka's chamber. There was an Olympic-sized swimming pool and a gym—everything imaginable.

Coming to his senses, G.W. nodded his head to the guards hopefully, as he stumbled towards them with suitcases in hand. It was at that moment that the huge mahogany doors opened and some figures emerged from the darkness within. When G.W. saw the President walk out of there, sandwiched between those two Secret Service bodyguards, it was as though something were tearing at his insides. Some monster seemed to be trying to rip its way out of him. His suitcases fell out of his hands and he stood there trembling as the murderous rage began to build within him again. The President's bodyguards, seeing him standing there like that, reached for the guns under their suits. They did not draw them out yet—they just reached for them and kept their eyes on the strange man who stood in their way with that startled expression on his face….G.W. wanted to draw the gun! His right hand was trembling violently; his every impulse told him to grab the gun and empty the clip into that bitch! As he looked at the President's grandmotherly face, all that he could think was that she had done this to him. She smiled instinctively, no doubt thinking that he was some awestruck worshipper, but she seemed like a beast to him now. *She* was the unknown enemy: she had done this to him; and the only way to rectify the situation was to kill her—*obliterate* her! He wanted to watch her squirm: to listen to her last gasps for air. She was walking up to him, still smiling at him…G.W.'s trigger finger flexed in anticipation, but then some voice—not exactly of sanity, but of self-preservation—held him back. The President and her bodyguards were coming straight for him, and with his last iota of strength and reason, he moved to the side and leaned against the wall, panting and clamping his eyes shut. He did not look up again until he heard the elevator open and the steps of the President and her bodyguards as they entered it. No doubt they were going to the roof, and the helicopter pad. G.W. sighed in relief when the elevator door closed, but he felt even more drained now.

While he had been struggling against the beast within, Shaka's guards had sat staring at him. Now, as if some unknown signal had been exchanged between them, the men came at him with metal detectors (which they seemed to produce out of thin air); he was frisked again, then his suitcases were taken away. It all happened in a whirlwind—he was literally spun around—then the door to Shaka's chamber was opened and he entered timidly, feeling slightly dizzy. To his amazement, he realized that the guards had left his gun—as though the thing had been overlooked in their scans and frisking. He began to wonder if the thing were only a figment of his imagination—perhaps a psychological crutch against a world that terrified him....

The chamber was dimly lit—which was to say that the blinds had all been drawn. However, with its spaciousness, and its scores of flashing TV monitors, it was like a way station in the universe. It was *huge*—perhaps 100 meters by 50 meters—with a ceiling that was so high that he could not even make it out in the darkness. A gigantic conference table was in the middle of the chamber, along with couches and a smaller working desk. The many TV screens were all set to different channels—and all showcased lives and conflicts and people babbling what seemed to be nonsense. As he glanced at the screens, he felt as though he were looking out on a hundred different worlds. It was disconcerting in fact: scores of people talking at once—in just as many languages and accents...people dying, people falling in love, people killing and hating one another, people making passionate love...there were the starkest news reports, the most fanciful stories...it was all there: a disconcerting window into their souls. As G.W. watched it all, he found himself thinking that Shaka could use the screens to attain not only cognizance of daily events, but some measure of omniscience....

After looking around confusedly, G.W. saw Shaka standing on the far side of the chamber, before a screen. The man's back was of course turned, and G.W. wondered if the man knew that he was there. He felt as though he had intruded somehow. But just then, the man turned around:

"Ah, Young Washington," Shaka said, his voice booming across the chamber. ("Young Washington" was the nickname that Shaka had used since G.W. told him that his full name was George Washington Wang—his immigrant father's gesture of appreciation to America.) "Come in," Shaka added.

G.W. nodded timidly, then swallowed deeply before he began walking over to the man. His footsteps resounded unsettlingly on the hardwood floors; over all the babbling voices, it was unreal—as if he were walking inside of someone's head, passing all her thoughts. Furthermore, there was always something unnerving about being alone with Shaka. To his alarm, a few weeks ago, G.W. had realized that he felt for Shaka the same discomfort that he felt when in the presence of unusually beautiful women. Indeed, around Shaka swirled a contradictory sexual aura that was probably attributable to all deities. The man seemed either asexual or hypersexual; he was either beyond the need for sex, or his every action and touch and word was inherently sexual. The man had never been married and was childless, but he was seen with a different young, beautiful woman every few weeks, like clockwork. He did not so much seem to date them as *consume* them. For a few weeks, these women would be the toast of the town, then they would disappear from sight and be replaced by another; and if these replaced women were ever seen again, they would seem wretched and haggard, as though the life and youth had been drained out of them. Of course, these spooky transformations all added to the belief that Shaka and The Company were not to be crossed. They were like the sun: they warmed the world and brought life, but if you stared at them too long, you were blinded; if you exposed yourself to their rays, you were burned.

Whatever the case, as G.W. drew close, he realized that Shaka was smiling at him. This of course made him uneasier. He felt self-conscious and unsure about everything in fact. He could not help thinking about his disheveled appearance—especially in contrast to Shaka, who was standing there in an immaculate white suit, with a clean-shaven, taut face that seemed ineluctably youthful and powerful. Also, even though G.W.'s buttock was not asleep anymore, he could not stop the waddling gait—

"Am I late for the board meeting, sir?" G.W. heard himself ask as he took the last couple of steps up to the man.

"No, you're right on time. I just finished my meeting with the President."

As he had reached Shaka, he instinctively went to shake the man's hand, but then he remembered in time that Shaka did not shake hands. G.W. put his hands in his pockets. "…Yes, I saw her," he said vaguely. That reminder of his murderous impulses left him feeling a little lightheaded. "Have you known her long, sir?" he went on, hoping that the banter would instill a level of comfort in him.

Shaka smiled in his usual enigmatic way: "When politicians think that you're rich and powerful, they are always eager to make you believe that you know them."

"So, she wants a favor?"

"She wants a cabinet secretary."

G.W. nodded uneasily when he realized that he had nothing to say on the matter. "…What about the board meeting, sir?" he asked, looking about the empty room.

"Like I said: you're right on time. All our meetings are broadcast via satellite, Young Washington. The cameras are ready."

"Oh…" G.W. said as he looked about uneasily and wondered where the cameras were.

Shaka again smiled enigmatically, then continued, "You passed by that little rally outside. What are they saying now?"

"Well…[G.W. cleared his throat anxiously] I suppose they think that everyone is selling his soul to you, sir."

At G.W.'s comment, Shaka laughed before responding: "One doesn't have to *buy* souls anymore, Young Washington. There's a glut on souls nowadays, and even the Devil can't be bothered to buy. Souls are lying in the fields, *rotting*, and no one can care less."

G.W. was always a little taken aback by these sayings; but feeling that he had to say something, he responded: "Don't these protests bother you, sir?"

"One can't let rats and ants decide one's actions…but," he went on thoughtfully, "that's the problem with the world: how high you can rise is always dependent on those who don't want to go anywhere. Man is the only creature who carries his own gravity around with him—carries it in the fear and ignorance of the masses….Escape velocity, Young Washington: we have to find some new way to utilize energy, so that we can blast off with so much force that we'll finally be free of gravity.

"Are you a nostalgic man, Young Washington," he went on quickly.

G.W. had been staring blankly, but he cleared his throat hastily, responding: "No, sir." And then, with a hopeful smile: "I like to believe that the best times are ahead."

"And so they are," he said with a smile. "They will be if we *make* them so, rather than sit around and hope for the best...Technology is our only hope for the future, Young Washington. In fact, technology is the only reason we are still alive as a species. [G.W. thought this was a good occasion to nod his head.] Take away even the most rudimentary microchip and society will be thrown into chaos; take away the computer and within a few days, 90% of us would be starving; entire countries would cease to exist. And yet all those fools outside sit around complaining that technology is killing the world and complicating their lives. On the contrary, every great technological advance has involved taking that which is complex and making it so simple that practically anyone can use it. The computer revolution started when the operation of the computer was reduced to pointing and clicking with a mouse. What does The Company do? Get rid of the mouse and turn point and click into look and blink: so simple that you become one with the computer—you don't even have to think about it. This is the way that technology, and the world, advances, Young Washington. There was a time when people were excited because the information of the world was at their fingertips. *Hell*, The Company is getting rid of computers as we know it. No longer is it a huge piece of machinery, taking up space on a desk. With the inception of our DreamVisors a decade ago, they now look no different from a pair of eyeglasses. And in two years, they'll be down to the size of contact lenses. With our Dimensional Portals, all the possibility of the universe is at the disposal of the masses. And when the Image Broadcast Complex goes online in a week, you'll no longer even need the Portals: all that possibility will be available wherever you are! Want a vacation? you can be in Tahiti in *nanoseconds*. Don't just see a movie: *feel* it. This is an age of biblical possibilities, Young Washington. With our technology, the blind can see; the deaf can hear; the old and infirm can run without pain and effort. We are performing miracles: changing the world and bringing hope back into the lives of billions of frightened, misled people; and the Pharisees, frightened out of their wits by our works, can only complain and pine for the good old days.

The Company has seen the promised land, Young Washington, and it is all here," he said, tapping his temple with his index finger.

G.W. nodded inanely.

"Talking of making the world better, the board is ready for your report."

G. W. nodded numbly, expecting Shaka to flip a switch or turn on an interface, but when the man simply stood there, looking at him, G.W. blurted out: "Can they see me already?"

"Of course, Young Washington," Shaka said nonchalantly. "They see everything that happens in this room."

G.W. felt as though his guts were clawing their way up his throat. He took a deep breath to calm himself, then realized that he had left the report in the suitcase—which was outside! Fighting his every instinct not to panic, he decided to "wing it." "Well sir," he began, his voice cracking slightly, "with the war between the Asians going on, we can expect our Asian holdings to dip still further. The entire region's a mess, sir—Korea, Japan, Indonesia... [When he looked up at Shaka's intent gaze, he got the feeling—as he always did when he talked to the man—that Shaka's mind was already made up, but that he was only asking questions to see how stupid G.W. was. He again cleared his throat nervously.] Besides lingering and deepening economic problems," G.W. continued, his voice again cracking slightly, "anti-Western sentiment is high there, and anti-Asian sentiment is high here."

Shaka looked at him with pursed lips, then continued: "The board wants to know if you believe that nuclear war will break out."

A creepy feeling came over G.W. as he wondered how Shaka was receiving questions—and where the cameras were in the room. There were rumors that Shaka had microchips inserted in his brain...G.W. shook his head: both to free himself of these thoughts and to answer the board's question. "...Stranger things have happened...but no, sir—*sirs*," he added quickly. "To me, it's mostly saber rattling. Not only would it be self-destructive, but they need one another economically. They may hate one another's guts, but they can't get around needs."

"Right you are!" he said, like a proud professor addressing a prized pupil. "Worse than the heathen who does everything differently from you, is the heathen who does the same things as you—but does it better than you.

This explains the relationship between most warring parties....The board asks if you still suggest that we get rid of our Asian holdings."

"I do, sir," he said, unconsciously scratching the nape of his neck.

"I see," he said, coyly. "And everything's a mess, as you say?"

"Yes, sir," he said with a rising sense of alarm, feeling that he was falling into a trap.

"—And Company stocks are due for a further dip as well?"

"Yes, sir…" And then, uncertainly: "You're not worried?"

"The board isn't worried at all, Young Washington," he said, straightening and looking as impeccable as in the commercial. "The board's view is that everyone else can run around like a decapitated chicken if he or she wants to. Stock prices should never be one's ultimate concern. Money comes and goes. Men who put all of their faith in money will never hold onto *power*. Just look at all the civil wars and rebellions in the world today [he pointed to the screen that he had been watching at G.W.'s entrance, on which guerrillas—South American indigenous peasants—were training in the jungle]. Anyone can make others act when he has something that the people want. The board believes that you can tell the powerful because the people follow them because they have no choice."

G.W. felt lost again—and, for some reason, taken aback. Still, feeling that he had to say something—to prove to Shaka that he *had* thoughts—he ventured: "Unfortunately wars aren't good for business, sir."

"That all depends on what your business is, Young Washington," Shaka said with a chuckle. "There is money to be made in everything; more correctly, there is *power* to be had. In fact, the more desperate and extreme the circumstances, the greater the power to be had. Always remember that, Young Washington."

G.W. nodded instinctively, but blinked slowly, with big cow eyes. He had absolutely no idea what Shaka was talking about anymore. In fact, every time he talked to the man, he had the feeling that they were having separate conversations. He opened his mouth to say something; but overcome by uncertainty—and needing to make sense of things—he ventured: "Then… we won't be selling our stocks?"

"Correct."

"Very well, sir."

At that, Shaka walked away a little bit and began watching another screen in silence. All at once remembering that this was how Shaka dismissed people, G.W. went to leave.

"Young Washington?" Shaka called.

"Yes, sir?" he said, stopping and turning around.

"The board wants to know what you would do if you knew that the world was going to end."

"I...I beg your pardon, sir?"

"If the world were ending, what would you do?"

"I'd be frightened, sir," he said, but was immediately ashamed of his response.

"Fear isn't an action, Young Washington: it's a *reaction*. What would you *do*?"

"I'd...I'd...There's no way to stop it?" he said, suddenly flustered, while Shaka stood there calmly with his hands in the small of his back.

"No."

"...I guess I'd get together with my family...say goodbye."

"You're an old sentimental heart after all," he said; a faint smile lingered on his face.

"I guess so, sir," G.W. said with a nervous laugh.

"What if you could save yourself by sacrificing your family—by ripping them to shreds?"

"*Sir?*"

"What if you could live by killing them and everything you profess to love? Would you do it?"

"...That wouldn't be living, sir."

"You'd be breathing, wouldn't you?"

"Well, yes, but—"

"Let me tell you something, Young Washington. There is hope and possibility in breath. If your wife had a car accident and went into a coma, would you want the doctors to immediately turn off life support?"

"Of course not," he answered instinctively; but then, remembering the vague fears he had had about his family upon awakening—and recalling that he had not been able to contact his wife in days—his heart skipped a beat. He opened his mouth to ask Shaka about his wife, but—

"*Exactly*—of course you wouldn't shut it off!" Shaka said triumphantly, "—because there is always the possibility that she'll come out of it. As long as she's breathing, there is hope. And she's pregnant, too, isn't she?"

G.W. went pale! He again opened his mouth to ask the question—

"So, let's say your wife was damaged beyond repair," Shaka went on, "but the baby was fine, and could be brought to term by keeping your wife hooked to machines and *breathing*, wouldn't you do it?"

G.W. was looking at the man in horror!

"—A family is a microcosm of the world, Young Washington," Shaka went on, either oblivious to G.W.'s expression or indifferent. "Just as you would keep your wife alive, would not you want to keep that comatose world on life support: feeding it via tubes, keeping its organs functioning with external machines?"

G.W. was trembling slightly now: "Sir," he ventured, "about my family—"

"Yes or no?" Shaka demanded. "Wouldn't you want to keep that breathing going?"

"I..."

"—The board is offering you an assignment, Young Washington," he began in a new voice. "We've always thought highly of your efficiency."

"...Thank you, sir," he said, utterly lost and confused again.

"Do you accept the assignment?"

"*What* assignment, sir?"

"A chance to save the world—or at least, the unborn baby it's carrying."

"I don't understand, sir."

"You'll have to leave immediately: we have one of The Company's private jets waiting for you."

"But sir..." He meant to protest with the fact that he had not seen his family in weeks...that he was exhausted beyond reason; for a moment, he was so desperate that he was even about to plead his *madness*. However, as he looked up at Shaka's calm, stern features, his voice was low as he bowed his head and said: "What do you want me to do, sir?"

"A situation has arisen in Africa."

G.W. again opened his mouth inanely. He went to ask what the hell was in Africa; but Shaka, feeling that the matter of G.W.'s trip had been resolved, abruptly went on: "Did you like Asia, Young Washington?"

"…No…not really, sir," he said, fighting to keep up—and to *focus*.

"Too many people, right?"

"Yes, sir." And then: "Sir, about Africa—"

But once again, Shaka's voice rose above his: "The reality of Asia—it *sickened* you, didn't it?"

"…Yes, sir," G.W. said, torn apart in too many ways to name.

"That is what the human race has become," Shaka began in a melancholy voice. "The height of technology, and yet more than half of the world has a standard of living worse than that of any other time in history. The height of technology, and half the world is starving, illiterate, *inveterate*. *Gravity*, Young Washington," he continued: "how can we possibly make progress carrying half the world on our backs? There will only be more wars in the future—more strife, more suffering…unless we do something.

"—The board wanted me to ask if you believe in God, Young Washington."

G.W. had a sudden impulse to hedge and avoid the topic all together—to run away and block out everything the man was saying! However, clinging tenaciously to self-preservation, he responded: "Not really, sir."

"You consider yourself a man of reason, then, Young Washington?"

"I try, sir," he said uneasily.

"Be careful in that, young sir," Shaka chastised him. "No matter what we profess to believe in, we all have gods. We all place our faith in someone or something"—he gestured vaguely to the revolutionaries on the screen again—"and all placement of trust leaves us open to loss and disappointment. Trust is an act of *war*, Young Washington," he said, staring at G.W. ominously. "Always be willing and able to kill those you trust."

Facts distort reality more thoroughly than rumors and lies,
because we are compelled to believe them.
VERSE 324:2 OF *The Teachings*

S omehow, G.W. made it back downstairs. The elevator doors opened
with a loud, off-tune ding, and he was staring out at the lobby again.
He seemed even more disheveled and lost now; and as he stepped into
the lobby, his strange waddling continued. It was probably a psychosomatic
reaction to all that was happening. He could feel a headache coming on…He
had a sudden urge for sex, but it was so panicky that it could not possibly
have been lust. There was something self-destructive in his longing. He
craved it the same way that an alcoholic reaching for a beer craved not the
drink, itself, but the unconsciousness that it promised. He did not want a
tangible body to caress; he did not want the human interplay, or even the
satisfaction that might come with the act. In fact, with all that had happened
lately, particularly in China, he no longer looked at sex the same way. The
notion of "making love" was unfathomable to him now—perhaps in the
same way that a fantasy left a bitter taste in one's mouth once it had been
shattered by reality.

The fact of the matter was that he had been with a prostitute in China—
quite inadvertently actually, if adultery could ever be undertaken inadvertently….The incident had happened about three days into his trip. It had
been like a dream within a dream: like everything that had happened over
the past month…After a long meeting with foreign dignitaries, in which he

had listened to the same panicky stories over and over again in different languages, he had returned to the luxurious suite that The Company provided. He had just finished taking a shower when there was a knock on the door. When he went to open it, he had seen a beautiful Chinese woman, who said that she was there to give him a massage. He had declined at first, but she had said that it was free: that it was all part of "the service"...Her hands had felt incredibly soft and tender on his skin. After spending so much time being bewildered by the harshness of the world and obsessing about inner feelings of doom (and all that might happen if he did not impress Shaka), it had been like heaven to lie there naked, feeling that woman's hands on him. Sexually, he had not been with his wife in months—since her pregnancy began to show. His wife had somehow reverted to the old Victorian model that women should be "confined" while pregnant, and had banished him to the nursery for the last three months. Of course, that was no excuse for what had happened; but again, with his bewilderment about the world, his utter loneliness in a nation of billions that was the home of his ancestors and loved ones, and the softness of the woman as she seemed to wring the tension out of his flabby neck and shoulders, he had literally been putty in her hands. As for the sex, it had been over quickly: he had reached orgasm from the shock of it—the sudden realization of what he was doing, and of what he had lost.

Now, he was off to Africa for some period of time that Shaka had not even bothered to specify. He would have to wait until he got back home to make amends to his wife. He would call her on his mobile phone and...he did not even know what he would say to her. Over the last two weeks, he had left the occasional voicemail message and passing update on where he was and where he was going, but he had not been able to *speak* to her. Now, with his strange dreams/premonitions of doom, and what Shaka had said...He was fighting to hold on. He had broken their marriage vows, and all that he could think was that he had to make things right. He had to put his little temple back in order before it was too late.

As he walked past the security console, G.W. nodded to Ernie; but as the old guard was still engrossed in something on the TV, the man barely acknowledged him. When G.W. got outside, the screaming tens of thousands hardly even registered in his mind. He felt slightly faint now; and with his headache worsening by the second, it was as if his entire consciousness were focused on the point of pain in his forehead. Shaka had arranged a corporate cab for him, and this was waiting when he exited from the revolving doors. He bowed his head and made haste to the curb, as though he were fighting against a cold, biting wind. The armed guards surrounding the perimeter again looked at him suspiciously, but he was far beyond them...

When he reached the cab, he threw his suitcases on the back seat and flung himself in after them. The driver was an obese Pacific Islander of middle age, in a dark suit that was too tight for his girth. The man looked back at G.W. uneasily, saying something that was lost in all the noise from the crowd. At first G.W. tried to understand, but facing the back seat of the cab there was another small TV screen; and at the sight of one of Dr. Mansmann's ubiquitous commercials, G.W. looked up at the man and groaned:

"Can't you turn that off?"

"Sorry, sir," the man said with a heavy accent, going on to explain that he did not have control over the screen.

G.W. groaned and told the man to take him to the airport. But even as he said it, and the cabbie started down the driveway, G.W. could not even conceptualize his going on another trip. Remembering his wife, he got out his mobile phone...but he did not even get the answering machine: the phone just rang. It rang 15 times. He hung up and called again...but there was no answer; and from deep inside, he began to wonder if he was even married: if that woman in his dreams was even real. It seemed as unlikely as everything else in the world. Remembering that he had her picture in his wallet, he got it out and stared at it vaguely for a while....

Africa...What the hell was in Africa? He did not even know what country he was going to. He felt ashamed that he had not asked: that he had been so cowed by Shaka that he had not tried to speak up for himself. And the things Shaka had said...! They left him even more convinced that something was very wrong. It all re-conjured the sick fantasy cum delusion cum obsession that he was in a post-dark pyramid world, dreaming it all. All the clichés seemed to be congealing: Shaka and the mysterious board—the power-obsessed industrial magnates, secretly bent on world domination; the crumbling, post-modern world, teetering on the verge of self-destruction. It would all be perfect if G.W. were a spy: some courageous freedom fighter—but he was a coward. He had never been so terrified in his life…and he remembered his strange murderous impulses. It was not only that he was a coward, but some kind of soulless monster—some automaton that had been programmed to kill. What had Shaka said about souls? "One didn't have to *buy* souls anymore—they were out rotting in the fields, and even the Devil couldn't be bothered to buy…" That G.W. had sold his soul was clear, but for *what*, was the question. He still had no idea what Shaka wanted from him. But that the man *did* want something (and had a project gestating in the back of his mind) was clear. The vital question was how he, of all people, could possibly fit into one of Shaka's plans. Indeed, for him to believe that the board needed him for something, he had to believe that he was special: that he had something that they could not get anywhere else…unless Shaka had picked him at random…to be some kind of fall guy: a scapegoat—*but for what*? to murder the President…? Who knew what The Company was willing to do? The gun was still in his holster…He *knew* he did not have a gun. He *knew* it! All of this had to be a…he did not even know what it could be…He shook his head in frustration. All questions led out to a no-man's-land; all efforts to use his mind to come to some kind of conclusion about what was happening to him only left him more confused and frustrated. And the realization of how ridiculous his conjectures ultimately were, only added to the feeling that it was all some farfetched, virtual reality fantasy. The only proof he had that he was not mad, was the gun. He had to keep reminding himself that it was not his: that it had been planted on him somehow. He kept repeating this in his mind until it occurred to him that he was conjuring madness itself….

When G.W. looked up at the TV, he realized that Mansmann's commercial had ended; but across the screen, flashed the usual litany of nonsense: the latest celebrity gossip…the latest news reports (filled with the same things they had been talking about yesterday, only with new criminals and lunatics)…And they were talking about that 10-year-old girl again. There were details, but dazed from everything that had happened, all G.W could do was stare at the fine contours of the girl's face. There was something magical in her eyes; and for whatever reason, G.W. felt himself relaxing. Even when the report ended, G.W. stared into the screen, thinking of the strange perfection of her. But these were not really thoughts, as feelings; and in a matter of time, he yawned and looked out of the window, having already forgotten about the girl.

As the cab drove along the city streets, he looked up at the brooding, Syntheline-polluted sky, and then the world of chaos below, in which people were going about their lives. Still desperate to make sense of things, he stared out on those people as though their existence might hold some clue to his own, but he did not feel like one of them anymore—if he ever had. In fact, it had been a while since he had felt like one of them. Shaking his head, he again tried to conjure the image of his family—of his wife and their unborn son. However, with the strangeness of time over the past few weeks, he felt as though it had been *years* since he had been home; and with this new, last-second trip, it seemed as though it would be years again before he saw them once more. He felt like a character in a Greek epic novel, compelled by the gods to be away from his home for decades—forced to battle monsters and outwit the evil and the powerful before providence would allow him to return to his family. He could not help thinking that he would return home to find it changed: as suspect as everything else in the world….

He rubbed his temples to soothe his deepening headache—but that was as ineffectual as everything else. With all the rush hour traffic, the cab ground to a halt the moment they entered the F.D.R. Drive. They were on the eastern side of Manhattan; and to his left, was the Manhattan skyline, lost in all the smog and pollution. To his right, were the East River and, beyond that, Queens. It all seemed so very ugly to him now…He needed rest badly—*he kept coming back to that thought!*—but like a soldier trapped behind enemy lines, he could not let his guard down.

Desperate to distract his mind, he looked down at the screen again, where an emergency report had come on. Some kind of bomb had gone off in

India. There was a correspondent on the site—in the middle of the chaos. The scene had a backdrop that seemed like hell, with flaming buildings and red skies. Remembering the board meeting, and the conversation on nuclear war, G.W.'s stomach convulsed—

"Fire's raining from the skies of New Delhi!" the correspondent screamed, coughing as she did so. And then the correspondent was describing how the thing had just lit up the entire sky. It did not exactly seem to be a nuclear bomb, but the aftermath was the stuff of nightmares. Camera crews were capturing the devastation. However, the reality of hundreds of thousands of deaths—perhaps millions (*tens of millions*) by the time it was said and done—could not really reach G.W. by now. There would of course be retaliation by India; and in the course of time, maybe Beijing would be nuked...China would retaliate...and the clouds of radiation would fly around the world, killing them all. G.W. sat there numbly, watching the scenes of hell on earth...but he did not really *see* them. By that time, all he could think about was Shaka saying, "Comatose world..."

The Devil tricks men not by granting them grand wishes,
but by satisfying their simplest desires.
VERSE 322:4 OF *The Teachings*

T hree hours after G.W. left Shaka's presence, he was in the air, headed
to a destination that was as unreal as everything else. Two of Shaka's
dark-suited guards had been waiting in the jet when he got there;
they disappeared into the cockpit with the pilot and co-pilot, leaving G.W.
alone in the posh cabin that was made out to look like an elegant office. He
sat alone in the silence, staring ahead blankly....

"A sensitive matter in Africa," Shaka had said....There was a briefing in a
sealed envelope lying on the desk before him. The wary feeling in his gut
intensified as the plane went supersonic. He thought about his wife again...
The throbbing in his head seemed to be passing another threshold of pain...
he rubbed his temples....

He opened the envelope, pulling at a string that made the entire thing
come apart with disconcerting ease. It was a full-sized sheet of white paper
with two sentences printed in the dead center:

Handle this situation any way you please.
Everyone has been instructed to follow your orders.

G.W. read the lines over and over again; then, confounded by it all, and
feeling the throbbing intensifying, he pushed the note aside and sat back in
the seat, closing his eyes.

He awoke an indefinite period later, with a sore neck and back—on top of his throbbing headache. As always, he was surprised that he had fallen asleep. The fleeting dream images and feelings of doom were there as well, but he was now more annoyed by them than alarmed. Looking up in the dimly lit cabin, he cringed at the sight of the nervous-looking man hovering over him—whom, more by his uniform than anything else, G.W. realized was the pilot. Over the man's shoulders were a short white man in his mid-thirties (whom G.W. remembered to be the co-pilot) and the two burly, dark-suited guards.

"We've arrived, sir," the pilot announced, looking nervously over his shoulder at the two guards. There was something unwholesome about the man's face, which seemed to speak of irreconcilable hardships. The pilot was a slim man of middle age, but the skin on his face sagged unnaturally, with jowls that made him seem like a bloodhound. Also, his eyes were red and lachrymose, like those of an old drunk.

G.W. sat up straighter in the chair, groaning as he did so. "Arrived *where*?"

"Angola, sir," the pilot announced.

"Angola!" And he thought to himself: *What the hell is in Angola?* There was a sharp pain in his forehead, and he rubbed his temples to soothe the pain....It was dawn outside. G.W. got up with great effort; and, as the two pilots obsequiously made way for him, he went to the window and bent down in order to look out. It was peaceful outside—wondrous in fact. A dense wall of jungle was before him; but between the trunks and leaves, he saw rays of the morning sun, which reflected off the dew and highlighted the dwindling patches of fog near the ground in pastel-like oranges and yellows. G.W. stared at it all for a while, aware that he should find it beautiful and peaceful—but that he could not quite achieve those states of mind. He was, in a sense, impotent....

"Why are we here?" he said, still facing the window.

"Don't you know?" the pilot said uneasily; and then, glancing hopelessly at the equally bewildered co-pilot, "They said you'd take care of everything."

G.W. straightened and faced the others, feeling light-headed from this simple effort. "Take care of *what*?"

"I've only been instructed to take you, sir," the pilot went on, while the co-pilot remained at his heels, looking on with a combination of curiosity and wariness. And then, as though to push things along: "The helicopter's waiting, sir."

"*Helicopter?*" G.W. said to himself. For some reason, the thought of further entanglements left him with the urge to sit down and rest again—

"Would you like breakfast first, sir?" This was the co-pilot.

"No…" And then, shaking his head distractedly, "—just tell me what this is all about."

The pilot swallowed deeply. "I've only been instructed to take you, sir."

"Take me *where?*"

"The village, sir."

"*What* village?"

"The village we've been ordered to take you to, sir—"

"Goddamnit!" G.W. screamed. [The terrified pilots jumped back!] "And stop calling me 'sir!'" he snapped for a reason that even he did not seem to know. Here he was, in the middle of the jungle, playing 20 questions with these fools. He felt as though he had totally lost control over the goings on of his life: that the outside world was simply something that kept acting upon him, shaping him in ways that he could not control. He rubbed his temples again, closing his eyes and inhaling deeply as he did so. When he opened his eyes, the pilots were still looking at him with the same terrified expressions. G.W. took another deep breath and repeated:

"*What* village?"

"That's all I can say," the man pleaded, again looking nervously at the guards. Just like before, G.W. was overcome by the impulse to scream at the man; but it was then that he realized that the terror in the pilot's eyes was not so much directed towards him, as the *guards*. *What the hell is going on here?* he wondered. The guards were huge men, with taut, elongated faces that reminded him of goats—including the eyes; and as they stared ahead with those godforsaken blank eyes, G.W. looked away, suddenly feeling uneasy.

"…Why all the secrecy?" he said at last.

"Shaka's orders, sir—*Mr. Wang*!" the pilot corrected himself quickly. "I'm supposed to bring you there, then you decide what happens, Mr. Wang, sir."

When the man realized that he had used "sir" again, he cringed, but G.W. put up his hand to signify that it did not matter. The pilot nodded nervously and went to open the door.

"Look," G.W. said at the door, "I'm sorry about yelling at you—I guess I got up on the wrong side of the chair this morning." He had tried to joke, but the pilot only nodded nervously. G.W. thought about calling his wife for a moment, but he suddenly could not see the use....

The outside world was warm and fragrant. As the sky was lit up in the pastel hues of dawn, the far-off cries of birds, and the sound of the wind gently rustling the leaves, made it all seem idyllic. The airport runway was a relatively short and narrow strip of asphalt, no more than 400 meters long, in the middle of the jungle. With its coating of nighttime condensation, the asphalt glimmered with the first rays of the day.

The only edifice seemed to be a shack directly across from them, which seemed to be too small to hold anything of consequence. The helicopter was perpendicular to the shack and the plane; and as the helicopter stood on its patch of gravel, it looked like a black vulture. As for the rest of the airport, there was nothing else: no refueling trucks, no control tower—nor did there seem to be an outside road. G.W. sighed to himself, thinking: *Why do I get the feeling that I won't find this airport on any map?*

The pilot was still looking back at him uneasily. G.W. felt the urge to reassure him, but then he again realized that the man's fears were not so much because of him, as the guards, who had positioned themselves just outside the doorway of the plane. G.W. was still in his suit, which was now a rumpled, smelly mess. With the heat, he wanted to take off the jacket, but he remembered the gun. He looked surreptitiously under his jacket and saw that the holster and gun were still there. This reassured him somehow.

The pilot gestured for G.W. to follow him over to the shack. G.W. felt faint as he walked. He needed to eat something, but this realization was not the result of a pang of hunger, but the recollection that people were supposed to eat. How long had it been since he had eaten? Days...and he had lost more weight. Feeling his chest, it occurred to him that his tits, as he had called the flabby protrusions on his chest, were gone now—completely. There was not even any loose skin. He could actually feel the muscle under the skin; and, beyond this thin layer, the bone.

The pilot opened the shack; inside, there were about half a dozen rubber suits, replete with headgear and breathing apparatus. They were the type of suits used in biological outbreaks, and when the nervous man handed one to G.W., he stared at the thing in horror!

Fifteen minutes later, G.W. and the pilot took off in the helicopter, leaving the others with the plane. Objectively speaking, the view was spectacular: unbroken jungle for as far as the eye could see, with the sun rising above it all and lighting the sky in brilliant hues of yellow and red. For the first time, it hit him that he was actually in Africa—in the middle of the jungle. But this was a global world, where one could be anywhere in 12 hours, no matter how remote. It was another of man's apparent victories over physical space and time. He would have been buoyed by the thought were it not for the strangeness of everything that was happening, and the obvious distress of the pilot. Added to all this was the reality that something had happened that required them to wear these suits.

G.W. was sitting up front, with the pilot, and the man kept looking at him uneasily. The suit had an unwholesome chemical smell, which was worse because he was now hermetically sealed in the thing. He tried not to think about it—*any* of it. The sun was to their right, which meant that they were traveling in a northerly direction. G.W. filed that away with all the other useless information....

They flew for perhaps 20 minutes. The pilot was about three-quarters of the way into his descent before G.W. realized that there was a village in the clearing below. The clearing was so narrow that if one had not known that the village was there, it probably would not have been seen. The landing was a bumpy one; when G.W. looked over, he realized that the pilot's hands were shaking. After they landed, they both just sat in the cockpit. The pilot did not even look over at G.W. anymore: he just sat there, as though implying that his job had been done and that the rest was now up to G.W.

G.W. was trying to come to grips with the obligatory confusion and uneasiness when he looked through the windshield and discerned, through the swirling clouds of dust, the dozens of unmoving forms on the ground. It was the fact that these forms seemed to be clothed that first got his attention. The unsettling feeling in G.W.'s gut intensified tenfold. He looked at the pilot, who glanced at him anxiously...and there was something unnerving about the way the clothes fluttered in the upheaval caused by the helicopter. Before his mind allowed him to admit what the forms on the ground were, he felt it within himself, and numbly exited the helicopter. Taking a few steps, G.W. saw the closest unmoving form for what it was: a maggoty lump of flesh—actually, a mother holding her child. He recoiled, taking a few clumsy steps back. Then, all at once, it seemed as though there were huge swarms of flies buzzing around him—notwithstanding the gust from the rotary wing. Dark clouds of flies were knocking into the mask of his suit: more flies than he had ever seen in his life! Just the sound of the thousands of tiny bodies colliding with his suit triggered some hysterical impulse in him to run and scream. His stomach churned as the full extent of it hit him. Perhaps a hundred clumps of flesh—*corpses*—lay rotting before him. His stomach convulsed violently and he doubled over; but as he had not eaten, all that there was, was bile. It reached about halfway up his throat, then retreated, burning the soft tissue. His stomach muscles ached; and they were still so tight that he could not stand up straight. Deciding to cut his losses, he kneeled down on one knee, again looking around at the 100 or so lumps of fly-infested flesh. Instinctively, he held his breath—even in the suit.

He looked up to see a man coming from one of the larger huts—also clad in a hermetically sealed suit. G.W. tried to stand; actually, he tried to flee, but realized that he did not have the strength. It was a middle-aged white man who looked at G.W. with the same imploring look as the pilot (who, by the way, had yet to leave the helicopter, or turn it off).

The white man helped G.W. up, then they stumbled over to the hut. G.W. was beyond numb—and sick. A Mozart concerto was playing on the stereo system inside the hut. However, the light, playful music was strangely unsettling. Inside the suit, the music had an airy, hollow quality that would always be linked with death in his mind. Also in the hut, there were desk computers, an examination table, a counter replete with microscopes, test tubes, Bunsen burners...*a dizzying array of equipment*...a huge refrigerator, a cabinet, a bed and a pair of chairs (both made out of bamboo); and of course, the stereo system. The man helped G.W. into a chair, but stood above him, still looking at him with the subservience of the pilots.

"You'll get used to it," the man said then, laughing nervously as he did so. He had an accent, which G.W. guessed to be of Eastern European origin. G.W. looked up at him—*stared* at him—but the man's words hardly even registered in his mind. Perhaps a minute passed. G.W. looked around the hut a couple more times before his gaze returned to the anxious face of the man. He suddenly realized that the man was waiting for him to speak, as if the things he had to say would make everything right.

G.W. tentatively opened his mouth, perhaps only to test his voice; but as his throat had been burned by bile and gastric juices, the first words were guttural and hoarse. He cleared his throat, willing his stomach to be still. "...What the hell happened?" he managed to say at last.

"—I was just following orders," the man said defensively.

"The Company's?"

"Yes," he said, nodding eagerly. "I didn't know this was going to happen," the man went on, his voice suddenly getting a hysterical edge. "All I did was administer the stuff and keep records—*they* sent it to me!"

G.W. again stared for a long while: "*Who* sent *what*?"

"...The Company...they send the latest samples to me, and I give it to the people..."

G.W. blinked drowsily, letting the words infect their meaning into him; then: "These people were *guinea pigs*? An entire village?"

The man twitched nervously. "Look, I didn't know, okay," he said again, the hysterical edge again entering his voice. Then, as if to speed things along, he ventured, "What do you want me to do, sir?"

"*Me*?" G.W. peeped. But it was all beginning to hit him now. Here he was, in the middle of the jungle, surrounded by dozens of murdered Africans...

innocent people destroyed by The Company with a kind of impunity that was beyond dehumanization...and he, G.W. Wang, was somehow presumed to have the power to make things right. He trembled with the burden of the thing: the weight of lost lives and souls—including his own.

"—They said that you'd take care of everything," the man whined. "Look," he went on, now twitching involuntarily every few words, "I just want to get out of here. Tell them I won't tell anyone. I just want to get out of here! I can keep my mouth shut!"

Watching the depths of the man's desperation was so unsettling that G.W. looked away. He tried to stand up, so that he could walk away (put distance between himself and the man's desperate, searching eyes) but the moment he was to his feet, his stomach convulsed and the bile made it all the way up to his mouth. He swallowed it back down (with the hermetically sealed mask, there was nowhere else for it to go) then he sank back into the bamboo chair. He was sweating in the suit, and the smell of his sweat, along with the chemical odor of the suit—and the bile in his mouth...he tried not to think about it. The man was still standing over him, staring with those imploring eyes.

"What are we going to do, sir?" the man repeated.

G.W. again had an urge to scream, *Don't call me, sir*! However, drained, he just sat back, staring into the dark corner of the hut. The Company was responsible for *mass murder*! Still, perhaps even then the horror of it was dulled by everything that had happened over the past few weeks. In fact, with the Asian war going strong, they all witnessed mass murder every day. He remembered the scene from the TV in the cab: the Indian sky lit up with the fires of hell. In the face of all that, what could the murder of a few dozen people possibly mean to him now—especially in a far-off African village? He looked towards the hemp cloth that was over the opening of the hut, trying to re-conjure the image—the *reality*—of a hundred dead people being devoured by maggots....

G.W. looked up at the man at last. A side of him wanted to yell for the man to sit down—to stop hovering over him—but he again could not see the use. His voice was low as he said: "When did all this happen?"

"Five days ago, sir."

"*Five days*!" he said in disbelief. "How long has this operation been going on?"

"Years, sir."

Years! he thought to himself, not exactly with disbelief—for that blessing was quickly being lost to him—but numbness. "...What's the purpose of all this?"

"Sir?"

"The drugs: what were they supposed to do?"

"I don't know, sir."

"How can you *not* know?"

"They just send the doses: I administer them and make reports."

For some sick reason, G.W. began to laugh a low, hollow kind of laughter that actually hurt his chest. Nobody knew anything, except that he should follow orders and the chain of command: it was the perfect bureaucracy. G.W. had been given the power to settle everything, and he knew even less than his supposed subordinates! In fact, the only people who probably knew everything were Shaka and the board. G.W. could not help admiring the efficiency of it. With enough planning and indoctrination, people could be organized to do anything: kill themselves, kill one another...*anything*... and nobody would complain, as long as he followed orders and was compensated for doing so. How many massacres and wars attested to this sickening human trait? The man now standing before G.W. had killed a hundred people, and yet he was as distanced from the decision as a night janitor in The Company's Singapore office. The man, whose name G.W. realized he had not asked—and would not—was now staring at him anxiously, especially in the wake of the strange laughter. *The poor fool*, G.W. thought to himself. The man had been sitting around for five days and nights, sur-rounded by rotting corpses and pangs of guilt....

Acutely sober, G.W. nodded to himself, perhaps acknowledging his new emptiness. Shaka had given him the power: not over life and death, but over the illusions that overhung them both. Shaka had purchased not so much a village of guinea pigs, as a village of walking, talking corpses, whom had long ceased to exist to the rest of the world. Then again, maybe this was just G.W.'s new emptiness—new *soullessness*—talking: his way of rationalizing what he was about to do. He now looked up at the European with a blank, drained expression:

"Why do I suspect there's some kind of self-destruct device in this village?"

The man nodded, then walked over to the cabinet in the corner of the room. G.W. followed, having to stoop because of his sore, tight stomach muscles. Inside the cabinet, there was an impressive-looking piece of equipment, with a complicated console and flashing lights. The man looked back at G.W. with the same nervous quickness:

"It's activated by palm print, sir…I don't have access."

G.W. went to place his hand on the sensor, but then realized that he was wearing the suit. "The thing that killed these people," he began, "—will it infect me?"

"I don't think so, sir. I'm only wearing the suit because of the smell."

"But you're not sure?"

"No, sir."

Numb again, G.W. unzipped the glove on his right hand and pressed his sweaty palm against the sensor. Instantaneously, the machine came to life. A computer voice came on, stating that the self-destruct option had been selected and asking how much time they wished to have. The cold efficiency of it made G.W. smile the same sick smile. But, at the same time, his inner panic increased exponentially, because it told him that he had been pulled deeper into this thing than he ever could have guessed. This operation— this village of guinea pigs—had been going on for years, while G.W. had only been Shaka's assistant for a month; and yet, in that month The Company had given G.W. access to a self-destruct device in a far off village. If the device could be controlled by remote control, which was more than likely, then why had they not set it off themselves? For that matter, why had they not given the European man access to the device? None of it made sense, unless the purpose of all this was to get G.W. to come here and take part in it. It was like he was being slowly indoctrinated into something. It was one of those logical leaps that came often to the paranoid—and yet he could not deny the *logic* of it. Just a day ago, just back from his "Pony Express" trip to Asia, he had thought that he was being nurtured as a kind of scapegoat in The Company; beset by murderous impulses, he had thought himself some kind of homicidal maniac in the making. If he set off this self-destruct device and incinerated evidence of mass murder, then he would be committing a criminal act every bit as evil as The Company's. This was the moment of no return for his soul; however, before he even acknowledged that he had made a decision, he looked at the European man, saying, "Do you have notes or anything else you need to get out?"

"No, sir. Everything is sent back to The Company via satellite."

G.W. nodded numbly. He placed his palm on the sensor once more, then requested 15 minutes....As he and the man walked outside, G.W. felt drained beyond reason. Seeing the lumps of festering flesh around him, his stomach convulsed again, but he hardly noticed. He spit the bile to the side of the mask, so that it oozed down the glass and his cheek. The man followed nervously behind him, like a dog afraid of losing its master. As soon as they were in the helicopter, the pilot took off; a few minutes later, there was a thunderous explosion, and the sky lit up as if it had two suns. The helicopter wobbled from the blast, but they were flying away from it all, and none of them even flinched.

Pleasure and pain are only sides of the same coin; but nothingness—
freedom from the arbitrary dictates of the body—is bliss.
VERSE 753:5 OF *The Teachings*

S trangely enough, the only thought that passed through G.W.'s mind was
that he was a good employee: that he had completed his job successfully,
and that Shaka would be pleased. Maybe a month ago, freshly promoted
in The Company, and idealistic about life and the future, he would have felt
something, but the man who would have been *sickened* by it was dead. True,
there had been initial surprise, perhaps—even disgust at the sight of the
rotting corpses…And it was not even that he was blocking it out: the images
were all fresh and vivid in his mind. It was the world, itself, and his existence, that seemed faded and dreamlike. As he remembered how he had
taken off the glove to operate the machine, he was acutely aware that his
life meant nothing to him. Maybe he had been infected with whatever had
killed those people; maybe he would go back to infect the world with some
horrible disease. What difference could it really mean? He was free in a
way that was utterly horrible, because, on some level, he did not care if he
lived or died. More to the point, he was beginning to accept the inevitability
of his own death. He was beginning to see his death not as an impending
horror, but as a loophole out of all he had seen and felt.

As for the corpses now being turned to ashes, they were nothing but people
who had never really existed. Now that they had been incinerated, their
nonexistence had simply been continued. And those exact arguments/ excuses
could be made for the people dying in Asia—and the world's failure to do

anything about it. Their entire society seemed to be in the process of killing dead, nonexistent things....

As the helicopter began its descent into the airport, the strange feeling in G.W.'s gut intensified. There was no going back now. The sight of the plane—the conduit back to so-called civilization—began to put everything in perspective: his life, his family, his soul…all the things that were lost. He was like a soldier that had gone into a foreign country and committed war crimes. A side of him did not want to go back home and face the loved ones that would neither understand nor accept the monster he had become....

The two goat-faced guards were still waiting outside the plane. G.W. was the first to get out of the helicopter. He practically tore off the suit. If he had been contaminated or not he could not really care anymore. It was good to breathe real air again—as opposed to the filtered, musty gas of the suit. The pilot and the European followed his lead and began taking off their suits as well. It was while this was going on that the two guards strolled over.

"You two," one of the goat-faced guards started, addressing the pilot and European in a tone that was at once menacing and indifferent, "—you have to wait here."

"What! We did everything you asked!" This was the pilot.

"Other arrangements have been made for your transportation—you'll have to wait." This was the other guard.

"But we won't tell anyone!" This was the European. He was looking back imploringly at G.W., as if for corroboration. G.W. looked away.

"We'll leave you some food," the guard continued with the same indifference. "You shouldn't have to wait too long."

The pilot and the European again looked at G.W. imploringly, but he only walked past them—back towards the plane. Of course, they were as good as dead. Maybe the food had been poisoned…more likely than not, they would never be picked up and would be left to starve and die in the jungle. Maybe authorities would come to investigate the explosion; but even if the men were picked up, they would probably only be blamed for the fire—which would rage for some time yet. By now, there would be no record of the men in The Company. All that the authorities would see was a fire, a helicopter, an airport…As he walked back to the plane, it occurred to G.W. that the airport would probably explode once they were in the air, so that none of it would ever have existed. He saw all this in a matter of seconds and accepted it, because he realized that he was also as good as dead. The co-pilot and the guards were only allowed to survive because they had seen nothing directly; G.W. would be allowed to survive for a while in order to...but that was the thing: the *why*? Why had he even made it this far? Maybe the plane would just explode in the air as well—

"*No!*" someone screamed. G.W. looked back to see the European fighting with the guards, which was to say that the man was trying to struggle and the guards were holding him with minimal effort.

"I won't let you do this!" the man was screaming now. In the meanwhile, the pilot was looking on indecisively. Finally coming to the conclusion that it was now or never, he threw himself at one of the guards, who caught him by the neck in mid air and threw him to the ground like a rag doll. The next thing G.W. knew, the guards had guns out; and after two reports of those guns, the pilot and the European were dead: both from gunshots to their foreheads.

The guards left the bodies where they were and started walking calmly towards G.W. During the guards' scuffle with the two men, G.W. had only looked on indifferently; but now, with the horrible echo of those guns rising in the air (and the sight, not only of the two men falling lifelessly to the ground, but also the menacing approach of the guards) G.W. felt something being triggered within him. The echo of the guns was opening him up to sensations that were so primal and immediate that the outside world ceased to exist for those few moments. It was as though a dormant instinct had been released, finally allowing his true self to awaken. His new instincts encompassed him totally, so that the effect was as disorienting as falling off an unexpected cliff. He plummeted over the edge, his stomach feeling as though it were forcing its way up his throat; he felt dizzy and sick, so that he could no longer even tell what was going on around him. All noises became slurred; everything became warped, as though he were moving faster than time itself. Still, even out of step with time and space, he could sense the menacing approach of the two guards; and as his newfound instincts reached their fruition, he grabbed his gun and, pointing it in the direction of the approaching guards (for he was still too disoriented to see), he emptied out half the gun's clip....There was something cathartic about pulling the trigger...but the disorientation only deepened as he surrendered his soul to the act. He could no longer even tell which way was up. And whereas the world had before been warped, it now became an inscrutable wall of darkness. He was careening though a void now, with nothing before him but the blackness of the abyss, and nothing to sustain him but the blind, self-destructive impulses that his newfound instincts conjured—

But then, out of the nothingness, there was a flash of light. For an instant, the world was illuminated—but the flash of light was too bright and momentary to allow him to see clearly. It was like an editing mistake in a movie—a scene placed horribly out of context...and then he was back in the darkness once more—again careening wildly, again nauseated from his fall through the abyss...and then the scene was back again—still too bright and confusing...but as the scene lingered a little longer this time, his body and mind were able to embed themselves in its reality. His eyes adjusted to the light; he realized that he was no longer careening through the void, and that there was solid ground beneath his feet...but he still felt strange— *displaced*. He felt as though he had not simply landed on solid ground again, but that he had crashed into it—been *splattered*. The abrupt change—from a dark void to a bright, tangible world—was like the bends in a diver emerging too quickly from the depths. His head throbbed, as though it had been split open; just the act of seeing—of trying to discern what was about him—was painful, as though his optic nerve had sustained damage. His body drooped and swayed as he stood there trying to make sense of the world...and shapes were beginning to come into focus now. He realized that there were walls around him—that he was somehow in a building. His eyes darted around wildly as the blurred shapes around him took on forms that brought both recognition and horror. And he realized that there was an eerie, resounding cry in the air. It was the same thing he had heard when awakening in the cab—a sound like the cries of a million madmen—except that it had been intensified somehow. On top of that, something else seemed to be in the air, causing reverberations not only though the space around him, but *reality*. Some force was rewriting time and space, itself—

the same thing that had brought him here…And something was moving in the room around him—a white blur on the ground which G.W. in time realized was a body! And there were more bodies before him on the ground! As the world continued to focus, he realized, with a jarring jolt to his system, that he was back at The Company somehow! He was in the lobby area of Shaka's penthouse; and looking down, he saw that what had at first appeared as a white blur was actually the white-suited Shaka! The man was writhing in pain…and there were five other bodies…but these lay still, in positions that brought to mind the fly-infested lumps of flesh back in Africa, as they were obviously dead. G.W.'s mind seemed to groan under the weight of all that was around him…and there was blood everywhere—*pools* of it. The front of Shaka's heretofore-immaculate white suit was bathed in it!

At that moment, while his mind was still struggling with the reality of what was before him, he looked at the other bodies, making out first the dark-suited guards from Africa, then, with more horror, *the President and her Secret Service bodyguards*! Still, even then, he did not grasp the full extent of what was before him until he looked down and noticed the handgun that he still held in his trembling hand. The echo that had been in the air was the lingering report of his gun—combined with the cries of his victims. He looked up slowly from the still-smoking gun, his jaw dropping…but Shaka's continued movement caught his attention…And there was something horrible about watching Shaka die. There was something inherently filthy and degrading about death—especially murder. However, in Shaka's case, it also seemed sacrilegious, as the man had been one of their gods. Frothy blood was now issuing from the man's mouth; his eyes were glossed over with a kind of pain that G.W. could not even conceptualize. They stared at one another for a while, but the reality of the terror in the man's eyes seemed to destabilize all reality. G.W. took a step back—was forced to retreat somehow from the realization of all that lay before him—*and of what he had done*! He looked at the gun again…and there was the President…and there was Shaka. He looked around in this panicked state and noticed the surveillance camera in the corner of the room, near the ceiling! Somewhere, a guard was watching all this; somewhere, an alarm had been activated, alerting armed guards, who would descend upon him with deadly force—

It was then that the elevator door opened with a loud, off-tune ding. Four guards ran out with their guns drawn. G.W. was lost—*trapped*! His doom was so complete that he wanted to cry. But then, while his mind was sputtering along, it came upon the last retreat of the helpless—the possibility that he was dreaming. It was the only thing that made sense; and if this was some nightmare, from which he would eventually awaken, then none of it—none of what he had done and nothing that he *would* do—could matter anyway. With this mindset, he squeezed the trigger twice, almost confounded when the first two guards dropped to the ground. G.W. stood there trembling as he thought, *So this is how it feels to kill someone*! The feeling was like being drunk: like saying to hell with everything. He felt enlivened—*emancipated*—but not so much by the murder, as by the recurring thought that there would be no consequences: that he could do anything and he would never have to pay.

It was while these thoughts were flying through his mind that one of the guards managed to get off a shot at him. It grazed his skull and he collapsed to the ground. Still, as he was falling, he squeezed the trigger again, shooting the guard in the chest. G.W. was amazed by the accuracy of his shots—the efficiency with which he killed. There was only one guard left, and he ducked back into the elevator as G.W. took aim. With the adrenaline pumping though G.W.'s veins, he leaped to his feet and bounded over to the fire stairway—which was in the opposite direction from the elevator and the final guard. As G.W. retreated, the final guard emerged from the elevator and took some shots at him....The blood from G.W.'s head wound was streaming down his face now; some of it went into his mouth and he tasted the slightly acrid fluid that had been in his veins just seconds before.

When G.W. opened the fire door and entered the stairway, an alarm went off. Orange emergency lights began flashing, making everything seem even more unreal. The door slammed behind him: the echoing noise was terrifying. Feeling slightly giddy, he stumbled into the railing, looking down the shaft at the crisscrossing stairs, going down and down. It made him giddy and sick; and as the stairs seemed to fade into eternity, an inkling of the task ahead of him made his resolve waver. For the first time, he thought about how he would get away—the impossibility of making it down 150 stories…but the thought of his SUV was like a beacon somehow. The idea of it parked in the garage was like a godsend to him—a fantasy that was irresistible—

It was at that moment that the fire door, which was at his back, burst open and the final guard flew out. G.W. instinctively whirled and punched the man in the jaw with his left hand; but as he was holding the gun, and therefore unable to make a real fist, he fractured his hand along with the man's jaw. Of course, with the adrenaline pumping though his system, he hardly even felt it. At the blow, the guard was thrown against the wall. The man screamed out in agony and held his eye, which had been ruptured by the barrel of the gun. G.W. did not know where he got the strength or the will, but somehow, he grabbed the guard and flipped him over the railing, so that the man fell down the shaft of stairs. The man's head hit a railing about three flights down, then another, until, about six flights down, his body came to rest in the stairway, broken and still. G.W. stood there numbly. He was never going to get away. He had killed the President! …And Shaka! …And the surveillance cameras had no doubt captured it all! There were dozens of guards in the building—not to mention the *thousands* still outside. Not only was it unlikely that he would make it down this interminable staircase: if he got on the elevator, they would surely trap him. Yet, there was still a voice screaming for him to escape; another voice, of pure insanity, was screaming that this was all a dream and that he would never have to pay the consequences. In a sense, it no longer mattered if this was a dream or the real world: he just wanted it to end. Possible consequences, whether horrific or palliative, were too theoretical in nature to affect his actions— to *guide* him. He felt as though he were in the midst of a schizophrenic attack. One side of him wanted to leap headlong into the abyss and end this. It craved violence and confrontation; it urged him to put the barrel of the gun to his head and put an end to it all—or to aim that gun at others and spread death to the world. However, the other side of him yearned for life and was desperate to hold onto it at all costs. Maybe this side was stronger in him now, because he suddenly remembered that there was a rarely used freight elevator on the 130th floor. It was so secluded that his pursuers would probably overlook it. He could run down the stairs…but *damn* it, there were surveillance cameras in here! Looking up, he saw one in the corner. There was nowhere to run: nowhere to hide. No matter where he went, his pursuers would always know where he was and send guards to cut him off. And the siren was still pealing: still boring into his head.

Looking down, he realized that the guard had dropped his gun. G.W. grabbed the gun now, somehow emboldened by the additional weapon. *To hell with it*! he thought. Besides, if this was reality, then he was as good as dead anyway, so what difference could it make? He started running down the stairs, but blood was still trickling down his face from the gash on top of his head; and after two flights, it was clear that he would not make it down another 18. *To hell with it*! he thought again. He exited the fire door and entered the floor's reception area. There were only executive offices on this floor; and given the time of night—and the situation in Company Square—there was no receptionist. G.W. stumbled to the elevator and pressed the down button. Instantaneously, the door opened with a loud ding. G.W.'s innards churned: it had to be a trick! Still, *To hell with it all*! One way or another, sooner or later, they were going to corner him; and when they did, not only would they put him out of his misery: he would empty the clips of his guns into them, taking out the last of his frustrations on the world before he went. Moreover, if this were just an escalating dream—or some fantasy in some post dark pyramid world—then when he awoke, it would not matter anyway….

Nevertheless, an eerie feeling came over him when the elevator doors closed and he was in the confined space by himself, listening to the airy, formless music and looking at his vague reflection in the shiny metal. There was a keypad for him to type in the floor he wanted, but he suddenly realized that he could not remember where he had parked the SUV—or even *if* he had! He had no bearings…he recalled how a few minutes before he had been in Africa. There was no way to know what day this was. He even doubted his trip to Asia…he remembered his wife all at once…but none of that seemed real either. The only thing that he had was the fantasy of his SUV; and in his desperation, he willed it to be there, waiting for him in the parking garage like a faithful lover. *To hell with it*! he thought again.

He pressed an arbitrary sub level on the keypad and told himself that if his SUV was not there, then he would just steal a car.

All the way down, he kept expecting the elevator to stall and a voice to come over the intercom, telling him that he had been captured. Maybe some knockout gas would fill the elevator—like they did in spy movies. All kinds of far-fetched ideas flew through his mind. He stared at the passing floor numbers on the digital display (140, 139...85, 84...62, 61...), becoming more horrified with each passing floor. The reality was that the closer he got to his goal, the more devastating it would be when he was captured. Maybe they were only letting him run for a while (like a fish caught on a line), only to exhaust him and have him hauled in with minimal effort. G.W. stared at the digital display (43, 42...36, 35...), waiting for the door to burst open and a hail of bullets to come in. He kept the guns pointed nervously at the door...The blood was still trickling down his face—though at a slower pace. He got out the handkerchief in his breast pocket and pressed it in the groove in his skull—making sure to keep one gun trained on the door.

He was doing this when the elevator door opened with its usual, off-tune ding. At first he leapt back in horror, but then he saw that somehow or another, he had made it to the parking garage. *It was all too easy*! He felt sick at the realization. Were the guards just letting him run a little farther? That had to be it. They were laying a trap for him...And then, looking across the dark expanse of the chamber, he saw his SUV! It was too convenient! He was trembling from indecisiveness and weak from loss of blood when the elevator door began to close. He leapt out of the closing door and entered the dark, mostly-empty chamber. The silence of it was horrible; the sound of the protesters outside was far-off and haunting. He again wanted to scream, *To hell with it!* in order to jumpstart his courage—or *blindness*—but he could not see the use of it anymore. The guards were laying a trap for him: he was certain of it! That was the only thing that made sense; and for a moment, he found himself thinking that he would turn himself in, just to thwart their plans....

His steps echoed horribly as he loped across the empty expanse of the place. He kept looking around nervously, as if expecting someone to leap out of the shadows. He was almost to the SUV when he realized that he did not have the keys! For a moment this caused a small earthquake within him. Everything seemed so useless: he was going in circles—and had been for months, maybe *years* now. He was trembling and indecisive again. And looking at the SUV, it occurred to him that maybe they had installed a bomb in it. Maybe, as soon as he started it up, a bomb would be triggered, and he would be blown to bits—just like in the movies! But then, when he reached the vehicle, not only did he see that the keys were in the ignition, but when he instinctively tried the door, he saw that it was open! He stood there like a leaf in the wind. *It had to be a trap!*

—But to hell with it! He was as good as dead anyway, no matter what he did. Whether they killed him now, or in an explosion ten minutes from now—or ten years from now—it made no difference. Surrendering to this mindset, he turned the key in the ignition and listened—as if from a million miles away—as the engine of the beast roared to life. And then, he stamped on the accelerator, still a million miles away as the vehicle lurched through the darkness. And then, the two guards came out of the elevator and shot out the back window; and then old Ernie appeared and disappeared; and then, he was before those screaming hundreds of thousands; and then, he was running over the guards in the driveway, listening to all the screams and gun shots and the sickening thuds that came every time someone was crushed to death beneath his tank; and then, somehow, he was on the smoggy street, crashing into a cab and running over yet more people in the intersection; but always, he was a millions miles away, thinking things that hardly even registered in his mind.

He realized that he had been shot (again) but it could make no difference now. The police vehicles and helicopters would of course be coming soon: what could be more conspicuous than a bloodstained, severely dented, bullet-riddled SUV? He waited for this event with the same numbness as everything else, promising himself that he would not give up, but would instead have to be killed—dragged out of the vehicle lifeless and bloody. He was a suicidal man in a suicidal world, desperate beyond reason to be put out of his misery. These were his thoughts just before he hit that tractor and everything went black.

The more we attain, the less we have; the more we know,
the less we understand.
VERSE 3923:16 OF *The Teachings*

Agent Respoli burst into the Dimensional Portal with his gun drawn. He was sweating and panting; his shirt was rumpled and damp with sweat. The Portal was still set to the beach scene at sunset. There was a man's body to the side, but Respoli's eyes went to the woman relaxing in the warm, fragrant water. She smiled when she saw him; Respoli pointed the gun at her as he stood there panting, but she seemed unconcerned as she emerged from the water, still naked. Her beauty—the perfection of her body and her movements—confused him for some reason, and he lowered his gun. The water was now streaming down her slim, tanned body as she stepped out of the water; and as the sun's rays reflected off of her, she seemed to shimmer in the sunset. Respoli stared at her, mesmerized; and yet, it was not so much lust that was in his eyes, as the strange feeling of finding something that one had not known one was looking for—and which one had had no conceptualization of before this moment. She was now walking up to him confidently; years of training told him to point the gun at her again, but still mesmerized, he stood there with the gun at his side, disarmed in too many ways to name. She was still smiling at him.

"…What do you want from me?" he asked at last.

"I want what you want," she said, "—to understand the will of the Goddess."

"How do you know what I want?" he said in a petulant, childish manner.

"Because I've been watching you…I see it all in your eyes: you've been chasing after her, but not so much to capture her, but because of the deep yearning in your heart—your *soul*—"

The mawkishness of what she was saying made a side of him want to laugh, but there was a side of him that knew that she was right. He had already given up everything to be here. He was supposed to be out looking for the President's assassin now—

"You've seen everything she's done," the woman went on, "—how people react to her, and how you, yourself, react to her—and you know her power: want to become one with it."

"…This is madness," he whispered to himself. He shook his head, again noticing the man lying in the sand: "What did you do to him…?" And then, half-heartedly: "I should arrest you."

"But you won't," she said with the same confidence. "And you came alone because you wanted to talk to me."

He shook his head again, as if fighting off a dream: "…I have to take you in and have you interrogated."

She smiled at him. "We are far beyond the stage of questions and answers, Agent Respoli. There are things that can only be comprehended by the soul—that are beyond words and the capacity of people to explain themselves. Such things can only be understood by the sharing of souls."

Her body was still wet: he looked at it as if just realizing that she was naked. He again shook his head to focus himself: "…What's all this about?"

"I want you to help me find the Goddess."

"…You don't know where she is?" he said, fighting to understand.

"No, that's why I need you—and you need me."

"…This is madness," he whispered; once again, he glanced at the man lying in the sand.

The woman was still smiling at him. "Only finding the Goddess will bring you peace."

"I want to *capture* her," he protested, but he looked away as to not see her smile.

"Very well," she said. "I downloaded something from a dimension a few weeks ago, Agent Respoli—one of her last thoughts before she disappeared. She used to post them for us. I have to give it to you."

He looked uncertain. "Now?"

"Yes. Take off your shirt."

He hesitated for a moment, then he took it off, letting it slip to the sand. She nodded, and he took off his undershirt. Strangely enough, there was something natural about getting naked before her. There was madness to it, but there was madness to everything. Moreover, for once, he was tired of fighting....When he let his pants slip to his ankles, he felt somehow cleansed. She touched him then, first caressing the sensitive spot on his abdomen, so that he shuddered, then she caressed his chest and neck and shoulders. Only when she kissed him and he pulled her to him, did the scenes begin to take shape in him—or *around* him. He could not tell the difference anymore. Everything was thought...The images came slowly at first—a trickle of sensations—then there was an overpowering surge of insight and godlike power that made his knees buckle and left his body shuddering, even as he gripped the woman's body—

And the strange thing was that he was not only seeing the world as the 10-year-old was seeing it: everything was framed with a kind of TV consciousness, as though the perspective were an omniscient one. He was not only experiencing a girl's thoughts, he was experiencing thoughts attuned to the movement of the earth—of tides and gravitational fields...of sunrises and sunsets...And yet, it was strange to see the 10-year-old sitting alone in a cramped bedroom in the South Bronx, surrounded by dark walls with crumbling plaster and peeling paint—

She is checking out her Internet site before going to school. In the next room, she hears the TV going full blast, as it always is...Respoli can smell the dank air of the room...The girl's attention is on the sound of the TV in the next room: she recognizes the theme music of her mother's favorite show—a celebrity gossip extravaganza—so she knows that she won't be interrupted for at least an hour. With a few taps on the keyboard, the program is up and running...Respoli can feel the warmth of the keyboard; she scratches her shoulder, and he feels not only the itch, but the fingers scratching the flesh. And now she is entering the strange world of the chat room, where anonymity opens up the illusion of intimacy. She is having fun with the people there—the ones who think that she is God. They give her the attention of lovers; they ask her advice on the movement of the world—of wars and life and death. They are as far away as Nepal and Swaziland and a side of her laughs at them and the fact that they come to her Internet site to hear her words…When she happens to glance at the time, she realizes that she is already half an hour late for school. She sneaks out of her room, and through the living room, where her mother's huge, slug-like form is asleep on the special bed designed to hold its girth. The bed is in front of the television, and the grotesque creature, whose existence has always shamed the girl, is sprawled on it like a beached whale, snoring and drool-ing with her mouth wide open. The woman is so morbidly obese that she has been on disability for nine years, and cannot walk ten steps without having to stop for a breath.

But the woman—the Creature, as the girl calls her—is sleeping now, in the kind of quasi-comatose state that usually follows her breakfast of eggs, bacon and a loaf or two of bread. In fact, the evidence of this smorgasbord is clearly visible in the greasy folds of her double chin and on the shapeless, curtain-like gown, which is the only thing that can cover her. The woman was one of those teenage mothers who became pregnant because she wanted someone to love her unconditionally—a fantasy that died with labor pains. Postpartum depression seized her; then, within a year of giving birth to her daughter, she was so fat that her groceries had to be delivered and contact with the outside world was virtually cut off. The 10-year-old girl has never known her father; and in a sense, she has never known her mother either. As she stands there, she finds herself thinking that her mother was only there because she had no choice: she was unable to run away like her father. Her mother had had to carry her in her womb, whereas her father had had no physical connection, and therefore had the wherewithal to abandon her….

Staring down at the Creature in the cramped space of the living room, a kind of formless rage grows within her. It is not only rage against her mother's circumstances, but somehow the circumstances of billions across the world, who are forced to live as animals—forced to give up dreams and, worse yet, comply with their own lack of imagination. Just once, she wishes that she can dream for her mother—*for the world*...be that sacred vessel that those on the Internet think she is.

She looks around as if seeing the ugliness of the place for the first time; and in a world where nobody sees how poor she is anymore—in a world where there is always an extreme case of poverty somewhere else (in some other neighborhood, some other city, some other state, or country) that is so egregious that all one could do is shake one's head and thank God for one's deliverance...in such a world, she is acutely aware not only of her own poverty, but also a kind of formless, social poverty, somehow embodied in everything that revolts her about her mother. She watches the Creature's open-mouthed breathing, and listens to the inevitable snoring that is barely audible over the uproar of the television and the outside world, suddenly wishing that her mother were dead. It isn't so much hatred of her mother, as hatred of the world—and all its intricate cruelties. She looks at her mother the way one looks at a freshly mangled dog on the side of the road: the only humane thing to do is put it out of its misery. Her mother is on the fringes of existence anyway, seemingly beyond the basic abilities that make life worth living—

But just then, seeing the DreamVisor next to her mother's pillow, the girl feels an unsettling jolt go up her spine....As she stands there, her mind goes back to a few months ago, when she surreptitiously put on the DreamVisor, instantly finding herself being groped and licked and penetrated by a phantom lover. All those months ago, even though she knew that it was not real, she felt the ghost world tightening around her so completely and wonderfully that she fled, lest she not want to go back to the real world, with all its pain and disappointments.

In actuality, her episode with the DreamVisor had changed her, like experimentation with heroin changed the chemistry of the brain. Every day since then she fought to resist the cries of the addiction—while all around her, on street corners, in the homes of friends and relatives...and in

Dimensional Portals everywhere, everyone else surrendered to the dreams conjured by machines—and the easy, all-encompassing pleasure that required nothing but surrender.

Even now, as she stands looking at the DreamVisor, she is terrified of the freedom—the utter lack of boundaries that the devices open up. She knows that it is good and healthy to dream: to conjure worlds out of the nothingness. However, her experimentation with the device has left her keenly aware that she had dreamed through the eyes of something inhuman—had allowed it to reach those inner places of pleasure and contentment that only love and trust and a lifetime of human understanding—and *struggle*—should have been able to reach. Through the DreamVisors, the ultimate in pleasure has been bottled and mass-produced, so that the pleasure itself became a commodity: an artificial flavor that was cheaper and perhaps slightly tastier than the real thing....

All these things she sees—feels on a spiritual level that leaves her trembling and weak. And in that strange moment, she turns and looks at the television screen, on which a news brief has come on. Some war or another has broken out or been escalated. Mangled corpses are lying about in a village, quickly decomposing—both on the ground where they lie, and in the minds of those watching them on television. It is the kind of thing that everyone has grown tired of hearing and seeing; but for once, a feeling of wild defiance grows in her heart. Somehow, she will stop these things—not by being a naïve, idealistic crusader, but a revolutionary—an *anarchist* if necessary. On the behalf of all the people being obliterated by possibilities they will never be able to grasp, she will take revenge on the world.

The girl—the *Goddess*—leaves then. She runs out into the world, desperate to get away from all the things she cannot reconcile. She is halfway down the block when the thing happens, and she is knocked off her feet by the explosion. The wave of hot air washes over her (even Respoli coughs as the smoke envelops him; he quails from the heat and the sudden terror of not knowing what has happened)....Perhaps a minute or two passes as she lies there groggily. When she regains enough of her faculties, she looks up to see that part of her tenement has been blown away—and that that region is where her home used to be. Still, even after they pull her mother's charred body from the wreckage, the girl is not horrified; even after the woman is declared dead, the girl's only thought is that her mother has simply been put out of her misery—and that the world lies out there: a universe of people incapable of dreaming their own dreams—

The vision ended and Respoli gasped, as though he had been holding his breath all that time. He felt, somehow, *devastated*. He was slow to emerge back into consciousness—to regain possession of himself. For a long time, it was as though he had no body—as though he existed only as a fragmented consciousness. He not only had the feeling that his world were crumbling around him, but that he, himself, were crumbling from within: that he was *becoming* something else—achieving some state of perfection that had before been elusive. And he saw it all then: images of wars and murders and frenzied mobs…images of all the peoples of the world—none of whom were able to grasp the possibilities of the world they inhabited. He felt as though he were still looking through the 10-year-old girl's eyes—still feeling her revolutionary determination to save a world that had already flung itself off a precipice. He looked around groggily then. At first, he was simply relieved that he seemed to have limbs and a body again. He could move his head and digest what was around him. He nodded his head when he eventually recognized the same beach at sunset. After a few moments, he realized that he was still holding the woman; but when he looked at her face, he saw the same blank expression that was on Dimitri's face. It was then that he recognized her voice within him and realized that she had somehow transferred her soul into him—and that he was holding a husk of a human being in his arms. There was no feeling of shock at this— nor was there surprise. Now, as she had said before, they could speak without words: show one another things that no words could fully convey. After a few moments of this conversation, the path ahead seemed clear. He now got to his feet with the determination of the Goddess and the faith of the woman. He left the woman's body lying in the sand—it was irrelevant now. Then, after putting on his suit and picking up the bag with the portable Dimensional Portal, he made his way to the door and the outside world.

The suicidal man is a superman, because even death cannot deter him;
but the man who wants to live—the man who has hopes and dreams
and things to lose—...such a man is an invalid.
VERSE 873:4 OF *The Teachings*

G.W. awoke within the confines of a posh, spacious bedroom. There was a momentary feeling of panic, which, seeming to run out of energy, quickly faded back into the nothingness. It was late in the afternoon—or so he guessed from the way the sun came into the window. He felt groggy and weak; and in the beginning, even the strangeness of the room meant nothing to him: he was just taking it all in—compiling a list of meaningless things to go with the dark, swirling mess that was his consciousness. He was in a huge, spacious bed. He tried to get up and groaned from the pain that came with the movement. His shoulder felt as though it were on fire; and when he moved his head, the throbbing pain emerged out of the nothingness and attacked him—like hornets swarming a foolish child that had disturbed their nest. As such, it took him a few more minutes before he was capable of moving again—or was courageous enough. He lay back down, closing his eyes tightly, as though trying to banish his demons. At last, he opened his eyes and looked around, making sure to keep his head still. There was an antique dresser in front of him: he was lying on his side, and the huge dresser was in his field of vision...he did not recognize anything. Gnashing his teeth, he sat up in the bed. His head felt as though it were too big for his body: his neck muscles were struggling to keep his head steady...There was a full-length mirror across the room and he saw himself. His head was wrapped with bloodstained bandages; his left arm was in a sling, and his face was discolored and swollen. He swallowed and realized how parched his throat was. Moreover, he still had no idea where he was. All he could recall was…fleeing from The Company: images of the President lying dead and bloody at his feet…and Shaka…and then himself racing down the city streets, running over people who could not possibly mean anything to him. The horror of it tried to confront him, but it was all so unreal: so much like a dream. Beyond those images, there were only vague, shady images of some man or men hovering over him, helping him. He wanted to say something—to call out and ask if anyone was there—but his jaw ached when he tried to open it…and his throat was sore. He managed to groan, but the resonance made his head hurt even more… He felt so very weak. He wanted to lie back down and close his eyes forever, but he remembered his wife then. He had not talked to her in…it seemed like forever. And he had to figure out where he was…what was going on… the questions went on and on, so that the urgency of the questions gave him the strength and purpose to get out of bed.

All his joints seemed to ache as he got up; his collarbone was definitely broken. He remembered that he had fractured his hand when he punched that guard in the face; but now as he looked at it and moved it, his hand seemed fine. His shoulder, where he had been shot, ached, but when he looked at it he saw no wound or scar—just a horrible bruise. Could he have healed already? Or maybe it was just that a great deal of time had passed— weeks, perhaps. He groaned and continued his quest to compile informa- tion—no matter how contradictory the initial facts seemed. He shuffled over to the mirror, looking critically and suspiciously at the gaunt figure before him. That man was a stranger to him. It was not only the bandages and the unnatural gauntness: he did not recognize the face—the red, searching eyes, the quivering, parched lips, the sallow complexion. It was not merely that he had wasted away—and that he was bruised and broken—but that he did not know that man: had no idea of his history. The only things that con- nected the man before him with his recollections, were the injuries. He unwrapped the bloody bandage on his head…there were several cuts and abrasions, but no signs of a bullet groove. He frowned. Even though he ached in the right places, he obviously had not been shot...his hand did not seem broken, there was no bullet hole in his shoulder. He rechecked himself before the mirror, still frowning. Maybe weeks had passed, he considered. However, there would still be scars....

G.W. called out then, to see if anyone was near; but with his parched throat, his voice was barely audible. He saw an attached bathroom and shuffled over, again marveling at the opulence of the place. Could this apartment possibly be his? Maybe all that had passed had been a dream, just as he had guessed from the beginning....He turned on the faucet; as he drank the water, it first burned his throat, then soothed it. He was so thirsty that he was gulping it down now, bending over the sink and sucking at the water as it pooled in his cupped hand. After drinking, he looked at himself again in the bathroom mirror, still trying to recognize the man before him. He felt as though he had awakened within someone else's body. Nothing seemed right....

He called out again. His head ached at the sound vibration, but he did not care. He shuffled back to the bedroom. For the first time, he noticed that the dresser doors were open. Some clothes had been thrown to the floor, as though someone had left in a hurry. The closet was open as well...some suits lay on the floor. He walked over and looked at a pair of pants on the floor: they were so small that they could not be his. But on a chair in the corner of the room, G.W. recognized the clothes he had been wearing: his corporate attire. They were bloodstained and ripped....

Confounded, he exited the room, calling out again. The bedroom emerged into a grand living and dining room. He saw, looking out of the window, that he was somewhere in Manhattan: the view was spectacular, notwithstanding the smog. The huge TV had been left on, but with the volume turned down. The usual scenes of violence confronted him: huge, angry crowds taking out their rage in all the self-destructive ways. G.W. shuffled over to the couch, which was in front of the huge screen, and sat down gingerly. There was a telephone on the coffee table; as he saw it, he again remembered his wife....There was a pang of longing and sorrow in his gut as it occurred to him that by now the world must know what he had done;

by now, his wife must know that he was a murderer. The FBI had probably taken her into custody. No doubt his home phone had been bugged in the event that he tried to contact her; but suddenly desperate for his wife, he reached down and grabbed the phone. It was only after he picked it up and put the receiver to his ear that he realized that he could not remember the number. In fact, it suddenly occurred to him that he could not remember exactly where he lived. As he scoured his mind, the only thing there was a generic idea of suburban bliss...a dutiful, traditional wife who stayed at home to raise his family...things that seemed horribly cliché—almost purposely so! Once again he returned to the thought that all of this was a dream...but then what about his injuries? He shook his head, not withstanding the pain this caused. Trying to retrace his steps, he concentrated on the idea of his wife and realized, with a debilitating feeling of shock, that there was nothing there either! In fact, he had no idea what she looked like! There was no picture in his mind's eye. He could not say if she had been a big woman or small, beautiful or plain...He remembered that he had had a picture of her in his wallet; and suddenly numb, and indifferent to the pain that came when he moved, he returned to the bedroom and rummaged through his bloody jacket. However, when he checked his wallet, all he found were his company ID and some business guards: nothing but evidence of his former corporate life....Who was he? How much time had passed? Where was he now? These were the questions which, when answered, would make sense of the world. Had he really killed the President of the United States? It seemed farfetched now. Obviously something had happened: something traumatic, which had left him bruised and broken...but he was beginning to doubt all his recollections. Had he really had a childhood in Chinatown? Had he really spent his evenings as a child on his father's knee, listening to far-flung stories of China's beauty and history? He had no idea. For those few moments, he was literally a man without a past.

Eventually, it occurred to him that the Image Broadcast Complex was no doubt up and running by now; billions of people, all over the world, were probably dreaming at this very moment, forgetting who they had been, what they had done...Maybe he was one of them! Maybe now, all over the world, billions of people were emerging from the initial fantasies conjured by the dark pyramid, all of them finding pale wastelands full of things they no longer recognized—and which bore no comparison to the vivid images that their minds had become addicted to. In the final analysis, there was something about his present reaction that was like the painful withdrawal that came after the high of a narcotic. A side of him longed for the world of his dreams, because even the horror had been vivid and *alive*, whereas everything around him—and everything he *felt*—seemed dour and intractable. Also, the prospect that he had been dreaming meant that he had not killed the President after all....

He shuffled back to the living room, still holding his wallet in his hand. He sat down absentmindedly on the couch, staring blankly at the TV before him. Scenes of chaos were still flashing over the screen....He looked around the apartment in bewilderment, trying to remember who he was. When he noticed the TV remote control on the couch beside him, he turned up the volume. It was strange to listen to someone talking again... As the reporter was screaming, and in the middle of the story, G.W. was confused for a while; but then, as he looked on in shock, he recognized his home—*his little oasis in the suburbs*! Not only was the reporter standing in front of it, but so were dozens of other camera crews and reporters—not to mention hundreds of police officers and Secret Service agents...and then the reporter said that the man that had murdered the President the night before was still holed up in the house, keeping his pregnant wife hostage. G.W. dissected these sentences painfully slow. The President was dead... the press was in front of his house...therefore, he had not been dreaming...but the last part did not make sense: he was here, in this luxurious apartment, not holed up in the suburbs. Certainly he had heard wrong. He did not fully begin to understand the scope of what had happened until the TV station played the surveillance tape from The Company: the scene from the lobby before Shaka's chamber, in which G.W. stood above the bloody bodies of his victims. As G.W. stared in disbelief, the man in the tape looked up and saw the surveillance camera. G.W. could remember just how it had happened; but somehow, the man who turned his face to the surveillance camera was someone else! It was an overweight white man with eyes full of madness—

"What the hell…?" G.W. whispered to himself, recoiling. He got up nervously, then sat down inanely. Now on the TV there were images from the gunfight with the four guards that had run out of the elevator. It was all as G.W. had remembered it—*except that the man in those scenes was someone else!* That man had been captured on surveillance cameras throughout the building—and then by network cameras when he got outside and started running over people…but in none of those scenes did G.W. see himself! The authorities had supposedly lost the man in the smog and had only found him at home after checking The Company's records. Now on the screen, was the picture from his work ID; but again, it was not G.W.—it was a guy that they were calling G.W. Jefferson. "What the hell…!" G.W. whispered again. How was it possible? Suddenly remembering that he had his work ID in his wallet (which he still held in his hand) he opened his wallet and stared at the picture. It was his picture, but the name was different. It said Xi Wang! …Not even G.W. Wang. He mumbled an epithet in Chinese. Somehow, he was not who he thought he was! Someone else had done the things he had…*dreamed*? Was that even what had happened? He stared ahead in bewilderment: it was obviously far beyond that. Somehow, there had been some disconnect in reality. Somehow, there was a man out there—a white man called G.W. Jefferson—whose soul and *existence* he had shared…but who was now separate from him again. Somehow, he had been split in two—as if through meiosis. But instead of the genetic material being split in half, his consciousness—his memories and self-concept—had been split in two. There was someone out there with half his memories— half his *soul*—and half his past. But that left only one question: who the hell was he? Who was Xi Wang? Yes, that was his picture on the ID…and certainly G.W. Jefferson had not had a Chinese father who told him homesick stories about China—certainly those were his memories…And this work ID verified that he had worked at The Company….He looked vaguely around the apartment: was this his place? Were these his things? He frowned: he had absolutely no recollection of them! His mind was working itself into a frenzy when his attention was captured by something on the TV screen. There were again scenes from in front of his house (he could not help thinking of it as such), and the reporter was still screaming in order to be heard over all the sirens and commotion. But then, all at once, someone screamed out and the camera zoomed in as flames appeared in the windows. The house was on fire! G.W.—rather, *Xi Wang*—looked on in horror! The house went up like a matchstick. In fact, within two minutes, the roof collapsed, so that it became obvious that the house had been steeped with an accelerant. Even the reporter was silent now. They had chased that murderous bastard—*the President's assassin*—to his home and he had killed himself and his family, cheating them out of their revenge....The reporter started crying—sobbing uncontrollably. But after the initial sorrow—or whatever it had been—she wiped away her tears defiantly. "That monster shot down two pillars of our country last night," she went on, "—the President and Shaka. But luckily for us, the American spirit lives on. Shaka is conscious and expected to make a full and quick recovery...."

After that, time became strange again. Xi sat back in the couch and stared at the TV for hours. He fell asleep like this and woke up the next day... there were scenes of huge crowds applauding as Shaka emerged from the hospital. The man was once again resplendent in his white suit....Xi Wang only nodded absentmindedly, eventually returning to sleep. After two or three days of this cycle of sleep and staring blankly at the TV, he awoke one afternoon to the sight of a reporter staring into the camera in shock:

"...another country confirms what was initially thought to be a statistical fluke: over 90% of the babies born in the last week have been boys! As yet, no one can offer an explanation...!"

Xi stared at it for a while, then he went back to sleep.

BOOK I
DEATH

III

Simply knowing something doesn't necessarily give one the wherewithal to manipulate it. This is why the saying "knowledge is power" is misleading. Knowledge by itself has no power, and is only like a Tower of Babel, which might easily collapse in the wind. The power resides in those who maintain the tower—not in the tower, itself.
Verse 9:12 of *The Teachings*

Bombs rained from the skies of Boston, just as they had rained from the skies of London the night before, and Bucharest the night before that. Over the last month, 87 of the world's major cities had been bombed. Whatever was bombing the cities made no demands and seemed to have no motivation but to destroy. The missiles came out of nowhere; as they had never been tracked to a source, there was no face that people could connect to the bombings. There was no culture or country that could be used as a rallying point to build up armies and defenses. Seven years after the apocalypse had brought history to the edge of oblivion, a powerful, faceless force was stamping out the last feeble fires of human existence. If the panicky news broadcasts were to be believed, then New York City would inevitably join the list of bombed cities. Maybe in a matter of weeks or days or *hours*, the last few conscious men of the city would look up in horror to see the strange new bombs that melted everything in lakes of fire and turned the sky a shimmering purple.

Sanity isn't a 'yes or no' proposition: it is a matter of degree.
Being too sane can be just as debilitating as being insane.
VERSE 1279 OF *The Teachings*

As it was the height of summer, the humid air of the city carried the odor of excrement, rotting trash and decaying flesh. Xi and two other wretches crouched in the darkness, staring anxiously into the gaping hole of an abandoned, fire-gutted apartment building. In fact, for as far as the eye could see, all the buildings were burned, leaving only charred brick facades and, in places where the buildings had collapsed totally, towering mounds of rubble. A few blocks away, some squatters could be seen standing around a bonfire; but besides that—and the huge clouds of flies that buzzed everywhere—there was no one and nothing else about.

Presently, as a faint noise came from the gaping hole of the apartment building, the frames of Xi and his comrades tensed up. Xi was wearing special goggles to allow him to see into the darkness. In his right hand, there was a remote detonator for an electric pulse grenade; his comrades looked at his thumb anxiously, as it hovered over the detonator's big red button—

"Are they coming?" one of the men whispered; Xi gestured for him to be quiet by raising his left hand, and the man looked nervously at the third comrade before scratching his grainy, lice-infested beard. The third man yearned to ask Xi as well, but only stared at Xi's stoic, goggled form for some clue; and then, when that seemed unfruitful, he gripped the barrel of his shotgun tighter and looked over his shoulder uneasily to survey the night.

His biggest concern was seeing that they did not get ambushed in the darkness—and crouching there with their backs exposed seemed to be an open invitation. He was not a man who liked to wait, but he was desperate; and given the nature of the world and what they had all become, Xi was his best hope....

Like most of the other men in the city, Xi was gaunt and filthy. They all had the bodies of men who had not yet recovered from their last illness; and with the tangled, greasy strands of the Luxuriant Hair reaching down their backs, there was a barbaric, unwholesome air about them. After all, seven years had passed since the news first broke that no more women would be born; seven years of riots and wars and madness...and yet even these things could not fully explain what Xi had become. In a sense, he was still that man whose soul and life had been taken over by another; his sins and fears and dreams had died with that other man and his family, so that it was as though he were beyond human existence. He did not feel like a man anymore; instead, he went about life as though he were a disinterested cosmic observer. Even seven years ago, when he sat groggily in that condominium, recovering from his wounds, he had been more curious about how the end of the world was going to unfold than horrified. He had looked on with that strange detached curiosity while whole blocks of cities burned and riot police and army units marched through the streets to combat the growing mobs. He had looked on disinterestedly while everywhere fools had begun to talk about governmental and international conspiracies to grab power— *through genes themselves*! He had stared ahead blankly as phone networks and power grids became unreliable, and reports from politicians and scientists became scant. In a matter of days, financial markets all over the world had lost 80 to 90% of their value. It had been a financial panic the likes of which had never been seen before. Everyone had just wanted to recover what he or she could and ride out the storm; but in their madness, they had only added to the storm's fury. No one had been able to stop and think...and so, banks had fallen, currencies had become worthless within hours; and as the scope of what had happened began to seep into the social consciousness, a new, all-encompassing kind of violence had risen out of nowhere. This new kind of violence had not been of the type that came and went and allowed fools to think about some return to normalcy: it had been of the type that seeped into the souls of men, changing them—corrupting that vital thing that made them human beings. As the social fabric unraveled, only the most brutal had risen to the top—and only those willing to pledge their total subservience to them had been able to survive. In the first year alone, half of the world's population had been reduced to refugee status, with billions of desperate, filthy wanders living out their lives fleeing from conflicts and searching desperately for food and shelter. New York City, like all major cities, became a Mecca for these wretches. Like a river bursting its banks, the city had spread out (consuming parts of New Jersey, Long Island and Connecticut) so that it now groaned beneath the weight of 20 million men.

But again, with Xi's detached curiosity, none of these things had really been able to horrify him. In the immediate aftermath, he had hidden in that luxurious condominium, still staring numbly at the sporadic news reports that had been able to reach him with all the power outages. He might have stayed there forever—might have been there still—were it not for the fact that the posh building had finally caught ablaze. Along with a quarter of the city, he had found himself thrust into the street with only the clothes on his back. He had stood across the street from the burning building, looking on in wonder as everything went up in proverbial and literal smoke.

It had been the early fall then, but it had seemed colder than it had ever been before. The world—not the one filtered through the screen, but the *real* world, with its sickening charred smell and filth—had confronted him at last; and for those few moments, the detached curiosity had left him. The people, seen without the buffer of the television screen, had been suddenly terrifying. Even the most pathetic of them had seemed imbued with amazing power...And they had all been pathetic by then. The chaos of the initial panic had been like a fire that burned so hotly that it quickly exhausted all of its fuel. In the wake of the riots, a new kind of listlessness had quickly overtaken the city. The people of the riots, spent of their anger and self-righteousness, had become shells of human beings. Xi had wandered about with these homeless wretches: there had been no avoiding them. He had been wrapped in a blanket like a child, scared of everything and everyone.

Like the rest of them, he had found food and shelter in the abandoned shops and supermarkets; he had become a scavenger, ripping apart the carcass of the country. A couple of times, gripped by a panicky kind of lust, he had even wanted to take a woman.

Indeed, by then, the act of taking a woman had become the new religion of the men. It had not been that the men found something sacred in the women that they raped. It had been the fleeting pleasure—the *pretense* of pleasure—that had possessed them. Maybe, in the pain and fear that they saw in the women's eyes as they raped them, there had been a reminder of the joy and pleasure that was already lost to them. Whatever the case, with all the rapes and murders, the great protective roundup of the women had begun. The terrified women had flocked to train and bus depots, forming long, impatient lines. More so than the men, there had been no place for the women by then. The world had rewritten itself in an instant, so that the women had stood there, confused and terrified by the gaping void before them. The places where they had once found love and companionship had turned, in an instant, into places of unspeakable horror...All that they had had was the hope that those who offered to protect them would do so. It had not been the government by then—that had been gone. It had been strange organizations that popped out of nowhere. The women had flocked to those organizations the way Xi remembered "starving Africans" flocking to United Nations aid workers. Driven to the extremes by their fear and desperation, they had seen nothing beyond the hand that proffered those few scraps of nourishment and comfort. The roundup of women, massive, almost *inconceivable*, in its scope, had in fact seemed so focused and purposeful that the people had rushed towards it as if it were a light in the darkness. However, by that time, even the Devil's hand, beckoning them into hell, would have been too tempting for them. Some men had even demanded that they, too, should be taken to safety. This little thing had threatened to once again ignite the riots; but those organizations, with their calm, efficient demeanors, had quelled it all. For space considerations, only the women may come for now, they had said with a parent's firmness; and the men, like children, had accepted it.

By then, Xi's detached curiosity had been back. He had only nodded his head, appreciating the brilliance with which the women were stolen away. They had not so much been lambs to the slaughter—for "lambs" implied that they were innocent. On the contrary, it had been their filth that was their undoing. The horror of what they had become had shocked them; and in their desperation to hide from it and block it from their conscious minds, they had been willing to go to any lengths. As such, as they got on buses and trains to unknown destinations, the women had been like the first Jews taken away by the Nazis in WWII Europe: their faces, while showing their uncertainty and fear, had betrayed a shortsighted thankfulness at being taken away from the front lines. Thus, within a matter of months, the women had all been gone from the city: gone to who knows where. Even those women that had chosen to stay behind had simply disappeared (like an early morning dream) or been picked off by the rape mobs. The organizations that had promised to protect them had taken them and disappeared back into the ghost fog of their arrival; and in time, the men—the lovers and fathers and brothers and sons—who had cried at the women's leaving, promising that they would see one another in time, had looked around the surreal landscape and wondered if the women had ever even been real. They had seemed dazed, as if just awaking from a dream: as if all that had passed before had meant nothing. Even to those who tried to remember—who carried pictures of their women in their wallets and told stories of their love—even to these men, the women became soulless caricatures of human beings.

Something devastating had happened to the very act of remembering and digesting information. And just as there had been a prehistoric period, now, with the passage of the seven years, men found themselves in a kind of post-historic period. After what they had done to themselves—and the women—memory became a useless appendage, there only to cause pain. Maybe all this had happened before the women were taken away, and their leaving had only made it irrevocable; but whatever it was, the men now seemed deprived of the capacity to see what was right before their eyes. Even Xi felt himself at the mercy of blind spots upon occasion. He figured that there had to be places where the women, prized as...well, *commodities*, were being kept. He suspected that the military and some of the more powerful corporations and syndicates had to be somehow involved, but as he could not conceptualize the logistics of moving and keeping hundreds of millions of women, he always experienced a kind of mental block when he tried to think of them. Undoubtedly, the fact that he had lost his soul and his life to another man only warped things further. His wife was the case in point. He knew now that she had never been his: that she had belonged to that other self; but beyond that woman, the abyss stretched to his mother, to his first girlfriend...In fact, the women of his history (like those viewed in video porno booths and those conjured in the men's corrupted imaginations) were like a sinkhole, sucking in *all* women, corrupting the *reality* of them.

Worse still, by the time the women were taken away, billions of men throughout the world had already surrendered their souls to The Company's dark pyramid. By the end of that first year of horror and tragedy, the cumbersome visors needed to interface with the dark pyramid were upgraded with luminescent contact lenses, called PinkEyes, so that people became one with the dark pyramid—and seemed forever disconnected from human consciousness. Xi sensed that their only hope was something shocking: some blunt force to put them off the easy track of their past actions. However, the only thing he believed could do that was the reality of a woman. With the PinkEyes and video porno booths and flawed memories, they conjured women every day; but a *real* woman, insusceptible to their will, whose body was her own and independent of crude, mass-produced fantasies...such a woman might be so shocking to their senses that she might jolt them back into reality—

Presently, as Xi and his comrades crouched before the gaping hole, there was another faint noise within the darkness; and with his infrared goggles, Xi finally saw what they had been waiting for. When his hovering thumb finally began its descent, the spirits of his two comrades perked up. The men now bubbled with the excitement seen in dogs waiting for their masters to throw their favorite stick. When Xi pressed the button, a blinding light flashed within the darkness, and dozens of eerie, high-pitched squeals rose in the air—

"*Now!*" Xi said, wrenching off the goggles and leaping up. The men at his heels turned on their flashlights then and bounded into the abandoned building after him (again like dogs chasing their quarry). They trained their flashlights on the ground; and there, flopping around in the rubble, were the dozens of squirming rats!

"We're gonna eat good tonight, boys!" one of the men exulted as they scooped down to collect the stunned rats. In fact, they were all laughing now, experiencing the kind of deep intimacy that men only expressed between themselves during sports, hunting and similar acts of conquest....However, it was while they were shoving the rats into a canvas bag, which Xi held open, that the apparition appeared. First, there was another flash of blinding white light, so that they were forced to turn their heads away and squint; and then, as they looked on in disbelief, that light turned from white to a wall of bright red flame. They could feel the heat on their exposed skin, burning their hairs...they coughed from the sulfurous smoke that billowed from the wall of fire; and as they stared into those raging flames, mesmerized by the way the flames highlighted the smoke, the apparition emerged— as if from another dimension. Xi's comrades cried out at the sight of the demon or ghost or whatever it was, and promptly began to fire their guns at it. And yet, while the apparition floated above their heads, all Xi did was stand there with his strange detached curiosity. The apparition was in a flowing white robe, and had the long hair that was characteristic of all the men; and as both the robe and the hair danced in the smoke and fire, Xi found himself thinking that it was just like a scene from the Bible. At the other end of the spectrum, Xi's comrades, terrified out of their wits—and unappreciative of Biblical references—emptied the contents of their guns into the creature in that billowing smoke and fire; then, when that seemed ineffectual, they leaped through the gaping hole in the wall and fled, leaving Xi standing there holding the bag of rats.

At this point, the most cogent thought Xi had about the apparition was that it had one of those too-beautiful faces that he attributed to homosexuality and the bizarre sex clubs that had sprung up to satisfy men's cravings for the illusion of a woman. The apparition was a boy—probably about 16 or 17 at the most. Xi looked to see if the boy had those hormone-induced breasts that had become "all the rage" among this subculture, but the boy was flat chested and had the gaunt body type common to all the men. Actually, the apparition had a mustache, which was trimmed down to a fine line above his lip, so that he seemed like one of those debonair Latino gigolos from the 1920s. A side of Xi wanted to laugh out from the ridiculousness of it; still, there was something in the boy's eyes that drew him in. The boy somehow had a face that seemed untouched by the last seven years. In those eyes, there was not the death that Xi saw everywhere (even when he looked into the mirror). The eyes struck him as some kind of bridge: not to a nostalgic time in days past, but to a future of honesty and openness. As Xi stared at the face, he did not know what to make of it. The Biblical entrance had meant nothing to him, but there was something about the eyes that he could not quite place: could not reconcile with what he had come to think of as human existence and *reality*.

The boy was smiling down at him; coming to his senses, Xi heard himself chuckle as he said, "You definitely make a good entrance, kid."

"You're not afraid," the boy said then. It was not a question, but a statement of fact. Yet, there was something about the boy's deep voice that drew Xi back into that place of confusion. It definitely did not match the boy's body and face. It had a confident masculine resonance that disturbed him for some reason. As such, he was a little defensive as he said:

"I've come across too many gods in my time to be traumatized every time one appears."

"I don't know," the apparition said with a snicker. "Fear can sometimes be a very healthy thing. Take your friends, for instance: they ran off thinking that I was some demon coming for their souls. Regardless of whether or not that's true, fear can sometimes lead to good choices—even in the absence of sound judgment."

As Xi looked up at the apparition, it occurred to him how far he had come. He saw himself standing there alone in that abandoned building, talking to a boy floating in a wall of fire. Either he was hallucinating or he was having an all-encompassing drug trip…or he really was talking to an angel/demon. In the final analysis, there was no difference between the options. Death was waiting out there one way or another. In a sense, he *was* death: he nourished it within his soul and saw the world in relation to it; he felt shielded from it, the way a fool was oftentimes too foolish to realize his own stupidity. For whatever reason, he smiled then, saying, "Maybe you should just tell me what you want, kid."

The apparition's lips formed themselves into an enigmatic, slightly coy smile. "What if your friends were right and I've come for your soul?"

"Then the joke's on you, kid," Xi said with a chuckle, "—my soul's long gone."

"—And souls are worthless nowadays, right—out rotting in the fields?"— *Xi looked up sharply!*—"...Why are you looking at me like that?"

"Like what?"

"Like you saw a ghost," the boy said, cheekily.

"...Someone I once knew...he said those words...something like them."

"Did you agree with him? Are souls so worthless that even the Devil can't be bothered to buy? ...There is that look again."

"...Did Shaka send you?" he said, surprised by how calm he was.

"Of course not," the boy said with a smile. "If Shaka thinks of you at all, Xi, he thinks of you as dead."

About five seconds passed before Xi could speak. "Who are you?"

"Who I am is irrelevant, but you may call me, Quibb."

"...Why are you doing this?"

The boy laughed again, saying: "Don't waste your time trying to figure me out."

"Then how do you propose that I waste my time?"

The boy laughed louder. "You have a good sense of humor."

But Xi was not laughing. There were two choices: either Shaka had sent Quibb, or Xi was totally mad....There were no good choices anymore. It was then that Xi noticed Quibb's hands—how long and slender they were; he looked away uneasily—

"There is another possibility," Quibb said with a smile.

"...What?"

"There is another possibility besides Shaka sending me and you being totally mad."

"…How did you know what I was thinking?"

But Quibb ignored him, going on in his confident baritone, "See, as you, yourself know, everyone is already mad; madness is the only way to process information in this world nowadays. Thus, your being 'totally mad' is meaningless. All these years, you have used madness to insulate yourself from what's going on around you. I am in fact the manifestation of your emerging sanity."

Despite everything, Xi found himself considering it—

"In actuality," Quibb went on, "I'm only a figment of your imagination."

Xi was considering this as well before he remembered his two friends; he opened his mouth to point out that they would not have run from a figment, but Quibb beat him to it, saying:

"Then why did your friends run away?"

Xi nodded uneasily.

"—Because they never existed either."

"What?" Xi said with a forced laugh.

"What if you are just a lonely man who hunts rats in an abandoned building and imagines friends who look to him with respect?"

Xi looked up blankly—

"You're going over your life with those men, thinking that you could easily settle all this by going to that hovel where you all hide out."

"…Why are you doing this?"

"I'm not 'doing' anything: I'm a product of your imagination, remember. I'm only here to give you the proverbial kick in the pants that your subconscious mind craves—so that you can get back on the right track."

Xi laughed uneasily again. Either he was very, *very* mad, or the boy floating in the flames before him was very good. In a sense, he was intrigued: excited to be having an actual conversation again—even if his mind had cracked. He had forgotten how good it was to interact intellectually with another human being—how satisfying it was to use one's thoughts for something besides hunting for food and fighting for survival. Still staring at the boy, he chuckled, saying, "And what is 'the right track'?"

"Killing Shaka, of course."

Xi's smile died.

Quibb laughed, saying: "There is that look again…and a little fear is beginning to creep into you as well. But that's good: as I said before, fear is very useful. Fear is the key to the soul—fear of death, of failure…fear of *something*. Unfortunately, you haven't been afraid of anything in years—especially not death."

Xi took a deep breath, and then he shook his head—as though trying to clear out cobwebs. "Let me see if I understand all this," he started. "I've been delusional, imagining friends, and you are some subconscious projection of my mind, which has come to get me to kill Shaka?"

"Basically." Then, when Xi smiled and shook his head, Quibb pursed his lips and looked at him critically: "The truth of what I say is clear to you on some level, Xi, but it is still being blocked by the fact that you don't know who you are. You still see yourself as G.W. Jefferson—not Xi Wang. The truth of who you are is back at The Company. You know that you really worked there—your ID badge told you that. You know that a person called Xi Wang really did exist, but you've been too afraid to figure out who he is."

"Why don't you just tell me?"

The boy stared at him earnestly for a moment, then smiled. "I'm going to do more than just tell you, Xi. I'm going to give you a great gift: I'm going to allow you to see the contents of your subconscious mind—see who you *really* are. Like I said before, you're still thinking of yourself as G.W. Jefferson; you're still horrified by the sight of the President's bloody corpse lying at your feet—and Shaka's death throes. You have to wash all of that from your mind. You've conjured a fantasy in which you've been separated from your 'true' self—all of that is nonsense. It wasn't you that killed the President; you did not shoot Shaka—it was G.W. Jefferson—"

Xi groaned; and while Quibb talked, Xi forced himself to look away from those eyes, where the key to everything again seemed to lie. He forced himself to stop listening: to stop allowing himself to believe that he was actually having this conversation. He took a deep breath and rubbed his temples. When he looked up, Quibb was still smiling at him:

"The time when you could have blocked out what I have to say has passed, Xi. I am *you*, remember?"

Xi could not even pretend to smile anymore. He opened his mouth to speak, but the flippant words he had wanted to say would not come.

Quibb's smile broadened. "This is a momentous occasion, Dr. Wang: you will look back on it as the moment when you emerged from the darkness."

"...*Dr.*?"

"Yes, Dr. Wang—*you*," he said, pointing at Xi with his long, slender index finger. "You were a scientist before all this. Your laboratory is back at The Company."

"My *what*?" Xi said, struggling to keep up.

"Your laboratory, Dr. Wang. Only by going back there will you realize who you were and how all of this happened. However, before that, remember that I promised you a great gift?"—Xi nodded absentmindedly—"To claim that window into your subconscious mind—and your true self—you must first acknowledge that your two friends never existed."

Xi instinctively shook his head. He had *lived* with those men. He had eaten with them and fought alongside them. Like someone catching himself being lulled into a hypnotist's trance, he shuddered—

"Why do you continue to fight me?" Quibb said, amused by Xi's stubbornness.

"—Because fighting is the only thing I have left!" he said. He unconsciously took step away from Quibb now, as though taking a step away from a cliff. "I *lived* with those men—"

Quibb chuckled at his foolishness. "Tell me something then: Where did you meet them?"

Xi searched his mind, then frowned when he realized that he had no idea.

"*When* did you meet them? Last week, last month...a year ago? When was it?"

Xi stared on, stunned!

"Exactly," Quibb whispered. "*Exactly*. You can't answer any of those questions because your mind has never needed to. It's like dreams: no matter how real they seem while you're dreaming, the unreality of them can always made clear by the fact that all the little details are missing. You can't answer any of my questions because your mind has never needed to formulate those details. Can you even tell me their names?"

Xi looked up, his frown deepening. "What kind of game is this!" he said in bewilderment. "You've just done something to my mind, that's all: hit me with one of those brainwashing rays!"

"Okay then," Quibb said with a sigh. "…I suppose that is possible. It isn't like 90% of the men in the city aren't delusional anyway, right? …But, look around you: your friends emptied two gun clips into me, and yet I'm unharmed. Do you even see any bullet casings lying around? Look at the surrounding walls: do you see any bullet holes? [Xi's head ached as he looked around!] Go home and check for some remnant of your friends—go back to that place where you lived with your comrades and see for yourself that they were never there." Having said that, Quibb disappeared—faded back into the darkness—and Xi found himself horribly alone: truly terrified for the first time in years. He dropped the bag of rats and ran!

Human beings are strange creatures: the more you fight them,
the more they want to fight you; but give them enough space,
and they'll fight one another.
VERSE 523:4 OF *The Teachings*

At the hospital, the age-old battle between life and death seemed to be at a strange stalemate. Few came to the hospital expecting to get better: few did. In fact, most of the men had been unconscious when they came in. The vast majority of them were workers from The Company that had fallen into the dementia that came with overuse of the PinkEyes. Through the largesse of The Company, thousands of such men could descend into contented stupors, neither having to worry about pain nor consciousness again. In two huge, dimly lit wards—one on the ground floor and the other in the basement—thousands of men lay out in the open, on old mattresses and worn blankets, without even the dignity or precaution of screens. The eerie luminescence of the PinkEyes meant that in the dark, silent chamber there were thousands of glowing pink orbs, which seemed to twinkle upon occasion as the men blinked their eyes. Sometimes a few days would go by before someone realized that one of those men on the floor was dead; and when these rotting corpses were finally discovered, they would be tossed into an incinerator at the back and set ablaze. As such, the stench of rotting, burnt flesh was always about the place. Most of the men were, in fact, nothing but skeletons wrapped in rags. In the summer heat, they baked, literally stewing in their own juices…and the flies feasted in this place: feasted on excrement and rotting flesh and all the filth that human beings produced as they drew closer to death.

Even the building seemed to be caught between life and death. It used to be a museum; and at a glance, it was reminiscent of the gothic period: of cathedrals and grand, grotesque architecture. It did not seem made for care and nurturing, but as a monument to decay. The walls, where they were stone, were worn, as if by the erosion of the sea; where they were cement or plaster, they were crumbling, leaving a sandy residue everywhere....

As he stood in the corner of the huge basement ward, Doctor Vincent Mansmann was grateful for the darkness. It was not merely that he did not want to see the state of his patients: he did not want to be *seen*. He stood with his back turned to the men, staring out of a window in the side door. He had hidden for seven years. He had called himself Ned Sullivan and shaved his head bald a couple times a week. Luckily, no one had ever come looking...except for Shaka—

Just then, someone cried out in the darkness of the chamber, but as those cries echoed eerily through the ward, Mansmann did not even flinch. With the PinkEyes, nobody really felt pain anymore. More likely than not, the crying man was merely caught up in a fantasy—an action/adventure extravaganza where he was the hero. As Mansmann yawned, he looked past the broken window of the side door and saw the vague outlines of the crescent moon beyond the smog. He stared at it absentmindedly for a moment, then transferred his gaze to the large, wall-mounted television to his right. The television's reception was horrible—as though they had a bad satellite connection—but this only made the images on the screen seem more disturbing. The reporter on the television was ranting again—screaming about how many of the world's cities had been systematically bombed over the last month. Mansmann squinted at the screen for a moment in order to understand. He had a vague recollection (from other nights of glancing at TV) that cities like London and Toronto had recently been pulverized by missiles, but knowing this fact did not bring him any closer to understanding it—or to *believing* it. Now on the screen, there were scenes from Boston: images of bodies being pulled out of burning and collapsed buildings. The cameras lingered over the dying, gravitating to those gripped by their final death spasms. There were images of a groaning, semi-conscious Bostonian who had a steel pipe stuck in his head…and there was something strange about the sky. He had noticed the same thing in other bombed cities: the skies were all purple and shimmering—like some kind of strange aurora borealis. This was why he suspected that those bombings had to be fake: either a publicity stunt or just the latest hoax in a long series of attempts to keep the men of the city—and the *world*—entertained. Mansmann yawned before returning his gaze to the night sky….

It seemed as if an entire lifetime had passed since that night seven years ago, when he headed home from his lab and got stuck in traffic…And then he had picked up that strange man, whom for a moment he had thought to be the President's assassin. Still dazed from the discoveries of his lab, he had looked at that supposed murderer and felt something like brother-hood. He had nursed the delirious man all that night—until, glancing at the TV, he saw a story on how the President's assassin had been cornered at his home. The proof, including a surveillance camera from The Company, had been irrefutable. Ashamed—and somehow heartbroken that he had not found a brother after all—Mansmann had left the condominium (and the man) and fled from the city. He had escaped to his little secluded cabin in upstate New York, hoping to disappear. It had only been a matter of days before stories of no more women being born began to appear. Staring numbly at the satellite feeds, Mansmann had watched it all crumbling. It had been just as he had foreseen. The world had lurched off wildly: without either a glance backward or into the future—where the repercussions lay. Whole cities had seemed to be on fire; the suburbs and places of wealth and luxury had crumbled even faster, as if the ease had been an accelerant of the madness.

Hiding in his cabin, Mansmann had gone days without eating or moving from in front of the television. He had just sat there, mesmerized by the flickering images of apocalypse, knowing that his hand had caused it. Like a fallen god, he had waited for his creations to come and deliver their justice unto him. Through the long days and nights, he had constantly clutched a gun in his bony hands, awaiting the inevitable standoff. He had put the nozzle of the gun to his temple a few times, only to collapse on the floor in tears. With each passing day he had gone a little more insane. The insanity had been like a daydream, which he had awakened from the way someone allowed a bad memory to fade away....When he had actually left his cabin and charged back to the city, he had no idea. He had simply found himself there, as if a beam from the heavens had transported him. He had reawakened into the madness, in one of those mobs. With all the fires, the sky had been one of those dream hues—a kind of reddish gray. Everything in that waking dream had had its counterpart, providing, in the face of the chaos, an almost soothing balance. It had been as if everything would take care of itself, and that all that he had to do was surrender to the dream.... Somehow he, scrawny and unassuming as he was, had become the leader of one of those mobs. With his gun clenched triumphantly in his hands, he had been at the vanguard, possessed, once again, by the cosmic joke. There had been things to be broken, women to be taken, men to be killed at whim...an entire *world* to be defiled. His only thought had been of what he would break next...and if he died along the way, then all the better. There had been no hope in it: no future—no *present* even. There had been, in reality, no joy, no sadness...During those moments, if he had had access to a nuclear bomb, he would have dropped it on them all, so that he could watch their horror with secret pleasure and longing....

However, in the end, it had been the waning of that horror that had awakened him. In the eyes of the ravaged women, there had not exactly been passivity to the act, but a kind of resigned acclimation. They had become used to it— to the *idea* of it—the way he, with foreknowledge, had been able to brace himself before the world lurched off wildly. And so, even those who remained pure in fact—those who did not rape or steal or butcher, or become victims of these acts—had carried the burden in their souls.

Only when it had reached that point had the bloodlust finally passed from his system. In his mind, this seemed to take a lifetime; in reality, it was probably only days...*maybe only a single day!* There was no way to recall it without risking bringing the madness back. He had looked around, dazed and ashamed like the rest of them, already closing himself off to shield his conscious mind.

In this way, regaining his sanity had required a level of insanity. They had all been guilty of such things. But Mansmann had remained just a little more self-aware than others because he, at least, knew what had brought the apocalypse upon them. To others, it had simply been a great cataclysmic rumbling, devoid of meaning—whereas he had heard his own name in that rumbling. He had caused it; and if he could find a cure, he would save himself. In fact, he had spent most of the last seven years at his uptown lab, searching for that cure. He only came down to the hospital to get a break from the frustrations and failures of his experiments. So far, everything he had tried had either led to a dead end, or backfired—as if some Divine will had mandated this genetic suicide....

In the darkness of the hospital, he sighed yet again. As his sleep-starved eyes wandered back to the screen, and scenes of Boston, there was the image of a little boy lying on the ground in shock. The boy's left arm had been blown off and half of his face had melted away. As Mansmann stared at the screen, he found himself thinking, on a vague level, that they all rushed towards death, no matter what they did. In fact, he had spent the years thinking of it, and had come to the conclusion that the key to understanding their self-destructive lives lay in the realization that their crimes could never be punished. What lurked behind their actions (his included) was not only a yearning for atonement, but *punishment*. They did not just want to make peace: they wanted to suffer, and to suffer at the hands of their victims. However, those victims, where they were men, could never bring them to suffer, as they only wanted to suffer themselves; and where they were women...well, that was impossible, as they were gone. Life meant nothing without some doctrine of right and wrong—no matter how vague or flawed—but what could be wrong where there was no punishment? More to the point, even if the women were to come back—or be *brought* back—that was no guarantee that the world could be saved. Not withstanding the fact that men could still only have sons, the world had simply gone too far to return to how it had been. Even when they had been only a year into the apocalypse, it had occurred to Mansmann that even if the women were to come back, the men would probably only stare at them, dumbfounded. At first, the men would probably even be revolted by those strange creatures. A disconnect now lay in that place where men had once sought companionship and love and tenderness. In those short weeks of madness, when they had run around decapitating women, raping them, raping men, dogs, *anything*...they had defiled the very notions of sex and pleasure. Now, with their PinkEyes, mind-altering drugs and cults, few of them even knew what was going on around them anymore. More troublingly, even those, like Mans-mann, who made attempts to understand the world, were too immobilized by the weight of their crimes to *do* anything. They all had that quick acceptance of fate that was seen with those who knew themselves to be guilty.

Mansmann nodded absentmindedly then, as he watched images of a decapitated man's body flopping about on the TV screen. Even the starkest news reports had about them an element of farce. The reporters were calling the thing that had attacked Boston The Purple Horde; and at the mention of the name, Mansmann felt a smile come to his face—just as it had when he thought about a murderous 10-year-old Messiah seven years ago. The Horde was being talked about in panicky tones now (the announcer was even saying that New York might be next!); but for some reason, it all seemed...*silly*. Boston ransacked? Maybe it had actually happened, and a thing called The Purple Horde really did exist; but in order for him to believe that, there were too many other things that he would have to believe. There was an information overload somewhere, and now the facts pertinent to their existence were being drowned in a sea of nonsense and lies and ill-conceived myths.

If one can make that which is real and obvious seem suspect, then one can make the unreal—the virtually impossible—seem plausible.
VERSE 121:1 OF *The Teachings*

By now the Goddess had lived four lifetimes. Her first lifetime was lost somewhere in the haze—in that other universe of possibility, where she was a 10-year-old Messiah. Like all things that had succumbed to the passage of time and *distance*, that former life now seemed inaccessible—if not irrelevant. It was like driving down a deserted highway on the darkest night, and zooming past a sign so quickly that all the words were a blur. At the speed that she was traveling, the sign was now too far down the road for her to even contemplate going back; and with the great distance—and all the strange, new signs that she was coming upon every moment—the sign was forgotten. Indeed, all that remained, and all that there was to contemplate, was her haphazard passage though the darkness.

However, in her second lifetime, a blinding light filled the entire universe, banishing the darkness. The light was so brilliant that even shutting her eyelids could not block it out. It was everywhere, as if it were bursting from within her—emanating from her innermost being. She tried to find some context for the light—something that would allow it to make sense—but it was so forceful that it burst through her, obliterating her...and another lifetime passed away.

In her third lifetime, the light dimmed somewhat, and her body and soul seemed to reconstitute themselves in the relative darkness. In this strange new place, she was able to see silhouettes and make out opaque shapes. She frowned at these weird figures, unable to find the references that would give them meaning. In the confusion and bewilderment that followed, another lifetime passed away....

But in her fourth lifetime, she was able to get vague glimpses of the world through a crack in her unconsciousness. At first, it was still too confusing to make sense. Yet another lifetime threatened to pass away; but then, one day, miraculously, she became aware of the fact that she was shuffling down a corridor. It was as if she had just fallen out of another dimension. She looked around frantically, but in her desperation to understand where she was—to understand *anything* in fact—nothing made sense. Although the concrete walls were white and sterile, and the fluorescent lights were almost blinding, everything seemed dark and morose around her. There were no doors or windows that she could discern; there were no people, no sounds...nothing that triggered a memory as to why she would be in this large, empty corridor. She felt so disoriented that she was amazed that she did not lose her balance and fall. As for where she had just come from, or where she was going, she had no idea either. All that she could dredge up from the murkiness of her memories were murmuring voices lost in the brightness above her, a painful, all-encompassing sensation, and then this.

Within her, there was a bizarre sensation, like having her body collapsing in on her soul. She felt smothered; yet, now that she looked down the corridor, an inkling of its size left her mind reeling! Maybe it was her disorientation, but staring down the corridor, she could make out no terminus ahead: it had to stretch on for *kilometers*!

What is this place? a voice within her whispered. And just then, inexplicably, a hollow, resounding sound rose around her. She panicked, like someone sensing the steps of her killer behind her. She went to scream...but then, with a confused frown, she recognized the lonely echo of her own steps. She was like someone just waking up, who could not recall when or where she had fallen asleep. And the strange thing was that despite her desperation to stop and get her bearings, she could not affect her steady, loping gait down the corridor; no matter how she quaked inside, she could not, for the life of her, *cease* walking. It was a strange kind of disembodiment—as if she were trapped in someone else's body, only peripherally aware of what her host knew.

Then, as she continued to survey her frayed senses, she barely discerned, above the lonely echo of her own steps, a murmuring voice—or voices. The murmuring seemed to come from everywhere and nowhere, maddening in both its ubiquity and in the concealment that made her wonder if it were only a figment of her imagination. It sounded just as random as the wind, and yet she was almost sure that it was composed of voices; and that those voices—as bizarre as it all seemed—were directing her to follow this corridor.

It was then that she saw something emerge from the haziness ahead. That double feeling—of excitement and dread—came over her again. Maybe she had been watching the thing's approach for minutes now—for *hours*. The thing came out of the nothingness and was soon there, confronting her. At first, with her confusion, it appeared as a multi-limbed monster—a hydra or an octopus—about to engulf her. The sound of its approach was like a stampede. Panicking again, she went to make way—but then she saw that it was only a group of 30 or so people...No: not just people, they were *women*. Something about that fact made her anxious—but only for the slightest moment. Those sensations were quickly lost in all the other jumbled feelings. She looked at the women, frowning. Their hair was closely cropped, and most of them were so gaunt that their breasts and hips had wasted away. Moreover, the way they marched phlegmatically down the corridor reminded her of prisoners of war. They seemed starved; their expressions were...they were difficult to gauge. There in fact seemed to be nothing tangible in their expressions: neither fear nor hope nor *consciousness*. They wore the kind of smocks that were worn by patients in hospitals, making her think that this was an insane asylum that she was in. Some were short, some tall and lanky; some were pre-pubescent...Nothing seemed to unite them but their clothes, their regimented gaits, and their blank expressions. She wished that they would look at her—would *acknowledge* her—but they just stared ahead, their eyes distant and glassy. She looked warily at them—at their haggard faces, their pale, anemic eyes—wondering how she, herself, must look.

...And how did she look? Her own appearance—her own *face*—it now occurred to her, she did not know. There was not even an image of herself in her mind's eye. In fact, she had not even been sure that she *was* a woman, until she looked down and saw her small breasts jutting out from the gossamer fabric of her smock. She felt like someone caught in a powerful whirlpool, pulled deeper and deeper into the vortex.

She searched her mind desperately again...but still nothing! Before this place in time—before this instant of consciousness—what had her life been? What had happened yesterday—a week ago? a month? a year? Her own name, it now occurred to her, she did not know. A family? A home? Nothing! And the strange murmuring was still unrelenting in the background! She felt like a leaf in the wind. It now seemed as if she had been walking forever. Time was hard to gauge here: each step seemed as the one before, taking her further into the nothingness. Peace and ease and understanding lay far off in some other dimension, where neither her legs nor the renderings of her mind could take her. In desperation, she tried to *will* memories to appear, but all that came was the realization that it was all useless.

By now the women had passed her; yet, despite her curiosity and desperation, she had never thought to stop and take note of their retreating steps. She had never thought to even call to them, and a taunting voice within her told her that she would never have been able to do even this.

I won't let this happen! she thought in a panic; but even her own voice, it now occurred to her, she did not know. She tried to say something, but she could not even open her mouth. The murmuring was there, enveloping her soul, its reins tight and unyielding. She was like a caged animal, driven insane by the confinement. She had to strike out: to do *something*—

But the more she tried to resist—if that was even the word for it—the more disoriented and giddy she felt. Beaten, she went on—for how long, it was again useless to conjecture. She went on because she could do nothing else...She found strange games to play with herself, like counting her steps and the interval between her steps and their echoes. Eventually, as she walked along, she noticed that every so often a placard would be emblazoned with a colorful insignia; and because a mind becomes hungry for new input in a desolate, monotone landscape, she focused all of her attention on it. It was a green sun placed against a shimmering purple background. It was the type of image seen in children's storybooks; but for some unaccountable reason it, too, seemed like the universe to her. Each time that she passed it, she felt a little closer to...understanding? She could not be sure.

She did not know *what* she was feeling, but the insignia was something verifiable—a benchmark that might be used as a reference point for further exploration. As she could not *cease* walking, she sped up her pace as best she could, until she saw the insignia approaching. Then, she slowed down as she passed it. However, the insignia inspired too many contrasting sensations for her to discern anything clear from it. There was a strange servile joy, and terror, and shame, and pride...Each time she passed the insignia, some new sensation seemed added to the list. For a while, this, too became one of her games. She seemed almost to become drunk on it, so that her mind seemed even more giddy and lethargic now. Then suddenly, like an explosion, something began to take form in her mind's eye. It was an image of men leading her away—*dragging* her away in fact! Something about them was horrible—as if they were not men at all, but nightmare creatures. Then, as her strange vision continued, she realized that the men were actually soldiers, and they were cursing her, slapping her...dragging her from her hiding place, out into the world that would destroy her. The vision was too chaotic for her to know for sure, but on the soldiers' shirtsleeves had been the same insignia that she now saw on the approaching placard!

Unfortunately, this image was so violent and shocking to her senses that the memory was almost immediately lost. It was the way a startled person dropped a plate that he had only moments ago been grasping firmly. She tried frantically to reclaim the memory; but like that startled person seeing the shattered shards, she knew that it was all beyond reclamation.

A voice within her, seeing everything going, told her to resist. But there was more fear and uncertainty in her now than either defiance or curiosity. The more she looked around, the less she seemed to understand, and, in turn, the more there seemed to be to fear. The world suddenly struck her as a huge beast that only seemed to need the slightest provocation to pounce on her. Safety seemed to lie in her total obedience; and as this mindset grew strong in her, she all at once began wondering why she was even resisting. Was anything so bad happening to her here? She again searched her mind, but could find nothing: neither good nor bad. There were still voices of defiance and panic within her, but they seemed almost irrelevant now—like whispers in a world of loud, jangling sounds. She was giving up by degrees, feeling less giddy now as her resistance ebbed. Even the murmuring was softer now—almost soothing. *What's the use?* she thought at last, like an exhausted swimmer surrendering to the tide...

When she happened to look up, she was startled to realize that her loping gait down the corridor had ceased. For how long, she had no idea: she could have been standing there for hours...To her right, there was an open door, leading to a dark, cramped chamber. She stepped in without thought, surrendering to the murky universe that commanded her. She was now in a square room—about five meters by five meters. Within the silence and darkness of the room, she became acutely aware of her own breath. It was harsh and hollow in the cramped emptiness of the room. There was only one window, which was nothing but a small aperture too far up in the wall for her to see the landscape. She did see, however, that it was night outside. A little piece of the moon was visible through some thick clouds...

She looked about the room again. The only embellishment in it was a mattress on the ground, which gave off the odor of urine and unwashed bodies. In the corner, there was a toilet which, from its stench, she guessed had not been flushed in a while. When she instinctively touched her own skin, she realized that it had a grimy residue about it. She had not realized it before, but she was actually sweating profusely. She had been so disconnected from her body that she did not realize how sweltering it actually was. It had to be at least 40 degrees centigrade. Her smock, she now realized, was so drenched with sweat that it was clinging to her body. Actually, she now felt as though she were *covered* with muck. Her breath came quicker, as if she were being stifled by the filth. The sight of this place made her soul rebel against the contradictory peace that she had been feeling only moments ago.

And the strange thing was that she suddenly felt as though she had been having this struggle every day of her life. It was like a dream which gripped her every night, but which was always forgotten upon awakening. Everything around her seemed not only orchestrated, but as though she had witnessed—

and *experienced*—it all before. No: there was definitely something unnatural here. Something powerful was warping everything. She sensed it in the air: a barely perceptible field of energy that made her skin tingle. It was in separating this field from herself that she at last began to grapple with her own humanity. Like a condemned inmate seeing the first glimpse of gallows in the distance, the passive shell about her cracked; and even in her confused state, she had the feeling that her life was meant for greatness—that her destiny was somehow being thwarted by this place: that out there, there was a wounded world, crying out for her touch. She sensed the world beyond these walls; she sensed unimaginable sorrow that cried out for her; and even then, she sensed the power within her. It was still inaccessible to her— an inarticulate whisper of things to come—but it was there nonetheless, at the foundation of her devastated consciousness.

Now, with a frenetic kind of resolve, she again tried to retrace her steps... only to again find nothing! It was the same old game, over and over again: her searching, only to find nothing. How long had it been going on! Something ran down her cheek and she realized that she was crying. She could hardly see the use anymore—of *anything*. Letting it all go, she collapsed onto the smelly mattress and lay there in the fetal position.

All of her struggle—if it could even be classified as that—had been in vain. She could already feel herself losing consciousness—losing that vague sense of defiance and curiosity that she had been feeling. She remembered the women in the corridor, and the way their eyes had seemed vacant when they shuffled past her. But even that was leaving her, disappearing into the nothingness. She panicked at first, like a dying person panicked. But she was now becoming too weak to care anymore. All of a sudden, everything seemed so arbitrary and disconnected in her mind that only apathy and forgetfulness seemed logical. At that last moment, she turned her head and looked up at the aperture, seeing the moon. Then, as her mind considered celestial bodies, she thought, strangely, of the green sun in the purple, shimmering sky...

Moderation is the extreme of extremism.
VERSE 419:5 OF *The Teachings*

In an age when everyone seemed devastated and confused by the changes that the world had undergone, Shaka took pride in the belief that only he seemed able to think clearly. In a time when people were unable to make sense of what was going on around them, only he seemed able to grasp the grand developments of human existence....

He was now being driven down the city streets. He sat in the back of a windowless armored vehicle that he referred to as his limousine. A thick sheet of bulletproof glass separated him from the guard that was driving the vehicle. A second guard sat next to the driver, clutching an imposing-looking machine gun in his hand. Instead of a glass windshield, which might be penetrated by a high-powered rocket, a huge screen was mounted against the armored plating. This screen was what the driver used to navigate the city streets. On Shaka's side of the bulletproof glass, there were some screens as well. One gave the same view as the driver; the other four were regular TVs, and picked up the shows being broadcasted to the men of the city—and the *world*.

Immediately outside the vehicle, the streets were packed, especially now as the vehicle was nearing Times Square. Even through the armor plating of the vehicle, Shaka could hear and *feel* the loud music of the nightly celebration. The celebration was part rock concert and part church revival.

The Company sponsored it—and broadcasted it throughout the city—but the entire thing was supposedly done "for the glory of the Goddess." A huge bandstand had been constructed for the nightly performers and preachers. Millions of men now stood before that bandstand, some of them dancing, some of them getting high on drugs, some of them screwing one another…but they were all supposedly there to worship the Goddess. Shaka watched the scenes on his monitor with a growing sense of amusement. He smiled and nodded his head; and just then, some crazed men ran up to the side of the vehicle and started banging on it with various club-like implements. In the forward area of the vehicle, the guard with the imposing-looking machine gun calmly pressed a button on the dashboard, causing an electric pulse to be sent out from the vehicle. Immediately, everyone within a 20-meter radius was fried and incapacitated. Those who passed out within the driving lane of the vehicle were simply run over where they lay. This amused Shaka for some reason—and reassured him as well.

His gaze again returned to the four TV screens. On two of them there were scenes from Boston—and panicky reports on The Horde—but on the other two screens there were images from Times Square. The square seemed especially packed tonight, and all the men within it were wearing PinkEyes. These were his people. They dreamt what he wanted them to dream—and saw what he wanted them to see. They acted as he deemed them to act; and even within the most chaotic and imaginative PinkEyes fantasies, they were dreaming within parameters that *he* had devised. Admittedly, for the slightest instant, Shaka was annoyed when the screen he was looking at showed a close-up of one of the revelers in Times Square. The man had the tattoo that millions of the Goddess' worshippers had started wearing: a few lighting bolts at the corner of the right eye, which they called, "Glory to the Goddess." It was supposed to represent the Goddess' mystic aura; but from Shaka's standpoint, it only detracted from the aesthetics of his PinkEyes.

Still, his annoyance was only temporary, because there was one unassailable fact: billions of men around the world were wearing his PinkEyes. In the face of that fact, even The Horde was irrelevant. *He* decided if those men were terrified or euphoric. He controlled their *souls*: what difference could The Horde's ability to destroy buildings mean to him? He was the epicenter of all thought and all possibility: when men had such power they tended to be arrogant—and to underestimate the danger that they were in....

The vehicle approached the bandstand from the back. When Shaka alighted from the vehicle, there were dozens of guards waiting there for him. None of Shaka's personal guards ever wore PinkEyes—he forbade it. It was suicidal to have slaves performing duties that impacted one's life. Life and death decisions were decisions that required *thought*. Slavery, on the other hand, was merely existence without thought; and while a slave might be ordered to guard him, only someone who could appreciate the consequences of life and death could be *controlled*.

The guards approached him with the strange combination of fear and decisiveness that he had come to expect from his subordinates. He passed them by without acknowledging them, then ascended the steps that led to the backstage area of the bandstand. As he walked, he had a slight smile on his face. The music was ear splitting now, but that did not bother him. He wandered through the backstage area, then stopped on the threshold of the stage, looking out first on the chaotic crowd, and then on what had become the headline act of these nightly celebrations: a band of teenage transsexuals who had the apt name of "The Dickless Bastards."

About seven months ago, when Shaka first got reports that the Goddess cult had started up again, he had thought little of it; but then, all of a sudden, hundreds of thousands of men had started gathering in Times Square. The lead singer of "The Dickless Bastards"—a tall soprano called, Circe—had been the center of it all. Circe was so incredibly beautiful that one could hardly believe that he was a man. With his long raven hair, shapely figure and assortment of thong bikinis, Circe was the embodiment of what men professed to want in a woman—which spoke volumes about the times. ...And Circe's songs were like nothing Shaka had ever heard before: words of archaic languages that nobody knew anymore, but whose meaning was clear—as if Circe had rediscovered the primordial language. Circe sang these songs to music that followed no style, and no discernible musical scale, but which had a logical rhythm that was unassailable—*perfect*. Even Shaka could not deny the effect of the music on him. Circe was now in the middle of an aria, seemingly oblivious of the chaos beyond the stage as his voice echoed throughout Times Square. There were thousands of flashing strobe lights, underneath which the millions of dancing and drugged-out men seemed as if they were caught in the throes of a fit. All of this pleased Shaka, so that his smile widened.

Circe was now gyrating his hips on stage provocatively; Shaka stared at the man for a while, as though mesmerized. Then, when he realized the nature of his thoughts, a feeling of revulsion came over him!

Saviors are a cop-out: they allow men to believe that all they need to do is wait and follow, when what they actually need to do is take the initiative.
VERSE 1631:4 OF *The Teachings*

Xi ran for his life, possessed by a kind of terror that he had not thought was possible anymore. Even when he was out of the burnt-out building, running down the dark, eerie streets where the streetlamps had not worked in years, he kept looking over his shoulder. He ran the way men ran in nightmares, never satisfied that he was moving fast enough. He passed through blocks of shantytowns, where tens of thousands of desperate men lolled about listlessly in the darkness. The stench of their excrement and death was overpowering. The way their bonfires highlighted their skeleton-like figures made them seem like savages—or the refugees of a devastating war. He ran on, picking up speed, as though these men were the things chasing him; and in a sense, maybe they were. Maybe he was running from seven years' worth of madness. Maybe what Quibb had said was true, and he was only now becoming sane again....He kept seeing Quibb's face: the disturbing beauty of it. He kept hearing Quibb's words: the confident, masculine resonance of the man's voice...Maybe all this was just a homosexual fantasy he was having; maybe, after seven years of masturbating in video porno booths like everyone else...He shook his head. With the women gone and the men trapped within their own stupidity and depravity, living in the city was like being in prison: men took pleasure any way they could; and when it came to sex, the human imagination was limitless. Xi would see men screwing in alleyways and street corners all the time. They screwed out in public, like dogs—but they did everything else in public as well: they died, shit, killed…

After a few minutes of running, he reached what used to be a major shopping district. Exhausted from his flight, and still numb and confused from his strange confrontation with Quibb, Xi stopped on the sidewalk and leaned against a lamppost to rest. Between his malnutrition and the fact that his body was not used to exercise, he felt lightheaded and sick. He was at the corner of 96th Street and Lexington Avenue, by what used to be the subway stop. The subway tunnels were still there for course, but no trains ran anymore. He looked around the block uneasily, as though he expected a monster to leap out of the shadows. There were no tangible monsters in sight, but he still had the feeling that he was watching something new and horrible. Seven years ago, this street had had the usual assortment of upscale apartment buildings, dry cleaning businesses, eateries and the like; but now the upscale apartments were wrecks populated by wretched men, and the businesses were mostly video porno booths, arcades and establishments specializing in hallucinogenic narcotics. There were flashing neon signs everywhere, and a few huge video billboards that thundered 3D advertisements from the sky in between glimpses of what was going on with the world.

In this case, the video billboards showed chaotic scenes from Boston. Xi looked at the scenes for a while, but he could make no sense of them. Like everyone else, he was used to seeing death and destruction. However, images of Boston, viewed in the context of his confrontation with Quibb, left him with the feeling that they were running out of time, and that they were all going to die horribly.…He was suddenly overcome by an urge to have sex—or at least to reach orgasm. He wanted to be preoccupied with an act—something that would leave him exhausted and slightly euphoric; and as his gaze returned to the billboard, it was as though death and madness were the new erotica of their times, because he felt strangely turned on by what he saw—*aroused*. It was as though his brain had been miswired somehow, and that stimuli that were supposed to trigger fear and revulsion now triggered sexual yearnings. He was certain of this now, because after the scenes from Boston, there were scenes from Times Square, in which millions of men were dancing and singing and surrendering to madness as they celebrated the Goddess. The millions of glowing PinkEyes made the scene seem like a place in hell, in which millions of demons were slithering over one another like snakes. As Xi looked on, there was the image of one man slitting the throat of another—all that, while millions of men danced and laughed around them, and mind-numbingly loud music filled the night.

As though suddenly coming to his senses, Xi looked anxiously about the street before him—both to assess any possible threats and to get his bearings. On the street, there were a few dozen men. Most were lolling about aimlessly; a few lay on the pavement—either sleeping, incapacitated in some way, or rotting. Across the street, there was a kid, no older than 11, who was lying in the gutter with nothing on but a pair of filthy socks. There were lesions all over his body where the maggots had eaten through the skin... and there were flies everywhere. Xi hardly noticed them anymore. Huge clouds of flies were always about the men. The flies were so brazen that they came and sucked the moisture out of your eyes and buzzed around your mouth, waiting for you to open it....Xi looked away from the boy's festering corpse, neither shocked nor repulsed, just fatigued by the realization of how they lived their lives—and how they died. He had become used to stepping over corpses; he had become used to seeing them and smelling them—as all the men were—but that did not mean that they were not a drain on his soul.

With all the running he had done in the humid summer air, the long, filthy tresses of his Luxuriant Hair were now damp with sweat. A few strands fell into his eyes; as Xi brushed them away, Quibb and a hundred other vague, self-destructive thoughts swirled in his mind....Quibb had known him: there was no denying that. Was it possible that Quibb was a part of him: some projection from a cracked mind? Yes, it was all possible. Too many things were possible in fact—that was the problem. Quibb had called him Dr. Wang; the man had talked about a laboratory back at The Company that would explain all this—but Xi's mind buckled under the weight of all these new, unfounded possibilities. Until he found something concrete—something that would allow him to differentiate the real from the unreal—he would never be able to figure anything out. Once more, he felt as though a moment of no return were approaching quickly on the horizon—and that he was running out of time to act. Yet, sensing himself at a crossroads, he could not help being intrigued—regardless of where those roads led. In a sense, he had gotten into a rut over these seven years. His survival may have required that rut; just as Quibb had said, he may have had to shield his mind and body and soul from the yearnings of a man—a *human being*—in order to survive, but he sensed (either rightly or wrongly) that something new was at hand. With this implicitly in mind, all he could hope was that this new thing was not just an escalation of madness.

As Xi sighed, three flies forced their way into his mouth. He spit them out absentmindedly and looked up at the video billboard across the street. Actually, the billboard had begun to flash in a neon orange color that was practically impossible to ignore—as it hurt the eyes. Now scrolling across the screen, in huge block letters, was a message that read: "Think for yourself: Shaka is a dickhead!" Next to that, there was a cartoon caricature of Shaka, with his head as a penis. As all the video billboards throughout the city were the property of The Company—and their programming was likewise at the discretion of The Company—the strange caricature was of course a pirate broadcast. The screen now showed a dancing cartoon Mexican (a desperado with bandoleers), which was the signature of the cyber-vigilante known as Tio Mendez. Xi was happy for the distraction—and the thought that there was someone out there trying to thwart The Company's will. However, even though these pirate broadcasts had been going on for about a year and a half now, Xi suspected that few others even noticed. Indeed, at that very moment, Mendez's broadcast was cut off, and perhaps the most popular show in the world, *Throw the First Stone*, came on the air. It was one of those reality shows that broadcasted from the streets of New York several times a day. The host was a middle-aged man who wore a top hat, tails and a bright yellow silk sash. He addressed the growing crowd like a carnival barker. As he announced that the show was about to begin, the men came around hungrily, grinning and giggling like hyenas. Then, as the barker's voice rose in the air, spouting gibberish that nobody ever really listened to, the object of the crowd's interest and hatred cringed on the ground. It was a scrawny, lice-infested boy who was no older than 15. His face was already scarred—disfigured by seven years of living like an animal. Someone in the crowd protested, saying something to the effect that he could not get a good look, and the boy was hauled up by some official-looking men who seemed to be some kind of mob stewards. The boy was thrown against a wall, where he drooped and cried. In the meanwhile, other stewards went around handing out the stones; and when the barker gave the word, a horrific cry escaped from the crowd as the stones were heaved and the boy was reduced to a heap of bloody, unmoving flesh. The next scene was one of the triumphant mob. The barker screeched something to the effect that another successful show had been completed, then that was that. A millisecond later, the screen returned to scenes from the Goddess' celebration at Times Square: images of Circe and chaos and revelry and men dying from their pursuit of reckless pleasure and forgetfulness. Xi had not realized it while he was watching *Throw the First Stone*, but he was shivering uncontrollably. All these images were drawing him in…*calling to him*; and just then, as he remembered Quibb—and the surreal sequence of events surrounding the man's appearance—he felt himself being pulled deeper into the abyss. It was only the prospect of finding out who he really was that brought him back to his senses. He remembered that he had been on his way home, to check and see if his comrades actually were a figment of his imagination. There was something ludicrous about the entire errand, but there was no point in trying to reason it out. He had to find out if he was crazy or not. More correctly, he had to find out just how crazy he was, since it seemed pointless to doubt his madness. After a final glance at the screen, and Circe's mesmerizing image, he set off for home.

He lived about two blocks away, in the basement of yet another burned out building. He thought it the perfect hide out, because the only entrance was hidden behind a putrid dumpster in the alley. Painted on the wall, above the dumpster, was a huge mural of the Goddess. Xi looked at it uneasily; he looked at the emanations around her right eye—the Glory to the Goddess—and was disturbed for some reason. The strange thing was that he could not remember how long the painting had been there. Either it had been there for years and he had never noticed it, or it had miraculously showed up within the last few hours—like some kind of evil omen. In fact, in that strange moment, he could not even remember how long he had lived here! As he stood in that alley, looking around confusedly, *none* of this felt like home. It was all *familiar* to him, but none of it seemed *personal*. Remembering Quibb's insane errand again, and desperate to push things to their conclusion, he moved the dumpster aside and entered the building. He quickly lit a foul-smelling tallow candle to provide light; but after looking around the basement, he realized that he had no idea what it was supposed to look like! It was small and practically empty. All there was, was a narrow cot against the far wall (which was perpendicular to him), a crate to his immediate right (which he guessed was for sitting on) and a rusty bike, which was leaning against the wall to his left. There was nothing that seemed to be inherently his: nothing that told him that this was home. Furthermore, if there was no proof that he lived here, there definitely was not proof that he had lived here with others. It was while he was thinking these thoughts that a voice called at his back:

"Now do you believe me?" It was Quibb. Xi did not even flinch: he just turned around and looked Quibb in the face. Even with the darkness and the flickering, eerie light of the tallow candle, Quibb face was remarkably beautiful. Xi's eyes went first to those earnest eyes, and then that slim gigolo mustache. There were no special effects this time: no walls of fire, no floating. And now that Quibb was on the ground, as opposed to floating in the air, Xi realized that the boy was actually shorter than he was. For some reason this assured him, because it occurred to him that he could bash Quibb's brains out. Nevertheless, there was still that thing in Quibb's eyes that Xi could not name. Even though Quibb was a boy, there was an ancient quality about his eyes—as though he had seen much; and yet Quibb did not seem like the other men of the city, who had seen much, yet been too blind and delusional and forgetful to *see*. There was a startling kind of perspicacity there. Quibb struck him as a vessel for the type of knowledge that not only shed light on ignorance—but *banished* it. Perhaps that was what made Xi uneasy: the prospect of yet another god. The search for a messiah was death: it was letting down one's guard and allowing oneself to believe that some external vessel of purity was a match for the corrupt, filthy places that they all held within....

Xi sighed, shaking his head. "...Why are you doing all this?"

Strangely enough, Quibb seemed melancholy just now, and sighed as well. "Now that you know the truth about your life, the road to sanity can begin."

"The road to sanity?" he said, unable to keep from smiling.

"Yes," Quibb answered, "—now you know that you're different from the other men."

Xi chuckled sardonically again: "I could have told you that...would have saved you the trouble."

Quibb smiled; then, seeming to see Xi in a new light, he pursed his lips before saying: "Let me ask you something, Xi: If the world were to explode tomorrow, would you care?"

"You mean I wouldn't explode with it?"

Quibb smiled again. "...I guess you would."

"Then it wouldn't make a difference."

"I guess not—unless you had the power to stop it."

"We're all going to die eventually, right?" he said vaguely.

"—But is *eventual* death *certain* death?" Quibb protested. "Human beings, like all living things, have always punctuated their lives with death, yet they still lived: built *civilizations*—"

"But we could have daughters then."

Quibb nodded his head: "...Maybe you're right." Then, seeming to come out of his reverie, Quibb smiled shyly. "I envy you, Xi," the man said then, looking at Xi earnestly. "Most people don't get the opportunity to forget their crimes. You had that chance for a while, but now it's time for you to remember again."

Xi looked at him uneasily. "My crimes?"

"You have to go back to The Company, Xi." When Xi shuddered and shook his head, Quibb looked at him with those same ancient eyes, saying, "This is your only chance."

"My only chance to do what—get killed?"

"The Company is the key to your mental block. You've gone down there upon occasion—but you've always turned away once you get within a few blocks of it. The Company terrifies you; the sight of its buildings eat away at something in you—but you have to go nonetheless. Remember: you're not G.W. Jefferson—nobody is looking for you—"

"What the hell do you want from me!" Xi said, before groaning in frustration.

"You have to go back to The Company."

"For *what?*"

"Turn away from all your delusions and fears," Quibb implored him, "—like this place. Leave them all behind and pursue Truth. Go down to The Company and reclaim your life. Besides, we both know that it's not capture you're afraid of—or death. Getting killed is irrelevant to you, Xi: at this point it's all about *how* you're going to die. Death is in fact your religion. You bow down to it: your prayers are to it. And when you pray, your great devil-god is The Company—and Shaka. The only way you'll ever be whole again is if you kill Shaka."

"*Stop saying that!*" he screamed, unable to help himself. ...And he remembered what had happened seven years ago: how some strange force had compelled him—or rather, compelled G.W.—to gun down the President and Shaka. He did not want to go through that again—even if only in his mind. He groaned anxiously, then placed the candle on the crate before going over to the cot. He sat down heavily then, so that the old springs creaked frightfully. "...I don't want to play this game anymore," he grumbled at last, waving his hand for Quibb to get lost.

"Don't you?" Quibb said sardonically.

"...I may be mad, okay," Xi conceded, sitting up on his elbows. "You may be some figment of my imagination or some bad drug trip...but I'm not stupid enough to go down there. Yes, I'm afraid, but I'm not stupid! *Kill Shaka?*" he said in disbelief, as the scope of it suddenly occurred to him—

Quibb laughed; when Xi looked up, he was again taken aback by the boy's too-beautiful face. "A little stupidity is just what you need now," Quibb began. "Look at where common sense has gotten you: living in a virtual sewer, eating rats and imagining two lice-infested men as your comrades. Your name is Dr. Xi Wang. You were a brilliant scientist seven years ago, not a jittery accountant from the International Finance Department…and what do you really have to lose? As you always say, you're as good as dead anyway."

Xi thought about it for a while. Rather, his mind drifted around the vague outlines of it; and finding himself equally confounded from all angles, he again looked up at Quibb. Suddenly curious, he asked, "What exactly do you want me to do?"

"First, you have to go to Company Square."

"You want me to just walk down there and kill him?" he said sarcastically.

"Of course not. I'm not trying to make a suicide bomber out of you. There is one way to peace of mind, Xi, and it's waiting down at The Company. Meet me down there and I'll tell you what to do." At that, the man faded into the darkness and Xi was once again left alone….

He did not want to think anymore. He was not even sure that he *could* think anymore. His thoughts rushed past him like the wind. He was more a victim of them than their master. After a few moments, it occurred to him that he could just go down to Company Square to take a look at things. Thus, pretending that nothing had been settled, he got out his bike and headed outside.

Sometimes one should ask questions not merely to receive answers,
but so that the respondent will be forced to listen to his own words.
Few people pay close attention to their own words.
VERSE 711:2 OF *The Teachings*

Mansmann was still standing before the exit of the basement chamber; for a brief moment, he could see the crescent moon beyond the small window of the door, but it soon disappeared behind the smog. He sighed.

Five years ago, when Shaka came to him and offered not only to fund his research, but also to make him the director of this hospital, Mansmann had hardly believed it. He had been sleeping at his desk in his uptown lab, drooling on the notes of his latest failed attempt to counteract the effects of his hair formula. He had been roused from sleep gruffly; when he looked up, Shaka and several of his attendants and bodyguards had been standing before him. All of them had been in the dark, monk-like robes that had become fashionable—except for Shaka, who had been in his trademark white suit. Mansmann had screamed at first, especially when he saw that the bodyguards had their guns trained on him, but Shaka had stepped up quickly, smiling reassuringly.

"Excuse the intrusion, Dr. Mansmann," the man had said.

The fact that the man had known his real name had left him with the feeling that he was *trapped—doomed.* "…What's going on?" Mansmann had managed to say after his heartbeat reached a rate that allowed speech.

"I wish to discuss two things with you. The first is that I would very much like to fund your research and provide you with whatever equipment you need."

Mansmann had cringed, glancing at his notes uneasily. "...What do you know about my research?"

"I know only that you have a great mind—and that in a former world you were able to use it to become a great success. You're the kind of man that I would like in my organization. In these dark times, all great minds should be supported—and should support one another. I'm trying to bring some civility back into the world."

"...Yes, I heard you were trying to run for mayor," Mansmann had said when he could think of nothing else to say; he had sat back in the chair, groaning as his back cracked.

Shaka had smiled at him. "Anyway, in my attempt to bring civility back into the world, I've started up a hospital."

"...Yes, I saw it on the news," he had said, gesturing to the screen playing on the far wall.

Shaka had laughed at him. "You still use a television?"

"I'm not a fan of PinkEyes," Mansmann had said without thought; he had grimaced as soon as the words left his mouth, but:

"Neither am I," Shaka had said with a wry smile, "—they give me a headache."

Mansmann had frowned.

"I mentioned that I wanted to discuss two things with you, Dr. Mansmann. The second is that I would like you to head my hospital—and to guide its operations in whatever capacity you wish."

"Me?" Mansmann had said, laughing uneasily. "I'm not a medical doctor." As he said it, he had remembered how he had made it through two years of medical school before he came to the conclusion that he hated dealing with people—and *sick* people in particular.

"Either way," Shaka had continued, "I would still like to fund your research; and there'll be no oversight from me—you'll be free to go in whatever direction you wish...."

Back in the present, Mansmann sighed. Five years ago, when he came down to look at the hospital, he had found that the doctors were actually only dazed men that wore PinkEyes programmed with various medical databases. Anyone could be a doctor now, because all the information was in the PinkEyes. Bums off the street could perform heart transplants; in this new era, all the knowledge of the universe was at their fingertips, so that intelligence, and even *consciousness*, was superfluous. More importantly—especially where this hospital was concerned—with PinkEyes, even health was superfluous. Why operate on a man with gallstones when by simply adjusting his Pink- Eyes, he would be unaware of the pain? Why check someone's abdominal pain, when a new fantasy would block out all discomfort? As such, many of the patients in the hospital were simply fools that had ignored minor cuts and sores and aches to the point where parts either needed to be amputated or cancerous growths bulged from their bodies and were inoperable. At first, Mansmann had tried to raise standards of care and have at least minimum sanitary protocols (like keeping men with various airborne plagues in separate wards), but it was pointless. Not only were medicines scarce or nonexistent: it was too easy to just block their suffering with the PinkEyes.

It was at that moment (while Mansmann was staring out of the door's window, up at the crescent moon) that a figure suddenly blocked out the moon. As Mansmann was in the basement, the side door he was currently standing before led out to some stairs—which ascended to street level. The figure stood on the top stair for a moment; then, as if receiving an order to charge, he bounded down the steps. Mansmann barely managed to leap to the side before the door burst open, banging against the wall. The crazed man flew into the room and headed straight for the bedridden wretches. Mansmann, still in shock, followed the man with his eyes; but as the crazed man leapt on the first man he came upon, and began to cackle, Mansmann suddenly recognized him. It was a demented necrophiliac that snuck in the hospital a few times a week. Coming to his senses, Mansmann yelled, "Kramer!" hoping that the guard was within earshot. He had met Kramer a few years ago, back at the lab. A gang of youths had charged into the lab one day (and had been on the verge of beating Mansmann to a pulp) when Kramer suddenly appeared and mowed them down with an Uzi. Since then, the man had been Mansmann's de facto bodyguard...but now, as Mansmann called for the man, there was no reply. "Kramer?" Mansmann called uncertainly as the necrophiliac began unzipping his pants. "Kramer!" Mansmann called more urgently...but then he realized that he had not seen Kramer all day—in *days* in fact. "Shit!" Mansmann cursed as the crazed man began to take out his frustrations on a wretch whom, palsied by his illness and PinkEyes fantasies, put up no resistance. Suddenly outraged, Mansmann yelled, "He's not even dead yet, you imbecile!" However, the lunatic was working himself into a frenzy now, his scrawny white buttocks visible as it worked up and down. "Kramer!" Mansmann screamed again. "Goddamnit!" he cried in frustration, finally realizing that he would have to do something. Still, just the thought of touching the lunatic made his skin crawl. The man was still giggling and cackling; Mansmann approached him tentatively, his face wearing a scowl of revulsion as the lunatic's scrawny buttocks began to work with more urgency. As though driven insane himself, Mansmann suddenly charged, screaming wildly as kicked the lunatic with all his strength. In a perfect world, the man would have been knocked unconscious—or at least sent flying—but the man hardly budged. Seeming to notice Mansmann for the first time, the lunatic's cackles and giggles ceased, and an enraged gleam shone in his eyes.

"Oh, shit!" Mansmann said, backing away. The lunatic left the wretch on the ground and started approaching Mansmann. However, as his pants were around his ankles, he promptly fell to the ground. Seeing his chance, Mansmann fled towards the side door. "Kramer!" he screamed desperately. The lunatic leapt to his feet and pulled his pants up all in one motion; in no time at all, he was chasing Mansmann. "Kramer, goddamnit!" Mansmann pleaded. When all hope seemed lost, and Mansmann's life was about to flash before his eyes, he suddenly remembered that he was carrying a stun gun. He pulled it from his pocket just as he reached the door; then, turning, he fired the gun at the lunatic. A wire shot out, implanting itself in the man; and as the electricity flowed through him, the man fell to the ground and began going into convulsions. Mansmann stood above the man for about a minute, still trembling. When the man ceased to move anymore, Mansmann sighed and leaned against the wall. He had that hypersensitive feeling that always came in the aftermath of the "flight or fight" response. His chest heaved as he gasped for air…On the TV, the reporter was still ranting about death and the horror of what had befallen Boston. Mansmann groaned and looked away.

Uncompromising brutality to that which is not immediately understood is the way to guarantee survival. Uncertainty leads to hesitancy, and that is tantamount to death. In an age when there is no guilt and no longing for what could have been, it is imperative to be quick on the draw— to destroy first and ask questions later…if at all.

VERSE 1534:6 OF *The Teachings*

The rusty chain on Xi's bike squeaked irritatingly—which made him uneasy, because it brought attention to him….As he went down the dark streets, riding through clouds of flies, the half-starved men of the city seemed even more alien to him. Of course, he had never been one of them, but now he felt total disconnection. As he watched them in the darkness, it occurred to him that more and more they were turning into a nocturnal race—especially in the summer. With the drugs, there were many that stayed awake for a days on end. In the winter, a great deal of them froze to death after they "came down" from their highs and fell asleep on the icy pavement. However, as Xi rode through a shantytown that had spilled into the street, it occurred to him that maybe it was not that they had become nocturnal, but that there were just so many of them that a large number of them were always forced to be out on the street. There definitely were not 20 million homes in the city, much less 20 million beds. All those men had to go somewhere, and the pavement was the only place. Indeed, there were shantytowns everywhere—some of them right down the middle of what had been major thoroughfares. What had once been the F.D.R Drive was now a major shantytown. There was not really any need for highways anymore. Not only was there no fuel for cars: no one was commuting to and from the suburbs anymore. As such, the precious space of the street was taken up by shantytowns. Some of the men built elaborate communities out of all kinds of discarded and pilfered objects, like cars and windows from what used to be department stores. There were also nomads, for lack of a better word, who carried their possessions everywhere with them. But as was the case with everything else, this had its drawbacks—namely that it made one easy prey. The trick was to have as little as possible, and have those possessions be so worthless and undesirable that no one would be bothered to steal them. Anything that could not be carried in a knapsack was a hindrance—and even carrying a knapsack made it too easy for the predators. That was why new arrivals to the city were always so easy to spot: they carried too much stuff. In all things, it was best to be a minimalist—which probably explained why Xi lived as he did. He had trained his palette and his mind to accept rat meat—as rats were an easy and plentiful source of protein. Then he bartered any surplus rats to eateries that specialized in "stew," so that he could get other staples. As there were neither banks nor standing financial institutions, the only way to acquire anything nowadays was through barter. The consumer economy was of course dead. The days of going into a store and purchasing a loaf of bread were over. Bread would be too expensive for an individual to attain anyway, especially in the city. There were still farms of course, but the logistics of getting the wheat to cities was too costly. In the initial upheaval of seven years ago, farmers would wake up practically every morning to find their fields raided and their animals butchered and roasted by bands of roving men. Thus, armed guards had had to be posted, which made the price of goods skyrocket. Moreover, with fuel stocks, like all stocks, being unreliable, some farmers had found that even when they managed to harvest, the crops rotted in silos with nowhere to go and no way to be transported. For all these reasons, most farmers had gone out of business within the first few years. Just like in the city, carrying too much had only attracted predators. Thus, the only way farmers had been able to survive was if they had a little dirt plot for themselves alone, out somewhere in the woods. In fact, today, the only entities that could undertake large farming operations were huge corporations that could afford small armies to guard the crops. Only they had the resources to purchase and maintain seed stocks, water supplies and fertilizer.

Only they could ship the crop to the cities, and only they could afford to buy. Accordingly, the only way for individuals to have something as seemingly insignificant as a roll of toilet paper was to work for a corporation. Heeding this inducement, millions of men had sold their souls to corporations in return for food and shelter. Most men were so desperate that it was not so much selling (which implied that they thought that their lives were worth something) as *surrender*; and after they surrendered, the corporations would get around the need to feed their workers by drugging them and brainwashing them and employing age-old "company town" tactics that had the worker being indebted for life after two or three loaves of bread. Suicide—either the direct kind, or the kind that involved drug use and the slow, inevitable deterioration of the human will to survive, were rife—

Just then, the billboard over Xi's head began to flash in that neon orange again, and he looked up to see another Tio Mendez broadcast. "Viva la Revolucion!" the caption read, again with the famous cartoon Mexican with bandoleers. However, too preoccupied and uneasy to care, Xi rode on....

It was about two blocks later that something peculiar happened: an old white woman suddenly appeared before him. He slammed on the brakes of the bike, then he toppled over the handlebars. Even as he lay on the ground, writhing in pain, the old woman remained there. He stared at her in amazement. She was not a real woman—this was certain because she was transparent, like a ghost, or an image projected on the world. Also, she seemed oblivious of him. She was naked and her skin and hair were wet, as though she were taking a shower. She *was* taking a shower, but the scenery of the bathroom did not appear along with her. All that there was was her naked body. Xi's eyes wandered over it in amazement; and as they did so, and he remembered what Quibb had said about allowing him to see into his subconscious mind, he suddenly recognized G.W.'s grandmother. He remembered it all now, but it was more than a mere memory, which had the passage of time to mitigate and shape it. He was viewing the scene as G.W. had seen it as a nine-year-old. G.W. had gone camping in the woods with his family and hidden in the bushes, in front of the outdoor shower. The reality of his grandmother's nakedness had mesmerized him: her pruny, sagging flesh; the drooping breasts that had long outlived their maternal purpose and now hung as useless, cumbersome appendages....The woman had propped up her leg on the wall to clean her vagina, and G.W. had been intrigued by the strangely contemplative expression that had been on her face as she stuck her fingers into herself to clean herself. It had been then that he realized the difference between the sexes—not the anatomical ones, for those had been known to every five-year-old by then, but the way those anatomical differences shaped their movements and self-concept. For weeks afterward he had watched the movements of women—the way they walked, their deportment...all the intimate little movements that shaped their lives—

G.W.'s grandmother suddenly disappeared. Xi got up from the ground confusedly. He looked around anxiously; some men on the street corner were having an argument—or at least talking loudly. Not knowing what he was supposed to make of the strange view into G.W.'s subconscious, Xi was suddenly wary of what else he might see—and what those things might say about him....And what did G.W.'s childhood voyeurism have to do with him? Xi's head was beginning to ache again. He got on the bike and continued to ride. He needed to *move*—to do something to preoccupy himself. He forgot about returning to The Company and simply followed the street.

The closer to midtown he got, the brighter the world got. There were actually some streetlights around here. There were also more video billboards in this area. Most of them were showing the festivities of Times Square. As Xi rode down the street, some of the men were actually laughing and joking with one another, so that for a moment the world seemed like a normal place. There were even hundreds of bicycle-drawn rickshaws, which gave this area an exotic, lively feel. On one block, there were dozens of tattoo parlors, where hundreds of men stood about to have the ever-present Glory to the Goddess tattoo. There were no corpses lying about here—The Company saw to that. Most of midtown, including Times Square, was in fact Company property. They had not put up gates and signs, like some of the other fiefdoms, but it was clear who the boss was. Even the swarms of flies seemed to have disappeared, as though The Company's influence extended even to vermin. There was even talk that The Company would get the subways to run again, and hold an election so that the city could rise up out of the stone age, but nobody really cared enough....

Circe was on the billboards, singing the most beautiful aria Xi had ever heard in his life. He stopped for a moment and stared up at the billboard. Circe's voice opened up things in Xi that he did not want opened. He did not want to think about beauty—even the illusion of it. Beauty made life worth living. Beauty gave men something to hold on to; and just like in Buddhism, the only way to live a good life and have peace of mind was to resist clinging to anything....

The last couple of blocks to Company Square were hard ones. Actually, the Image Broadcast Complex, like the towering skyscrapers of The Company, had been visible since 96th Street. The 150-story skyscraper was lighted in neon lights with a kind of phallic pride. Around Company Square, there were always hordes of men wrangling for sympathy from The Company, like sinners trying to get into heaven. Many were just men looking for work: waiting on line to replace the hundreds of men that inevitably died each week. There was also a nascent cult of the Image Broadcast Complex, whose pilgrims came from all over the world by the thousands in order to touch the dark, nonmetallic material that covered the structure. Unfortunately for them, unlike seven years ago, when hundreds of thousands had been allowed to gather inside Company Square, now only the select of heaven were being allowed up into that super-world. The rest had to wait at street level, behind spiked metal barricades, stretching their hands out pitifully as they begged the indifferent guards for a chance.

Because of all the men, Xi had to get off his bike and walk with it; and even then, he had to stop about a block from the gate, as the throng was just too dense. He craned his neck then, and looked up at the entire length of the main skyscraper. As he did so, he remembered fleeing from The Company that night seven years ago. His mind flashed with images of running over all those people...doing anything in order to escape. Quibb had said that those recollections were not his; nevertheless, the realization that he was on the verge of returning to this place made his stomach twinge. Like Quibb had said, he had avoided The Company at all costs. He had avoided it the way pagans avoided a bedeviled patch of the forest.

Looking at the guards at the gates, and the splendor of The Company's buildings, it occurred to Xi that simply getting to Shaka was an impossibility. The man appeared on the air every once in a while, but no one had really *seen* him in years. Like all great things, he was more myth than man; and now, as Xi looked at all the men desperate to sell their souls to The Company, he knew that he was mad for even allowing Quibb to imply that he could occupy the same plane of existence as Shaka.

It was while he stood there craning his neck that it occurred to him that he had not thought about Quibb during his ride down here. He had not thought about the madness of dreaming up friends and forgetting what his home was supposed to look like. He had not thought much about anything in fact—as though he had been somnambulating. Now acutely awake, he started backing away. He felt as though Quibb had cast some spell on him, which was now wearing off. Eager to be free before Quibb could return and recast his spells, he began turning around (which was difficult to do with the encumbrance of his bike and the crowd). Unfortunately, when he finally turned around and looked up, he saw Quibb waiting on the periphery of the crowd.

Xi walked up numbly, like a condemned man. He remembered the thought he had had back at the basement—that he could bash Quibb's brains out…but that seemed out of the question now. It was not that he was utterly passive to Quibb, but that dealing with Quibb seemed to require resources that he did not have. At every instant, he felt himself outplayed.

By the time he finally reached Quibb, a feeling of wariness and inevitability had just about settled about him. It was then that Quibb smiled a strange, bittersweet smile and said: "Tell me something, Xi: have you ever been in love?"

The question took him off guard; he stared at Quibb for a while, as they stood there on the periphery of the desperate men. And then, employing the kind of self-defensive sarcasm that men used when they were ill at ease, he scoffed: "If you really were part of me, then you would not have to ask that."

Quibb smiled again: "Sometimes one asks questions not merely to receive answers, but so that the respondent will be forced to listen to his own words. Few people pay close attention to themselves—and their words." Having said that, he gestured with his head for them to continue walking, and Xi complied. There was a strange silence between them now, as Quibb's question lingered in the air.

"…Who the hell are you, Quibb?" Xi asked once again.

Quibb smiled but looked straight ahead—not at Xi. His voice was calm and resonant as he said, "I'm a man who wants to know about love….Have you ever felt it?"

"Yeah," he blurted out last, as though frustrated with the question—with the idiocy of the situation and love, itself. And yet he continued, "I *think* I was…"

"You're still thinking about G.W.'s wife?"

"…Yes." He went to ask about seeing G.W.'s grandmother, but Quibb went on:

"Would you die for someone you loved—or for *something* you loved?"

"…I guess," he whispered as they walked along. "I would be willing to, if I found something like that…."

Quibb nodded then, as though deep in thought: "…Maybe you're right."

They walked along in the midst of another strange silence. It was as though each had forgotten about the other. Xi was startled to realize that he felt almost comfortable with Quibb at his side. About a block and a half later, Quibb stopped and faced him:

"Here we are."

Xi looked around confusedly. The block was empty. They could still hear sounds from the revelry in Times Square—for those were everywhere— but with the exception of some nondescript buildings, which had been warehouses seven years ago, there was nothing else about. It was then that Quibb pointed to the manhole cover at their feet, revealing that that was their destination. Then, gesturing to Xi's rickety bike: "Leave that: you won't be needing it anymore."

"What do you have in mind?" he asked anxiously.

But Quibb only pointed to the curb: "Beneath that dumpster, you'll find a crowbar. Use it to open the manhole cover." Xi went over; just as Quibb had said, there was a crowbar. He got down on his knees to get the crowbar, then he returned to the manhole cover. Quibb was smiling at him. "…Time is of the essence," he said when Xi seemed uneasy.

"…What's in there?" Xi said, gesturing to the manhole.

"It's an entrance to The Company."

"Look, I'm not sure I want to do this."

"But you are still curious, aren't you?"

"…You said if I met you down here, you'd tell me what the plan was."

"I won't have to tell you anything: it will all be self-evident once you open that cover and climb down there."

It was not exactly a satisfactory answer, but once again overcome by that "what the hell" mindset, he shrugged his shoulders and pried the manhole open. Quibb nodded his head encouragingly; Xi, like a fool, descended into the darkness. At the bottom of the rungs, there was a corridor about 25 meters long. At the end of the corridor, there was a dull light and a door. He looked back up through the manhole opening to see if Quibb was coming; but just then, someone hemmed at the end of the corridor (by the door); when Xi looked, he saw Quibb waiting for him.…Xi walked up with the same feeling of being trapped within a plot-less fantasy. It was all so surreal that he once again could not help thinking that he was dreaming and that he would not have to face the consequences of his present actions once he awoke from this. Besides, there was still an element of detached curiosity about him. A side of him yearned to know what was going to happen next— even though another side was terrified and bewildered. Quibb was still smiling that disconcertingly beautiful smile; as always, Xi did not know what to make of it. Eventually, he looked away uneasily, and it was as his eyes went to the ground near the door (which had before been cast in shadows), that he noticed that someone was lying on the ground. The door was actually held open by a man's body!

"—What the hell…?"

"This is the worker you're going to replace."

"What!" And then, looking down at the body: "…*Replace*? What the hell are you talking about?"

"After you put on his PinkEyes, the sensors won't know you aren't him."

"Put on the PinkEyes…!" Xi said in alarm. And then, "How did you know he was going to be here?"

"He's here because I made him come here. I made him disconnect the sensors around the door, then I overloaded his PinkEyes, so that the last of his will would be lost."

"*You?*" he whispered, as though not quite able to follow.

"He's brain dead now, but all his vital functions are going, controlled by the PinkEyes."

"—And you expect me to wear them!"

Quibb smiled, saying: "That's a strange reaction, seeing as how you invented them?"

"…What?"

"You invented PinkEyes, Dr. Wang—except that you called them Portable Dimensional Interfaces or something like that."

Xi looked on with the same sense of bewilderment. The detached curiosity left him for good then, and all he wanted to do was get away—*flee*. Quibb smiled then, saying:

"Why would I bring you all the way down here just to kill you now—or to *get* you killed?"

As Xi looked at the dead man on the ground, it suddenly occurred to him that if Quibb had actually killed that man, then he could not be a figment of his imagination! Xi retreated a step, as though beaten back by a cold breeze; he looked around as if seeing the world for the first time, then he stared at Quibb with new suspicion and understanding. This morsel of logic and common sense brightened Xi's spirits; he felt as though he had figured out a complicated puzzle, so that he smiled, saying: "…I admit that you had me going for a while: all that 'I'm a projection of your mind' shit. I don't know who you are, or who you *think* you are, but there is no way I'm putting those things on—no way I'm doing anything else!" However, it was then that Quibb spoke up, saying:

"Maybe this will impress you then." As he said it, Quibb brought his soft, warm hands to Xi's temples. The touch was like a bolt of lightning going through him. There was again a flash of white light, in which Xi was lost and disoriented. For those few moments, he did not know if he was still standing or not. His body seemed to evaporate around him, leaving only his essence. And now, building all around him, there was a scene from his past: a distant world from another reality. He was back in Chinatown, a teenager in love—and there was the white girlfriend that his parents would never approve of, with her perfect little pear-shaped face and her soft, red lips. He could even smell her delicate, flowery perfume now. They had gone out for a month or so, with him sneaking out to meet her...to touch her and hear her say a few whispered words. It was a whole other lifetime; he had been a whole other person, looking at the world with hope and that all-encompassing, cataclysmic love known only by the young and young at heart....His father had come upon them holding hands in the subway station and slapped him across his face with so much force that the man's hand-print had been on his face for two days. Xi had never seen her after that—

Xi collapsed to the ground as he emerged back into the present. The present, juxtaposed to the wonder and vividness of his past (or at least his past love) seemed dour and depressing. Moreover, that fragment of his history was perhaps too bright: everything else was either blinded or cast in shadows; and to a certain extent, his sudden recollection of what he had been was perhaps worse than ignorance, because it gave him something to lament and pine for. Quibb had opened his mind to things that could only exist in that bygone world of youthful dreams. Xi suddenly felt bereft— as devastated by the loss of his love as he had been when he was a teenager. He lay in the moldy filth on the ground, cringing, looking up at Quibb in desperation as the world of the present began to focus around him:

"...Who the hell are you?" Xi managed to gasp.

"I'm whatever you need me to be...whatever you allow yourself to believe I am. Now, get up," Quibb commanded. "*Get up*," Quibb repeated more urgently, so that Xi clambered to his feet, like a drunk who had just been kicked out of a bar. "Remove the PinkEyes from the man," Quibb instructed him presently. Xi reached down and tried taking out the man's PinkEyes—

"Pull harder!" Quibb instructed him. "They're fused to his corneas—*pull harder!*"

With Quibb's exhortations eating away at him, Xi was now clawing at the man's eyeballs with his grimy, jagged fingernails—

"*Pull!*" And then, as Xi sank his nails into the man's eyes, grunting as he pulled with all his strength, the man's eyes ripped apart, so that the jelly of his eyes squirted out over Xi's hands. Xi squealed out; he looked down at the gelatinous ooze that now covered his fingers, realizing that although the PinkEyes were in his hands, so were the outer covering of the man's eyes—

"Put them on quickly!" Quibb commanded him, "—before the sensors realize that he's dead."

Quibb's orders were so decisive and overpowering that Xi, in his anxious, benumbed state, brought his trembling hands (and the gory PinkEyes) up to his eyes. The instant the PinkEyes touched his eyes he was rocked back, as all the information surged through his mind. As he blacked out, he heard Quibb screaming at him, saying: "Don't gulp it down, *concentrate!*" But Xi was drowning in the information and easy pleasure.

IV

*In a sense, men don't really fantasize about women—but about
themselves with women; all sexual yearnings are not so much about
one's lovers as they are about one's idealization of oneself as a lover.*
VERSE 309:1 OF *The Teachings*

Xi awoke as he had awakened so many times before—in a panic,
totally lost…He gasped and sat up in bed, panting. For those first
few moments, there was nothing but darkness, so that it was as
though he were floating in a void. Then, all around him, pink, glowing
orbs began to appear. He instinctively went to scurry away in horror, but
then he was possessed by the feeling that he was *supposed* to be here. That
was the strange thing: he was overcome by the feeling that he was home. It
did not come from within him: it felt *imposed* from without—especially
since he had no idea where he was. It seemed to be some kind of huge
dorm—but the vastness of it left his mind enfeebled. The men around
him—*thousands* of them—were all wearing PinkEyes. He, like the rest of
them, was sleeping on a bunk bed that had four levels. He was on the top
level, able to survey the entire chamber…but he still had no idea where he
was, nor did he know how he had come to be there. He groaned, then massaged his head, as though hoping to jumpstart his thought processes. As he
took a deep breath to calm himself, his throat burned from the musty odor
of the men. He coughed….

Everyone seemed to be emerging from sleep now. Some were screaming
out and panting like Xi, but all of them were awakening now, confused and
devastated that their PinkEyes fantasies had been disrupted. When Xi real-

ized that he too was wearing the PinkEyes, he felt as though a miasma were sweeping over him....He had no idea how long he had been in this place: it could have been days or weeks...*years*...even all his life. Now, as he looked around, Quibb and the other facts that explained his existence in this dorm were like a farfetched dream that no sane man could take seriously. On top of that, wearing PinkEyes made it practically impossible to concentrate. It was difficult to explain. It was like being able to glimpse into the mind of God. Xi only had to think of something and it opened up on a screen before him—or in the *world* before him. Everywhere he looked, there were ghosts in his field of vision—information constantly streaming...dates, times, bits of historical data. Every moment, there was the temptation to exercise all the power at his command and conjure something out of the nothingness. Quibb had told him that he would be able to see into his subconscious mind, but the PinkEyes intensified everything to the nth degree. He could be anywhere in the globe in nanoseconds, just as Shaka had promised years ago. In fact, wearing the PinkEyes was like being everywhere at once—and seeing everything at once. It all swirled before his eyes, beckoning him like a temptress; and with his consciousness spread across what was practically an infinite plain, he had instantaneous access to things that his conscious mind could not even digest as yet—elements of theories that were understood only by an esoteric few, calculations to mathematical proofs far beyond his comprehension...and for some reason, he kept getting visions of the outside world: grainy images of bombed cities and purple, shimmering skies. Those things were all hovering on the periphery of his mind, like a tidal wave ready to rush in and wash away his consciousness.

He groaned in the darkness, feeling dazed and restless. The image of a naked, gyrating woman suddenly popped into his field of vision. He realized that he had been dreaming about her or conjuring her—or whatever men did when they wore PinkEyes in their sleep. As he watched her, he realized that she was faceless—that her face was literally a blank slab of flesh. He shut his eyes hard as not to see; he conjured images of war and hate—anything to free his mind of the faceless woman that was somehow the embodiment of his fantasies—

The man on the bunk next to his began screaming gibberish; Xi stared at him uneasily, until he realized that the man was praying—babbling something about the Goddess' love. Xi looked away and massaged the back of his neck with his trembling hand, still hoping to soothe his worsening headache. As he sat there in the darkness, trying to make sense of his existence, he miraculously remembered that all the men of this dorm (himself included) were workers at the Image Broadcast Complex. Even then, all that he could remember of his stay here were vague images of himself sitting alone in a small, dark windowless room. In that room, he had sat at a console with hundreds of flashing lights; on cue, he had found himself pushing buttons and changing circuit boards. He did not even know why he had pushed particular buttons or replaced particular boards—he had just fallen into it, following the directions programmed into the PinkEyes. PinkEyes gave men the ability to perform complicated surgeries, build technological marvels...even speak ancient Greek if the urge hit them...but he shook his head as he again accepted the fact that he had no access to the *knowledge* behind these great and wondrous acts—any more than a computer had knowledge of what it was doing.

Xi rubbed his temples again. He could already feel the PinkEyes taking over—not by forcing or eroding his will, but by giving him everything he wanted. In actuality, it was wrong to say that any of the men had been enslaved by the PinkEyes. The PinkEyes were whatever you wanted them to be. The men in the dorm with him—and the billions more around the world that used the devices—were like people drinking in a bar. Some wanted to get drunk—to forget, or to convince themselves that they were having a good time; some probably had no intention of getting drunk, but were swept up by the merriment and lost track of time and the number of drinks; still others, had one drink and called it quits. True, there were men who went around probably never seeing what was before them. These unfortunates could be seen in the city's gutters and in the special wards set up by The Company; but if they were enslaved, they were enslaved by the freedom and the power of being able to conjure anything. Since he had been wearing the PinkEyes, Xi had had at least one mind-warping PinkEyes fantasy. In it, he had been a great lover—an adonis with a harem of millions. The only disturbing thing was that all the women had been faceless....

His mind wandered to Quibb at that moment; but again, that only set him down irrational paths—into fanciful places, where men had too-beautiful faces and long, slender fingers. He remembered that Quibb had told him that he had invented PinkEyes. The man had called him Dr. Wang, and told him about his laboratory. However, those things were still as incomprehensible and groundless as they had been when Quibb first told him. In fact, he now could not help thinking that Quibb—and even the events of seven years ago—had been nothing but a fantasy conjured by the PinkEyes. He remembered the gigolo mustache and smiled to himself—albeit nervously. Maybe he had always worked in the Image Broadcast Complex. Maybe all the elements of his past were just a dream...maybe they had all dreamed their pasts and were nothing but mindless automatons whose only moments of freedom came when the dark pyramid dreamed for them.

Presently, he wondered what time it was; and as the time magically appeared before him, it occurred to him that they had all been summoned for their shift. Some of the men were talking to one another now, discussing their fantasies. They seemed so very alien to him now. All the other men had already surrendered to their PinkEyes—whereas Xi could still hear Quibb screaming for him to resist the easy pleasure of the devices. Even as the hundreds of men began to descend from the bunk beds and line up for showers, Xi's mind returned to the prospect of Quibb. He could still remember the extraordinary feelings and images that had come when Quibb touched him with those warm, soft hands; his heart still ached from those recollections of teenage love; and in the final analysis, he was desperate to believe that he had once loved and been a human being. Quibb's touch had done all that; and on some level, Xi was desperate to be touched again— even if only in his fantasies....

To find out the greatness of a place, one should not go to the enclaves
of luxury and refinement, but to the place where the despair is greatest.
Only there can one see the true nature of the society, since it is in the
enclaves of suffering that the true nature of those in power—
the great ones—can be seen.
VERSE 1193: 4–5 OF *The Teachings*

The city was so huge that only those on the periphery of the great behemoth were as yet aware of what had already begun. Out of nowhere, thousands of lights streaked across the heavens. At first, the sight was inconceivably beautiful. Some of the men, dazed from whatever intoxicants they had managed to concoct or procure, smiled at the sight, thinking of how good this batch of drugs was turning out to be. Also, there was something mesmerizing about the way those streaking lights turned the sky a shimmering purple. It was only when the first of those streaking lights fell to the earth and exploded that the men began to scream out in horror.

God is a creation of pain and hardships.
VERSE 3433:23 OF *The Teachings*

On the TV, another successful episode of *Throw the First Stone* ended— which was to say that another unfortunate fool had been stoned to death. After a few days of tinkering unsuccessfully in his lab, Mansmann had returned to the hospital. (Shaka provided him with an armored vehicle for such trips.) At the hospital, there were not even any other doctors anymore. Nobody bothered. There were at least 20 corpses in the hospital, but even Mansmann did not really care anymore. The necrophiliac he had hit with the stun gun a few days ago was still lying on the ground—and was now a festering pile of maggots. Mansmann looked over at the corpse absentmindedly. Remembering Kramer's strange disappearance, it occurred to him that everyone he had ever known—and had the slightest connection with—had disappeared. It was at times like these that he found himself wondering why he did not just put a bullet through his head and end this entire farce.

Mansmann yawned, then waved the flies away from his mouth. After a few moments, he stared out of the window—up at the sky. In the chamber behind him, one of the men cried out again, but that was too common an occurrence to draw him totally from his reverie. On the screen to his left, there was another report on the Purple Horde, but those reports had long ceased to register in his mind. Mansmann was thinking his usual jumbled thoughts when he saw dozens of lights streak across the heavens. He stood watching them abstractedly, thinking, through the process of association, of biblical fireballs falling from the sky. During those dreamy moments— that is, before those streaking lights hit the ground and shook the earth— it did not occur to him what they might be. Only when the earth was rocked by their impact, and his shrill cries of panic rose above the explosions, did he know.

If one no longer knows what is real, then nothing matters.
If one can dream away all fears, then courage is banished from the world;
if one can live the unreal, then the real becomes superfluous.
VERSE 1124:23 OF *The Teachings*

The Goddess opened her eyes and arose from the mattress, panting as if she had just run from the horrors of a distant dream world. However, that was the strange thing: the dream had been almost soothing. She tried to analyze it, but it was quickly lost as she tried to retrace her steps. For a moment, she did not know where she was. She looked around anxiously, a side of her already expecting the worst. It was then that she recognized the cramped room from her previous moments of consciousness. Also, the murmuring (the *power*) was still there. It was a dull field of energy around her. She could sense it gathering its strength so that it could punish her for waking up. As for now, however, she felt something new and puzzling: the feeling of self—that she, for the most part, was in control of her body. This moment of reorganization seemed to be all that she had before the power reached full strength. She looked desperately around the room, not quite sure what she was looking for. Then, her eyes at last came to the door, which she was shocked to see was still open.

She got up from the mattress, overwhelmed by the feeling that it was either now or never. She could already feel the power settling about her, preparing to strike. She shuffled towards the door, feeling spent beyond reason. When she peeped out of the doorway, she again had to brace herself against the realization that the corridor seemed to have no terminus—in either direction! And which direction had she come from the last time she was conscious? She searched her mind, but quickly gave up the struggle. It all seemed so hopeless. Was there even a way out of this place...? But she resisted these thoughts with all of her strength. She walked into the corridor, randomly picked a direction, and began walking. She tried to run, but was too weak. She had only taken a couple of steps, yet she was already out of breath. Suddenly, an all-encompassing pain gripped her, and the murmuring seemed like bombastic ringing in her ears. But even then, she only gritted her teeth and went on, knowing that this was the punishment to be paid for her resistance. It now seemed that her senses existed only to cause her pain. She could not hear anymore—all that there was, was that ringing. She could not see anymore—all that there was, was that painful blur of light and motion. After a while, she was so giddy that she did not even know if she was still standing. All that she knew was that motion was her salvation: everything else was death. She kept repeating this to herself, so that it became like a guru's chant, putting her in a trance—

Then, out of the chaos, a scene suddenly appears. In the vision, she is hiding in a dark place, watching a TV. She watches images of war and self-destructive violence...and there always seems to be a story on TV about a young girl who has killed her mother and blown up buildings. Around this girl there is always talk of God...and the vision goes on, now showing a world of smoke and fire. All of these images flash in her mind, like scenes on a TV when the viewer flips from channel to channel, seeing part of one show and part of another. And yet, this manner of viewing the world is her way. Hers is a kind of TV consciousness, rendering disconnected bits of a million shows into a stream of logic that only she can conceptualize. As her consciousness expands, she sees herself hiding in terror, looking out on the world with fearful revulsion. With all the fires, the sky is a disconcerting vermilion hue. Outside, soldiers are marching again—in riot gear—but people do not seem to care anymore. This is probably why she has to hide—this sudden carelessness. Everywhere, there is a new kind of laughter—shrill, mirthless...*insane*—

Another scene takes shape before her: men, imbued with a kind of rabid sexuality, rampaging down the streets. But on those streets, too, is a middle-aged woman whose shocking dishevelment—with ripped, grimy clothes from days of hiding—makes the girl shudder. The sudden debasement of things once idealized—once held as indissoluble—makes her want to cry out to the woman to run. She watches all this from behind dark curtains in her hiding place; she bites her bottom lip as she sees the mindless, amoeba-like way the men of the rape mobs move and engulf their victims…The middle-aged woman sees them too late; she turns and is swept down…down into the filth of the gutter. The men are there, chanting as if the woman were a sacrifice to their god. One of the men, the girl notices from her hiding place, wears the tattered remains of a police uniform. He is their nucleus: their god. His face is full of suffering as he draws the woman down; and in those eyes is the kind of pain she imagines on the face of Jesus when he suffered on the cross. The man's eyes are Jesus' eyes, looking down on the defiled world that has condemned him to death. And all about him, men gather, chanting like the first Christians must have chanted when they realized the ascension of their human-born Jesus into God, free of frailty and lust—free of compromise and uncertainty. All around, men gather, chanting with their fundamentalist vigor as the woman's voice whines eerily above the commotion of their religion—

The vision continues, now showing images of the President being gunned down and chaos spreading all over the world. She sees that the White House is now ransacked and burned, so that the soot and ashes have turned it black. All these images swirl in the Goddess' mind, seemingly devoid of meaning. However, it is then that she hears a TV announcer's voice—another byproduct of her TV consciousness—saying, with a kind of horrific solemnity: "…the end of woman." Hundreds of voices are saying it in fact, so that the chorus thunders from the sky and seems to be a pronouncement from God. The end of woman—the end of *her*? She feels even more disembodied—as though her body were dissolving—

And then, miraculously, her vision ended, and she again found herself alone, stumbling down the endless corridor. Replacing the chaos of the vision, was the pain rendered by the murmuring and the power. These, however, she could deal with, as they were old companions. The things that she had just seen were too much for her. They had filled her with the kind of awestruck revulsion and terror that a monk praying alone in the darkness for decades would have had to the sudden appearance of God's enigmatic face. After her long search for answers, all that she could do was let the visions fade into myth, and then recede into nothingness. In fact, she was so terrified of what she had seen that she almost groped for the old pain and disorientation. When she felt those things settling over her, immolating her senses, she reveled in them. There was something almost suicidal about her now, as if the vision had been something beyond pain and death.

However, there was still a thought resounding in her mind: her guru's chant about escape. It confronted her like an old lover, shaming her. Escape? Yes, she remembered at last: saw the cramped, sweltering room. That was another death to be avoided. The terror and confusion were still there, but the choice ahead was clear: she had to get out of here, because staying was death. Her pace, slowed by her confusion, picked up again as she felt a new single-mindedness building in her. The details of what she had seen—like the emaciated shells of the women shuffling down the corridor, and the insignia on the placards—were forgotten for now. She let everything else be taken and warped—her senses, her memories—but she held fast to the simple and vital knowledge that she had to escape.

By now, the pain, as best as she could describe it, was "thick" around her. She had to fight to move through it, as if she were in a quagmire. Still, motion was her rebellion, so she concentrated on the movement of her limbs, letting everything else fall away. The ringing in her ears was like a jackhammer drilling into her skull; her senses were so frayed that she closed her eyes, only taking brief glimpses every so often. She went on like this maybe for minutes, maybe for hours…But on one of her glimpses into oblivion, she saw something that at first she did not understand. She looked up and saw the end of the corridor standing no more than five paces ahead of her. More than that, at the end, there was what looked like an open door and a staircase! She would have tried to confirm what she saw, but just then the world began to swirl before her once again, so that she quickly closed her eyes. Did she dare hope? Maybe the power was simply playing with her senses: giving her hope only to take it away and despond her. Now trembling, she opened her eyes and peeked out at the world again, but what she saw was so disorienting that she could make nothing out. She could feel herself beginning to waver—

I have to get out! she thought defiantly, in the face of all that was lost to her. She again tried to talk—to yell out to hear her voice—but her voice still belonged to the power. The ringing in her ears was now maddening; and even behind closed eyelids, the world was still swirling. She could not feel her legs anymore—she could not even tell if she was still moving! Her senses were either too numb, or too wracked with pain—

Five paces...

She shuffled along the wall, blind, deaf and dumb, her only hope being that she would be able to escape before even movement was lost to her. There was a wall ahead of her, impeding her! Was this, too, a trick? She opened her eyes, challenging the strange vertigo; she let her hands roam the wall, challenging the numbness. A doorway! She could not believe it. She saw the outlines of it faintly though the swirling landscape. She had to go, and quickly, before the power became complete! She thrust herself headlong though the opening and almost immediately found herself toppling down a flight of stairs. Through the numbness, she felt the blows against her body. It seemed to go on forever; but at last, she lay still at the bottom of the flight of stairs. Where there had been numbness, there was now painful throbbing; where there had simply been pain, there was now something almost sublimely excruciating.

She would have cried out, but she still had no voice. She lay there in silence, with her face contorted by the pain and madness. And now *everything*, she suddenly realized, seemed silent and still and dark. The ringing was gone; and when she opened her eyes and looked around, she realized that the overpowering sense of disorientation was quickly fading away. The murmuring was still there; however, it was so faint that it was as if its place in her soul had been jarred out of place by her fall.

She looked around, dazed. She was lying on a platform, between the ascending staircase she had just fallen down, and a descending staircase.

Above her, she saw where she had come from: the doorway that led to the bright corridor; below her, she saw a flight of stairs descending into darkness. For her, there was only hope in the darkness...

She got up, trembling as if she were an old woman...maybe she *was* old. But this was not the time to consider all that was uncertain. Now was the time to consider only what she knew to be true: that she had to escape. She hied down the stairs as recklessly as she could without toppling once more. She now felt the blood trickling down her forehead from when she had fallen; her left hand throbbed mercilessly, so that she wondered if it was broken. Still, she could nurse those things later: she could not waste this respite from the murmuring. All hope lay in the darkness ahead; all that she had was this flight of stairs, going down and down, deeper into the darkness. It was now so dark that she could see nothing: she had to stretch out her hand for guidance—

Ahead of her was another wall. No, it was a door! She stood there, trembling in the darkness, hearing her harsh breath echoing in the silence. Her hand searched the surface of the door: it was one of those doors that...she was not quite sure how she knew this, but it was a pressure door: the type seen in submarines. There was a thing to be turned, and a lever that had to be pulled in order to release the door. For a moment, she stood there uncertainly, wondering how she knew these things. And what if she was underwater! How would she escape then? Maybe she would open the door and drown!

But again stricken with the wild defiance, she turned the lever to loosen the pressure seal—until she heard the lock click open. She paused for a moment, then pushed the door open with all her strength and will. There was a sudden, disorienting whoosh of air, which pushed her from the back. It was so powerful that it almost pushed her through the open door. She was squinting her eyes, fighting the rushing air until she could see what she was being pushed out into...but she could not fight it anymore: she was being pushed through the doorway!

After she was pushed through, she almost fell to the ground, but managed to keep her balance. She stood there, mesmerized. Was she dreaming?

Immediately in front of her, there was a lawn, which stretched for about 50 meters in front of her; beyond that, there were dark woods. She took a tentative—almost unconscious—step. Looking down, she realized that the uncut, calf-high grass was wet from a recent rain shower. The moon's rays highlighted the grass and all that was around her. Indeed, everywhere, for as far as her eyes could see, there was a verdant world, not so much highlighted by the moon's rays, as *glowing*. The air that she now breathed was fresh and cool. It revitalized her as it blew against her sweat-drenched body; and her thoughts, so long unfocused, suddenly seemed lucid and unencumbered. The murmuring, and the power, and all that had enslaved her, she felt receding. She giggled at this sensation—at this *freedom*—and was startled to find that she could laugh now: could force air from her lungs and open and close her jaw as she wanted.

She stood there laughing as she lost herself in her new powers. But then, she perceived something beyond the now faint murmuring and her own laughter. When she acknowledged the clangorous noise in the air, she realized that her opening the door had set off an alarm! When this occurred to her, she stood petrified for a moment. All her old uncertainties reclaimed her. She probably would have stayed there forever, unable to overcome this one last hurdle, were it not for the old thought of escape. Driven by the instinct—almost the *madness*—of escape, she ran across the lawn, towards the thickness of the woods. Her feet, she realized for the first time, were bare. The wet grass tickled them. She almost giggled at this new sensation as well; but just then, a gruff voice commanded:

"Stop!"

It seemed to be a computerized voice. Either way, she was so used to taking orders that she froze. She turned towards the voice and stood petrified as she saw what had called her. At first she only stared at the four or five figures that marched towards her with a robot-like stiffness. They were wearing a kind of non-metallic armor, replete with visor-enclosed helmets. She stared helplessly at these robotic soldiers, too terrified to scream or *move*...and then she suddenly noticed the insignia on their chests: the same one from the corridor! She took a terrified step backward, shaking her head. It was then that she chanced to turn her head and see the true dimensions of the building she had just exited. It rose at least fifty stories, so that its height was lost in the heavens. As for its width, it stretched at least 400 meters on either side of her. So incredibly huge...and no windows, no lights...It seemed like a sarcophagus of steel and concrete. She could not even make out the door from which she had just come: everything was lost in the shadows. That other world, locked behind the steel and concrete, seemed like another dimension. While she was now breathing this fresh air and reveling in this verdant world, she remembered the stuffiness and the unending corridors. Her entire insensate existence within that place once again triggered the demand that she escape—

But the robots were only about ten meters away from her now, ambling steadily towards her. Frozen by the reality of their approach, she saw no choice but to prepare herself for death. As such, when a projectile suddenly whizzed past her ear and hit the first of the robots in the torso, she only blinked confusedly; when two other guards fell, she looked towards the tree line, where there were men with machine guns. The men were waving eagerly for her to come. She watched it all as if in slow motion. She looked back at the monsters: only two of them were still standing; however, the others were still functioning: with their protective armor, they had only been knocked down. They were beginning to rise now, and something about that was more terrifying than their presence. Before she even realized it, she was running towards the woods—and the men with the machine guns. She was still uncertain about the men, but they were preferable to the certain death that would come if the robots brought her back inside that sarcophagus of a building. She looked over her shoulder: the robots were all on their feet now—like corpses that had risen from death. The men with machine guns were screaming insanely for her to run faster now, and yet she still felt as though she were moving in slow motion: that no matter what she did, she would never get away from her pursuers.

At last, she was in the woods; a man grabbed her hand and began to run with her, but one of the robots' bullets quickly brought him down. She did not stop. Behind her, the firefight seemed to intensify. It seemed as though grenades were being thrown now: as though the very earth were being torn apart behind her. Now mad with terror, she ran through the woods. From behind, she heard the thundering reports of guns that she instinctively knew to be those of the robots. She heard the men with machine guns crying out then—screaming in terror, so that she knew that they were done for: that she was the only one left. She was now on a declivity, slipping in the damp sod, getting entangled in vines, scratched and bruised by unseen boughs and trunks...She could hear the robots following her—there was not even a firefight anymore: the men with machine guns had been wiped out. She ran for her life! Fear charged her, and she ran like people ran in nightmares: single-mindedly, with all the purpose that it was humanly possible to conjure.

She heard her heart beating from far away; and the way that she was running, it was almost as if she were running towards her heartbeat. The escape alarm of the building—the *fortress*—was still pealing in the background, sounding like a hysterical woman. She wanted to strangle that woman with all the rage that eventually came of fear. The hope of escape was now far off in the distance, too complex and confusing to be of use to her. Once again, all that she had, was the thought of escape, itself: a sort of animalistic, instinctual impetus. She surrendered herself to it, running even more recklessly and blindly; so that in a way, she lost her soul to the thought of escape—

She hit her foot against something and found herself toppling to the ground. She rolled and slid uncontrollably down the muddy slope. In the darkness, it was like being devoured by a creature: rocks cut into her like jagged teeth; the slippery ground was like a throat...From behind, she heard the blaring alarm; the robots were still calling out, trying to discern where she had gone. She was beyond disorientation: beyond even thought—

She landed with a splash in a deep pit, and lay there, dazed, wallowing in the mud. She was too terrified to cry out at the pain. She could still hear the footsteps and the computerized yells of her pursuers. They sounded like ogres, uprooting baby trees and trampling whatever lay in their path as they charged down the declivity. And the alarm was still there, crying out.

Like the voices of her pursuers, and the pain, the alarm seemed to follow her everywhere: find every hidden spot she tried to conceal from its all-seeing eyes. She clenched her fists as the pain, both physical and psychological, coursed through her. Her breathing, harsh and irregular, sounded hollow in the darkness of the pit—

Something leapt at her from the mud of the pit; she went to cry out as its slimy body slid down her arm. A toad! The pit was littered with them; to her horror, she saw one on her stomach, and one between her legs, one on her thigh...How did she keep from screaming! Her pursuers were almost upon the pit. If they fell in, too, then everything would be lost. She clamped her eyes shut and endured it all. The footsteps seemed to thunder within her head, like bombs; the alarm was still pealing...the slimy, bumpy bodies continued to clamber against her warmth...She gritted her teeth and lay rigidly in the mud and filth—

The alarm suddenly stopped, but after how much time, she had no idea. She had been so intent to lock herself off that she had lost track of time. Scanning the air, she now heard nothing: not even her pursuers' steps! In the pit, the toads still croaked and clambered against her warmth; but her attention, for the moment, was elsewhere. She tried to breathe shallowly, so that she could scan the air for any sound. Was it a trap? Would she look out, only to see them waiting there for her! And what had happened to the alarm? Strangely, part of her missed it; in those moments of chaos, it had become an ally to her, keeping her company. Whatever the case, all the contradictions and uncertainties were too much for her. She found herself sniffling in the darkness of that pit, unable to hold back her tears. It seemed as though she would always be running—always be terrified—even if she got away from this place. And that was the horrible thing about it: it was not only that she did not know what she was running from, but that she did not know what she was running to—where she could find safety.

Cast in this light, even escape seemed meaningless now...She still did not know how much time had passed: maybe five or ten minutes, maybe an hour. She sat in the filth of the pit, scanning the air for any clue: some twig breaking, or a branch snapping back...there was nothing but the incessant croaking and the hollow sound of her own breathing. A toad, she now realized, was on her neck, clambering towards her face! No longer able to stand it, she leapt up and flung them all from her! She clambered up the muddy sides of the pit then, her temporary insanity winning out against the fear of her pursuers.

Clawing at the slippery sides, she finally reached the top of the pit. Holding her breath, she peered over the side: nothing. Were they only waiting out there, like cats, she wondered, playing with their prey! She looked out on the dark landscape, thinking of all the things that might be there, right before her eyes. She crouched there for a minute or two, scanning the darkness...but still nothing.

Could she dare hope that they were gone? She climbed totally out of the pit, still staring warily out into the darkness. No one seemed around, but there was something new in her, warning her that it had been too easy. Her mind went back to her escape: *They leave the door open in that place?* she wondered. Her mind was still hazy, yet she knew that no security for a... what was that place anyway? a prison? Whatever it was, the security should not have been so conspicuously lax. Another quiver of uncertainty cascaded through her. Everyone had had dreams like that: finding himself removed from the source of his pain and suffering, only to awaken—just at the moment of greatest exultation—to find it all a dream. She was paralyzed by that fear for a moment. She would die if she woke up in that cramped cell now: the thought of it made her legs tremble. But something new occurred to her. That they had done something to her mind and the minds of those other women was certain. Maybe with all of that, they did not have to lock the doors. Still, that idea, she knew, was a child's syllogism. Her escape had simply been too easy—too much like a dream. She could not help cringing at the sensation. Or maybe, if not a dream, she would walk on a bit farther only to find her pursuers waiting for her: walk on a bit farther to find that this was only another trick to break her spirit....True fear was about being confronted by possibilities that could neither be proved nor disproved; and at the moment, the entire world was so new and blank that there was possibility and mystery everywhere—

The wind blew then, and the leaves rustled and shed themselves of some of their accumulated raindrops. She stood in the darkness, cowering beneath the mock shower. *What now?* she wondered. The realization of how disconnected she was from the world again drained more precious life from her. It all seemed so inevitable: one day she would be drained of everything and find that both her fears and hopes had been equally useless. She waited there, as if death itself would come: a hulking figure to strangle her...but nothing came. Suddenly gripped by another bout of temporary insanity, she cried out, screaming until her lungs burned and her throat was dry and sore. Out of breath and giddy, she collapsed to the ground, grabbing her head as she listened to the echo of her madness. *Let them come*, she thought at last. *I have nowhere else to go.* She waited, but still nothing: no approaching steps. *Why won't they come!* she thought, almost angry. She wanted it to be over with—she could not stand to be toyed with. But nothing...! She cried then, not just with tears, but with her entire body, so that even with all of her bruises and cuts, every one of her muscles seemed sorer afterwards. Yet, even after this outburst, she could hear no steps. She frowned: did she dare hope that they were not coming? She stood up on unsteady legs; she took a couple of short, uncertain steps down the declivity, hearing nothing but the sound of the wind, the distant cries of an owl, some crickets and the toads. She did not know what to think...but at least there were trees here...and the air was fresh and pure. This openness and freedom once again triggered the intricate process of emancipation and hope. Instead of thoughts of pursuing robots, she lost herself in the rustling of leaves and the scent of the decomposing vegetation on the forest floor. She had glimpsed freedom and now she wanted to be free.

As she came to her senses, she looked down the declivity, finding something engrossing about the darkness in its depths. There was again only hope in the darkness...She found herself walking along, as if pulled by a beacon. She felt sleep snuggling close to her; but deep in her, there was the feeling that something vital lay undone. As she walked along, she saw brief images of her night of flight and rebellion; but these things, though recent, seemed too extreme to be real. Worse, if those things seemed unreal then how could she possibly make sense of anything else? Who was she? How did she come to be in that place? Who had done this to her? All these questions rose up in her mind so that she again found herself on the verge of giving in....

She walked on in silence; after a while, she discerned the purl of rushing water and smiled unconsciously to herself. It was like a gift from a forgiving god. She walked to the sandy bank, still smiling. She could hardly believe it: this, too, seemed like a dream. The water glistened in the moonlight, seeming to dance on the moon's rays. It seemed so pure...Before she had given it any thought, she waded into the cool, gently flowing water, to the point where she was about waist deep. The current tickled her as she stood there. The smock that she had been wearing had been torn to shreds by now. She took it off and surrendered it to the river. She was naked now...had been naked for a long while. She immersed herself totally in the river, enjoying the feeling of sudden weightlessness and thoughtlessness. She felt everything leaving her: the dirt and grime and filth...and she was free—but only for as long as she could hold her breath—

When she looked up from that watery world of dreams and freedom, she saw dozens of dark figures waiting on the bank for her. They were more of the dark-suited soldiers that had originally beckoned her into the woods. Before she even knew what was happening, two of them took her by the hand and led her out of the river. They all had the gaunt, effeminate frames and long flowing hair of their times, which was why she was at first a little unsure about their sex; and there was a youth there, probably no older than eight, who struck her as a reincarnation of Shirley Temple, with dimpled cheeks and a mass of blond, curly hair—

"Don't be afraid, Goddess," one of the figures said, stepping up, "we have come to take you back to the world." She was convinced that this one was a woman, because of the timbre of the voice (and because the figure was in a gossamer summer dress)...but it was the man formerly known as Agent Respoli of the FBI. It had been seven years since his merging with the woman from the Dimensional Portal, so it was probably incorrect to call him either a man or a woman. He was something new now—Respoli-Priestess—and the Goddess immediately found herself startled by his movements. He now held her hand delicately and reverentially as he smiled at her. "The world awaits you, My Master," he whispered. At this, the rest of the men bowed down before her, mumbling benedictions that she could not decipher through her stunned disbelief.

Unsurpassed strength is the greatest weakness.
VERSE 328:3 OF *The Teachings*

Circe was onstage at Times Square, twirling before the crowd in nothing but a thong bikini. Behind the stage, there was a huge holographic picture of the Goddess, replete with the emanations from the eyes. As the hundreds of colorful stage lights reflected off the smooth, sweat-covered surface of Circe's body, a stunning kaleidoscopic effect was produced. Shaka was once again watching from just offstage, enchanted. There were rumors about Circe: stories that the man actually was a woman—some kind of bioengineered experiment "born" seven years ago when followers of the Goddess stormed into the laboratory and freed her—that is, Circe—from her growth chamber. Shaka dismissed these stories as nonsense. However, his investigations of Circe had all been inconclusive, and even he could not deny that there was something incredibly compelling—and *unusual*—about the man.

Anyway, when Circe's aria ended, the man stayed on stage for a while, casting the mandatory benedictions from the Goddess. When he blessed the men, they screamed louder and flailed about more wildly, as though reaching orgasm. As Shaka watched these antics from offstage, he could not suppress his sarcastic smile. He waited patiently for Circe to finish, always respectful of the ability of men to manipulate others. As for Circe, he came off with his face flushed with pleasure and energy, and his body drenched with an almost oily-looking covering of sweat. His eyes were bright—especially when he looked up and saw Shaka.

"Have you been thinking over my offer?" Shaka asked at once.

When Circe smiled, his Glory to the Goddess tattoo seemed to sparkle. Shaka looked at the effect, mesmerized—

"I don't like people making demands on me," Circe said then.

"No demands will be made," Shaka said with an endearing smile. "You like to sing: I have the wherewithal to broadcast your concerts (not to mention your religion) to billions of people around the world. That will suffice for now—"

"And later?"

"There is no later, my dear," Shaka said with a slight bow, "—just *now*."

"Yes," Circe agreed, his face thoughtful, "—just now...."

Circe and Shaka were just about to walk backstage together when Shaka happened to look over his shoulder. First, he merely glanced out on the crowd as they danced in the open air of Times Square, but then he looked up at the sky. His initial thought was that the streaking lights were stars— which would have been strange in itself, since stars could rarely be seen though the thick clouds of smog. He turned around completely, pursing his lips as he tried to resolve the non sequitur. It took a few seconds, but at last he knew exactly what they were. In fact, if not for the bright, multi-colored stage lights and the mind-numbing volume of the music, he would have noticed the lights in the sky minutes ago—not to mention the rumbling that came with their impact. Circe, seeing him stop, stopped as well. He followed Shaka's eyes to the skies, but seemed more interested in Shaka's reaction to the lights than the lights, themselves.

"What do you think they are?" Circe asked then.

Shaka nodded with a smile: "The Horde has come at last." Presently, two muscle-bound men in dark suits appeared in the tunnel entrance that led backstage. They nodded to Shaka, but he did not take any notice of them. Circe looked at them with the same curiosity with which he had regarded Shaka's reaction to the lights. It was then that one of those descending lights zoomed above their heads and disappeared over the tops of some neighboring buildings. A millisecond later, the earth shook and a red gleam lit up that corner of the night sky. Some of the lights were even coming straight for them; and yet, through it all, Circe's attention remained focused on Shaka and his reaction to the strange lights.

The revelers were still dancing in the night—as though oblivious of what was going on around them. At last, one of the descending lights exploded into a building across the street; Shaka looked on as the building crumbled, burying thousands in the rubble. Another of the flaming lights landed in the middle of the crowd, exploding with so much force that Shaka and the others were forced to stagger back. And yet, through it all, Circe's first priority seemed to be observing Shaka and making sense of the faint smile across his face.

Some of the men in the crowd were starting to come to their senses now; instead of dancing and cheering, many began to scream and run. However, they were packed in so densely that they only trampled one another in their attempts to escape. Bombs were raining from the sky now—another one landed in the crowd and thousands of men disappeared in a blinding ball of fire. The heat forced Circe to turn away. There was smoke everywhere now, which gave off the acrid odor of sulfur and burned fresh. Then, when the power went off and the music stopped, all that there was, was the sound of exploding missiles and screaming, terrified men.

When Shaka turned around, he realized that Circe was still staring at him intently. He also realized that there was no terror in the man's eyes: that there was nothing but curiosity. He went to say something—to commend Circe in some way for not falling into the idiocy of the others—but when the agitated bodyguards began pleading with him to flee, Shaka shook his head in annoyance, saying, "One cannot run from death—"

A missile crashed into the huge screen behind the stage! Still, even while the guards screamed, paralyzed by fear, Shaka barely flinched. Ever the gentleman, he turned to Circe, who was still watching him intently, and said, "Here: take my hand." Circe smiled, again causing his Glory to the Goddess to sparkle. When Circe took Shaka's proffered arm, the man turned to the cowering guards, saying: "Walk calmly now: death is like any other wild beast—when you run from it, it begins to think that you're prey."

It is hope that leads men to hopelessness…
VERSE 234:12 OF *The Teachings*

The night embraced them and held them with the acceptance of a mother. As Xi and the hundreds, perhaps *thousands* of men walked along the wide underground corridors, he found himself wondering when was the last time he had seen the sun. He thought about that while images of sex flashed before him. The faceless woman had returned, gyrating seductively before him like a Siren calling him to his doom. She was in a thong bikini…her breasts were huge and her hair was blond. He tried to ignore her, but he realized that he had an erection. Actually, he had had it since he woke up; when he showered, most of the other men had worn erections as well—some had even masturbated right there. Xi had watched a man out of the corner of his eye, the latter's gaunt body tense and straining as he eked the pleasure out of his body; some of the men had even started groping one another….

As Xi walked along with the thousands of men, his mind kept flashing back to Quibb's long, slender fingers. He shook his head to drive away those thoughts, and focused on the teenage girl from the memory Quibb had allowed him to see. He was relieved that he could see her face; he could still remember the perfume she used to wear, and the way dimples used to form in her cheeks when she laughed. He remembered the first time he had felt her breasts. They had been small and soft…She had hugged him, pulling herself to him so that her breasts had squashed flat against him. That had been after their first date. They had stood there hugging and he had not wanted to let go. Minutes had seemed to pass. He had kissed her then, half mad with desire as he cupped her breasts and felt her nipples through her bra. She had smiled and gone into her apartment....Even now, his head swam as he thought about that simple pleasure—that *genuine* pleasure. He would give anything now for something that real.

This was what he thought about as he walked along with the thousands of men. They were all dressed in the same gray overalls that smelled of grease, grime and the industrial detergent used by The Company. Their dour expressions were like those of zombies. Not all of them were dour of course, but even the laughing ones—the ones talking excitedly or making the lewd jokes that were compulsory—even these men seemed hollow: like teenage boys whose sexual experiences were limited to beating off to videos from their father's porn collection, but who were nonetheless always talking about what great lovers they were....He had a sudden desire to see the sun: to feel its warming rays on his skin. There was the momentary fantasy that he would somehow be purified by the light—and that everything would be made clear in the light of day—

All at once, the world before him flashed in that mind-altering neon orange again, and another Tio Mendez pirate message played itself out before him...but he hardly noticed—nor did he care. It was all useless information...He looked around at the massive underground chamber that they were now in, and thought of the countless more in which thousands of men slept and showered and ate and then went off to work and die. The corridor had cement walls, a high, curved ceiling and was lit by yellow-hued fluorescent lights. It had to be at least 30 meters wide, and was a model of efficiency, with those on the right going in one direction and those on the left going in the other—just like on a highway. As Xi marched along with them, he found that the trampling of their many feet had a strangely soothing effect. However, the faceless woman was still in his field of vision—and his erection was still there....

They were now coming upon a huge, oval-shaped chamber that Xi had heard was right beneath Company Square—and the 20 ten-story buildings. The rhythmic clanking of the huge machines within the chamber created a song that was as hypnotic as it was deafening. It was all power generators and computer image sequencers and transmitters for the massive video billboards throughout the city. The men who worked in this chamber peeled off and went about their duties; but those, like Xi, who had assignments elsewhere, continued on. There were giant screens on the walls and the chaotic images that flickered on them—unconnected sections of commercials and television shows and news reports and computer-generated dreamscapes—produced an eerie strobe light effect in the dimly lit chamber. Somehow mesmerized by it all—and the hive-like quickness of the workers tending to the huge, noisy machines—Xi separated himself from the stream of men and stood watching it all. The faceless woman had started massaging her huge, jiggling breasts—

He looked past her, putting his hand in his overalls to keep his erection at bay. He thought about the men again, and their work in this chamber. Looking up at the huge screens, he found himself thinking that it was these images, sent out to thousands of billboards and billions of PinkEyes, that kept them going. This place was both the release valve and social coagulant of their civilization. Thus, placed in this light, the work of the men seemed almost sacred. Yet, at the same time, it all looked like an insect colony. The men seemed like drones; the dark metal of the machinery seemed like one massive structure: seemed, at times, like their queen. They were the machine's legs, its eyes, its hands…while in return, the machine pumped out more like them, whose only purpose would be to serve the machine—

Just then, as Xi stood beyond the stream of marching men, one of the power conduits blew with a loud explosion, shooting flames into the air. A worker, who had just happened to be passing that spot, was caught in the blast. His clothes must have been seeped in some accelerant, because the flames soon consumed the entire length of his body. Panicking, the man backed up, into one of the coolant pipes; and like a duped child's warm tongue against a freezing pole in winter, the man's body bonded with the pipe. The pipe held him up, in a pose that was too erect, burning. Xi could not explain it, but there was something incredibly beautiful about the flames as they flickered over the man's body: something almost *enchanting*. He looked at it all past the image of the faceless, gyrating woman. The flickering flames were like an escaping spirit dancing over the man's rigid body, and something about it was strangely erotic. If the man would have screamed out, then maybe that would have broken the spell; but he just stood there rigidly, burning like a match. There was the illusion of life and vigor and magic in the burning. Even the stream of men marching at Xi's back turned to watch—even though they did not stop their marching. It was only after about 20 seconds that the men who worked in the chamber (most likely alerted and directed by the PinkEyes) finally came around to douse the flames covering the man; and even then, their priority seemed to be dousing the blown conduit, not the man. Xi came out of his trance then. As the fire retardant sizzled on the man's burnt flesh, his charred, lifeless body finally slid from the coolant pipe. After the fire in the machinery had been put out, the men gathered around and stared at the burnt corpse. In the dim lighting of the chamber, their gathering was solemn, but seemed to lack genuine compassion. Something about the flickering screens of the gigantic chamber made it all seem dubious. On one of the screens, there was a commercial playing—but for a product that most likely did not even exist anymore. A Disneyesque cartoon man was dancing merrily through the countryside, accompanied by cartoon bears and deer and raccoons. Those scenes, towering over the men, seemed like a mockery of the thing that had just happened. On the floor, the men all seemed locked in time— *inept*—and it all seemed to be the work of the cartoon man. Xi had a sudden impulse to break the screen. A panicky voice within him was shouting that they would all be destroyed if the cartoon man did not stop his dance. The voice was blaring in his mind, above the clanking machinery. It was like pressure building in his head: he felt as though he were going to explode! However, just as he went to cry out, the commercial drew to a close, and the brand name of the fictitious product, Crazy Loops Cereal, was displayed against a still frame of all the grinning characters. The still frame hovered on the screen; on the floor of the chamber, the men gathered around the corpse; but for those few moments, on neither the screen nor the chamber floor did anything move. Xi stared into the grinning cartoon faces, trembling, once again feeling himself being overcome by the certainty that they would all die if the scene did not change....And then, in another moment, the grinning faces flickered away. It again seemed like a reprieve; but for the *slightest* instant, in the interval between commercials, there was something else—something *worse*. Xi was not sure, but for a millisecond, there was what seemed to be a green sun, placed against a purple, shimmering sky. It seemed too momentary and trivial to have a lasting effect on him, and yet, even while another fictitious product was advertised, the image of the green sun in the purple sky stayed with him. It was triggering sensations in him that were too disparate and chaotic to make sense. He did not know what it meant, nor did he know where it had come from, but one feeling rose above the chaos, incapacitating him. It was what he had felt when the cartoon man danced: the certainty that they were all going to die, and die horribly. Almost half a minute had passed, and yet he was still staring into the screen, seeing the vast purple sky with its glistening green sun. He could not escape the feeling that he had seen it before—in one of his PinkEyes fantasies, perhaps. Yes, that seemed right. But in what context? It was important that he remember—they would all die if he did not! The feeling of death cloaked him, suffocating him. He wanted to scream out like a madman at the confinement...but then, in another millisecond, he was free. He was panting and sweaty as he emerged back into consciousness. He looked around confusedly then, just getting ready to retrace his steps, when the imperative of the PinkEyes took over, reminding him that he would be late for his job. The faceless woman had disappeared at last, and he was happy for it. With the blown power conduit, there would no doubt be problems with the steady transmission of the images. Soon, the colony would be whipped into a panicky haste, the way ants charged out when someone stepped on their hill. He, himself, ran ahead and found a place on the stream of marching men, so that he could make it to his monitoring post with all due haste.

Once you have been pushed off a precipice, your resistance
becomes superfluous: you must fall.
Verse 932:1 of *The Teachings*

Xi was shoulder-to-shoulder with thousands of agitated men now: they were all jogging along, still following the imperative of the PinkEyes to fix the machinery that was their master. His mind went to his work post: the small, windowless room where he sat alone for hours on end, staring at screens and the flashing console. On those screens, images of the men in the city would be juxtaposed to commercials for products that nobody had money to buy—and which more often than not no longer even existed anymore. Images of nonsense like Crazy Loops Cereal would be shown next to things that were supposedly real—like *Throw the First Stone*; but after a while, there would seem to be no difference. He and hundreds of other technicians made sure that it was kept going. A flashing red light told them when something was wrong; they either pressed a button or replaced a fuse or changed a circuit board. It was the same old realization, made trite and annoying by repetition: they were in fact living parts of the machine, as self-aware as ants....

After a while, the corridor opened into another chamber—a kind of roundabout to other chambers. All of it seemed new and overwhelming to Xi; but with the PinkEyes guiding his actions, he turned into one of the corridors as though he had done so a thousand times before...and maybe he had. He ran down more corridors; eventually, he found himself going to the right, jostling with hundreds of men who were going in the opposite direction. It was not until he was practically to the door that he realized that he was coming upon an elevator. A sensor scanned his PinkEyes as he approached, and the elevator opened. After the cavernous corridor, he felt trapped as he entered the small elevator—but this was all overcome by the panicky ant colony feeling that was still rising to a frenzy in him....The elevator door began to close. There were no buttons to press. There were no displays to tell him what level he was on. Once his PinkEyes had been scanned, the elevator automatically took him to his floor. Now, as the door slammed shut, Xi suddenly wondered about the worker he had replaced. He wondered how long the man had been working in this place...but then he again found himself thinking that all of that had been part of his spy fantasy, and that he had always been here. In the final analysis, nothing was important but following the imperative of the PinkEyes—

The sudden movement of the elevator left him with the feeling that his testicles were hovering somewhere near his belly button. Even then, the ant colony feeling guided his thoughts and actions. He had never felt this way before. It was obviously something programmed by the PinkEyes, but he almost wanted to cry—as though he had just lost a loved one. He had the sense of being insignificant—and yet being given this one chance to prove his worth. He was desperate to prove himself: to perform his duties well for the advancement of The Company.

He was panting for air when the elevator door opened. Before him was a narrow hallway, which stretched for about a hundred meters and led to a dead end. There were about two dozen doors down the windowless corridor, and Xi could only guess that each opened to a cramped, window-less, monitoring post. There was something claustrophobic about it all: he tried not to think about it. His door was the fifth one on the left—even though he did not know how he knew that. His steps echoed eerily as he ran up to it....

Still following the silent imperative of the PinkEyes, he wrenched the door open. He was about to dart in and begin his duties, when he looked up and saw a figure sitting at his post. For a moment, he thought that he had made a mistake and entered the wrong room—but then he recognized the delicate features of Quibb's face! *He froze!* The existence of the man left him shuddering with the realization of everything else that might be possible—that he might be Dr. Xi Wang, inventor of the PinkEyes; that he might have had a whole other life, which was now somehow lost to him—

Quibb, seeming agitated, gestured for him to enter. When Xi did not move, but instead stood there staring blankly, Quibb got up and pulled him in. Then, the man slammed the door. The room was about 12 meters by 7 meters; Xi could not keep his eyes off Quibb—

"We have to act quickly," Quibb said with a kind of unease that seemed out of character for him. "…It's up to you."

"Me…?"

"To hell with it all, Xi," Quibb said in frustration. It did not sound like him at all; and he still seemed agitated—nothing like the god hovering in the wall of fire. "—Are you happy?" the man asked abruptly. "I mean, are you content with this idiotic life, or are you willing to risk it all—like you said you'd risk it all for love?"

"I…" He did not know what to say—where to begin—

"I want laughter in the world," Quibb went on, looking desperate: looking, thought Xi, like a human being for once. "I want laughter—*real* laughter, just like I had with you."

"With me?"

"What's the use of winning when there's nothing real?" Quibb went on. "Will you fight with me, Xi?" he implored him.

"Fight what?"

"Fight everything—and *nothing*—…this stupid existence. We probably can't do anything, but let's die as human beings."

For some reason, Xi nodded.

"No more power grabbing! It's time for honesty, Xi. Honesty so pure and simple you want to cry from the beauty of it—"

Just then, something rumbled overhead: they both looked towards the ceiling—

"Oh, God," Quibb whispered, grimacing, "it's started! We have to get out of here!"

"*What's* started?" Xi whispered back. All at once, an alarm began to blare.

Instinctively, Xi looked to the console, thinking that a button had to be pressed or a circuit board had to be changed. But then his eyes went to the monitors, where there were images of bombs falling from the sky...men screaming in terror all over the city! An episode of *Throw the First Stone* was playing, and for once the well-dressed barker in the top hat looked horrified—

"The world's going to end now," Quibb revealed, "—end again...and it'll keep on ending unless we stop it. Come on!" Quibb screamed, grabbing his arm. They took a step towards the door when a loud blast rocked the world and made part of the ceiling come crashing down. The lights went out; Xi looked around in a panic. With the darkness and the dust from the crumbling ceiling, the world was as dark as pitch. He stumbled backwards as another blast hit, banging his arm against the console. And then, when the most powerful blast yet made his knees buckle, he fell to the ground and covered his head with his trembling hands as more of the ceiling collapsed. He must have been hit in the head, because it seemed to explode; his eyes burned, and he cried out—partly from pain and partly from terror—

And then, a new kind of madness seized him. He would later rationalize this, but he was suddenly overcome by the feeling that a monster was in the room with him. It was more than a feeling: his hair stood on end; he seemed to hear footsteps approaching. As he lay shivering on the ground, clamping his eyes shut in a futile attempt to keep the pain and horror at bay, there was the momentary image of a creature moving in the darkness, its elongated paw reaching out for him—and then, the emergency lights came on. He screamed out again and cringed on the ground as the world was illuminated. With the siren, dust and smoke—not to mention his retreating terrors—the world was a confusing mess. He lay in the fetal position for a few seconds, as though still expecting to be attacked; but distant rumbles—and the prospect of the weakened ceiling collapsing on his head—prodded him into action.

He was too dazed to stand up (he felt as though he had been mugged— *brutalized*) so he got on all fours and scanned the room feebly. It was then that he realized that the PinkEyes were offline: that the Image Broadcast Complex had probably been blown to bits and that they were all alone now. A feeling of panic came over him again, so that he wanted to return to the fetal position and cry. His eyes were now burning, so that he had to fight the instinct to claw out the PinkEyes…but then he saw Quibb lying unconscious on the ground, bleeding from a gash on his forehead. Xi went over to the man, still on all fours, as though the blast had taken his humanity. When he touched Quibb tentatively, part of him was amazed to see that the man was real. Quibb was flesh and blood; the man's chest rose and fell as he breathed—just like any other man. Quibb groaned then, and Xi stared down, mesmerized. However, another blast made the world shake again; and suddenly sobered and energized by the prospect of the collapsing ceiling, Xi stood on two legs and hauled Quibb up. He supported the one-time angel-demon's frail frame in his arms now. With the adrenaline pumping through his veins, he rushed to the door with his cargo. His only thought was escape: images of monsters reaching out from the darkness left him for the moment; the pain and panic that had come with his withdrawal from the PinkEyes were secondary for now. When he opened the door and went to flee, the sight of the chaos in the hallway left him frozen. The siren was louder in the hallway—seemed to be boring a hole in his head. Also, all the other technicians had emptied out of their rooms and were crammed in the narrow hallway. All of them were yelling at once; some of them were fighting with one another in their desperation to escape. Xi thought of the machine then, without its workers. There was an anxious, devastating feeling at this, but he resisted it—*spurned* it. How quick they all were to give everything up! It went back to something he had thought before, about only the extremes being able to move them. Either everything was perfect, or everything was ruined and in disarray. There was no center….

The men in the hallway were fighting to get into the elevator at the end of the corridor. They seemed like animals. They were all on their own now. Indeed, without the Image Broadcast Complex, *billions* of them were now on their own, unable to turn to the easy, all-encompassing fantasies of the PinkEyes. As Xi looked at the men in the corridor again, he found himself thinking that there was something horrible and shortsighted about their impulse to survive. They seemed like crabs, clambering over one another to get out of the fisherman's basket: none would escape. A massive throng had formed at the mouth of the elevator. The men on the inside of the elevator were fighting those on the outside; some of the men on the outside, having squeezed themselves in, found themselves having to switch allegiances. The opposite also happened; so that in time, everyone ended up fighting everyone else. Xi was still standing in the doorway of his post with Quibb in his arms. There was no way that he was going to join the melee. Moreover, it occurred to him that without the PinkEyes to tell the elevator's sensors where to take the elevator, the elevator would not operate anyway!

Looking around, he remembered the fire door at the opposite end of the hallway. In their panic, none of the other men had remembered it. He moved towards it now. On the door there was a sign in huge red letters that read: "Do not enter! No reentry!" He looked warily over his shoulder, at the fighting men, and knew that he had no choice. Shifting Quibb's weight in his arms, he turned the knob—but it was locked! He looked from the melee to the locked door, feeling trapped. Just then, another blast shook them all, causing more plaster to fall from above. He would have gone mad with the sensation of being entombed, had he not noticed how crumbly the plaster around the door had become. The blasts had no doubt done that. Putting Quibb down, he rushed against the door. It gave a little, but held. Bracing himself again, he rushed it once more. *It gave!* He entered quickly, then dragged the wheezing Quibb in after him. The staircase was suffused with a dull orange emergency light that made everything seem unreal. To his immediate left, there was a thick metal grating that blocked the descending flight of stairs. There were dim lights below…he looked down the shaft, seeing the crisscross of staircases, going deeper and deeper. There had to be at least 50 stories below this one! The size of it took him aback for a moment. It had never occurred to him that there might be that many sublevels in this place. He would have stood there forever, reeling from the shock of it, were it not for the alarm, which was still blaring.

Coming to his senses, he looked up, seeing the dozen or so flights of stairs that went up. The ground shook again. Knowing what he had to do, he took Quibb's frail body in his arms and rushed up the flight of stairs. Quibb's breath was warm on the nape of Xi's neck; the man's blood was dripping down Xi's shoulder…but it was then that the strange feeling came over Xi again: the inner certainty that a monster was reaching out to grab him from the shadows. Too terrified to look back, and suddenly infused with a massive dose of adrenaline, he found himself bounding up the steps. He was so terrified that he could not tell if what he heard was actually the sound of pursuing footsteps or the sound of his erratic heartbeat. At the top of each flight of stairs, he would glance back. There would never be anything there but darkness, and yet the feeling's grip on him would always intensify. He was so terrified that he seemed to reach the top of the stair-case in no time. In his haste, he threw Quibb to the ground—he had actually forgotten that he was carrying the man—and went to the door. The door was locked—and he dared not look back at the approaching face of the monster, whose claws he seemed to hear scratching against the steps as it galloped up the staircase. Xi began banging on the door; he was so numb with terror that he was on the verge of beating his fists into bloody nubs—anything to escape this staircase and the monster closing in on him! Beyond the door, he could hear the men rushing past; he heard men screaming out—and things breaking. He looked at the casing of the door, but it was solid steel and cement. Quibb was lying on the ground, gasping like a fish out of water; but again, Xi had long forgotten about him—

A growl sounded right behind him: he shuddered, already opening his mouth to cry out—

But suddenly, the door burst open; and as the door opened into the stair-case, it banged against Xi's shoulder. It was only by grabbing onto the railing that he did not fall down the stairs. First he stared confusedly down the empty staircase; he listened, but there were no growls and no approaching footsteps. Then, still numb and bewildered, he looked to the open doorway, where a florid, antagonistic face appeared, framed against the chaos of the front lobby. Right over there was the console where old Ernie used to sit—

"What you doing in there! You should not be there!"

The man seemed preternaturally clean. He was in a suit: one of Shaka's official guards. Xi found himself groping for an explanation: "The elevator: it was not working, so I took the stairs." His voice sounded pathetic—*childish*.

"You shouldn't be there!" the man thundered. And what was strange was the man's clarity of purpose in all the chaos. Hundreds of men were rushing past, screaming; the city was being rocked, and yet the man stood in the doorway, reprimanding Xi for something that seemed, in the face of every-thing, irrelevant. And now, the man was reaching under his jacket for something! The moment seemed to take forever; Xi, with a faint feeling, saw the butt of the gun come out. With an instinctual revolt, Xi pounced on the man. A hard elbow to the man's neck left the man stumbling into the rushing crowd. As Xi looked on, the man's eyes grew wide with shock as he grabbed his crushed trachea. The crowd, already mad, saw nothing. Xi stood by the door, which had automatically closed behind him, watching as the man went through paroxysms of agony on the ground, suffocating from the crushed windpipe. Added to this, the crowd was trampling him. As his gun was still in his hand, he began to fire at the crowd in desperation, but it was already too late. It took only a little while for him to be trampled to death by the rushing men. Those men, made insensate by their fears, probably never even knew that he was there, beneath their feet. Xi stood there staring for a moment, watching all the madness—then he remembered Quibb. He remembered Quibb the way someone emerging from a violent dream remembered some little facet of the dream. In short, he was curious to see if Quibb had been real or part of the dream.

He turned back to the door, but then remembered the monster—and his newfound fears. He looked at the door anxiously, and yet he also felt possessed by that strange self-destructive curiosity of people in horror movies, who felt compelled to investigate noises in the darkness....The door, itself was one of those plain, nondescript doors that did not even have a knob. All that there was, was a keyhole, from which still protruded the guard's keys. Xi looked at the dozens of keys on the key ring, unsure. He had not seen a locked door in years now. Something about it was unnerving. Locked doors implied secrets...he almost did not know how to conceptualize it anymore. His hand trembling, he turned the key slowly—cautiously—as if he expected a grand world to appear beyond the door...or the monster. However, when the door opened, it was the same staircase that he remem-bered. He felt silly, and relieved....Quibb was still lying on the ground, hardly breathing. It was actually Quibb: he had to let that thought dissolve in his mind for a moment. The things Quibb had said before the ceiling collapsed were forgotten for now: all that there was, was the reality of the man. Before venturing into the corridor, Xi craned his neck and stared down the staircase to make sure that there was no monster. Then, using his foot as a doorstop, he quickly pulled Quibb out, taking the man in his arms again.

The front lobby was enclosed by glass, so that he could see the men running about in Company Square. In the sky, he could see the lights descending; and across the square, the dark pyramid seemed fully engulfed by huge red plumes of fire. That sight seemed particularly unnerving to him somehow. What did it all mean? Was this the end of the world at last? For a moment, he was overcome by a new sense of panic; he wanted to run about like the rest of them, yelling that the sky was falling. Still, as he looked around, it occurred to him that it probably was not even the end of the world that terrified them, but the end—or at least the curtailment—of the PinkEyes. His head still ached from the withdrawal, and a side of him could not help thinking that they were doomed. Yet, as these thoughts crossed his mind, he saw that not all of the men were running around in a panic—and that not all of them were leaving. Some of the men—like those that had been waiting outside the gates before all hell had broken loose— were now rushing into their heaven, too stupid to see what it had become. Thousands of them were now congregating in Company Square, believing, with relief and thankfulness, that the long ordeal was coming to an end at last. How could the same thing mean two such totally different things?

Xi stood there indecisively for a while. He definitely did not want to go out into that chaos. However, as one of the nearby buildings exploded in a huge orange cloud, making the ground buckle beneath all their feet, Xi looked up at the heavens—*truly* looked up at them—noticing that they were now a shimmering purple! He had not noticed it through the rose-tinted glass of the lobby, but some of the men had broken the glass of the lobby to get out, and he now saw the sky clearly. It was just like his vision— or whatever he had had back in that chamber. What did it all mean? He looked around in bewilderment, but when his gaze came to Quibb, who lay almost peacefully in his arms, something new and unsettling suddenly came over him. For the first time, maybe even ever, there was someone dependent on him. Something about this responsibility required too much of his energy: too much of his *soul*. For an instant, he rebelled against the feeling of altruism, wanting to throw Quibb to the ground and run away like the rest of the men. However, as he looked down at Quibb's angelic face, he was undone. The man was breathing faintly in his arms now, and Xi found himself thinking that if the man had been awake—if he had been writhing in agony, or begging for help—Xi would have been able to leave him. However, the man lay there with his eyes closed—*helpless*. Even with the congealed blood on his bruised face, the man radiated a childlike innocence that filled Xi with a kind of paternal responsibility. As Xi stared down at the face, he felt the sense of anxiety growing. Remembering the keys, he took them from the lock—as a thief would do it. Then, with a panicky resolve, he moved on.

Lying should never be used as a last resort.
Deception works best from a position of power; therefore, if you lie
and cheat to begin with, even if your victim does not trust you,
at least he won't be sure—and uncertainty is the key to deception.
VERSE 5678:2 OF *The Teachings*

S haka made his bodyguards get flashlights from his limousine, then they left the armored vehicle behind: even an armored vehicle was too conspicuous a target for death. They walked down the sidewalks with two nervous bodyguards in front of Shaka and Circe, and three behind. Shaka and Circe still walked arm-in-arm. The eerie cries of the men being blown to bits in Times Square echoed down the streets; in fact, everyone seemed to be screaming and/or running about in a panic. Rickshaws were colliding with one another and overturning; in many instances, the men left the rickshaws and ran off. The men ran in all directions, like chickens with their heads cut off. Only Shaka and Circe seemed calm.

Presently, a group of terrified men ran ahead of Shaka and his group; in mere seconds, a cult of half-naked men leapt out of the darkness and cut them down with their tomahawks. The cult's faces were painted in a bizarre pattern that made them look as if they had huge, lemur-like eyes and gaping mouths. Something about it was ridiculous, so that Shaka and Circe looked at one another and smiled. Clad only in loincloths, the cultists seemed like demented cannibals as they leapt around the dead bodies. Still convinced of the ridiculousness of it all, Circe and Shaka walked on steadily, unperturbed. The cultists whooped threateningly when they saw Shaka and his retinue approaching. They went to pounce on them, but Shaka's bodyguards pulled out their machine guns and wiped them all out with a kind of overkill that could only come from terror.

Shaka looked at Circe's eyes then, where there was a gleam of excitement the likes of which he had never seen before; when Circe smiled, the Glory to the Goddess again seemed to sparkle. It was as if everything going on about them—all the destruction, all the death—were a game...and of course it was; but up to now, it had been a game that Shaka had only played by himself. He had never had a partner before; and when Circe looked at him and smiled, with that self-confidence and ease that seemed almost to rival his own, he suddenly felt unsure.

Circe laughed at him. "You're wondering about me: asking yourself why I'm not afraid."

"Am I now?" Shaka said in a droll manner.

"Yes, you're reminding yourself to do a more extensive investigation of my background—find out what I did before I miraculously showed up in the city seven months ago."

Once again he chuckled, saying, "What makes you think I haven't already found out about your background?"

"I suspect you've *tried*, but there is nothing for you to find—or at least nothing that will satisfy you."

He smiled: "Yes, I know what your worshippers say: you were 'born' seven years ago—were some kind of bioengineered experiment that escaped with the help of the Goddess."

"You sound unconvinced."

"It's easier to believe that you're just a teenage transsexual with a nice voice."

They walked past the slaughtered cult as though the incident had never happened; in the meanwhile, the surrounding men continued to run around in a panic, and the bombs continued to rain from the sky—

"I never took you for one to put stock in easy answers, Shaka," Circe said. "Why is that?"

"Those willing to believe in easy answers are the easiest to deceive."

Shaka laughed at Circe's reasoning. "That implies that convoluted answers are more trustworthy."

"I only wish that you would keep your mind open to possibilities."

"Possibilities like what?"

"Like maybe all the stories spread by my 'worshippers' as you call them, are actually true."

"You mean that you really are a woman?"

"Human perceptions have become so warped that no one can see what is standing right before him."

"Is that so?" he said playfully.

"Yes. It's time that we all see things for what they are. And I'm not just referring to myself," Circe said, gesturing to the sky, "but what's happening to the world."

"And what's that?" Shaka said coyly.

Circe smiled. "Someone or something has come to threaten your hegemony, Shaka."

"Do I look threatened?" he said, chuckling again.

"No, not yet, but with all this bombing, it's only a matter of time before the Image Broadcast Complex is blown to bits and the PinkEyes go offline—if they haven't already."

"And?"

"Well, you have been their god for years now—through the PinkEyes, that is. The PinkEyes ordered their lives; without the PinkEyes, the semblance of order and reason will be lost—perhaps forever. Nothing is more dangerous than millions of wretched men losing their god—and that's just in this city alone."

Shaka smiled again: "No need to worry: the men have you and the Goddess to fall back on."

Circe looked at him earnestly for a long while. "Do you believe in the Goddess, Shaka?"

"The *Goddess*?" Shaka said with an amused frown. "…And that's another strange thing about you: you come out of nowhere and in a few months you manage to get *millions* of men—perhaps 70% of the men in the city—to flock to what had become an obscure cult."

"Stop changing the subject," Circe scolded him playfully, "—do you believe in the Goddess or not?"

"No," he said with a smile, "…but I believe in you."

"That explains it then."

"Explains what?"

"Why you've been coming to see me under the pretext of a business arrangement, when you could have easily sent one of your minions; why you've been going about the motions of pandering to me and haggling with me when, with all the power at your disposal, you could have easily crushed me beneath your thumb—like you do with all who defy your will."

Shaka stared at Circe blankly for a while, before laughing uneasily. He had received an unexpected response from someone, and this was the first time in years that that had happened. For the first time in years, someone had seen him clearly—perhaps seen him more clearly than he had seen himself. A voice of inner panic told him to kill Circe, but this voice only made him uneasier. Eventually, he cleared his throat, saying: "Assuming that all you say is true, what conclusion is one supposed to reach?"

Circe looked at him and smiled: "That you're in love with me." ·

Once again, Shaka stared for a while before his nervous laughter rang out. It was so loud that the fidgety bodyguards looked back at him uneasily. By this time, Circe had joined in his laughter.

Stupidity is one of the most dangerous things in the world.
Sometimes, it is merely self-destructive; but at other times,
in its blindness, it destroys the best-laid plans of the wise.
VERSE 689:3 OF *The Teachings*

The barrage from the sky continued. Whole buildings—whole *blocks*—were melting in what seemed to be lakes of fire. The fires spread as if the streets had been steeped in gasoline. The fleeing men would sometimes find themselves trapped on all sides by walls of flame; blocks of burning men could be heard howling like wild animals. Now that the PinkEyes were offline, the men had nothing to guide them. Over the years of the apocalypse, 20 million men had flooded into this city to hide; they had been like tiny fish, schooling in the shadows of the reef to avoid the predators. Unfortunately, in a single night, they had discovered that the tactic that was their primary means of survival was flawed. On top of that, with the PinkEyes gone, most of the men were so confused by their sudden emergence into reality that they had no idea what was going on. Men ran and screamed and killed...and sometimes killed themselves when they realized that the easy pleasure of the PinkEyes was lost to them. Nowhere was there logic; everything was chance: *random*...due to the prevailing winds. Sometimes, those who sought shelter within already dilapidated buildings were destroyed for their foolishness; sometimes those who saw this danger and rushed out into the streets were destroyed for their rashness. Sometimes a bomb fell just two meters away from men cringing in the street, yet they escaped without harm; sometimes it fell four hundred

meters away, and the resulting fires and cave-ins killed those who had foolishly thought themselves spared. Something new was being born out of this
chaos. New life was coming into being; somewhere, monstrous muscles
were contracting, pushing the new creature out into the world....

The hospital stood out in the night, highlighted by the fires of the buildings
burning across the avenue. It seemed inevitable that one of those descending
missiles would strike that huge, grotesque edifice. Yet, the wounded men
continued to flock to the hospital, joining the hundreds of dying men that
had before been anesthetized by the PinkEyes—but who were now writhing
in incomprehensible pain. For the most part, the wounded brought themselves in. There were no ambulances. Those without the strength and ability
to walk had no chance of making it; and in actuality, it was probably the
case that the wounded men came upon the hospital by chance than because
of any true purpose. The men ran in all directions, and into all buildings: it
was only inevitable that a few of these madmen would run into the hospital.

These terrified dozens joined the hundreds already inside the hospital.
There was no help for Mansmann—as he had been the only one on duty
when the bombing began. The men clawed at him in their desperation. As
there was no anesthesia, the men shrieked in agony as he sawed off their
limbs, sewed up their wounds and tried futilely to treat/bandage severe
burns. Burns were the most prevalent injury among the newcomers—and
the most sickening. There was a nauseating bar-b-cue smell in the air—an
odor of half-cooked meat. That was on top of the usual smells of death and
excrement. In the chamber, five hundred men now yelled out for the old
doctor. Their arms were outstretched like zombies in the darkness. Most of
them would die—if not from their wounds and Mansmann's hackneyed
operations, then from infection. Bandages were being made out of the
unwashed sheets of the sick and dead. Mansmann had used the same
bloody instruments on all of the men. He tried not to see...not to think:
two quick cuts and an operation was over...time to move on to the next
one. He was walking in a pool of blood and entrails and extricated limbs. In
a moment of madness, he had killed a man: cut his throat and held the pillow
over the agape mouth. He had not realized it until about six patients later,

when the ghost images of the murder had filtered back into his consciousness. He had looked over his shoulder, at the bloody pillow, trembling.... But an inexhaustible sea of zombie hands were raised to him, so he went on killing them with the brutal efficiency of the damned....

The men's eyes did not glow anymore—which made sense, as the Pink-Eyes were offline—but Mansmann instinctively found something unnerving about it. It was more evidence that they had lost their souls—the proverbial luster in their eyes—and were now some kind of walking dead, trapped between life and death. With regard to Mansmann, as long as the zombie hands were raised to him, he did not think to stop—nor did he *think* for that matter. In time, he would collapse into the filth and be done with it; he worked harder, probably even pushing himself to that point. If he had help—a few dozen other doctors and assistants—he might have had a chance, but he was an island in a sea of death. Shapes appeared blurred before him; sounds had an airy, unreal quality. He was standing, but he had the sensation of being enveloped by a dense liquid, like quicksand. The sensation was not entirely disturbing. He surrendered himself to it; his breath came softer—

"You the doctor?" a man was asking him.

"What?" Mansmann had to strain to look up: to *see*. It was a man holding another in his arms. There was something about the way the man held the other that made Mansmann look twice; but even as he stared at Xi (and the unconscious Quibb), he did not see Xi as the man that he had taken home that night seven years ago. He saw only that this man was somehow different from the mass of desperate, self-deluded men. Of all the men that had run into the hospital that night, perhaps only Xi had done so purposefully. He had carried Quibb all the way up from Company Square: through 15 blocks of death and chaos. He had looked over his shoulder every few steps, still sensing something stalking him from the shadows....In the morning, he would shiver and wonder how he had survived—how some missile or fire or apocalyptic dreamer had not gotten him; but for the moment, he was blinded by something else. Mansmann noticed it and frowned. There was a carefulness about the way Xi held Quibb that seemed somehow anachronistic—

"Can you do something for him?" Xi said then. His voice was not panicky and loud like those of the other men. He did not claw at Mansmann. He just stood there, holding Quibb and staring back at Mansmann with an expression that the old doctor did not seem to have the wherewithal to decipher.

Mansmann, still fighting to focus, looked more closely at the unconscious Quibb. "Where's he hurt?"

"He was hit on the head."

Mansmann put his gory fingers to Quibb's neck. "He's still alive," he said with a fatigued nonchalance. A missile exploded nearby and a man to Mansmann's left squealed out particularly loud, so that Mansmann looked over at the man absentmindedly. Xi panicked a little at this and stepped into Mansmann's line of sight; his voice was more unsteady and suppliant as he cried—

"Please, sir, can't you help him?"

For some reason (most likely it was the pressures of the night) something within Mansmann exploded then and he screamed: "What the *fuck* do you think this is! Look around you! I've got arms to saw off…guts to sew up!"—strangely enough, he was almost on the verge of tears—"and you want me to play nurse maid to your little lover boy!"

Xi twitched uncomfortably at the reference; something about Xi's look of shame and unease brought Mansmann back to his senses. They stood staring at one another, both uncomfortable.

"You hurt?" Mansmann asked at last.

Xi shook his head.

"…I could use a pair of hands." They stood staring at one another again. There was an uncomfortable silence. "…You gonna help or what?"

Xi nodded at last, numb to it all.

"Put him down somewhere," he said, gesturing dismissively at Quibb, "—he'll be fine when he wakes up." Then, he looked up at Xi with narrowed eyes:

"Can you stand the sight of blood?"

After looking around anxiously, Xi nodded.

There is money to be made in everything; more correctly,
there is power to be had. In fact, the more desperate and extreme
the circumstances, the greater the power to be had.
VERSE 23:2 OF *The Teachings*

After 15 minutes of walking down the street, Shaka's agitated body-guards had finally managed to convince him to find shelter in the subway tunnels. Once within the tunnels, they had begun walking downtown—towards The Company. The thundering explosions of the bombs dropping overhead had still been audible; and a couple of times, the explosions had caused tunnels to collapse and become blocked. Still, through it all, Shaka had seemed unconcerned as he walked arm-in-arm with Circe.

Now, as they walked, the only illumination came from the flashlights of the guards walking ahead of them. Every once in a while, someone would trip over the train tracks. On top of that, Moles—people who had taken to living in the subway tunnels—occasionally looked at them warily from the darkness. The stench about these men and their dwellings was unimagin-able: the acridity of festering urine and feces, along with musty dampness and death. The Moles looked at the light-dwellers suspiciously—as though they were responsible for whatever was thundering overhead; Shaka's men held their machine guns ostentatiously....

The rumbling above their heads continued. After a few hours of walking, there was no conversation—no idle banter. Something about walking down the tunnels was hypnotic, so that time seemed to stand still. Once, the light from one of the bodyguards' flashlights fell on a sickening scene: hundreds of huge cockroaches swarming over the bloody, bloated carcass of a rat. Shaka stopped and stared down, his eyes brimming with a kind of primordial pleasure as he laughed and said: "Evolution has a strong stomach. Just look at rats and roaches: they can live anywhere—will eat their own shit if they have to...."

V

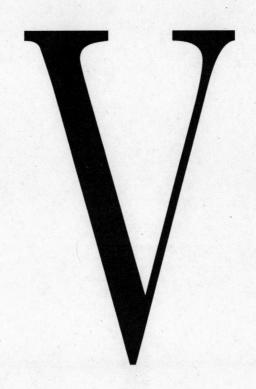

Politics is the civilized incarnation of social violence;
civilization is the euphemism for the brutality metered out by society.
VERSE 3741:2-3 OF *The Teachings*

Halfway across the world, in a nebulous region that was once either Nepal, China or India, the approach of dusk was hastened along by an entrenched fog bank. In the fog, the heavily fortified mountain complex seemed like a dark, fairy tale castle—the abode of an evil witch perhaps. As General Vishnu Gupta's helicopter began its descent into the complex, he looked down enviously at the well-equipped private army. Below him, the soldiers were now training their guns on his helicopter. Some search lights had been turned on to guide his helicopter into the complex; and as the blinding lights shone skywards, General Gupta could make out the dozen or so missile launchers that lined the stone battlements.

A short, plump man in his late 60s, Gupta was a man of practicalities. Forty years in the Indian army had left him keenly aware of the essentials of self-preservation. Seven years ago, at the onset of the apocalypse, he had had the foresight to commandeer two battalions and barricade himself (and as many munitions and provisions as possible) in a huge underground bunker. Now, as there was not a country called India anymore, Gupta could not really call himself a general. It was more appropriate to call him a strong-man, as his existence was totally dependent on his ability to brutalize and subjugate others. He had learned that the only way to keep people in check was through the constant reminder of where the power lay. The roving men beyond his battlements were like rats that would do anything to sneak into his house and consume his provisions. Self-preservation required ruthlessness and almost paranoid watchfulness against outsiders. In fact, it was not only the desperate men outside that he had to worry about: there was always someone else waiting in the wings of his own troops. He had gotten rid of several ambitious lieutenants for this very reason; he set up showcase executions of soldiers so that dissension became a mortal sin in a religion were he was God and Priest and Inquisitor, all wrapped in the person of a short, paranoid wretch. Of course, his constant vigilance had left him on the verge of a nervous breakdown. It was for this reason that Gupta now smiled as he looked down on the complex. All that he wanted to do for the next day or so was retreat into pleasure and lose himself in a bacchanalian orgy with the heavily pampered whores within the complex. He had a mistress at home; but as he had grown tired of her, he had consigned her to his troops' harem….

After the helicopter landed, the proprietor of the complex (a perpetually grinning Korean man) came running out. Actually, Mr. Cho seemed like a woman himself as he came out clad in a flowing silk gown. Gupta felt a twinge of revulsion as he shook the man's soft, manicured hands. Cho would not stop talking for a moment as he led Gupta into the complex. The man bowed every few steps, so that his gait was a kind of unseemly lurch. Gupta felt like hitting him; for a moment, he pondered raiding this place and taking all the women and armaments. Maybe later, he considered….

Cho led him to a huge chamber that had satin cushions and flowing silk curtains everywhere. With the back lighting, the room was several dreamy pastel shades. On top of that, it was also so heavily perfumed that Gupta felt slightly dizzy as he entered. It was a place for the dainty, and Gupta's brusqueness was out of place there. Cho's face unconsciously soured as Gupta stomped in with his heavy, mud-encrusted army boots, but he said nothing—or at least, nothing about the boots. In truth, Cho did not stop talking for a second: he talked about everything, from the weather to the price of food, not even stopping so that Gupta could respond. It was while Cho was prattling on in this manner that five women glided into the room.

They were veiled, and came in with that shy affectation that Gupta found so annoying. To him, all seduction was a ploy by nature to get him to pass on his genes. All flirtation, all love, was just a hollow shell; all cultural sexual norms were meaningless. Nature did not care if there was love involved in the act or if it was done according to custom; nature did not care about perfumed flesh and silk sheets. All that mattered was that the act was done, and that genes were passed on. Of course, given what had happened to the world, even genes were irrelevant to the process now—it was merely a matter of power, just like everything else connected with survival. As the women sashayed up to him and stood posing before him, Gupta could not help smiling at the idiocy of it all. The women were dressed as belly dancers; and watching their gossamer costumes, Gupta laughed, saying:

"Why do they have veils—is it so that I will not see how ugly they are?"

Cho's toothy grin widened: "Ah, it is all part of seduction, sir."

Gupta grunted noncommittally, his expression telling Cho to commence with whatever he had panned. Getting into his sales pitch, Cho gestured to the first two women, who were buxom and shapely. He began talking about how they were versed in all of the means of pleasing a man; when he nodded, the two women took off their veils with much fanfare. Squinting in the dim lighting, Gupta saw that they both had to be at least 45 years old. More likely than not, they were from a middle-eastern country, because they had the characteristic generous growth of facial hair, replete with eyebrows that were a single patch of unruly follicles across their foreheads. Gupta first cringed, then cursed out loud, stammering as he spat: "I wouldn't set these hags on my worst men!" Unperturbed, Cho glibly tried to explain that some men liked facial hair in a woman; but seeing that he was making no headway, he shrugged his shoulders and gestured for the two women to leave. The next couple of women were all right, but not much more attractive than any of the women in Gupta's troop's harem—or his old mistress, for that matter. Gupta had come here for something spectacular—not something he could have gotten at home. Still, Cho's eyes had a pleased gleam to them as he came to the last woman. She was a little slighter than the others, and a great deal shorter, so that Gupta was ready to reject her as well. But when the veil was finally taken away, and Gupta saw the smooth features of a 13-year-old Laotian girl, he could not help smiling. There was a subtle perfection to her—she was not plotting and bawdy, like the others. Cho came up to Gupta side and narrowed his eyes cabalistically as he whispered:

"She's a virgin!"

Gupta's eyes opened wide as he looked from the girl to Cho, suddenly intrigued by the idea that the girl had never been touched. All at once, as he watched the bowed head of the girl, he realized that it was not really physical pleasure that he wanted—not *sex*, really—but, *ownership*. Young women were rare—a 13-year-old virgin was even rarer still. It was like buying a priceless vintage car that was more something to be ogled than driven. Cho was already rubbing his hands together, counting the money in his mind. Surreptitiously, Cho waved for the other women to get lost—they had served their purpose. It was all in the presentation, he thought to himself, masking his widest grin yet by pretending to scratch his nose.

"A virgin!" Gupta said, dreamily. The girl looked up shyly and smiled before looking away.

"Five pounds of pure gold and a ton of rice," Cho cooed while Gupta smiled at the girl. Talk of money brought Gupta to his senses.

"How do I know she's a real girl!" he demanded. Gupta knew all too well that young boys were often castrated and sold off as girls. Cho's smile faded away for the first time—but even this was affected.

"You can check for yourself," he replied, "—with your *eyes*, that is."

Gupta swallowed deeply, then nodded quickly.

"Right this way, then," Cho intoned, leading the couple to another silky chamber. This one was more intimate. Actually, it did not even have a door: the arched entranceway was covered by a sheer fabric, which Cho held to the side for them to pass. "I'll be right outside," he said with another smile—and a meaningful look to the girl, whom he intended to keep pure until money had changed hands.

Gupta followed the girl in, then stood in the middle of the room, feeling like a young man on his wedding night. He suddenly remembered his own wife, whom he had not bothered to take into safety after the apocalypse.

The last he heard, some escaped convicts had taken her and his two homely daughters into the woods. *C'est la vie*—and good riddance! he thought.

There were French doors on the far side of the room, which led outside; and as they were slightly ajar, the silky curtains that covered them danced slightly on the breeze. It was so much like a dream, he thought. "What is your name?" Gupta managed to ask, but as the girl could not speak his language, she only smiled. Ah, how perfect she truly was, thought Gupta: a woman that he would not have to talk to! He sat down expectantly on the edge of the bed as the girl began to undress. There was a knowing seductiveness to her as she smiled and untied her bodice, revealing her budding breasts. Watching her, Gupta giggled at her perfection. The girl was a little confused by his laughter, wondering if she was doing it right—but this was how that experienced old crone, who had been a consort in Bangkok, had taught her. Her undressing like this was quite natural to her. She was somewhat curious of the effect that doing it in front of a man would have, but it was all business to her—all practicality. This was the way to survive in this world, she thought as she let the bottom of her outfit slip to the floor. This was what the dozens of other women kept here had told her. Freedom was useless to all of them: freedom—the ability to go anywhere— was necessarily circumscribed by the reality that in most places they would be raped on sight. Their "enslavers" were their protectors—as well as their only hope for survival. That was the reality. Now, as she walked up to the man and let him touch her breasts, and that place between her legs, all that she could hope for was that she would be imprisoned behind some huge, protective wall. Once safely within that place, she did not care what happened to her. She just wanted that little pocket of air in which to breathe....

She had been six years old when the apocalypse came. Her first memories had been of wandering the roads with hundreds of other refugees. She could not remember her name, but she remembered that they had called her "boy" to keep her safe. She remembered feeling beset upon and harassed— and constantly being hungry. And then, she remembered, with a troubling vividness, hiding in the nook of a tree as she watched the others being decimated by bandits and rapists. And then, she had been alone. If she had had parents, she could not remember them. All that she could conjure were vague feelings: a nurturing kindness, which she took to be her mother; a playful protectiveness, which she took to be her father. How she had survived by herself, she had no idea. She had come upon a monastery, and that had afforded her a few months of safety and survival. Those months had been spent watching the monks fighting off wave after wave of attackers. The monastery had been a pocket of sanity in a world of madness; but then, one day, the place had been burned down in yet another attack, and she had been forced to flee. She had wandered about the countryside for days, making sure to stay out of sight of the wandering men. She had been like a beast herself, existing on berries and roots. But it had been on one of those forays for food that she had stumbled upon some troops. She had looked up at the gruff men, sure that she would die; but just then, their smiley-faced leader had come up—it had been Mr. Cho. "What is your name?" the man had asked with a knowing glance. "Boy," she had answered without thought—and that had been that.

For six years, Cho had been like a father to her—like a *protector*. Some of the women said that he had several other installations like this throughout Asia, all stocked with thousands of women, and that he was rich beyond conception. Whatever the case, she now watched the Indian man's smiling face as he fondled her, thinking only that she would have a new father to protect her. She looked at the old, Buddha-looking man, and thought only of business. She had never dreamed of love or some wonderful Prince Charming sweeping her off her feet. She had never dreamed of anything but the bare necessities. The man that would be her new protector was inserting a finger into her now—it was nothing new: some of the women liked doing that to her, too. As long as her hymen was not broken, and she kept her value, she did not care. She wiggled away when his finger went up about a quarter of the way—that was enough for now.

It was while the Indian was looking up at her in appreciation that there was a powerful explosion outside the complex. The French doors blew away and a wave of fire threw them to the ground. As the flames flowed into the room, they melted the curtains and sheets. Mr. Cho burst into the room, looking around in horror. There were now gunshots and the sound of mortar fire outside. Gupta, coming to his senses, got to his feet, leaving the girl named Boy cringing behind the bed. Gupta and Cho went over to the opening left by the French doors, taking in the destruction for themselves. Gupta's helicopter was churning in a sea of flames: that had been the first explosion. He and Cho could only stare in shock. But then, as a mortar shell fell a few meters from where they were standing, both were blown back like ragged dolls.

Cho landed only a few feet away from the girl—she was sure that he was dead. The Indian man was moaning in the corner of the room, badly burnt. The girl looked on in horror at what was becoming of her protective world; but still, she did not scream. The women had trained her to never scream in the presence of a man—except to feign ecstasy. She huddled mutely in the shadows as the battle continued beyond the gaping opening in the wall. She could differentiate the combatants by the sound of their weapons.... And then, beyond the opening, she saw a helmeted figure. It seemed like a robot...actually, its suit reminded her of a lighter version of one of those early space suits. Whatever the thing was, she was mesmerized by it. She stooped there silently as it walked calmly into the room with its stiff gait.

The thing saw the Indian man writhing on the ground and shot him twice in the head with a kind of precision that convinced her that it could not be human. It stood watching the man for a moment, but then it looked up so suddenly that she knew that it had seen her. She was frozen in horror. In three steps, it was in front of her. It stood watching her for a long while, as if its CPU were computing something. She was beyond fear now—and hope. She was a girl of practicalities, and these practicalities told her that she was dead. She stooped there, staring up at the towering figure, suddenly noticing, by the light of the fire raging outside, that there was an emblem on the robot's chest: a strange sun, placed against a shimmering background. The last thing that she remembered was a blinding flash of light.

The true gauge of power is the ability to bide one's time.
VERSE 19:7 OF *The Teachings*

After hours of navigating the subway tracks, Shaka and his party walked out of a midtown subway station, and towards The Company's 150-story skyscraper—where Shaka still lived. The strange dawn, with its shimmering purple sky, hardly registered in their minds as they walked towards The Company. Sometime during the last hour or so, the bombing had ended as mysteriously as it had begun. The men were aware that the bombing had stopped, but to most of them, it made no difference. They were like victims of a mugging, lying semiconscious on the ground. On some level, there was a feeling of relief that the beating had stopped; but on a deeper level, they were too devastated by the lingering effects of the blows to celebrate. There was a strange new listlessness about the city, like that tense moment immediately after birth, when the mother was exhausted from the effort, and everyone else waited for the baby to cry, to see if this was to be a time of happiness or of mourning.

There were again guards in front of The Company's buildings, along with supplicants eager for entry. Once recognized, Shaka and the others were allowed to pass. They walked wearily past the guard post. Shaka's once-white suit was in filthy shreds. He had given his jacket to Circe as to protect him from all the stinging insects of the subway tunnels. Circe stumbled along, his stiletto heels broken off....

When they finally got up into Company Square (they had to take the stairs to get into that super-world), they saw that the dark pyramid was in ruins. Much of the front had collapsed, and it was still smoldering. Thousands of men were acting as firemen; thousands of others, who had succumbed to the fire or various injuries, were lying about in various stages of animation. On the other side of Company Square, lazy plumes of smoke rose from the upper floors of the main building—the 150-story skyscraper— where missiles had exploded. Circe watched Shaka closely again, but he could see no reaction. It was almost as though Circe had come all that way just to see Shaka's reaction to all of these ruined things, because it was then that he smiled and announced:

"I think this is where I'll take my leave."

"What?" Shaka said

"I suspect you have pressing matters to deal with," he said with another smile; and as he said that, he gestured to the man that had detached himself from the crowd in front of the Image Broadcast Complex, and was now running up. The latter was short and bony, wore wire-rimmed glasses, and had a bloody bandage wrapped about his head. He was dressed in a kind of monk's robe—a *cassock*—that flicked around his legs as he ran; and as he came towards them, he seemed like a half-starved priest fleeing from a war zone—

"Where is Dickerson?" Shaka demanded as the man ran up.

"Dead, sir," the aide answered, diverting his eyes obsequiously as he panted from his effort.

Shaka narrowed his eyes: "You are Stein, are you not?"

"Yes, sir," the man said, looking up hopefully.

Shaka looked over at the main building: "Is it salvageable?"

"Yes, sir: most of the damage is just to the outer shell: the structural integrity is still sound, and the fires seem to be contained. As for the Image Broadcast Complex, most of the machinery is fixable, sir—but it will have to be offline for a few days."

Shaka was staring at the building; he nodded at last. "You will take over Dickerson's responsibilities, Stein."

Bowing: "Yes, sir."

"Arrange to have the repairs done as quickly as possible," Shaka went on. "Have the men work around the clock."

"Yes, sir."

"What about my penthouse?"

"It sustained some damage, sir…It's probably not safe to be on the upper floors until we make all the repairs. We have another suite prepared for you, sir."

Shaka nodded. Stein was looking at him uneasily—as though he had something to say, but did not know exactly how to broach the subject; seeing Shaka's impatience rising, he plunged ahead: "Sir, there has been an incident!" He was so nervous that his voice was too loud; Shaka looked at the sweating man with growing annoyance. Stein looked surreptitiously at Circe, who was still looking on intently, then looked at Shaka with a gaze pregnant with meaning.

"You can talk freely," Shaka assured him.

"—There's no need," Circe said, smiling again. "I'm leaving, remember. But here's something to remember me by," he said, producing a videodisk, which he must have been carrying in his thong, since that was all he had been wearing when he got off stage. Shaka did not consider this legerdemain as he took the disk.

"What's this?" Shaka said as he took it.

"It's the access code to a special Dimension—the place that will convince you of the existence of God." Saying that, he smiled enigmatically (still with those sparkling Glory to the Goddess), turned and walked back the way he had come.

Shaka wanted to ask Circe when he would see him again, but the realization that he would sound like a lovesick fool made him uneasy, so he turned away. Stein was still looking at him.

"What's this about?" Shaka asked, more annoyed than ever.

Nodding, Stein took a palm-sized screen from one of his pockets. "There has been a security breach, sir," he said, handing the report to Shaka.

Shaka stared into the screen with unmoving eyes; for the second time in the last few hours, something totally unexpected had happened to him. When he looked up, there was a brutality about him that was horrible. Stein instinctively took a step back and stood there trembling. Shaka stared into space, his mind working frantically; finally, he said in a low, menacing voice: "Find out everything you can about the whereabouts and dealings of Xi Wang—then find out who's that he's carrying away; if they are still alive, then bring them here to me."

Stein bowed; Shaka and his bodyguards moved on.

When governments and corporations talk of self-sacrifice, the reality is
that while you sacrifice, they reap the benefits of your labor and stupidity.
VERSE 765:5 OF *The Teachings*

At the hospital, the work continued. If there was any waning in demand, it was only because those who had waited for hours to be treated, had died. As they had been doing for hours now, Xi and Mansmann tended to the men that had come into their charge. A passerby might have taken them for scavengers, as they hovered over the supine bodies for a moment or so, and then moved on. Presently, Xi was holding down a screaming man, as Mansmann set the latter's broken arm. Xi could see the bone moving beneath the skin…he was beyond sick. Yet, mentally, he was so dazed that he felt barely connected to the act—and himself. The congealed blood of the men had become sticky on his hands; his clothes had become stiff with clumps of blood; and at that moment, Mansmann's "patient" was screaming in agony at the old doctor's brusque, jerky attempts to set the bone. Many times during the night, Xi had looked up and wondered what he was doing in this place. They had all been fools to come here. As for himself and Mansmann, their work seemed due more to madness than altruism. The men died no matter what they did. At that moment, Mansmann's patient's screams reached a new pitch as the old doctor twisted the bone beneath the skin—

Xi looked away. He wanted to scream, himself, so that his voice would block out all the sounds of the world. He wanted everything to cease, so that he could catch his breath. As such, he was amazed when he looked up and realized that that was exactly what had happened. Mansmann, and the hundreds of wretched men in this chamber, were all frozen in place, as if time had stopped. There was not a sound in the world; but in that world of stillness, Mansmann's patient moved then; and looking down, Xi gasped as he realized that the patient was Quibb. Quibb smiled then, and sat up.

Xi's mouth gaped. Quibb's smile broadened.

"Quibb…" he managed to whisper at last.

"Don't worry, Xi. You are either having a delusion, or you are finally beginning to see the truth."

"…Everyone's frozen," Xi whispered, looking around uneasily.

"They are all irrelevant to your life—everyone, except for him," he said, gesturing to Mansmann.

Xi looked at the old doctor's sweaty face helplessly. "What's so important about him?"

"You'll figure it out in time," Quibb said simply.

Xi stared at the man, a side of him wanting to beg the man to give up his secrets; at the same time, another side of him was just thankful for the silence of this moment—this respite from Horde bombs and screaming voices. He looked at Quibb then, realizing that the man's head wound was gone.

"You've healed already?" he said in amazement.

Quibb smiled: "You saved me, Xi. You saved me—treated me as a friend when I needed you—and now I want to save you. This is the only chance I will give you."

"…Okay…what am I to do?"

"The choices must be yours, but I am here to offer you options. You can either flee from the city: get away from Horde bombs, and Shaka—*who is even now starting a search for you*! You have to get away from this city—and even *me*—and try to forget everything you've seen and felt. In this way, you'll probably survive the onslaught that is destined to wreck havoc on the city over these next few days, but…"

"—But what?"

"But you'll never be alive that way. You'll only ever be alive again if you stay, Xi, and *risk* death. That's the paradox. If you stay in this city, you will experience things no human mind was meant to experience: horrors that will make you question the stability of the universe. You'll experience pain no man has the stamina to bear. That, by itself, might be worse than anything The Horde could do to you; but if you stay, and take a chance, all the secrets you've ever wanted to know—like who you are, how you switched places with G.W. ...how people *really* lost the ability to have daughters— ...all these answers are waiting for you, if you're willing to risk it."

"...I'm willing," Xi said at last.

Quibb stared him for a while—stared at him *earnestly*, and with compassion; and then, smiling, he lay back down. "You're even now evolving, Xi—I knew you wouldn't turn back. Your mind has seen too much already. Enlightenment is always a brutal, one-way process," he said, lost in thought. "...Anyway," he said, coming back to his senses and smiling shyly, "remember what I said. This is either a delusion, or you are finally beginning to see the truth. Your future actions will determine which it will be." As he pronounced these last words, his face changed back to that of Mansmann's agonized patient, and the surrounding world once again erupted with motion and sound. Xi looked at it all in amazement. The pocket of peace and silence was swallowed up by the chaos; already, he felt himself harassed by the world, and swaying from the fatigue of the night's efforts. Still, Quibb's words remained in the back of his mind: a far-fetched hope that was his only chance for life—

At last, with a sickening, grating sound, Mansmann set his patient's broken bone in place. Looking down, Xi felt the revulsion enveloping him; he felt a little giddy...and it was not only the conditions, but also his own fatigue— all that Quibb had said, and all that seemed to lie on the horizon. At the very least, he needed a break in order to catch his breath. He and the doctor stared at one another then. Xi looked into Mansmann's emaciated features, his lips already forming the words of his plea. The old man looked across at him too, but as if not seeing...no, that was not quite it. In Mansmann's eyes, there was a hint of the same revulsion he sensed in his own; but for the old man, there was an added feature: something monstrous that made

Xi twitch. It was as though Mansmann had overcome the horror by embodying it. Somehow, he had become the incarnated pain and suffering of the hundreds of men that he had butchered throughout the night. Something about his bent, willowy frame cut Xi's plea short; and just as Xi began to wonder how that waif of a man even managed to remain standing, the old man collapsed into the filth on the floor.

The zombie-like groans of the men seemed to heighten with Mansmann's collapse. And then, as the strange despair spread throughout the chamber, there was a noise like that of monkeys shrieking in the treetops. Xi looked about the chamber anxiously, seeing the hundreds of desperate faces. That was the moment when it occurred to him that the bombing had stopped. He had no idea how long it had been. A feeling of elation tried to take hold of him; looking out of the window, he saw that the sky was brightening, and that a new day was at hand. However, just as the feeling of joy began to make inroads into his psyche, he was again overcome by the strange certainty that something was looking at him from the shadows—*stalking* him. He could feel it moving closer: the hair on his arms stood on end; and just as a new milestone of internal terror was reached, a few of the chamber's zombie men reached up their hands and tugged beseechingly at his pants. One of the men inadvertently grabbed at Xi's crotch, so that he cried out. He instinctively kneed the man in the face; then, for some reason that was beyond him, he took Mansmann in his arms—just as he had taken Quibb—

Quibb! He remembered that he had brought Quibb here! He could not even remember where he had placed the man; but panicking, he knew that he could not think about that now. As he took Mansmann in his arms, more zombies reached up to grab him. Xi kicked one of them in the chest. He had to escape! His carrying away the old man seemed altruistic; but in reality, he was using the old man as a shield. The zombies were clawing at his arms and legs: the only thing that saved him was their weakness. He was shoving them out of the way, kicking them…hitting them with Mansmann's frail body. Where he was going, he had no idea; at first, he merely went in circles, trampling the same wretches. But then, looking towards the corner of the room, he saw that a door was ajar there. It seemed placed there by a divine force. He rushed towards it now, as if it were his only hope. He was not only walking over the sick, injured and those that had just been operated on, but also the dead. He did not bother to differentiate: all kept him from his goal.

When he reached the door and pushed it open, he saw a small chapel. At first, he thought that the windows were stained glass, and that they were what accounted for the strange light; but then, after realizing that all the windows were in fact shattered, he remembered the purple, shimmering sky of the previous night. He stood on the threshold of the room for a few moments, just staring at the strange morning sky. It *terrified* him: it had since last night. A side of him wanted to give up right there; but coming to his senses (or rather, subverting one terror by embracing another, more manageable one), he remembered the zombies at his back. He scanned the room to see if it was safe: there were two rows of scratched, graffiti-laden pews in the chapel. There was also a television on top of the altar. That seemed appropriate somehow....After this quick survey, he placed Mansmann on the first pew, then he barred the door and listened to the droning protests of the zombies on the other side. Looking around again, he realized that there was no other door. After the surge of panic that came with the feeling of being trapped, he felt stupid as it occurred to him that if anything happened, he could just escape through the shattered windows. He took a deep breath at last, feeling secure enough to try to retrace his steps—and to rest.

The bombing had really stopped. He listened to make sure…but did not know if the end of the bombing really meant anything to him—it was just another milestone in a litany of meaningless milestones. Images of Quibb and The Horde bombing went through his mind; he thought, on a vague, anxious level, about his premonition back at the Company: about a green sun in a purple, shimmering sky like the one outside the window. His mind seemed to groan under the weight of it all. Luckily, it was then that Mansmann began to regain consciousness. The old man moaned like one of the wretches outside, and Xi went over to him, kneeling down at his side.

"Rest now, old man," he said as Mansmann's strained eyes opened.

"…Not ready yet," Mansmann protested, trying to get up.

"Not ready for what? [He smiled for some reason.] What you waiting for, death?"

"Can't rest…" the old man moaned.

Xi held down the man's frail body with minimal effort. It occurred to him that Mansmann was delirious; the old man's eyes were wandering the room, and yet they did not seem to see anything—not even Xi. Xi was kneeling there, staring down at the man's vapid expression, when Mansmann's wandering eyes suddenly focused on him. The old man frowned then. He was just about to speak, when a voice suddenly blared behind Xi! Xi jumped, expecting to see the sea of zombies at his shoulder. He slipped to the floor as he swung around, already preparing to scream as he stared up at the source of the disturbance: the television. A test pattern was showing, but someone was talking over it—

"The Devil is upon us," the resonant voice was saying, "—but we must not give in to the evil!"

At first, Xi only frowned at the weirdness of it. But then, his jaw dropping, he realized that it was Quibb's voice! Unable to understand it, he stared into the colors of the test pattern, as if therein lay Quibb—

"For six hours the Devil has bombed us! Tens of thousands of men have lost their lives this night; entire sections of the city have been destroyed, and all of this with neither warning nor provocation. We are at the vanguard of history! We must fight this Devil! We must *defeat* this Devil!"—Xi felt sick—"An entire world lies in the balance. The Devil calls itself *The Horde*!" Xi cringed at the name. He was shaking more visibly now, horrified by the possibilities as he remembered how Quibb had rambled on about fighting the night before—

"The Horde has been terrorizing the great cities of the world, bringing destruction like a plague of locusts. It wants to destroy what we have created. We must not allow that. Our great city, which was last night tossed into the filth by the Devil, must rise! Through the will of the Goddess, it is mandated that we should! We are the final army of Heaven! [Xi's face creased with confused horror!] We are a force of righteousness in a universe of sin! We must not lie still! Feel the power of the Goddess and rise! Rise! *Rise!*"

Xi could *feel* the words! Quibb was inside of him, ravaging him with thoughts of hope and rebirth…and *war*. Still trembling, Xi stood up and took a step closer to the TV before realizing, with a heightened sense of shock, that Quibb's words were being heard in the streets as well. He meandered over to the window and looked out in disbelief. Like a fool, he had thought that the words had been for him alone. The voice was coming out of all the video billboards. The hospital had a public announcement system, and he realized that Quibb's words were playing over it as well.

Still numb, he walked to the door with a rigid gait; Mansmann watched him closely, still frowning. Xi unlocked the door and stood in the doorway, hearing Quibb's resonant voice echoing throughout the chamber. "Quibb!" he whispered. He had wanted to yell it out, but his throat was dry. Where had he left Quibb? He wanted to rush to that spot and check now, but his mind was too chaotic to remember. Had he ever really brought Quibb here? It seemed doubtful now. He knew, without even the necessity of verification, that Quibb was gone: that Quibb was beyond them all.

"...The Goddess will not stand for this!" Quibb was saying now. Xi listened to it all, but was lost. What could Quibb possibly have to do with the Goddess? That fact seemed ominous somehow. It was a new development in a complex tapestry of schemes. And then, as he looked at the men, he found himself wondering what Quibb had done to them! Their zombie moans had ceased; throughout the chamber, there was only Quibb's voice. Xi looked into the eyes of the men, shocked to see that they were listening: that they were being *moved*. Quibb was telling them of the emergence of the thing that would destroy them; collective hatred and fear of that thing had calmed them, where everything else had failed. For the first time since the putative apocalypse, the men were actually concentrating on their collective lot—seeing the world as it was!

Mansmann, who had been watching Xi closely, pooled his strength and walked up next to him.

"You know what this is all about?" Mansmann said, looking at Xi suspiciously.

Barely hearing, Xi shook his head.

There was something unnerving about Xi's reaction to the strange voice. "You are not like the others, are you?" the old man said, still frowning. It was not a question to be answered; it stayed in the air, acknowledged by neither of them. Then, as Mansmann followed Xi's frantic eyes, he asked, "What are you looking for?"

"...I don't know yet," he whispered in bewilderment.

Mansmann nodded vaguely, then they stared at one another full on. At first, there was a hardness there—the defensive sizing up that had become a prerequisite for survival over the past seven years—but then that wore away and they looked at one another uncertainly, realizing, on a vague level, that they were connected somehow, and that that connection made them brothers.

For God to live and become part of people's souls, all of the prophets and apostles that first brought Her to the people must first die. In the long run, no God can flourish if there is too much ready evidence of Her existence. About God, there must always be mystery and speculation.
VERSE 455:5 OF *The Teachings*

I n those moments before Quibb's voice roared throughout the city, Shaka walked into the suite by himself. He was still in the same soiled, torn clothes that he had worn in the subway tunnels. He wanted to get clean and rest, but he was gripped by an overpowering sense of restlessness. He looked around the suite as if lost. The suite obviously was not as posh as his penthouse, but there was a king-sized bed, a mahogany desk, an en suite bathroom, and a huge video screen that took up a great deal of the far wall. The men had even managed to restore some emergency power.

The suite was four stories above Company Square, and Shaka found it strange to be so close to the ground—especially after all the years he had lived in the penthouse of the tallest building on earth. For some reason, he was left with a melancholy feeling as he looked out on Company Square and the throng of workers. The lingering smell of smoke burned the back of his throat and he was annoyed that he should be forced to breathe it. He was not yet prey to that sense of hopelessness that came when men realized that their lot was not entirely in their hands, but for once he felt stripped of his invulnerability. The man that had walked from Times Square fearlessly the night before was gone. It was not that he feared death, but that he was irresolute. He felt as though he had failed to account for possibilities that might have very grave consequences. In the interim, all he could do was build up his defenses. There were four guards posted outside; Stein was posted down the hall, there to see to Shaka's beck and call, and yet Shaka felt the kind of vulnerability that even an army of millions could not negate.

After a deep, tired breath, he took another step into the room. His mind kept drifting to Circe and darting away uneasily, playing a strange kind of flirtation with the man's stunningly beautiful image. Shaka did not like it at all. He kept reminding himself that he did not want Circe as a lover and felt relieved by the realization that a tryst with a teenage transsexual was repulsive to him—just as all sex was....And yet Circe's image was still there. He kept seeing those eyes—not only the man's Glory to the Goddess, but also the way Circe had looked at him directly, without the subservience he had come to expect....He no longer knew if the kind of shameless servility that the other men showered him with was something he wanted or something that just was. Everything suddenly seemed uncertain—except for the fact that he wanted to know the thing behind Circe's eyes. He wanted to know the source of that self-confidence—that slightly mocking intentness. He wanted these things, even while he was aware that he was being infected by this curiosity. It was leading him astray—into things not entirely germane to his self-preservation...and Circe had been so right: Shaka could have easily sent one of his minions to negotiate with Circe; he could have bent Circe to his will at any moment....His mind drifted to Xi Wang. Once again, there was the feeling of being taken off guard—this time by the realization that the man was still alive. Xi Wang had disappeared off the face of the earth seven years ago, right before the world erupted into chaos. The man's showing up again after all these years could not possibly bode well—especially as he had been seen coming out of that door. As was the case with Circe, Shaka felt himself bedeviled by a frantic urge to immolate Xi and all the unaccountable things. He reminded himself, with an unconscious nod, that uncompromising brutality to that which was not immediately understood was the way to survive nowadays. Uncertainty led to hesitancy, and that was tantamount to death. In an age when there was no guilt and no longing for what could have been, it was imperative to be quick on the draw—to destroy first and ask questions later...if at all.

...His mind, despite his inner protestations, drifted back to Circe. He remembered Circe's videodisk then, and what the man had said about proof of the existence of God. Those words made him smile sarcastically, and this pleased him. He took the disk out of his pocket and stared at it with the gnawing curiosity that seemed to be a threat to his very existence and peace of mind. He was just about to walk up to the video screen, where there was a Dimensional Portal, when the screen suddenly flickered on, showing a test pattern. Instantaneously, a booming voice issued from the speakers, exhorting him to rise and have courage. First, he stood there frozen, mesmerized and unnerved; but then, coming to his senses, he called to Stein. Initially, Shaka's voice was calm; but by the third time he called Stein, he was screaming. The strange voice booming over the speakers continued to rant, seeming to rise to counter his voice. He felt somehow as though he were being stifled. The voice was talking about The Horde now, screaming that they had to stand strong against it. Shaka could barely hear his own voice anymore; then, after some threshold of panic and frustration was reached in him, he picked up a chair and smashed it into the screen. Even when that was done, and the speakers had all been punctured and wrecked, he continued banging the chair against the shattered screen. When the guards rushed in with Stein in tow, they found Shaka slumped on the ground, panting and weak. The madness returned to his eyes when the guards stood in the open doorway, and Shaka heard the booming voice issuing from the intercom in the hallway. *The voice was everywhere...!*

Life is the most deadly and destructive phenomenon in the universe.
VERSE 834:2 OF *The Teachings*

"I am the voice of conscience!" Quibb's voice declared over the public announcement system, the way Jesus had said, "I am the way and the light." The entranced men stepped out into the world, nodding their heads as Quibb's homily continued, and the path to salvation was made clear to them. Now that The Horde had come, and they had experienced the devil's wrath for themselves, they were easy converts to Quibb's religion. Nothing made men flock to God, as much as the fear of the Devil; and on this particular day, the men of the city had never been more afraid.

The self-declared Voice of Conscience was there to channel their fears. As many of the men were still withdrawing from the PinkEyes, they probably thought of this as a new dream, from which they would soon awaken if they waited patiently. Even then, Quibb's voice was setting a strange dynamic in motion. The Voice of Conscience was engaging them—refusing to let them seep into despair and passivity. There was a war to be fought, and they were to be soldiers. There were fires to be put out, and men to be rescued, and they were to be firemen and rescuers, respectively. Even to the delusional and insane, The Voice of Conscience was there, slowly entwining itself in their souls.

"—Mobilize against stagnation, my brothers!" The Voice screamed then. "Stand firm because *The Horde will be back again tonight!*" Some of the men gasped; some began to cry; some laughed uneasily; others were too embedded within their neuroses to react at all. The Voice's homily continued, telling them about the strength of the Goddess: the power that came when one submitted unflinchingly to Her will. The key to reforging civilization lay in the will of the Goddess; the future existence of man—and overcoming The Horde—depended on the men's faith in the Goddess. Xi listened to these strange commandments of their times, still wondering what a 10-year-old black girl could have to do with Quibb and the thing that had happened to them last night.

Whatever the case, as The Voice's commandments took hold of the men of the city, dozens of volunteers began to stream into the hospital. They asked Mansmann what was to be done, and he set them to the grim work ahead. As for the old man, while he had seemed dead to the world a short while ago, he now seemed rejuvenated. The volunteers were put to work heaping all the dead bodies from the hospital into a pile on the front side-walk. Xi joined these volunteers, and was presently holding his breath as he carried an old man's carcass from the bowels of the hospital to the sidewalk. It was good to work: it kept him from thinking and seeing. The feeling of being stalked from the shadows was still there; more than once, he had shuddered and peered into a dark corner that either turned out to be empty or populated by a half-dead bastard....

Some of the buildings across the street were still on fire. More of The Voice's volunteers were trying to put out the flames, but the water that came out of the fire hydrants trickled, rather than gushed; and with no hoses, the men's attempts to put out raging infernos with buckets and tin cans seemed more insane than anything else. Xi watched the flames across the street disinterestedly for a moment, then his gaze returned to the purple, shimmering sky....Purple Horde: it made intuitive sense, but the name was the only thing about this that made sense. Now that Xi thought about it, what The Horde had done to them last night went beyond what was necessary for conquering and enslaving them. With its unrivaled power, The Horde could have driven down to the center of the city and declared that it was in charge, and nobody—*perhaps not even Shaka*—would have gone against it. In fact, with their PinkEyes and delusions and masochistic psyches, those that had not been oblivious of The Horde while it enslaved and butchered them, would no doubt have *worshipped* it. The Horde was using resources that it did not need for the simple purposes of conquering men and their territory. If what Quibb had said was true, and The Horde was really destroying all the great cities of the world, then either it had motives that could only be understood by the gods, or it had no motives, and was only the purest form of self-destruction. Something about The Horde brought to mind the sterility and efficiency of machines. The fact that the bombing had stopped at sunrise seemed to be proof of this. The beginning and ending of The Horde attack had been pre-determined—not out of any strategic purpose, but because those were the times programmed into the machine. Some kind of war game was being conducted on a computer somewhere; a machine had inadvertently been left on and forgotten; and over the seven years of the apocalypse, the programming had become corrupt, churning out the code that would eventually destroy the human race....Xi sighed and shook his head. If there had been Horde soldiers on the streets right now, then things would be different; if there had been some evil Horde dictator—or *country*—that they could all direct their hate or terror towards, then they would be able to put what had happened to them in some kind of logical perspective...but there was nothing but the lingering reality of death: smoldering buildings, corpses...and the ever-present madness that had been there since the apocalypse. The only thing that kept him going was the thought that Quibb had come to him in a vision, and made a covenant with him. He would finally have answers to all the questions that had haunted him for the past seven years. All he had to do was withstand the horrors of the next few days.

One builds empires by giving one's enemies—and those one is to rule—freedom to operate. Most will become drunk on the illusion of power and destroy themselves—the rest will panic and demand to be ruled.
VERSE 1687:3 OF *The Teachings*

As the girl named Boy opened her eyes, she did not merely seem to be awakening from sleep (from a natural process that was attuned to the body's rhythms). On the contrary, regaining consciousness was like being released from the grip of a monster. Her muscles ached; her head felt groggy. Even when her eyes began to focus in the dim lighting of her surroundings, it took her a moment to realize what she was seeing. She was lying on what she would come to realize was a cot. She sat up uneasily. Then, as she looked around, her mouth gaped. This place, as incomprehensible as it seemed, had at least 10,000 other cots in it—each with a supine figure. The cots were all placed in row after row, side-by-side, in the inconceivably huge chamber. The ceiling had to be at least one hundred meters above her. She looked around in a daze, trying to get her bearings. There was a horrible stillness about the place, so that she wondered if everyone else was dead. She looked at the person lying on the cot to her right, realizing, with a feeling of shock, that it was a woman. They were all women, it seemed! She tried desperately to think back, finally remembering Mr. Cho and the robot. All of that seemed as if it had happened just a millisecond before; but deep within her, she felt that a much greater amount of time had passed. Maybe hours, maybe days, weeks...months, *years*. She panicked at the vagueness of everything. But just then, as she looked towards the far wall, she saw the strange emblem she remembered from her last moments of consciousness—the sun against the dark background. It was painted on the wall. It was *huge*…! She stared up at it in awe, suddenly wanting to cry—to scream out like the scared child that she was. For the first time in her recent life, she had absolutely no idea what was happening, or what she was to do in order to stay alive. After a while, she realized that a harried-looking African girl about 15 years old was sniffling in the cot to her left. Instinctively, they hugged one another in the horrible, death-like silence of the chamber.

Religion is like masturbation: by itself, there is nothing wrong with it, but when it is foisted upon others, the act becomes indecent.
VERSE 4542:8 OF *The Teachings*

Quibb's voice was still ranting about The Horde and the Goddess. Xi was now carrying another corpse from the hospital to a pile in front of the building. However, as he listened to Quibb's rant, he suddenly found himself wondering if that was even Quibb's voice. He knew that it was a real voice, because other men were listening to it and were being moved by it. However, was it *Quibb's* voice? He searched his mind, but could come up with nothing concrete. It could just have been someone that sounded like Quibb—or maybe The Voice of Conscience did not sound anything like Quibb at all. Maybe Xi was so obsessed with the man that he was projecting his voice everywhere. He still was not even sure that he had brought Quibb here last night. The images in his mind, of him taking Quibb in his arms and entering that stairway, then seeing all those hidden subterranean floors...and then being confronted by that murderous guard... None of these images were verifiable. Indeed, if not for the wreckage around him, he would now be doubting the existence of The Horde.

Xi plopped the carcass onto the pile of corpses, then he retraced his steps to the hospital. His steps were timid and stiff. ...He did not like the purple, shimmering sky at all. Something about it made his skin crawl. He had definitely seen that purple sky and green sun back at The Company (between those commercials). There was no point in trying to deny it...but even his possible clairvoyance seemed irrelevant in the face of all that had happened—and all that seemed on the *verge* of happening. Now, as he walked along, he could not overcome the feeling that there were vital facts staring him in the face—but that he was too stupid and preoccupied to grasp the grand conclusions. On top of that, looking up at the strange sky was like staring at an unfocused screen—it hurt his eyes and made him dizzy, so that he looked away—

"The Horde will attack again tonight!" Quibb's voice declared, "—but we are the final army of the Goddess!" Xi groaned and rubbed his temples, inadvertently smearing clotted blood and filth on his face. He could not even begin to conceptualize what Quibb could have to do with all this. Xi listened to Quibb's voice for a while, trying to make sense of it, but one could not *just* listen to The Voice: the words were like a parasite. One felt them working within, eating away at one's insides...And Xi had always been wary of that Goddess cult—even at times when he had laughed at the antics of its members. He feared it because he realized that on some level he had always believed...but he believed in the Goddess the way a child afraid of the dark believed in ghosts and monsters. His belief in the Goddess negated all joy and hopes for the future. The Goddess was for him the Anti-Christ, in a universe where Christ was embodied by reason and order and common decency.

Xi went back into the hospital to get another corpse; but then, after looking around absentmindedly, he returned outside. His eyes were red and watery from all the smoke in the air. As he looked at the men around him, he realized that their PinkEyes were still fused to their corneas. As a consequence, all of them had gray, metallic eyes. Xi remembered that he, too was wearing the devices...he could not remember if it was possible to remove the devices or not—that is, while one was still alive....Down the street, he could hear men screaming...perhaps burning to death—

A tingly feeling went up his spine! He shuddered, peering over his shoulder uneasily. A cry was already forming on his lips as he stared into the shadows; and as he stared into the darkness—into an empty place by the wall—he was certain that he saw something moving there: a monstrous paw retreating into the nothingness. He brought his trembling hands to his face, clenching them over his agape mouth as he tried to reconcile what he thought he had seen, with what was *possible*—

There is nothing there! he said to himself, not because he believed it, but because, like a terrified child, he was desperate for it to be so. After a minute or two of waiting for the paw to reappear, he clamped his eyes shut, bowed his head in exhaustion, and leaned against the outer wall of the hospital....

Xi was in this position when Mansmann walked up. He opened his eyes wearily when the old man stopped in front of him.

"You okay?" Mansmann asked.

Xi looked around vaguely (as though he had forgotten where he was) before returning to Mansmann. "No," he whispered at last.

"What's wrong?"

He rubbed his temples in frustration—and partly from the growing headache. "...Something's after me," he said, like a terrified child telling a parent his bad dream.

"What?"

"Since The Horde came, something's been stalking me."

"...Something?"

"Everywhere I go, I feel it—*sense* it."

Mansmann tried to reassure him: "It's just the bombing—posttraumatic stress."

"No," Xi said, standing up straighter, but still staring out on the world uneasily. "Something's out there, waiting to kill me...something *knows* me... it's like a part of me—" He caught himself and laughed anxiously. Mansmann was staring at him uneasily. "...I'm sorry," Xi said at last.

"No—it's not a problem...talk to me. What are you feeling?"

Xi looked at the old man as one would look at a torturer—at someone who promised paradise when all he had to offer was the hell of disappointment. He wanted to talk, but after seven years of trying to insulate himself from the insanity of others, and constructing an internal fortress in order to keep his vital truths and fantasies for himself alone, he did not want to *risk* talking. He had learned that it was hope that led men to hopelessness.

It was hope that made men venture out onto the farthest limbs, in search of the succulent fruit that their hopes represented. Xi did not want to venture out onto that limb, and expend resources he did not have, in order to just crash to the ground, or find that the fruit was actually sour. Yet, in Mansmann's eyes, there was something that called to him: an earnestness that he had probably never seen before. Also, he still felt their strange connection. "...I don't know," he began after a sigh, his voice low and contemplative. "...Maybe it's the stress like you say...but everything is wrong....It's like we're already dead and don't know it." He looked at the old man hopefully; Mansmann looked back uncertainly, but nodded his head in encouragement. Xi went on: "...That Voice—the things it says"— he could not explain his fears and this frustrated him further—"...it's just not right. It's like a cat's caught us and is playing with us...letting us run a little, so that when it pounces on us again our terror will be that much greater, because for a little while we thought we were free—that we had escaped death....I mean, why the hell did The Horde stop bombing us all of a sudden? It's like it's all a game—a sick trick someone's playing on us—"

But just then, there was a huge explosion in one of the buildings across the street, and several of the volunteer firemen disappeared in the bright red flames. Xi and Mansmann were forced to stagger back from the force of the blast. Some of the men across the street were fully engulfed in flames (and running around wildly); after the initial shock, Mansmann left Xi and ran across the street to help the men. Xi took a step in that direction, but faltered—not from fear, but from the renewed feeling that it was all irrelevant, and that there was something else out there. He felt suddenly lonely— and *drained*.

Quibb's voice was still screaming that The Horde was going to be back again tonight. Xi had a sudden impulse to escape, and turn his back on everything Quibb had promised in the vision; but as Quibb had said, he had come too far already to turn back. Moreover, he was suddenly overcome by the feeling that if he found Quibb (and managed to understand the man's place in all this), then he would not only be able to save himself, but also the *world*. A strange religion was building strength within him now, with

Quibb as God and High Priest, and himself as God's anointed...but he shook his head uneasily as the full extent of these thoughts began to register in his conscious mind—

"The Horde want only to destroy us!" The Voice screamed then. When Xi sighed and looked up, the shimmering heavens again made his head ache. He closed his eyes for a moment, desperate for a quiet place to rest and think, but The Voice was still screaming about war and destruction— and *revenge*. Xi now clamped his eyes shut and brought his trembling hands to his ears. Even then, The Voice reverberated through him. He was not just hearing the words anymore: he was feeling them—*living* them. How could he doubt Quibb's covenant with him when he was listening to Quibb's voice at that very moment!

"—The Horde destroyed others because they were not strong," The Voice was saying now. "But we are a great city, fortified by the indefatigable spirit the Goddess. Don't stand there in silence! If you will fight, shout your defiance, so that your enemy will hear! Yes, I said, *shout!*" At this, a few men cried out pathetically. "Let them hear your anger!" The Voice urged them on. "Let them know that you are men!" At this, the defiant voices of the men—at first dozens, then hundreds and thousands and *millions*— began to rise in the air. It went on for what seemed like *minutes*, cresting like a wave over all of their heads. It was deafening, terrifying...an entire city of madness. Xi was forced to sit down on the ground. He felt weak— *spent*. What did it mean! What was Quibb doing to the men! The only thing that made sense was again that he had to find Quibb. Even if the man was just a delusion, he was the only thing that Xi had: the only thing that gave him the *hope* that he would find peace and understanding. Only Quibb had the answers; only Quibb could lead him to safety. Xi started looking around then, as if making sure that Quibb was not right before him, and then it hit him: *the Image Broadcast Complex!* That was the only place that he could think of that had the technology to broadcast *simultaneously* over multiple media. Quibb would have to be in such a place!

The men were still shouting their madness. When Xi looked up, he saw the old doctor staring at him from across the street. The intensity of the man's gaze at first took him aback—but then he again felt the connection between them. After all, the two men had been bound in blood by their night's work. While the other men succumbed to Quibb's voice and screamed their wild defiance, only Xi and the doctor remained silent and unmoved by the madness. This, too, proved their brotherhood. They stared at one another, still unsure. But then there was a moment of mutual understanding and thankfulness that neither tried to account for. After nodding to the doctor, Xi simply arose from the ground and took his leave; when he was halfway down the block, he heard the men in front of the hospital cheering. As he looked back, he saw that the pile of corpses on the sidewalk had been lit....

He was filthy, but he was not so much disgusted as annoyed by the sticky mess that covered him. Down the block, there was an open fire hydrant. He washed his hands, face and neck under the cool stream of water—but trying to wash the congealed blood off his clothes only made it worse. Now was not the time for cleanliness anyway. The stench of carrion would be with them for a long time to come. As it was the middle of summer, the thousands of bodies trapped beneath the rubble would start to smell by the end of the day. There would have to be thousands of corpse bonfires across the city....Maybe there would be another epidemic—

"*They will attack again tonight!*" Quibb's voice yelled again. Xi cringed, fighting not to be overcome by it all. The men's caterwauling had finally ceased, but the sound of their wild defiance continued to ring in Xi's ears. Just then, he was passing a building that had perhaps been gutted for years now. The glass of the windows was long gone, and the strange light of the day cascaded down, creating odd shadows in the gutted structure. At first, he thought that the shadows were only another byproduct of the light. For some reason, he stopped to make sure, finally making out the men dancing inside. It was yet another cult. About 20 men were dancing naked around a flame as they chanted an indecipherable refrain. With the highlights from the flame, and the strange light, they seemed horrible. Their eyes were glossed over—no doubt from drugs. They seemed like deluded pagans performing a heathen dance—and yet, they seemed suddenly powerful to him: free of doubt and concern. They would die if their leader told them to—and would not question the order for a millisecond. That state of mind was just as horrible as it was powerful; and at the moment, yet another troubling realization grew within him as he listened to Quibb's voice. The Voice of Conscience was still ranting about preparing for The Horde. That the men were nothing against The Horde was obvious and terrifying, but that the men were listening to Quibb's voice—and were following it with the same unquestioning faith as the cultists before him followed their master—made Xi shudder. He was witnessing the beginnings of the Cult of Quibb.

The world is full of fools pretending to be stronger than they are—
who have no idea about the extent of their weakness.
Verse 1892:3 of *The Teachings*

As the new day spread across the horizon, Respoli-Priestess looked down at the Goddess, who lay sleeping on a soft patch of moss. They had hiked through the forest for the past few hours, pulling the dumbfounded woman behind them. They were now actually on the old Appalachian Hiking Trail. Energized by all that was before him, Respoli-Priestess was the only one that did not seem to be exhausted. Except for some vigilant foot soldiers, who kept a keen eye out for any sign that they were being followed, he alone stood. Most of his men either lay on the ground or slumped against tree trunks and boulders. They were on top of a mountain now; and as a new day was at hand, the sky was painted in delicate pastel shades. Down in the valley, he could see the river shimmering through the trees; through the bushes, he could hear the soft purl of a stream.

Respoli-Priestess took a long, deep breath and smiled, thinking not only that a new day had come, but also a new era. At that moment, a hawk cried out overhead; and as the high-pitched sound reverberated in the air, those resting on the ground were all roused from sleep. However, the Goddess was in a place that was beyond sleep. As she inched herself closer towards consciousness, she saw flashes of her escape from that place on the mountain… and then it was as though she took a wrong turn, into one of her mind's secret eddies of possibility. At first, she saw one of those Horde robots step out of the nothingness. In the darkness, she retreated a step and screamed, but then there were robots *everywhere*—like a plague: like a bacterium multiplying exponentially. Soon, there were *billions*, and even the universe seemed too small to encompass them. She was being squeezed now. She felt them against her—like billions of rats squirming in the sewer. Eventually even that barrier wore away, and she felt them *within* her; she felt their *consciousness*—the deep darkness of soulless monsters. She screamed—not just in terror, but as a secret admission that she was willing to sacrifice her very *soul* to escape them. It was then, as she felt their darkness filling her, that she realized that her soul and theirs were made of the same stuff—*as if she were their mother*: as if they were coming back home to her—

And then, that was all gone. Her mind scurried away—like a rabbit released from a bobcat's paw. Her flight back to reality—or at least, away from her oneness with The Horde—was a brutal, haphazard one. As she emerged into consciousness, she was totally lost—like someone waking up without the sense of sight or hearing or touch. That, combined with all her displacement and confusion, made it impossible to discern the subtleties between the waking world and the dream world. In this semi-conscious state, she now remembered her flight from that place on the mountain in a burst of images and fears that did not so much mark it as an event from her past, but as a faceless, nameless horror. She sprang upright from sleep, involuntarily grimacing as sore and lacerated muscles protested. Her eyes burst open, but the glare of the morning sun was so bright that she shut them almost immediately. Trembling, she put up her hands to shield her eyes. Horrified to muteness, she glimpsed the two dozen or so nebulous forms standing before her. They stood with their backs to the sun, so that the only thing that she saw was their outlines against the painful glare. Even while she had hiked with them the previous night, she had not wholly been conscious. The world had simply been a place of terror and confusion, in which strange creatures had directed her motions. Dazed from everything that had happened, she had had no idea where they were taking her—nor had she been *capable* of caring.

Accordingly, now, as she looked up at the figures still lost in the glare, some of that old helplessness came over her again. She was beyond running: she knew that instantly. She expected to be attacked at any moment, yet the forms just stood there; with their backs to the light, they seemed to be without faces—without expressions, or *souls*—that she could discern. She opened her mouth, her lips trembling as she fumbled for words. But—

"Goddess be praised!" she heard one of them say in a euphoric whisper. There was awe and hope in the voice; it seemed to mean everything and nothing—she could not even tell the sex of the voice. However, that name— *Goddess*—must have had some significance to her, because, as she heard it, a debilitating feeling of dread came over her. Like everything else, the name seemed connected with horrors too unspeakable to name. She grasped her head, as if in pain; as the figures continued to tower over her, she was so desperate for things to reach some kind of conclusion that she almost wished that their assault would begin. Instead of this silence, she wanted to hear loud, screaming voices: feel gruff, callused hands hauling her away...But then, the forms stepped in closer to her, so that they blocked out the rising sun, and she saw them taking shape—as if by magic. They stood against a morning sky suffused in a crimson hue, and the reality of their gaunt, effeminate bodies began to put things in perspective: to connect these men to the ones that had greeted her after she emerged from the river. She looked at their faces now: most of them were wearing makeup—the gaudy, excessive makeup of old women who refused to acknowledge that their "beauty" was behind them. On some of their faces, the makeup was in dark clumps and splotches around their eyes and mouth, as though not to highlight beauty, but to inspire horror and disgust—

"Goddess be praised!" someone exulted again; and looking up, she noticed the machine gun slung over his shoulder. Most of them had guns in fact... and she recognized the black fatigues of last night. Looking down, she realized that she was now wearing a long, flowing summer dress. They had dressed her in it after she emerged naked from that stream. And now, stepping up to get a closer look at her, was the child with the curly blond hair that reminded her of Shirley Temple. The child seemed like an idealized TV version of girlhood, with blond curls and dimpled, rosy cheeks. The child even had a frilly dress with a big bow at the back. The Goddess stared at the child for a moment, both enchanted and sickened by the cloying sweetness. There was also another of the band that confused her. The others all seemed to be staring at that one—

as if waiting for guidance. It was the one that had held her hand last night and told her not to be afraid. The way that the others regarded this one—with a kind of religious reverence—he (or she) seemed like the center of their dreams and hopes and fears—

"Do you know where you just came from?" Respoli-Priestess asked her then, his voice soft and gentle. Maybe it *is* a woman, she thought to herself, especially after again noting the dress—

"Can you understand me?" Respoli-Priestess asked, while the others gathered around and stared down at her. Even she was mesmerized by Respoli-Priestess; fear was superseded by the same reverence that she saw in the eyes of the others. His figure was slim and supple; his eyes where clear and radiant, with long, dark lashes. All about him, there was the suggestion of natural beauty. He wore no makeup—at least, none that she could discern. Even his shoulder-length hair seemed perfect, as it accentuated the smooth curvature of his face—

"Do you know where you came from?" Respoli-Priestess asked again. There was so much compassion in his eyes...it was almost unsettling; but she was coming back to her senses now. She looked around confusedly for a moment, then back at him—

"You don't know who you are, do you?" Respoli-Priestess asked with an encouraging smile.

She shuddered, suddenly remembering the things she had felt as the emerged into consciousness—*her maternal oneness with The Horde*. She shook her head absentmindedly and helplessly, feeling the darkness enveloping her again. She opened her mouth to say something—to protest against the darkness perhaps—but she could again find nothing to say. She looked away then, ashamed. But:

"You are *God*!" Respoli-Priestess exulted suddenly. The others, hearing this, began to cheer amongst themselves.

"God?" she whispered, almost mechanically, like an automaton. Then she listened to the word in the air, finally connecting it with meaning. What went through her mind then? the startling immensity of it? the ridiculousness of it? She frowned; she went to shake her head—

"Yes, *you* are the one!" Respoli-Priestess declared. "You have come to save the world, My Master! We've searched for you for all these years—and *waited* for you! I *knew* you were in that place—I knew your enemies were keeping you from us," he said, looking around wildly at his followers, who nodded their heads. "But *The Teachings* told me to wait for you—told me that one day you would outwit your enemies and emerge from that huge tomb, like Lazarus escaping *death*!" As he said this last word, he raised his arms up and struck a kind of transcendent pose; and at that signal, the others cheered and began capering about like children at a party. Those in front kneeled down and started bowing before her, mumbling prayers that were too jumbled to hear. It was beyond sense; panic again tried to seize her, but she was suddenly impervious: insensate, *stunned*... Scenes from her visions— of the ascension of that man into God as he raped that woman—flew through her mind. And yet, everything was still *off*: still too much like a bizarre dream—

Something brushed her calf; as she looked down, she saw that two of the kneeling men, ostensibly overcome by their awe of her, were caressing her exposed ankles with mesmerized gleams in their eyes. The men had the odor of cheap perfume and motor oil. Their gaunt, grime- and makeup- encrusted faces were unsettling. Their hands, as they stroked her ankles, had a man's hardness to them. Yet, their touch did not exactly seem threat- ening. There was a solemnity to their caresses that calmed her, so that while the others bowed, mumbling their benedictions, and the purl of the nearby stream harmonized with the morning birds and the wind, she sat there wondering what it all meant. But suddenly—

"Away from there, you demons!" Respoli-Priestess squealed, just now seeing the caresses of his minions. With a lighting quick agility that took even their newfound God aback, Respoli-Priestess leapt up from his genuflections and was soon applying the back of his hand to the scruff of the two worshippers' necks. They tried to dodge blows, but there was no avoiding Respoli-Priestess' wrath. Like repentant dogs, the two scurried away, whining and bowing.

As she sat there, the Goddess looked on in stunned amazement. She looked at them all—their gaunt, grimy faces, their clumsy cavorting and their obvious madness—and, for some reason that was beyond her, she put her head back and laughed. Her laughter shook her entire body uncontrollably, almost painfully.

"Forgive us, Master!" begged Respoli-Priestess, while the rest of the band looked on with a kind of repentant horror. But all that they did was make her laugh harder. Only the child with the curls—the Shirley Temple clone—joined in her laughter, jumping about like a grasshopper. At that moment, youth seemed unspeakably wonderful to her. She smiled at the child then, grateful for...she did not quite know what—nor did she care. All that there was, was laughter; and whether it was prudent or not, she found herself coming to the conclusion that Respoli-Priestess and his cult were harmless. Her acceptance of their madness had its own sweet madness to it.

"Who are you?" she asked at last, with a casual glance around the group.

"We are yours to command, Master," replied Respoli-Priestess.

She frowned, like a tired mother frowned at a child's silliness: "But *who*—"

"Praised be your will, My Master," Respoli-Priestess said with a smile of ecstasy. "Now that you have come, we are washed clean. You will make with us as you will!"

She shook her head, frustrated and fatigued by the inability to communicate. She was like a tourist in a distant land, and Respoli-Priestess was like an over-eager tour guide who did not realize that she could not speak the local language. However, it was then that her stomach growled. For the first time, she acknowledged her own gnawing emptiness and hunger. Her laughter died away then. "Food?" she asked.

Bread, a cheese-like substance and a syrupy beverage were brought before her. All of it tasted and smelled artificial, almost unwholesome. Images of industrial production and processing flew through her mind. But she was hungry, gripped by the need to eat, itself. She did not really taste the food as she engulfed it. She ate like an animal, ripping at the food, rather than chewing it.

The others watched her closely, smiling and nodding as they observed her hunger. When she looked up and saw their eager eyes, she felt a little self-conscious, so that she blurted out:

"I'm not, you know—*God*, I mean." Her mouth was full of food; she tried to act at ease.

"You *are*!" Respoli-Priestess said with a confident smile; the others nodded again.

"How can I be God?" she said with a nervous chuckle, "I don't know anything."

"That only proves it!" Respoli-Priestess rejoiced. "That is how you will save us!" She went to shake her head, but Respoli-Priestess talked as if drunk: quickly, on the brink of incoherence. "—As Jesus, you came down to Earth [she tried to stop him, but the man only talked faster]...you came down to earth to suffer for us and save us from sin, but our sin remained. Yes," Respoli-Priestess went on, "it remained, because no one can really suffer if he knows that he is God, soon to return to Heaven. Suffering is about not knowing; *humanity* is about not knowing; so as an omnipotent Jesus coming down to earth, you could neither suffer nor be human. But this time, sacrificing your *Godhood*, you have come back to us as an innocent girl; and *this* time, it will be decisive: we will either be saved or perish. Either way, we will be cleansed!"

She looked at them with blank cow eyes. "...What?" And then, "What will I save you from?" she asked at last. Words seemed weird to her again; she felt suddenly anxious, almost nauseous—

"The end of the world!" Respoli-Priestess said triumphantly.

She sat staring at them in horror! Whether it was the morning dew that had settled on her, or the dawning realization of what Respoli-Priestess had just said, she shivered. Keenly attuned to her needs, Respoli-Priestess ordered more clothes. They handed her a gaudy pink robe that made her think of herself as some kind of bimbo Jesus. She arose to put on the garment, grimacing once more. She felt a little giddy, too, and had to lean against a boulder for support. Two of her new followers stepped up to support her, still trembling with their strange awe of her.

"Yes, this is just as *The Teachings* foretell!" Respoli-Priestess exulted again.

"Teachings?" She felt her disorientation building—maybe it was only the standing...

"It is said that after you have cleansed us, you will bring the women back."

"The *women*?" She looked up anxiously, her stomach twitching… "Where'd they go?"

"Praised be your will, *My Master*! Your enemies have taken them. But even that is part of your will. They have been taken away from this world—this place of sin—leaving only the men to atone."

She looked on incredulously. "…So you're a *man* then?"

"Praised be your will," Respoli-Priestess went on quickly, "you took the women away because we didn't understand the gift. That is why we dress like this: to honor you: to show you that we understand." There was an endearing earnestness of faith in his eyes: a kind of intoxicating insanity. Yet, Respoli-Priestess seemed only like a caricature to her; this world, which she roamed without bearings, seemed like a caricature of the real world. Nothing seemed real. As before, answers seemed further off every time she tried to understand. Today, she was to figure everything out—that was what she had said the night before. However, now, she found herself wrestling with something even more entangling. She felt as though she were floating away and would never find herself…but then something new occurred to her, and she rushed towards it for dear life.

"—A mirror?" she blurted out. One of the drag queens in the back did have one, and she trembled as the rhinestone-sprinkled hand mirror was passed to the front. What would she see? Now, she almost did not dare to look. She held it tentatively in her hands; she glimpsed down: *the eyes*! Eyes of a crazed woman…! Hair closely cropped and nappy—just like the others from that place on the mountain…! Her full lips were chapped and bleeding from dehydration; her nostrils were slightly flared, seeming uncentered on her bruised, scratched face. She seemed to be in her late teens or early twenties, but she seemed without youth: without time…*without a soul*! And the *eyes*, with their searching vapidity, were huge and bulging! She looked away from the face then, overcome by the sudden, debilitating sensation that she was ugly—but ugly in some mystical, *spiritual* sense: in a sense that went beyond adolescent vanity and social convention about beauty. She could not help thinking about The Horde as she looked at her face. She could not help thinking of herself as the nexus of a ruthless hive mind.

As she stood there shaking, she once again had recollections of her flight—and saw images of men rampaging through the streets. All of these images hovered before her, and she could not turn her eyes away. With what she had just heard, it was no use trying to deny that something colossal and *catastrophic* had happened to the world. Her past was lost to her, but if *this* was the real world, then this was the place where her *history* was. This was the place that had terrified and traumatized her younger self. While logic told her that she would one day have to return to that place on the mountain (in order to confront The Horde and sever its link to her soul), instinct told her that before that final battle, she had to discover as much about the world and herself as possible. This piece of reasoning sobered her up. However, in light of her strange, selective amnesia, and the things she had seen, she found herself wondering, with a kind of insane courage, what if she really *were* God! It was just as sane as everything else that she had thought and seen in this world. She looked at the drag queens around her, again overwhelmed by the possibilities: overwhelmed by the scope of Possibility, itself. She cleared her throat, trying to calm herself: trying to claw her way back to her sanity. A speck of that old defiance gathered within her, and she groped at it savagely, blurting out:

"I'm not God!" She trembled as she said it, but the men only smiled, as one smiled at a fool who refused to acknowledge the obvious.

"Will you come with us anyway?" said Respoli-Priestess, smiling.

After the defiance passed from her system, she felt lost and devastated again. She felt herself on the verge of drifting away once more; but with a new resolve that seemed just as insane as her followers' faith, she stretched out a desperate hand to the world. "Do you know what my name is?" she said, almost pleading for something to hold onto. However, Respoli-Priestess only laughed, saying:

"God is beyond names, My Master." At that, he gave her his arm and they began to walk down the trail.

VI

The same uncompromising mindset required to counteract injustice and wrench power away from tyrants, is the same mindset demonstrated by the tyrant, who is willing to do anything in order to keep his power. This, incidentally, is why there will never be revolutions.
VERSE 234:2 OF *The Teachings*

Tio Mendez, the famed, yet anonymous, pirate of the airwaves, sat alone in a dark basement apartment in Harlem. The place was silent and still, except for the sound of fingers clicking keys on a console. The console was used to control the elaborate telecommunications device within the chamber. Beyond the clicking of keys, the crisp words of The Voice of Conscience's ongoing rant could be heard over the device's speakers. The device was actually so complex that its component parts were spread out over several rooms of the basement. It had its own power source and rendered so much information that four screens were needed to incorporate it all.

As for Mendez, he was a spindly man in his late forties, who seemed like a demented hermit that had lived alone in the hills for decades and gone mad from the isolation. His basement apartment was like a cave. As hygiene had long become an unacceptable encumbrance in his life, his apartment was like a pigsty. Furniture was only a magnet for garbage, so he had gotten rid of everything but his chair, his console and an old mattress. He tried to keep everything to the basics. Clothes were pretty much unnecessary—especially with the summer heat—so he went around naked. This, of course, was not to imply that he had actually reasoned any of this out. On the contrary, his present state seemed to be more a product of intellectual laziness and indifference than actually planning. His fingernails, for instance, were each at least three centimeters—which was incredible, since he spent most of his time typing at the console. Whereas most men would have cut their fingernails from the inconvenience alone, he simply worked on, as if stopping to cut them would have been too much of a distraction. Also, whereas most of the men had long hair, his reached down to the ground. Sometimes he forgot about his hair when he went to use the toilet. A couple of times, he had even flushed the toilet with his hair still in it. But even after pulling his shit-coated hair from the toilet, he had not thought of cutting his hair. Like all geniuses, he seemed inept in everything but that area where his genius lay. For Mendez, that area was technology.

To call him a computer nerd was a crude understatement. Of the four screens in front of him, one was a view from an old NASA satellite; one showed some esoteric information on Indonesia, which was constantly being translated into English by a subroutine that he had created; another showed the present position of the gulf stream; another, glistening with scores of purple stars, showed all the places on the globe where The Horde had attacked. From his little console, he had the ability to find virtually anything—like a god of information. Unlike the wearers of the PinkEyes, who had had access to all the information of the known universe, but little wherewithal to grasp it and inculcate it into their lives, he had always been able to possess and manipulate *knowledge*. In this respect, he was a member of a dying breed—

Someone laughed in the darkness behind him. It was one of those non-sequiturs that took time to register in his mind; but when it did, he wheeled around, a muffled shriek already escaping from his throat—

A man stepped from the shadows; Mendez jumped in his seat! He wanted to scream something, like, *How'd you get in here*! but he felt as though his heart were stuck in his throat.

…Silence. There was only the slightest impression of a smile on the man's shadowy face. It was Quibb.

Mendez looked at a steel pipe that was lying on the floor, but he judged that it was too far to grab. "…Who are you?" he managed to squeak through his terror. He was like a worm hiding under a rock, sent squirming when the rock was turned over, and the light of day destroyed the universe of soothing, dank darkness. That Mendez was sitting naked did not even register in his mind yet. For now, he was still being undone by the man's calm demeanor.

That demeanor was somehow more unsettling than if the man had been ranting and raving, brandishing a club. The man stopped about three meters from Mendez, seeming to tower over him. Mendez kept squinting, but the man's face remained in the shadows. If he could only see the face…! "Who are you?" he peeped again, his voice tremulous.

"Don't you know my voice?" the man asked in a calm, resonant tone.

"—The Voice of Conscience!" he said with a gasp. Mendez had thought that The Voice was just a computer spurting nonsense. Those whose lives were less dominated by technology than his had looked to spiritual sources: he had looked to technology. He had thought that The Voice was anything but a man; and now, somehow or another, that thing, whatever it was, had taken human form and manifested itself before him. On top of that, Mendez looked over at the speakers of his computer in amazement: The Voice was still ranting on the airwaves, telling the men about The Horde and the war to come. Mendez looked up at the man in the shadows again, with new horror shining in his eyes: The Voice was *everywhere*—like *God*! From the dim highlights provided by the flickering screens, Mendez could see that the man was still smiling. It was not a vindictive smile, but an amused one—

Mendez had an impulse to go crazy—to dash at the man and beat his brains out—but something unaccountable was holding him back: *the awe of men towards God*. His strange ineptitude in the face of the man's presence brought with it its own terrors. "What do you want?" Mendez managed to say at last, still trying to catch his breath.

"Ah, *finally*," Quibb said with a satisfied air. "…Down to business. Very good… I'm here so that you can take your rightful place in society." Then he added, somewhat desultorily: "Religion and politics are the means through which men are civilized. The Goddess will provide the religion; you will provide the politics."

Mendez had to think for a while before he realized what the man was talking about. "Politics?" he said suspiciously.

"Yes, you wish to rule other men," The Voice said in the same even tone that had been playing in the streets all day; once again, Mendez glanced uneasily at the computer speakers. "Everyone wants something," The Voice continued, "—you want power. You already have some of it: you are able to find out things that no one else in the city can. You know many things that most won't even begin to suspect. But that isn't enough. You want to get out of the shadows—out of this filthy hole you hide in. You want more than just information: information is useless unless you can *use* it. Furthermore, you don't just want people to laugh at The Company and Shaka—and all those men who are dwarfed by your intellect. You don't want to be just another satirist. You want to move men *positively*, not just negatively and satirically. You want them to cheer for you: to *love* you—not simply to hate and deride others. This is the power that drives you. I know how to get it for you."

Mendez stared. There was nothing to be said—nothing to *do*. He felt lost—*overwhelmed*. In time, he nodded, feeling even more ashamed by his admission.

Quibb smiled. He looked around with the same confidence that he had had from the onset, diverting his attention to the screens. Noticing something, he chuckled, saying:

"So, you think you know where the women are, do you?"

Mendez felt naked—he *was* naked! But the screens were *his*; only he should have been able to know what they meant…And yet it seemed useless to hide from the…*The Voice of Conscience*. He felt like a class nerd realizing that the new boy was smarter. He squinted his eyes again, still trying to see that face…! In time, he grew defensive. "Yes," he averred to counter Quibb's smile, "…I know where they are."

Quibb looked at Mendez's information once more, before chuckling to himself—the way someone chuckled at a child's foolishness. Then, in a tone that told Mendez that their meeting was over, Quibb concluded: "I'll send you some help in a day or two—when The Horde's attacks stop." Still smiling confidently, the man walked into the shadows (what was actually the corner of the room, where there was no exit) and disappeared. Mendez stared into the empty darkness for a while, unable to believe his eyes! Some people screamed when terrified; others, in a contradictory manner, tried to laugh their terror away. Mendez was of the latter sort and laughed a high-pitched squeal that echoed horribly in the cramped basement. Trembling uncontrollably, he spent the next few hours gnawing his fingernails down to the cuticles.

*No great plotting is needed for fishing: just the arbitrary
casting of lines, and patience.*
VERSE 2099:5 OF *The Teachings*

B y now, Shaka had washed up and changed into a robe that resembled
Stein's. He was standing before one of the windows of his suite, staring out on the strange morning sky. Below that, lay Company Square
and the most salient evidence of The Horde's power: the wreckage of the
dark pyramid. While the sight of the thousands of men working on the
Image Broadcast Complex filled him with satisfaction, nothing seemed
right anymore. He still could not get used to being so close to the ground:
he felt like a god banished from the heavens. More troublingly, he could
hear the eerie echo of that strange voice down the corridor. The reality of
how the sound of it had driven him mad was somehow a reminder of his
mortality. Those words had infected him with the fear of death; even after
regaining his composure, and making the guards clear away the rubble from
the smashed screen, the specter of death had been on him. The only thing
that had been able to distract him was the thought of Circe. He had had the
guards bring him a portable Dimensional Portal to replace the one he had
smashed; and now, as he had been doing over the past few hours, he took out
the videodisk that Circe had given him and looked at it longingly—

There was a deferential knock on the door; when Shaka bellowed for the
person to come, Stein entered, still huffing and puffing from all of his errands.

"We still don't know where that broadcast is coming from, sir," Stein
informed him. "The men are calling it, The Voice of Conscience. Somehow,

it's everywhere—broadcasting over speakers that don't even have power in them."

Shaka turned to Stein with a frown: "How is this possible?"

Stein shrugged: "I don't know, sir, but I heard that some of our engineers might have been working on the technology."

"So you're saying that this could be our technology?"

"It's possible, sir," Stein said, sorrowfully.

"Are you sure it's not coming from here?"

Stein cringed before venturing, "We don't know, sir, but it doesn't seem likely. We don't even have power in the complex yet." When an expression of dissatisfaction remained on Shaka's face, Stein shuddered; then, desperate to palliate the man: "—But when we do get power, we could easily jam it."

"…No," Shaka said absentmindedly, "—someone has stepped forward to take power: that, in and of itself, is nothing of consequence. Besides, the more you try to countermand something, the more of your own power you give to it."

Stein nodded timidly once again.

"—Tyrannies never last, Stein," Shaka went on, still with that air of abstraction as he stared dreamily out on the devastated world. It was almost as if he were not even listening to himself: as if he were merely saying things that the Shaka of old would say, and that none of it was relevant anymore. Images of Circe and Xi, and the devastation wrecked by The Horde, joined with the mystery of The Voice of Conscience; and suddenly desperate to believe in his words, he looked at Stein with tired eyes, saying, "You build empires by giving your rivals, and those you are to conquer, freedom to act. Many will become drunk on the illusion of power and destroy themselves; the rest will panic and demand to be ruled."

When Shaka paused, Stein hesitated for a moment, wondering if he should broach the logical subject. At last, he cleared his throat: "What about The Horde, sir?"

"What about them?"

"The Voice of Conscience is saying that it will be back again tonight…in a matter of *hours*. Is there something we should be doing?"

"What is there to be done?" Shaka said, but with a certain amount of defensiveness—like someone in denial. Stein saw this and nodded compliantly.

"What about Xi Wang?" Shaka demanded next.

"There is no sign of him, sir. With all the chaos last night, nobody saw him after he left the lower floors. With all the disturbance, and the power outage, none of our cameras were able to capture anything."

"How much does he know?" he said, looking off into the distance.

Stein took a deep breath: "There is no way to tell. It seems that he was working as a monitor for a few weeks. We think that he pretended to be someone else in order to get close."

"So, it was all a ruse."

"It seems so, sir."

"Find him, Stein," Shaka said in a low, menacing voice. When Shaka turned back to the window, Stein bowed and exited the room with the same nervous haste with which he had entered it. Alone again, Shaka remembered the videodisk. The portable Dimensional Portal was in the middle of the room. He was eager to put in the disk and enter the Dimension, but a side of him was wary. In fact, both his curiosity and his wariness worried him, because both were evidence that he was allowing himself to be led by outside forces. Yet, the disk was in his hand and the Dimensional Portal was before him....

A second after he inserted the disk, the room around him turned into a tropical beach at sunset. There were neither people nor edifices around him, and the majestic sun hovered just over the horizon. He smiled, having forgotten the power of his technology. He took a deep breath of the sea air then, listening to the waves softly hitting the beach. And then, as he looked up, he saw Circe emerging from the water, his body glistening from the water and the rays of the setting sun. Circe was naked and all Shaka could do was stare. As Circe smiled, Shaka thought about how incredibly beautiful the man was. In fact, he could not think of him as a man anymore. Masculine pronouns seemed like a desecration of the perfection before him. Circe was a *she*—Shaka surrendered himself to it. She was still smiling—still coming towards him. Shaka tried not to look at her perfect breasts...not to look at that beautiful smile. And it was not even that he was aroused by these things: even as Circe walked up to him in that highly charged erotic setting, it was impossible for him to view her as a sexual object. In fact, if he had, he would have merely laughed at the artfulness of his technology. On the contrary, it was just as Circe had said: this Dimension provided him with proof of the existence of God, because Circe was for him an object of worship. She was in front of him now, and her closeness made his skin tingle; she reached out and held his hand at that moment, and he shuddered at the softness of her skin. Then, all of a sudden, the wind began to pick up, blowing her hair wildly and erotically. She smiled again, and in that smile, there seemed to be everything that Shaka had ever wanted: answers to questions that his crude mind had yet to even conceptualize. It was all there, waiting for him to surrender...and he *wanted* to surrender—to dive headlong into the depths of those possibilities and spend an eternity in worship—but just before that instant of no return, a savage instinct of self-preservation seized him; the face and reality of God came into conflict with his own brutal will; and before he even knew what was happening, he wrenched his hand away from Circe's softness and took a few desperate, shambling steps backward, eventually collapsing into the sand—

When the guards rushed in to investigate the sound of something hitting the floor, they found Shaka trembling on the ground like a scared puppy. However, Shaka was the kind of man who was made more brutal by the realization of his weakness; and by the time Stein came running into the room, Shaka was already to his feet:

"Find Circe!" he said, his eyes shining with rage, "—bring her to me!"

"You mean, *him*, sir," Stein corrected him before he had thought better of it.

"Yes...him," Shaka said, turning his back on them and waving his hand for them to leave.

Sometimes death becomes so entwined in one's soul that only by facing it head-on and challenging it recklessly can one live.
VERSE 3939:23 OF *The Teachings*

The time until the next Horde attack was counting down in everyone's mind. Xi trudged on, still searching for the elusive thing that would save them from annihilation. Everywhere he went, he was confronted by the harsh realities of last night's attack—and the even more disturbing sight of men being directed by Quibb's will. Xi was still being lured by the fantasy that he could save himself and the world by finding Quibb, but more and more, he felt like a fool that had followed a mirage into the desert. Even as he began to see the mirage for what it was, he realized that he had already come too far into the desert to turn back. In that insane way that people's actions became more uncompromising and extreme when they began to realize that their beliefs had led them astray, Xi could now think of nothing but finding Quibb. In fact, he could not even think anymore. All that there was, was the act of searching—of *walking*—

"They will attack again tonight!" Quibb's voice repeated for the thousandth time. Xi's pace slowed. He found it difficult to concentrate on anything—especially with that strange sky giving him a headache. He did not know what to make of it—or even if there was anything to be made of his vague thoughts. …Over the minutes and now hours of his search for Quibb, he had had the feeling that his PinkEyes were working—that he was seeing things that were not really there…and that the sky was responsible for it all. He stopped now and stared at the sky, defiant of the disorientation this

caused. His headache seemed to grow exponentially—like a noise growing from a low hum to a screeching blast. He stumbled backwards, ready to clamp his eyes shut; but as he looked on, he realized that the shimmering patterns of the sky had changed into something even more miraculous. The sky now seemed to pulse with energy; as he looked closer, he saw that the flashes of light were mathematical formulas: millions of calculations that scrolled by too fast to be read, but which seemed, like everything else, tantalizingly familiar. He stared up at the sky, transfixed and helpless. His mind was like a heavily laden old truck now, groaning as it made its way up a long, steep hill; and then, as he continued to stare at the pulsing, scrolling heavens, he saw something in the western corner of the sky that seemed unspeakably ominous: a huge digital timer was floating in the clouds. The timer was counting down—like the one above the dark pyramid seven years ago. It was now at nine hours and thirteen minutes. As he did the calculations, he realized that that was when the night, and The Horde's bombs, would once again cloak the city—

And then, the hairs on the back of his neck stood on end! As the familiar feeling of being stalked from the shadows seized him, he looked around anxiously; and now that his mind had been attuned to the pulsing heavens, he just managed to see a dark form slip back into the gutted remains of a building. He stood there trembling, staring at the place where the form had disappeared. He could *sense* it there, beyond the rubble, waiting for him to join it in the shadows. He was more terrified than he had ever been in his life! That shadowy form had been something horrible—he was sure of it, even though he had not seen it clearly. He retreated a step, and then another, but there did not seem to be anywhere to run. He could feel that creature of the shadows everywhere now. It was in the air, like a foul odor. He was breathing it in, choking on its vileness…and yet, his terror, like the purple, shimmering sky, was opening him up to new possibilities. He had the feeling that there was a dark place within him, where terrible secrets lay—debilitating traumas that had sealed themselves off from the rest of his mind with scar tissue. His mind was beginning the process of clawing through the scars—opening up wounds that he suspected would never again heal;

and now, as he stood on the sidewalk trembling, staring into the rubble in case the dark form returned, all that he could think was that he had glimpsed the demented form of the Devil—

He gasped…then he took some deep breaths, as if coming out of a trance. When he glanced up at the sky, he realized that it was again shimmering: there were no scrolling calculations; the digital timer had disappeared…He clamped his eyes shut, wondering if those things had ever even been there. He groaned in frustration; when he opened them again, he felt so disoriented that he was forced to lean against a lamppost for support. He looked in the direction of the rubble and the departing form of the Devil; but as always, there was nothing there besides the shadows….

His stomach churned with acid at that moment, and he belched, tasting the hot, bitter gas. He realized that he was hungry—*starving* in fact. He wondered how long it had been since he had eaten. It seemed like *weeks*—even though that did not seem possible. There was talk that The Company gave its workers drugs to negate their hunger…Xi did not want to think about that…

In time, he found what remained of Broadway and headed downtown. Quibb's voice followed him everywhere, blaring from the ever-present video billboards. Despite going for hours now, The Voice did not sound tired. In fact, the more Xi listened to it, the more he found himself thinking that it did not sound human at all. It seemed like a recording—not only in that it repeated the same things over and over again, but also in that it seemed to do so without having to take a breath, or swallow, or succumb to the hesitancy and imperfection that marked human speech. The incessant rant seemed somehow *perfect*—laid out with a god-like precision. Xi tried saying one of those long phrases to himself and found himself out of breath halfway through it. The Voice literally seemed to exist without the demands of a body: as pure intellect.

…Xi's gaze kept returning to the sky—despite the fact that his headache worsened as he did so. He wondered if the scrolling calculations had meant anything; he wondered if he had actually seen that digital clock. The clock in particular kept eating away at him. The idea of it left him thinking that he was running out of time—that they were *all* running out of time. The Horde would be back in nine hours. That was all the time he had to find Quibb and make sense of the universe before they all died. On top of that, the purple tint of the sky was still making everything, especially time, seem warped. His headache reached a new threshold then, so that he groaned and leaned against another lamppost. He clamped his eyes shut again, as though doing so would banish the pain. Quibb's voice was coming from a video billboard overhead. Xi had a sudden impulse to scream: to do anything to block out the words that seemed to be boring their way into his skull and his *soul*. When he opened his eyes, he found that his vision had gotten blurry. He blinked again, hoping that that would correct the problem, but his vision was getting worse by the moment—and he was beginning to feel sick. He eased himself to the ground, fearful that he would faint and crack his skull on something. Totally exhausted, he lay on his back, among all the rubble and filth, hoping that the fit would soon pass. Still, he only felt himself being drawn in deeper. It was as though he had not slept in weeks, and that his body, unable to stand the strain any further, was shutting down all systems. The effect was not totally unpleasant. It was like surrender after a long period of suffering and strain. The sounds of the world—and the men—took on an airy tone. Even Quibb's voice began to seem far away, so that Xi began to think that he had been given a respite. It was only when he tried to open his eyes that he realized that he now had absolutely no control over his body! He did not even feel as though he *had* a body. The substance of him seemed to be gone somehow—as though he were dead! Now desperate to know what was happening around him, he fought to open his eyes—to embed himself in whatever reality existed beyond his clamped eyelids. Even when his senses returned to the point where he began to feel the effects of gravity working on him again, he still felt powerless against the world. He suddenly realized that he was swaying from side to side—and that he had been doing so for a while. The motion was deepening his sense of nausea. The drive to open his eyes seized him, possessing every last iota of his strength and will—

And then, miraculously, his eyes popped open. He looked around frantic-ally, but the things that he saw were so incredible that even as he saw them, he was unable to make sense of them. All around him, the world was zooming past in a blur—and he was still swaying. Before he was able to accept where he was and what had happened, he looked around with the panic and horror of seven years ago. In fact, it was that feeling from seven years ago (that something was wrong with the nature of the universe) that alerted him to where he was. A horn was honking impatiently behind him; he turned his head to look back; then, taking a huge sweep of the landscape and his immediate environs, he returned his gaze to the front—and grasped the steering wheel of the SUV.

...Somehow, he was in that SUV again. When he grasped the steering wheel, the swaying stopped—but his mind still rebelled against all that he saw and felt....He looked around slowly. He was on the highway: thousands of other cars were driving along with him. He was in a suit and tie; he looked out of the window—at the car passing on his left—and saw a woman driving along in a minivan, with her kids in the back seat! He stared on in shock. The woman happened to look in his direction; when she saw the intent—almost *demented*—way that he stared at her, she zoomed off. The feeling of not being real was beginning to build momentum within him again. Trying to put everything in some kind of perspective, he noted the facts: he was in this SUV again, driving down the highway; he was in a place where women existed and where there was rush hour traffic. Thus, he was in a place where the apocalypse of the last seven years had not taken place—or had not taken place *yet*. Moreover, from his dress, the direction he was driving, and the time of day, he knew that he had just come from The Company. Instinctively, he adjusted the rearview mirror to get a look at himself and gasped: it was G.W. Jefferson that looked back at him! He grasped the steering wheel tighter—as though controlling the vehicle were the key to controlling his existence. His swirling mind offered up three possibilities: either he was dreaming now, he had dreamed the last seven years, or he had somehow been transported back in time. The second possibility—that he had nodded off while he was driving and conjured a nightmare—was of course the most soothing one; and with all that he now saw and felt, it seemed like the most realistic one. Furthermore, remembering his wife and his unborn son, and realizing that he was on his way to see them, he felt everything else fall away. He was on his way home now, and the thought of hugging his wife was like a panacea for the madness of whatever nightmare he had just awakened from. He was not Xi Wang—there was no Quibb, no apocalypse, no creature stalking him from the shadows…

Indeed, the already vague life of Xi Wang disappeared as he embedded himself in this reality. There was a kind of madness to it—or maybe he was only now becoming sane again. Besides, it was impossible for Quibb to exist in a rational universe. A city of 20 million wretched men and Circe and The Horde…none of these things could exist in a rational universe. His mind was like a computer that had crashed after receiving a contradictory and irreconcilable command. Like that computer, his existence was being rebooted now; and with that re-initialization, all the old contradictions were lost in cyberspace—along with strands of meaningless, corrupt data. He was G.W. Jefferson reborn, free of Xi Wang and his madness. He was a loving husband returning home: that was all that he was and all that he had ever been. Fully reintegrated into his present life, he glanced at the back seat, unconsciously nodding to himself when he saw his suitcases. He had just returned from his trip to Asia. He had had his meeting with Shaka and the board…and he was on his way home—not to Africa, as had been the case in his dream. Africa had been another part of the fantasy—the *nightmare*.

Suddenly reassured, he turned on the radio and listened to the news. The Asians were still killing one another; celebrities were still being embroiled in scandals….He was on the exit ramp now. Soon, he was slowing down as he entered his neighborhood. Now coming into view, were dozens of identical three-bedroom, aluminum-sided houses. G.W. opened the window then, smelling the slightly rancid, slightly acrid odor that was always in the air. The housing development had been built on a landfill, but that was the only reason why he had been able to afford it. An entire neighborhood comprised of neo-bourgeoisie, all of whom were grasping for the American Dream—or at least some affordable version thereof…

After he parked in his driveway, he practically leaped outside. Home at last: the well-tended lawn, the quiet streets where the neighborhood children played the last games of the afternoon…it was incredibly solemn and beautiful.

He stopped for a moment, taking it all in with the vestiges of a smile on his face. He remembered his trip to Asia then—and his adultery—but he was home at last, and he would take his wife in his arms and hug her; and when he told her that he loved her and the son that was to come, they would all be made anew: be *purified*. Maybe all that was a fantasy in itself, but it was a fantasy worth striving for and deluding oneself about. He was walking quicker now, practically running up to the door. He fumbled with his keys for a while, still smiling.

However, when he opened the door and looked in, the lights were all off and there was a kind of lonely silence that made his spirits drop. The house was dead quiet. Remembering the vague feeling he had had when he woke up at The Company—that something had happened to his wife—he called out her name then. When there was no reply, a feeling of panic began to stir within him…but then his exhaustion re-exerted itself and he sighed in resignation. Even the maid/attendant, who had been hired to help his wife through her pregnancy, did not seem to be around either. Maybe his wife had gone to visit her parents on Long Island, he thought to himself. The fact of the matter was that with all his traveling, he had not been able to contact her in the better part of a week. As such, she would not have known to expect him. In all likelihood, she had gone by her parents in the interim. G.W. called out to his wife again, but there was no answer—and he did not really expect one. He left his suitcases in the foyer and headed upstairs, to the bedroom. With his wife gone, he would be able to sleep in the master bedroom tonight—as opposed to the cot in the nursery, where his wife had banished him since her "confinement." He was so very tired. For the first time in a long while, he felt as though he would sleep well. Accordingly, his mind was on thoughts of sleep when he entered the bedroom and saw his wife lying on the bed. He immediately stopped in his tracks. She was on top of the covers, in her nightgown, lying rigidly—the way a corpse was laid out! Something about it was unnatural—especially with the protuberance of her abdomen; and as G.W. rushed over to take a look in the dwindling light, he saw that she was wearing something over her eyes: one of Shaka's DreamVisors! It was one of the sleek, new ones, which were to be used when the dark pyramid went online. They were not really available to the general public yet, so that was stranger yet. Growing more anxious by the second, he called out to his wife, but she remained corpse-like. He bent down and touched her, but with a timidity that made it clear to him that he really did think that she was dead. Even after he shook her warm shoulder, she remained unresponsive. Growing desperate, he shook her harder; and then, when that proved ineffectual, he screamed out her name and took her by both shoulders, shaking her even more violently. At last, he snatched the DreamVisor off. It was only then, while he stood above her panting and wide-eyed, that she frowned and showed the first signs of life.

"Mary?" he called her again, now lowering his voice. He caressed her head as she stirred into consciousness.

"G.W.?" she said, groggily; and then, checking her temples: "Where's the DreamVisor?"

G.W. looked at the thing in his hand: "Where'd you get it?"

"Shaka brought it for me."

"*Shaka* brought it?"

She nodded drowsily.

"He *came* here?"

"Yes."

G.W. sat down heavily on the side of the bed, with his back to her, staring off into the darkness.

"What's wrong?" she said with a giggle.

G.W. groaned equivocally.

For some reason, she giggled again; and then: "What day is it?" she said with a yawn.

"What?" he said, looking around.

"What day?"

"Thursday."

"*Thursday*? Wow!" she said, giggling yet again. "I've been in the dream since Monday night!" As her giggles rose in the air, G.W. suddenly remembered this strange new behavior from her last few phone calls—at least from the times he had been able to reach her. Had she been using Shaka's Dream Visor all this time? And what had she been dreaming? She had to be picking up a broadcast from somewhere. Was Shaka broadcasting specifically for her?

"It feels like *weeks* have passed!" she said. Then she laughed and looked up at him with a rapt expression, saying, "It's so wonderful in there! It's so real: so *beautiful*. [He groaned again, becoming uneasier.] You can smell things, taste things...*feel* things. Try it," she said then, taking it from his hand and trying to place it on him—

"No," he said, moving his head out of the way. She tried to put it on again. "Stop it—*stop* it!" he screamed, grabbing her hand. For some reason, he was panting again, looking at her with a wildness she had never seen before. "Promise me something, Mary!" he demanded then.

"What?" she said, regarding him confusedly.

"Promise me you'll never use it again."

"*What*! Why not?"

"Just promise—until I know for sure."

"Know what?"

"Until I know *more*," he said, obliquely.

"You saying it's not safe?"

"I don't know *what* I'm saying," he said in frustration, getting up and turning his back to her, in order to look out of the window at the dwindling light of the day. "I don't know anything anymore," he said, ashamedly. "Things don't seem right, that's all...It's all weird. I mean, *everything*: Shaka picking me out of nowhere to be his assistant...him coming to see you...and the things he says—there's something not right—"

But when he turned back around, she was sleeping. She looked incredibly exhausted: perhaps even more so than himself. It was too abrupt to be normal—especially with her excitement and giggling just moments before. More anxieties assailed him; and as he stood above her, he suddenly wondered what the thing was doing to her mind—her *soul*. He took the DreamVisor from her hand and looked at it in the dwindling light. For the first time, he found himself thinking that the protesters in Company Square might be right about Shaka and the dark pyramid. His free hand went to her stomach then, caressing it softly; after that, he put a sheet over her and left the room, feeling horribly alone....

He should have gone to bed, but he knew that he would not be able to sleep. His thoughts were like a faucet steadily dripping in his mind, driving him mad. He went back downstairs, to the living room, and turned on the wall-mounted television. On one of the news channels, there was another report on that 10-year-old black girl. G.W. stared at it dreamily until, five minutes later, he realized that the report had ended four and a half minutes ago—and that he had no idea what it had been about. Now on the screen, there were more reports of the Asian war: army officials on both sides hurling threats and accusations at one another. There had supposedly been a poison gas attack in Shanghai, which had easily left ten thousand people dead. G.W. went to the kitchen while this chatter went on in the background. He made himself a heaping sandwich, stuffing it with cheese and leftover bacon and salami—and whatever else he could find. However, when he returned to the living room with his concoction and a huge mug of apple juice, he knew that he had no appetite. They were showing the victims of the poison gas attack: many had been burned by the chemical reactions, their skin literally dripping off. Even those that survived would be left blind and scarred: *perhaps 50 thousand people...!* He felt sick. He changed the channel and lay back against the couch, breathing shallowly...

When, six hours later, his wristwatch pager began vibrating, he was surprised—as he always seemed to be nowadays—that he had fallen asleep. As he awoke, the retreating ghost images of his dream left him with a vague feeling of doom. Still groggy and confused, he looked at the number he was to call; and when he recognized it, his stomach suddenly churned with alarm: *it was Shaka!* The usual numbness came over him again. He turned off the TV—on which the same army officials were screaming recriminations at one another—then he turned on the light. It was a little after 1:30 in the morning. He picked up the phone and dialed the number like a condemned man.

"I need you to come to my office," was all that Shaka said when he answered. The sound of the man's deep baritone was unnerving. The power of it— even over the phone—made G.W. quake inside. For a moment, it was not merely that Shaka's words were reverberating within G.W.'s head: it was as if the man were in there, seeing through him with impunity.

"...Now?" G.W. said, looking at his watch again.

"This is a global world, Young Washington. It is morning in Europe and afternoon in Asia."

"Okay, sir," G.W. said quickly, "—I'll be there in an hour…" But Shaka had already hung up.

G.W. groaned as he got up from the couch: partly from stiffness, partly from the hovering cloud of dread that always seemed to be with him nowadays. He walked back upstairs with a shuffling gait that was not far from his previous waddling. He went to the hall bathroom to avoid awakening his wife. When he turned on the light and looked at the harried face staring back at him, he cringed. His skin was an unhealthy pallor, seeming loose on his face; his eyes were red-rimmed with huge bags, and the hair on his head was a tangled mess. Even his beard's growth seemed to be more than that of a day: it was as though he had been sleeping for *days*. He was still wearing the same rumpled, smelly clothes….Slowly, he undressed, watching the unwrapped body as if he were seeing a stranger. He had indeed lost weight; but again, he had lost it the way a starving man lost it. His clothes were all loose on him, and that had probably added to his disheveled appearance. He stood staring at himself for minutes on end, trying to come to grips with the stranger in the reflection….

In time, he showered and shaved. He needed a haircut, but that was out of the question at this hour. When he went into the bedroom to get some fresh clothes, his wife was sleeping in the same rigid position as when she had been wearing the DreamVisor. Actually, he went over to make sure that she was not wearing it—and, again, to check that she was not dead. She was breathing shallowly, but frozen, as if in a dream. Strangely enough, seeing her like that conjured images of Shaka saying, "comatose world." All at once, that horrible conversation returned to his mind; and when he looked at his wife more closely (he had to see by the light from the hallway), her face wore a look of ecstasy that he immediately found disturbing. He remembered her seeming rapture as she described the world of Shaka's DreamVisor…

Fifteen minutes later, he was driving his SUV down the highway, his mind in the obligatory daze. He had practically run out of the house; and now, with the emptiness of the highway before him, he was again rushing—

doing well in excess of the speed limit. He was not rushing to Shaka: he was just rushing—getting it over with, whatever "it" was...

His mind was on nothing in particular when he drove up to The Company. The protest was of course still going on; and with only a week or so left until the dark pyramid went online, the protest was growing both in volume and intensity. There were now at least 200,000 people gathered within the square. They came from all parts of the world to protest, yelling in dozens of languages. The chants did not have the thunder and vehemence of earlier that day, but the hatred and threat of violence were there nonetheless. Moreover, in the darkness, it had an eeriness that made it seem more sinister than chaotic. With the backdrop of the dark pyramid (which The Company had lit up with spotlights for security reasons) it again seemed like a heathen gathering—a human sacrifice, perhaps—to a god who lay laughing somewhere in the darkness.

The protesters had set up permanent encampments in the square—which were of course illegal—but Shaka was either unwilling to have them disbanded by force, or could not care less. More likely than not, it was the latter. What could the madness of millions possibly mean to a god? The Company was already shaping the lives of billions. It seemed as though Shaka were allowing the chaos of the protest just so that his triumph would be more spectacular when the Image Broadcast Complex went online. The smooth introduction of the dark pyramid, juxtaposed to this chaos, would make him seem more godlike: would only manifest the greatness of The Company and every-thing that it did....

G.W. was thinking these vague thoughts as he entered Company Square. Moreover, with him locked up in his tank-like SUV—not to mention his lingering thoughts about his wife, and his uncertainties about the world—little of what was going on around him really registered in his mind. He could barely hear the chants of the crowd through the windshield and closed doors. He was so distracted that he did not even see the danger signs of the mob. He was honking his horn languidly, inching his way through the crowd, without realizing that there was something ominous about the crowd being in the driveway—especially in such numbers. The angry protesters had actually overrun the phalanx of guards. Some of the protesters were even struggling with the guards as they tried to storm into the main building. G.W. stared ahead blankly for a moment, still not quite comprehending—

Then, all of a sudden, a glimmer of light right outside the vehicle caught his attention. When he turned to the left to look, he was so stunned by what he saw, that he did not even recoil at first. It was a crazed man swinging an aluminum baseball bat. The first swing cracked the glass, but did not break it; with the second swing, glass from the point of impact flew on G.W.'s face, but he still sat there, too stunned to move. On top of that, dozens of people were coming about now, chanting and yelling encouragement to the crazed man as they overran the guards posted on the perimeter. With the crazed man's third swing, half of the window shattered. The glass seemed to rain down on G.W. like Biblical hail from the heavens. He realized, too late, that he had to get away; but unfortunately for him, with all the protesters filling the driveway, there was nowhere to go. G.W. was so terrified that he could not even move an inch. Now that the glass was shattered, he could hear the maddening din of their chants and yells. Then, the next thing he knew, he was outside the vehicle—wrenched out of the door. He looked up just as the man with the baseball bat raised the thing in the air to bring it down on his head. G.W. did not even feel the blow as the world was replaced by a curtain of darkness—

And then, he felt himself drifting away. The old feeling of being without substance—without a *body*—came over him again. As time became warped once more, he found himself enshrouded in vague scenes: images of himself in a white room. It was either daytime or the overhead lights were blinding— he could not tell which. His vision was blurred; a man was hovering above him, but the man's form struck him as a glowing shadow. Everything the man said sounded slurred—or just nonsensical. G.W.'s head felt as though it had grown to five times its previous size—he could not even raise it…but he guessed that he was in a hospital. The man (the doctor, G.W. assumed) came closer to him now. The man checked G.W.'s eyes by parting his eye-lids with his fingers; G.W.'s pulse was taken. There was something about the man's touch that was unnerving. His hands were so cold that they seemed to burn G.W.'s skin…and the sound of the man's voice seemed to thunder from the heavens. G.W. strained his eyes to see the man's face; as he squinted, the face eventually became clearer. G.W.'s entire consciousness now seemed concentrated on the slowly focusing face of the man above him; then, at last, in that instant just before he totally lost consciousness, the face made sense to him, and G.W. Jefferson stared into the smiling, self-assured face of Dr. Xi Wang—

The next thing he knew, he was transported back through time and space. When he emerged into consciousness, he was lying on his back again, staring up at the sky. There were again calculations scrolling in the heavens; as he turned his head languidly to look, there was again a huge digital clock floating in the clouds. It told him that there were now less than eight hours left until they all died—and that he was again Xi Wang, surrounded by the grim proofs of The Horde and the apocalypse. The Voice of Conscience could again be heard in the background…Xi looked around in a daze, but could no longer be surprised by what he saw and felt.

Somehow, he had been given a glimpse into G.W. Jefferson's soul. He vaguely remembered Quibb's promise: that he would be given the ability to see into his subconscious mind…But then he remembered, with equal vagueness—and uncertainty—the reality of Quibb. As always, Quibb was a mental block, which led only to a no-man's-land….And why had he again been shown something from G.W.'s Jefferson's life? What about Xi Wang's life? As always, he had no idea. In fact, the more information he was able to gather, the less he seemed to *know*. A side of him was desperate to analyze the retreating images of his vision or recollection or whatever it had been, but he knew that he did not have the stamina. On top of that, his mind was still in shock—still reeling from its trip from soul to soul.

Some nearby men were clearing away the rubble of a collapsed building. When one of them saw Xi lying there, he called out to his comrades; and following the altruism that Quibb had implanted in them, they came over to see if he was hurt. Xi was soon helped to his feet; he found something about their attentiveness disturbing; he thanked the men effusively, but only so that they would see that he was well, and leave him alone. When he could take it no longer, he left them and walked off quickly. He was still a little dizzy, but his only thought was to be alone so that he could forge some kind of meaning out of what had happened.

...He still could not keep himself from looking up at the sky. It called to him—like a lover. When he looked up, he saw that the calculations and clock had again disappeared, and he was happy for it. He walked more quickly, with a kind of shambling trot, but he still could not escape the pull of the sky....G.W. Jefferson had never gone to Africa: the man had gone straight home after the board meeting. That thought popped into his mind: it was one of the few things he was able to salvage from the shipwreck of his mind. Xi was not sure if it was relevant—especially after seven years. Maybe nothing mattered anymore....What the hell was he to do now? As he listened to The Voice of Conscience's ongoing rant, he remembered that he had been searching for Quibb; but as his mind now recollected the man more as a delusion than as an actual human being, his search for Quibb could not really mean anything to him now. Accordingly, he walked on more in a daze than with a true purpose in mind.

History is a god; among us all are the faithful, the heathen and the agnostic.
VERSE 182:3 OF *The Teachings*

As the Goddess walked through the woods with her worshippers, she suddenly realized that she was in love. These were her first moments of life and awareness. She was in love with breathing—with savoring the aroma of flowers in the air. For the first time, her thoughts were her own and she allowed her mind to concoct fanciful scenarios—the way a child playing alone could change the inanimate objects of her playroom into grand realms. More than that, she felt the giddiness of a teenager who realized, with sudden fascination and empowerment, that she could bring smiles to the faces of the boys around her—that the movements of her body were bewitching to them. She found, as she bent down to caress flowers and drink from streams, that things seemed more vivid when she touched them. It was almost as though she were fertilizing the world—bringing life to all the faded, dying things. Even the weird prophesies of Respoli-Priestess and his cult were forgotten for now. Everything was subsumed within her game of bringing life to the faded things. She was like Dorothy now, traveling to the Emerald City to meet the Wizard and make things right. The overgrown path that they now hiked down was the yellow brick road; Respoli-Priestess, the Shirley Temple clone and the drag queens were her Tin Men, Scarecrows and Cowardly Lions. They would all be completed through this journey; and after the preordained happy ending had come to pass, she would be returned home, where she would forever be secure in the love of her family.

One way or another, slavery always makes slaves of those who set out to be masters, and fools out of those who presume to be gods....
VERSE 1641:3 OF *The Teachings*

After walking a few blocks, Xi was so exhausted that he was forced to lean against another lamppost. He felt horrible—not only physically sick, but as though his soul were dissolving. This was what Quibb had warned him about during their covenant: pain that no man had the stamina to endure...and yet, even that brief glimpse into G.W.'s life had set him on the path to enlightenment. He was *certain* of it. He nodded his head absentmindedly; and despite how much he tried to resist, he still felt compelled to look up at the purple, shimmering sky. By now, he was certain that his vision—or recollection, or whatever it had been—had probably been a psychotropic reaction to the purple sky...*yet he could not stop himself from looking*! He was panting for air now...and he was sweating....Dr. Xi Wang had treated G.W. Jefferson seven years ago—a week before the dark pyramid went online. That was another of the thoughts that popped into his mind. He tried to conjure a recollection of himself as Dr. Xi Wang, but it was pointless....

Thousands of men were still about, clearing away the rubble. That act seemed horribly futile all of a sudden. In less than eight hours, The Horde's bombs would be dropping again, turning more buildings to rubble, and the existing rubble to dust. Yet, the men were undeniably upbeat. Quibb's words were working their minds over, probably like the purple, shimmering sky was working him over....Xi was still leaning against the lamppost; but with so many of Quibb's converts around, he became worried that some of them would notice him leaning there and again come around to ask if he was okay. He was just about to move on, when he looked down the street and saw what first struck him as a column of robots. About 20 of them were marching up the middle of the street in some kind of suits that brought space exploration to mind. All the figures had helmets with reflective glass for visors, so that Xi could not see their faces. They were carrying weapons and what seemed to be some kind of scanning devices; and when Xi looked at their chests, he saw the insignia: the purple sky and the green sun! He looked on numbly—the way a pedestrian watched a speeding car that was only milliseconds from plowing him down. However, it was then that he realized, with perhaps greater horror, that none of the other men seemed to be noticing the column of robots! There were hundreds of men in the street, and yet nobody else was noticing! Xi wondered if he was imaging this. Of course it was possible—just like everything else in this godforsaken world. However, it was then, while Xi was staring at the column intently, that one of the robots seemed to notice him observing them! Terrified out of his wits, Xi looked away. He started walking again—down the sidewalk; he glanced back once to see if the robot was still observing him, but the column continued its trek down the middle of the street....

Xi walked on with his head bowed. The purple, shimmering sky was still calling to him. He was addicted to the sky somehow. The sky was a drug, changing his blood chemistry so that he craved it—was on the verge of doing *anything*...He shook his head. His mind skimmed the surface of some more of the things he had seen in the vision....What if something had happened when G.W. Jefferson got clubbed in the head and that doctor (rather, *himself*) somehow got connected to G.W. In the face of everything else, it was plausible, but how was it *possible*? There seemed to be no way to know for sure, and trying to make conjectures from strange visions (which might themselves only be delusions spawned by the shimmering sky) was only driving him mad....He wanted to forget all he had seen and thought. He wished that he could be like the other men and be a blind, soulless follower of whatever was put before him. He suddenly wanted to get drunk—or to take a psychedelic drug that would make him forget all his troubles—

Suddenly, the creepy feeling of being stalked came over him again! It was more powerful this time, so that he knew that something had changed: that he was about to cross some terrible new threshold. Even before he wheeled around, he *felt* it. An immense wave of negative energy—*of pure evil*—seemed to blow past him, so that he was forced to squint his eyes as he wheeled. And then, he was hurtling through the air. Something huge had tackled him; he opened his mouth to scream, but nothing came out. All the air seemed to be sucked from the world. The force of the collision was so powerful that he felt nothing for the few seconds that he was sent flying. It was only when his body hit the ground that the pain encompassed him—*seized* him. He landed face first. After the initial disorientation, he suddenly realized that whatever had tackled him had never let go: he felt powerful muscles squeezing him; hot, smelly breath, like that of a panting beast, blew on his neck, making him shudder; claws sunk into his flesh as the beast's muscles tightened. He tried to breathe—to scream out, or even to move—but he seemed paralyzed! He was being crushed against the ground by the weight of the thing on him. It had a hot, musky scent, with an undercurrent of burnt, rotting meat. Xi clamped his eyes shut—*he dared not look!* The heavy panting was still at his neck; he felt the hot, slimy saliva dripping down on him; the creature's mouth moved closer to his ear—

"I'm going to kill you like you killed me!" That was what it said. Xi lay on the ground trembling, listening to the words echoing inside of his mind like a bean rattling in an empty pot. Minutes seemed to pass—maybe even hours. In retrospect, he was sure that he had passed out, because when he opened his eyes, the sun's place in the sky seemed to have changed: the shadows seemed different; and when he cringed and glanced over his shoulder, the creature was gone. He was alone; instinctively, he caressed his neck, and the congealed residue of the creature's saliva was there; bloody, newly-formed scabs were on his skin, in those places where he had felt claws; and in the heavens, the digital clock was there, telling him that there were only six hours left....

Quibb's voice was screaming the same nonsense: something about the Goddess' will allowing them to stand strong against The Horde. These words were how Xi finally began to get his bearings. He got to his feet and looked around. Men were still working further down the block, but nobody had noticed him—perhaps because they assumed that he was already dead. A few meters away, a headless corpse was lying on top of a heap of corpses. An iridescent swarm of flies danced around the pile, like electrons zipping about the nucleus of some new, monstrous element. ...Xi commanded his legs to move. He had nowhere to go, but he knew that he had to move. To distract his decimated body and mind, he listened to Quibb's exhortations to the men. Supposedly, there was a call for soldiers by Shaka and some of the other industrial leaders; Quibb's voice was urging all the men to enlist and take up "defensive" positions around the city. Factories that had yesterday churned out eating utensils and PinkEyes were today making machine guns and mortars. Quibb's voice was telling them what to do—and where to go. As Xi stumbled along (and looked at blocks and blocks of rubble and death), he again wondered what they could possibly do against The Horde. It was not an enemy they were up against, but a *force*—like gravity and the creature that had tackled him to the ground....

Human history is the story of the movement of people and resources.
Verse 1736:7 of *The Teachings*

The Goddess smiled and the universe smiled with her. However, after a while, she began to grow tired—at first physically, then mentally. The flowers that she touched no longer seemed to grow more vivid; the surrounding world began to seem dour and *tainted*. …And she began to sense it out there—The Horde. She sensed The Horde the way wafting smoke alerted someone of fire. …And in her mind's eye, she began to get glimpses of things that were still too jumbled to make sense: ruined cities, bombs dropping upon horrified men, and an interminable column of robots amassing on all the frontiers of civilization. By then it was the middle of the afternoon. The Goddess and her cult began to come upon little villages, which were either empty or populated by pathetic men who only stared, barely seeming able to hold up their heads. The population grew the way a waterway grew: little streams became loud, rushing rivers, which they had to ford in order to keep from being swept away. They came upon farms with thousands of gnarled, sunburned men toiling away under the gaze of dozens of armed guards—who were either there to protect them and the crop, or to make sure that the men worked…maybe both. The Goddess and the drag queens passed once-fine mansions, which were now gutted and surrounded by shantytowns that had been created from their salvageable parts. In fact, there were shantytowns everywhere, all of which were populated by tribes of men that reminded her of stray city dogs. Every time she looked at them, she had the impression of master-less beasts cast into a harsh world. Compassion kept telling her that the only humane thing to do was to "put them down." However, her yearning for life could not be so easily stifled. There was still love within her: she still felt that she had the potential to give meaning to all the faded things—even though the things she saw in her mind's eye left her cowed and anxious. Those images were getting more vivid now. She saw buildings exploding; she could hear the bombs—*and even hear screaming voices*—as faraway cities faced The Horde and obliteration. The images were changing her, like pheromones during mating season. She felt her body reacting to them, pulling her to the extremes of all creatures in estrus....

At the same time, she was like a young animal that had not yet reached sexual maturity. While the brutal mating rituals went on around her, and the adults fought amongst themselves for the right to pass on genes, all she could do for now was wrestle with the other juveniles: hone skills that would one day be necessary for life and the continued existence of her species.

It was then that some crazed men jumped from behind the rusting husk of a car, and rushed at them with crudely fashioned knives and clubs. The warriors of her cult shot at them, chasing them away. A few of the crazed men even dropped...but corpses and skeletons were everywhere by then— just another element of increasing urbanization and sexual maturity. After a while, the dead became too commonplace to be noticed; she, too, stopped seeing. Instead, as her sense of inner alarm grew, she kept reminding herself that the Emerald City was drawing closer with every step that they took down the yellow brick road.

Crime is easy to fight. "Criminals" are easily jailed and gunned down. However, injustice is harder to fight, because more often than not the perpetrators of injustice are people no different from ourselves, whose manner of living is the basis of our way of life.
VERSE 502:8 OF *The Teachings*

Xi reached Company Square a little after three o'clock. When he remembered that he had come all the way here in order to look for Quibb, he wanted to curse himself for his stupidity. His head ached horribly now. He had to squint to see....There were still guards at the gates—and thousands of workers were busily removing the rubble—but the huge crowd of supplicants was not there anymore. With so much work needing to be done, all able-bodied men were being taken up to the super-world. Actually, in this case, Xi did not think that the men's diligence was totally Quibb's doing. The workers were again insects tending to their queen—the dark pyramid—deferring their needs and humanity to the only thing that could block the reality of what they had become. It occurred to Xi that with security being so lax, he could easily slip in; but as he looked up at those huge buildings again, an inkling of The Company's size killed some of his resolve. Besides, looking up forced him to look at the sky; and as he did so, his mind got a taste of its drug....There was something about The Company that had always left him queasy. His reaction to it was still that of a pagan frightened by an evil omen. Once again, he recalled what had happened the night before, with the guard at the top of the staircase, and the dozens of hidden subterranean floors. The keys that he had taken from the man seemed suddenly heavy in his pocket. They were a reminder that the event had happened: he tapped his pocket for confirmation now, feeling nauseous. Moreover, with his mind still being rocked by the eddies of the vision—or recollection, or whatever it had been—it suddenly occurred to him that those subterranean floors would be the perfect place to keep the women—

An inflection in The Voice of Conscience made him cringe! As he came back to his senses, he forced himself to move. He glanced at the sky and his head pulsed with pain; the world became blurry again. He clamped his eyes shut, cursing himself for having given in to the urge to look up. However, he was so weak and disoriented by now that he was forced to kneel down. There was too much information to digest—too many possibilities and fears for rational contemplation. He could not see the point in resisting anymore—if that was even what he was doing. He wanted to surrender to his visions, and the pull of the purple, shimmering sky, and let fate direct him wherever it pleased. However, it was at that moment that two men detached themselves from a work detail up the street, and walked directly towards him. Thinking that they were again going to ask him if he was all right, Xi forced himself to stand up. What made Xi more uncomfortable was that as the two men neared him, they pasted fake smiles on their faces—as if they were going out of their way not to scare him. And then:

"Aren't you Xi Wang?" one asked.

Xi froze; they stared at him, still smiling their pasted-on smiles. Self-preservation demanded that he lie; panic told him to run; and yet, as Xi stood there pale and stunned, he found himself nodding. It was only when the men's smiles widened—this time with genuine joy—that the full extent of it hit him. He had been found out! No doubt Shaka had told his men to be on the lookout for him. Yes, such a thought was paranoid, but in the face of all that had happened, it seemed logical. Xi felt naked before the men—*trapped*. Moreover, in a time when nobody knew anybody—not even his closest associates—there was something terrifying about being *known*. Besides Quibb, Xi could not name five other people. His mind fluttered with images of the old doctor from last night, and his two comrades. However, he had not asked the former's name; and according to Quibb and prevailing evidence, the latter were delusions.

"What's this about?" Xi managed to whisper. His voice sounded pathetic—as it had the previous night when he was confronted by the man with the keys.

"Do you mind coming with us?" asked the other man. "Shaka wants to see you."

"*Shaka*!" Xi gasped. As he heard the word—the *name*—instinct took over; and before he was conscious of having moved, Xi bolted. He did not realize it until seconds later, when he was hurdling piles of rubble. He darted down alleys and between crevices in the rubble. Maybe it was another two minutes before he even looked back. Whether he had lost them, or they had never followed, he had no idea. He hid behind the charred husk of a car, panting. Why the hell would Shaka be after him? But then he reminded himself that he had been Dr. Xi Wang seven years ago; according to Quibb, he had invented the PinkEyes—maybe Shaka was looking for him in order to fix the dark pyramid. But no: his mind went back to the subterranean floors and the thought that had left him reeling: that that would be the perfect place to keep the women! Maybe someone had seen him exiting from that door—or seen him carrying Quibb away. His mind was about to rebel against all the "ifs" but he patted the keys in his pocket again, then he nodded absent-mindedly to himself. Were the women really on those subterranean floors? He did not even know if it made a difference....He sighed.

In time, he emerged from his hiding place. Instinct told him to keep moving—even while paranoid thoughts of secret cameras and spies fluttered through his mind. He slunk around corners like a thief in the night, then darted down side streets. He wanted only to lose himself. He once again had to go around entire blocks because fires and collapsed buildings made them inaccessible. Maybe another two hours passed this way....

Eventually, he reached what remained of the old financial district, in lower Manhattan. The purple, shimmering sky was still calling to him, but his terror and the drive to hide distracted him to the point where he was able to keep functioning. Lower Manhattan was not as crowded as midtown Manhattan, but there were still thousands of men trying to clear away the rubble. Quibb's voice still roared over the speakers of billboards....The building that used to house the New York Stock Exchange was now a kind of homosexual cathouse. Prepubescent boys and transsexuals were often seen parading in front of the institution that had once shaped and stabilized world financial markets—

Suddenly, one of the functioning billboards on the block flickered on. The men gathered around: the broadcast was something on The Horde—images of what it had done to Paris and Nairobi and Kuala Lumpur and Melbourne: and all of that just last night. In fact, as it was night in some of those places, some of those attacks were taking place right now! It was too much to comprehend. The Horde seemed to be everywhere: some kind of rogue god of destruction. The men gathered around and stared up at the gigantic screen like pious servants. They came like Muslims called to prayer; and while those images flickered across the screen, Quibb's voice was there, still inculcating them with the sacred gospel of the Goddess' will, and The Horde attack that would come that night. In a sense, The Horde had not been real until it made its way onto the screen. The screen seemed to validate the men's feelings in a way that the surrounding reality never could. Their gods were resplendent in all the flickering complexity of the screen—as were their devils. Moreover, with the PinkEyes still offline, they were building their new religion slowly: starting first with the sound of The Voice, then images on the screen; and sooner or later, they would once again achieve the height of worship and surrender their souls to whatever holographic heaven was conjured before their eyes. As for Xi, he again yearned to surrender to their blind acceptance—their blind *faith*—but it was not in him. While the new religion gained strength in the souls of the men, he stood on the periphery, like an unrepentant sinner denied the Grace of God. At the same time, he shook his head: he wished that he could believe that television and the PinkEyes had made people stupid and pliable. He wished that he could blame it all on technology; but as he looked around, he realized that people were the way they were because of people: because of flesh and blood—because of human frailties and desires. In the final analysis, the worst kind of slavery existed within the yearnings of the flesh.

He looked up at the screen again. He was just about to nod his head at the vague conclusions that his mind had achieved, when a face suddenly appeared on the screen. He had to stare at the face for a while before it finally made sense to him. He stepped in closer then, as if mesmerized. *It was his picture!* That was his face hovering up there on that huge billboard—but it was a picture from seven years ago, when he was Dr. Xi Wang. In fact, that name was now scrolling under the picture. Quibb's voice was still talking about The Horde and rebuilding, but Shaka controlled the imagery; and after Xi's name had scrolled across the screen, there was an announcement that there was a $50,000 reward for information on Dr. Xi Wang's whereabouts. Xi stood there frozen and helpless. Shaka had thrown down the gauntlet, and now there was nowhere on earth that Xi could hide.

When one has no legacy—nothing worth passing on—
children are only a sexually transmitted disease.
VERSE 135:3 OF *The Teachings*

As evening approached, the Goddess' sense of adventure waned with her energy. She no longer cared where Respoli-Priestess and his cult were taking her, as long as they stopped soon to rest. The shoes they had given her to wear were too big, and a blister had developed on the sole of her left foot. Respoli-Priestess was walking them deeper into the woods now. The Shirley Temple clone was holding the Goddess' hand. He smiled at her from time to time, but they were all exhausted now. No one was talking anymore; after a while, the Goddess began to wonder if they would ever stop: if they even had a destination in mind. It was at that moment that they came upon a dilapidated wooden building. The jaded sign in front of it said that it had once been a forest ranger station, but now nature was reclaiming that which men had foolishly thought was their own. The windows and doors were all gone; moss and creeping vines covered most of the edifice... and the gaping black holes left by the missing windows and door seemed like the eyes and mouth of a monster. The travelers all stopped and stared up at the structure, unsure, but then Respoli-Priestess beckoned them on. Two of the drag queens cut away the vines that barred the doorway, then they all entered. The wooden structure was slowly turning into dust. Many seasons of leaves had accumulated and biodegraded on the floor, so that grass and moss were growing on some patches of the floor. Termites and other insects had eaten away at much of the structure, and the mold-covered walls were being leached of the minerals necessary for their structural integrity. On top of that, in the air, there was a dank, musty smell, as though this were an animal's den. In fact, it was at that moment that something began hissing in the darkness; when they looked, they saw several raccoons emerge from the shadows to defend their territory. The warriors of the cult stepped forward and easily slaughtered the animals; and then, still wordlessly, others came forward and began to skin the creatures. When the Goddess gleaned that they were preparing their dinner (*and hers*) a sick feeling came over her and she stumbled towards the entrance to get some fresh air. The Goddess wanted only to get away. She was fleeing towards the dwindling light of the day, and the outside world; but as she drew closer to the light, she experienced an anomaly: a moment when her awareness seemed to expand exponentially. Her immediate environs became irrelevant, and she had the feeling that she had the eyes of God. Unfortunately, she still had the mind of a woman—*a human being*—and was unable to digest what she saw. Her mind rebelled against all that was being demanded of it; then, as if by instinct—as if returning home to the thing she knew best—she saw The Horde. She saw *millions* of them: those robots. They were in cities all over the world, butchering millions of people at that very moment. As she stood there helplessly, she saw bombs dropping and hapless men being blown to bits. She saw buildings disintegrating…and she felt unimaginable pain: the suffering of *billions*. For whatever reason, her mind zoomed in on one scene. It was nighttime in a far-away city. There were people huddling in the darkness—in a bunker somewhere; overhead, in the outside world, explosions could be heard. Then, suddenly, Horde troops were there. The machine guns of the troops were being raised in the air, and the people huddling in the darkness were screaming. A few men jumped up to make a stand; they drew guns of their own, but the robots gunned them down with their computer-guided efficiency. Then, as the robots stepped up to survey the dark chamber, the Goddess saw that all the people in the chamber—at least, those still alive—were women. The Goddess did not realize this until now, but she was seeing through the eyes of The Horde's soldiers. The robots took another step closer to the terri-fied women—whom screamed out—and the Goddess screamed with the horror of those women. The screaming women were hugging one another in their panic and hopelessness; and when, by instinct, the Goddess' mind sent out a desperate plea for the robots to stop, she was amazed that all those Horde troops stopped and lowered their guns. In fact, it was not only the troops in the dark chamber that stopped, but the millions of them all over the globe! For that moment, she was again at one with them. It was like a gnat discovering that it could control a herd of elephants. Their actions were byproducts of her will—her *consciousness*. Now that she had this new-found power, she almost wanted to laugh triumphantly. It occurred to her that this was the moment when all the secrets of the universe would be revealed to her; she accessed Horde troops back in that place on the mountain, where she had been held captive. However, when she tried to advance from merely seeing out of the eyes of The Horde, and attempted to assess its consciousness, she gasped. There was nothing there but an abyss. The nothingness opened up before her like a trap door. In her desperation to escape the nothingness, she fled from The Horde and everything she had seen; and unfortunately, like a clumsy person tripping over a computer's power cable, she lost all the data that had been on the screen. The god-like link she had had to The Horde's troops was severed, and all she was left with was the realization that she had been on the verge of something horrible: of seeing The Horde *completely*. When she came back into consciousness, she was lying on her back, and Respoli-Priestess was kneeling by her side, asking her why she was screaming.

*Intelligence is the ability to see the nature of one's ignorance; power is
the ability to manipulate and exploit the ignorance of others.*
VERSE 3:4 OF *The Teachings*

A s Xi stared up at the screen—*and his face*—he was still being rocked by
the realization of how totally Shaka had trapped and bested him. On
top of that, there were only a couple of hours left until The Horde
returned. Xi was trapped on all sides: even if he survived tonight's onslaught,
Shaka would surely capture him in the morning. He retreated a few steps
from the screen, as if in a futile effort to escape from the reality of his doom—

But suddenly, his heart skipped a beat! Up ahead (from the group that had
gathered beneath the screen to see the report) one man was walking away.
The man was headed away from Xi, so all that he saw was the man's back; and
yet, Xi was sure that it was Quibb! He could not believe it! He was running
now, a wide smile coming over his face. He ran all the way up to the guy, and
then tapped him on the shoulder; the guy turned…it seemed to take forever.
Xi stared deeply into the features; in his daze, he had to check several times
before he was sure that it was not Quibb. It was yet another of those gaunt,
longhaired clones. The anorexic man smiled at Xi; there was a brazen sexuality
about the man's gaze. Xi unconsciously backed away; looking down, he saw
that the man was one of those transsexuals that had had breasts surgically
added: the rigid cleavage could be seen above the man's deep v-neck collar.

"S-Sorry…" Xi stammered. "—Thought you were someone else." Before
the man could even respond, Xi was running again. Halfway down the

block, he looked over his shoulder, horrified to see that the man was still standing there, smiling at him. He felt sick again. What did his chasing after Quibb mean...? His mind ached with all that was being demanded of it....When he was out of breath, he started walking. He meandered down to nearby Battery Park. ...*What do I want from Quibb?* he asked with a bluntness demanded by the situation. Was Quibb a lover forged out of his desperation and loneliness: a fake woman—*the fake goddess of his fantasies?* He trembled in the silence of his mind, but then breathed easily. The thought of sex with Quibb was revolting to him; the thought of sex, itself— of *closeness* with another—was revolting. Their sex was something for private video stalls rented by the half minute, not for touching and closeness. His mind went to how the men would crowd into hundreds of thousands of these little stalls across the city; breathing in the overpowering stench of stale semen, they would watch the latest holographic pornos and insert their penises into the disposable, latex-coated vibrating sleeves. That was their sex: a technologically rendered release....And yet, he still chased Quibb....

The pungent odor of river sludge brought him from his reverie. Exhausted, he sat down on a park bench and looked out on the polluted, slow-moving river. He leaned forward, resting his elbows on his thighs, so that he could prop his head up with his hands. He could make out the graffiti-coated Statue of Liberty from where he sat. It had once represented the Goddess of Democracy; now, it was just another testament to decay. It occurred to him, all at once, how androgynous the statue had always seemed to him. There were elements of both masculinity and femininity in the towering figure. The face was hard and angular, but there was just the hint of breasts beneath the soft contours of the long, flowing gown....*And what use would a penis be to God?* he thought with a slight smile—or a vagina, for that matter? The gods were all androgynous: their sexuality was as ambiguous as the yearnings that had spawned them.

*There can be no self-preservation in hell: even if one manages
to survive, just the process of survival breeds death.*
VERSE 102:14 OF *The Teachings*

When the girl named Boy woke up, she saw the same cavernous chamber before her. She had no idea how much time had passed, but she felt somehow that she had been sleeping for *years*. The noise within the chamber was great now—because many of the women were whispering fearfully amongst themselves. It was still dim in the room; looking around, she realized that there were no windows—only a few fluorescent lights. She looked up at the emblem again—the green sun in the purple, shimmering sky—trying to decipher what it might mean. As all of the cots were facing it, it occurred to her that it had been placed there for them to see. There were a couple of doors on that side of the room, beneath the emblem. She wondered, with both fear and curiosity, where they might lead. The African girl was still sleeping on the cot next to hers. Looking at her sleeping figure, and those around her, Boy suddenly realized that they were all, herself included, wearing purple jumpsuits. Moreover, as she chanced to look down, she noticed that on her wrist, there was a bracelet of some kind, which had some numbers on it—like those of a serial number. How all of these things had gotten on her, she had no idea. Then, frowning, it suddenly occurred to her that the air had a strange haze to it—everything was a shimmering purple. The more she looked around, the more dazed she felt. It was then, while her mind was flying about for answers, that the robots came in. The doors beneath the emblem opened, and dozens of the helmeted figures came into the room with their guns held at the ready. At the sight of these figures, a pall came over the chamber once again. Some of the women were standing at attention now—these were the veterans. The reaction of these women told her that this was nothing new; and just as a puppy could learn the master's tricks from watching its parents, so, too, Boy and the other newcomers quickly followed the veterans and stood up. As Boy rose, she tapped the African, whom, even while she rubbed the sleep from her eyes, followed her new friend. The robots spread themselves out—about one to each five or so rows; with the shimmering purple light cloaking them, their movements seemed distorted and disjointed—as though they were not even there. They seemed like ghosts— some of them actually moved so quickly that they appeared as a blur; some of them seemed to be going in slow motion—as if they were undersea. Even when they took up their positions and stood facing the women, the distortion continued. Indeed, just like ghosts, after a while they disappeared all together; but by that time, the women in the room had stopped seeing and stopped thinking. They waited compliantly for their orders, and when the murmuring told them to sleep, they returned to their cots and did just that.

> *The fool professes to understand herself completely—*
> *and she is usually right.*
> VERSE 1232:45 OF *The Teachings*

Xi was still sitting on the bench in Battery Park. He sat there for about 15 minutes, just staring at the river and looking across occasionally at the Statue of Liberty. The sky was still calling to him...he was so tired of fighting it. He looked up at the sky for a moment and experienced the usual effects: dizziness and loss of self-control. However, on the periphery of these disturbing influences, he had the sense that there were answers to his many questions—just as Quibb had promised. No doubt there were more visions out there; and for the first time, it occurred to him that the only thing that mattered to him anymore was getting an explanation of what had happened to him seven years ago. Besides, what did he really have to lose? his freedom? his mind? his life? ...all these things were gone already....

The park was deserted—save for a few men who were too insane to be influenced by Quibb's voice and The Horde's impending attack. Knowing that he would not be bothered by more altruists, Xi lay supine on the park bench and stared straight at the sky. The shimmering purple encompassed him at once, but he did not fight it. Somehow his surrender made things easier. His sight became blurry again; like seven years ago, when he had been transported from Africa to the lobby in front of Shaka's chamber, he had the feeling that he was watching an editing glitch in a recording—a TV program that ended too soon, giving him a glimpse of things he was not supposed to see. When he looked around, he felt somehow as though time had stopped: the wind did not seem to blow; the calls of the sea gulls, which had been sounding in the air just moments ago, ended abruptly. Indeed, the constant sounds of the city—the voices and *chaos*...—all came to an end. He, himself, did not feel like a man in the world, but like a contrivance floating through space. It was as though he were witnessing the end of the universe; then, all at once, a strange feeling of calm—of *knowing*—came over him, and he brought his hands to his temples and grabbed hold of something that should not have been there. When he pulled that thing away, the world dissolved before his eyes, like a television losing its power. For a moment, he was in a dark, formless place; but a millisecond later, he found himself lying in a bed, in a small, too-bright, windowless room, holding one of Shaka's old DreamVisors in his trembling hands....

He was G.W. again—he knew that at once—and this seemed to be the same place from his last vision: the all-white room where he had come in contact with Dr. Xi Wang. Now, however, there was no one else in the room with him. He lay in a daze for a minute or so, staring blankly at the DreamVisor in his hands. He realized, with a jolt to his system, that he had been dreaming about the events of Africa! Lingering feelings of horror still gripped him; he still saw the pilot and the European scientist being gunned down by the goat-faced guards; he still heard the echoes of those gunshots... but he had no idea what it all meant. In the last vision, G.W. Jefferson had gone from the board meeting to his home: maybe the events of Africa had never happened; maybe it had always been a dream....

He looked around the room as though a clue would be found within it. The room was clean and fresh-smelling: he had forgotten how it felt to be in clean, bright surroundings. The sheets had the fragrant aroma of laundry detergent and bleach; the walls were white and free of the cracks and accumulated grime that were to be seen everywhere....He had to keep reminding himself that this was a vision; like before, there was the urge to forget that he was Xi Wang: that he was actually lying on a park bench, staring up at the purple, shimmering sky. He was desperate to hold onto those vital pieces of information; still, he felt himself losing ground. More and more, he found himself thinking that if he was in a clean, orderly hospital, and this was the present, then the last seven years could not have happened. There was an appealing kind of madness to the thought that was perhaps impossible to resist. The madness was weaving itself into his soul, so that he had no bearings: no idea what was real and what was not; and looking at the DreamVisor again, it occurred to him that if one no longer knew what was real, then nothing mattered. If one could dream away all fears, then courage was banished from the world; if one could *live* the unreal, then the real became superfluous. Everything was suspect now: the good, along with the bad. The only thing that he trusted was his growing distrust: his *wariness*....

When he turned his head to look around the room, he realized that his neck and head ached horribly. Touching his head, he realized that there was a bandage on it. He remembered the man with the aluminum baseball bat; he remembered all the ghosts of his previous vision.

It was while he was lying there, feeling totally lost, that he looked up, seeing a wall-mounted television. "TV on," he called, then sat up eagerly (despite the spike of pain that came from this sudden movement). Violent images flickered across the screen: the Asian war was still on. A million people had been killed in some Chinese province or another....There was news of the latest bombing by the 10-year-old Messiah/terrorist. G.W. was about to change the channel, in order to see what else was going on with the world, when the nurses came in. They were two middle-aged white women with affable faces, and the fact that they seemed to match his mind's idea of "nurse" so perfectly left him thinking that he might still be dreaming—

"Oh, Mr. Jefferson," one started in a singsong voice, "you're awake. Good: Shaka is waiting for you."

"...I'm G.W. Jefferson," he said to himself.

"Yes you are," the nurse said with a smile. Then, while Xi, or G.W. or whoever he was, looked on in bewilderment, the other nurse went to the closet and brought out a suit. G.W. could not remember if the suit was his or not. Desperate for answers, he ventured:

"How long have I been here?"

"Shaka will tell you everything himself, sir," the nurse cooed to him. Then, the next thing G.W. knew, he was being coaxed out of bed. His hospital gown was taken off, then he was dressed in the suit—which seemed slightly too big for him. The women's faces wore blank smiles as they dressed him....

They placed him in a wheelchair; after a trip down a long, white-walled corridor—which, strangely enough, did not seem to have any other doors—they entered the elevator. G.W. was again trapped in that no-man's-land, where his mind was moving so quickly that it did not seem to be going any-where. The ever-present voices of panic and confusion tried to seize him, but even they just seeped into the convoluted mess that his thoughts had become. He felt like a tired old man with a mind addled by age and infirmity; he found himself thinking that maybe, in some far-off waking world, he was. He still could not help thinking that this was a dream within a dream within a dream...

The three of them rode up in the elevator, listening to the eerie, formless music and watching the floor numbers passing by on the digital display. The only thing that seemed real was his emptiness. In a sense, it was the only thing of substance that he had: the only thing that he could trace back and receive an inkling of who he had been and what he had done....By the time the door opened, G.W. felt as though he actually did need the wheel-chair. As he was wheeled out of the elevator, and again came face-to-face with the huge wall/window of Shaka's penthouse, he realized for the first time that he was at The Company! That realization made him panic for some reason. He saw that it was again nighttime outside. However, with the smog, he could not make out the Manhattan skyline. All that there was, was darkness, so that G.W. found himself thinking that maybe even the world did not exist anymore. Maybe the entire universe was restricted to himself, the nurses, the guards, and whatever lay beyond the doors of Shaka's chamber.

As the nurses wheeled him up to the chamber door, the guards looked at them indifferently, then went back to whatever they had been doing.

"We're here," one of the nurses announced to G.W. when they wheeled him up to the door; before he knew what was happening, G.W. was coaxed out of the wheelchair. One of the nurses opened the huge mahogany door. As G.W. was about to step into the dark chamber, with its hundreds of flickering screens, he glanced back at the guards, who were still sitting at the console; and as he did so, he felt as though his heart had become lodged in his throat! He choked and reeled, recognizing two of the guards from Angola: *the goat-faced guards*! They were cleaning their handguns: taking them apart and oiling them. About five guns lay on the console, most of them in pieces. As G.W. stood in the doorway, forcing air into his lungs and thoughts into his mind, the men again glanced up at him disinterestedly, with those inscrutable goat's eyes, then went about their business.

G.W. seemed to lose track of time again, because the next thing he knew, he was inside the chamber, walking the last few steps to Shaka. He felt as though he were walking in his sleep; and with all that had happened, he could not put it beyond the pale of possibility…Shaka was talking to him now. G.W. listened, but then realized that none of it was registering in his mind. Shaka seemed to realize this as well, because he stopped and waited patiently for G.W.

Maybe 30 seconds passed; G.W. looked around vaguely—at the scores of screens that lined the walls of Shaka's chamber. A porno was playing in one of them and G.W. found himself thinking of how ridiculous human beings were: how ridiculous their sex and lust and love—and everything that went into their procreation—were. However, thoughts of procreation brought him to thoughts of his own wife and son. He was G.W. Jefferson and he had a wife and a son on the way. Xi Wang and Quibb and all the rest of it were lost by now. The last seven years were again just another part of the dream within the dream. As he tried to retrace his steps—and resume the life of G.W. Jefferson—the entire litany of madness (from his trip to Asia, to his rise in The Company and the horrors of Africa) flashed before his eyes. In fact, the images of Africa seemed unusually fresh in his memory; and if those images were real—and were not just a sick DreamVisor night-mare—then dozens of decomposing, maggoty mothers and children really had been lying on the damp sod of Africa…and he really had set off the explosion that destroyed the evidence. Acutely aware that he did not have the wherewithal to confront those possibilities, he looked over at Shaka and asked the most honest question he could think of: "Who am I?"

"You are G.W. Jefferson," Shaka replied.

G.W. thought about it for a while, but he realized that this was meaningless to him. He could have been named John Smith for that matter—

"Why was I in the…the [he searched for the right word]…the infirmary?"

"You got caught in the protest outside: you were clubbed in the head."

"When?"

"The day you returned from the trip to Asia."

"…How long ago?"

"A week."

"I've been here for a week?"

"Yes."

Fighting to put things in perspective, he ventured: "…That's when you decided to put on the DreamVisor—when I was unconscious?"

"Yes, the DreamVisor has certain healing properties—especially for severe concussions. Your brain was actually hemorrhaging—you were about to die."

"…So, I've been dreaming for a week?"

"Correct."

A week! he thought in disbelief. He went to ask if he really had a wife; but instead, "Am I really your assistant, sir?"

"Yes, Young Washington," Shaka said with a smile. "Don't worry—you're just experiencing the effects of your injury: the lingering disorientation."

"…I dreamed that you sent me to Angola."

"I know."

"…You mean, you made me dream those things?"

"Yes."

"The events in Angola," he found himself going on, "—they really happened, didn't they?"

"Yes," Shaka said, matter-of-factly.

"…How long ago did it happen?"

"Two years."

"…I wasn't your assistant back then," he said, trying to make sense of it.

"Correct," Shaka answered him.

"…I didn't really go then?"

"Correct."

"...If I didn't go, then who did?"

"One of your predecessors."

He thought about it for a while, but could come up with nothing definite. He again searched his mind like an alcoholic with a hangover trying to piece together what had happened the night before. Then:

"...You had those Africans killed on purpose—it wasn't even a mistake."

"And what if I did?" he said, again with that disconcerting frankness. He laughed then, going on, "We both know that you could not care less about those people. Your only concern is why I showed you all those things...and why I picked you in the first place to be my assistant."

"...Yes," he admitted after searching his mind.

Shaka pursed his lips. "And what do *you* think I am after, Young Washington? Why do you think I picked you?"

G.W. shook his head in frustration: he could not even begin to guess.

Shaka nodded patiently. "Okay. Answer this then: What did you get out of the images from Angola? Why do you think The Company killed all those people? More importantly, why would I *show* you?"

G.W. stared numbly, as if seeing more than he actually wanted to see. He blurted out: "You did it because...because you can."

"Good," Shaka said, pleased. "My faith in you wasn't misplaced."

"...When you sent my predecessor to Angola it wasn't even about making a report or organizing a cover up: you had settled everything before you sent him....Is he still alive?"

"*She*, actually—and she committed suicide."

"—Two years ago?"

"Yes."

A strange feeling, either of courage or profound helplessness, came over G.W., and he looked at Shaka intently, asking, "Are you going to kill me?"

Shaka laughed, saying, "Why would I have you nursed back to health if my only intention had been to kill you?"

"...I know things now," G.W. pointed out, "—Africa."

"What do you really know?" Shaka said after a chuckle. "Let me tell you something about knowledge, Young Washington: You have information for questions that haven't been asked, and that no one has any intention of asking. That sort of information is useless."

"And that village doesn't exist anymore," G.W. whispered, nodding drowsily. "None of it exists anymore."

"So, then," Shaka continued, "tell me why I sent your predecessor to the jungle—and why I showed you something so seemingly incriminating?"

"You...you showed me so that I could see it—*learn* from it...Just as you sent me to Asia."

"Correct again."

"This was all a game—some test you're putting me through. You put my predecessor through it, but she failed."

"She failed herself," Shaka corrected him.

"It's all a game—an experiment," G.W. whispered.

"Yes."

G.W. stood there thinking his usual vague, pointless thoughts. A few seconds passed; Shaka stared at him as if waiting for him to figure everything out. Something about it was reminiscent of a father waiting for his child to say his first words. However, G.W. only shook his head, looking totally distraught. He felt pathetic and useless. His mind was so sluggish that he would never be able to make sense of the swirling mess within it. He was totally at Shaka's mercy; but strangely enough, with that thought came a kind of peace. He did not really fear death anymore. Death was a meaningless concept—because life meant so little to him now. Shaka had done that: the events of Asia and Africa had shaped him, either by distorting his conceptualization of life, or clarifying the horror and filth of it....

Shaka was still waiting patiently, like that parent hoping for those first words; but then, seeing that G.W. was not up to the task of figuring out the mysteries of the gods, he sighed, saying: "Okay, I guess you've earned this." He pursed his lips for a moment, then continued, "Tell me, Young Washington, what did you learn from your trip to Asia? What is the one impression you came away with?"

"...Too many people."

"Exactly, Young Washington," he said, proud again. "There are too many people in the world: too many people competing for finite resources; too many wars over these resources: too much degradation of the natural world and the social fabric—not to mention the souls of men...and all because there are too many people in the world."

G.W. looked on warily—

"I took a bold step, Young Washington," Shaka went on. Remembering the African village, G.W. blurted out:

"You're going to wipe them out!"

"No—not in the way you mean."

"...Which way then?"

"What would happen if nobody had any children for 20 to 30 years?"

"*What*?"

"What would happen if for 20 or 30 years no new children were born? The world's population would dip drastically, wouldn't it?"

G.W. forced himself to nod.

"It would give nature a chance to catch up," Shaka went on, "—adjust to all those billions. And in that time, people might come to see the error of their ways. *I* took the initiative, Young Washington," the man continued, while G.W. stared on in stunned disbelief. "Just over one year ago, a compound was released into the atmosphere: a tasteless, odorless, virtually undetectable compound. It was supposed to—"

"That's what you were working on in the jungle."

"Yes."

G.W. remembered the daunting efficiency of the jungle operation—and his thought that given the right organization, men would go about destroying themselves and the world, and give no thought to what they were doing, as long as the bureaucracy rewarded them and told them that their jobs were secure. The European man, who had administered the experiment on the people, had had no idea what he was doing: had died ignorant of the implications of his actions. G.W. saw the perfection of what Shaka had done and nodded his head. However, Shaka was staring at him oddly—with an intentness G.W. had never seen before—and G.W. instinctively blurted out:

"Something's gone wrong, hasn't it?"

"As you so eloquently put it, something has indeed gone wrong, Young Washington." He pursed his lips again, before continuing: "The compound was bastardized, producing unforeseen consequences....Are you familiar with Vincent Mansmann?"

"...The hair guy?"

Shaka nodded. "His hair formula combined with the substance I released and now, instead of being infertile, people will be able to have children, but only sons."

All at once, G.W. remembered what Shaka had told him about keeping a comatose person alive until she regained consciousness and health. He looked at Shaka with new understanding and horror then. "That's why the Image Broadcast Complex is going online," he whispered.

"It would have come online anyway," Shaka corrected him. "...There will be no brainwashing, if that's what you mean. That's one of the great lies of human history: that human beings have the power to make other human beings do things against their will. The complex will be there for those who require it....A long, dark night is coming, Young Washington. We must now provide it with light and direction; at the very least, we have to keep the comatose patient alive until the light comes again."

"How many people know about this?"

"A handful."

"What about the board? Do they know?"

"There is no board," he said with his usual curtness. "There are people who *think* they are on the board, but there is no board."

G.W. looked around in bewilderment. "...Are you sorry, sir?"

"Pardon?"

"Are you sorry for what you've done?"

But Shaka only laughed.

G.W. bowed his head, feeling foolish; when Shaka's laughter died down, he looked up timidly, saying: "What are you going to do with me?"

"I'm offering you a choice that most won't have, Young Washington. I'm offering you knowledge, pure and unadulterated. You can either show up for work tomorrow, or run away and hide."

"…What about the people outside? What are you going to do about them?"

"I'm not going to do anything." And then, as G.W. looked at him incredulously: "They are no threat to me, Young Washington. I've allowed them to protest on Company property for months now, when I could have easily thrown them out. Human beings are strange creatures: the more you fight them, the more they want to fight you; but give them enough space, and they'll fight one another."

G.W. opened his mouth, but nothing came. He just stood there like an old man.

"Go home and get some rest, Young Washington," Shaka said in a voice that almost seemed compassionate, "—tomorrow will be a busy day."

G.W. stood there for a while, looking lost. He felt as though he should say things, but he did not know what they could possibly be. In the end, he nodded and shuffled way. The way he was walking, it was as if the weight of the ideas gestating in his skull had set his balance off kilter. And yet, just like Mansmann (who was at that very moment stuck in a traffic jam, contemplating the end of the world), despite the blow to his soul, there were some things that were acutely clear to him. Shaka would of course have him killed now: this was plain. Maybe there would be an accident on his way home… or maybe Shaka was counting on him to kill himself—like his predecessor had. He looked at the maddening precision of it and was cowed. As for himself and the rest of the world, he had been shown how death, when it came, would be a dream; and how life—in whatever form it took on— would be like death. Still, he was even then falling into delusion, finding himself thinking that if this was a dream—some *fantasy*—then he had to believe that he was the hero, and that somehow events would so conspire as to make him victorious over his enemies. He was drunk on this spurious reasoning now—

However, when he opened the chamber door, he was again stunned by the presence—the *reality*—of the goat-faced guards. Instantaneously, all his fantasies—or at least those involving his invulnerability—died away, and he was left only with his fears. The goat-faced guards did not even seem like human beings anymore, but as some kind of supernatural sentinels. He stopped abruptly in the doorway of Shaka's chamber; the men again looked back at him indifferently before continuing to clean their guns. G.W. could not move; he tried conjuring his spy fantasy—and the feeling of courage that had come with it—but all that nonsense fell away now. The only thing he could do was stand there; the lobby and the elevator were before him, but he was now overcome by the fear that the guards would shoot him in the back when he walked to the elevator.

It was then that Shaka's door closed automatically behind him, knocking him into the world that was suddenly so terrifying to him. Thrown off balance, he stumbled into the console, bumping into the back of one of the guards; as he came in contact with one of those supernatural sentinels, it was either as if the spell that held him had been broken, or that a new, more powerful and self-destructive spell had been cast. With everything that Shaka had said still percolating in his mind, he was suddenly beset by a pang of longing for something real and pure: something to love and have faith in. He wanted to see his son born, talk to his family…if those people even existed to begin with! And if he was dreaming all this, then there would be no consequences. He was about to back away from the console—and the guard over whom he was still hanging—when one of the goat-faced guards inserted a clip into his gun. At the sound of the snap, something was triggered in G.W. He did not want to die: not in a dream, not in the real world, not in a world made meaningless by dreams and fantasies; and before G.W. could even think, he reached over the guard's shoulder and grabbed two of the assembled guns. He trained the guns on the men then, telling them to freeze…but they started to rise—as if they were automatons. G.W. went around to the other side of the console, so that it acted as a barrier—but still the men continued to come! In fact, they did not seem agitated at all: it was as if they had expected him to grab those guns…It was then that the elevator opened and the President filed out with her bodyguards. Time suddenly seemed to speed up—as though he were watching a movie that was being fast forwarded; and in no time at all, the President, the guards and Shaka (who had come out to investigate) were all lying in bloody pools at his feet—

The vision ended abruptly, again leaving him with the feeling that he had been splattered against the ground after falling from a cliff....As the world of G.W. Jefferson faded away, the grim reality of Xi Wang's existence began to take shape. He gasped, as though emerging from a deep dive, and sat up, panting. However, he had no time to rest! Night had come while he was away in the world of his vision; and as he looked up, he saw dozens of missiles streaking across the heavens! The Horde was back! Xi jumped to his feet. Panicking, he took two steps in one direction, but something over there exploded, so he turned and ran off in the other direction. Actually, he could not really run: he was too stiff. His muscles were tense and unresponsive—but as his terror seized him, he made do.

There is nothing more dangerous than a man losing his God—especially if he loses it through the revelations of another man. At such times, that other man in fact becomes his Devil, and the attempt to hold onto his God becomes a struggle between Heaven and Hell.
VERSE 627:5 OF *The Teachings*

Mansmann was standing absentmindedly in the huge basement ward of the hospital. Over the intercom, The Voice of Conscience was in the midst of another rant on The Horde. It was then that a siren suddenly began to peal. Within the hospital, the men all paused. Everyone was going through a kind of posttraumatic stress, which was made more harrowing by the realization that the trauma had never really ceased. The men took deep breaths, as if preparing themselves for a tidal wave. It was only Mansmann who stood around, hoping, with a child's heart-felt earnestness, that a missile would descend on them all and blow them to bits. He was thinking this when a missile landed on the building, and the front wall suddenly exploded. He was blown to the ground, joining his terrified patients. Glass and brick flew through the air. The explosion was like the screaming voice of a madman. While the men of the hospital were blown back—and blown apart—the madman's voice bounced around inside of their heads. There was something transcendental about it; for seconds after the blast, they seemed to float, as if free of their bodies. Men who had already lost one leg found that they had just lost the other. Fire from the explosion was now dancing over the living and dead, alike. Men were crying out again; and yet, all of those voices raised together could not match the madman's shrill voice.

Mansmann got up from the ground groggily. Part of the front wall had collapsed, leaving a gaping hole. He felt cheated somehow—that was his first reaction. He had wanted something stronger—more *powerful*—to immolate them all. There was madness in the thought, and madness in him. The newly injured were already beginning to cry out to him. Mansmann looked around at them all, sickened by their desperation and their need—particularly of him. *Fuck you all*! he thought to himself as he ran towards the gaping hole. He did not run quickly, but steadily. He was fleeing, and he had never felt such bliss before. As he ran, it was the same feeling he had felt when the apocalypse first began. This time, however, his hands were not dirtied. He could be like the rest of them, running scared. He wanted to revel in their animalistic, instinctual innocence; he was tired of being, or *pretending* to be, a god amongst these wretched men. As such, he found himself chuckling when he reached the opening. After clambering over the rubble to make it outside, he looked out at all the new destruction with a smile. More missiles could be seen flying across the heavens. Most of the destruction was in fact quite superfluous: a redundant apocalypse in a land that had long been destroyed. Still, rejoicing, he ran out into it, welcoming death and, in his own sick way, celebrating life.

*There are men who are so deeply defined by what they fight against
that they mourn the deaths of their enemies more deeply than
the deaths of their loved ones.*
VERSE 847:4 OF *The Teachings*

Shaka, Stein, several aides and Shaka's bodyguards rushed into a dark, dank underground bomb shelter, then slammed the thick metal door behind them. They were panting and harried from their efforts. Even Shaka had found himself running to the shelter—*the same Shaka that had walked from Times Square the night before!* Indeed, he had led the flight, pushing past some guards that had been going too slowly for him. Shaka's resolve and clarity were gone, and this was debilitating to him—like it would be to a man waking up to find that he had lost his sight. They could hear the distant rumbling over their heads as The Horde's bombs continued to rain down on them. There was a restless quality about Shaka; even after he sat down on a plush lounge chair, he twitched uneasily in the seat. Mocking thoughts of Xi and Circe joined newfound fears and uncertainties about The Horde. For the first time in recent memory, he looked and felt tired. The ageless quality about him was gone. He did not exactly seem old, but his youthfulness had withered away. Stein and the others looked at him uneasily....

"Sir?" Stein began.

"Yes?" Shaka said, an annoyed frown already coming over his face as he transferred his gaze to his aide.

"I've had men monitoring The Voice of Conscience's broadcasts," Stein started. "—Just as you requested, sir."

"Have you figured out where the broadcasts are coming from yet?"

"No, sir...but—"

"But *what*?" he asked, impatiently.

"Well, the monitors have reported that The Voice has mentioned Tio Mendez several times."

"Tio Mendez?"

"Yes, sir. It's been talking about how we need leadership—someone who is willing to speak the truth and do what has to be done."

Shaka grunted then pursed his lips.

"...Sir, I was thinking that maybe The Voice *is* Mendez."

Shaka thought about it for a while, then: "That would explain a lot."

Stein felt proud—and *relieved*; reinforced by these sensations, he ventured further: "And then there is more. Maybe Mendez is a tool of The Horde's propaganda machine....Then again," Stein cut himself short, plaintively rubbing his scaly cheeks, "if The Horde is as powerful as they seem, why would they bother with propaganda?"

Shaka chuckled, then shook his head at his aide's naiveté. "You have made the dire mistake of both underestimating The Horde *and* overestimating them....No," he went on, shaking his head again: "The extent of The Horde's violence—the *mindlessness* of it, in fact—tells me that they are even now dying. After all, they are the byproducts of their evolution: they are obviously as mindless as their violence."

Stein did not follow, but prudence demanded that he nod anyway.

"You ever watch someone drown, Stein?" Shaka went on, staring dreamily into space.

"No, sir," Stein responded cautiously.

"The moment they realize that they are going to die, they start thrashing violently, spending up the last of their energy, when staying calm and conserving energy would have saved them. In some cases, when you try to help them, they are so violently insane with dying that they drag you down with them: kill you, all because they had seen the shadow of death. You've got to leave those alone—just let them die."

"So," Stein said, tentatively, "The Horde isn't a problem?"

"*Fool!*" Shaka screamed, "haven't you been listening!"—Stein was trembling like a scared rat!—"The Horde is a killer, but a *stupid* killer. Stupidity is one of the most dangerous things in the world. Sometimes, it is merely self-destructive; but at other times, in its blindness, it destroys the best-laid plans of the wise. Don't take your eyes off The Horde for a minute! In the interim, get as many men armed as possible and wait!"

Capitalism often saw people as less than they were, but it keenly understood the crucial elements of human nature. Communism saw people as more than they were, but had no idea what people wanted the most. The lesson here is that regardless of whether an aspect of society is good or bad, the key to its success is whether or not it accounts for what people really want.
VERSE 2908:7 OF *The Teachings*

Missiles were still descending around Xi; off in the distance, he heard men screaming! As he neared the outskirts of the park, he remembered the subway station at Bowling Green—he had passed it when he walked down here. He could hide in there for the duration of the bombing. He shuffled on faster. Life was beginning to enter his muscles again, and he was happy for it. He would analyze the vision after he was safe—

Unfortunately, as he neared the subway station, he realized that others had also looked at it as a safe haven, because hundreds of men were fighting to enter the station at once. He joined the throng, no longer concerned about keeping himself separate from their madness. The Horde was back, and they were all terrified. The Voice of Conscience had been right about The Horde and now none of them would ever question it again—especially not Xi....

After much struggle, Xi finally made it down to the subway platform. *Tens of thousands* of other men were already down there. There did not seem to be any air here. It had to be at least 40 degrees centigrade. As there were no lights in the place, Xi could not help thinking that this was only a coffin that they were in...but more men were pushing at his back. There did not seem to be anywhere else to go; and maddened by all the jostling, he leaped onto the subway tracks—which, for some reason, the other men had avoided—and began to move to the other end of the subway station.

Quibb's voice could be heard coming from the public announcement system, urging the men to have courage. However, as a louder inner voice was telling Xi that one well-placed Horde bomb would bring the ceiling crashing down on their heads, he found himself thinking that if he got out of the station, and into the subway tunnels (where there was less open space), then he would be safer. He ran along quicker now, tripping a couple of times on the ties of the tracks. It felt good to run—to be free of the other men. After a few minutes, he was out of the Bowling Green station, walking in the dark tunnel. The next station was Wall Street—he could see it, and thousands of other men, in the darkness ahead. Needing to be alone, he sat down in the darkness of the tunnel, between the stations. Even though he could still hear and feel the bombs dropping overhead, it felt good to be alone again. He was thinking these thoughts when he suddenly had to clamp his eyes shut!

Something blinding had appeared before him. He put his hands up, trying to shield his eyes from the light—and yet, there was something enchanting about it. He felt as though he were being enveloped by the light—*protected* by it. He felt all of the madness that had just gripped him ebbing, leaving only a feeling of profound peace. He felt the way one did when in the midst of a good buzz. He had the sudden impulse to laugh. And just then, out of nowhere, a resounding voice told him not to be afraid. It was beyond sense, but it was glorious! Something was floating above him—in the light. He squinted up at the shimmering form, his jaw dropping. *It was Quibb!*

"Don't lose faith in me," Quibb said, smiling down at him.

"Quibb—" All that he could do was whisper the name, awed, and, for the life of him, thankful beyond reason! He was trembling uncontrollably, wondering if he actually *was* drunk. Quibb's voice was resounding in the cavernous subway; the light was blinding, and he wondered, in a panic, if the other men would see and hear. At the thought that this was a delusion fed by madness and desperation, he was devastated, but the strange bliss of the light soon enveloped him again. He could not take his eyes off Quibb. He was trembling uncontrollably, struggling against the possibilities. "Quibb," he managed to say then, "—what *are* you?" But there was only a smile on that other face. That face was calm, knowing, at peace with everything…Xi sat staring in amazement—and then, suddenly, it was all gone. There was no light, no resounding voice…No Quibb. The world seemed empty—and irrevocably so.

"*Quibb!*" he whispered into the darkness. He remembered how only days earlier he had laughed when Quibb first appeared in that wall of flame. Now, as he found himself on the verge of tears, he marveled at how far he had fallen into the abyss—and at how far there might still be to fall.

VII

Never waste time worrying about the approach of danger:
either make a plan of action to combat it or prepare to meet your fate.
VERSE 3435:34 OF *The Teachings*

An entire day passed them by. The earth turned on its axis, so that the sun rose on the eastern horizon and disappeared into the west. Since the beginning of history, men had gauged time by these movements; but a new era had come, in which men watched the heavens not for the moon and stars, but for purple skies and descending missiles. These signs were the new markers of time and history. New religions rose up to encompass these things. New folklore and customs came into being, all to explain the purple, shimmering skies and the coming of night, when the missiles came from the heavens, and God unleashed his fury on all those who had sinned during the day.

As another evening approached, the Goddess and her band neared the core of the city—*Manhattan*. They were actually in New Jersey now, walking down a six-laned highway. Upon occasion, when there were gaps in the tree line, they could see upper Manhattan across the Hudson River. For the last day or so, they had been walking through the vast outskirts of the city. The Goddess, by her own estimates, was in a kind of walking coma. She had *known* The Horde—had been at one with it. Yet, she had known The Horde the way dishonest lovers knew one another—without sharing their true selves. The only truth was that The Horde had *touched* her. With that touch, something of The Horde had stayed with her, like a sexually transmitted disease whose effects would only manifest themselves when her body, or the body of her next lover, began to fall apart...and maybe she was already experiencing those effects.

She felt somehow pregnant: as though her dealings with The Horde had fertilized something in her. At times, as she felt the thing growing in her, she was overcome by the joy of an expectant mother; at other times, she felt the moroseness of a cancer victim. Now, however, after walking for so many days, and coming upon so much grim evidence of death and disaster, she was too exhausted and dazed to care. In her mind's eye, she was still getting glimpses of what The Horde was doing; but now, they were only like flashes of blinding light, which instinctively caused her to close her eyes to protect her senses....

Earlier on, she had looked up and realized that the sky had a strange purple tint to it. Light did not seem to follow the laws of physics here: there did not seem to be shadows or highlights; objects seemed to be suspended in the air; noises seemed hollow...At first, she had tried to understand it and give it meaning; but like everything else around her, it had only drawn strength from her. Eventually, she had cut her losses and concentrated her will on walking.

The odd thing was that the closer they got to Manhattan, the less people there seemed to be around. Over the last two days, they had passed streams of terrified men. Sometimes the men had come thousands at a time, dragging themselves along like refugees from the front line of a battle. Only her little cult of militant drag queens had been going towards the city. A couple of the refugees had told them to turn back—had kept babbling about the end of the world and bombing—but Respoli-Priestess had only smiled, his peace still undisturbed as he pushed the cult forward.

The Goddess had noticed the eyes of some of those retreating men: the metallic husks of the deactivated PinkEyes and the Glory to the Goddess tattoos. She had asked Respoli-Priestess what the tattoos meant, but he had only waved his hand in a dismissive manner and said that it was a mark of idolatry—that millions had been misled, but that the true religion would soon wash away all the lies. Halfway through his sermon, her mind had wandered off...

There was now a harsh solemnity to everything: parts of the landscape seemed ravaged by man; parts seemed ravaged by the unchecked encroachment of nature, with weeds and shrubs proliferating in what used to be concrete sidewalks and tended yards. There were craters in the roads once more—some of them fresh!—and some of the buildings were still smoldering. Yet, in the face of all these new developments, she could not overcome the feeling that they were all trapped in an unchanging dream. She found evidence for this in their walking, which seemed as if it had been going on forever—and always would. Things seemed simultaneously locked in place *and* thrown wildly out of balance. The paradox left her dazed and feeble… and that strange sky was doing something to her. She could not explain it, but she now found it impossible to concentrate. No doubt some of that was due to her exhaustion, but there was something about the sky that left her uneasy…and a little sick as well. It was almost as though the sky were infecting her soul somehow….

They were still walking down the six-laned highway. The Hudson River was about half a kilometer to their left, beyond some trees; to their right, there were warehouses and industrial buildings. The absence of other people began to eat away at her again. Her mind suddenly flared up with thoughts of the Emerald City. She needed that fantasy desperately just now—the way an alcoholic needed a beer. A building to her right was still smoldering: she coughed on the smoke; her eyes burned…but all that day, she had been in the midst of such things: things that had been touched by The Horde, but which her clouded mind saw only as shadows in the darkness. She had passed the bombed remnants of bridges; on the highways, there had been evidence of collisions that had never been cleared away: rusting corpses of cars and huge, 18-wheeled tractor-trailers. These pile-ups had stood in the middle of the highways like pieces of modern art. They had unnerved her at first, but now they were merely part of the thing that hovered on the edge of her consciousness.

She did not have the wherewithal to digest information anymore—to *cogitate*. Perhaps later, when she had recovered her faculties, she would try to figure out the mysteries around her. For now, all she could do was hold on.

After so many days of walking, her entire body was sore. She was existing from step to step. Worse than that, since her communion with The Horde the day before, she had been left with the unsettling feeling that that communion had gone both ways. The Horde, she was increasingly convinced, had gotten a whiff of her scent, and was closing in on her at this very moment. Somewhere, the robots were being dispatched; coordinates were being triangulated…and it would only be a matter of time before the robots emerged out of the nothingness and gunned down Respoli-Priestess and the others—just like the people she had seen in that dark bunker the day before. She looked at Respoli-Priestess then, knowing that he and his cult would be slaughtered if those Horde robots confronted them…so the only thing to do was to continue running, until they reached the safety of the Emerald City.

The six lanes curved to the left, around a patch of trees; and as she contemplated the road ahead, she knew that she could not go on much longer. She cleared her throat timidly, looking over at Respoli-Priestess:

"How much longer?" she asked. It sounded like a child complaining from the back seat of the family sedan. She focused her eyes on Respoli-Priestess' serene face, almost ready to beg; but just then, he smiled, saying:

"We are here."

She turned to look with a violent, twitching movement. She gasped, almost toppling from the blunt force that came when she got an unobstructed view of the city. Unfortunately, considering the state of her mind, she was unable to make sense of what she *saw*. They were on the New Jersey side of the Hudson River, looking across at the behemoth city. The six lanes led to what remained of the George Washington Bridge. Part of it—the far end—had partially collapsed into either the river or the bank. It was impossible to tell with the thick purple smog, which lingered in brooding plumes over the city. The smog, itself, seemed to be mostly from the smoke, but she could not tell if the smoke was actually purple, or if it was only being tinted by that strange, shimmering sky. Under that sky, the city looked like an entangled heap of metal and brick and glass. The river continued past that place; but there was no gentle purl now, only a dour, swamp-like stillness. Sludge—back flow from the city's sewers—now overflowed the banks, and swarms of flies darted around in an iridescent cloud of pestilence. The stench was impossible to describe: the excrement of *millions*...that was how she got a sense of them. She reeled; she coughed, her eyes watering...

She looked up at the sky, her frown deepening. The purple was deeper here—*richer*—and she felt its pull more strongly. How come she had not realized it before now? *The purple smog of the sky had given the sun a green tint!* It was the same picture from that placard of that place! She felt so stupid! She had been walking beneath this purple sky all day, and yet she had not put it all together. As for the city, she had thought that the stench she had smelled all day had been from the men in her cult, but she had been wrong. The air—its smell, its taste, its tint...—the feel of the land beneath her feet... *everything* seemed corrupted. Even the offal floating down the river seemed somehow...tainted. Everything had the smell of industrial production, as if there was no longer a difference between products and industrial waste: as if the products of this society were muck and filth. Then, as her gaze went to Respoli-Priestess and his band, it again occurred to her that this was their world, and that this was what they had brought her to fight. Before her, in that crumbling wreck of a city, was what they loved and hated: what they had become, and what they were becoming. All of their truths and lies...their secret hopes and fears—everything that made them real and unreal—...it was all there. However, as she looked out at the city, her mind finally churned out a piece of logic: if she was to be God, then out there, there was a Devil—an entity whose existence and eventual ascension depended on her death. That Devil was now cemented in her mind as The Horde. She did not know it by that name, but she knew it, again, the way that a dishonest lover knew her mate. She knew the harshness of its touch, its brutality—

She shuddered. She could still sense The Horde out there, amassing on all the frontiers of civilization. Yet, as she watched the city, she had the feeling that the purpose of her existence was becoming clear. Looking out on the city, she knew that this was the true beginning of her consciousness. These moments of revulsion were attuning her to her true self—uncovering tools that would be necessary for future survival. Before, she had been like a new-born baby, reacting to the introduction and removal of stimuli. Hands had appeared from (and disappeared into) the darkness that lay just beyond her stunted consciousness, and she had watched those hands with awe and dread and amusement. Before, all that she had been able to do was cry and whine and coo, in hopes that her protectors in the adult world would take care of her. Now, at last, she glimpsed the thing lying off in the distance and knew that her cries were meaningless.

The colossal place back in the woods, from which she had fled, was some- how connected to what had happened to this place; the sky of this place had been on its placard. She kept coming back to that thought....Respoli- Priestess was still holding her arm; he grasped it a bit harder to pull her out of her shock.

She looked at him—into his beautiful eyes—lost for a moment. "When did this happen!" she asked at last, her eyes wide.

The serenity was still with him: "The war has begun, My Master."

"War?"

"It is the final phase of the prophecy," he said with an unsettling kind of joy.

As she glanced over at the city, his meaningless prophecies were terrifying just now. She was being pushed forward, and yet she still had no clue of what was to be done.

"Everything has been put in motion," Respoli-Priestess rejoiced once again. "You have come down from heaven—"

She gnashed her teeth: "*I'm not God*! Stop saying that!" She felt giddy and frustrated—on top of her previous exhaustion. "Don't you *see*," she went on, looking desperately into their eyes, "there's no prophecy here. I was trapped in that place...with women—and it wasn't *God* who took them! There were men in the streets, and..." But they just stared at her, no closer to comprehension than herself. And then she saw, all at once, that they had had the same battle that she was having: the one between myth and reality. For them, however, myth had won, and this was what had become of them. She looked at them—at the *ridiculousness* of them—feeling suddenly guilty. They seemed like confused children to her again.

"Let us go, My Master," Respoli-Priestess said at last, still smiling con- tentedly.

She stared at him for a moment, confounded and appalled, as if he had just beckoned her into hell. But then, just as quickly, she nodded. For some reason, she knew that there could be no retreat now—no rest; destiny, either demonic or angelic, could not be denied right now. And with a strange combination of courage and fear, she started walking over the bridge with them, venturing further into the filth and the unknown. The little Shirley Temple clone, perhaps sensing her fears, grabbed her hand....

They walked on, dwarfed by the mammoth bridge that had been meant to allow the movement of millions. They were still the only ones around. She once again had her old feeling of being a gnat on the back of an elephant... if only she could fly away! The bridge had been through an ordeal, but she could not tell if the worst of it was recent or from years of neglect. Some of the cables of the suspension bridge had snapped; the huge structure moaned sorrowfully, as a wounded person would. It seemed as if it would topple at any moment, taking them all with it. Every step that they took seemed foolhardy. Ahead, off in the distance, the collapsed end of the bridge disappeared into the purple abyss. And now that they were over the river, the stench of raw sewage was unbearable. She tried holding her breath, but that only made her giddier. Respoli-Priestess, seeing her stumble, took her free arm—Shirley Temple still held the other. Appreciative of all help, she closed her watering eyes and let herself be led. Her only hope was to shield her senses. However, it was then that she had another of her flashes. This time, instead of images, she had a single, horrible feeling: that she was being hunted by the Devil; and then, even before the city's sirens began to peal in the air, she knew that The Horde had arrived—that they were coming for her. Her legs froze up. The others looked back at her confusedly, but it was then that the sirens began to blare. They sounded eerie in the silence; and by now, Respoli-Priestess and the others had walked her so far across the bridge that the smog of the city had totally surrounded them. She could only see about 20 meters in each direction. Everything else was lost in the smog, so that she found herself thinking that The Horde was using the smog to sneak up on her. It was using the siren to mask the approach of its steps! Unable to stand it any longer, she went to run back the way they had come— this time with the little boy in tow—but Respoli-Priestess restrained her.

When she turned to protest, she noticed that Respoli-Priestess and the others were craning their necks, as though trying to discern something beyond the thick smog. "It is beginning!" Respoli-Priestess shouted suddenly. It was then that something streaked through the heavens, leaving a white smoke trail. She watched it abstractedly, until it disappeared into the smog of the city; and then, a second later, there was the explosion, which turned the purple a bright orange. She again went to run back the way they had come, but Respoli-Priestess still held her firmly. Besides, some of those streaking missiles had just exploded into some of the warehouses behind them. The bridge shook beneath them!

"We have to get to the other side!" Respoli-Priestess yelled, not in panic, but so that he would be heard over all the explosions. He was so decisive that she found herself running towards the city with the others. The bridge seemed like jelly beneath them. The city was being riddled with missiles now; with each explosion, clouds of smoke were lit up in countless bright, violent hues. From the city, the impromptu soldiers sent a barrage of mortar fire into the heavens—but they did not seem to connect with anything, nor did they seem to be aiming at anything for that matter. Then, no more than 40 meters from where they were running, one of those wayward mortar shells dropped, rocking the bridge. The Goddess and her followers all fell to the ground. More of the suspension cables could be heard snapping. Metal from the bridge was dropping into the river. It seemed only a matter of time before the bridge collapsed! Dust rose up into the air; and now, the smog was so heavy around them that they could hardly see. Shells were raining down all around them. Luckily, most were only falling into the river, but the resulting turbulence seemed too much for the fragile bridge. Once again, Respoli-Priestess urged them on. She felt hands on her, pulling her, dragging her: she ignored the parallels with the vision she had had while back in that place on the mountain! She was like an animal now, wanting only to survive. She ran along with them, blinded by the dust and smoke— and by the horrible certainty that The Horde had found her. And now, she heard men screaming out in agony all around her. It seemed as if every other second she would hear a nearby explosion, followed by more eerie cries. She held tight to Shirley Temple's little hand: he was her vital link to reality. With the unstable bridge, and the stench of the river, she was feeling sicker—

Then, just in front of her, there was an explosion, and the man who had been running ahead of her was catapulted up into a cloud of smoke and dust. A second later, another man was catapulted into the air! The bridge was rigged somehow—*mined*! She faltered, her innards turning cold; but Respoli-Priestess, who had all the while been yelling for them to keep going, wrenched her behind him. Her soul had been sapped of its strength; all that kept her going was the growing madness. She did not want to die, and yet every step that she took held the possibility of death! There was nowhere to go, and yet she had to keep going...!

They went on like this for what seemed like an eternity; she waited every moment for her own yell. She would hear cries and wonder if they were hers. Once or twice, she cried out, just so that she would know her own voice when the time came. They were at the partially collapsed end of the bridge now, descending into the thick smog ahead. It was insane. There might not even be a bridge there anymore. She expected every moment to find herself falling into the flowing scum of the river. The George Washington Bridge was easily a couple hundred meters high: the fall would kill them! But just then the bombing ceased. This too, she had sensed before it happened. Out there, she felt The Horde was reorganizing—confused for some reason. It wanted to capture her, not kill her; realizing that it was employing the wrong methods, it stopped the attack abruptly. Somewhere, new battle plans were being made; new instructions were being sent out to the millions of robots worldwide, whose prime directive was now to capture the Goddess.

She ran on for a few seconds before her mind was able to encompass these thoughts. A side of her was of course thankful that the bombing had stopped, but the screams of the men that had fallen remained in the air, draining her sanity and sense of purpose. Their cries were a horrible dirge in the dust and smog. The Goddess ran down, down the collapsed end...The siren, which grew louder as they approached the city, chilled her soul; the sound of their many harried steps—and their harsh gasps for air in the dust, smog and smoke—left her numb. Now that the shelling seemed to be done, Respoli-Priestess beckoned them on harder. This new eagerness made the sounds of their flight seem even more horrible. She pulled Shirley Temple along as if he were a sack; she forgot that she was even holding him. Everything seemed far off...*warped*. Then, through the smog and dust, she at last made out a wall. She did not realize this until well after they had all fallen the remaining five meters to the muddy filth of the bank. The wall was a levee for the frequent floods that had begun to plague the city. She lay groggily on the ground for a while, but Respoli-Priestess made them keep running until they reached the levee. When they did, some of the exhausted men leaned against it, panting; some collapsed to the ground: she joined these. She almost smothered Shirley Temple as she dropped. Everyone was exhausted beyond reason. They were like vanquished soldiers after the battle, drained by the terror, and yet relieved beyond belief to still be alive.

She could feel the siren reverberating through the levee. She tried not to think about it...Their numbers seemed to be cut in half by their dash across the bridge. There were only about ten of them left—if even that. She could still hear some far-off moans; she shook her head to chase them away, almost sure that they were ghost voices. As she looked back the way they had come, the bridge still seemed to be tottering—

Suddenly, the man lying next to her shrieked out in agony. When she looked, she saw him going through spasms on the ground. His arm had somehow been blown off, leaving only a bloody stump below the armpit! He, himself, had not noticed it until the moment before, when he cried out. She went to scream herself; she recoiled at the sight of the spurting blood, but then Respoli-Priestess came over and started caressing the man's face; and suddenly, the man's cries died away to almost childish simpers. He was mumbling something about sweet oblivion, and Respoli-Priestess kneeled before him, smiling down approvingly.

She sat there, confused and appalled. Why was no one getting a tourniquet? They just stood around with their insane faith. It was at that moment that the simpering man sought out her eyes and whispered, with a final, strained breath, "I'll be with you soon, My Master..." And then he was dead, as easily and senselessly as that.

She trembled, horrified by the icy words! Nobody died that easily: it was ridiculous. It was almost suicidal: no, it was beyond the mere ending of life. There was something unsettling about his peace: about the content smile that remained on his face. What had they become! Why had they run to this place while the bombing was going on—and through a minefield at that! They had run through it as if death meant nothing. The madness of their faith left her sick. She looked around at the men then—at what they had *become*—realizing, all at once, that one day she would probably have to flee from them. Their faith was so strong that it seemed certain that they would eventually destroy her. She did not want to end up like a crucified Jesus, whose triumph lay in a torturous death. She wanted to *live*...!

Now that death had sanctified his minion, Respoli-Priestess stood up with satisfaction shining in his eyes. "Let us go," he said.

"But what about him?" she asked, gesturing to the corpse. And what about all the others, who had fallen on the bridge?

"He is beyond us now," Respoli-Priestess answered, the way someone spoke of another's great achievement.

She nodded tentatively, perhaps too dazed to probe further. Respoli-Priestess helped her up, then they began to walk along the wall. The siren continued to peal. They walked along the filthy bank, staying close to the wall as it skirted the river. In a few places, gaping sewer pipes, large enough for a man to crawl through, protruded from the wall. From these pipes a steady stream of raw sewage dropped into the river. They had to walk beneath these things, their backs pressed against the wall to avoid being splashed—but even this was futile. They were all, to various degrees, covered with filth by now...and then there were the flies—the *swarms* of them.... Luckily, she was too dazed to know the true extent of it. She could hardly smell by now. The stench that had before nauseated her, was now somehow lost between her synapses and her consciousness. She was not even too appalled when Respoli-Priestess, whom had led them on steadily, stopped before one of those gaping sewer pipes, telling his followers to enter it.

This pipe seemed stuffed up from the inside, but that was no consolation. A kind of crusty black scum had congealed on the rim. She locked herself away; and when it was her turn, she entered on hands and knees, crawling into the putrid darkness. She focused on the barely perceptible form of Shirley Temple's buttocks ahead of her. Their breathing, echoing harshly in the darkness, again seemed unreal. She, herself, breathed shallowly. It was not even the stench by this time, but the lack of air and the heat. She knew that she would faint in due time—it seemed inevitable. For now, however, she tried to keep moving. The pipe began to take on many turns, like a maze. The feeling of being lost was again overwhelming. A budding kind of claustrophobia also took possession of her. She thought about being stuck in this metal tube forever. Her breath was coming quicker now—which was doubly terrifying, as there did not seem to be any air to breathe. And the siren was still blaring; with the darkness and the echo, it seemed more urgent now...

Somehow, her limbs were still moving. She did not know if it was her lightheadedness or not, but she thought that she perceived a light ahead— as from an exit. The light was getting brighter; she moved faster now— they all did, as if possessed by the same madness. An exit! She could hardly believe it! There was an open grate, and those ahead were escaping through it!

The most mysterious thing in the world is the obvious.
VERSE 234:4 OF *The Teachings*

They had all fallen into the rhythm of the rapist. Sundown had become a time of growing apprehension for the men. Thousands went insane with the waiting—on top of those who were already insane and/or in withdrawal from the PinkEyes. Moreover, as the bombing had never started this early before, many of the men had been taken by surprise. Even though the bombing only lasted a few minutes, the men were so on-edge that they did not really notice. Thousands of them were flooding into the subways right now—on top of the millions who had taken up residence down there as a precaution. After two nights of bombing, they seemed to hear the explosions in their minds. Last night, some of those hiding men, maddened by the rumbling of the bombing overhead, had gone on rampages, killing hundreds. Men armed by The Company had cracked under the pressure and fired their guns and mortars into crowds of their brethren.

Xi now sat on a subway platform in Harlem, with his back resting against the side of an ascending staircase. Over the last 24 hours, he had followed the subway tunnels uptown, wary of the outside world—and the purple, shimmering sky in particular. He sensed somehow that he had to regain his strength before he would be able to withstand more visions and revelations; and luckily for him, without the strange influence of the sky, he had not sensed the creature of the shadows all day. The tunnels had given him a break, but it was like trying to rest in hell. He was now at the 175th Street subway station, on what used to be the A-Train line. There were at least fifty thousand men around him. It was stiflingly hot. Unfortunately, the men were packed in so densely that Xi could not even think about going outside (had he harbored such notions). In truth, his settling here had been more because of the impossibility of moving farther than because he was comfortable here. He was trapped by the wretched men—there was not even space in the tunnels. The man to Xi's left began to snore; a moment later, the man's head fell on Xi's shoulder. Xi nudged the head away and sat there, wondering how much more he could take.

Believe it or not, there were actually men sleeping; some were lolling about in semi-conscious stupors; many had passed out from heat and dehydration—not to mention panic. Of course, some were dead and dying. Even though the bombing had stopped five minutes ago, panicky voices could still be heard squealing all throughout the chamber. The echoes of these voices were maddening, especially with the heat and confinement. Furthermore, as the trains had not run in years, rats and roaches had taken over what man used to call his dominion. The rats, some of them as big as half a meter, crawled amongst the men with a boldness that made them seem tame. Every so often, a man would cry out; others would look to see one of those beasts with its fangs deep in his flesh. Only Xi seemed to be vigilant about chasing the beasts away. As for the roaches and the clouds of flies, however, there was nothing that could be done. He was sure that he would lose his mind down here; and yet, he, like most of the others, was too terrified to leave….He could not even begin to guess how long it had been since he had slept. Sleep was yet another thing that had been made superfluous by the ongoing apocalypse.

Quibb's voice was still playing over what had been the subway's P.A. system, telling the men to have courage. Xi pulled his knees to his chest and stared into the darkness….It had been almost a day since he had seen Quibb floating above him. Every few moments of the last 24 hours had been spent with him asking himself if it had really happened. It was no longer a question of if he was mad or not—only of what he had seen. Furthermore, even when he tried to convince himself that Quibb was just a figment of his imagination, he could not deny the many truths of what Quibb had told him. Specifically, he could not deny what Quibb had made him *feel*. Even if Quibb was a fantasy, at least he was a fantasy that had opened his mind and brought him, at least remotely, in touch with his soul—

A fight suddenly broke out farther up the subway platform. Some new arrivals from outside were trying to find space; someone stepped on some-one else's hand and now dozens of men were jostling with one another. It was like a ripple in a calm lake, so that even Xi was getting jostled now. Men were trying to flee from the fight; others were trying to get closer to it, or starting fights where they were. Men were getting to their feet now. A sense of panic came over Xi, so he balled himself up on the ground and waited for the riot to be over. Minutes seemed to pass before some sem-blance of calm came over the subway tunnel. Men were milling about now, staking out new territory, like dust settling back to the ground after a heard of stampeding cattle had passed. When Xi looked up, a man was staring down at him—

"Hey!" the man said in surprise.

Xi frowned. Even when he recognized the old doctor from the hospital, his frown deepened. He could not believe in chance encounters anymore—not since Quibb. Thus, as he looked at the old man, he found himself wondering what place the man could have in the schemes of the gods. At the same time, despite what his visions had shown him about Mansmann's part in the apocalypse, it still did not occur to him that the old doctor might be Mansmann. In a sense, they were all stripped of their pasts. "…Hi," he said at last. He felt shy: they both did. For some reason, it was as if each were naked before the other man; yet, it was a kind of nakedness that obfus-cated the truth and kept them from seeing what was actually there.

Whatever the case, Xi had a little space beside him: he gestured with his head and the old man sat down. They sat silently for a while, staring off into the darkness. Then: "What are you doing all the way up here?" Xi asked. Somehow it felt good to talk: to think about something besides Quibb and the creature of the shadows; but unconsciously, Xi touched the scars on his arms, where he had felt the creature's claws the day before—

"I have a lab a few blocks away," Mansmann started, "—I figured the subway was the safest place to spend the night."

"…Unless the ceiling collapses," Xi said, looking up.

Mansmann nodded: "Yes."

That strange ease was built up between them again; some more moments passed with them staring into the darkness ahead.

"…Still feel like something's chasing you?" Mansmann started cautiously.

After a moment of confusion, Xi remembered their conversation back at the hospital. That seemed like years ago. Yet, in light of all that had happened—and the growing feeling that there were no chance encounters in the universe—Xi nodded his head. He looked at the old doctor thoughtfully then: "You believe in destiny—that everything's preordained?"

"…Of course not. We all have free will."

"Maybe free will is only the universe's way of softening the blow of destiny. When we think we have a choice, our enslavement seems more bearable." They stared at one another for a moment, then they both smiled for whatever reason. It was good to talk. Xi felt real again—at least for a little while; and as he reveled in this respite, he looked at Mansmann with that strange combination of hope and anxiety that came when lonely people began to think of a stranger as a potential friend. "Maybe our meeting is fate," he ventured.

Mansmann smiled, but shook his head: "Our previous meetings were chance: if we meet again, it will be fate."

Xi could not help smiling. "It's only fate after we have three chance encounters?"

"No, it might have been fate since the first time, but we will only know for *sure* after the next time. You can only assess fate in retrospect."

Men have found a strange kind of solace in the idea of a scheming Devil, who plants evil in their hearts and tricks them into selling their souls, when it is obvious that no such trickery was ever needed, and that the evil was theirs alone.
VERSE 1935:1 OF *The Teachings*

The Goddess tumbled out of the pipe, joining the panting, entangled pile that had come out before her. She, like the rest of them, gulped the air, becoming almost drunk on it. The purple smog seemed like country fresh air in comparison to what she had just breathed. For those few moments, she lived only to breathe the air: everything else seemed far off. She could not even feel the bodies around her; she was so dazed that it was almost as if she were floating in a purple cloud. She could tell neither up nor down. And the sirens were still there with her, blaring so loudly that they seemed as if they were coming from inside of her.

It was a few moments before she even had the strength and will to look up; but even then, maybe it took whole minutes before she began to understand what she saw. At first, all that she could make out were dancing rectangles of light in the purple smog. It was only when she managed this that she realized that the rectangles of light were actually screens—video billboards—which had been fastened to buildings. She strained her eyes, looking up at the flickering screens. There were images of people smiling and capering about; there were images of love and peace and war and...*everything*. It was as if this place were a monument to that strange TV consciousness that she had been struggling with. It was a flickering, senseless world: images with no context, or a context that was to be supplied by the viewer's unstated understanding of the syntax. The quickly changing scenes on the billboards seemed only to accentuate the lack of movement everywhere else. From where she lay, she could see down three wide avenues. She was now lying on the curb of one of the avenues (which hugged the wall), and the other two formed an oblique intersection across the street. Because of the blaring siren, she had expected to find scenes of chaos: people running wildly and screaming; ambulances darting down the avenues, tending to the many prone bodies. She had been unconsciously preparing herself for a throng of millions…but there was no one else about. She looked at the billboards again. The smog, she realized all at once, acted like smoke at a laser show, helping to highlight the colors. If there was any audio, it was being drowned out by the siren. Yet, she did not even need that: her mind supplied the announcer's voices and the melodic jingles that made it all make sense. She felt, somehow, at home. The flickering images were somehow her language— even if the only message they communicated was madness—

A stray hand in her face reminded her that she was actually on a pile of men. The realization made her feel silly. She rolled off the pile and onto the sidewalk. Presently, Respoli-Priestess emerged from the pipe, his face, too, betraying the madness of confinement. He dropped on top of a man that had just been about to stand up, then he tumbled down beside her, panting. Seeing him, the Goddess' old questions returned once again.

"Where's everyone?" she asked, tentatively—almost afraid to know.

"I guess, hiding," he said, panting.

"—From the bombs?"

"Yes."

"So there're people then?"

He looked up slowly, still catching his breath: "Millions," he said.

She looked around once more, wondering about the bombs, the thing that had sent them, and the place that she was to have in it all. She scanned the world again. The city, with the tops of its crumbling buildings lost in the smog, was like a forest that was choked with fog: there was something eerie about it. The siren was like an unseen wolf's howl. With that smog, the danger might come at any time, yet she would never know—until it was too late. Her unsteady eyes returned to Respoli-Priestess:

"...What exactly do you expect me to fight?" she asked again.

He stared at her blankly. That particular question had not actually occurred to him. "I don't know," he said.

She frowned. "*You don't know*? Then why'd you bring me here?"

"The prophecy—"

"*What* prophecy? Who wrote it?"

"No one wrote it—*The Teachings* are a communion of souls, My Master, working together to reveal the secrets of the universe—"

She screamed in frustration!

"I've hidden *The Teachings* away, My Master, so that future generations will know of you—"

She screamed again! "You brought me here, yet you haven't told me *anything*—"

"You are the one who will tell us what to do."

"Enough of this!" she yelled, getting up from the ground. She backed away from them a little, as if she were preparing to defend herself. "You're driving me crazy!"

"My Master," Respoli-Priestess pleaded, urgency sounding in his voice for once as he rose from the ground, "this isn't the time or place. We have to get you to safety—"

"Safety from what! That's the thing: what are you so afraid of? Bombs and mines obviously don't scare you!"

"Our safety means nothing; only yours—"

"Enough!"

"My Master...!"

"And stop calling me that!"

"My Master," Respoli-Priestess entreated her again, "we *must* get you to safety! [She went to scream something] They'll *kill* you!"

"...*Who* will?"

"The nonbelievers."

"That doesn't—"

"Please, My Master! A mouse is a timid creature; but millions of them, driven mad by an outside, unreachable force, will take out their frustrations on those around them. We have to get you to safety: they might be out at any moment!" He stood there entreating her with his eyes; there was so much dread there that she lost her momentary defiance. Seeing the uncertainty in her eyes, he took her hand and they started running again. They ran across the street and down one of the avenues that began at the oblique angle. There were discarded rickshaws everywhere....Running into the smog, they came upon blocks of bombed out and burning buildings. She gauged her own fatigue by watching Shirley Temple, who was still at her side. The little boy seemed on the verge of collapse—just as she knew she was.

As she ran with them, she looked up in awe at the buildings—even the crumbling ones. It was all new to her; and yet, there was still the faintest inkling of a bizarre homeyness.

As usual, Respoli-Priestess took the lead, beckoning them with an eagerness that did not leave much time for clarity of thought. It seemed that she would never catch her breath in this place. Every time she looked around to gather her bearings, she found herself being forced into wild, aimless flight. They were now taking many turns down the city blocks; it seemed like madness to her that Respoli-Priestess could possibly know where they are going, and yet she had nothing to battle her fear but trust in that madness—

Suddenly, the siren ceased; everyone stopped, horrified and confused by the silence. ...But there was not really silence: The Voice of Conscience was there, screaming about standing strong against The Horde. There was a billboard directly above the Goddess and her cult, and The Voice was blaring over it. The Goddess shuddered when she heard it: she *knew* that deep, baritone voice—there was no question about it. She knew it and *feared* it. In her mind, it was connected with horrible things. She probed these thoughts for a moment, suddenly realizing that she had heard that voice back in that place in the mountains! She was *certain* of it. The Voice of Conscience was the voice of The Horde! She retreated a step, but as she looked up at the billboard and saw the commercial that was playing, she found herself mesmerized. She forgot about The Voice of Conscience for the moment, and stared at the bright, flickering colors on the screen, losing herself in the quick, yet deceptively smooth editing. It was all entrapping her. She and the others were now in a kind of outdoor mall; stores and restaurants lined the block. The smell of food cooking (and burning) permeated this place; yet, all that she could think about was what was playing on the video billboard. On the screen, there was a clown parading in front of a store on stilts. He was saying something, but the only audio was The Voice's rant on The Horde. Still, as this was The Goddess' world, she knew exactly what the clown was saying. It was the company slogan, "Harlequin supermarkets don't *clown* around!" with a strained overemphasis on the word "clown"—as if it were an inside joke. She even heard the jingle in her mind—the playful, cloying music. On the screen, the clown was balancing on stilts. Then, something strange: suddenly, he lost his balance; and then, the next moment, he was falling. But he was not just falling in the screen, but falling *out* of the screen. His gigantic body was toppling towards them. She screamed; in a futile gesture, she put up her hand—as if that were going to protect her from the gigantic body; but suddenly, the clown disappeared, only to reappear in the screen, along with the corporate logo of the supermarket chain (which of course did not exist anymore).

The drag queens stared at her confusedly: they had not even flinched. It was all some kind of holographic technology. She looked around warily at all of it, finally understanding. It was then that Respoli-Priestess, who had been sidetracked by the ceasing of the siren, beckoned them again. He gestured to an alley halfway down the block, and they all ran for it. Still, even as she ran along with them, she wondered about the images on the many screens. There were images of women: some in a priggish 1950s mode, some in a porno mode. Images of women, warped; images of men, warped...of love, of kindness, of sexuality, of the landscape...so that everything was assumed to be false: *a projection*. That was the unsettling thing about this world: it was not that there seemed to be some domineering entity trying to shape reality, but simply that unreality, itself, seemed to have been broadened. After a while, she would not flinch either: she would just stand there, reassured by the realization that it was all fake.

All at once, The Voice echoed through the streets, saying, "The bombing has stopped for now! Rejoice, my brothers, there will be no more bombings today, nor tomorrow! Rise from your places of shelter, my brothers!" it thundered. "Rise! Rise! *Rise*! We have won a victory in the war today! We showed courage against evil! But the war continues! The enemy sends missiles to Moscow and Bucharest; the enemy destroys and pollutes cities in Holland and Nigeria! We must be the shining light of the world! We must show the others how to fight evil! We must continue to grow strong so that when they come back, we'll obliterate their evil from the world once and for all…!"

What it all meant, the Goddess could not even begin to fathom. Following Respoli-Priestess and the others, she ducked into the alley at that moment. They hid behind some putrid-smelling dumpsters and waited, holding their breaths. She hugged the little boy, both of them trembling. All around them, there were loud, screechy sounds, like cellar doors opening. She heard people talking as well—and she knew that those voices were not coming from the billboards, because they did not have that mindless, high-energy seller's intonation. The people—*the great multitudes*—were arising from their sleep, like disturbed giants. She did not want to be caught stealing around in their midst, like a tiny Jack from the fairy tale. This was what Respoli-Priestess had feared….Minutes passed; the din of the giants grew more penetrating—*maddening*. It seemed as if they were right on top of them, looking down.

When Respoli-Priestess gauged that the time was right, he stood up, gesturing for them to walk with him towards the street—back the way they had come. No one moved. Once more, Respoli-Priestess was telling them to go towards the thing that promised the most danger. There was a moment of hesitation, but then the other drag queens obeyed him. Only the Goddess and Shirley Temple remained crouched. The others, looking back, waited for them to comply, then they all set off together.

"Walk naturally," Respoli-Priestess told them.

The Goddess felt sick to her stomach by now—she had been sick to her stomach all day in fact…She glanced at the sky, then looked away as her head began to ache. She had been doing that all day, but had never given thought to what it might mean…She was still holding Shirley Temple's trembling hand. It seemed to be her only link to reality. The great multitudes could be seen now. Respoli-Priestess was taking them back towards the outdoor mall. Tens of thousands of men were about—and *only* men. She again trembled at the realization. She was the only woman here, out of all those millions. But no: there had to be others out there. If there were no women in this city, then certainly there were in that place from which she had fled. Thinking of that place again made her stomach twinge. She could not deal with that now; that realization, as it had all the other times, was quick to come. She had to deal with this first: this city of men—this *world* of men—from which her kind had been banished....

The band's easy pace towards the mall continued. The Voice of Conscience was still echoing through the streets, talking about victory and courage. The closer the Goddess got to the mall, the more she found herself thinking that surely the men would notice a group of drag queens walking down the street. However, as she looked at the men walking past the mouth of the alley, she saw their bizarre variety and knew that a band of transvestites in army fatigues would hardly be noticed. She had wondered about the wisdom of wearing something as conspicuous as her dress, but she saw men in the crowd who, like Respoli-Priestess, were more beautiful—and *feminine*—than she. Indeed, as she looked into the mall, she found herself thinking that the entire gamut of human existence was being showcased for her. Some of the men were in rags; some were in robes that were reminiscent of the Old Testament; some were in nothing but their underwear. There were even men running down the street pulling rickshaws. It seemed as if anything and anyone might hide in their midst. Moreover, they were celebrating: they saw little. There was an ease—*a careless acceptance*—about the men that was unfathomable. As she looked at them—and their reaction to their bombed, wrecked world—it was almost as if nothing at all had happened.

The cult was approaching the mouth of the alley. The Goddess still gripped the little boy's hand. She seemed almost as his mother now. They stepped into the stream of pedestrian traffic, virtually unnoticed. Respoli-Priestess led them on at a calm pace.

It was at that moment that she heard a disturbance at the next intersection. An angry crowd could be seen running towards them! Everyone in the band froze. Her innards trembled as the mob descended: it seemed silly to think that they would not be noticed! She could curse herself now. And what was descending on them was just like the mob of her vision. Trembling, she went to give herself up to their brutality; but just before the mob reached her, they grabbed a gaunt old man. In her terror, she had not noticed that the man was fleeing from them. He had seemed just as insane as the rest of them.

As the man was collared, an official-looking man in a yellow sash came to the forefront. Now that the billboards were back online, and the men were in a celebratory mood, *Throw the First Stone* had been resumed. The barker, with his top hat and sash, stood before the crowd and his camera crew now, announcing that the old man they had collared had been stealing while they hid from The Horde. The mob—it seemed as if everyone was a part of it now—booed. Thousands of people now crowded in, all yelling like monkeys—like *animals*. There was an almost infectious excitement in the air now; if she had not been so terrified, even she might have been swept up by it. As she looked, she saw that even her followers were gripped by the thing. Respoli-Priestess was whooping wildly, his delicate hand waving indignantly in the air; the others followed suit. Previously, the men—*all* of them—had struck her as jovial and carefree; now, they seemed gripped by the darkest passions. She saw vengefulness and hatred in their eyes. It was all so precipitous that she wondered if what she had seen of them before had been an illusion. Only she and the condemned man, who struggled and pleaded ineptly at the hands of a huge, cackling brute, seemed impervious to the madness.

Thousands of excited men were still flooding in. The hatred spread throughout the surrounding blocks, like a wildfire. She would be burned alive with the rest of them, God help her. There was nowhere to go now: the multitudes were packed in densely all around her, blocking any retreat. The condemned man was heaved against a wall, then the mob stewards started organizing the crowd, so that the men made a semicircle around the man. The man tried to run, but was thrown back into the semicircle by the crowd. Next, some people went about with a demented kind of gleefulness, distributing stones to those closest to the front. The Goddess was close enough to the front to be one of them. Her stone came from a teenager who had the face of an acolyte—except for the hatred gleaming in his eyes. When the stone was proffered to her, she only stared blankly, until the heard Respoli-Priestess telling her to take it. She took the thing; it was the size of a lemon, weighing about half a kilogram. It felt like a ton in her clammy hand.

She had not realized it earlier, but the billboards, which had previously showcased advertisements for products that no longer existed, had switched to the scene around them. People, as they held their stones, looked up at the gigantic screens. It was all a show, she suddenly realized! It was then that there was a yell from the barker and the stones began to fly. It was horrible! The condemned man's skull, in those first few seconds, was busted open; his teeth were shattered; he charged like a wild animal, but was sent back by a wave of stones. The Goddess stood there frozen. In the chaos, she looked down at her stone and saw a slogan on it: "The Company believes in justice!" Other people's stones had other slogans and corporate logos on it. And they were not even real stones at all, but mass-produced cement pellets.

About 10 seconds had passed since the barker had given the signal. Almost everyone had depleted his store of pellets by now. It seemed as if she were the only one who still held onto one.

"Throw it!" she heard Respoli-Priestess say; she looked over, seeing the eyes, where there was a grim earnestness. Unnerved, she threw it, but lackadaisically, so that it missed. The man was lying in a pool of blood by now, unmoving. All around, there were still the animal calls; and then, when the last stone was thrown against the prone, unmoving body, a monstrous cheer shook the world. She felt weak and nauseous; she could not help it: she threw up; and too light-headed to stand, she fainted. Her minions held her up; but even if they had not been there, the mere pressure applied by the surrounding bodies would have kept her up. Strangely, now that the man was dead, the crowd was disbursing, talking excitedly—like kids after a Saturday matinee. When enough people had departed, her followers took her unconscious body away, unnoticed in all the merriment.

VIII

If events occur with sufficient gradualness, then, through that great fallacy of human reasoning, they will be presumed to be natural.
VERSE 2343:5 OF *The Teachings*

The initial minutes after The Horde's departure—and The Voice of Conscience's announcement of this fact—were pure bliss. In the subway, men jumped to their feet, some dancing with one another. Their cries of joy rose up in the air, drowning out The Voice's warning that the enemy would eventually come back, and that this ultimate battle lay ominously on the horizon.

As the other men celebrated, Xi and Mansmann looked over at one another incredulously, again realizing how different they were from the others.

"...You have somewhere to stay?" Mansmann asked at last. "—My lab is only a few blocks away from here...if you need somewhere to stay." Then, noticing the scars on Xi's arms, "I could clean those up for you—they look like they're getting infected."

Xi glanced at the hideous scars on his arms absentmindedly, but his mind was elsewhere: on Quibb and all the incomprehensible things he had seen over the last few days. He looked up at Mansmann helplessly: "...You afraid to die?"

Mansmann stared at him for a long while. His first impulse was to hedge—to pretend not to have heard and to ask Xi to repeat the question... anything to avoid answering—but this impulse passed and he found his mind going to the question. "...No," he said after a while.

"Do you believe in God?"

"...I don't know," he said after a sigh, "but if He or She exists, I believe that God has long ceased to believe in *us*."

"Then what is left to us?"

"...We have to believe in ourselves—in one another."

Xi nodded his head at the correctness of what Mansmann had said. "What about happiness? Do you ever believe in God then—at moments when you're so happy...when things seem so perfect that you find yourself thinking that some powerful force has to be in charge?"

Mansmann shook his head: "God is a creation of pain and hardships. People offer up praises to God when they are happy, but it's desperation that makes men *love* God."

Once again Xi nodded at the correctness of what had been said. Quibb had told him of the old doctor's importance to his life—and his quest for enlightenment—and in light of the man's words, Xi was now convinced of it. He took a deep breath and looked around with a new clarity in his eyes, as if just awakening. "Where is this lab of yours?"

"In an old church building around 169th and Amsterdam. Shaka set up a clinic on the ground floor, but it's just filled with squatters—I'm on the second level."

Xi nodded; most of the men had exited into the streets by now, and the uproar of their joy seemed distant as it echoed from the streets. Mansmann looked towards the exit himself, before looking down at Xi quizzically: "You coming?"

"There's something I have to do first," Xi said, averting his eyes from the old man's glaze.

Mansmann nodded and left him....

When Mansmann got outside, he could not help smiling as he watched the impromptu celebrations that had started up. For the first time in a long while, the men seemed alive to him. At the same time, they seemed like sloppy drunks, who had imbibed too much of what The Voice was telling them, and were now just embarrassing examples of excess and stupidity. The functioning billboards showed scenes of felicity and triumph, and played music that seemed fitting for courageous war movies. Even Mansmann had to fight to keep himself from being swept up in it. It was the kind of congeniality that existed at New Year's Eve parties. For those few moments, there was immeasurable hope—the illusion that something arduous had passed, and that something new and wondrous was on the horizon—

"Doctor Sullivan!" someone called. It was a few moments before Mansmann recognized his alias. There was a moment of shock and panic, when he wondered who could possibly know him—

"Doctor Sullivan! Doctor Sullivan—*wait*!"

Mansmann looked around to see two drag queens running towards him. They ran all the way up to him—he took a step back.

"You must come with us, Doctor! Thank goodness you're here!" It was a middle-aged man with so much makeup that he looked like a demented clown. The other one actually looked like a woman. Mansmann frowned for an instant, but the demented clown was grabbing his arm so that he would follow—

"Get the hell off of me!" Mansmann snapped, pulling his arm away violently; but then, frowning, he finally recognized his one-time bodyguard. "*Kramer*?" he said, his eyes wide. "What the hell…! What you do to yourself!" He hoped Kramer had not gone to the extreme of having himself castrated; once in a while, Mansmann got requests for that sort of thing—

The other one was speaking now: "It's an emergency—*please*!"

Mansmann diverted his shocked gaze to the other one. Once again, he was a little unnerved by the other one's beauty. He could not quite place it. Maybe it was only a reminder of femininity: not that thing illustrated clumsily—and grotesquely—by Kramer, but something essential and unaffected.

"You're the only one that can help us!" Kramer was saying again.

"Come, *please*," the feminine one was saying. "It's not too far."

Mansmann looked into those soft eyes again; unsettled, he nodded. At that, the two drag queens set off at a trot, and he jogged along with them—back the way they had come. The men of the city were still celebrating. He was again keenly aware that he was out of place—that he would never be one of them. However, he did not want to think about that. Now panting, he called to Kramer, asking:

"How much longer?"

"Not far."

"What's this all about?"

"Someone…you must help," the man said, flustered and desperate.

"Someone hurt?"

"Yes," the feminine one answered.

They jogged for about half a block, and then into the alley, where about eight other drag queens were standing over a supine body. Mansmann initially classified the Goddess as a plain-looking young man with closely cropped hair. However, there was something about the face that caused Mansmann to look more closely—to be drawn into things he had not felt in years. It was disturbing in fact: he was unable to move—to *think*. When the feminine-looking drag queen hemmed, he was brought back to his senses. He looked over the other drag queens uneasily; then, almost forcing himself not to look at the person's face, he bent down and checked the pulse at the wrist.

"What happened?" Mansmann asked.

"He collapsed," Respoli-Priestess said.

Mansmann nodded: "It seems like exhaustion." He should have examined the eyes to check for a concussion, but he was still unnerved about the face. Besides, even a concussion was nothing compared to what he had seen in the last few days. He was still holding the Goddess' almost dainty wrist in his hands; he put it down anxiously, then looked up at the others: "It's probably malnutrition…over-exertion. Let him rest and get him something to eat…" He could not help groaning at the cliché stupidity of the statement. He wanted to rush away: to get away from them all…but there was still something about the unconscious man—*the Goddess*—

"Can we go to your lab?" Kramer was saying now. "If you take care of her, the rest of us will work for you."

Her? Mansmann thought to himself; Kramer realized his mistake and watched Respoli-Priestess uneasily. Thinking it over, Mansmann merely attributed it to one of their bizarre cult rituals. Nevertheless, looking at the Goddess again, he frowned, saying, "All that for him?"

"All for…him, yes," Respoli-Priestess said.

Mansmann was staring down at the supine body when he noticed that the front of the dress was damp with blood. "Did you notice this wound?" he said, bending down again. He raised the dress up, seeing the bloody thighs… the pubic hair…*It was menstrual blood*! Respoli-Priestess grabbed his arm gruffly with one hand, then pulled the dress back down with the other; the grip was soon eased, but remained firm. Mansmann's mind was numb; his breath got caught in his throat. He tried to smile—to do anything to shield himself from the blow…the *shock*!

He got up nervously from his crouch; the others were looking at him closely, and that only unnerved him further. "…Ah, I guess we can go," he said at last, dazed and out of breath. "…Lots to do," he said, trying to smile again. He started off, his gait tense, his mind still being rocked by the aftershocks. One of the men took the Goddess in his arms, then they all followed Mansmann closely.

Only those who insist on thinking themselves blameless
in their oppression are truly oppressed.
VERSE 2789:2 OF *The Teachings*

X i still sat on the subway platform. Only he and some sleeping—most likely dead—men had remained: everyone else had rushed out into the streets.

Suddenly, Quibb was there; Xi did not even flinch. "…I waited for you," Xi spoke up quickly. "I knew you'd come."

Quibb smiled down at him: "Good, then we're beginning to understand one another."

Xi nodded, fighting not to fall into the all-encompassing awe of the last time. He realized that The Voice's rant was still playing over the P.A. system—even though Quibb was standing before him. That suddenly seemed miraculous to him…but he reminded himself that these moments were precious. He had spent the hours compiling questions; he blurted out the first one, almost afraid that he would not have enough time:

"Why are you doing all this, Quibb?"

"I'm doing it because you made me laugh once."

He stared at Quibb helplessly. "…The men are willing to *die* for you."

"Yes, I know," he said. For a moment, there seemed to be slight hesitation and uncertainty there, but then his smile returned and he continued, "They have to be willing to die for something before they realize how precious life is."

Xi was not sure if that was true or not, but he nodded his head anyway. And then: "What about The Horde?"

"They'll attack again in a week or two."

Xi stared for a moment, then he nervously raked his fingers through the filthy strands of his hair: "How do you know all these things?" he said in frustration. "Why'd they come…why'd they *leave*—it's not as if we were putting up resistance?"

Quibb looked at him knowingly, then smiled. "Maybe they haven't left. Maybe they are here now—have *always* been here….Because you don't see roaches doesn't mean that your house is free of them."

"…But *how*?"

"You know how."

Xi thought about it for a while, then nodded his head: "…I think I saw some of them," he said, his eyes growing wide. "They were marching down the middle of the street, and I was the only one who could see them…Why are they doing it, Quibb? What are they after? And why are you telling all those men that they won—that they can even *fight* The Horde?"

"Like I said, I tell the men to fight because if they don't, then they're already dead. As for The Horde, it's simple: A body that's wounded will direct blood to the brain and the vital organs."

"What the hell is that supposed to mean?"

Quibb only laughed, saying: "I've answered it very simply: A body that's wounded directs blood to the vital organs. The wound has already been made: now, The Horde is waiting to see what the body does."

Xi thought about it for a while; then, looking up at Quibb sharply, he blurted out: "This is how they look for women, isn't it? They bomb, then they see what the men protect."

"Yes," Quibb said, matter-of-factly.

But Xi frowned: "Doesn't make much sense—seems like they might accidentally blow up the women they're after."

Quibb chuckled, saying: "Your assumption is that The Horde values the things it seeks to acquire."

Xi nodded in resignation, then he looked up at Quibb helplessly again: "I think I know where the women are—where they're hidden in the city."

"Do you really?" Quibb said with a smile.

"Yes, I have these keys…" he tapped the pocket with the keys; but when he looked up, Quibb was again smiling at him the way one did when enduring a child's foolishness.

Quibb laughed at Xi's expression of confused disappointment. "…Anyway," the man said with a sigh, as though talk of The Horde and women were inconsequential, "have you heard of Tio Mendez?"

"…Yeah…of course."

"He's going to lead a social revolution. The only way to fight The Horde is through organization."

Xi stared wearily for a while before nodding.

"You are going to help him, Xi," Quibb went on. "He lives in the basement of a building on the corner of 116th Street and 3rd Avenue. It will be the only one standing. Go see him—he will be expecting you."

Xi was staring up at Quibb. It was then that he noticed the tattoo around Quibb's right eye—the Glory to the Goddess tattoo—

"You believe in the Goddess?" Xi said in amazement. As he said it, he unconsciously touched the corner of his eye.

"Of course I do, and so do you."

"Me?"

"Of course."

Xi searched his mind; but as always, he could come up with nothing definite. "How long have you had that tattoo?" he asked then.

"I've always had it."

Xi shook his head: "I would have noticed it before."

Quibb was laughing now.

"What's so funny?" Xi said in annoyance.

"You haven't looked at your face in the mirror lately, have you?"

"…No."

"What if I told you that you had the Glory to the Goddess tattoo as well?"

Xi shook his head timidly.

Quibb laughed heartily. Then, he brought out a mirror—produced it out of the nothingness, like the magician of the shadows that he was—and held it up for Xi, so that he could look at his face. The tattoo was there, under layers of grime. Xi had to wipe away the grime with the palm of his hand, but the tattoo was there, mocking his sanity.

"You always believed in the Goddess," Quibb went on, while Xi sat there in shock; he glanced in the mirror again—first looking at the tattoo, then at his strange, metallic eyes— "You were one of the first to put your faith unquestionably in Her," Quibb continued. "Even seven years ago, you loved the Goddess—were willing to do *anything*."

Xi groaned and shook his head. There was no use in questioning what Quibb had said, because the tattoo was incontrovertible. However, even then, he still could not *believe* it. There was a logical sinkhole there and he *knew* it. If a man woke up without his leg, and was told that space aliens had stolen it during the night, the undeniable fact that the leg was gone might lead him into believing in space aliens, when there was a more mundane, earthbound answer for his lost leg. As such, incontrovertible facts sometimes led to faulty conclusions. ...And yet, the Goddess was within him. Just as Quibb had said, whenever he saw Her face, he had felt a jolt in his system; his mind had gone blank, as though attuning itself to divine states of being. He searched his mind—his recent past—and acknowledged that every time he saw a Glory to the Goddess tattoo, something had been sparked within him. He could not deny that...but he would have noticed if Quibb had worn that tattoo before this moment! He sighed in frustration. As he sat there helplessly, it was as if the effects of all his days of sleeplessness and mental exhaustion came crashing down on his head. His body slumped from the weight of it. He took some deep breaths to regain his strength and composure; but as always, he seemed done for. It was then that he looked up at Quibb's smooth, earnest face and remembered all that he was supposed to say to Quibb: all the questions that had percolated in his mind as he hid in the subway tunnels.

"...I've been having visions," Xi said at last.

"Yes—you've been seeing into your subconscious mind."

"But it's all been G.W.'s life."

"I know."

"How can my subconscious mind be someone else's life?"

Quibb smiled enigmatically. Xi looked away, then took a deep breath, reminding himself to remain calm: to use this time wisely. He looked up at Quibb again:

"...I think the sky is triggering my visions somehow."

"Yes it is—"

"*Damnit, Quibb!*" Xi screamed, unable to help himself. "What is it all supposed to mean!"

"It means that after you help Mendez, you still have to go back to The Company and find out who you are—who Xi Wang was and what role he played in the end of the world."

"...The end of the world," he repeated anxiously. He sat silently for a while, deep in thought. When he looked back up, Quibb was gone. Yet, as Xi looked around and listened in the silence, he was sure that he heard the man's voice whisper, "Find Mendez...."

"They" is the most terrifying term in human language.
VERSE 3939: 3 OF *The Teachings*

Once Mansmann had situated the drag queens in some basement rooms of his clinic, he went up to his lab and returned with some tools to diagnose and treat the unconscious one. He told himself that it could not have been menstrual blood: maybe it was just a botched sex change. Yes, that seemed more likely…but he was anxious when he began his examination in the dim lighting of the room. Actually, he was probably happy for the dim light, because he could not see the face clearly. He first opened the person's eyes and used a flashlight to see if a concussion had been suffered. All the members of the band were now crammed into the small room; they stood solemnly, staring over Mansmann's shoulder. He kept looking back at them uneasily….When he took out a syringe, the head drag queen demanded to know what he was doing.

"I'll need some blood to make a diagnosis."

Respoli-Priestess thought about it for a while, then nodded.

When Mansmann began to draw out the blood, he first thought that the dim lighting had produced an optical illusion. To counter this, he turned on the flashlight he had used to check the person's eyes, and gasped when he saw it for himself. The blood had a yellowish hue! It was more like bloody pus, so that he thought he had stuck the syringe in a sore—but it was clearly in the vein. He turned off the light quickly—both to stop himself from seeing and as to not alert the others to what he had seen. His mind pulsed with dozens of harrowing possibilities: some new plague, perhaps....He left the room without a word to the others—he *fled* from it, his mind still pulsing with possibilities too terrifying to name.

Any man can seem godlike if his subjects are wretched enough.
VERSE 1543: 4 OF *The Teachings*

Xi hopped off the subway platform, onto the tracks, and began to make his way downtown—towards Tio Mendez's lair. Quibb's voice was still encouraging the men to come out onto the streets in celebration of their supposed victory over The Horde. Xi could hear the men of the city through the ventilation system—their laughter, their raised, excited voices. Already, the logarithmic music of Mardi Gras was blaring from the streets. The Voice was now telling them where to pick up weapons around the city. It was telling them how to train themselves and how to instill all the madness of war within themselves. As he walked alone in the darkness, Xi could sense the men overhead being worked into a frenzy. Even he felt the strange mob instinct calling to him, warping everything that he saw and felt. The only thing that saved him was the recollection of Quibb's image floating in the darkness before him. Quibb had come to him personally; Quibb had called him by his name, just like God had called Abraham and Muhammad by name and sent them off to do His work.

Xi was now certain that his existence depended on following Quibb's will and finding Mendez. Mendez was part of the puzzle that Quibb was slowly revealing to him. At the same time, like an overburdened apprentice, he felt as though the more he saw, the less he understood…and then he remembered how dismissive Quibb had been when he told the man about the women at

The Company. Maybe there were no women there and Xi had come to a faulty conclusion; maybe there were women there and that was irrelevant to Quibb....

He left the subway station and entered the tunnel. It was pitch black—a kind of darkness that seemed not only to entail an absence of light, but also a disassociation from the world of mortal men. His steps faltered; his thoughts, which had before been on Quibb's plan, were now overrun with the irrational fears of little children. The darkness before him seemed to be not only physical, but also *spiritual*. He had a visceral reaction to it: his skin crawled; a tingly feeling spread over his hands and feet, as though they were on fire. The darkness had been an ally just hours before; within it, he had hidden from the shimmering sky and all the horrible things spawned within his visions. However, this new darkness was the place of childhood nightmares. He was overcome by the urge to run away—flee back into the light: out onto the streets, where there would be safety in the numbers of the other men...but the adult in him rebelled against all this; for some reason, he had to prove that he was not afraid. He thought of it as a test that Quibb was putting him through. Now strangely defiant, he took a few bold steps into the darkness, stomping his feet against the ties of the track, as though that would chase away the monsters hiding within. Yet, even then, he remained on edge. When a rat squeaked in the darkness, he jumped....

He walked about 200 meters in this manner; after a while, his bold steps grew timid. The rhythm of his breathing was harsh in the darkness. He stopped then, and turned back hopefully towards the train station. He had wanted to see a familiar sight—a reminder that the world of men still existed—but there was only darkness, and *silence*. Amazed, he realized that he could not even hear the men's celebrations anymore, as though they had been sucked into an abyss. Even Quibb's encouraging words were nowhere to be heard—

And then, that old feeling came over him again! A muffled squeal escaped from him as he realized that the creature of the shadows was close—and that he had unwittingly wandered into its realm—

A voice chuckled behind him—so near that he felt the chuckle reverberating inside of him! *He ran*! His leg got caught on a tie, and he almost toppled to the ground, but he somehow managed to keep his balance. He could hear footsteps behind him now—the galloping of a beast, not a man—

"You thought you could hide from me in the darkness?" The creature laughed at his stupidity. The creature's voice was horrible—guttural, growly; the words were slurred, as though all the long, jagged teeth in its mouth made it impossible for its lips to form words correctly. Xi could hardly breathe by now; on top of that, he was not entirely sure that he was still running in a subway tunnel. The ties and tracks that had been so treacherous before, now seemed to be gone; on top of that, he was running so wildly—and *heedlessly*—that he would have banged into the walls of the tunnel by now, or broken his legs on the uneven ties. No, he was not in the tunnel anymore; and just then, he felt something sharp slash across his back! He screamed out! The creature had swiped at him with its claws—

"You can't run from me!" the creature gloated. It slashed him again—it was toying with him: making sport of its prey, like a cat. The creature's laughter echoed through the darkness again; in his terror, Xi felt as though the creature's laughter were something tangible—a weapon that would rip through him—

"I'm going to kill you like you killed me!"

"I *didn't*!" Xi pleaded as he ran.

"—*You* killed *me*!" the creature screamed, enraged by Xi's denial. The claws slashed Xi's back again, but went deeper this time. Indeed, the claws entered him so forcefully that he lost his balance and plopped onto the ground. It seemed to be a concrete floor—not the ties and tracks that should have been there. After the initial spike of pain that came when he collided with the ground, numbness spread throughout his body. He waited to be mauled by the creature, but there was nothing—no claws, no sounds of footsteps closing in. He looked up hopefully; but ahead, he saw the creature emerge from the darkness. Rather, illumination miraculously appeared—a dim band of light, as when dawn brightens the horizon. The creature was standing about 12 meters from him. At last, Xi saw it clearly. Its form, amazingly, was that of a man, but Xi knew at once that it was not human. It was naked, and was covered from head to foot with running sores.

Its face in particular was *hideous*—a mass of erupting pustules. It stood hunched over, as if its bones would not fit within the decaying flesh that covered them. Xi wanted to run, but running—getting to his feet and fleeing from the creature—seemed like too complex a procedure. He could barely even force air into his lungs now—much less run—

"*I'm going to kill you like you killed me!*" the creature announced again. Its teeth were all rotten—*jagged spikes of decay*—

Xi opened his mouth, desperately trying to form out the worlds of his denial/plea, but his jaw was trembling so violently that he could not speak. Indeed, he could do nothing but wait there for his fate. It was then that he noticed the creature's eyes. They were the only things that were not rotten—which still had a connection to the world of men. Xi *knew* those eyes. He had seen through those eyes. Indeed, his own eyes bulged in horror and amazement as the realization seized him: *the creature was G.W.*! Life seemed to drain from his body; and then, he was screaming at the top of his lungs, because the creature was galloping towards him again. It was running on all fours, and Xi forgot about G.W.'s eyes and everything else but the fact that he was now going to die!

Hope is the possibility that one's imagination has not lost sight of reality.
This is what differentiates it from delusion, where the imagination
loses all connection with reality.
VERSE 4367:13 OF *The Teachings*

After a night of experimentation and discovery, Mansmann did not know what to believe anymore. His mind was at once chaotic and sluggish as he sat in the darkness of his lab. All the blinds had been drawn and he really had no idea what time it was in the outside world. He had been locked in his own little world for the last few hours. He had spent that time running tests on the blood he had drawn from the person downstairs. The blood was like nothing he had ever seen before: if he had not drawn it himself, he would not have believed that it came from the veins of a living, breathing human being. He had known that something was very wrong the first time he saw the blood; and now, after examining it through a microscope, he felt as though he had glimpsed upon the thing that would destroy them all. The blood was a super pathogen: an unstoppable, virulent cancer—

He groaned and shook his head, coaxing his mind away from the wild conjectures that would only threaten madness, and towards the few things he knew to be facts. To begin with, it had that yellowish hue—which turned red when exposed to air. That was probably why her menstrual blood had appeared red the first time he saw it....Yes, the thing down in the basement was a woman: he had done a genetic analysis and seen for himself, but it was a woman the likes of which had never before existed on earth. Also, the blood did not have a *type* per se: it was not Type O, or A or *anything*. There were compounds in it that he had never seen before—which seemed structurally impossible from a physical standpoint. Whatever the case, the blood was changing the woman's physiology, the way a retrovirus bioengineered its victim. She was becoming something new and horrible—something that seemed beyond the crude definitions of life and death. In a moment of whimsy, he had experimented on the blood, trying to infect it with syphilis and half a dozen other illnesses—but the super pathogen had wiped out these illnesses within seconds—as if it were some kind of defense mechanism. He had kept repeating this same experiment for hours, unable to believe his eyes. The woman should be dead; the super pathogen should have killed her a million times over, but it seemed to be protecting her. As far as he could tell, the only reason she was unconscious was because of some kind of shock: some kind of mental palsy, triggered by trauma or strain. Besides a lack of nutrients and an iron deficiency—which, for all he knew, could be natural byproducts of the woman's physiology—the woman had some kind of homeopathic immunity to disease. She carried within her veins the ultimate disease—*pure, flowing death*—the way that someone who had been vaccinated carried antibodies….He did not know what to think anymore. What he felt now was similar to what he had felt seven years ago, when he looked through the microscope and saw the absence of X sex chromosomes. There was no doubting the cold facts of science, but he could hardly believe what he *saw*….How was it possible! Part of him wanted to rush down to the basement and demand answers, but he did not even know what questions to ask. There was a woman down in his basement that seemed impervious to disease—*perhaps even to death*—and his mind became sluggish with the possibility of what else she might be. Every time his mind tried to explore those possibilities, he felt a little more drunk. A city of twenty million men—maybe less since the bombing—…and one supernatural woman….A *woman*—this fact began to come into focus as well. Maybe there were others—*of course there were others*! But where…and *how*? His mind raced on; he was drumming his fingers nervously now—

He got up from in front of the microscope and paced around his lab. What should he do now…? Suddenly anxious, his mind went to what would happen if the men of the city found out about the woman. Would they run in here, ripping her and the building apart in their eagerness...or would they shrug their shoulders? Would they even react? After all, there was The Horde now....

There were too many questions. Sighing, he walked to the window and opened the Venetian blinds. He was almost stunned to see how bright it was outside. Looking at his watch, he saw that it was almost half past seven in the morning. He had spent an entire night in that trance....He took a deep breath, trying to clear his head. He frowned: maybe it was only the morning sky, but the purple seemed a little fainter. The sky did not shimmer anymore...and that fact left him relieved. He probably had not realized it before this moment, but the purple, shimmering sky had terrified him— perhaps more than the bombing. The sky had triggered a kind of primal fear in him; he had not been able to think straight, as though the distortion in the sky had been implanting something in his soul....

The Voice was still blaring down the street; despite the earliness of the day, there were hundreds of men on the street, clearing away the signs of destruction. More likely than not, many of them had been working all night...and dozens of men were walking around with machine guns over their shoulders. As The Voice's rant turned to The Horde and plans for its return, a few of these armed men screamed out in defiance and fired their guns into the air....Since the bombing ended yesterday evening, there had been a strange kind of hopefulness in the men—but also a growing bestiality. On first glance, it seemed like a contradiction; but as Mansmann stared down at the men, he saw that there was a horrible kind of perfection to what they were becoming. As he listened to The Voice's latest rant, and saw the effect on the men, he suddenly realized that The Voice of Conscience was some kind of God of War—a modern-day Ares—bestowing mortals with the wherewithal to destroy civilizations. His mind tried to go to it, but he had neither the time nor the patience to think about it. Also, at that very moment, something began to chime within the room. After looking about confusedly, he realized that it was the videophone. When it occurred to him that the caller could only be one person, his innards convulsed so violently that he was forced to rest his hands on his knees to keep from falling. The videophone was in the corner of the room; with his stomach muscles so tight, he walked over to it with the shambling trot of a chimpanzee.

When he answered the device, Shaka was staring back at him. There was a strange intensity about the man's eyes that made Mansmann look away timidly—

"Good morning, Shaka," Mansmann found himself saying. "How may I help you?"

"Nothing in particular—just wanted to know that you made it through the last few days safely."

"…Thank you, sir."

"No need for thanks—I'm just protecting my investment," Shaka said with an equivocal smile that seemed layered with meaning and malice.

"…I'm all right," Mansmann said at last, when he could think of nothing else to say.

"The Company has contributed a lot of resources to your research efforts, Dr. Mansmann. Have you made any notable discoveries lately?"

As Mansmann watched the gleam in Shaka's eyes, his blood ran cold! *Shaka knew about the woman!* There were probably spying devices in the diagnostic tools Shaka had furnished him with. He felt weak—trapped and undone. The faint, menacing smile was still on Shaka's face. Mansmann forced himself to speak:

"I'm looking at some promising data now—nothing certain yet."

"Very well," Shaka said. "Tell me when you have something definite."

"Yes, sir." Then, when the call ended, Mansmann was left with a horrible feeling of bereavement and vulnerability—as though someone had come into his house while he was away, and stolen all that was precious to him. Outside, The Voice was still ranting and the men were still toiling away. Mansmann walked over to the window, looked out on the world uneasily, then closed the blinds.

Beware of anyone who asserts that the most intractable of problems
can be fixed in a few easy steps: that man is either a fool or a con artist.
The primary reason that problems persist is that people insist on
believing (wrongly) that they have the solutions. Logic dictates that if they
actually had the solutions, then the problems would not exist.
At the very least, they would not be intractable.
VERSE 1121:34 OF *The Teachings*

After his videophone call, Shaka turned his mind to some paperwork. He was sitting at his desk, staring down at some printed figures Stein had given him, when the door suddenly opened. The entrant walked right up to his desk and stood there patiently. When the affront of this intrusion registered in Shaka's mind (the entrant had not even knocked!) Shaka looked up with rage already bubbling in his eyes…but Circe was smiling at him.

"The word on the street is that you want me dead," Circe said.

For a moment, Shaka was lost: caught between the vengeful impulses he had been nourishing all these days, and the simple shock that Circe was actually standing before him, smiling in that way that he remembered from that dimension with the beach. It was only when his gaze wandered over to the open doorway that he came to his senses.

"Guards!" he called.

"I sent them to get something to eat." Then, with a laugh: "Don't tell me you're afraid of me?" When Shaka looked longingly at the door, Circe continued: "They'll be back any moment, Shaka—no need to worry."

"…Why are you here?"

"I'm here because you've been trying to find me."

Something about the entire exchange was maddening—especially with Circe smiling at him like that—and he snapped: "Then why didn't you come sooner?"

"You didn't want me to get hit by any Horde bombs, did you, Shaka?"

Shaka stared at Circe for a while; as always, he was unnerved by Circe's twinkling Glory to the Goddess tattoo. He almost had to force himself to look away—it was as though his thought processes were being eroded by the power of Circe's stare. Shaking his head confusedly, he again looked to the open doorway. Circe chuckled.

"Still looking for your guards?" Circe teased him. "Very well....Guards, you may enter now!" At that, the two robed men entered the room, their faces wearing puzzled, anxious expressions. Their gaits were weird, as though they were fighting with their legs. They walked up in this strange manner, then stopped when Circe put up her hand and gestured for them to do so.

Circe laughed again, saying: "Feel more secure now, Shaka?"

"Get her!" Shaka screamed to the guards, but the men were frozen in place. Circe gestured with her head then, and the men immediately began to perform a bizarre kind of striptease.

"What the hell is the meaning of this!"

"You're right, Shaka," Circe said, grimacing at the men's hackneyed gyrations. "It is somewhat stomach-turning." Then, to the guards, "Leave us for now, gentlemen." At that, the two men, freed of whatever enchantment had held them, pulled their robes over their exposed nakedness and shuffled out of the room.

Shaka first watched it all with a sense of outrage, but then he suddenly found himself smiling. "Congratulations, Circe. *Congratulations*. First you sent me to a dimension that almost wiped my mind, and now you're making fools out of my guards. Well done."

"You misunderstand me fully."

"Do I?"

"Yes. First of all, you misinterpreted the dimension I sent you to. Few men get the opportunity to glimpse the face of God."

Shaka laughed heartily, saying: "The only face I saw in that dimension was yours; and despite your parlor tricks, I'm not yet ready to consider you God. Besides, I don't like people messing with my head."

Circe smiled. "'Messing with your head'? Is that what you call it? Men who think that they can meet God and not be stripped of their power and sense of self are fools. Like most men, your problem is that you want a God you can control."

Shaka smiled. "...And what kind of God do you want?"

"One who will see me as I am."

"As you are? And how is that?"

Circe smiled and took a step closer. "Have you ever seen me naked, Shaka?"

"Of course I have," Shaka said, strangely flustered, "—you were always dancing naked at your concerts."

"And what did you see when I danced naked?"

Shaka opened his mouth, but all he could think to say was, "Skin."

"What if I were to tell you that I've never danced naked at my concerts?"

"What are you trying to say?"

"What if that was just a projection of your mind?"

Shaka shook his head at the weirdness of it all; he instinctively glanced at the open doorway for the guards again—

"See me now, Shaka," Circe said then.

"I've played enough games today," Shaka said, going back to his paperwork and waving his hand dismissively at Circe, but—

"See me as I truly am," Circe said again.

When Shaka looked up, he was mesmerized by what he saw—which was strange, because what he saw was so simple. He seemed to stare for minutes on end. His mind seemed to travel the entire gamut of perception, from shock and confusion, to the most profound levels of enlightenment. At last, he frowned and said, "What are you?"

"Like I told you before, I'm the product of science. When men look at me, they see what they want to see—"

"They also see what you want them to see." And as he said it, he was startled to realize that he was looking at the old, mesmerizingly beautiful Circe again.

"Yes."

"...Why have you come here?"

"I'm here because I need to be seen for what I am—if only for a little while. As you, yourself, must know by now, it's exhausting to make men see things that aren't there."

There are things that can only be comprehended by the soul—that are beyond words and the capacity of human beings to explain themselves.
VERSE 2321:3 OF *The Teachings*

The Goddess' mind drifted in the nothingness. It was so dark that she could not tell if her eyes were open or closed. She only knew that the darkness was somehow tangible—as if she were wearing a heavy shroud. She could hardly breathe from the weight of it; when she tried to move, she realized that she could not—that she was bound somehow—

And then, there was an explosion of light and motion. The images were blurry at first; but soon, everywhere she looked, she saw those Horde robots—*millions* of them—roaming over the landscape like ants. And what made it all so disorienting and terrifying, was that it was as if reality had been ripped apart, because those millions of robots had millions of backdrops behind them—devastated wastelands within cities; towns that were still on fire; even dark forests and underground bunkers. The robots were marching in their battle suits, gunning down men, dragging away screaming, terrified women…but they were just ghosts, she realized. She had been about to scream as one of them approached her, but then it walked right through her. The sensation this caused was eerie: like having a cold breath blowing down one's neck. Worse, she felt as though being in this place was diluting her consciousness: flooding her soul with the reality of The Horde, so that soon there would be nothing of *her* left.

This has to be a dream! she reasoned. However, even in dreams people wanted to stay alive. Even in dreams people feared pain and death. Moreover, while dreams were things that people conjured, she got the sense that this place was conjuring *her*; and that if anything happened, it would be she, and not this place, that would fade away forever—

"You're right to be afraid," someone said at her back.

The Goddess whirled around and saw a figure emerge from the nothingness. *It was Quibb*; the Goddess retreated a step. She opened her mouth, fumbling with words that refused to come.

"—This isn't a dream," Quibb clarified. "This is the consciousness of The Horde." Quibb stopped about three meters from her, and stood watching her critically.

"How..." She ran out of breath. "...How did I get here?" she said when she could breathe again.

"You can be anywhere you wish—you're the Goddess."

The Goddess frowned as her eyes roamed over Quibb's face. "I *know* you."

Quibb smiled. "You know me as well as anyone can know me."

The Goddess frowned deeper: "I can't remember anything about you, but I *know* you. You were in that place on the mountain. I recognize your voice."

"Yes."

For a moment, the Goddess was distracted by something on her left: some Horde ghosts had just literally blown a man's head off; the severed head lay on the ground, where its blood-splattered lips seemed to gasp for air—an involuntary neural response perhaps. The Goddess forced herself to look away. She blinked deeply, then looked at Quibb again. "...How did you find me?"

"I've always known where you were."

This confirmed something that she had always known, and her spirits flagged. "...I was allowed to escape," she said after a moment.

"Yes. Having you here in the city serves The Horde's purpose."

"What purpose is that?"

"It's important to them that the men believe in you."

"Why?"

"They think that will make things simpler for them after they take over. If they control the men's god, then they control the men—"

"*They?*" she said, annoyed by the semantics. "You speak as though you don't have anything to do with it. It was *your* voice that I heard back in that place, telling me what to do, what to *think*..."

"I was there, but now I'm here."

That answered nothing, but the Goddess moved on. "...What do you want from me?"

"There will be a rally at Central Park in a few days. I want you to go."

"What if I refuse?" she said, still combative.

"You won't," Quibb said with a smile, "—and not because I'm forcing you to go, but because you want to go. You'll *need* to go, just to clarify things in your own mind."

"Why should I believe anything you say?"

"Your beliefs are irrelevant. What God believes doesn't matter—only what men believe She believes."

"You don't believe that I'm God," the Goddess said suspiciously.

"What I believe is also irrelevant. What matters is that the men believe in you and that their beliefs will demand certain things of you."

"Things like what?"

"Courage...self-sacrifice, maybe. You're going to have to ask yourself if you're willing to die for them."

"...And if I'm not?"

"If you're not, they may just kill you anyway," Quibb said with a shrug. "Either way, the path to life and enlightenment will begin at that rally in Central Park—

"Anyway," Quibb began in a new, more urgent, voice, "Time is short, and I have to leave now, but there is something I need you to remember before I leave. Take my hand," Quibb said, walking two steps closer to her and extending his hand.

The Goddess hesitated.

"Take it," Quibb whispered, encouragingly, stretching out his long, slender fingers.

The Goddess stared at his hand uneasily, but her own hand was stretching out now. And then, when their hands touched, there was a flash of light and the Goddess felt the universe re-writing itself once again—

She screamed out; in the real world, her bloodcurdling cries brought Mansmann and the drag queens to her bedside. While she saw images from her past—of men holding her down and imposing their will on her—Mansmann and the others called to her and held her, asking her what was wrong.

As for Mansmann, thinking that she was having some kind of seizure, he was just about to look around for something to shove in her mouth (so that she would not bite her tongue) when a shiver suddenly went up his spine. It was the same feeling from seven years ago—when he drove home from his lab and stared at the face of the 10-year-old Messiah on the TV. In fact, that exact image flashed in his mind. Mansmann backed away from the bed, realizing that the person before him was *the Goddess*. His mind seemed to erupt with every kind of madness then. He had before laughed at the woman's cult, thinking them fools; but remembering her strange, yellow blood and its invulnerability to disease, he could not stop himself from considering the possibilities. He seeped into the abyss of those thoughts— losing himself in them. It was only when the woman—*the Goddess* screamed out again, that he finally came to his senses.

As for the Goddess, she was still trapped within the murky horrors of her past. The blurry figures above her—the *men*—were still holding her down. She could not make sense of her surroundings, and this only escalated her terror. All that she could do was fight, and yet even fighting seemed futile. Their vise grips were unbreakable—

Her head was strapped down now; more restraints were applied to her wrists, ankles, and around her midsection, so that it was now impossible to move. Something was put over her eyes, so that she was trapped in the darkness! Her breathing became harsh and irregular: it had an echo that disturbed her for some reason. Then, while she waited for something to happen, she heard a high-pitched noise. It seemed to come from far away, but then she felt a point of heat in the back of her neck; instantaneously, the sound seemed to increase a thousandfold, as did the heat. After a moment of shock and confusion, she realized that something was being drilled into the nape of her neck! The pain was impossible to describe! A piece of metal with a serrated edge was revolving in her neck. She could feel the drill's reverberations throughout her entire body. The drill seemed to be in her head now—*in her brain*! She arched her back then and, gathering up the last of her strength, she screamed!

This was how she returned to the real world. Initially, she did not differentiate Mansmann and the drag queens from the figures of her past. All that mattered was that she was free now; and still traumatized by the recollection of the thing inserted into her neck, she slapped Mansmann's hands away and began clawing at the back of her neck—

"Get it out!" she screamed. They tried to restrain her, thinking that she was delirious, but by the time they managed to pull her fingers away, they were already bloody—

"*Get it out!*" she screamed again—this time as a plea to them, or maybe just a plea to the universe. Mansmann, still flustered from his epiphany about her, told the others to turn her over, so that he could treat the wound. The Goddess was still screaming; Mansmann shone the light into the wound, but then frowned when he saw something metallic within the bloody flesh. He grabbed his medical bag. Then, getting out some tweezers, he ordered Respoli-Priestess and the others to keep her still as he pulled out what seemed to be a microchip. Mansmann stared at it in amazement. There was a tiny blinking light on it, which seemed to mesmerize him. Then, overcome by a queasy feeling, he tossed it on the nightstand and smashed it with the heaviest thing he had at hand—the lamp. He was trembling; they all looked at him in horror, then they looked at the Goddess, who had passed out by then. Seeing her open wound again brought Mansmann to his senses, and he got sutures and bandages from his bag.

There is not a man alive who, given the chance to be God, would not avail himself of the opportunity to rule men's souls. This simple dynamic has accounted for most of the world's evil since the dawn of time.
VERSE 2331:5 OF *The Teachings*

Now, on all the video billboards and screens, there were images of what The Horde had done in Buenos Aires. It was as though the cameras were showing images of a desert, because all that there was, was a wasteland. There were corpses everywhere—many of them smoldering; there were images of wild dogs pulling at limbs, gorging themselves on carrion... and there were images of men in shock. Some of them walked around with mortal wounds and did not even know it....

Xi screamed out! His eyes burst open, and somehow the sun was there. The glare made geometric shapes dance before his eyes; he clamped his eyes shut, feeling the burning pain traveling up his optic nerve and into his brain. He groaned and lay like that for a few moments, too groggy to move—to even make sense of where and who he was....Maybe two minutes passed like this. Eventually, he remembered the subway tunnel and the creature: *G.W.*

He looked around: the morning sun was rising over some gutted tenements a few blocks away. He, himself, was in an empty lot. In fact, there were no standing buildings within blocks of him—nor were there any people about. A recent fire had seared the ground where he lay. The charred smell of the earth made him want to retch—especially on an empty stomach. He remembered the purple, shimmering sky and glanced up uneasily; but somehow, the shimmering was gone. That was a relief—but the mystery of how he had gotten here, and what had *happened*, left him feeling as lost and vulnerable as ever. Pooling his strength, he sat up...he felt different: as though his body had been systematically stripped, and then reassembled. Even as he sat there groggily, looking at the barren landscape, he struggled to get used to his new body. Instinctively, he looked at his arms—where there had before been infected wounds. Now, there was not even a scar! He caressed the skin meditatively. He remembered his back—where the creature had slashed him in the tunnels. He inserted his arm under his filthy shirt; but again, there were no wounds! How much time had passed...? Then, for the first time, he wondered how he had gotten outside—how he was still *alive*. He shook his head: maybe none of the events of the tunnel had happened; maybe the creature of the shadows had been nothing but a figment of his imagination—like the men who had been hunting rats with him. He was about to add Quibb to that list of hallucinations, but he needed Quibb: needed the fantasy desperately, so that the actions of his recent past would make sense. In his new fantasy, Quibb had done all this. Quibb had *saved* him from the tunnels; Quibb had cured his wounds; Quibb was *God*. Xi suddenly yearned to go out there and proselytize: spread this wondrous feeling to all the people still wallowing in ignorance and idolatry.

It was then, as if on cue, that the premonition flashed before his eyes. The wasteland before him was replaced by the relative verdure of Central Park...and there were hundreds of thousands—perhaps *millions*—of men cheering. At first, their cheers seemed without meaning and without an object, but then Xi saw a man standing on a platform before all those cheering millions. It was Mendez, and his words were filling the men with the rapture that Xi now felt! Xi had never seen Mendez before, but he *knew* the man on the stage was Mendez. This information was supplied by the vision—programmed into the imagery, so that when the vision ended, Xi knew exactly what was to be done, just as Moses had known what had to be done when he descended from Mont Sinai with the Ten Commandments. Xi was shaking now—not with fear, but with *rapture*: thankfulness that Quibb had furnished him with such clarity. Suddenly imbued with great energy and drive, Xi rose from the ground. He surveyed the landscape—all 360 degrees of it. On the corner, there was a street sign. Xi, whose muscles were still stiff, shuffled towards the sign. …He needed something to drink: his mouth and throat were parched, and the charred odor of the earth did not help matters. However, when he arrived at the street sign, he stared at it for about 30 seconds with a smile on his face. Somehow, he was at 116th Street and 4th Avenue—only a block away from Mendez's lair!

Quibb's will had done it all—had taken care of all contingencies—so Xi put his faith in him and continued shuffling down the street. As there were no standing buildings nearby, there were no video billboards around—which meant that there was no Voice of Conscience. The landscape was ugly—seemed scarred and diseased. Whether the surrounding buildings had been destroyed in The Horde's bombing, or by the neglect characteristic of poverty-stricken communities, he could not tell. Whatever the case, without The Voice to guide the men and prod them into clearing this area of rubble and filth, the surrounding blocks were a kind of dead zone in the city: an empty wasteland within an overpopulated wasteland. There was something eerie and lonesome about it, but Xi's mind was still being numbed by thoughts of finding Mendez and bringing Quibb's glory to fruition….

Soon, he reached the intersection Quibb had specified; and just as Quibb had said, there was only one building standing at the intersection. Even then, the upper stories had been burned out a long time ago. Beneath the stoop, there was a basement door. Xi walked down to the door and knocked on it, then stood there with the same strange feeling of euphoria bubbling within him. Soon he would meet a living part of Quibb's plan. He almost wanted to laugh out—

Xi heard steps coming up to the door. He smiled as he was watched through the spyglass.

"What do you want?" a man screamed from the other side of the locked door—both threateningly and uneasily.

"Qui…" Xi smiled at his mistake, "—The Voice of Conscience sent me with your destiny."

There seemed to be a moment of hesitation, then the door was unlocked and opened. Xi smiled again when he saw Mendez. Before him, in rumpled, too-tight clothes that were strangely clean looking—as if they had not been worn in a while—was a middle-aged Latino with hair reaching down to the floor. Mendez looked back at him shyly—*uneasily*—and Xi smiled, coming to the conclusion that the man obviously had no idea what his destiny was.

After a moment of uncertainty, Mendez nodded, gesturing for Xi to enter the small, dark apartment. Xi complied. An odor redolent of mildew and dirty socks pervaded the place. Mendez led him into a back room that was desolate, except for some sophisticated-looking computer equipment. The only real embellishments were some pornographic posters on the wall. Quibb's voice was playing over the speakers of the computer; on several computer screens, the images being broadcast on the billboards of the city were showing—

"You were expecting more, weren't you?" Mendez said with a nervous laugh.

"…It doesn't matter what you are now," Xi said after thinking about it objectively, "—The Voice knows what you will be in the future."

Mendez's forced smile died away, and he looked at Xi gravely. "…Who is that Voice guy anyway," he whispered, as if he feared being overheard. "How does he do all that stuff?"

Xi thought about it for a few moments, then smiled contentedly. "He understands power."

Mendez nodded. It did not entirely explain things, but at least it was something to work with. He looked up at Xi with narrowed eyes, then: "How are you going to help me?"

"Pardon?"

"The Voice said you'd help me become a leader."

"…Oh." He thought about the vision again and another smile came to his face. "There is going to be a great rally at Central Park," he began. "You will be on a podium, before *millions*, and they will be cheering for you."

Mendez grumbled anxiously, then went to his desk and lit a joint. He stood uncomfortably in the middle of the room, holding the joint with a trembling hand. Xi stood back and looked at the man critically.

"Don't be afraid of your destiny," Xi reassured him. Now that Quibb had remade him, he had no worries. In fact, Xi had just been about to smile once more, when he glanced at one of the computer screens (where the broadcast from the billboard was being shown) and saw his picture! That reminder of the world of men momentarily washed away his feeling of euphoric invulnerability; then, as his jaw dropped, and he stared at the screen with anxious, unbelieving eyes, his name was shown beneath the picture. After that, in bold, scrolling letters, there was the message: "$100,000 REWARD FOR INFORMATION ON THE WHEREABOUTS OF THIS MAN. CONTACT THE COMPANY FOR FURTHER INFORMATION."

It was then that Mendez laughed out, saying, "Dr. Xi Wang: *that's you!*"

Xi shook his head feebly—

"Shaka's after you too, huh!" Mendez said, laughing out again. As an amazed grin came over Mendez's face, Xi had a wild impulse to leap at the man and strangle him: claw out those eyes that were now seeing though him; beat his head in, until his brains oozed out…but then Xi remembered that Mendez was part of Quibb's plan; and when he realized that his mindless rage had left him on the verge of threatening his master's grand design, Xi bowed his head in shame.

IX

Some say that the ultimate goal of science—and mankind—will be realized when man can create life, but all of man's research into life has ultimately only taught him how to better destroy himself.
VERSE 3432:10-11 OF *The Teachings*

As always, the days passed quickly and disappeared in a blur. It was the third day since Xi had introduced himself to Mendez. On the first day, The Voice of Conscience had mentioned Mendez's name—and his virtue—a couple of times during his hourly diatribes on the advancement of society. By the middle of the afternoon (about half an hour after The Voice revealed Mendez's location and his need for volunteers) dozens of men had flocked to Mendez's door. At first, they had looked to Xi to know what to do, and he had told them to go out into the city and spread the gospel that a change was needed—and that in four days Mendez's vision for the city would be laid out in a speech at Central Park. However, within a matter of hours, by which time The Voice seemed to be talking about Mendez almost exclusively, it had been beyond Xi. Hundreds of men had showed up at Mendez's door to offer their services. Guards had posted themselves at doorways; the surrounding streets had been cleared of rubble; and everywhere one looked, all remnants of the "dead zone" began to disappear. On top of that, equipment for Mendez's great speech began to appear spontaneously—like speakers and amplifiers. Men with technical expertise showed up and put themselves to work; men showed up with food and clothes and machine guns, so that Xi began to feel unnecessary and overwhelmed and *jealous* that he was no longer the vital cog in Quibb's plan.

That first night, Xi had fallen asleep in a corner of Mendez's basement apartment—or passed out there. When he woke up, it had seemed as though *weeks* had passed. Mendez had washed, gotten a haircut, and changed into a brand new suit. With this new ensemble, he had looked like a prototypical conservative politician—with one of those plastic-looking hairdos and an equivocal smile that seemed unable to convey warmth, no matter how far it stretched across his face. Xi had opened his eyes to find reporters from Shaka's networks interviewing Mendez in his "humble beginnings." The basement was so cramped that one of the reporters had actually stepped on Xi's hand as he lay on the ground. Xi had gotten groggily to his feet, overcome by his old sense that the universe was mad. Mendez had been standing before the cameras with a news anchor's ease. He had been glib and witty; men had laughed and given praise and signed on to the struggle after hearing him. Indeed, as Xi looked on, he had found himself thinking that if there had been women, then they would have flocked to the man. However, perhaps more advantageous in this age, Mendez had exuded the kind of sex appeal that drew *men* in droves—that strange combination of being able to promise sustenance and threaten death at the same time, seen for instance among the alpha males of wolf packs.

…Now, on the third day, with both Shaka's networks and The Voice of Conscience describing Mendez's Central Park speech as the seminal event of civilization, there were so many men about, that Xi stood around ineptly, trying not to get in the way. The volunteers and converts literally cluttered the streets around Mendez's tenement. Tent communities and shantytowns had sprung up amongst the surrounding vacant lots. There were now huge video billboards on the block, just like most other places in the city. Images of The Horde's worldwide campaign of destruction were continually shown, so that the men were now actually *consuming* death. Everything was coming together now, so that Xi no longer had any doubts that they would defeat The Horde when it returned. Quibb had said that they would win, and it was now impossible for him to think otherwise.

As for Mendez, by now there were men to groom and outfit him, and men enlisted to be his bodyguards. There were "yes men" and men who thought it all a party. There were men marching around with the adversarial gleam of generals in their eyes, as well as moralists bent on restoring the moral standards of yesteryear. Mendez's campaign commercials were blaring everywhere by now; his smiling face adorned hundreds of thousands of buildings and screens. ...And tomorrow, at last, was the day when his great speech would be given. For the men of the city, Mendez's words would be their words; Mendez's thoughts would soon become their actions; and once the grand designs of his speech had been implemented, there would be peace and rebirth.

Xi sat in the corner of the cramped basement and watched it all with awe. Of course, by now Mendez had forgotten all about him. Presently, needing some fresh air (and having no reason to remain), Xi went outside and began to wander the surrounding shantytown. By now, it had grown to encompass tens of thousands of men: true believers who would *die* for Mendez; and in the strange way of the brainwashed, the men had not only begun to believe that their only choice was to follow Mendez, but also that they had *always* followed Mendez. Through Quibb's will, the solar system had changed its orientation, so that Mendez became the sun, and all the other stars and planets seemed pale in comparison. Only Xi seemed to remember that three days ago, Mendez had been nothing. Yet, even Xi did not think it relevant anymore: all that mattered was tomorrow, and the day after....

Around noon, the men began to queue to get some greasy-smelling soup being concocted in several huge steel drums. As such, there were about half a dozen quasi-parallel lines snaking to the drums. Xi got on one of those lines—but more because he had nothing else to do than because he was actually hungry. The smell of the concoctions was sickening. He was actually holding his breath when he looked over to the line on his left and noticed that two men were staring at him—looking at him as though he were a ghost. At first, he thought that they recognized him from Shaka's advertisements, but the intensity of the horror in the men's eyes told him that their reaction had nothing to do with the potential cash windfall of capturing him. In fact, they seemed so agitated that he became convinced that they were looking at someone or something else. He looked away and was ready to forget the entire thing. However, he sensed them looking at him from the corner of his eye, and when he looked up at them again, the men jumped. He frowned. The men began mumbling to one another; one of them pointed to Xi with a trembling finger. Xi looked at them more closely. He had thought that they were strangers, but there seemed to be something familiar about them. In fact, he was now convinced that he knew them. Something about them called to him, so that he unconsciously stepped off the line and took a step towards them. Unfortunately, seeing him approaching, the men became more agitated; and when Xi was about five meters away, one of the men screamed:

"You're *dead*! We saw you die!"

As Xi froze, the terrified men ran off in the opposite direction. Xi stared at them in bewilderment; he replayed the man's cryptic words in his mind, able to make no sense of them. But then, as his mind returned to their faces, he felt as though he had just been clubbed in the head! He could hardly believe it, but somehow or another, those were the two men he had been with when Quibb showed up that first time! Their names were Clem and Steve! Their names popped into his head all of a sudden, along with all the things that Quibb had stumped him with that first night. Yes, their names were Clem and Steve, and he had met them about five years ago. He had been cooking rat stew in an abandoned building, and they had come up and asked for some. That was the extent of it. Xi suddenly laughed out. *He remembered*! However, when he looked up, he realized that the two men had disappeared. Xi took off in their direction…but they were gone. They had run as though they had seen the Devil….It took Xi about another minute to realize that if Clem and Steve were real, then Quibb had lied to him. This realization had to break down his defenses—to overcome the antibodies that Quibb had implanted in him—and when it finally managed to infect its meaning into him, his body literally slumped. Quibb had lied to him! Quibb was a fraud—*all of it had been a scam*! The realization left his muscles quivering. Quibb had brainwashed those men—just like the man had brainwashed *him*. Memories had been wiped from his mind—maybe others had been put in their place…*but why*? Damn it, that was always the thing: the *why*!

After the strange scene with Clem and Steve, all the surrounding men were looking at Xi oddly. When he realized this, he felt suddenly shy. The old feeling of being out of place came over him again. He had to get away from this place—away from Mendez and the thousands of converts…away from *everything*. He scanned the area one last time for Clem and Steve. However, when his eyes came to one of the billboards, they stopped and he stared at the screen with a blank expression. Once again he was staring at his old work ID; but now, it had been computer enhanced to show how he looked now. The reward for information on his whereabouts was now up to $500,000!

…Xi wandered off. He did not look to see if anyone noticed him: he could not really care anymore. At first, he merely shuffled through the sprawling shantytown aimlessly. Quibb was just a man—not a majestic god. Worse than that, Xi, by helping Mendez, had been duped into setting something in motion that for the first time seemed *ominous*. For once, the image of Mendez standing before a cheering crowd of millions seemed terrible…and Mendez's rise to power would only be a minor milestone in Quibb's master plan—Xi was sure of it. Xi felt stupid and weak; nevertheless, after a few moments, he reached a place of mental clarity and inner peace that he had not felt in years. He nodded to himself: there was no choice now but to go to The Company. Now that he no longer had the delusion of Quibb to give him false hopes, he had nothing to lose. Perhaps worse than that, there was nothing else to be gained from life—nothing that could be done to him that had not already been done. On the edge of the shantytown, someone had left a bicycle lying around; without thought, Xi got on and pedaled off—towards The Company.

Never trust people whose only virtue is their innocence—and who never pass up the opportunity to point out their innocence. True innocents, by their very nature, would not be able to make the distinction between innocence and corruption, as they would not have any point of reference— any experience with corruption whatsoever. As such, those who continually flaunt their innocence are not only deceiving you, but themselves as well.
VERSE 1132:3 OF *The Teachings*

The Goddess had spent the preceding days in a stupor. After the thing in her neck was removed, it was as though her body's natural rhythms and mechanisms for maintenance were thrown off balance. First, her temperature soared, so that she had to be immersed within a bathtub full of ice and cold water. Then, after it seemed that her temperature had stabilized, it dropped radically, so that heat packs had to be used. Through it all, she remained unresponsive, or mumbled a few cryptic words from whatever dream she was having.

Earlier that day, during the hourly ritual where Mansmann and the entire band gathered around her bed to assess her health (or to pray, as was the case with the cult) the Goddess had reached out her hand. In her delirium, she had pulled the little boy—the Shirley Temple clone—into bed with her. She had done it unconsciously, but the little boy had seemed content to be with her, no matter the circumstances. The men had stood around watching her hold the little boy as though he were her favorite teddy bear—or her *son*. They had all felt the longing for a woman in their hearts at that moment, because what was the maternal instinct, as expressed by girls playing with dolls or mothers snuggling with their children, if not a manifestation of female sexuality...?

As for the Goddess, through it all, her mind had been like her body:

struggling to regain some measure of stability. It vacillated from devastated dreamscapes, where Horde robots inhabited the shadows, to teaming metropolises within which millions of suffering characters rushed towards self-destruction. Her mind was conjuring all of human history—everything from the Big Bang and the dawn of time, to the last fleeting hours of human existence. Only when it reached this final stage, did she suddenly realize that she again had a body. It was not the body of a woman, but a girl's body, growing into fullness and sexual maturity. It was a body beset by mysteries and yearnings—which cried out for caresses and exploration. The memories of puberty, which for women came in the form of first boyfriends, first menstruations and first furtive sexual experiences, were absent for her. However, she had the body, itself. Its impulses and yearnings were her memories; when she touched it, she felt real. But more than that, when she touched it, the earth moved around her; the sun rose and fell in the heavens; ocean tides ebbed and flowed. In fact, now, the entire universe seemed to be attuned to the movements and rhythms of her body, as if she were the conduit of all possibility. As her fingertips caressed her skin, new realities came into being; as blood flowed through her veins, new strains of thought were brought to fruition. Her menses brought cataclysms to the world; her laughter brought sunny days and peaceful sunsets. She was the receptacle and the engine of all that ever was and all that would ever be. With this realization, her body shuddered, and she lay on the bed, exhausted, helpless and at peace, still clutching the little boy to her body....

*There is the illusion of power in thwarting God,
even if in so doing one destroys one's self.*
VERSE 344:9 OF *The Teachings*

Xi looked ahead blankly as he rode towards The Company. *Quibb had lied to him.* The thought almost made him want to cry. Quibb was just a man after all, with a man's motives; worse than that, an inkling of what those motives could possibly be, made Xi's skin crawl. Through Quibb's orchestration, an army of millions was being organized. There were soldiers everywhere now—or at least men with machine guns. All the factories were now making them around the clock. Heavy guns and tanks were being churned out as well, and distributed throughout the city. They were all falling in step with Quibb's masterpiece. The man was like an octopus, but with millions of tentacles—into millions of souls. Presently, Quibb's voice was reminding them of tomorrow's Central Park rally. As Xi listened to it, he had no doubt that Mendez would be running everything within a matter of days. Militias were already reporting to him; remnants of corporations, with the notable exception of The Company, were already casting their lot to him (and even The Company tacitly supported him by broadcasting his campaign commercials over the billboards!). Mendez would be running everything; and through Mendez, Quibb would be their master....

Xi felt dead inside. He pedaled the bike for about twenty minutes, but hardly saw what was about him. When he reached midtown, he saw that the thousands of rickshaws were out again, leaving the streets a chaotic swirl of colors. The men were still repairing the city, following Quibb's voice. In fact, whereas other areas of the city were still being cleared of rubble, the closer he got to Company Square, the more it looked as if it had never even been bombed. The windows were all new; the sidewalks and streets seemed to gleam with their newness. Even the people who strolled down the sidewalks seemed freshly made. The holographic billboards here were state of the art. The images looked so real that for a moment he was taken aback by the hulking 20-meter figures that danced above his head. He gasped when he saw the Image Broadcast Complex. It had not only been rebuilt: it seemed twice as large as before. It seemed like a glittering crystal palace, stretching 30 stories into the sky and taking up at least an entire city block. He stood across the boulevard from Company Square (actually, the street had been widened as well) gawking at the hulking structures up in that strange super-world. As the afternoon sunlight glistened off the dark pyramid, the light seemed to refract and bathe the nonmetallic alloy in all the colors of the rainbow. The effect was almost hypnotic. It did not seem possible that such a place could exist—that such a place could even be made by the hands of men—and especially in only a matter of *days*!

It was at that moment that Quibb's words confronted him: *A wounded body directs blood to the vital organs.* He looked around, seeing the sparkling newness. As he remembered the first night of the bombing, and that door leading to those dozens of subterranean floors, he once again came to the conclusion that this *had* to be where the women were being kept. Women were the only resource valuable enough for a worldwide consortium, such as The Horde, to expend so much effort…but he kept remembering how Quibb had laughed when he tried to tell him about the women. Was there something out there more valuable than women…?

He was just about to sigh in frustration, when a pack of five men surrounded him. It was not done with hostility, but with the efficiency of an amoeba. "Dr. Wang!" one of them said gleefully, "we've been looking all over for you!" Looking up, Xi recognized two of the men from his last visit. Their menacing smiles were still there, and that seemed appropriate somehow.

Knowing what one cannot do does not necessarily tell one what to do.
Coming to a dead end only means that one has come the wrong way—
it does not tell one the correct route.
VERSE 875:8 OF *The Teachings*

When the Goddess finally opened her eyes, there were murmuring figures above her, lost in the blinding light that now shone directly into her eyes. She panicked instinctively, because what she now saw was what she had remembered when she shuffled down those unending corridors that first time. She was overcome by that old fear again: that she would wake up and find that her escape had all been a dream. And just then, the light began to dissipate, and the murmuring voices became louder— more urgent. She quickly checked her body to see if she could flee; but she knew, instantly, that she was too weak. She prepared herself for the worst. She was already gasping to scream when the world, and the figures above her, suddenly came into focus. An old man was staring down at her, deep concern showing on his face. The drag queens were at his shoulder, looking relieved. Their presence was a relief to her, because it meant that she had actually escaped…but then she remembered Quibb: all the things she had been told within what Quibb had called, "The Horde's consciousness." …Her mind could not deal with that now. She had to catch her breath first, so she concentrated on the things in the room with her: the old man, Respoli-Priestess and the others. The murmuring that she had heard before was their prayers. She saw that they were all in a room now, and that she was lying in a bed, holding the little boy—who was still fast asleep. There was a window off to her right, and the faint rays of the evening sun shone through it. She stared longingly out of that window—forgetting about Respoli-Priestess and the others for the moment. Quibb's voice—*the voice of The Horde*—could be heard outside the window. She listened to it now, shuddering within herself as The Voice mentioned tomorrow's Central Park rally. It was just as Quibb had told her. For a moment, she closed her eyes, resigned to whatever fate Quibb was planning for her—whatever schemes The Horde was constructing around her; and at that moment, residual images of what The Horde was doing in far-flung corners of the globe left her feeling weak and helpless. She could still sense it amassing out there. Worse than that, she could feel it closing in on *her* in particular—hunting down her scent like a pack of rabid beasts. ...Yet (and this was the strange thing) she suddenly felt as though there were something out there that could combat The Horde: something out there which, when combined with the secrets she held inside, would be able to rid the world of The Horde forever. As she listened in the silence of the room—attuning her senses to the *world* around her, not just Quibb's words—something out there called to her. She realized that she had always sensed it; but now that she had her new awareness, she was *certain* about what she sensed. In the air, she could taste and smell something, like pheromones. The sensations aroused within her seemed too complex and powerful to have been initiated by a creature of flesh and blood—and yet she conceptualized the thing calling to her as a man that could come and *claim* her and open up all the secrets within her. She had a sudden impulse to leave this place—to search out that lover—and complete her awakening...but the drag queens were still murmuring. She looked at them confusedly, as though just noticing them. The back of her neck burned as she turned her head, but the explanation of that burning was still lost in the haze.

The little boy was snoring slightly; he felt warm and good in her arms. Mansmann took one of her arms cautiously, as though she would break, then checked her pulse. The blinding light of her awakening had been from a flashlight that he shone into her eyes. Respoli-Priestess and the others were still mumbling their prayers. Those prayers did not make sense at first, but then she remembered, with a kind of annoyed grimace, that she was supposed to be God. She lay there, thinking: *What good are your prayers? If I'm your God, I certainly can't grant them.*

The doctor's frown deepened after taking her pulse. As she and the old man stared at one another, something inscrutable was exchanged between them. There was something in his eyes that was not unlike that of the drag queens. It was not worship actually, but awe. *He knows I'm a woman*, she thought to herself. He seemed almost terrified of her. His hands shook a little as he checked her vital signs....

Coming to the conclusion that she was in no immediate danger, she again turned her head and stared out of the basement window. The sky was getting dark and she felt a little drowsy. As she lay there, The Voice repeated the name "Tio Mendez" in three successive sentences. Even while the reality of The Voice still made her uneasy, there was something soothing about the melody of the words, *Tio Mendez*; more than that, there was something about the melody of those words that was like a lover's name, bringing a lump to her throat and a knot to her gut—

But at the moment, Respoli-Priestess began moaning some gibberish. As his cries rose in the air, the doctor glared at him; but when the entire cult joined in the chorus, the doctor just shook his head and tried to concentrate on his patient. The Goddess smiled at his reaction; Mansmann's frown lessened; and as simply as that, their little pact was formed.

The truth does not become any less truthful because it is said by your devil.
VERSE 1532:4 OF *The Teachings*

Shaka's men were still smiling at Xi like demented Jehovah's Witnesses. As he watched their faces, he found himself thinking about how it would feel to kill them. He had recurring dreams of being a martial arts master—like in those Chinese movies where 20 bandits surround the hero, laughing and taunting him...not knowing that he is the hero—a *superman*. The first fool steps up, but after a blow to the head, the man is sent flying. The laughter dies; the camera pans to the faces of two outraged bandits; they nod to one another, then, pulling out their swords, they rush the hero. However, two lightning quick blows later, they lie on the ground holding the small of their backs and groaning. The rest of the bandits, a little scared now, decide to rush the hero en masse...but his Kung Fu skill is too great. He knocks them senseless before they can raise their hands. His deadly fists are moving in a blur; with one athletic kick, four hapless fools are knocked to the ground. He is swirling like a top now. Bandits are falling left and right; at last, the final bandit rushes him, but after a vicious blow to the mid section, there is a lingering camera shot of the bandit's surprised face, frozen by incomprehensible pain and the realization that he is facing no ordinary man, but the greatest Kung Fu master of all time....

Back in reality, two of the smiling men took Xi by the upper arm, and coaxed him off the bike. Another man took the bike, while the others led him on. Xi went without protest and without thought. When they all walked through the huge gate, Xi felt strangely relieved: one way or another it would all be over soon. There would be no more running and hiding—no more delusions and lies to lead him astray. Still, as he walked along, a strange thought began to percolate in his mind: Would Quibb allow him to be taken like this? Like an alcoholic at a moment of weakness, Quibb was again his God—his protective guiding spirit. Even as a man that had lied to him, Quibb was nonetheless The Voice of Conscience: the entity that had its tentacles in the souls of men. Suddenly putting faith in that horrible image, Xi felt strangely insulated—almost at ease. Was he not like Moses, shielded from the power and evil of Pharaoh by God? For a few moments, he was buoyed by the thought…but then it made him sick.

They bought him to an elevator, which took them all directly to the lobby of the 150-story skyscraper. The lobby looked out on the super-world of Company Square, and it was even more impressive than Xi had remembered. Within Company Square, Xi could see thousands of workers—along with the dark pyramid. Up close, the pyramid was even more of an awesome sight.…The Jehovahs were taking him through the lobby now. It was bustling with workers putting on the finishing touches of the repair effort: painting the walls and other such tasks. Xi and his entourage passed by the secret door, through which he and Quibb had come. He remembered that he still had the keys in his pockets! He glanced at the Jehovahs anxiously then. For the first time, he wondered if he should have come—but it was too late for that, so he retreated to the numbness that had brought him this far.

Eventually, Shaka's men led him to an elevator that was being guarded by two burly guards. The latter smiled when they saw Xi and the Jehovahs approaching—as though it had been their collective directive to entrap Xi. They all piled into the elevator and headed up to the penthouse. Xi was beyond thought: during the elevator ride, his mind seemed to abandon him. There was a plush burgundy carpet when they got out. The entire floor of Shaka's penthouse had been remodeled. The huge window was gone—or had been walled off. Instead, the dim lighting made the cavernous anteroom seem luxurious. On the walls, there were paintings arrayed in an eclectic style. A dapper-looking young man was stationed at a desk against the far wall; as Xi and his captors walked towards the receptionist, the plush carpet muffled their many steps. It was at least a 20-meter walk from the elevator to the receptionist. The latter looked at their approach quizzically, then grinned when one of Xi's guides told him that this was the man they had been searching the city for.

The young receptionist pressed the intercom as if there were not a moment to waste. "Shaka!" he yelled into the intercom, "I'm pleased to tell you that your men have found Dr. Wang! They've brought him here."

"Well show him in then!" the voice on the other end rejoiced.

Xi observed all this with a kind of numb fascination. Then, he felt an arm on him as the Jehovahs took him to the left—towards the gigantic wooden door of Shaka's chamber. Xi could hardly think anymore. If they were going to kill him, then why go through with this stupid act? Maybe they wanted to figure out what he knew first. Images of torture flew through his mind….

Shaka's chamber was *grand!* Most of the screens that he remembered were gone. Instead, the entire side of the wall was glass, so that the huge room was suffused with the evening light. Shaka, clad in something that looked like a religious robe, was behind a desk at the far end of the room. The man looked like a gentle parish priest—but then Xi suddenly remembered his vision, and the realization that Shaka had caused all this. Instinct told him to not see the man as a human being, but instead to shun him, like the Bible told them to shun Satan and his works…but it was hard. There seemed to be a preternatural glow of health about the man. Xi frowned then, noticing another figure lying on a couch in the corner of the room. The figure smiled at him. It was Circe—

Shaka stood up and grinned as Xi approached. "Ah, Dr. Wang," he started, "you have no idea how difficult you were to locate." And then, to the others:

"Where did you find him?"

"He was right outside, sir."

"Ah, fortune has shined on us all!" Shaka rejoiced.

Xi swallowed hard. His throat felt *charred.*

Shaka looked at him askance: "You look rather pale, Xi, you must not have been eating well."

Xi nodded.

"Poor thing!" Shaka lamented. But his expression changed quickly as his smile returned. "Rest assured that those days are over. Do you have any idea why I've been searching for you?"

Xi looked warily at one of the Jehovahs, who was still holding his upper arm. He shrugged his shoulders.

"We will need men like you in the rebuilding, Xi….I'm curious," he said with a frown, "seven years ago, you just disappeared off the face of the earth… And the men tell me that you fled from them once."

"I was…" his voice sounded pathetic. He swallowed with effort once again. "I was…busy."

"Just the kind of man I knew you were," Shaka said vaguely.

Xi nodded—it was all he could think to do.

"Yes," Shaka went on, "it's just as The Voice of Conscience says: we have to rebuild! We are nothing but the byproducts of our evolution. We must do that which the times demand. Men of knowledge, such as yourself, are in great demand. We are at the vanguard of history here!"

Feeling suddenly nauseous, Xi clamped his eyes shut. What was all this! Surely they were baiting him. He kept waiting for the knives to come out. It was driving him crazy! He glanced at the weird robed figure on the couch again, his unease growing. Circe seemed as beautiful as ever, but Xi had the strange feeling that the man's face was changing as he watched it. He had the unsettling suspicion that he was not seeing what he thought he was seeing—

"At any rate," Shaka said, summing up, "we need your technical expertise. Your lab is still where you left it," Shaka said with a smile—to which some of the men laughed along.

Xi stared for a while, then nodded—it was again all he could think to do. He stood there, still waiting for the knives to come out, while Shaka continued to praise him and delineate the benefits of working for The Company. Xi waited, still trembling, while Shaka told him to report for work in a day or so (after he had gotten some rest and a good meal). Shaka then handed him a wad of bills—actually, it was the script used by all Company workers—along with a small device he said he would use to contact Xi. Xi was not listening:

he shoved the bills and the device into his pockets without thought. He waited, wanting to scream, as he was led back to the elevator and to the street. *They are going to attack now!* he kept telling himself. He braced himself for their blows while they prattled on about things his mind could not decipher anymore. Even when they handed him his bike and said goodbye to him, he walked tentatively out of the gate, looking back at the waving men every few seconds. Finally mounting his bike, he rode off wildly and recklessly. He again took to the alleyways, riding as fast as he could for about five minutes.

At last, when he could go no farther, he huddled in an alley, crying. It was all a trick: it *had* to be! He felt as if it were only a matter of time before they killed him. They were simply toying with him. That was the true gauge of power: the ability to bide one's time. Even if they really wanted him for his "technical expertise," he was not Dr. Wang anymore! He did not have any technical knowledge whatsoever! Thus, one way of another, he was done for....

The horrified faces of Clem and Steve suddenly popped into his mind; he remembered how Mendez had laughed when he realized that Xi was the man in Shaka's "wanted" poster. All these things bubbled in his mind, along with the realization that Quibb's machinations were responsible for his predicament—

"I have not forsaken you," someone said. There was a sardonic air to it, but Xi did not notice as he looked up to see Quibb step out of the shadows.

Xi stared at Quibb with a strange new intensity: the expression made Quibb's smile fade. For a moment, Xi's face expressed pure hatred—and not even hatred between man and God, but between men. The recollection that Quibb had lied to him—that Quibb was just a man with schemes—made Xi's blood boil. Gone was the awe and subservience of yesterday. A side of Xi wanted to leap at the man—to strangle him with his bare hands!

"...You've changed somehow," Quibb said, frowning.

Xi sat up and faced him. He continued to stare; but for once, it was with a knowing glance. "Shaka wants me back," he said at last. For a moment, he considered telling Quibb about Clem and Steve, but decided against it for now. Quibb was still looking at him oddly. For some reason, Xi smiled; and then, instinctively: "You can't read my mind anymore, can you?"

"…What?"

Xi laughed, still looking at Quibb knowingly. His new mindset—his lack of awe—must have been blocking Quibb's mind control. Xi felt possessed by a horrible kind of power now—the madness that came when men realized that they were doomed, and that all they had left to them was violence and revenge. A smirk came to his face as he ventured, "Why exactly are you here now, Quibb? You have another errand for me I assume? I helped Mendez like you asked: now the men are ready to give their souls to him."

Quibb continued to stare at him suspiciously; then, as though remembering why he had come: "Yes, there's something I would like you to do."

"Command me then, master," Xi said in a low, cryptic voice.

Quibb frowned. Apparently Xi's sudden self-assurance was unnerving, because Quibb cleared his throat uneasily before explaining: "Tio Mendez is going to have a rally tomorrow."

"I know—*everyone* knows: you've been blaring it for days now."

"Yes, but you have to be there. You were not going to go, were you?"

"No, I wasn't."

"…Trust me just a little longer, Xi. I want you to understand—"

Xi could not help laughing. "It's my *understanding* that you want now? I thought you just wanted an audience."

There was silence; Quibb looked at him helplessly. For the first time, Xi realized how tired Quibb looked. Maybe all those days of babbling nonsense over the airwaves was finally taking its toll on him. "—Everyone wants to be listened to," Quibb continued desultorily, as though just recovering from Xi's jibe. "…You want someone to listen to you—same as me. There's nothing shameful in that."

Xi stared at the man, and then he shook his head again.

"…Trust me just a little longer," Quibb almost seemed to plead. There was a strange earnestness to his voice that Xi had never heard before. A side of him wanted to laugh and go about his business, but something in the timbre of Quibb's voice kept him there. He almost felt sorry for the man. Common sense told him to resist; but at last, he shook his head and looked up, his voice faint:

"What am I to do?"

"Just go to the rally. I want you to see it—to *understand*….Look, Xi," Quibb went on, as though fighting some internal battle, "things don't always go as planned…Do you believe that people can change—or that who they are is branded on their souls?"

"…I don't know," Xi said with a groan, realizing that he did not have the patience.

"Just keep that in mind," Quibb went on. "…Does the term 'hand of evolution' mean anything to you, Xi?"

"Should it?"

"It will, and when it does, you'll be given a great opportunity: the chance to decide who you want to be."

…But Xi was too exhausted mentally to try to figure out Quibb's riddles at the moment. Instead, he sighed and nodded his head. He looked away then, because he knew that Quibb was going to leave, and he did not want to go through the ritual of seeing the man fade into the shadows.

A religion is in its greatest peril until it reaches its second generation of believers. The faith of those who come to a religion upon hearing of it (and accepting it into their hearts) will always be susceptible to the calls of other religions. However, the faith of those who are born into a religion will be strong, in that even while they may hear the calls of other religions, those calls will always be jarring and discursive to their ears.
VERSE 521:9 OF *The Teachings*

The Goddess was having a tumultuous dream, the contents of which were vague—but so intensely pleasing that the overload of sensations seemed on the verge of being painful. Her body shuddered with the contradictions. And then, as the strange pleasure seemed to burst from some dam within her, and rush out—over all the plains and valleys of her consciousness—she bit her lower lip and emerged from sleep. Her body felt drained and devastated; in those first few moments, spasms coursed through her body; but in time, all of that passed and she lay still and helpless…and at peace.

It was nighttime outside. All was dark and still within the room; beyond the window, Quibb's resonant voice again said, "Tio Mendez." The melody of the words still seemed to caress her body like a lover; but as she came to her senses, she realized that the little boy was still in bed with her, and that during her tumultuous dream—and the explosion of pleasure that had ended it—she had wrapped her legs around his waist, and her arms around her neck, pulling him to her breasts. She released him guiltily, but he was sound asleep; and even in the relative darkness of the room, she could see the contented expression on his face. She sighed—a side of her had thought she had suffocated him. The thought brought a whimsical smile to her face….Outside the window, beyond the melody of The Voice, the strange music of Mardi Gras could be heard. There was a careless sensuality about the music that appealed to her present state of mind—and the warmth of her body. She again yearned to be out in the world, seeking out something that her stunted consciousness could only conceptualize as a lover, but which her ever-evolving instincts told her would be so much more.

She had no idea how long she had been lying in this bed, but it seemed like weeks. Her mind started down the path that encompassed her flight from that place on the mountain and all the shadowy recollections of her past. However, she did not want to become trapped in those dead ends just now. The mysteries of her past were like a parasite, sucking life from her. The lover she sensed was her future, and he was out there—on those streets with the careless, sensual music. She had to get out into the world and seek out that lover with all the hormone-induced single-mindedness of a jungle creature. There was obvious madness to it, but it was a kind of madness whose purpose had been honed by millions of years of evolution. Human beings tried to act as though they were more than beasts—that their lives were somehow beyond the crude calculus of sex. The city was the culmination of their gender-neutral nirvana. In her current state of mind, she felt as though it was her destiny to strip them of that myth—to devastate their civilization culturally and sexually, in the same way that The Horde was devastating them physically. She was a seed, gestating within the earth, changing the pH of the soil, adding nutrients to the despoiled earth...so that in the future, new life would be able to grow. New ecosystems would be able to arise where before only the hardiest weeds had been able to prosper. And maybe the urge to procreate was just the body's budding awareness of its own mortality, because more and more, there was a sense of recklessness growing within her. In that strange way that terminal patients began to live more desperately—and to take more chances with their lives—she felt an urge to explore and gain new, verifiable experiences, regardless of the consequences. She could not just *exist* anymore: she had to find out what she was existing *in*. Also, instinct told her that she had to begin the process of separating herself from the drag queens. There was a world of horror out there; and even while Respoli-Priestess and his band had insulated her from it somewhat, she sensed that in order to reach her true potential—and to make sense of all the things Quibb had said to her in The Horde's consciousness—she had to see the world with her own eyes, free of cryptic religious prophecies. She had to find out the truth *tonight*—before tomorrow's rally in Central Park. In fact, at that very moment, Quibb's voice was talking about the rally and Mendez again. The Goddess nodded her head, now more certain than ever that this was the time to step out on her own, in order to see and feel and *taste* the world around her.

This was her mindset as she watched the little boy yawn and stretch and emerge peacefully from sleep. She stared at him intently for at least half a minute before he discerned her gaze in the darkness. He smiled shyly.

She smiled back, reminding herself to keep her expression and voice calm. "I have to know some things," she started. "Is there a library or…some place where they keep old information?"

"I know a place," he said, seeming proud.

"Take me there," she said, trying to reign in her eagerness.

He looked unsure—he had not counted on that. "I don't know—"

"It's important."

He seemed tortured by a private fear; but then, as she put her hand to his face, he gave in reluctantly. "I'll get the others—"

"No…just us."

"Why?"

She searched her mind for something to say, then: "Don't you like being with me?"

"But they'll be angry with me," he pleaded.

"How can they be angry," she reasoned, "am I not their God?" She felt both proud and ashamed of her newfound ability to lie. The little boy was so guileless that she almost felt sorry for him.

"Well, if *you* say," he said with a sigh.

They rose from the bed then. There was a sharp burning sensation at the back of her neck, where she had clawed out the microchip, but she was so excited by the prospect of getting outside that she was able to push it to the edge of her consciousness. The little boy still seemed unsure; she rushed

443

him along before he changed his mind. She looked towards the window, but there were iron security gratings barring it. Next, she tiptoed across the wooden floor, holding the little boy by the hand. However, when she opened the door a crack, she saw the outlines of two drag queens in the darkness. They were posted at her door, sitting on chairs! She faltered, but when she looked again, she saw that they were asleep. They were snoring, and their heads drooped to their chests. Charged into action, she rushed back to put on her shoes (which were at the bottom of the bed). The little boy followed her example. Then, again holding the little boy's hand, she returned to the door, snuck past the two snoring guards, and tiptoed down the dimly lit hallway. She hated corridors! This alone almost made her turn back....But it felt good to walk. The prospect of being free fed her muscles....She had never really smelt the stench of this place before. It almost made her vomit. In a couple of rooms, she saw stick figures of men lying on the ground. She was sure that they were dead—and had been dead for a long time....

Shirley Temple crept along with her, seeming more horrified than herself. At the end of the hall, just before the staircase, they came upon a room with a light on inside. Peeping in, she saw Respoli-Priestess and the others! She ducked back. Peeping in again, she saw that they were all kneeling on the ground, praying. Taking Shirley Temple in her arms, she darted past the door and up the staircase. On the ground floor, the horrible stench of the clinic almost made her knees buckle. Both the stench and the exhaustion that came with carrying the little boy up a flight of stairs made her put him down. Through double doors, she saw hundreds of men lying still in the sweltering heat. She backed away. There was another door at her back; opening it, she found herself face-to-face with the outside world. She again had the feeling of déjà vu as she fled from the building. The little boy seemed desperate to get away as well. He had the expression of someone who knew that he had done wrong, but who was trapped in the wrongdoing. He took her hand and they jogged off, down the block.

She was surprised at her strength. It felt good to be moving about again. The little boy was taking her towards the music—the logarithmic beat blaring a few blocks away. She was nervous as she watched the first men that they came upon. She was horrified to see their smiles and ease. She and the little boy turned the corner: thousands of men dancing in the night! She wavered. As Shirley Temple looked up at her, her indecisiveness fed his.

She shook her head: she had to do this. She smiled down at the little boy, trying to reassure him. They walked on, through the crowds of dancing, drunken men. Many of the men had the Glory to the Goddess tattoo, and the Goddess suddenly remembered Quibb's words—that The Horde needed the men to believe in her. The recollection made her queasy; and just then, one of the men tried to take her hand and dance with her; she pushed away the tottering drunk and rushed through the crowd, once again pulling the little boy behind her.

After about five minutes of this, the little boy took her down a side road. When she was free of the crowd, she finally allowed herself to acknowledge the true extent of her terror. A side of her wanted to rush back to the clinic then. She did not have the courage to find lovers and uncover the mysteries of the gods. She was panting and trembling now…but the relative calmness of this block soothed her. It was amazing how the city changed from block to block. One block was overflowing with men, and pulsating with music; another was dark and deserted, with only the Voice's omnipresent homilies to keep them company.

They walked down these side streets for a while. A couple of times, drug users stumbled from the shadows and they had to run on. How much longer until they reached the place that the little boy knew…? Doubts were confronting her again. And would it even be worth it? Shirley Temple seemed so clueless: what if he had misunderstood her? They had been going for at least 45 minutes now. It seemed too late to go back; and yet, all of the twists that he was taking her on were making her doubts grow.

They were walking down a major street again. Men were everywhere, but seemed intent to hurry to the party, which seemed centered down the length of Broadway. The Voice of Conscience was there too, like the moon following her throughout the night. As always, it was talking about Mendez—and that rally….The little boy and she had been going for almost an hour now. They were far away from the relative safety that that strange clinic had seemed to engender. She quaked inside as they passed through blocks littered with the remains of skyscrapers. Those that had not been bombed, just seemed to stand in disrepair. Just when she was about to tell the little boy that she had had enough, he took her towards one of those buildings. Looking up, entire floors of the glass-skinned structure were...*skinless*— window-less. It seemed like a burned-out ghetto building—except for the fact that it was in the heart of what clearly used to be the business district. In front of the building, there was a huge abstract sculpture: geometric shapes teetering end-to-end. With the dim lighting, it seemed like the toy of a monstrous creature....

Where the entrance used to be, there was a graffiti-laden slab of marble. It was actually on a kind of counterbalanced hinge, which locked in place somehow. The little boy, with a deft movement, pushed the slab to the side, letting her pass. She faltered as they entered the dark, empty lobby. She expected to see guards in such a big place—or at least hundreds of squatters— but there was no one. The emptiness unnerved her. Also, the stale smell of disuse pervaded the place: a pungent mildew smell. She looked down at the little boy quizzically. He seemed preoccupied—*nervous*. He moved quickly; she followed closely behind.

In one of the open elevator shafts, there was a ladder that led up to the first floor. At first, she was wary of entering the darkness—she was sure that she heard rats squeaking within—but the little boy moved quickly, as if oblivious of her doubts. Clambering onto the first floor, she found the little boy waiting. A few light bulbs hung from wires in the ceiling, casting an eerie glow on everything. The little boy's sweaty face seemed terrible below the lights. He still looked around nervously, and that unease was wearing away at her. She bent down to him, whispering:

"What's wrong? What is it?"

He was nibbling at his lower lip, scanning the darkness warily: "My father," he whispered, "...he lives here."

"Your *father*?" she whispered, now taking her lead from him. His obvious discomfort made her doubts grow—

"Go down that hall and turn left," he said, sidestepping her question. "There's a big room with news things."

She looked in that direction, then frowned. "Aren't you coming?"

"You go first," he whispered, "I'll come later." Why was he acting so clandestine all of a sudden—and so mature? She went to say something, but with his strong urging, she left him. She took a couple of steps; when she looked back, he was gone. She wavered; she went to call out to him, but the uneasiness she remembered in his eyes stopped her. What to do now…? She looked around the airy, dimly lit floor. There were still cubicles and shattered computer consoles: all the old reminders of office work. It was that suggestion of normalcy and the past that motivated her to go on. She would find the little boy later….

She followed his instructions and came upon a huge room filled with videodisks. There was something unnerving about the place—especially with the darkness. There was a switch on the wall, but when she turned it on, only about five of the dozens of fluorescent lights in the huge chamber came on. Rats and cockroaches darted into the shadows when the light disturbed them. With the dim lighting, it was impossible to tell what else was in there. She wavered; her mind returned to the little boy for a moment, but her attention soon went to the shelf immediately in front of her. She stepped up to it timidly and randomly pulled out a videodisk—it was a news broadcast. There was a date on it. While she was not entirely sure what year it was now, from her calculations, the videodisk seemed like ancient history—stuff from at least 20 years ago. She pulled out the disk to the left of it and saw that it was for the following week. She concluded that each of the disks had to hold a week's worth of news. Turning her head to the right, she saw that there were some consoles for viewing in the corner of the room, but she needed something more recent to tell her what had happened to the world. There had to be hundreds of thousands of videodisks in this place. This building (or at least this floor) must have housed a news service of some kind. Becoming increasingly eager by the moment, she stepped farther down the row. The videodisks were all so dusty that it seemed as if no one had looked at them in years. She roamed the dusty rows for about five minutes; finally getting her bearings, she walked down to the last row and got a videodisk from the latest date that she could find. If her calculations were correct, the videodisk fell in the general area of seven years ago. Her heart beat chaotically in her chest as she brought the disk back to the viewing console and inserted it. She waited impatiently. The images came on the screen as they had accosted her in her nightmares. There were images of chaos and riots. There were not even reporters as such, but panicked people screaming into the camera. The cameramen seemed always to be running and fleeing. She watched the scenes for about five minutes before stopping it. She would have to go back a bit further to get answers. The chaos had already taken control on the videodisk that she had just watched. She took it out and went back to the shelves. This time, she took a disk from a month prior to the one she had just watched. She rushed back and inserted it into the console. There were scenes—less chaotic, perhaps—but just as unsettling. There were still people yelling at one another—and yelling in a manner that made it almost impossible to decipher what they were yelling about. The more she watched it, the more she realized that no one seemed to know what was going on—they were all just panicking about something that they seemed to sense more than see. She fast-forwarded the disk in frustration; when she randomly stopped it, she heard the voice over that she remembered from her vision. It was a man saying, "…The end of woman." Her heart skipped a beat as the story continued:

"…more doctors have confirmed the mutation. They are not sure how it happened, but they confirm that men can no longer produce X sex chromosomes. All spermatozoa carry the Y sex chromosome…"

She struggled to keep up. Luckily, the reporter was explaining it all. Sperm were the male things. Women's eggs only carried X sex chromosomes; men's sperm were either X or Y, and it was they that decided the sex of the child. She felt excited at finally getting answers….She lost track of time as she watched the report…there was speculation about radiation and the poisoning of food and water. Somehow, it was *worldwide*! There were reports mentioning the ozone layer and global warming. There were reports of men going around wearing ice packs on their testicles…There was so much information—*too* much information. She watched and fast-forwarded through about four successive days' worth of news, digesting about five percent of it. She felt suddenly restless. She was just about to stand up, when the news report changed to a story on...*the doctor from the clinic!* She gasped when she recognized the face—

"...Some scientists think that there might be a connection between the inability of men to produce X sex chromosomes, and Vincent Mansmann's Luxuriant Hair Formula...." It was really the doctor from that place—or at least she thought so! The hair had been longer then (and blond) but the face seemed the same. The reporter was talking about how Mansmann had disappeared—how the government was hunting him down. The man seemed like a kind of scapegoat of fate and history. They showed one of Mansmann's commercials: on screen, the man was perpetually jolly—nothing like the dour old man from the clinic. She suddenly felt that she understood what she had sensed in his eyes: the horrible burden that seemed to weigh him down....

She stopped the disk, then inserted the first disk she had watched. She felt that she now had some kind of basis for understanding what she saw. After inserting it, she again randomly skipped ahead. The story on the disk was a report on women going to camps for their safety. She saw women going into armored vans: strange prisoners of the times. People were crying and hugging. There were reports of rapes...images of crazed men *butchering* women.

The images were beyond horrible and graphic. She felt as though she could see into their souls. She felt *polluted* as she watched the images. After a while, it was almost as though the images were violating her—she forced herself to look away just for the sake of self-preservation. She was just about to stop the disk, when her face appeared on the screen! It was from *years* ago, but it was unmistakably her face. Now on the screen, there were images of the Army and National Guard in a shootout with crazed men— *and women*—whom claimed that she was *God*. After the shootout, bloody, gnarled cultists were seen being hauled away. There was madness in their eyes—something that went beyond faith and religion. Those that could still talk, were yelling that the apocalypse was proof that the little girl they followed was God—and that this was the moment of rapture; at the same time that God was punishing man by taking women from the world, He had incarnated Himself in the image of woman. He had been reborn as the metaphorical and actual conduit of future life; and by descending into man's midst in the form of a vulnerable girl (whom men could either destroy, sealing their doom, or nurture and safeguard), God had given man one last chance to redeem his soul. A reporter demanded that the cultists divulge the location of the girl, but the crazed followers screamed back that they would never tell where she was. They had hidden her away to protect man from himself; they were the Disciples of God, empowered Heaven....As the report went on, she suddenly realized one very vital thing: there was not *one* cult, but competing sects—all of whom claimed that only they could protect her from the infidels. They were like drug gangs, killing one another for territory and the right to control her—

She stopped the disk and got up anxiously. She wished that she could remember all this—that she could see her own place in it. She wished that she could hear her voice in one of those news broadcasts—see herself talking, so that she could know that she had been a real person. All that she was was a myth that only the most insane claimed to have seen—like Bigfoot. Besides her picture, there seemed to be no other evidence that she had ever existed—and even her picture did not exactly seem concrete. It seemed like a computerized depiction of her face. She sighed. As she stood there in the silence, it occurred to her that she had perhaps never been a human being: that she had always been a supernatural conduit for madness and brutality.

It was while these thoughts were draining strength from her, that she realized that the little boy had been gone too long. She remembered how nervous he had looked—and the strange way that he had told her that his father lived here. She returned to the hallway with a growing sense of uneasiness. Actually, searching for the little boy was a way to block out what she had just seen. She had to let her mind acclimate itself to those images— and the reality that others' belief in her had led to so much bloodshed and insanity.

Perhaps forty-five minutes had passed since she and the little boy parted. The entire floor was dark and still; only the far-off squeaking and rustling of rats—and the muffled words of The Voice of Conscience over the broken speakers of the P.A. system—seemed to tell her that she was not alone. She walked back the way she had come, straining her ears for any sign of the boy. Suddenly, around the next corner, she heard someone grunt—as if in pain. She did not know what to do—*she froze!* Was it the boy? She strained her ears again, hearing sniffling in the background. The boy was in trouble! She rushed around the corner. There was a room with a light; she ran to the open doorway. There was a strange scene. A man was sitting in a chair; Shirley Temple was kneeling before the man, as if he were praying to him. But that did not compute: she looked again, gasping. She realized that the man's pants had been pulled down. He was leaning back in the chair, breathing hard. Her gasp made them both look up at her. As the little boy looked up, she saw his tears, and the muck of the man's semen dripping down his face. They both seemed shocked to see her; but the little boy, seeing her, seemed to die. In a flash, he was running. He burst past her, darting down the corridor; she ran after him, almost toppling down the ladder in the elevator shaft.

She finally caught up with him beyond the building's entrance. She grabbed onto him while he cried—

"But you said you wanted to know...!" he whimpered. "You said you wanted to...!"

She hugged him with all her strength; she tried to calm and reassure him, but she felt ten times more ashamed and distraught than he did—

"...You said you wanted to know...!" he whimpered one last time.

"...God," she whispered, wondering what the world had done to him—to *all* of them.

As the little boy continued to cry, she took his hand and they walked slowly down the street. The Voice of Conscience was babbling the usual nonsense about the strength of collective action: it began to eat away at her. They moved on. Everything was bubbling in her head. She had answers at last—but what conclusions was she to draw...and at what cost had she gotten those so-called answers? She held Shirley Temple closely as they walked.... What was she to do now? For a moment, she felt her old confusion reclaiming her. She might have lost herself to them forever, if the images from the videodisks had not confronted her again. The world all at once seemed like a place of extremes. At one extreme, was the nightmare world within which she and everyone she had met was trapped. Here, everything was muddled and confused and reactionary. They did not live: they *survived*... maybe not even that. They existed the way dust existed, blown into the crevices and gutters. They took up space, like filth that people were too lazy to clean away. The only thing that could save them was the other extreme: they had to forge change—be *revolutionary*! What that entailed, however, she could not even begin to fathom. There was so much to change—and so much that seemed beyond anyone's ability to change. She felt suddenly helpless...but she had to do *something*. She could not just sit around anymore, waiting for...for God knows what. Everything seemed to be eating away at her...and The Voice of Conscience was blaring from a speaker that had been hoisted onto the upcoming lamppost. The incessant babble was like the murmuring that she remembered from that place on the mountain: it was driving her insane, not leaving her a moment's peace. A combative streak surged within her then. She looked down at Shirley Temple, suddenly offended by the frilly little dress that he was wearing. She shook her head: "Is this you?" she said, pulling at the dress. He looked up at her, shrugging his shoulders. The blankness of his face frustrated her for some reason; and just then, as they passed beneath the lamppost with the blaring speaker, she whirled, grabbed a stone from the ground, and threw it, with deadly aim, at the speaker. After the deafening crash, there was silence: wonderful silence. There was a video billboard down the block, but she could not hear it clearly; so for a moment, it seemed as if they were the only two people in the world.

The little boy's eyes were wide as he stared up at her. There was suddenly a gruffness about her: a *hardness*. Her mind was resolving all the paradoxes: constructing her as she had to be in order to survive what was before her. She looked down at the little boy: "Be what you are," she said, pulling at his clothes again. Her voice sounded strange in the silence. "No more of this," she said, still tugging at his clothes. "No more *pretending*!" He seemed on the verge of tears again; but catching hold of herself, she bent down to hug him and reassure him—

"Hey you!" yelled a voice down the block. They turned to see some soldiers running towards them. Images of the scene from *Throw the First Stone* popped into her mind; she took off with the little boy in tow; there were gunshots behind them; they ran down an alleyway, losing the yelling men down a side street. Actually, the men seemed to get caught in a gun battle behind her, but she was too locked within herself, and the act of running, to notice. The strange thing was that as she ran, the feeling of indignation waxed high in her. This frightened her: her relative lack of fear—her sudden recklessness. Recklessness? Was that it? Or was it natural outrage—*necessary* outrage—in the face of the times? No more women? Was the world really lost? Was this the end? No: she remembered that place in the mountains again. There had to be other such places. And she knew from her visions that in some of the other cities the women lived with the men; maybe elsewhere, this unnaturalness did not exist. There was so much to ponder and so much to *do*. Yet, there was a strange sense of responsibility rising in her. Somehow, it was all up to her; and as she ran on, still pulling the little boy behind her, she found herself thinking (this time with an openness to possibilities that was like madness, itself), *Maybe I am God...!*

With these thoughts in mind, the air seemed surprisingly fresh. She felt revived somehow, as though she had just freed herself from a horrible burden. Whatever the case, she was reveling in this feeling now. She could not be cooped up like an animal anymore. She jogged down the relatively empty blocks, still reveling in her newfound freedom. Even when she came upon some men, they slunk nervously past her, as though sensing her power. She was heading back to the clinic, but she felt as though she were headed out into unexplored territory. Looking at the men around her, she saw that they were blinded as she had been blinded: were burdened and incapacitated by their own lack of imagination and their *cowardice*. She was almost giddy with power now. It was not until five more soldiers swaggered out of the shadows of a doorway that she knew that she had lost herself in her delusions.

"What y'all running from!" one of the youths demanded. She could do nothing. The sense of freedom darted away so quickly that she was left frozen and inept. The youths were approaching, yelling something that terror would not allow her to decipher. The nozzles of the youths' guns were coming up. She still could not move! It was over! She felt as though she would faint; and all at once, gunshots started blazing all around her. She clutched the little boy close and crouched on the ground like a bizarre statue. She prepared herself for the pain of hot metal entering her flesh. However, the little boy was tugging at her sleeve. When she looked down at him confusedly, she suddenly realized that the gunshots had stopped— and that there were footsteps behind her. She turned to see some men running up. She sucked in a lungfull of air, so that she could scream with all her might, but then she recognized Kramer and some of the other members of the cult. Kramer asked her if she was all right; the others clambered around her to see if she was wounded. Fighting to understand, she looked ahead, to where the five soldiers lay dead....

"Let's get back home," she whispered at last, feeling suddenly drained— not only of strength, but *power*. This time, they walked, as to not attract attention to themselves.

Freedom is the ability to choose one's prison.
VERSE 983:2 OF *The Teachings*

Shaka stood before the window—rather, the glass-enclosed side of his suite—staring out at the nighttime skyline. It was good to be back in his penthouse suite. It was like finally being back home after a long time away. As he looked out on the city from 150 stories in the air, he felt (for the first time in a long while) as though he genuinely loved the city. The men of the city had really done a good job making repairs. Even he had to admit that The Voice had been able to move the men in ways that his PinkEyes never could. Moreover, after days of rebuilding, the thought of The Horde returning with its bombs made him feel sick.

Circe was lying on the couch near him, and he suddenly felt relieved by her presence. They had just had a long conversation about nothing in particular. The topic of the conversation had faded away, and they had settled into the comfortable silence. As he stood there looking down on the city that he suddenly loved, it occurred to him that this was the first time in his life that someone else's presence had not seemed like a burden on him. He looked across at Circe then; as they were alone, she had transformed herself once more, and was again the simple being he had viewed before. For some reason, he smiled before looking back out on the world.

"Is Shaka your real name?" she asked him suddenly.

He stared at her for a while, then laughed, saying, "No, it's Joe Sanders."

Then, introspectively: "No one has asked me that in 20 years—no one has even *dared* to ask."

"...But you wanted that terror," she said with a smile. "You wanted them to fear you."

"Yes...I needed it," he said, deep in thought. "...I built The Company on it. People were too frightened to ask questions."

She nodded, looking off into the distance with a wistful smile on her face. However, just then, Stein's usual deferential knock sounded at the chamber door.

"Yes, Stein," Shaka yelled, even before the door had been opened. With the strange new intimacy that had been built up between he and Circe, the prospect of Stein's presence was even more distasteful than it usually was. Stein walked up and stood there with his usual subservience. "Have you completed the arrangements for Mendez's rally tomorrow?" Shaka demanded.

"Yes, sir." Stein's voice was cautious and uneven.

"It won't be traced back to us, will it?"

"No, sir. I saw to it myself."

Shaka nodded—his way of both showing Stein that he was pleased, and telling the man that he could leave. However, Stein maintained his position, as though he had something else to say; when Shaka looked at him, the man looked at Circe uneasily, as though to imply that it was not safe to talk—

"What is it?" Shaka groaned.

"Sir," Stein began, speaking quickly, "some of our operatives in other cities think that The Horde might be trying to collect the women."

Shaka stared at him for a while, an expression of indifference coming to his face: "And?"

"Well, sir," Stein said in a panicky voice, "shouldn't we be worried?"

"Never waste time worrying about the approach of danger, Stein," Shaka chastised him. "Either make a plan of action or prepare to flee." These words pleased him, so that he looked at Circe with a smile; but when he did so, he realized that she had again transformed herself into the glamorous illusion. Remembering what she had said about it being exhausting to keep up illusions, and seeing Stein looking at her oddly, he exploded:

"Stop staring at her! Get out of here!"

Stein almost tripped over himself in his haste to get out of the chamber!

X

*The flawed presumption of most conspiracy theorists is that
they are worthy of being conspired against.*
VERSE 2:45 OF *The Teachings*

As another hot summer day emerged on the horizon, the men of the city awoke to the realization that today was the day of Tio Mendez's great speech. In the news, The Horde had once again attacked Denver. At least, people thought it was The Horde. It was some kind of lightning-quick attack force. Onlookers described big—almost *superhuman*—men leaping from half a dozen things like jump jets, arbitrarily subduing a few men in a generally abandoned district of the city, and then moving on. In less than half an hour, it had all been over; and the corpses of The Horde's victims, now stiff with rigor mortis, lay on the ground like collapsed statues....

In New York City, the news no doubt ate away at them—but it did so on a subconscious level. It was almost as though The Voice would not let them acknowledge it. Instead of fear, they evinced a strange kind of defiance and joy. After all, this was the day of the great rally, when Tio Mendez would lay out the plan that would save them.

By eight in the morning, thousands of men were already setting off for Central Park; thousands more had spent the night there, staking out their positions. How far Tio Mendez had come in only four days....

Xi set off for the park around 10 in the morning—two hours before the rally was to begin. He had not slept the night before. He had gone to another subway station, still not ready to go back to The Company and put himself at Shaka's mercy. The sick thing was that he was even considering going at all…and yet, running seemed out of the question. He was not even sure that he *wanted* to run. The only thing that mattered was solving the mystery of who he was and what he had done. Maybe Quibb had lied to him, but one thing remained certain: the truth of who he was, was back at The Company—just as Quibb had said.

…He had needed to be alone last night. He had needed to come to those conclusions by himself. In fact, in an effort to make sense of things, he had spent half the night writing down all the things he knew to be facts. He had diagramed his and G.W. Jefferson's experiences at The Company, as well as all the things happening in Quibb's plan. He had drawn flow charts and made lists, trying to figure it all out…but he had gotten nowhere. That old realization—of the daunting complexity of everything unfolding around him—had left him frustrated and restless. Even when he tried to sleep, thoughts about the women beneath The Company, and the trap that Shaka seemed to be setting for him, had eaten away at him like acid.

Now, as he looked at the thousands of men (who were now talking excitedly about Mendez and his plans for the future) Xi found himself returning to an old thought: only the women could save them now. And he did not mean that in a passive sense. It was not about what the women would do *for* them, but what they would do *to* them. They needed an act of violence upon their souls—something to reach that place they had all closed off seven years ago. What the men of the city—and of the *world*—all needed, was the shock that would come with the reality of a woman. Granted, even with the return of the women, there might still be wars and everything else that had plagued humanity. There might be riots and gang fights to secure the women, but at least they would be fighting for something concrete— not some shadowy, self-deluding construction like Quibb's voice—

He shook his head: he was going mad with thoughts of the women beneath The Company—and with the fear that such thoughts were just a red herring, keeping him from the truths staring him in the face. He was still constantly plagued by the feeling that he was overlooking something obvious—*and of course he was*: it was an inevitable byproduct of his strange existence….He had to do something—*talk* to someone. He felt as though he would burst if he did not tell someone what he knew, or what he *thought* he knew…but there was no one. Once in a while, his mind wandered to that old doctor from the hospital, but as he had not seen the man in a while, he felt as though he never would again….Time was strange in this place: so much happened in a week….

What now? he thought with a frown as he approached the park—and even more excited men. He felt out of place as always; but remembering Quibb, he pressed on. He would go to the rally and wait for the great revelation Quibb had promised, then he would return to Shaka and The Company tomorrow. A side of him kept telling him to run, but there was a kind of sickness growing within him. The part of him that was positive that it was a trap, kept telling him that he was so embroiled in the plans of great men that they would not readily kill him. Quibb wanted him; Shaka wanted him: the two great forces of their universe had gone out of their way to meet him and had spoken to him by name. Of course, none of this made him impervious to pain and death, but at least he had what men had craved since the beginning of time: the assurance that his movements and daily struggles were being closely observed by the gods.

He continued on towards the rally, joining throngs of tens of thousands. He looked at the hopefulness and childlike anticipation that gleamed in the men's eyes, secretly awed by how thoroughly Quibb had worked his magic. Xi seemed to be the only one who still struggled with Quibb's spell…. Maybe that was why Quibb had chosen him: for the challenge—*the ultimate joy*—of breaking him….

The morning sun was already high; but as always, it was lost behind the smog and haze. The summer heat was like a steaming shroud descending on them, stifling them; on top of that, the air seemed charged, as when two powerful weather systems were about to combine into a monstrous storm…. Xi was walking in the park now—through grassy meadows that he suddenly realized had been mowed and cleared of weeds and trash for this event. Most of the larger trees had been burnt in a forest fire a few years ago; but between the burnt stumps, shoots of new growth could be seen. For a moment, that seemed like an adequate metaphor for all that was happening to the city.

His first glimpse of the great lawn of Central Park—and of the hundreds of thousands of men—at first made him hesitate. It reminded him of how Company Square had been seven years ago. Since that night, the sight of the restless multitudes had always unnerved him. Still, the recollection that Quibb had *personally* asked him to come here, left him again wondering about the grand thing that the man had planned. That thing would be viewed by *millions*. It would be the coup de grâce of all Quibb's machinations—Xi was certain of it. As his mind drifted back to the women, he wondered how they might fit into Quibb's plan. He was thinking these thoughts, again wishing that there were someone he could talk to, when he came upon Mansmann. The latter had been walking along nervously and clandestinely, his attention trained on a group of men about fifty meters away—

"Now it is officially fate," Xi joked, as he came upon Mansmann's shoulder. Nevertheless, it was a joke with an undercurrent of uneasiness. Mansmann stared at him in amazement, as if shocked and uneasy as well. "The universe must have a plan for us," Xi tried to joke again, "—it keeps throwing us together like this." Yet, even while he laughed, he seemed unsettled. With all he had seen and experienced—*and what Quibb had said*—he could no longer believe that the universe allowed random events. As he looked down at the old man, his mind went off on wild, unsustainable tangents, with thoughts of the possible roles that the old man and he could play in the schemes of the gods.

Mansmann smiled shyly. At last, as if feeling compelled to explain why he was there, he began, "I was just keeping an eye on…" but then, realizing that he could not reveal that he was spying on the Goddess, he laughed anxiously.

Xi looked ahead, to the group of six or so men that Mansmann had been observing; but as the old man seemed to become anxious as he did so, Xi shrugged his shoulders, letting it go.

Since Mansmann had taken that microchip—or whatever it had been—out of the woman's neck, he had grown increasingly paranoid. On top of that, it had been practically pointless to ask the drag queens direct questions—as they either responded with the drivel of their religion, or that combination of recalcitrance and antagonism seen among those who were themselves paranoid. Forced to rely on his conjectures and observations, Mansmann had come to the conclusion that the thing in her neck had been some kind of tracking device. That, combined with what he knew about the miraculous properties of her blood/physiology, had brought him to the conclusion that the drag queens had stolen her from someone or something; and that when that thing came to reclaim its property, it would be with the wrath of wronged, vengeful gods. More troublingly, he had to convince himself that Shaka did not know about the woman—that the man's call a few days ago had been nothing but a coincidence. He held fast to this assumption, because the alternative was too horrible. If Shaka knew—and was even now receiving data from all the experiments Mansmann was running on the woman's blood—then he was lost....

There was a huge, colorfully decorated rostrum set up about 500 meters away from where Mansmann and Xi were currently walking. Over the structure, there was a flat canopy, on top of which were situated three gigantic screens. Even from this distance, Xi recognized some of Mendez's campaign commercials. By now, the crowd was so thick that it was difficult to move closer to the rostrum. Xi was content to stay where he was; but Mansmann, whose eyes had remained trained on the group of six as it advanced towards the rostrum, seemed eager to walk on. Instinctively desperate for company, Xi moved along with him.

Maybe augury is nothing but a dim recollection of something long known, but only recently forgotten...
VERSE 3933:34 OF *The Teachings*

The night before, when the Goddess and the others walked back up to Mansmann's lab/clinic, Respoli-Priestess had been wildly distressed, until something in the Goddess' eyes curtailed him. The entire band—at least, those that were not still out looking for her—had flocked around the Goddess like dogs greeting their returning master. She had only stared at them all, then told them, with a firmness they had never heard from her before, to follow her back to the basement. There, she had told them how things were going to change. To begin with, from then on, they would all dress like men—even her. They could not be muddling through the world anymore. They had to forge change, instead of simply being reactionary and—as she saw it—*indifferent* to the forces acting on the world. They had been terrified of her—of the *new* her; they had stared up at her, wide-eyed and silent, wondering what had happened to their God. Still, some, seeing her new manner as the fulfillment of prophecy, had been filled with joy.

This morning, when she awoke to the sound of Quibb's voice, she had nodded to herself. Maybe Quibb's invitation to the rally had been nothing but a trap, but there was no point in hiding anymore. One way or another, this rally would tell her more about the world and what she was to fight—and that was all that mattered anymore. The experiences of the night before had cemented this belief in her. That morning, she had rounded up the cult and told them to get ready. Respoli-Priestess had of course protested against her going, but there had been no stopping her. In line with her edicts of the previous night, she had made them all dress as men. Even she had donned some old clothes that the doctor had brought from his closet.

Now, the Goddess, Respoli-Priestess, the little boy and some of the warriors walked towards the canopied rostrum in the distance. Strangely enough, as they walked shoulder-to-shoulder with thousands of excited men, she felt their excitement coming over her. It was the same atmosphere that she had seen on the streets the night before; but with the heat and humidity of the day, it seemed more intense and *unreal*. There were vendors selling candy and various other items. On her way to the park, she had seen street performers dancing and singing—and receiving wild applause from passersby.

Inside the park, the crowd seemed to glow: maybe it was because they were all sweating from the heat; maybe it was something else. As she walked along, it was almost as though the oppressive heat of the day were being generated by the men's bodies—by some kind of furnace of possibility within them—and not the sun. On top of that, the sound of all the excited men was becoming deafening. The Goddess and the masculinized drag queens were still moving through the crowd, closer to the brightly decorated rostrum. "Mendez is becoming a god to them," Respoli-Priestess said as he looked around at the men. At the sound of his sonorous voice, she looked up at his face—at the serenity that had always seemed to be there, and which had always had the strange effect of both calming and unnerving her. The clothes that he was wearing were too big for him. He looked like a woman trying to impersonate a man. However, to some extent or another, they all did. Even the soldiers of Quibb's army seemed to be nothing but girls playing at war. There was something farcical about it all....

A network of wireless speakers had been set up throughout the great lawn. Dozens of three-meter-high poles, each with four speakers on top, were organized into a grid. The deep baritone of The Voice was playing over the speakers, enumerating all of Tio Mendez's strengths to the point where the Goddess again felt love for the man growing in her heart. On the three screens above the rostrum, images of last week's destruction were playing, juxtaposed to images of the men standing defiantly. A patriotic song was playing, over which The Voice was saying: "We will not be deterred from our destiny!"

It was all contrived, but the men were being swept up in it. In the air, there were words like brotherhood and unity. And then, as The Voice went on a rant about rebuilding and standing strong, a picture of Tio Mendez came upon the screen. There was a monstrous cheer throughout the crowd! Even the Goddess felt herself on the verge of joining those cheers, but battled the impulse savagely….

Her little cult threaded itself through the crowd, moving even closer to the rostrum. They were perhaps sixty meters away by now—and that seemed to be about as close as they would get with the crowd being as dense as it was. It was then that something on the screens caught her attention. There was an image of angry, defiant men burning something. It was a flag of some kind…No, more than that, it was the green sun placed against the purple sky. She faltered, feeling herself being bombarded with all her old fears and insecurities. And she was seeing the same phantasmagoria again: men in the streets, ravaging everything in their path, Horde troops pillaging civilization…It was again too much to comprehend. All of that flickering madness churned before her eyes, and she suddenly felt defenseless….She had not realized it before, but she was trembling uncontrollably—and sweating profusely. The sun was high, and the day was hot and humid, but what she felt could not merely be attributed to the effects of heat. Her senses seemed frayed, like an unraveled rope. Everything was flying in the wind…*aimless*. Around her now rose a wailing noise. At first, she stared at the speaker closest to her, certain that the noise was coming from it, but then she realized that the entire world seemed to be wailing. The grass and the wind and the sun were all wailing. She could hardly breathe by now; a mindless kind of desperation was growing within her—and yet she was suddenly overcome by the certainty that the flag burning on the huge screens was responsible for it all. Now, as she looked up, it was almost as if the flag were singing her to sleep—draining her will and her *consciousness*. She was now convinced of this, because the more she tried to focus on the colors of the banner, the more blurred they become before her eyes. By the time she realized that she was in the middle of a seizure, she could do nothing but surrender....

Somehow, she was lying on her back, staring up at the puzzled faces above her. She found herself drifting away, and it felt wonderful at first. When the shaking started, she hardly even felt it. It was like someone else was shaking, and she was only feeling the vibrations....

From far off in the distance, she heard a parade: shrill trumpets and the deep thud of the drums. She heard it, and the applause and cheers of the crowd, the way someone heard something under water. In fact, maybe it was only in retrospect that she knew what it was. Everything was jumbled; everything was unreal. People around her seemed like caricatures of people: scents like imperfect derivations of scents. It was all like a disjointed slide show: a movie where she saw only every tenth frame. People and things jumped about like puppets on strings, and she feared them—even though she was the one out of control. Respoli-Priestess, who had been taking lessons from the doctor, stuffed something into her mouth, and she felt as though she had been bridled: as if she were being ridden by something merciless. She was just about to retreat into herself and surrender to the pain, when her mind offered something stable and indelible: the image of a woman. The woman's face did not seem familiar to her, and yet the woman seemed strong, bold, pure...and a thousand other characteristics that left the Goddess cowed. The woman's eyes were resolute; her face was stern but soft, as she looked out on all the surrounding chaos. The woman stood there, unperturbed and steady against all the churning madness. When the woman's image faded away, her departure seemed to rip apart the very fabric of reality. However, that rending was like a huge explosion: a Big Bang, seeding the universe with the atoms and energy that would nurture life. As that life energy enveloped the universe, the Goddess felt herself being invigorated. Her body felt warm and virile...*that* was the thing that confused her at first: the fact that she felt possessed by a kind of masculine potency. It was like nothing she had ever felt before. As a woman she had had visions and dreams of an outside force pleasuring her. She had reacted to that pleasure with childlike wonderment. However, with the strange masculine potency coursing through her, the pleasure seemed to be hers to command and initiate. The pleasure was out there to be *seized* and she was to be its master. On top of that, it was again as though she were the conduit of all possibility and pleasure, because around her she saw the reality of what their sex had become. She saw sex being performed, just as she had seen countless other mundane acts performed; and as she compared those mechanical acts with what she felt pulsing through her body, she realized that sex had been co-opted somehow—*corrupted*. Her mind was still swirling, and yet she saw this clearly. Sex had become something that people had *done* to them, not something that they, themselves *did*. They needed props and pornos and all the other appurtenances of modern technology just to engage in the thing that the beasts of the jungle fought and died over, and seemed not only genetically but also *spiritually* programmed to engage in. The world was full of bored lovers, who had been entrapped by their lack of imagination and *stupidity*... but she had pure, life-giving sexuality within her: enough for the entire world. Her healing touch had the power to initiate a chain reaction in the imaginations and souls of the bored multitudes. Her sexuality would be a new Big Bang, seeding the universe with life and possibility.

...The middle-aged woman's face had done all that, but the seizure was beginning to take a toll now. It seemed as though her insides were being ripped apart. Her mind, too, was beginning to dissipate in the pain. When she lost all hope, and began to believe that these would be the last moments of her life, she returned to her old thought: that screaming one last time would be a victory over her unknown enemies. She gathered the air in her lungs and screamed as best she could. A shrill, pathetic noise came out, and her lungs and throat hurt from the effort, but the seizure was over.

Her first breaths were harsh and deep, again hurting her lungs. As she inhaled, she smelled her foul-smelling sweat. It was so pungent and nauseating that it seemed like somebody else's. Even the blood in her mouth seemed like somebody else's. Only the pain seemed to be hers—

Just then, there was a cheer from the crowd as the parade entered the field.

Still, all that she could do was wait to be rescued from this strange place. She felt numb beyond reason. The first face she discerned was that of the little boy. As she looked at him, there seemed to be an entire universe in his sorrowful eyes. But soon, the other forms, which had been so densely packed that they had appeared as a solid wall, began to take shape before her. She recoiled from the stares and gaping mouths, but Respoli-Priestess cooed to her as if she were a baby. She had not realized it, but Respoli-Priestess had been holding her all that time. The man was sitting on the ground with her: her head was lying on his lap. Respoli-Priestess was caressing her head like a mother would. She looked around, dazed. Dozens of men were staring down at her, and all that she wanted to do was get away. She felt ashamed somehow. It was the loss of control that she hated: the feeling that she was a slave to some other self...But the parade was coming, bringing their beloved Tio Mendez. From the ground, she heard people excitedly calling his name. Respoli-Priestess, imbued with a kind of maternity that she had never known, managed to smile, telling the onlookers that her fit was over. The onlookers, perhaps unnerved by his maternity— by his *caring*—nodded and tried to direct their attention to the parade; but they kept looking back, unsure.

Her newfound mother told her that he would take her away from here, but she shook her head. This was all that she could manage. Every muscle felt as if it had been shredded; all that she could do was lie there, waiting to heal....The marching band and the cheering still sounded as though she were hearing them from under water. Lying on the ground, surrounded by a forest of feet, it was certainly difficult to get her bearings. The marching band was just slightly out of tune, like the rest of the world. The sun, as it peeked out from behind the smog, was a strange burgundy hue that she had never seen before; the sky seemed dark orange...

The front of the parade was almost to the rostrum. The parade was marching straight through the crowd. The men around her were jostling with one another to make space for it...and the band seemed only a few meters from her. Suddenly, like an excited child, she had to see.

"Pick me up," she told her new mother in the loudest voice she could muster. Respoli-Priestess looked quizzically at her, pleading with his eyes; but when he saw that it was no use, he gestured for two of the warriors to help. Her head whirled as they picked her up. The two warriors each held one of her arms, and her new mother held her around the waist, from behind. She looked around her, again startled by the realization of how huge the crowd was. The band was marching to her left, followed by a few floats; at the end of the procession, on a flat bed truck, Tio Mendez and some aides stood and waved to the cheering crowd. The men raised their triumphant hands and shuffled along to the song of the marching band. For some reason, she wanted to join them, but the impossibility of that left her feeling sorrowful and inept.

The cheering was deafening now. The marching band had reached the platform. As there was nowhere to go, they made a corridor, so that the cortege of cars, floats and the truck carrying Mendez could make it to the platform. Her mother asked her if she was okay, and she leaned back against the warm, smooth fabric that covered his soft body.

Tio Mendez was clad in a new suit that looked so clean that it seemed like a supernatural cloak. He was still gesticulating to the crowd from the truck, working them into a frenzy. He was no more that 20 meters away from her now. Everything seemed close. And Mendez had never looked so...*awesome*. He seemed tall and powerful; his smooth, bronze skin seemed to glisten preternaturally in the sun. In comparison to the gnarled, wretched men around her, Mendez was everything. He seemed imbued with that magical power little girls always attributed to their fathers. He walked as if he were attacking the very air that he was walking through. He seemed like a universe onto himself: an omnipotent being, sucking up the essence of their universe like someone inhaling the air in a paper bag. Furthermore, there was a certain agelessness about him. At times, he seemed only thirty; at times, he seemed ancient—although, without the decrepitude. He seemed to be constantly shifting before one's eyes, like a chameleon changing from branch to branch.

The truck rolled up to the platform; the song of the marching band reached a blaring crescendo as Tio Mendez and his aides began to walk up the stairs. Everyone was clapping loudly as the men ascended the steps. Considering the way that they clapped, she thought that he must be a father to them as well. She wished that she could clap, too, but she was still out of sync with the world.

Mendez's aides and bodyguards took up positions behind the podium. A seat was reserved for Mendez; he took it while another man (one of his aides) went up to the podium to announce him.

"I'm fine," she felt compelled to whisper to her mother; and for a moment, the latter held her just a little tighter.

The band's song was still at its blaring climax. As Mendez settled into the seat of honor on the rostrum, the men cheered even louder as if they, too, sensed that he was the universe. When the marching band's song ended, the cheers came full blast. She was almost rocked back by it, but her mother's arms were there, shielding her from harm.

The man who was to introduce Mendez was speaking now: "We gather here today," he started, a pained timbre in his voice, "the last of the true believers." And there was suddenly silence, as if his words were the only things that existed in the world. As the Goddess' mind was still cloudy, the words were like the wind, blowing through a crevice in her body. They whistled, reaching unexpected highs; they startled her at one moment, then soothed her at the next, so that she was lost in the uncertainty, not knowing whether to panic or rejoice. The people in the crowd seemed to be overcome by this paradox as well, as they stood in awe and stared.

"Yes, brothers," he said, his voice quickening, "rejoice that we won a victory on the field of battle; but know that the true battlefield is in the hearts and minds of those who would reject the Goddess, their Merciful Mother!"

As the Goddess listened to these words, and remembered Quibb's revelation—that The Horde wanted the men to believe in her—she shuddered inside, shaking her head unconsciously.

"We live in a world of sin," the man at the podium bellowed, "within which world governments and family structures, and even common decency, have been torn asunder!"—He paused here dramatically—"Only one realization—that the Goddess is *all* that we have, and have *ever* had—can save us!" He nodded here, knowingly; and the men of the crowd, who had heretofore stared up at him, mesmerized, clapped wildly—*suddenly*. It was difficult to explain. It was not only that their cheering did not seem commensurate with the tone of his words, but that it seemed to be more than cheering: more than the mere voicing of joy. It was pure energy; it was their *souls* that they gave to the man. She felt their essence rising in hot waves; she was jostled by it. She, too, felt what the man must feel: a sort of excitement that left her skin tingling—

"As the last of the true believers, in a world of idolatry and heresy," the man resumed, "we must make this place of filth and degradation pure for the Goddess' return. Others challenge us, but it is not just us that they challenge!" he yelled, his voice bellicose, whipping up the crowd. "Yes, these heathens attack like wild, uncaring animals. But it is not us that they challenge, my brethren! No, it is the word and will of the Goddess! It is that thing that is beyond their bungling actions and idolatry! How dare they think that they can challenge us—can ever defeat what we are!"

The men's joy and pride were overflowing! And it was again as if the world were nothing more than their cheers. She turned her head and looked out on the great multitudes of men, seeing their many hands waving as they shouted their chants. She felt herself being rocked by it. It felt as if it would never stop: as if they would always be in this place, celebrating the man's words. At his seat of honor, Mendez had a content smile on his face. He did not even have to clap, as the others did. The words were for him: he was only letting the rest of them share in them—

"Hear us heathens!" the man at the podium shouted suddenly, inspiring more wild chanting. "Tio Mendez will make you kneel before the will of the Goddess!" And his voice was like thunder, warning them all of the lightning, which seemed destined to come down from the heavens and tear into anything that dared to stand tall...And that was what she thought it was at first. The Goddess was staring up at the man, waiting for lightning, and was not surprised as something flashed before her eyes and exploded with a resounding clap. All at once, the world became fire and light, and a bombastic blast that left everything vibrating. For a moment, she thought that this was hell that they had all fallen into. The flames swept over everything, so bright that they did not illuminate, but instead *blinded*. She felt her hair and clothes melting in the heat.

And it was as if the outside world suddenly disintegrated in the blast: as if the world were suddenly swallowed up, leaving only a girl dependent on the strong arms of her mother. All at once, she realized that Respoli-Priestess and herself were being lifted through the air. They soared as easily as things in a fairy tale; they disappeared into the smoke and flames, as if disappearing into another world. She wanted to laugh at the sensation; but just as the fairy tale began to take shape around her, her putative mother and she hit the ground as if tossed from Grace. She landed first; as they had flipped in the air, her mother landed on top of her; however, considering the size of the crowd, they landed on top of a heap of people. As these people seemed less disoriented by the blast than she was, they were soon fighting to extricate themselves from the pile. She, on the other hand, just lay there, fighting to hold on. People were inadvertently kicking her now, in their desperation to flee….Soon, the people in the pile with her had fled, and it was only she and her mother—and one or two burnt corpses that had landed on top of them. Her mother was on top of her, pinning her to the ground. Her right cheek was being crushed against the hard earth. The earth smelt metallic, like rust. She felt sick; she wanted to cry again: not because of the pain, itself, but because it seemed as if it would never stop. Her mother's arms were tight around her diaphragm: she could hardly breathe. She tried to move, but could do nothing but let the pain flow through her. She coughed and squinted through the smoke, but she could discern nothing; and with the smoke, and its harsh, sulfurous smell, it was again as though only she and her mother existed in the world. Partly deaf from the explosion, it was as though time stood still—

But all at once, after some indefinite period of deafness and numbness, the chaos began as three-quarters of a million voices rose up in terror. Gone was the courage and defiance that had sounded in the men's voices when they cheered for the man on the rostrum. Beyond the smoke, she heard them running and screaming, trampling one another. When the smoke finally began to dissipate, she looked around wildly; but still dumbfounded, and pinned to the ground, she was unable to understand the odd music that was produced by their screams and the ensuing stampede. All that she knew, was that her mother was still there: that his arms were still securely around her. She stared ahead in a daze; that is, pinned on her right side, she stared ahead, level with the ground. There was something next to her. With the smoke, and her lightheadedness, she could hardly tell what it was. At first, it danced before her eyes like a child's rendition of things: a stick figure, cast against a surreal landscape. But then more of the smoke cleared, and she squinted at the figure no more than half a meter away from her. She squinted at the face, with its agape mouth, from which a last, agonized cry had escaped; she looked at its eyes, which were frozen in time, looking towards the menacing thing approaching on the horizon. It was one of the warriors, who had only moments ago been holding her arm! For some reason, she went to cry out to him: to force air from her lungs and call to him; but just then more of the smoke cleared, and she saw his neck, which was bent at a ludicrous angle from his body!

More screams littered the air! She thought that some of them surely had to be hers, because she looked around, seeing more ludicrous things. She tried to make sense of it, but nothing made sense anymore. Finally, however, she looked up to where the rostrum should have been—she looked up as if in slow motion—and saw that it was now only a pile of rubble, which was still smoldering from the explosion. Everything that was once there was gone now: the fine bunting, the people...And with the strength granted to her by her fear of the unknown, she somehow managed to lift her mother's torso and look back, over her shoulder. She had to stare for...perhaps for an eternity, before she began to understand that half of her mother's face was gone. Flying debris had taken it. A few centimeters to the left, and it would have taken her own head. She stared, hardly able to comprehend it, because the rest of the face was fine, still staring back with the inexhaustible calmness of mothers.

Time became strange again. She fell in and out of consciousness; every time she looked around, the sight of the hundreds of prone, unmoving bodies made something in her recoil. It seemed as if hours passed...*days*, in fact. The sirens came—it seemed like thousands of them—at first sounding like fanfare. Lying there on the ground, attached to the husk of her mother, she looked around as if expecting another parade. In time, soldiers and the altruistic ran past her, checking to see if anyone could be saved from the rubble of the rostrum; some went around, scavenging from the corpses and dying. As the corpse of her mother covered her, they did not see her. She just lay there and watched. This too—this period of waiting—was like a dream. Mangled things that had once been human beings were extricated from the rubble of the rostrum. Arms and legs that could not be traced to any one corpse were tossed in a pile, to be matched up later—if even that. *Everything was so strange!* The sky was a dirty color, like the browning pages of old pulp novels. The billowy clouds seemed somehow "angry—"

But some men were coming about now—scavengers, it seemed. She cringed as they got closer; their steps seemed to thunder in her ears. They were moving her mother; she screamed out—or at least tried to. The scavengers were rolling her and her mother over, so that she was now on top. She did not want to be in the light—to be *seen*. She put up her arm in a feeble attempt to guard her face from their attacks; but just then, with a frown, she recognized Mansmann....

After the bomb went off, those too close to the front had been killed instantly; those at a certain distance, had been caught in the stampede after the blast. The old doctor and Xi had been far enough back to avoid the blast, and yet close enough to avoid the stampede. At first, Xi had wanted to run too, but the old doctor had gone the other way; and still gripped by his strange yearning for companionship, Xi had followed the man. In actuality, the old man had hardly even known that he was there.

Now, the old man seemed to have found what he was looking for. "Are you all right?" he asked the Goddess. Xi looked on confusedly. Similarly, it took the Goddess a while to decipher what the old doctor was saying. At first, she only stared, still numb. When she seemed unresponsive, the old man began trying to pull Respoli-Priestess' arms apart. Mansmann did not have the strength and looked at Xi imploringly, so that he joined in the old doctor's (seemingly strange) endeavor. The two men were groaning now, their muscles straining as they tried to gain leverage. At first, this appalled the Goddess as well. She wanted only to lie there, secure in her mother's arms; but with the snapping of tendons and joints, she was finally freed. The old doctor pulled her away from Respoli-Priestess' corpse, checking frantically to see if she was hurt.

She could breathe at last. She looked back at the mangled frame now, with its arms bent back at impossible angles. She looked at the bloody remains of the face. Her own body was covered with that blood. That was probably why Mansmann seemed so frantic. He kept asking her if anything hurt, but she was still getting her bearings. She looked around at the broken frames of the warriors—

The little boy! She had forgotten about him. His frame lay prone about a meter from her. Suddenly revived, she rushed over to the little boy. The old doctor and Xi followed her over. While she bent down to hold the little boy, Mansmann and Xi stood above them. There were no visible wounds, but the little boy was not breathing. She looked back pleadingly at the doctor. Mansmann, satisfied that she was fine, bent down to the little boy, beginning CPR. He worked on the little boy feverishly for a while, then, shaking his head at the Goddess, he gave up. She stared at him, at first not comprehending. But then, she nodded and bowed her head. Taking Mansmann's place above the little boy, she caressed his face. As she looked down at that face, something began to grow within her. At first, it seemed like mere grief, but she knew that she was beyond that. It was the same feeling of power she had felt before—but now somehow refined and perfected within her. She bent her head and kissed the little boy on the forehead; instantaneously and inexplicably, he moved. They all looked on in amazement as the boy opened his eyes and looked up at them. He looked first at the old doctor, then Xi; when his eyes came to rest on the Goddess, he smiled. Suddenly laughing out, she hugged him tightly. As Mansmann and Xi looked on, they did not know whether to be unnerved by the way the boy had come back to life, or to be relieved that a life had been spared. They did not even want to acknowledge what they had seen—or to define it in their minds as miraculous. In the end, they put aside the unexplainable and smiled at the simple sight of the Goddess hugging the little boy. As for the Goddess, she once again felt herself opening up to new possibilities. She looked out on the world now, suddenly feeling at one with the sky and the earth and the wind. Seeing the way she looked at the world, Mansmann and Xi stared at her, unsure. The two men seemed out of place—cowed by her power and the strange new sense of certainty that shone in her eyes—

But just then, there was a great gasp from the men looking through the remains of the rostrum. Xi and the others looked over at the smoldering wreckage to see someone being pulled out of the rubble. Xi's heart leaped in his chest! *It was Mendez*: he was alive! Not only was he alive: his suit seemed untouched; there did not seem to be a hair out of place. How was it possible? Mendez was alive—and *whole*. Yet, this alone was not why Xi felt as if his heart would leap out of his throat. One of the excavators was supporting Mendez by the shoulder; and when Xi looked closer, he realized that it was Quibb! Mendez seemed to realize this as well, because he stared in disbelief and horror. The man looked like he had just realized that he had sold his soul to the devil. In the meantime, onlookers suddenly began to cheer. A mobile news crew, which had before been focused on the corpses surrounding the remains of the rostrum, rushed over to capture the proof of Mendez's immortality. As they had a live feed, Xi suddenly realized that this scene was reaching every pocket of the city. Those who only moments ago had been crying at the horror of it all, were now screaming out in joy. The sound of the city's joy was thunderous. It rose up suddenly— louder than anything Xi had ever heard before. They had all witnessed a miracle. No one else from the rostrum—and no one within 50 meters of the rostrum—had survived. The cheering rose up like a tidal wave, cresting above their heads. Only Xi and Mendez—*and the Goddess*—seemed horrified; only they stared at Quibb, realizing what he had done, and what he could do. At that moment, Quibb, who still held the quivering Mendez, looked down at Xi and the Goddess. He did it deliberately, his satisfied smile seen only by them.

As millions of men cheered throughout the city, the Goddess' mind could only churn out one thought: Quibb had made her come here so that she could see the true power of The Horde—its ability to manipulate the men and herself. Quibb had manufactured those cheers; and all that the Goddess could conclude, was that she was another manufactured icon to be used when the time was right. The men were cheering for Mendez, thinking that he would help them fight against The Horde, when The Horde had set up Mendez! The precision of it was maddening.

As the initial wave of cheers began to subside, the soldiers seemed to come to their senses. They rushed to surround Mendez now; in the process, they looked like seraphim surrounding the Messiah. Only Xi, Mendez and the Goddess knew where the real power lay; and then, in the scramble of the soldiers to surround and protect Mendez, Quibb disappeared without a trace! Again, only the trio realized this, but the horror of this secret awareness was seen clearly on their faces.

The men of the city were already creating scriptures around the miracle. Xi was numb....Two miracles in one day...However, Quibb's was of course grander than the one involving the little boy....

The soldiers were taking Mendez off in an armored van. Seeing Mendez disappear, Xi felt something quake in his heart: perhaps the realization of how deep he was in this thing. He stared at the hastily retreating van as it drove through the sea of dead bodies. In their haste, the soldiers were literally driving over the dead and dying. Xi felt sick; he watched the retreating vehicle for a while, then he shook his head and looked away.

Excited by the cheering multitudes, the little boy began hopping about. The child looked as if he had never even faced death—something about it was unnerving...*unnatural*...and it was not only that they were still surrounded by hundreds, if not *thousands* of burnt, broken corpses. It was more proof of how meaningless life was. Xi and the doctor made eye contact then. The old man was frowning at him: the man had always been intrigued by the secrets that seemed to lie behind Xi's eyes—

Someone off to their left was moaning on the ground. The Goddess went over to help. Xi, Mansmann and the little boy instinctively followed her as she knelt down beside the suffering man. Xi and Mansmann exchanged a glance again, but now it was Xi who was in search of secrets. There was something amazing about the strange person that the old doctor had been so desperate to find—and it was not only the ostensible miracle with the little boy that intrigued him. Xi could not take his eyes off the man—off the *Goddess*. He watched the softness, the attentiveness: the things stereotypically thought to preside mostly in women—in the *feminine*. There seemed to be an energy—a *glow*—emanating from that person. *Could it be a woman?* he asked himself. *Of course not*. Xi felt like laughing the thought away; and yet, he could not stop looking....

The boy was still hopping merrily about the corpses. The old doctor went over to the Goddess; Xi followed. They did not even know one another's names, and yet they were bound in this thing. The Goddess was holding the moaning man's hand, whispering something that made the man's screams subside. There was nothing but a touch and a smile, but the man seemed at ease. He died that way. They moved on to other men, with her in the lead. It was as if the men's screams of pain called out to her alone. Still, there was something about those screams that seemed vital—*humanizing*. Something drew them in closer, when they should have been repulsed. The screaming men, touched by her gentle hands, seemed, if not at peace, then pacified by something that neither Xi nor the doctor could begin to fathom....

Soldiers were beginning to come about. The old doctor, watching them over his shoulder, became antsy. He had a sudden urge to cover the Goddess and hide her. He felt, all at once, that if anything happened to her, then he would die. He stood around nervously, formulating how he was going to get her to safety—

She looked up at him then, just having quieted the cries of a man with a broken back. "You're the one, aren't you?" she said, her eyes narrowing: "...Mansmann." That image from the videodisk had been playing in her mind.

Mansmann stared as if not seeing: as if not *hearing*...He nodded, feeling numb.

"You caused all this?" she said, her voice as gentle as her ministrations to the dying.

He could not move; he felt himself on the verge of tears—as though his moment of absolution were at hand. He nodded again, feeling suddenly relieved by his admission.

In the meantime, Xi, who was still at his side, frowned, feeling left out of their secrets. He had not really heard what she had said....

A truckload of solders was coming up, its siren blaring; Mansmann came back to his senses. "We have to get you out of here," he said to her, "...we've done all we can."

She stared at him, then she looked at Xi, as if just noticing him. Xi had to fight to keep his eyes on her: she was like something so bright that he wanted to divert his gaze. He did not know what it was, but for the life of him, he did not want to leave her. In that moment, as strange as it sounded, he would *die* for her, with neither hesitation nor questions.

She called to the little boy and held his hand, then she looked at Mansmann. Finally, her gaze rested on Xi.

Mansmann glanced at Xi, and then nodded as if to say that she could trust him.

Xi felt lost again—left out.

She spoke up then, her voice rising above the question implied in his eyes. Her voice seemed to rise above the world, with its sirens and screams of agony (and residual joy). "...This can't go on," she said, looking around. "It's too unnatural....You need the women."

Xi stared at her, his eyes growing large. "*You're a woman!*" he said, his throat dry. The old doctor seemed horrified at Xi's words; he looked around nervously to see if anyone had heard.

She looked at Xi, her eyes having a clarity that he had never seen before. There was a strength there—a *power*—which he had sensed, but which now seemed beyond his comprehension. "Yes," she answered, simply.

"But *how*...!" He could hardly breathe—

Mansmann seemed as if he would go insane! Xi looked from the old man's nervous exasperation to her calmness. He had to know—

"There are more like you?" he blurted out.

She looked around the landscape as she talked, not at him. "There have to be," she mused. Then she looked him straight in the eyes again: "If there aren't, then the world is over."

Xi nodded. He was once again possessed by his old thought: only the women could save them. He could not believe it: someone else had finally said those words, and it was a woman! He felt giddy; he was shaking—

"I know where there are other women," he said—he almost *screamed*. The words reverberated through him and he felt relieved that they were finally out of him. "I know where they are," he said again, both horrified and relieved to hear his words. Mansmann and the Goddess stared up at him, frowning, not knowing if they should take him seriously. "They're in the city—"

"The city?" the other two said in unison.

"Yes," he said, both enlivened and horrified that he had told the secret.

More soldiers were coming around. "We have to leave here *now*!" Mansmann whispered frantically.

Nodding, they walked off together.

XI

It is how people view death that defines how they live their lives—
and ultimately if their lives are meaningful.
VERSE 2312:3 OF *The Teachings*

Shaka stood before a screen in his suite, watching the events of the rally. His body was rigid, as though being forced to endure an invisible burden. As he stared at the screen, it was almost as though he were seeing something past it—events that had yet to unfold. Circe walked up behind him and stood watching the screen with him. After a while, she sighed, saying:

"You have made a dangerous enemy today, Shaka."

Shaka still seemed caught in his trance: "...There is no way he could have survived the explosion...*no* way."

Circe smiled, "—Unless he has the power of God behind him."

Shaka turned and looked at her uneasily; she laughed at his expression:

"No, I don't believe that either, but the men will believe it."

Shaka thought about it for a while. "Yes."

"Every God needs a Judas, Shaka, and you're going to be it when they discover that you set that bomb."

"...I have to kill Mendez."

Circe chuckled, saying: "You've tried that already, and look where it's gotten you." She looked at him closely now: "You're tired of all this, aren't you? ...All this plotting and back-stabbing."

"...Yes," he said absentmindedly, still staring at the screen.

"In that other world—seven years ago—you used to enjoy this game, but it's not fun anymore."

"Fun?" Shaka repeated with a laugh: the phrasing seemed ridiculous in the face of what the world had become.

"Let's get away, Shaka," she said, stepping around him and standing in front of the screen, so that he was forced to look at her. When she did so, he blinked drowsily, as though just realizing that she was in the room with him. He stared at her for a while, noting the strange excitement in her eyes, then he laughed, saying:

"You mean we should go to Tahiti?"

She ignored his sarcasm: "Some place better—where we'll never have to worry about other people again: where there'll be no schemes…no power struggles."

"—A fairy tale," he instinctively scoffed, even though his voice lacked passion.

"Do you trust me, Shaka?" she asked then, still looking at him closely.

He stared for a long while, amazed to find that he actually did trust her. The realization was debilitating—or enlivening. He was not sure which. The only thing he knew was that he was tired of it all—just as Circe had said. Circe smiled then, as though reading his thoughts:

"I'll be back tomorrow morning."

"*What*?" he said, an anxious edge suddenly entering his voice. "Where are you going?"

"Just trust me. I have to get something that will allow you to rest—allow us *both* to rest. I'm tired too." When she hugged him, he was so amazed by the way her body felt in his arms that he did not want to let go.

Sometimes the best way to hide is to reveal oneself.
VERSE 23:10 OF *The Teachings*

Since the beginning, everything had been spiraling out of control. As the men from the rally spilled out into the streets, Xi, Mansmann, the Goddess and the little boy fled back to Mansmann's lab. Now that they had found one another, they felt suddenly vulnerable—especially in the midst of so many agitated men. They felt conspicuous—especially Xi and Mansmann. After seven years, it was strange to walk with a woman. The thought of something happening to her made them sick to their stomachs; and yet, surrounded by so many armed men, who were themselves paranoid and insane, the dangers to the woman seemed infinite.

It was about one in the afternoon, but it seemed much later. A storm was on the horizon. The wind had picked up, whipping refuse across the streets and sidewalks. As the wind began to howl, the men started yelling in order to be heard. As for the men, they seemed possessed by two contradictory demons. The first one filled them with a strange kind of intoxication; everywhere, men were laughing, talking about what had happened at the rally: the *miracle*! Those who had not been there listened, with childish wonder and excitement, to those who had. The witnesses rose to a kind of celebrity status, like the religious prophets of yesteryear. On top of that, the screens and billboards were all flickering with images of Mendez's ascension: of the miracle that happened before all of their eyes. The reporter kept repeating that everyone within a 50-meter radius of the rostrum had been killed instantly—except for Mendez, who had survived without being scratched. The men of the city looked at it all and cheered.

However, the second demon filled them with the madness of war. Men brought out their guns and looked suspiciously at those around them—*even while they celebrated*. Yes, Mendez was God's anointed—some were even making the leap and saying that Mendez was God, Himself—but even Jesus had had his enemies; even Jesus had been brought low by the schemes of petty men. This being so, a new kind of self-righteousness rose in the men. Those already preparing for The Horde's return now prepared themselves for a holy war. The Voice had been framing the upcoming fight in these terms for days now, but with Mendez's Lazarus-like ascension from what had seemed to be documented, certain death, a ragtag force of millions now became unified under what they thought to be the banner of God.

Presently, as Xi and the others neared a particularly crowded intersection, they looked ahead and noticed that a column of armed men—*soldiers*—had set up a checkpoint. The men ahead of them were now slowing down—as there was a bottleneck at the narrow corridor of the checkpoint. The men were being forced to go through the checkpoint single file—all under the watchful gaze of two-dozen armed brutes. When Xi saw this, he felt as though his blood had turned to ice in his veins; he looked back at Mansmann in horror: they both looked at the woman with the same expression. Around them, the men were talking about saboteurs—and so were the video billboards. A dragnet was supposedly being set up to capture this fifth column; there was speculation about The Horde planting spies; soldiers were told to mobilize and defend the homeland. It suddenly occurred to Xi that there would be no Mardi Gras tonight—and not out of some sense of mourning or seriousness, but because Mardi Gras had taken place during the rally. The rally had been the ultimate sideshow attraction: the hero had faced peril and come out unscathed—and supernaturally so. On top of that, millions of men were being enlisted to join the show.

It was at that moment that Xi realized that Quibb's voice was not playing down the streets anymore. He had not heard Quibb's voice since the bombing at the rally. His first instinct was a primal kind of panic—like a child in a crowd suddenly realizing that he had lost sight of his mother. However, the prospect of getting the woman to safety brought him back to his senses.

Looking at the soldiers in the intersection, he knew that having the woman go through the checkpoint was an unacceptable risk. The soldiers were not making everyone submit to strip searches or anything like that; still, there would be too many dire consequences if they discovered her. Seeing no other choice, Xi and the others turned and went against the stream of men. When they reached the next intersection, they turned onto a side street that was mercifully less crowded. Then, once free of the throng, they began to run. They ran almost without noticing it; and again, for Xi and Mansmann, the reality of the woman brought on strange new anxieties. Xi kept looking back at her, wondering, in the back of his mind, if this was all a dream. The world was certainly taking on a dream-like hue now. The sky, which had before merely been overcast, was now filled with quick-moving, charcoal-colored clouds. The clouds had appeared out of nowhere, as if God were venting His fury for their attempted treachery against Mendez. As always, anything seemed possible; and as Xi ran, he returned to his old thought that Quibb was the secret mastermind of their destinies. In fact, everything that he had been unable to account for, was now attributed to Quibb. Changes in the sky and the wind were all Quibb's doing. The souls of the men and his own pointless existence were all due to Quibb's machinations. Guiltily, he remembered their last meeting, when he had laughed at the fact that Quibb seemed confounded for once; he had rejoiced that Quibb seemed dismayed by his newfound sense of freedom—but all of that was contradicted by what Xi had seen today. He forgot about Clem and Steve—and all the things that went against the reality that Quibb was operating with the precision of God. In fact, he now found himself thinking that Quibb's apparent confusion and vulnerability at their last meeting must have been part of his master plan. Yes, in the back of his mind, the doubts remained, but when one had been hit by a truck, one did not stand around analyzing and moralizing. In fact, one did not stand at all: the force of the blow directed one's fate, so that it became a simple matter of physics. Even if one managed to survive the initial blow, the only thing that consciousness allowed was shock. Moreover, in just the same way that a religious man countered his doubts with deeper and more stringent prayer regimes, Xi prayed to Quibb in the way he always had—through awe and confusion and a dawning sense that he was willing to do anything to be part of Quibb's greatness.

Now, as Xi ran along with the woman, it suddenly occurred to him that Quibb had sent him to the rally to find her. Who was he to doubt Quibb? Quibb was up there in the heavens, mastering their lives; and as Xi acknowledged this, he felt the security of a child. He was almost insane with his love for Quibb now. For a moment, his soul swelled with the joy of being Quibb's slave—*God's* slave. After all, it was so easy: all he had to do was surrender and let go of all doubt…but somehow, the reality of the men around him kept him from achieving this state. He had always thought of the men as fools, not brothers. Their mindless cheering now seemed to mock him. Their obvious madness inevitably made him question his own sanity. Maybe if Quibb had been before him at that very moment, smiling in that enigmatic way of his, things would have been different. However, it was then, as his strange struggle with Quibb's religion reached its climax, that he happened to look back at the woman, again feeling that jolt of wonder and anxiety…. No, even while his awe of Quibb remained high, he could not totally surrender to Quibb while being confronted by the reality of a woman. Just as he had always thought, the reality of a woman was a dose of clarity for addled minds….

An hour later, Xi was still leading the procession; but when he reached the next corner, he stopped abruptly and darted back. The woman and the boy, who had been following closely behind, bumped into him. Mansmann was a good 15 paces off and came up to them wheezing and panting. On the next street, about 30 soldiers were making another blockade. The soldiers walked with a macho swagger that told everyone that they would not hesitate to shoot. With Xi's anxieties reaching new limits, the soldiers seemed more like trolls setting up a toll bridge, than human beings; and yet, with their gaunt frames and long tresses of Luxuriant Hair, even they seemed like girls playing soldier games. If the soldiers followed any chain of command, it was hard to tell. Most of them were youths who, in years past, would have comprised the city's murderous youth gangs. Now, they were placed in the contradictory position of keeping order.

Xi again looked back at the woman uneasily. If one of those thugs even spotted them standing there clandestinely, they would be undone. He thought about crossing to the other side of the street, which was still clear, and walking past. However, he realized that that would probably attract too much attention. They backed away. They were only five blocks away from Mansmann's lab. Xi, turning, looked at the woman closely for the first time, surprised at how calm she looked. There was something soft and comforting about her. There was a beauty there, of the type he had not thought about in seven years—maybe longer than that—and that troubled him. Glancing at her baggy shirt, he noticed how its contours delineated her small, perky breasts. It was one of those maddening things that one only saw if one looked. Every day, he passed dozens of men more feminine—more *beautiful*, in fact, than her—and thought nothing of it. Now, it seemed obvious that anyone seeing her would immediately know that she was a woman. He looked over at Mansmann helplessly. The old man was still catching his breath; as the exhausting prospect of another dash seemed to manipulate his judgment, he panted:

"I say we just walk past them."

Xi thought about it for a while: they might walk around the block only to meet up with a worse band of youths. The prospect of the dire consequences to be borne if the youths found the woman still ate away at him, but he nodded to Mansmann's suggestion anyway. The quicker they got out of the streets, the better—at least, this was what he told himself to keep his fears at bay. He and the old man looked at the woman anxiously—she nodded as well.

Xi took the lead again. He tried to walk slowly, but not so slowly that he looked like he was trying to hide something; he tried picking up his pace a little, only to find himself panicking at the idea that he might be walking too quickly. It was maddening! He could feel the tension on his face. What if they asked him a question! He would be undone in a second. His throat was dry. He felt as though he had guilt written all over his face. He wanted to rush back, but it was already too late. He felt like a condemned man taking his final steps. The youths were talking excitedly amongst themselves. Xi hoped beyond reason that they would not notice them. He could feel his leg muscles tensing up: they would cramp soon!

It was at that moment that one of the youths turned and looked at them. The youth's comrades were still joking, but he stared suspiciously at Xi and the others. Xi unwittingly made eye contact with the youth; but then, terrified, he did not know whether to maintain it or look away: both seemed like indictments! Xi and the others had not even walked to the center of the street yet, but they were already attracting attention. If they had thought this through, they would have tried to talk naturally amongst themselves: tried joking and laughing like many of the other men were doing. That would have taken attention from them. Like fools, they walked silently, single file, with the guilt showing on all of their faces. It was over! The youth was saying something to his comrades. They all turned and looked at Xi and the others as they approached. Xi thought that he would faint. He kept telling himself not to run: that would be a death sentence. Still, it seemed to be the only logical thing to do; rather, it seemed to be the last *instinctual* thing to do, for his logic had abandoned him a long time ago. He was sure that he was trembling—he could not even tell anymore. Also, he still did not know whether to look at the youths or to look away. As he tried to make up his mind, his eyes seemed shifty and dishonest—

"Hey, you!"

Xi almost toppled at the words. *God*, he was shaking uncontrollably!

"Where'd you come from?" It was a pug-faced youth with a scar over his left eye. He had the face of a boxer—and a very unsuccessful one at that. The youth hopped over the barricade and was soon right in Xi's face. He seemed to be the youths' leader; the others were following, encircling Xi and the others. It was over! Xi's lips were trembling—

"Hey, want a blowjob?"

For a moment, Xi thought that he had said the words; but with a frown, he realized that his lips were still fumbling to open. He looked to his side: the woman had said it!

"I do it real good," she was saying in a throaty voice. She was unbuttoning her shirt, the protuberance of her small breasts showing. Xi was numb. He looked over at Mansmann, who stared back just as unbelievingly.

"I've had all my parts fixed," she was saying, a kind of demented sexuality gleaming in her eyes. Her shirt was open, the small cleavage showing. "Just for a few dollars—"

"Fuckers!" the pug-faced youth screamed in disgust, his face becoming a mass of contoured frowns. "I can spot you people a mile off!" He looked at Xi, his repugnance deepening:

"You just fucked him, didn't you!"

Xi stared blankly for a moment, but then he took his lead from the woman. For once, his nervousness worked for him. "A guy gets lonely," he heard himself saying—

"You people should be shot! If I had my way, you'd all be floating in the goddamn river!" The youth looked over at the woman again: "Cover that fucking chest! Goddamn freaks! [He seemed unsure of what to do next, and this seemed to frustrate him.] Get the fuck out of here!" he yelled at last, trembling with rage and some unacknowledged sense of ineptitude.

The woman was leading the way now; Xi and Mansmann followed, looking pathetic in the wake of her brazen, confident stride.

"Goddamn shit packers!" the youth yelled after them. He was laughing now—first nervously, then with a sense of relief. The other youths joined in as well, hurling other epithets. Xi and Mansmann, still trembling, could hardly believe it. Only the little boy seemed unconcerned as he skipped along merrily by the woman's side. Had they actually escaped? Xi had the urge to look back, but he did not dare. It was not until they had reached the next corner that he sneaked a glance back. The youths were talking amongst themselves once again, not even looking in their direction. A sliver of a nervous smile came to his face.

"…How did you know?" he whispered.

She looked back at him at that moment. That wonderful calmness still showing in her eyes as she said, "Sometimes the best way to hide, is to reveal yourself."

The thing about conspiracies is that to keep them going, one constantly has to be constructing one's possible adversary—one's scheming devil—into an all-knowing god.
VERSE 232:23 OF *The Teachings*

After its showy prelude, the storm finally descended upon the city in earnest. Rather than simply raining, it was as if water were being pelted from the sky. It hit the ground with a drumming sound more characteristic of hail than rain. The men all ran for cover. They stared out with wonder from doorways and beneath awnings. There was something wonderful about a good shower. It enlivened the soul and quickened the senses—just like the first snow of winter. A couple of the men, overcome by a strange childlike joy, leapt out into the rain and began dancing about. Some leapt into puddles, giggling like little boys that knew that their mothers were too preoccupied to notice their naughtiness. There had not been a storm like that in a while....

Mendez was in a room by himself. It was a posh midtown suite, in what used to be an exclusive hotel. Supposedly, the bed he was lying on had once been slept in by the President—that is, the last one before the apocalypse. Still, given his state of mind, a pile of bricks would have afforded him the same comfort. The wind and rain were coming through the open window, making the gossamer curtains dance like a specter. The carpet was getting soaked; and with all the wind, a floor lamp near the window seemed on the verge of collapse. Nevertheless, he was too drained and preoccupied to notice those things. His mind kept returning to the events of the rally.

After getting to the podium, the only thing that he could remember was a moment of disorientation, a blinding light…and then The Voice of Conscience pulling him out of the surrounding rubble. The sequence had literally passed like that: in milliseconds. After that, he had felt out of place as the men sorting through the rubble stared at him in awe, and camera crews rushed over to capture the entire thing. Initially, he had been so dazed that he had not realized why they were staring. Only when he looked around at all the rubble—and then, finally, out to where the crowd had been, seeing the thousands of mangled corpses—had he realized. He had stood there ineptly, finally getting an inkling of The Voice's mastery as he stared into the man's twinkling eyes. Worse than that, there had been something about touching the man—about being supported by the man's warm, stable arms—that had left him undone. His skin had crawled…and then everyone had begun to cheer for him. People that had been running away from the blast, had turned and come back. The cheers had crested in the air, so that it became apparent that people outside the park had been cheering as well. The scenes of his emergence from the rubble had been carried live, broadcasted to every video billboard and TV in the city. *Millions* had cheered for him; in that moment of euphoria, those millions had implicitly pledged their souls to him. It should have been a moment of triumph, but he had felt dead inside as he stared at The Voice's calm, confident smile…and then, during the commotion caused by the soldiers rushing to protect him, The Voice had miraculously disappeared….

Mendez sighed. After what had happened today (and reports he had seen on TV) he was certain that his ascension was complete—and yet, he had never felt so low in his life. For the first time in his memory, he felt as though he were out of the loop of information. Although thrust to the vanguard by The Voice, he was acutely aware that he was just a pawn. All about him, he felt the harsh wrenching of The Voice's puppet strings. He felt enslaved and *doomed*….With a pang of remorse, he found himself yearning for the quiet solitude of his basement apartment on 116th Street…but all of that was another lifetime away now—

The floor lamp finally lost its battle with the wind, and toppled to the ground with a loud crash. Mendez, barely emerging from his daze, looked about the room. As he blinked drowsily and looked around, he suddenly realized that somebody else was in the room with him! Just then, a man stepped out from behind the dancing curtains, but remained in the shadows with only a silhouette of his face showing. Mendez went to scream out, but it was as if his vocal chords had been taken away; and then, sitting up in bed with a jerky motion, he realized that the man in the shadows was The Voice of Conscience. Mendez stared into the shadows in mute horror. The Voice took a step closer to him, and the light from the window illuminated the man's face. So much seemed to lie behind that calm, confident smile…and Mendez's mind suddenly erupted with thoughts of how it had felt to be held by that man. As a ghost, The Voice had been terrifying; but as flesh and blood, the man seemed more horrible—seemed to somehow transcend the boundaries between fact and fantasy. The Voice was a ghost with substance. He had both the power to dissolve into the ether, and to shake the very foundations of the world. He entered men's souls with the same ease that his voice traversed the airwaves. On top of all that, Mendez felt his will and courage eroding in the silence of the room. Only the distant rumbling of thunder told him that there was still an outside world—and that other men might actually be out there, living their lives. The silence ate away at him like some kind of ravenous beast; and instinctively coming to the conclusion that hearing his own voice would be the first step in reclaiming his soul, Mendez cleared his throat and forced himself to speak. His voice was unsteady and hoarse as he ventured: "…Did you plant the bomb?"

The Voice chuckled. "Of course not."

Mendez was encouraged somehow: he had spoken and he was still alive. "…But you knew it was there?" he ventured again.

"Of course."

"Then why didn't you stop it?" he blurted out before he had thought better of it.

"For what?" The Voice chuckled with an incredulous expression. "It has obviously fit nicely into our needs….The bomb was set by one of your adversaries—Shaka."

"Shaka," Mendez whispered. He felt suddenly cold. As a pirate broadcaster, he had led a campaign against Shaka for years—from the shadows at least—but now he was out in the open. He felt suddenly vulnerable—like a crustacean that had molted its exoskeleton, and which had to hide from predators until its shell hardened again. As he again looked up at The Voice's calm, confident smile, another surge of helplessness and horror came over him. Such horror triggered the body's fight or flight mechanisms, making men either cowardly or murderous. At that moment, he had an impulse to rush The Voice and leap out of the window with him. He did not just want to kill: the shame of what he had become, made him want to destroy himself as well. It was pure madness; for a moment, a wild cry grew within him as he tried to scrounge up the courage for the dash; but just then, The Voice laughed. It was a horrible, cackling laugh. Mendez shuddered, his momentary madness fleeing back to its nether regions. The Voice took a few steps closer to him then, his eyes intent, his mordant smile seeming like a scowl on his face.

"Mr. Mendez," he started in a calm, deliberate voice, "it is the nature of men that they try to destroy that which has created them. Men, ever contradictory, want two things above all else: to *become* powerful and to *succumb* to the Ultimate Power. Ever confused, when they glimpse the Power that they've been searching for, they forget all that has passed before, and hunger only to destroy it. They think that they can destroy that which has created them—that which has been the center of their lives—without being destroyed themselves. *Look at me, Mendez!*" he screamed, pausing so that Mendez's feeble eyes could take him in. "I cannot be destroyed!" And at that, he faded away. He did it slowly, deliberately, staring into Mendez's eyes so that there could be no doubt where the power lay. Mendez hid his face and cried.

Democracy and free will are the ultimate tools of oppression.
VERSE 12:2 OF *The Teachings*

The last three members of Respoli-Priestess' band surrounded them when they got back to Mansmann's lab/clinic. One of the men had stayed behind because he had cracked his ribs in the mad rush across the George Washington Bridge; another was just now recovering from a stomach infection; the third, Kramer, had stayed behind to watch the other two.

"The others are dead," the Goddess told these three men, simply. The men hobbled along after her, clinging to her rain-soaked clothes like frightened children. The woman turned around and stared deeply at her three followers as they entreated her for some kind of comfort and assurance. "I won't leave you," she whispered at last. And then, when their cries became too much for her: "Go back to your rooms. Tomorrow we'll figure out what to do." While the woman was talking to her followers, Xi and Mansmann stood by the side, watching the weird dynamics of cult worship. Indeed, by then, they found themselves being drawn into that state of mind themselves. Whatever the case, at her urging, her last three followers reluctantly but dutifully left her. She nodded to the doctor and Xi then, and they followed her and the little boy to her room.

In that small, dimly lit room, she and the little boy sat on the bed; Mansmann and Xi found chairs. They all sat down with their damp clothes.

She addressed herself to Xi first; she was blunt: "You say you know where the women are?"

"Yes, but...[there seemed to be so much to say—and so much to *ask*. Also, there was something in her eyes that made him unfocused and uneasy. There was something about her face that wore him down. Mansmann observed him closely, wondering if he was going to figure out that she was the Goddess: if he was going to be pulverized by the possibilities when he figured it out. For the moment however, Xi was still trying to grasp the realization that she was a woman. He found himself looking at her the way a 13-year-old boy looked at a beautiful girl. She was sitting with her legs open—like a man—and that pose made his stomach twinge. As he stared at her, he felt a panicky kind of lust rising in him. He forced himself to look away. Refocusing his mind, he cleared his throat and began again.]...They're at The Company," he started, "—I think they're hidden underground."

"Have you seen them?"

He had not expected that: "No, but...I figured it out, see: The Horde... that's why they bombed. They wanted to flush out where things were. Under The Company, there are dozens of underground floors that nobody knows about: that's where the women are. [He danced about the issue of Quibb: the woman and the old doctor seemed dubious enough as it was.]

"—But you've never actually *seen* them, right?" she asked again.

He felt ashamed and deflated. He had instinctively wanted to impress her; he spoke up quickly, a hint of defensiveness in his voice: "I haven't *seen* them...but something's down there. It all makes sense..." He remembered the keys in his pocket; suddenly desperate, he stood up and pulled out the keys, so that he could show them. "*See*: these are the keys to the secret entrance. On the night of the first bombing, I got them." [He danced around the details with the guard and his first murder, too.] He tossed the Goddess the keys.

She twirled the keys before her eyes, then sat back on the bed with her back against the wall. She seemed deep in thought for a moment. Then: "We have to find out for sure," she mused.

"I'm going back to work at the complex tomorrow," Xi spoke up, desperate to make up: to *prove* himself. "I'll figure out a way." He sounded pathetic: like a dog that wanted to please its master. She stared into him: her eyes were resolute and clear. He looked away....

Mansmann had been quiet during all this, staring at them both intently. He had waited for his turn with a kind of rapt patience. Seeing his chance now, all the questions he had always wanted to ask her now bubbled to the surface. He had to restrain himself in order to focus his mind:

"...So," he started, almost sounding out of breath, "where did you come from?" She looked over at him abruptly; there was something unnerving about the eagerness in his eyes. Also, for a moment, she seemed lost and terrified by the memories that he had triggered. To calm herself, she unconsciously caressed the little boy's head as she talked; in response, the child lay his head on her thighs like a contented cat. "I escaped from some kind of prison in the woods," she began, still in awe of that place. She remembered what Quibb had told her, about being allowed to escape, but she did not know how to explain that dream/vision, so she omitted it. After a pause, she continued: "It seemed to be filled with women...I think The Horde ran it [both of the men's eyebrows raised]. I escaped somehow... The leader of the cult [she still did not know Respoli-Priestess' name, and this frustrated her: seemed *shameful*]...he said that they had been waiting for me to come out. The Horde was using some kind of mind control in that place—I guess The Horde kept all the women dazed....Somehow, I got out—had a brief moment of awareness, and I escaped. I ran through the night: down a mountain, through the woods...the cult was waiting for me at the bottom of the mountain." She looked up uneasily then:

"...They think I'm God," she said, plainly. "They brought me to the city to save the world."

Still stung by his failure to impress the woman, Xi had been following the conversation only halfheartedly. However, when the woman talked of God, he remembered her miracle: how she had brought the little boy back to life with her touch. Even now, he could sense her power—and it was like nothing he had ever felt before. In years past, Shaka had been a brutal, terrifying God to him; Quibb had come along, with mystery and contradictions; but now, in the person of this woman—this *genuine* woman (not a surrogate version of a woman, like Quibb, or some asexual god of technology, like Shaka)—he sensed something pure and *real*. All at once, his mouth gaped!

"You're the Goddess!" The words flew from him before he could restrain them. He stared at her the way one would stare at Santa Claus—at a walking, breathing myth!

She stared at him for a moment—as though taken aback; in the silence, Xi felt ashamed again. For a moment, the Goddess was trapped in the images from the videodisks: scenes in which insane men shed blood in their battles over her. She grappled with the reality of what men did in her name once they became convinced that she was to be the savior of their lives and souls. She shook her head then, deep in thought. When she looked up at Xi, she noticed the tattoo around his eye.

"That tattoo," she asked, pointing, "—what does it mean?"

"Oh," Xi said, suddenly shy. "…It's the Glory to the Goddess tattoo."

"Do you believe in me? That I'm God?"

"…I don't know what I believe," he said after a moment of uneasiness. "I don't even know how I got the tattoo. I can't remember anything. Quibb—" He was going to talk about how Quibb had pointed it out to him, and told him how he had always believed, but he faltered.

The Goddess shook her head as he sat there silently. "Saviors are a cop-out," she began. "They allow men to believe that all they need to do is wait and follow. Look at what Mendez—and that Voice—are doing to the world. *Men* need to act…not to wait for commandments…"

Xi felt a little ashamed, because what she had said was true. Yet, as he stared at her face, there was no doubt that she was the Goddess—and that the sight of her seemed to bend reality: to *beatify* it somehow. Seven years ago, she had been a 10-year-old version of the beautiful sophisticate that appeared in The Company's ads; now, she was that woman. It was eerie, and yet watching her had a strangely calming effect on him—almost an inebriating effect. Xi had to force himself to look away—he could not think while he looked at her. He seeped back into the abyss of himself. In the meanwhile, Mansmann was wondering how he was going to broach the subject that had almost become an obsession to him over the last few days. At last, he cleared his throat premonitorily; when the others looked up at him, he was staring at the woman intently:

"—I've been running tests...*experiments.* You're not like any other human being I've ever seen."

"What do you mean?" she said, a certain uneasiness creeping into her voice.

"...Your blood: I can't even begin to explain it—what it is and what it can *do*. I took some samples out of you, and they were yellow."

"What do you mean?" she said again.

"I mean...you should be dead, but you're not. You have some kind of super disease within you"—the Goddess seemed horrified; Mansmann rushed ahead, to allay her fears. "I ran some tests, and you're impervious to disease— to *all* sicknesses as far as I can tell—"

"What do you mean?" she demanded, frowning.

"Well, to begin with, you don't have...well, your genes aren't corrupted like ours: you don't have the thing in your veins that stopped men from having daughters. You're the *antidote.*"

The others still stared at Mansmann as though not understanding. He took a deep breath and went on more slowly:

"I ran some tests, as I said before. I took some of your blood and injected it into some of the men in the clinic: some of the *really* sick ones. Men with inoperable cancers were cured within hours; men with tuberculosis soon began to breathe freely; and when I checked their blood, they were *cured*: *they can have daughters*! You have within you the power to resurrect the human race. Either you were born like this, or someone with an incredible amount of expertise—*someone with The Horde*—cured you...or created you as some kind of...I don't even know what..."

She was breathing shallowly. Her mind returned to one of the images from the videodisk, in which one of her crazed followers had screamed that she was to be the last hope of the human race. She did not believe in prophecy or destiny, but there was no denying the facts. She shuddered almost imperceptibly. "You think The Horde did this to me?"

Mansmann looked at her gravely: "Unless you were born this way." Then,

"...I wonder if The Horde even knows about your blood. If they knew how precious you were they would never have let you escape—and would have left no stone unturned once you had." However, as he said those words, he remembered the microchip in her neck—the possible tracking device! He shuddered.

As for the Goddess, Mansmann's revelation made Quibb's ominous words within The Horde's consciousness come back to her. The Horde had wanted her to escape: maybe the blood was just part of their scheme—a trick to get the men to follow her...but then why was Quibb setting up Mendez. She pursed her lips, deep in her thoughts....

Mansmann was staring at her again, still trying to scrounge up the courage to ask the vital questions. "You say you escaped from The Horde," he began. "Can you tell us anything about them?"

Her mind flashed with images of her flight from that huge sarcophagus of a building; she was staring at the floor now, seemingly in a daze. "...Nothing that makes sense," she said at last. Then, looking up at them in bewilderment, "I don't even know my own name...I can't *remember*."

There was silence for a while.

"...Carolyn Smith," Xi said at last.

"What?" she said, looking over at him.

"Carolyn Smith," Xi repeated. "That's your name—I remember."

"*Yes*," Mansmann said in amazement. He remembered from all the TV coverage of her cult—and the manhunt for her.

"Carolyn Smith," she said meditatively. She let the name echo in her mind, but she realized that it did not really have any relation to her—it did not *mean* anything to her. It was while she was deep in her thoughts that Mansmann remembered what she had said back at the rally. He now looked at her with a certain amount of anxiety:

"...How did you know my name—that I was Mansmann...what I had done?"

It took her a while to put his words in their proper context—to realize what he was talking about: "...I saw it on the videodisks—old news programs." She looked down at the little boy then, who had fallen asleep on her lap. She caressed his head once more.

Mansmann nodded, but when Xi finally digested what the old man had said, he laughed. "—*You're* Mansmann?" In his mind, that name was connected to a glitzy pop icon—nothing even remotely close to the old doctor. He stared at the man in disbelief, but then an amazed smile came over his face as he suddenly realized the resemblance.

With the attention on him, Mansmann felt suddenly self-conscious, but Xi felt a deep propinquity with him then: a bond that seemed almost spiritual.

"—You were not responsible for any of this, you know," Xi said then.

Mansmann looked up, frowning. "What?"

"It was Shaka. He had this plan to curtail the world's population by drugging everyone, so that they would not be able to have children for 30 years."

"*What?*"

Xi took a deep breath; hearing the words with his own ears, the story sounded too bizarre to be real. He refocused himself: "Shaka released a compound into the atmosphere about a year before the apocalypse. It was undetectable—but then it combined with your hair formula somehow. It was supposed to make people sterile for 20 to 30 years, but when it combined with your formula, it only cheated them of the ability to have daughters."

Mansmann stared in disbelief. "How do you know all this?"

"I worked for The Company."

Mansmann shifted anxiously in his chair. In one sense, discovering that the woman's blood was the antidote to the strange infertility had lifted a great deal of the burden from his soul, but hearing Xi's words now almost made him want to cry. He was a penitent realizing that he had never sinned... but then he frowned:

"You say *Shaka* did all this?"

"Yes. He told me." He suddenly realized that Shaka had told G.W., but he did not have the patience to go into that.

"...Why'd he tell you?" Mansmann went on, desperately needing a concrete reason to believe this farfetched story.

"I used to work with him....I invented the Image Broadcast Complex... and the PinkEyes."

Mansmann looked at him in amazement; for some reason, Xi felt compelled to add:

"My name is Xi Wang." He felt awkward: it was the first time he had spoken his name in years.

"*You* invented the PinkEyes?"

"Yes," Xi said uneasily, especially when it again occurred to him that he no longer had that expertise. He was the shell of a great man: a confused fool inhabiting the body of a one-time genius. Both he and Mansmann had been men that had touched the world profoundly, only to find themselves separated forever from the source of their power.

For a moment, there was plaintive silence, in which they all attempted to digest what they had heard. Then, as though just remembering something, the old man's eyes narrowed as he looked over at Xi: "You know who The Voice is, don't you?" There was a bluntness there that took Xi aback. He was pathetic again: all of his defenses seemed breached; but seeing no use in hiding, he shook his head:

"I have no idea who he is—or *what* he is—but I've met him…[The Goddess nodded her head unconsciously, because that was her description as well.] He just showed up one day—appeared out of nowhere," Xi went on, his words coming quicker; and now that the topic was out in the open, he found that he could not stop. He let the words flow from him; he felt the burden of the secret being lifted from him, but instinctively panicked at the thought that there would be nothing left when he was done. He grappled with this for a while, but the words went on, no longer under the power of his will. He looked up at the old doctor then: "He was the one I brought to the hospital that first night of the bombing [Mansmann searched his mind, but realized he had been too dazed that night to remember.]…I brought him there and you asked me to help you. With all the death and blood, I lost track of where I had put him. He disappeared…and then he was The Voice of Conscience. He *knows* things…he *does* things. He sent me to help Mendez—he's behind Mendez's rise…and he was somehow involved in the bombing today. He was there today, at the rally, pulling Mendez from the rubble.…He will know about her," he said, gesturing to the woman. "He seems to know everything I know—or at least he *did*," Xi added. As he said it, he realized that some of what he was saying might not be making sense. Nevertheless, he continued, "We're connected somehow, he and I. He wants me to go back to The Company for some reason. [He looked at both of them helplessly.] Something big is going on: he knows what it is and he's trying to make me part of it. He seems to know everything…" But he stopped at that, feeling suddenly weak and disoriented. Then, as he looked up and saw their discerning eyes, a wave of guilt went over him. He felt somehow as though he had betrayed Quibb. Quibb was no longer his god, per se; still, he felt like a Judas: a man without honor. He even felt disconnected from Mansmann and the woman now: as though he were not to be trusted with other human beings. He retreated into himself….

The Goddess remained silent through all this. Her realization about the connection between Quibb, the Horde and Mendez's rise seemed too horrible to admit. Mansmann seemed to be battling his own demons as well. When Xi revealed that his connection to The Voice meant that The Voice would know about the woman, Mansmann was forced to confront the thing still hovering in the dark recesses of his mind: the possibility that Shaka knew about her as well and was receiving all the data from his experiments. He glanced at the woman nervously, but he was too ashamed—and *terrified*—to tell her….

It was still raining outside. The wind must have shifted, because some droplets of rain suddenly began to pelt the window. Those in the room all looked towards the window at the noise. Mansmann sighed; Xi nibbled his lower lip; the woman, who had allowed them to talk uninterrupted, now looked at them with a certain amount of alarm. She sensed them seeping back into a kind of stupor—like hypothermic hikers falling asleep after getting lost on the trail. She spoke up quickly:

"What do you guys want to do?"

They looked at her confusedly, then glanced at one another blankly.

"…I'm tired of being in the dark," she went on, "—of not knowing why things are happening around me. I feel as though I've only been alive for a few days—everything before that is lost. In my short life, I've looked around and understood little of what I've seen. I want to *understand* the things I see. I'm tired of fleeing with my life: if we have to sneak and scheme, let's act so that we'll be able to solve the mysteries around us."

"What do you propose?" Xi ventured.

"You said that you think there are women beneath The Company. Are you willing to find out?"

Xi nibbled on his lower lip again—

"It has to be something *you* want," she told him, "not something you do for me, or to *belong*. Do you want to find out?"

"Yes, of course…but how exactly? I can look around when I return to The Company," he proposed unenthusiastically. Yet, now that he had found the Goddess, the suicidal resolve to return to The Company was less palatable. For once, he wanted to *live*. He wanted to be around her—to *talk* to her.

Mansmann joined in: "If we do anything, it will have to be before The Horde returns. If there really are women in The Company, then that's the first place The Horde will go—"

Xi frowned: listening to them now, this all seemed insane. He had wanted to impress the woman with his secret about the subterranean floors, but now that it was the time for *action*, the fantasy and glamour of knowing faded away. In their stead, he saw all the grim, immutable realities: "There'll be guards everywhere—and cameras. Even if we manage to get in the building—and down into those floors—we'll never get out." When the Goddess looked at him with a certain amount of resentment, he struck back, "Do you want to know more than you want to *live*?"

In the silence that followed, he felt ashamed again: like a *coward*. To redeem himself, he proposed: "If we go, we'll have to think it through…" but it still sounded cowardly in the silence.

"Maybe we just need a good night's sleep," Mansmann said to make peace.

"Yes," Xi said, rubbing his temples.

It is one thing to be a faceless member of the masses (and to look up with fear and trembling at the powerful), and another thing to know that the powerful know your name and are keeping an eye on you.
VERSE 5112: 3 OF *The Teachings*

It was strange how things changed. Equations that had held only moments ago disproved themselves as time went on....That night, panic invaded the city; and oddly, it seemed to sneak in on the warm vapors of the summer rain. The same rain that had had the men playing in the streets seemed to bring madness. Throughout the torrent, a childlike joy had soothed the men; but as the rain died down to a drizzle, the men began to take to the streets. Stories of The Horde were on all the billboards—along with the same scenes of Mendez's ascension. The billboards reminded them why they needed Mendez. According to the billboards, The Horde was re-invading all of the cities it had attacked. There were satellite feeds from all over the world. Cities like Johannesburg and Rome, already in ruins from years of looting and the unrestrained chaos of their collective nightmare, were now ablaze, churning eerily in the night. Everywhere, there were strange reports of The Horde—or something like them—making surgical strikes and leaving. There were reports from remote parts of the world, like the Falkland Islands, where the surviving men had revealed they had had women. Still shaking, the survivors had talked about how The Horde had come in, stolen the women and killed a great deal of the men before setting off. It had all been lightening quick. There had been no stopping them—no compromise...no hope....

Back in the city, the news ate away at them. Men who had only hours ago been celebrating their victory, now began to panic again. They took to the streets as those old feelings of anxiety and dread returned. The soldiers— rather, the roving bands of armed youths—shot at anything that moved. All of a sudden they seemed convinced that bums stumbling from alleyways and men sodomizing one another on secluded streets were commando regiments of The Horde. In the chaos, bands of youths shot at one another, wiping themselves out. Over their heads, the screens showed the destruction that was to come; those apocalyptic images, along with their own memories, pumped a steady stream of madness into their veins.

The day man acquires the ability to banish all evil from the world will be the day that he corrupts the last piece of goodness in his soul.
VERSE 1832:5 OF *The Teachings*

Shaka was still in his suite, staring at the screen. He looked around the huge chamber absentmindedly then, as though to re-confirm that Circe was gone—and that he was alone. He hoped she would return soon; but as he considered what was happening to the city, and saw images of two groups of paranoid youths wiping one another out in a gunfight, it suddenly occurred to him that it had been foolish of him to allow her to enter that chaos. He had never really feared death before; and in a sense it was not death that he feared now, but the prospect of death alone. He saw death off in the distance, after some immeasurable period of loneliness.... His mind was on the fairy tale place that Circe had mentioned, when Stein's knock sounded at the door. As Shaka came to his senses, he was understandably disturbed by the nature of his thoughts....

Stein ran up to him—across the wide chamber; then, panting from his efforts: "Sir, the Image Broadcast Complex is ready to go online."

Shaka pursed his lips as his thoughts began to churn, then he walked off a short distance by himself. Circe had talked about running away—*escaping*—but the thought of running, and leaving everything he had built, seemed suddenly out of the question. On top of that, the realization that he was waiting around for Circe opened up for him just how vulnerable he was. He was *waiting* for her, making his existence and his *future* dependent on her return. There was something self-destructive in that—and unmistakably shameful. Moreover, the thought that Circe might never return—that she might be killed, or change her mind and keep going by herself—ate away at him. As had been the case before Circe came to him the last time, he reverted to the one thing that soothed him: the promise of taking revenge against his enemies. In this frame of mind, the challenge that Mendez posed to his hegemony—if not his very existence—seemed to trigger his old self to return and defend him with all the brutality and connivance at its disposal.

When Shaka turned around he seemed almost surprised to see Stein waiting obediently. Remembering what the man had said about the Image Broadcast Complex, a gleam suddenly came into Shaka's eyes. The men had bowed to his power once, and they would do so again. Mendez and The Voice had been mere usurpers: once the PinkEyes came back online and the men felt that old power coming over them again, they would know their master and rise up to follow his will—

"Bring it online," Shaka said, then nodded to Stein to signify that the man could leave.

If God created Man thinking that he would be a faithful servant,
then She had obviously miscalculated.
Verse 397:6 of *The Teachings*

Xi awoke as he had awakened seven years ago: in a panic, certain that something horrible had either happened, or was in the process of happening. He burst upright in the basement room that Mansmann had given him, already gasping to scream. However, as he looked around in the darkness, his breath got caught in his throat. Weird shapes were flashing before him; he clamped his eyes shut then reopened them—like a man with a hangover trying to clear his blurred vision. In the air, there was a high-pitched noise that left him feeling as though something were drilling into his soul—penetrating all the intimate places within him. Before it occurred to him that the PinkEyes were back online, he thought that he was having another of his strange visions—or that he was still dreaming. However, when his mind—and his visual cortex—began to pulse with the familiar rhythm of the PinkEyes, he again clamped his eyes shut, wondering how much more his mind could possibly take.

The sound of his breathing was harsh in the small room...but the strange, high-pitched noise was still drilling into him. He opened his eyes slowly and warily: the blurred shapes and figures being generated by the PinkEyes were still dancing before him. However, after a few moments, they cleared up somewhat, and he recognized human faces gripped by horror and madness. The men of the city were killing one another—but in a peculiar frenzy that made it evident that they had lost their minds. The images being conjured by the PinkEyes were beginning to give him a headache—and to *sicken* him. He closed his eyes again; he wanted to lie down, but the high-pitched noise seemed to be growing in intensity. Only when desperation drove him to clamp his hands over his ears, did he realize that the noise was not coming from the PinkEyes—but was instead something blaring in the room. He looked around warily—and it was strange to again have to filter out the ghost images of the PinkEyes in order to see the real world. He looked around deliberately, having to concentrate to see what was around him. At last, he realized that the high-pitched noise was somehow coming from his person. He tapped his pants pockets, then brought out the device Shaka said he would use to communicate with him. Xi had forgotten all about it! He was holding it as though he expected it to explode at any moment. Nevertheless, there was a flashing button that Xi instinctively pushed; and when he did so, a holographic image of Shaka's smiling, confident face suddenly appeared before him. Xi gasped—

"I hope I did not awaken you," Shaka said with a smile.

Xi could only stare—

"Good," Shaka said without waiting for a response, "—I require your services, sir."

Xi swallowed deeply to lubricate his parched throat. "…Now?" he managed to whisper—and the disturbing thing was that he was suddenly reminded of the vision he had had where Shaka called G.W. in the middle of the night—

"Yes," Shaka responded plainly. "Now, more than ever, I require your technical expertise."

—But just then, the PinkEyes conjured ghost images of men setting fires to shantytowns. There was one image of a man with a flame-thrower—surrounded by several other men—*his blazing victims*. The latter were running about wildly, like some kind of fire monsters. "…What's happening?" Xi asked in bewilderment.

"It's the PinkEyes—they don't seem to be working properly. I was hoping that you wouldn't be affected by whatever is doing this to them."

Xi's head still ached, but that discomfort seemed to increase tenfold when it again occurred to him that he was not Dr. Xi Wang anymore—that he had no technical expertise whatsoever. He was on the verge of confessing this to Shaka, when the man announced:

"A helicopter will pick you up in a few minutes."

"…What?"

"A helicopter is en route to you now."

"…But how?" he said before he realized that the device he still held in his hand must have some kind of tracking device! Shaka did not even bother answering the question: he just smiled when he saw that Xi understood. Then, the man's image disappeared.

Xi was frozen by shock for a moment. He tried to think, but he could not get his thoughts past the realization that Shaka's helicopter would arrive within *minutes*! On top of that, ghost images of the men going crazy made it impossible to concentrate. Shaka had been tracking him all that time! Xi's mind seemed to falter as it offered up the possibility that the device had been sending audio back to Shaka: that Shaka had heard the conversation with Mansmann and the Goddess! Even if that were not the case, one thing was certain: he could not be in this building when the helicopter came! The Goddess was sleeping right down the hall from him! He jumped up from his mattress, and was at the door in two steps. His feet were bare, but he did not have time to find and put on his shoes. Plus, getting up so quickly made him feel lightheaded and queasy. He had to lean against the door to regain his balance. After a few deep breaths, during which his mind kept blaring its alarms, he opened the door. The basement hallway was dimly lit; the shadows cast by the lone bulb hanging from the ceiling seemed to metamorphose into monsters right before his eyes. He entered the hall and turned to the right; still fighting to regain his strength and equilibrium, he groped along the walls. The woman's room was two doors down from his. After he passed it, the only thing was to walk up the stairs, to the ground floor. As he walked, his muscles did not merely feel sapped of strength, but as though they had been dead for a while. It was almost as though he had to overcome the effects of rigor mortis. His legs had been ravaged by all the running of the previous day—and he obviously had not been supplying his body with the minimum nutrition required to maintain muscle mass and stamina....

He burst out of the side door and entered the night. He was panting horribly—almost gagging. He could hear gunshots in the distance—more proof of the men's madness. He took two steps towards the street before he tripped on something—or just ran out of strength. Desperate to distance himself from Mansmann's clinic, he crawled along on his hands and feet for a moment, before his strength returned and he was able to stand. At that, he jogged out into the street (it was wide and empty) then he ran down to the next block. He was halfway through the second block, when a blinding light suddenly appeared in the heavens. Before Xi even realized what was happening, the helicopter landed soundlessly before him. Now beckoning him to enter the helicopter, was one of those demented Jehovahs from Company Square. Xi walked to the passenger side of the vehicle like a cornered criminal accepting his fate. The Jehovah grinned at him unnaturally—as though set on showing him every tooth in his mouth. Xi looked away.

Once within the vehicle, the Jehovah took him to dizzying heights. Xi did not like the look of the city from the air. It seemed like a huge ants nest: he got the impression that a deluge would come and wash it all away....He closed his eyes and the Jehovah laughed at him....Strangely enough, Xi was surprised by how stable his mind felt. His headache seemed to be ebbing— even though a sense of bodily discomfort and fatigue remained. It was almost as though his mind had adjusted to the PinkEyes. Opening his eyes, he realized that he did not feel the confusion he had felt the first time. There was no power struggle: no flood of information that he had to fight to keep at bay...but the helicopter was taking him on a stomach-churning ride. After taking him up to dizzying heights, the Jehovah now seemed to be on a kind of kamikaze dive. They zoomed through a smog bank; when they emerged from it, The Company's 150-story skyscraper appeared— as if by magic. If the rest of the city had looked like an anthill, then the 150-story skyscraper was a tower of light and magic. It seemed to glow and pulse with energy. Xi looked at it in awe; below the massive structure, seeming indecently small now, were Company Square and the Image Broadcast Complex.

The full weight of what was happening probably did not occur to him until the helicopter began its descent. He was going back to The Company! Shaka had called him—or at least called the man he thought to be Dr. Xi Wang; and in a matter of moments, his fate would be sealed. His old fears about Shaka planning some intricate death for him again took hold; in a moment of panic, Xi was almost overcome by the impulse to knock out the Jehovah and fly them both into the skyscraper....

The helicopter landed softly on top of the 150-story building. The entire ride had perhaps taken 45 seconds. Xi's feet were wobbly beneath him when he stepped out of the vehicle. A robed man was waiting for them on the roof. The Jehovah laughed at Xi's wobbly gait and helped him up to the waiting man.

"You still haven't cleaned up, Dr. Wang," was the first thing Stein said. The man sounded like a mother who had come back home to find her child's room still a mess. Xi felt a little ashamed. Stein addressed the other man:

"Take him down to his lab—he can get cleaned up there." And then, giving Xi one last disdainful look, "Shaka will expect you in an hour—make sure you're ready."

Fear is not about that which is, but about that which might be.
VERSE 3823:1 OF *The Teachings*

The Goddess was again in that strange place between the waking world and her dreams. She panicked at first, because she thought that she was in the midst of another seizure. She felt herself again succumbing to a shameful loss of control, but this state was heightened somehow—more vivid than any fit she had had. It was as if she were a spirit, floating above the shell of her body. Her room was dark and still; but all around her, were the same phantasmagoric images she had seen during her seizure at the rally. The strange images flashed before her eyes too quickly for her conscious mind to decipher them, but residual sensations stayed with her. She was being jostled by hope and subservience and powerfulness and dozens of other seemingly unconnected sensations. She felt as though she were grappling with some monster in the darkness; and just when she thought that it would drag her into the depths of its pit, a final image appeared, seeming to give meaning to all that had passed. It was the image from her fit at the rally: the *woman*—strong, powerful, standing above everything…The woman seemed ageless, her features beyond time and its effects. There was an imperviousness there that left the Goddess awed. She wanted to cry out to the woman. She wanted to give praise and thanks and *die* for the woman. She stretched out her hands to the ghost hovering above her…And then, it was gone, and there was only the room and the living world. The little boy was snoring on the bed beside her. She looked around anxiously in the darkness and frowned, as one was likely to frown after such an episode.

The time is quickly approaching when men will find nothing else to believe in—when they will see their gods for the devils they are, and their truths and philosophies for the flimsy lies they have always been.
VERSE 412:3 OF *The Teachings*

X i and the Jehovah took an elevator down the entire length of the building. There was no airy elevator music anymore, but the long ride in the silence was torture. Xi was still amazed by the power he seemed to have over his PinkEyes. There were two possible explanations: either the dark pyramid and the PinkEyes were not as potent as before, or he was somehow immune to their effects. Shaka had no doubt called him so that he could find out the problem; but as he watched more ghost images of the men of the city, it occurred to him that their reaction might be a kind of immune response as well. The last time the PinkEyes were online, the men had been passive consumers; now, the men seemed to have evolved to the confusion and maddening frustration that Xi had felt the first time he put on the devices. Of course, unlike the men of the city, Xi had not gone on murderous rampages, but the effort required to keep all the information of the known universe at bay had been madness itself. As he looked at more ghost images of the rampaging men, he saw that they were not even attempting to hold their madness at bay. They had lived so long in a world without limits and self-restraint that the freedom allowed by the PinkEyes became a license to kill....

Xi was taken to a sublevel with long, white corridors that reminded him of the vision he had had where G.W. woke up in the infirmary. He and the Jehovah seemed to be well in the bowels of the building; they walked down one corridor then down another, until Xi began to feel lost. At last, the Jehovah stopped in front of a door that had a daunting-looking security panel at its side. When Xi looked at the flashing console confusedly, the Jehovah laughed at him, saying:

"You really have been away a long time." The man then went on to tell Xi that the console was a DNA scanner, and that he was supposed to breathe on it. When Xi blew on the thing tentatively, the door opened. The room on the other side was huge—perhaps 50 meters by 30 meters. The air was stale, as though the door had not been opened in years. Impressive-looking supercomputers were running against the far wall. Other pieces of complex equipment still seemed to be running as well. There were flashing lights and pulsing orbs and microscopes and displays that flashed complex algorithms—and a myriad other things that reminded him of some mad scientist's laboratory. He stood timidly in the open doorway, seeing scanners and diagnostic tools of all conceivable types...chemistry sets that still somehow had reactions going, with liquids automatically being siphoned from huge, temperature-regulated containers, then directed through a complex network of tubes....All of this equipment was crammed in the middle of the room; off to the side—to Xi's right—there was a bed, a couch and a door that led to a bathroom. When Xi saw this, it suddenly occurred to him that he used to live down here. Just as Shaka lived in the penthouse, Xi had lived in the basement: two men at the opposite poles of the universe....

As he again looked at the daunting array of equipment in the chamber, he was cowed by the fact that he had no idea what any of it was...but there was something in the room that called to him. There was something in there, like a familiar scent, opening up the passageways of his mind. Seeing the mesmerized expression on Xi's face, the Jehovah smiled his amiable—but ultimately condescending—smile one last time, then left. By now, Xi had forgotten all about him. The room was calling to him—*drawing* him in a way that was not only irresistible, but which also left him with a vague sense of euphoria...as though he were finally home. He did not even attempt to make sense of it. He stepped into the chamber—was *pulled* in....And his PinkEyes seemed to be going crazy. They literally pulsed with information—as though they were downloading something into him. He took another loping step into the room; the door automatically closed behind him, but he did not notice. He was looking around wildly now, but he was seeing things beyond the room: an entire lifetime of memories. Somehow, it was all coming back to him: the truth of who he was, and what he had been. He felt the usual disorienting effects of a vision coming over him again. At first, he thought that he was going to pass out; but after the immediate disorientation and pain, a feeling of calm settled over him. Even the PinkEyes were calm now. He saw more ghost images hovering before him, but they were not images being broadcasted from outside, but from *within*.

He stepped farther into the room: there was a kind of examination table in the middle of it, and he saw G.W. lying on it—but as a ghost from years past. All around him, there were now such ghosts. G.W. was delirious, still bloody from his confrontation with the man with the aluminum baseball bat. Two other ghosts—Company guards—had just brought the man in to Xi— to *Dr. Wang*....Dr. Wang tells the guards to leave. A feeling of exuberance fills him as he looks down at G.W.'s cracked skull. He is so arrogant that it does not occur to him that G.W. might die—or that the man might be better off in a hospital emergency room. What he is about to do is all about science. His only reason for being is to make advances; he wants to push the boundaries—regardless of the law and so-called ethics, and all the other things that men of vision allow to keep them back. The question of *if* he should attempt this experiment was settled when Shaka called down to say that he had found a man to help him prove his theories. In fact, as he watches G.W., his concern is not for the man, but his experiment. He makes some last-second alterations to his machine by pressing some buttons: everything is ready now. Dr. Wang nods to himself, then smiles as he takes one last look at his machine and the man who is to help him prove his theories. Actually, G.W. is not lying on an examination table at all: the slab is part of the machine; and like an MRI scanner, the machine has a hollow center, into which G.W. and the slab are to be inserted. Dr. Wang unconsciously caresses the machine as he presses a button to start it up; a few moments later, G.W.'s body is inserted into the machine headfirst. G.W.'s mind is to be downloaded into a special Dimension while the machine heals blood vessels in his head and re-establishes links between nerve endings and so on. It is actually all out of Dr. Wang's hands now—the machine will take care of everything; and then, after the hardware of the mind has been reconfigured and stabilized, the software of the mind will be reinstalled into G.W. The entire thing will take a couple days....

Dr. Wang grows restless after a few hours. The machine has lots of data and interesting displays for him to look at, but he wants more. He wants to be more involved. In a sense, he wishes that this were a surgery requiring him to make incisions and literally get blood on his hands....It suddenly occurs to him that he can amuse himself and pass the time by visiting the Dimension he had sent G.W.'s mind to. There is a kind of voyeuristic streak in him. He likes looking at other people's struggles and pain and unhealed wounds—so that he can ultimately feel justified in staying out of the world and contenting himself to this lab in the nether realms of The Company....He enters the Dimension, ready to amuse himself with all of G.W.'s private longings and sorrows. However, G.W. is with his family. The man's wife is there; and in this world, their son has not only been born, but is a toddler that is just taking his first steps. The proud parents look on, clapping and giving encouragement to the laughing child. They are having a picnic in the park, on what has to be the most beautiful spring day ever. Trees are bursting with pink, yellow and orange blossoms—even the sky seems to bloom with life and promise. Dr. Wang initially finds something cloying about the scene. There is something about it reminiscent of those Christmas specials that belabor the moral that family and love are the true wealth of a man. However, the fact that Xi loves his wife is not only self-evident, but *overpowering*. His love for his wife and child is almost a kind of madness. In the Dimension, Dr. Wang feels all that G.W. feels; these new sensations swell up in him, inhabiting places that had lain barren for years. Indeed, he is probably susceptible to the cloying nature of the scene precisely because of all he has blocked out and turned his back on. Seeing G.W.'s family, Wang realizes how profoundly he misses home. His parents had not lived in Chinatown—those were just more flawed memories. He had never had a father that took him on his knee and told him epic stories of China; his mother had never looked at him in the way of doting, self-sacrificing mothers—all of these things were not only flawed memories, but also fantasies from his deepest longings....In reality, he had been an orphan by the time he was ten. Those two people in Chinatown had been his aunt and uncle. Instead of supporting and nurturing him—as in the fantasy—they had taken every chance to show him how much they resented having to take care of him. They had pushed and prodded him to a degree that was inhumane at best and criminal at worst....Yes, it was all coming back to him now. He had moved in with them when he was 10. His real parents had actually been gnarled Chinese peasants...and he had lived in China with them before events forced him to move to New York City. Instead of loving him and taking a personal hand in his upbringing, his father had gone off to the city to find work when he was seven years old, and had never returned. After that, his mother had beaten him at the slightest provocation—as though trying to take revenge on all men. Still, he had loved life then. In that strange way of children, his life had been a living fairy tale, in which horror and pain had only been plot devices necessary for the fulfillment of the grand, cinematic happy ending. In this fairy tale, he had seen China as a place of unrivaled beauty. He had somehow overlooked the open sewer that wound its way through his neighborhood, bringing disease and death and an overpowering stench that seemed to seep into his very molecules. He had not seen the brutal way that poverty wreaked havoc on the souls of his neighbors—and his own family. In fact, on those few occasions when his consciousness allowed him to glimpse these things, he saw them as proof of his goodness—as all fairy tale heroes seemed to be poor and wretched. As for his mother, one day he had come home from school to find that she had committed suicide. She had stripped naked and hanged herself from the rafters of their hovel. Her nudity had been strangely mesmerizing to him—and it had not been as though he had never seen her naked before. After all, they had lived in a cramped, one-room place where only a curtain had separated him from his parents when they were in the throes of their passion—and often times they had not even bothered with the curtain....He had stared at his mother's naked corpse as it swung gently to and fro, twirling in a slow orbit that eventually gave him a 360 degree view of her. When her pale, discolored face came into view, with her tongue hanging out of her mouth like some slaughtered farm animal, Wang had screamed; but strangely enough, it had not been out of the horror of seeing the face—but some dark realization that his mind had refused to reconcile. He had thought about it for years, confounded by the strange scream that had brought the neighbors running. Only now, as Xi Wang of the present looked at that woman's face and body, did he realize that his mind had projected her as the prostitute from G.W.'s adulterous affair in China....

Xi was finally beginning to understand it now: he saw how his mind had become entwined with G.W.'s. He had gone into G.W. Jefferson's mind that day, carrying all his pent-up frustration and hatred: the view he got of G.W.'s life had not only opened him up to things he had long tried to bury, but also seemed to challenge the very foundations of his self-denial. G.W. had in fact just returned from China; and with the horror of what China had become lingering on the fringe of G.W.'s mind, Xi had been forced to confront his past—and *reality*. There was nothing more dangerous than a man caught in the process of losing his god—especially if he was losing that god because of the revelations of another man. At such times, that other man in fact became his devil, and the attempt to hold onto his god became a struggle between heaven and hell. Moreover, just as Dr. Wang had hated G.W. for his conclusions on China, he had hated the President for her stance on China: for the fact that she had called it a pariah state and was every day proposing to go to war with it. He had hated her with the unstable mind of a child in self-denial....And he had hated Shaka too. He had resented the man to an extent that did not even seem humanly possible. From his point of view, he, Dr. Xi Wang, was the brains of The Company: he did all the work—made the discoveries upon which the foundation of their society seemed to be based—but Shaka always got the attention. Shaka appeared on TV; Shaka dated all those beautiful women that Xi could not even bring himself to talk to....For years, he had told himself that all that mattered was the science, but once within the confines of G.W.'s soul, confronted by an image of what seemed to be a full, content life, Xi's soul had rebelled, infecting G.W.'s soul with his childish hatred and insecurity. He had lashed out, like a toddler unable to get his way....In effect, Xi had created the maniac that gunned down the President and Shaka, then went home to rape and murder his wife. Xi had done all that. Yet, the struggle between G.W.'s soul and his own had not been a one-sided affair. While Xi had passed on his hatred and self-loathing, maybe G.W. had passed on some measure of compassion and human feeling. Their souls had fought and scavenged one another; in the end, Xi's darkness had probably won out, but it had been a pyrrhic victory at best....Days had passed; the machine had automatically put an end to the struggle between their souls when it completed the repairs to G.W.'s brain. However, not having the sophistication to separate G.W.'s struggling soul from Xi's, the machine had chopped the convoluted mess in two, indiscriminately sending one part to Xi's body and the other to G.W.'s....Xi had emerged first, dazed and insane from his corrupted, half-soul. The phone had been ringing. More out of instinct than anything else, Xi had picked it up. It had been Shaka's secretary asking if G.W. was ready: the woman had been calling on Shaka's behalf for days, trying to get an update on the procedure. The woman had let her annoyance be known over the phone, but Xi had been so dazed that he had understood none of the sarcasm—and few of the words. He had in effect been operating with half a mind—or half of his mind and half of another man's; worse than that, the two halves had been mixed beforehand, so that none of the reference points seemed to be where they were supposed to be....G.W. emerged from the machine while Xi was standing there holding the phone. Somehow, when each saw the other, the madness of the Dimension gripped them again. They flung themselves at one another like two beasts...but when they touched, it was strange. Each could feel what the other felt. It was as though they were two bodies sharing one soul. Still dazed and insane, they realized their strange consanguinity the way two ants realized that they were from the same nest: not with true consciousness, but though chemical and biological signatures that were hot-wired into their being. Like those ants, each went his separate way then—fumbling away in confusion. G.W.

managed to open the door and leave…but as they were one soul inhabiting two bodies, when G.W. wandered off by himself, the link between them became unstable; and when out of range of one another, so to speak, the strain became so severe that they both passed out. G.W. was found in the corridor and taken to the infirmary (and shown the events of Africa through the DreamVisor)….When G.W. awoke in the infirmary, Xi still lay on the ground of his lab, unconscious. In effect, he had been the passive side of their soul….G.W. had been taken up to see Shaka; when he killed the President, Xi had finally awakened. The stress of being one soul inhabiting two bodies, plus G.W.'s flight, had had the strange effect of making Xi mirror G.W.'s actions. He had fled like G.W. had fled. When G.W. jumped into his SUV, Xi had taken a similar-looking vehicle on another sublevel of the parking garage…but while Xi had exited through a street-level exit, G.W. had gone out through Company Square. G.W.'s vehicle had been the one that was shot up by the guards in Company Square. It had been his murderous rampage that garnered all the attention…but both vehicles had gotten lost in the smog; and with two reports of a huge, rampaging vehicle, the police had lost track. When Xi crashed into that pizzeria and lost consciousness, G.W. had again had the entire soul—and all of its madness— to himself; and when Xi woke up at that strange condominium a day later, G.W. had just been about to kill himself….

As Xi came back to his senses, he realized that he was lying on the ground. He had no idea when he had fallen; and at first, he was so disoriented that he had no idea where he was. In the wake of what he had just seen and felt, everything seemed different to him now. As he looked around, he did so as a new being, with all of Xi Wang's memories and all of G.W. Jefferson's. Everything came back to him at once, in a rush of facts and figures and recollections that his mind could not possibly have the wherewithal to sort out. His mind would have to re-forge links between the trillions of disparate facts and recollections before all that information could become *knowledge*. Nevertheless, the grand schemes of his former life came back to him first. He found that he understood the theoretical constructs underlying the PinkEyes and the dark pyramid (as well as the device that had entwined his soul with G.W.'s); he understood how they worked, in the way that most people had a rudimentary understanding how a television worked, even though the ability to *build* a television, or even to just maintain the infrastructure responsible for a television broadcast—was beyond their purview....As he looked over at the device that had entwined his soul with G.W.'s, he saw it for what it was: a soul catcher. It had been left on all this time; and some-how, it had held G.W. Jefferson's corrupted soul after the man killed him-self and his family. When Xi entered this room, it had joined them again. He had no idea how this was possible—but then he remembered that he was wearing the PinkEyes. Only the PinkEyes (and through them, the Image Broadcast Complex) had the sophistication to complete the task that his machine had attempted seven years ago. He and G.W. had gone from being two separate men—two *strangers*—to being two men sharing one soul; then, after G.W.'s death, Xi had been left as one man with half of two men's souls. He was whole now, but whole in the sense that he had his own soul as well as all of G.W.'s memories. Mercifully, G.W.'s consciousness did not enter him again. After all, the two men were in fact murderer and victim....

Xi again marveled at the power that the PinkEyes seemed to give him—and at the new clarity that he had while wearing them. They were a part of him now—not something alien to be resisted. He got up from the ground gingerly. His side was numb, so that he began to wonder how long he had been lying on the cold floor. Now that he was whole again, his PinkEyes went back to showing ghost images of the city. The men were still acting on their madness; and with his newly reacquired expertise, he suddenly realized what was happening to them. As if by instinct, he went to a console in the rear of the chamber, which was connected directly to the Image Broadcast Complex. After he made a few adjustments, a burst of calm and well-being was broadcast over the PinkEyes. Within seconds, the worst of the rampages stopped. There were of course still men butchering one another; voices of panic still cried out in the night, but the worst of it seemed over.

Everything seemed so simple to Xi now: he laughed at the sensation. He was like a boy waking up to discover that he had superpowers—that he could fly and move heaven and earth. *That* was the kind of power he felt at his command. Filled with this new confidence, he allowed his mind to explore the possibilities that the PinkEyes (as conduits to all the information in the known universe) opened up to him. All at once, he knew why The Horde had used that purple, shimmering sky—and why that sky had caused his visions. *It was all his technology*! It was all coming back to him now. He had developed the shimmering sky for the military—or at least set them in that direction. Just as he had previously guessed, the shimmering sky had made The Horde soldiers invisible when they invaded the city—which was to say that it had made them invisible to everyone but *himself*. As The Horde had used the same technology as the Soul Catcher, he had been somewhat immune. The shimmering sky had actually begun the process of separating the souls within him....This of course all meant that The Horde was somehow connected to the U.S. Military, or what was left of it. It also meant that Xi Wang, through The Horde's actions, was once again responsible for mass murder....Quibb...the man had known all this somehow. Xi looked at it all with a sense of logic that he had not had in years; he analyzed the data, adding in Clem and Steve, and Quibb's machinations with regard to trying to get him to believe that he was something that he was not; his mind, aided by the PinkEyes, processed Quibb's actions with regard to Mendez and the men of the city, and he came to one conclusion. Xi's stomach muscles tightened then. He now went to the security system he had installed seven years ago. After typing in his password, he instructed the computer to show the last person that had entered this chamber before him. The computer replied that there had been no one, but going on another hunch, Xi made the computer scan for a specific wavelength of the light spectrum. It was the wavelength used by his holographic technology, and after rescanning the data, the computer returned an image from a month ago: there were two figures entering side-by-side—one was Quibb; the other was Circe.

Cynics are at heart the greatest idealists—it is only that they use cynicism to shield them from the pain of their unrealized (and seemingly unrealizable) ideals.
VERSE 84:1 OF *The Teachings*

Before Xi sent a pulse of calm and well-being over the PinkEyes, Circe had walked the dark city streets as a ghost. The men she passed had not been able see her, but as they fired off their rounds, and allowed themselves to sink into paranoia, the reality of their madness had left her feeling sick. For the first time, being alone with the men—*being in their midst*—had been disturbing.

It was probably about five in the morning when she finally ducked into the hideout. It was a burnt-out apartment building; the entrance to the basement was an ingenious trap door that appeared when one knocked the wall in the right place. Only when the trap door closed behind her, and she was descending the steps into the dimly lit basement, did she make herself visible again—

"Quibb," she called as she descended the steps, "—I've come for the device." However, there was no response. The basement was *huge*. At the bottom of the steps, she looked around as if lost—as if she had wandered into the wrong basement. It was only after a few moments that she realized what was wrong. All the broadcasting and holographic equipment was gone! Save for some cots in the corner, and an overturned couch, the chamber was *gutted*. She stared in disbelief, wondering what it could all mean. "Quibb?" she called again, uncertainly.

It was then that two figures stepped out of the shadows in the corner of the room. Her first thought was that it was Quibb, but when the figures stepped into the light, and the visors of their helmets glistened, Circe froze. They were Horde soldiers, and they had been waiting for her.

If one spends life attempting to account for all that is possible,
one will lose sight of what is probable.
VERSE 483:2 OF *The Teachings*

Mendez woke up suddenly. Actually, he had not really been sleeping, but stuck in that deep lassitude that came when one thought oneself out of options. Looking over at the windows, he sensed, rather than saw, that a new day was at hand. However, the bluish gray tint of the pre-dawn sky only seemed like an indictment. Thoughts of killing The Voice again gripped him, but that seemed silly now. He still did not know what The Voice *was*, much less what it wanted. He had to think! If The Voice's motive was to have him as a puppet, then he would rather die now. For a moment, he found himself thinking of how he could thwart all of The Voice's plans by leaping out of the tenth story window now. A wonderful feeling of power rose up in him. He imagined The Voice's shocked face, the smug smile finally gone. Buoyed by these thoughts, he got up and walked to the window, the fantasy of ending his life playing in the back of his mind like a mesmerizing tune. Pulling the damp curtains aside, he looked out on the city, surprised by how beautiful it in fact looked in the pre-dawn light. After the rain shower, the air seemed fresh; the essence of the world seemed revived. Moreover, as he had hidden in the basement for years, he had not been up this high in a long while. He remembered what The Voice had told him that first night: that he wanted to be out of the darkness and up in the light, where the power was....The carpet was still damp beneath his feet. The cold dampness, finally penetrating his senses, made him step away from the window. He frowned, perhaps only then realizing what he had been about to do. He retreated back to his bed and lay there sullenly, his mind returning to the question of what The Voice wanted. Why prop him up when The Voice could have easily ruled himself? It did not make intuitive sense. And yet, if The Voice was sophisticated enough in his machinations to set him up as a puppet, then surely his plans had to reach far. The possible scope of those plans reawakened that old side of Mendez: the side that had hungered for information. In the days since The Voice had whisked him away from his basement, he had lost all connection to his old self. In effect, he had lived in a world of The Voice's making. Nodding to himself now, Mendez knew that slowly, as to not alarm The Voice, he had to reconnect himself; instead of the toadies that flocked to him because of The Voice's influence, he had to find his own men: men loyal only to him. That would not be so hard now. His mind went back to the rally, and what The Voice had done. Now, the men were not only amused by him: they were in *awe* of him! He got out of the bed again and walked to the window. A triumphant feeling rose in him as he stared out on the city. As that vast city sparkled in the morning light, it seemed like a ripe apple—his for the taking! All that he had to do was outwit God.

With all of the evil, cunning men in hell, it is foolish to believe that any one entity—even the Devil—would be able to control them indefinitely.
VERSE 2532:3 OF *The Teachings*

Xi was still staring at the image of Quibb and Circe on the monitor. He suddenly remembered his appointment with Shaka; but with all his visions and catharses, he had no idea how much time had passed. He was certain that the allotted one hour given to him to "get cleaned up" had passed, and the idea of Shaka waiting for him instinctively left him queasy. His first impulse was to rush to get ready. However, as Dr. Wang's attitude towards Shaka was still settling within him, jostling for space with all the other contradictions and self-destructive impulses, the idea of Shaka was *loathsome* to him. He *hated* Shaka. Yet, like Dr. Wang of old, it was hatred of a type that was untapped and unfocused. Like all cowards, Dr. Wang had ultimately been terrified of the object of his hatred—which had in turn fed his hatred, so that it grew within him like a poison that his body was unable to metabolize and excrete. Also, as he could not yet totally divorce himself from the flawed memories and attitudes of the last seven years, on some level, he continued to view Shaka as a kind of demon-god. Once one got a taste of power, as Xi certainly had since entering the lab and reclaiming his memories, the powerful became more of a threat: they ceased to be just impersonal objects of fear, and instead became *rivals*. It was one thing to be a faceless member of the masses (and to look up with awe and trembling at the powerful), and another thing to know that the powerful knew your name and were keeping an eye on you....It suddenly occurred to him that

Shaka had probably set up spy cameras in here. He looked around uneasily, again feeling himself brimming with resentment and hatred; but ultimately, the power at his command joined with his hatred of Shaka to insulate him from the boundless fear he had felt welling up in him. After all, he was a new being: he was more than Dr. Wang's brilliance, and more than the street-smart Xi that had managed to survive the last seven years. For once, the whole was more than the sum of its parts; and in the cosmic battles that lay ahead, all the knowledge of the universe was available to him. Yes, there were still obstacles and mysteries, but he felt uniquely endowed with the wherewithal to take on the universe. Delusions about demon-gods left him for the moment; flawed memories and self-destructive, unfocused calls for vengeance began to lose their potency and pass from his system. He nodded to himself, then went to the bathroom.

He did rush to get ready, but it was not with a sense of panic. As he stripped off the rags that clothed him, that act seemed to be a metaphor for his new state of mind. When he stepped into the shower, there was hot water. He had to make a conscious effort to pull himself away and not succumb to the easy pleasure. The soap was fragrant and soothing—unlike the harsh industrial detergents the men had been using over the last seven years. As he washed himself off, the water was literally black. All the grime was leaving him now and he rejoiced. He knew that there were battles ahead; but for those fleeting moments, he wanted only to revel in the simple pleasure of being clean.

When he was finished, he returned to the outside chamber (where he had a clothes closet) and got out a suit. As his body had wasted away over the seven years, the suit was too big for him. On top of that, it seemed as though it had been out of style even when it was new. Still, it was clean, and it was his.

When he exited his lab, he did so with a sense of peace. True, the Pink Eyes were still pumping out a sense of calm and well-being to the men, but Xi's peace came from within; and again, while his PinkEyes allowed him total access to whatever information he wished, he was in total control. He smiled again....The corridors seemed to go on forever. After a few minutes of walking, he realized that he was lost—that the floor plan seemed to have changed from what he remembered. An elevator bank that he always used to take was not there anymore. He called up a blueprint with his PinkEyes, but it was an old version; besides, he did not have any point of reference to tell him where he was now. With all this, when he finally found an elevator, it was not the one that he and the Jehovah had taken from the roof of the building. The elevator was huge, able to carry at least 50 men comfortably. He felt dwarfed and uneasy as he entered it; when he looked at the console, he saw that the elevator did not have any buttons. Before he could get out, the doors closed behind him. He felt trapped; as the seconds passed, he looked around with growing unease.

Actually, the elevator ride was so smooth and silent that he was not aware of having moved. About five seconds after the elevator doors closed, the doors opened suddenly. Instead of the empty corridor he had just left, he saw a dark, subterranean chamber with thousands of workers. A shift change seemed to be in progress, because men were going in every direction. As he looked around, he realized that he was below the Image Broadcast Complex. He had walked through here as a worker a few weeks ago: in the middle of the chamber, there was the huge machinery that powered the dark pyramid. The sight and reality of these things—along with the thousands of workers moving listlessly in the relative darkness—was jarring to the senses. Also, as he was newly clean, the stench of the men—along with the dank odor of the chamber, and the pungent industrial grease of the machinery—was nauseating. There was something disturbing about the silent, soulless way that the men walked. The last time Xi had been here, some of the men had at least been joking and talking to one another…but that was gone now. The commands he had just programmed into the PinkEyes (in order to control the men's violence) had stolen even this semblance of humanity from them. In the entire chamber, there were no voices—nothing that implied the presence of human beings or *life*. Still, there was something about the men that called to him. He was curious about them: wanted to see for himself if they really were soulless. With this impulse guiding him, he stepped out of the elevator. Unfortunately, the chamber was so packed that in order to keep from being trampled, he was forced to stand with his back against the

wall. Moreover, now that the PinkEyes were back online, the eerie glow of the thousands of devices in the chamber again conjured images of demons in hell. He searched their faces anxiously, but there was nothing sinister on the men's faces—just the blank obedience and soullessness of hive insects....
For the first time, he was confronted by what he, as the inventor of the PinkEyes, had done to them; and yet, as he used his PinkEyes to see what was going on with the rest of the city, he found himself thinking that maybe it would be simpler if they were all enslaved by the PinkEyes.

He now estimated that after The Horde attacks (and the purges of the previous night) perhaps only 60% of the men in the city wore PinkEyes. However, of those 60%, there were various gradations of subservience: 25% were perhaps totally enslaved by the PinkEyes—as the men around him were. The workers in this chamber were being given the most potent dose of the dark pyramid. Like a radio transmission, the signal strength diminished the farther one got from the epicenter of the broadcast: the dark pyramid. The men closest to the Image Broadcast Complex would do whatever the PinkEyes demanded of them, and do so with neither pangs of conscience nor *consciousness*. Theoretically, there were PinkEyes wearers who felt as Xi felt: who were in command of all their faculties and were *empowered* by the devices. However, the vast majority of them existed somewhere between total subservience to the PinkEyes, and an equally devastating state, where the insufficient (but corrupting) dose of the dark pyramid freed them from all connection to reality.

Moreover, what Xi was beginning to realize, was that in time, even the men within this chamber would become unstable. As propagandistic images of The Horde were broadcasted over the PinkEyes, it occurred to Xi that his pumping out a feeling of peace to the men had set a volatile reaction in motion. As the dark pyramid drove them towards madness, their consciousnesses would all begin to act in ways that were impossible for the PinkEyes to predict and account for. As Xi thought about it now, it occurred to him that he had only been able to curtail the violence of last night because the most violent members of the rampaging mobs had also been those most susceptible to the PinkEyes. With the unstable reaction building in strength every moment, it was only a matter of time before their minds either crashed from the contradictions, or madness set them on another rampage. Until that time, they would grow more unruly...So yes, it would be simpler if they were all slaves—especially with men still out there killing one another, and the cult of Tio Mendez building momentum in the city—

Mansmann and the woman suddenly popped into his mind. They did not seem real to him anymore, but as a fantasy: an oasis of possibility and hope in a world of death. He did not want to think about them too much—and build up his hopes. He almost wanted to hate them—and hate everything in the world—so that he could again be free. Strangely enough, at that moment, he looked at his years of rat eating and amnesia with a kind of nostalgia. He had been free back then—in just the same way that the wretched masses of the world, who suffered and died without even the faintest idea of what was destroying them, were free...And what was the use of being able to see clearly in a world whose existence seemed dependent on blindness and illusions? What was the use of being clean in a world of filth? Men were still fools and murderers....He did not know what to think anymore. In truth, he was probably thinking too much...It occurred to him that he could just leave now—find the exit and forget about Shaka and the schemes destined to play out over the last days of their race. For a moment, he was buoyed by that thought. After all, what did he really have in this place? Maybe Shaka needed his technical expertise for the time being (and this would insulate him from the man's treachery) but there were no long-term prospects in this place—and there was no *life*. Ahead of him, he saw nothing but pointless struggle. He would have to battle Shaka and Quibb—and there was still The Horde, butchering the world with his technology....

And now, the realization that Quibb and Circe had to be Horde spies, left him feeling even more empty inside. Xi still stood against the wall, staring at the men; but now, increasingly bewildered with his place in the world—*and the world, itself*—Xi began to walk along with the men, as to burn off some restless energy.

The stench of their unwashed bodies was still foul, but somehow this made them more real—more *human*. Also, as he walked along with them, the idea of Mansmann and the woman inevitably began to fill him with a sensation that approached hope. He could not put any faith in the world anymore—in *men*—but the fact that there were women out there—or at least *could* be—gave him something to hold onto: something which seemed tangible and worthwhile. Women seemed almost sacred to him now. He remembered his mother then—and the weird incestuous yearnings that had churned in him over his lifetime. He was aware that there had been a profound sickness in him—particularly when it came to women. …*What were women for?* he suddenly wondered, as men had wondered throughout the ages. It was not only a question of purpose: it was inevitably a question about himself. What did he need from them, and what did they need from him? He recalled, again, that he had never really loved a woman. But in his fantasies, he had always loved; in his fantasies, he had been a great lover—as all men were in their fantasies. In a sense, no men fantasized about women—but about *themselves* with women; all sexual yearnings were not so much about one's lovers, as they were about one's idealization of oneself as a lover. In his case, his fantasies had not so much been about beautiful women, as they had been about the man that those beautiful women wanted—the superhuman Adonis whose name those beautiful women called out in their moments of ecstasy. Presently, he remembered what Quibb had shown him in the sewer entrance to The Company—the fleeting love affair he had had with that white girl. He was relieved to find that it had really happened; but as he also found that he could remember neither her face nor her name, it occurred to him that maybe even she had been nothing but a kind of living mannequin, on which he had projected his yearnings. All his life, he had lusted after fantasies. With his newfound clarity, it now seemed evident that it had never been a human being that he had wanted at all, but a god: a thing to worship and place (untarnished and pure) on a pedestal. That realization now sickened him, especially as he was certain that that god of fantasy had manifested itself perfectly in the form of Quibb.

XII

Nothing makes men flock to God, as fear of the Devil. This is why it is said that the Devil was God's most effective creation.
VERSE 3545:2 OF *The Teachings*

By six that morning, the news was blaring over the screens and Pink Eyes. Last night, The Horde had again attacked Boston. It was only a matter of time—days, *hours* maybe—before they were back. While those totally enslaved by the PinkEyes were compelled to do The Company's bidding, those still free to vent their paranoia and desperation flocked to Mendez. In fact, if these men had been buoyed by thoughts of Mendez before, they now seemed on the brink of ecstasy with thoughts of him. In their passion, they amassed in front of his hotel, offering to sell their souls for the protection that only he (as the man impervious to death and Horde bombs) seemed able to provide. In fact, there was almost a riot in front of his hotel as thousands of men gathered to give praise to him. Mendez was their king—and king by *Divine* mandate....

Deciding to acknowledge his subjects, Mendez descended from his suite and gave a speech in front of the hotel. It took half an hour alone for him to get the tens of thousands of men to be quiet. Some of the men cried at the sight of him, as young girls cried at the sight of a rock star. Mendez stood there, waving and nodding, his confident smile making them giddy—as though it were proof that he would save them. When Mendez was finally able to speak, he said little—certainly nothing of substance. Instead of revealing how he would defend them against The Horde, he told the men that they were strong; instead of telling them what they would do tonight (or whenever The Horde attack descended upon them), he made oblique references to his rise from the flames and rubble; he talked about saboteurs, those disloyal to the ideals of his kingdom, and all the other Judases lurking in their midst. Still, in a sick sense, that was what the men wanted to hear. It was his voice alone that they needed—*especially now as the Voice of Conscience was no longer there to guide them.* Mendez's voice was steady and confident, and they felt it filling them. He talked for about a quarter of an hour—about 90% of which was interspersed with applause. At the end, he said: "Within all of us, we must forge our *own* voice of conscience, so that we won't be misled by our oppressors." It was deliberate; he had sat down thinking about it as the men began to gather in front of the hotel. Now that it was said, a side of him panicked at the realization that there would be no turning back. However, another side of him exulted in the sudden feeling of freedom. It was the same feeling that he had had the night before: there was the illusion of power in thwarting God, even if in so doing one destroyed one's self. Either way, his words filled the men with wild love for him, and that was all that mattered. As he waved his hand at the cheering multitudes, all that he could think was that he was the only one up there now: he, not The Voice....

He returned to the suite and sat down at the grand desk in its living room, waiting for The Voice to come. He closed all the blinds (so that the entire room was cast in darkness), and waited by himself. It was all a kind of perverse test: God would either come and punish him for what he had said in his speech, or turn away in disgust, leaving him to remake the world in his own image. He sat at a desk with a buzzer in his hand (so that he could signal the five heavily armed guards waiting outside his door); even then, as he stared into the darkness, it suddenly dawned on him that he was not afraid. He only wanted to know where he stood: if he was to be a man of power or just a puppet of God. In time, he decided that he would give God an hour to act: he was so presumptuous that he now believed that everything—even God—adhered to his timeline. He kept staring at his watch, counting seconds and minutes. Every far-off noise seemed to be a prelude to The Voice's vengeance. He expected The Voice's icy features to appear at any moment—but *again*, not with any true terror, but with perverse curiosity. He even found himself wishing that The Voice would come, so that he could press the buzzer, and his guards could rush in to blow the bastard to bits....The hour seemed to take forever to pass. *Just a few more minutes*! he kept telling himself, the way a marathoner racked with pain was able to coax himself along....When the hour finally passed, Mendez laughed out loud and leaped up to celebrate his freedom. He danced about the room like a child. Then, he yelled for his guards and lieutenants to attend him. Now that this victory over the heavens had been secured, he had work to do. In the wake of his euphoria, the first impulse that gripped him was the impulse to kill as many people as possible. He commanded his troops to go out into the world and bend the men to his will. He had already directed lieutenants to bring the most powerful technologies to him—satellite communications, holographic projectors and the like. He now went to the adjoining suite, where all these technologies had been amassed. The daunting array of flashing consoles made him feel as though he had entered the gates of heaven—not merely as a man that had proven his virtue, but as a man that had triumphed over virtue and *God*. Now that God was dead, and the mysteries of man lay bare before him, he would have to take on the Devil, who rose fancifully in his mind in the form of Shaka and, beyond that, The Horde.

If God is like language, and can be acquired merely by listening and
observing and taking part in society, then religion is like a dictionary,
which comes into being because one group presumes that it knows how one
should speak. The purpose of language is to facilitate the communication
of thoughts and intentions; the purpose of the dictionary is to decide
how one should communicate. While both may be necessary,
never confuse one with the other.
VERSE 897:5 OF *The Teachings*

X i was still in the bowels of The Company. However, he had his bearings
now, and was marching slowly but surely towards his meeting with
Shaka. As he walked shoulder-to-shoulder with the soulless men,
there was something almost hypnotic about the sound of their many feet
trampling the cement floor. He felt stifled—*trapped*. The urge to escape
came over him again. With another Horde attack imminent, he wanted to
flee the city now—get out into the woods somewhere…but the image of
the woman back at Mansmann's clinic called to him. He was not entirely
sure that he thought she was God (somehow, his newfound reason refused
to allow him that indulgence), yet, he feared her disapprobation. His futile
attempt to impress her (by telling her about the women on the subterranean
floors of The Company) had only trapped him. He was *obligated* to her—
and to the idea of saving the world. Also, in a sense, she had power over him
precisely because she was so vulnerable. One videophone call from him,
and she would be taken away to be experimented on. It occurred to him
that he could have her as a guinea pig; within the hour, he could have her
on his examination table—sliced open and dissected….He did not want to
think about the woman anymore.

From the fringes of his mind, came the realization that Quibb's voice still
was not playing—that their putative god had disappeared. Xi did not know

what to think about it anymore—if he had ever really thought about it to begin with. With The Horde coming back soon—*maybe even today*—they probably did not need The Voice of Conscience anymore. More likely than not The Horde had already accomplished what they had set out to do....

These were his thoughts as he walked up a flight stairs, and through a gaping doorway. Before he even realized it, he and the tide of soulless men were outside, looking out on a new day. They were up in Company Square again; the sun was rising on the horizon, but the morning seemed somehow corrupt and suspect. All throughout Company Square, other men—*soldiers*—were amassing in columns...*tens* of thousands of men. Xi saw that there were no generals and lieutenants—the PinkEyes were the only chain of command. And now, the men closest to him were moving to the left and standing at attention. Something about the entire thing was creepy, intensifying Xi's previous urge to flee. He was pushing past them now; in his desperation to get away from them, he punched one of them in the face. The man did not even flinch. His head went back from the force of Xi's blow, but the man's eyes were straight forward, like some kind of zombie—

Xi's mind went blank. A strange fit of claustrophobia came over him; his fists were moving wildly now—he did not even know what he was hitting: he just knew that he had to escape! ...At last, somehow, he was free of them. He was panting for air...and his knuckles were bleeding from all the punches he had thrown. Yet, even when he was free of the men, he retreated about 10 steps from the amassing columns, looking at the entire thing in horror. Now, as he looked around Company Square, he saw that in conjunction to the men coming from inside of The Company, thousands more were coming from off the streets. Xi analyzed the message being broadcasted over the PinkEyes, and saw that the men—or at least the percentage totally enslaved by the PinkEyes—were being compelled to mobilize to protect The Company from the imminent Horde attack. There was a horrible stillness and solemnity about the city now. The PinkEyes had ensnared them—were stealing the last of their souls; and yet, with The Horde coming, Xi again found himself wondering if there were any other options. Only the hive mind seemed able to save them now. Only the unanimity that came with tyranny could save them. Yet, Xi also knew that a stable system of slavery was itself a contradiction: a fantasy of the powerful. One way or another, slavery always made slaves of those who set out to be masters, and fools out of those who presumed to be gods.

He sighed. After looking up at the 150-story skyscraper, which sparkled majestically in the early morning light, he began his own solemn trek across Company Square. Shaka was still waiting....

Xi came out of his reverie just after he entered the lobby of the skyscraper. As he walked by the door that he and Quibb had emerged from the first night of The Horde bombing, there was a familiar twinge of anxiety in his belly. It was as though an entire lifetime had passed since that night....A security desk was now positioned in front of the door, manned by two guards. Remembering that he had given the woman the keys, Xi was relieved that he would not have to worry about them finding the keys on him. There were a few hundred men in the lobby (most of whom were heading outside to Company Square). He turned around now, and looked back at Company Square and the tens of thousands of amassing men. At the moment, machine guns were being distributed to the men. Xi stood there for a moment, again wondering if anything could save them besides enslavement to the hive mind—

Suddenly, he realized that he was being led away. Someone was holding his upper arm and leading him farther into the lobby. Looking up, Xi saw the Jehovah. The man's condescending smile was still there; and for a strange moment, Xi was so exhausted by all he was forced to account for, that he found himself hoping that the man was leading him away to kill him. He needed to rest....

The elevator was in a secluded nook. The Jehovah looked over at Xi once they were free of the crowd, explaining, "This elevator will take you to Shaka's office, Dr. Wang." The man was still holding Xi's upper arm. There was not anything particularly menacing about his grip, but it represented a power relationship. The man held Xi the way someone held an old woman to guide her across the street. It made Xi acutely aware of how frail he must seem.

The elevator opened as soon as the Jehovah pressed the button. The man helped Xi on the elevator, reached in and pressed something on the keypad (there were actual controls in this elevator), but he stayed outside.

"Aren't you coming?" Xi asked like an insecure child.

"Me? No," the man said, smiling again. The door closed on his smiling face....

Xi stood stiffly in the immaculate elevator. He stopped trying to think: it only seemed to drain him of vital energy. Just then, his stomach groaned with its emptiness. He had no idea when was the last time he had eaten. He was sure that he was developing an ulcer....

The door opened; he was again in Shaka's luxurious foyer. He remembered that there was no guard post anymore—just a receptionist. The latter smiled grandly when he recognized Xi.

"Go right in," the receptionist was saying. "Shaka is expecting you."

Xi nodded uneasily, then walked towards the door with a gait that was so stiff that he was sure that he would cramp up and topple. Touching the glistening, golden knob, he faltered. Uncertain, he looked back over his shoulder; the receptionist smiled back, nodding encouragingly at him. He knocked feebly, but he barely heard the knock himself. His turned the knob with a trembling, clammy hand, then peeped in. He had to squint again, as the huge windows—the glass wall, in fact—acted as a prism for the brilliant rays of the morning sun. Streams of reds and blues and greens—*all the colors of the rainbow*—rained down on him. It again seemed like a place of magic and wonder.

Shaka, who had been busy at his desk, looked up to see Xi peeping at him. "Come in!" the man boomed with the characteristic smile of his minions.

Xi tried to smile back, but his facial muscles thwarted his intention with a spasmodic grimace. He stepped in.

"Ah!" Shaka beamed, getting up from his desk and coming around to greet him, "You look good in fresh clothes!" As Shaka was arrayed in a flowing white robe, he suddenly struck Xi as a black Charlton Heston playing "Moses" in the classic movie, "The Ten Commandments."

When Shaka shook his hand and patted him on the back, Xi looked on in bewilderment. From what he remembered, Shaka *never* shook hands—never touched others. Something about the man's touch was actually unnerving; Xi locked himself away....

"...You fixed the PinkEyes!" Shaka was laughing now, seeming oblivious of the tense way that Xi carried himself.

"...Yes," Xi said when he could think of nothing else. A side of him wanted to inform Shaka of the explosive chain reaction that had been set in motion, with the men being force-fed both a yearning for peace and jingoism, but he felt somehow that this explanation would take too much out of him—

"It is men like you who have to step to the forefront of society!" Shaka went on. "It is something demanded by evolution: all that has brought us to this place in time. I need a right hand man like you: a man who has experience in what it means to organize men and command power."

Xi looked on warily: "Me?" he said.

"Such modesty!" Shaka said with a chuckle. "I have big plans for you, sir!" Shaka exulted then. The man was laughing again, but Xi suddenly found that there was something horrible about Shaka's voice. The man did not sound and act like Shaka at all—but like a second-rate game show host. Gone from Shaka was the understated self-confidence and *power* of seven years ago—or even their last meeting! Now underlying his actions and words was the kind of demonstrative congeniality that was always used to mask desperation and anxiety—and *artifice*. Xi did not know the madness that had gone through Shaka during his night of waiting for Circe's return, but he *sensed* it. In Shaka's eyes, there was the madness of a man who was searching for something that seemed to be lost forever—

Xi's stomach must have groaned then, because Shaka moved to the subject of food. There was a table to the side, on which a smorgasbord had been set up. There was fresh fruit and wholesome, fresh bread and omelets and pitchers of various juices. Shaka led him over, chuckling again as he saw Xi's salivating expression. Shaka nodded encouragingly to Xi, then stood to the side and watched Xi put eggs and a few slices of bread on a plate. After the first few bites, Xi forgot that Shaka was even there. He had not tasted food like that in *years*. It was food that did not taste as though it had been rendered through a complicated industrial process, but like *real* food. There was no aftertaste of machine oil and smoke. It *filled* him. He was eating with his fingers, slurping at the juice...Shaka's laughter brought him back to his senses.

"...You disappeared from your lab this morning," Shaka said when Xi looked up. There was something sinister in his eyes, but it faded away so quickly or *expertly* that Xi almost immediately found himself wondering if it had ever been there. Whatever the case, the renewed reality that Shaka knew his movements—and was no doubt keeping track of him—made him twitch. Shaka still had an air of desperation about him, but now Xi found himself wondering if it had been an act; worse yet, he found himself thinking that maybe that desperation really was there—was *boundless* in fact—and that the man was willing to do *anything*....

Xi nervously wiped the food away from his lips with the sleeve of his suit: "I got lost," he said. "The floor plan has changed."

"I see," Shaka said with an enigmatic laugh. "Anyway," he went on, "from the way you eat, I can tell that you've been famished."

Recalling how he had eaten—*like an animal*—Xi felt suddenly self-conscious. There was something disarming about letting others know the extent of one's hunger, because it showed them how easily one could be manipulated. Luckily, the intercom on Shaka's desk rang then. As Shaka diverted his attention and walked back to his desk, Xi again wiped his mouth with his sleeve. However, remembering that one was not supposed to wipe one's mouth with one's sleeve, he felt uneasy again. By the time Shaka told the secretary to send the call through, Xi had retreated into himself somewhat.

Just as Shaka seated himself behind his desk, the call went though; and from a holographic projector on a stand beside Shaka's desk, which was perpendicular to both Shaka and Xi, Mendez's torso appeared. Xi froze!

"Ah! Senor Mendez, how nice of you to call!" Shaka was saying, leaning back in his chair.

Xi could not breathe!

"Thank you for taking my call," Mendez said.

"Nonsense!" Shaka protested. "A man of your importance should expect people to be happy to take his calls. How may I help you?"

"I was wondering if you would consider taking a position in my government. The city needs men who know how to organize the masses."

"I was just saying those exact same words," Shaka said, looking over at Xi with a smile. Xi still had not moved.

Mendez looked over, visibly surprised. For a moment, there was an uncomfortable sensation between them. After all, they had both been cowed by Quibb's will—and were the only men who knew the depths of the each other's shame. Moreover, as these were the last days of man—a time when the powerful were busy trying to gather the last scraps that could sustain them—Mendez had his hackles up. When he saw that Xi was with Shaka, the hatred flashed in his eyes. For an instant, it lingered there, grotesque and horrible, but he forced it down into his gut, and smiled in the same blank, menacing way that Shaka smiled. Mendez looked at Shaka then, saying: "...I see you've found Dr. Wang at last."

Shaka frowned: "You two know one another?" he said, looking from one man to the other.

"We have an associate in common," Mendez started, "—nothing important. *Anyway*," he said, returning to the matter at hand, "will you join my government, Shaka?"

Shaka's smiled yet again. "I would be delighted," he said; and then: "I would consider it my civic duty!"

Xi still had not moved.

As soon as Mendez and Shaka ended their conversation with fake smiles and effusive declarations of good will, Shaka's smile died. The man looked up at Xi with a new horrible intensity shining in his eyes, then walked over to him. Shaka placed his hand on Xi's shoulder then; Xi stared ahead— blankly into Shaka's eyes.

"We're at the precipice of history, Dr. Wang," Shaka began. "What we decide in the next hours and days may very well decide if the human race survives or dies out. The question of life and death is one beyond morality and conscience. It is one which simply asks: What is to be done? Continued existence is its own justification—its own moral compass. We must place ourselves at the vanguard of evolution, Dr. Wang, and take those steps that will ensure our continued existence....

"Before you disappeared seven years ago, you were working on a special project for me."

Xi had been staring at the man's face blankly; but at those last words, something horrible was triggered in him. As if more by instinct than in response to Shaka, Xi said the words, "The Hand of Evolution." As he said it, he remembered Quibb's final words to him: that when he understood what the hand of evolution meant, he would be presented with the opportunity to decide who he wanted to be. He felt weak—

"Yes," Shaka went on, his face stern—like the Shaka of old. "It is time that we institute The Hand of Evolution and bring the Image Broadcast Complex to its full potential, so that *all* men, regardless of whether or not they are wearing PinkEyes, will be subject to its will. It is a matter of them or us. Either we subdue The Horde and Mendez's fools with The Hand of Evolution, or they'll overrun us....I know that you were close to completion."

Xi hedged: "I was, but that was seven years ago."

"Complete the project, Dr. Wang—you have a day at the most: *hours* maybe. It is the only thing that will ensure our safety against The Horde. If The Horde comes before you're finished, then we're all dead."

*The more powerful one becomes (and the more one relies on
his power over men) the more one hates his fellow men.
At base, the powerful are probably all misanthropes.*
VERSE 2733:3 OF *The Teachings*

The word spread like wildfire—especially now that the PinkEyes
were again online. Somehow, a few soldiers had managed to shoot
down one of The Horde's planes. Actually, this was a baseless conclusion, as no plane had been found—and none had even been seen. What
had been seen, however, was the enemy....The two Horde soldiers walked
away from Quibb and Circe's hideout with their robotic gaits. The first
men to see them knew that they were the enemy because The Horde's
insignia—the green sun against the purple sky—was emblazoned on their
chests. The Horde soldiers walked out in the open: there was no hiding—
no clandestine behavior whatsoever. As the alarm went out over the Pink
Eyes and billboards, men rushed from the surrounding streets to block off
the soldiers. They approached the figures with their fingers on the triggers
of their guns; when they were close enough, they shot wildly, but the enemy's
body armor was impervious to their bullets. The enemy only walked on:
upright, deliberate...Some of the men yelled for the figures to stop...to raise
their hands in the air...to drop to the ground with arms outstretched...but
their words were to no effect. Dozens of men are coming around now, still
shooting and yelling; some were caught in the crossfire and dropped lifelessly to the ground. The enemy walked on: the men were the ones who
stopped and hedged; they were the ones who formed a defensive wall to

fight off the seemingly unarmed enemy….The men stopped firing eventually. Some of them realized that if they surrounded the enemy troops from the back, then they could subdue them by hand. This was what they had all dreamed about: a chance to see the enemy. Each wanted to be the one to subdue the troops; each wanted to have stories told about him for years to come. This was how heroes were made….

Indeed, seemingly pulled by that fantasy, more men were coming up all the time. The moment of reckoning seemed to be close at hand. Five hundred men now had their eyes and guns trained on the enemy; like wolves around a powerful buck, they waited for their time to pounce. Some of them were licking their lips. They kept reminding themselves that if they waited a few seconds more, then their moment of greatness would come…But then, suddenly, the enemy stopped and let out a high-pitched sound that seemed like laughter. The sound took the men aback, so that hundreds of them now stood their ground and stared warily at the figures that already seemed beyond the power of men and guns. The sound the Horde soldiers made was like nothing the men had ever heard before: a kind of dirge—but not so much with sorrow, as pride. Something about it made them all shudder. Some of the men were instinctively backing away now: most of them had forgotten about subduing the enemy and gaining glory. But one of the men— either the bravest, or the most insane—snuck up behind those soldiers and raised his trembling gun to the head of the enemy. The others watched him, already praising him. But just then, the hidden explosives that had lined the enemy's body armor went off, killing 200 men and maiming another few dozen. The enemy's wail seemed to echo in the explosion, mocking the men of the city and their illusions of power….

Time is the ultimate weapon—there is no defense against it.
VERSE 3121:7 OF *The Teachings*

Mansmann was making his rounds though the clinic—if "rounds" was even the word for it. Since the woman had come, he had all but abandoned the men—except of course for the few wretches he had experimented on with her blood. He walked slowly through the doleful chamber, once again wondering what he was doing there. He came upon at least 30 dead bodies, some of which had been there for weeks. Dozens of men were so sick that they would not last a week. There was of course the woman's blood, but not only did she not have enough blood to cure them all: the entire thing would be a waste of time, as the men's lives seemed pointless to begin with. Beyond their illnesses, they were simply wasting away from starvation and neglect. As Mansmann watched them, he was glad that he was not deluded by thoughts of compassion. The closest he came was a feeling of relief that the PinkEyes were again online, and that none of the men was feeling pain.

Just then, two men in robes entered the chamber. As soon as Mansmann saw them, he knew that they did not belong there. In fact, the men seemed almost supernaturally healthy—*robust*. There was a quickness to their steps— a youthful spring—that annoyed Mansmann for some reason.

"Who the hell are you?" he demanded as they walked up to him.

"We're from the United Brotherhood," they said in unison, seeming to puff out their chests.

"Congratulations," Mansmann grumbled. "What do you want?" he said, transferring his attention to one of the comatose patients on the ground.

"We're here to check up on you," they again said in unison, like annoying twins.

"...*What*?" Mansmann said when he realized what they had said.

Their smiles broadened; the twin on the left took the lead: "We have to make sure everyone is giving his best for his brothers."

"What's this about?" Mansmann demanded.

"Look at these deplorable conditions," the other one went on, "—men dying on the floor—"

Mansmann exploded: "How the *hell* do you expect me to take care of 500 men by myself! What the hell is wrong with you people!" He was about to tell them to get lost when the men smiled—

"You misunderstand us, sir: we're here to help."

"You?" he said, confused and dubious.

"We were both doctors before all this: the Brotherhood sent us over to assist you. In fact, more will be coming: you'll have at least two new doctors per three-shift rotation."

Suddenly remembering his fears about Shaka, it dawned on him that maybe the man had sent them to spy on him. All he could do was stare at them.

The power of God is not a matter of what She can do, but of what the people are willing to do in Her name. Indeed, the most powerful gods don't do anything at all—their followers, gripped by the name of God, move heaven and earth with nothing but the inference that they are following Her will.
VERSE 643:2 OF *The Teachings*

As Xi stepped away from his meeting with Shaka, the possibilities hovering on the horizon confronted him like monsters hiding in the darkness of a child's room. As he stepped into the elevator and started the lonely trip down the length of the building, his only thought was that the last days—if not *hours*—of the human race were at hand. Given what Shaka demanded of him, his only choices were betraying humanity by stealing the last of men's souls, or reconciling himself to The Horde. The power he had felt before, when repossessing his knowledge and memory, now seemed unwieldy and unresponsive. It possessed him and weighed him down, but he did not necessarily feel as though he could *command* it. In a sense, the most cogent thing that had come with the return of his memories, was a deeper sense of mistrust and insecurity. He understood the powerful now: saw them not from the vantage point of a bewildered weakling, but from the perspective of a peer. Worse still, The Hand of Evolution was a mammoth beast on the periphery of his mind. He dared not approach it; and yet, like a patient predator, it waited in the darkness for him to advance within pouncing distance. They played this game with one another, each holding his distance, waiting for the other to betray his weakness and impatience....The fact of the matter was that he had finished The Hand of Evolution seven years ago. He had finished it weeks before he experimented on G.W.; but realizing the total power it would give Shaka, Dr. Wang had encrypted it and stored it away in an inconspicuous file, within a database that held countless teraquads of data. He had hidden it away not because of any moral qualms about being able to rule men's souls, but because he had not wanted to give that power to Shaka. He had finished the project and kept it secret, so that he could use it as a bargaining chip: something to hold over Shaka's head....

Xi scratched the nape of his neck anxiously as the elevator made its way down the building. He kept telling himself that if he could only rest and figure things out, then he would be fine—and the *world* would be fine. However, given all that lay before him, the flood of information/memories that his overworked mind had been able to convert into knowledge seemed negligible—*useless*. Most of the grand schemes had probably been revealed to him by now, but the details and inner workings were still lost to him. Yes, it was all coming back to him—drop by drop—but that trickle was *maddening*, especially with the moment of no return approaching so quickly on the horizon. In a sense, he was probably a bigger fraud than he was when he had no memories whatsoever. Furthermore, he had to admit to himself that even it he reclaimed all that knowledge, he would probably still be powerless to stop what was coming. Now, of all times, he did not want to delude himself into feeling that he had power when all of his movements were in fact due to the manipulations of others. He could not allow himself to see his puppet strings as emanations of his power....All his life, he had created power for others. Shaka's empire, and The Horde, had been built on his inventions; Quibb had sent him about like a fool, so that he could help in Mendez's ascendancy. Indeed, he was singularly responsible for the rise of all their gods and demons—and yet, he had *nothing*. Even his so-called technical expertise seemed like a curse to him now—a mark of weakness. Some people said that knowledge was power, but knowledge was only powerful to the powerful. Simply knowing something did not necessarily give one the wherewithal to *manipulate* it. Astronomers, for instance, had no power over the heavens: they could not bend stars to their will, nor could they change the orbits of planets; but as an astronomer, Xi had mapped the universe so that all the gods could navigate the heavens....

The elevator doors opened, and Xi again looked out on the lobby. After the chaos of the morning's shift change, the relative emptiness of the lobby now made it seem deserted. As he stepped out into the lobby, he imagined the men down in the bowels of the complex, working their lives away like the automatons that they were. Looking out on Company Square, Xi saw that the thousands of solders were still standing at attention. When The Horde came and blew them all to bits, they would be oblivious. He looked away....The Jehovah was still posted in the lobby. The man came up with his perpetual smile, wishing Xi a good day, but Xi only grumbled and moved on.

Two guards were still sitting at the desk that had been placed in front of the entrance to the subterranean floors. Xi looked away uneasily, but then he remembered Quibb, and the way the man had laughed at him when he told him about the women beneath The Company. Had Quibb laughed because there were no women under there, or to throw him off track? It had to be the latter. As Horde spies, Quibb and Circe had no doubt entered his lab looking for The Hand of Evolution. When their search came up empty, they had probably set out to find him and brainwash him. Rather, Quibb had concentrated on him, while Circe had taken Shaka. Xi remembered seeing Circe on Shaka's couch, and the way that the man's face had seemed to be changing as Xi watched it. Who knew what Circe really was under all those illusions—and what the man had made Shaka see!

Xi wondered how long Quibb had observed him before he and Circe realized that he had lost his memory. Maybe they had scanned his mind somehow and seen the jumbled mess that it had become—and guessed that the key to his becoming whole again was back in his lab. After scanning him, it would have been child's play for Quibb to manipulate him into coming back to The Company. Quibb had gotten him to wear PinkEyes, perhaps hoping that they would trigger his memories. Maybe they figured that once he remembered who he was, he could tell them where The Hand of Evolution was...but then Xi found himself wondering what the point of The Voice of Conscience had been. Also, he still could not figure out why Quibb had propped up Mendez. Maybe Mendez was a Horde spy as well.... Xi shook his head: a more likely conclusion was that The Voice and Mendez were simply ploys to destabilize Shaka's power base. Maybe The Horde had bombed primarily to get the PinkEyes offline, so that they could get a foothold in the men's souls in the power vacuum. Xi nodded his head: it had only been in the absence of the PinkEyes that The Voice and Mendez had been able to rise. It all made sense, yet the only meaningful conclusion that Xi could come to, was that he was still a pawn in the schemes of gods....

He made it back down to his lab in a daze. Yet, despite his jumbled thoughts, it was increasingly clear that nobody—not Shaka, not Quibb and The Horde—could ever be allowed to possess The Hand. This realization was a step in the right direction, but knowing what he could not do did not necessarily tell him what he *should* do. Coming to a dead end only told one that one had come the wrong way—it did not tell one the correct route. As such, he felt horribly trapped—*helpless*. When the door of his lab closed behind him, he stood there anxiously. Operating under the assumption that Shaka had planted surveillance devices in his lab (and knowing that if there was even a chance of him surviving this, then it was imperative that he make Shaka think that he was diligently working on The Hand), he went and sat down before a computer console. He sat there for about ten minutes, just staring at the screen and pressing buttons as to keep up the illusion that he was actually working. In the interim, his mind searched frantically for the scenario that would save his life.

Actually, as Xi sat at the console, it occurred to him that his knowing where The Hand of Evolution was, was probably the only reason he was still alive. Just as he had sensed seven years ago, it was the bargaining chip that had ensured his life. He had no doubt that once he gave The Hand to Shaka (and the man became God and master of their souls) he would be disposed of....All at once, Xi found himself thinking that he could bring The Hand of Evolution online now, brainwashing Shaka and everyone else. After all, he was the only one who knew how to make himself immune to its effects. *He* could be God; *he* could rule men's souls....He got up and walked around restlessly, then he returned to the console. On second thought, there was no way he could even risk opening the project: if Shaka really had surveillance devices connected to the console, then his opening the project would give the man total access—and *power*. Moreover, it was just as likely that Quibb and Circe had planted surveillance devices in here. The project was safe where it was…but what was he to do now? He just could not sit there indefinitely. If Shaka began to suspect something (and this was inevitable if he really was monitoring this console!) then Xi was done for. He would have to decide on a course of action soon. He got up uneasily again, then sat back down….Shaka had been right about one thing: The Hand of Evolution was the only thing that could control The Horde. Xi found himself being intoxicated by this fact. He wanted to resist it—and the course of action it demanded—but he had gone too far already. The time for half steps was over: it was all or nothing now. As such, everything was reduced to one simple question: Did he want to live? If the answer was yes, then he had no choice but to use The Hand—to bring it online for *his* use. It was a choice between dying as a slave or living as a god. The decision seemed clear, but he instinctively felt himself on the verge of something *horrible*: a step that once taken would be the end of his life—*if not all existence*.

No, there *had* to be something else. He did not entirely know what it was, but he sensed that he had to get away from The Company—put space between himself and Shaka—in order to think things through. He remembered The Goddess and Mansmann again. He remembered the woman's decisiveness—her *power*; and being essentially a coward, it occurred to him that he could get her to decide what to do. Thoughts of seeing the woman were again like a kind of madness…and then it occurred to him that with his PinkEyes, he could access The Hand of Evolution from anywhere, at anytime. He could get the woman's counsel about The Hand; and if she told him to bring it online, he could shield her, himself and Mansmann from its effects, so that they could be safe until they decided what to do with the human race. This realization gave him the illusion of power—and the courage needed to go about the task of fleeing from Shaka and The Company. However, in the final analysis, courage was nothing but a kind of cowardice: the ability to act with blindness, when the consequences to be paid were so obvious.

Never trust a god who hates your enemies—and whose primary
reason for being seems to be to take revenge on your enemies.
Such a god has been corrupted by the hand of man and is only
really a refection of your own desperation and powerlessness.
VERSE 3444:6 OF *The Teachings*.

Over the PinkEyes and screens, there was a scene from The Horde's raid on Providence, Rhode Island. Some men had actually managed to get footage of some of the troops. It was dusk. Clad in body armor from head to foot, The Horde soldiers nonetheless moved with a stunning degree of agility. It was some kind of warehouse district: some-place with old industrial buildings. The five or so soldiers were looking about, trying to discern something. There were only about five seconds of actual footage. The cameraman, perhaps trying to get a better angle, had foolishly moved from his hiding place. But just then, on the screen, there was a flash of light, and then static. That was it. It was reminiscent of a big foot sighting on video: there was something dubious about it all. It was too blurry: too fleeting for anything resolute to be gotten from it. Yet, the men, who existed between a panicky dread of the eventual attack, and a blind hope that Mendez would protect them, were believers. They had seen their devil; now, they waited for God's protection.

A mouse is a timid creature; but millions of them, driven mad by an outside, unreachable force, will take out their frustrations on those around them.
VERSE 942:8 OF *The Teachings*

When Xi exited the elevator and stepped out onto the 150th floor, Stein was manning the receptionist's desk. When Stein recognized him, a look of deep, almost *insane*, hatred came over the man's face. He sat at the desk, staring up at Xi without even trying to hide what he felt. Xi stepped up uneasily, suddenly realizing that the man was looking at him the way one woman looked at another whom she suspected of having designs on her man. When Xi realized this, he was caught between the horror of it and the ridiculousness of it. He shook his head instinctively, as though on the verge of explaining himself, but Stein grunted then, demanding:

"What do you want?"

"I need to see Shaka."

"Is he expecting you?"

"No—I don't think so…But it's important."

Stein grunted again, then called up Shaka.

When Xi entered Shaka's grand suite, the man was standing on the far side of the chamber, before a screen. It was just like the scene from seven years ago…Xi tried not to think about it. As he walked up to the man, he gave himself a desperate pep talk, reminding himself that if he only managed to do this, then he, Mansmann and the woman would be safe….

"Why are you here, Dr. Wang?"

"I need to get something—can I use your helicopter?"

Shaka stared at him as though seeing right through him—both literally and figuratively. "...What is it that you need, Dr. Wang?"

"Notes on The Hand and other breakthroughs I was working on."

"Oh?" Shaka said in a calm but inherently menacing tone, "you've been keeping up with your work over the years?"

"Yes," Xi lied.

Shaka pursed his lips: "...You know, you've never really explained why you did not come back to The Company over the last seven years. I was under the impression that we were allies: that your discoveries were solely for the use of The Company."

"They are, sir," Xi said, fighting to keep his tone even—and to maintain eye contact with the man.

"Allies don't desert one another and play games."

"I didn't, sir," he said in a panic. He felt doomed: he had an insane impulse to rush Shaka and bite and claw at him like an animal. He could not help shuddering when the thoughts registered in his mind.

Shaka looked at him closely—still as though seeing right through him. He nodded his head, as though coming to some conclusion, then: "Is there anything you want to tell me, Dr. Wang?"

"...Pardon?"

"As my ally, is there anything you think I should know?"

"Like what, sir?"

"Anything that might affect The Company and its continued existence?"

"No, sir."

"Nothing at all?"

"No," Xi said with a suddenly hoarse voice.

"...I understand." Then, nodding towards the screen he had been watching on Xi's entrance, "Look at what is happening to the city. Look at what the men are becoming."

Xi turned to the screen; the same images had been playing over his PinkEyes, but he had been blocking them out....There were reports of people being shot in the streets by soldiers that wore Mendez's banner—a red strip of cloth—around their arms. At first, Xi did not understand what he was seeing, but then he realized that what he had feared was taking place: the contradictory messages being pumped out over the PinkEyes were making the men more unstable. Still, this was perhaps beyond the PinkEyes, because Mendez's supporters came exclusively from the ranks of those that were not *totally* enslaved by the PinkEyes (as they would have been following Shaka's will) and those that had never worn the devices. There was an image on the screen of a man sodomizing another in a burned out building; as a mob of Mendez's supporters came upon them, the lovers squealed out like pigs before being shot down. Shaka chuckled sardonically at this. Xi looked at the man uneasily; and worse than Shaka's reaction, was the fact that the butchery on the screen was practically being reported with joy! Men were being shot in the streets like rats, and yet there was jubilation. The reporter was saying some gibberish about strengthening their body and weeding out saboteurs. There were flawed analogies about warding off viruses and purging one's system of cancers. Still, all that Xi saw were scenes of pathetic men being shot, while the rest of the population was whisked along by the thrill of the hunt. It was a new version of *Throw the First Stone*—a *purified* version of it. Mendez was clearly going mad—and yet Xi realized that that madness was exactly what the men wanted, and *needed*. The victims cried out for more blows; the extent of Mendez's brutality was seen as proof that he could defend them against The Horde. Indeed, if Mendez could kill them like The Horde had killed them, then that was proof that he was a match for it. The men now existed in a place where they *needed* the impossible, because their consciousnesses could not face the possibilities before them. Their continued existence seemed to *depend* on the impossible—and so Mendez rose up as a god whose only purpose was ultimately to guarantee the continuation of their fantasies....Xi sighed. Believe it or not, there was still a side of him that wanted to believe that this was all part of Quibb's plan—*even The Horde's plan*—because it would mean that there was some purpose to it...but there could be no purpose in this. There was no plan—no *God*...not even a scheming man. Mendez and Quibb and Shaka—even *he*—were simply fools that had started a fire that was now beyond all control.

For some reason, Xi looked over at Shaka then. He forgot about why he had come here—about the Goddess and Mansmann and escaping the horror that was even now descending on them all. These things seemed pointless somehow. Instead, he stared at Shaka as the man smiled at the events on the screen. Then, as Xi's alienation and bewilderment became complete, he ventured, "Do you like Mendez, sir?"

"*Like* him?" Shaka chuckled, incredulous. "What do you mean?"

"Well," he started, already wishing that he had kept his mouth shut, "...you could have...disposed of him a long time ago...and yet you keep broadcasting his message—*publicizing* him."

Shaka laughed out loud, as if the assertion were a silly one. "We have passed the era where likes and dislikes are relevant to existence, Dr. Wang. What men believe—what they agree with or disagree with—is of no consequence to me," he went on. "A heart does not know why a man is running—it does not care: it *cannot*, in fact. When a man runs, a heart only knows that it must pump more blood. The Image Broadcast Complex is the heart of the city, Dr. Wang. The blood that it pumps out is what you see on the screens and PinkEyes. There is nothing moral in blood—nothing *political*. There is no like or dislike in blood: it is simply a necessary element of continued existence."

Xi nodded abstractedly. Something about Shaka's calm, resolute voice was horrible just now. Suddenly eager to leave, Xi was about to bring up the topic of the helicopter once more, but Shaka was again looking at him closely. Once again, there was something menacing about the man's smile that made Xi look away. Luckily for him, a buzzer went off on Shaka's desk then. When Shaka walked over, Stein informed him that he had a call....It was Mendez. A painful spasm went though Xi's gut when the man's image again appeared on the videophone. Xi felt frozen in place, but Shaka smiled and called him over.

Mendez's image did not even seem human anymore. Oftentimes the most powerful men—the men able to move heaven and earth—were those who had uncompromisingly sacrificed their humanity. Mendez's face seemed harder; when he spoke, his voice was guttural and harsh: as uncompromising as the power that had stolen his soul.

"What do you think of my recent actions?" Mendez asked. He was smiling, but all about him, there only seemed to be rage and madness. There was a confident, yet sociopathic, gleam in his eyes that was reminiscent somehow of Stalin's. He stared deeply into Shaka's eyes, still smiling his dead smile as he repeated: "What do you think?"

Shaka smiled, glancing at Xi, who now stood at his side: "We must all do those things that ensure our survival."

"I agree," Mendez said, his dead smile widening to a grin. "We have to weed out all the cancers and parasites. [His eyes narrowed then.] Since we are in agreement, do I then have permission to use your broadcasting apparatus?"

"Of course!" Shaka said, gleefully.

Mendez nodded to someone out of the range of the videophone, then smiled to Shaka: "We put together a report on saboteurs: it should be coming on the screens at any moment."

Both Xi and Shaka turned and looked at the TV screen. During the usual scenes of the rampage, an official-looking message came on, announcing a special report. A smart-looking reporter was standing in Central Park—at the sight of the rally bombing:

"We at last know who it was that set the bomb," the man said, menacingly. "First," he continued, "observe the breakthrough images that were captured a few nights ago. Here, you will clearly see the bandits killing some of our soldiers."

The scene changed to show two people—a man and a little boy—walking down the street suspiciously. It had been taken from one of the thousands of cameras that were set up all over the city. Xi remembered them well from when he used to be a monitor in The Company. The camera was zooming in on the bandits now. Xi's knees almost buckled: *it was the woman and the little boy!* Xi unconsciously took a step forward, his mouth gaping.

"Now look what happens," the reporter went on. Just then, some soldiers accosted the two figures on the screen. Something was yelled; then, all of a sudden, some more men (the woman's cult!) appeared. In no time at all, the soldiers were mowed down by bullets, then the attackers, the woman and the little boy ran off together. The reporter went on: "Here are pictures of the murderers' faces." Now on the screen were digitally enhanced versions of the cult members' faces, which differed only minutely from their actual faces. Xi was numb—*drained*; just when he thought that it was over, the reporter reappeared on the screen:

"And now," he said, indignantly, "here is the evidence that they set the bomb."

On the screen now appeared the pug-faced youth that Xi remembered from the barricade after the rally! He could not help gasping.

"Yeah, I saw them," the youth was saying. "They was acting suspicious. I saw them guys right off. They come walking from the rally: three homos and a little kid. They smelled of explosives. They had an evilness about them. It's these weird freaks," he said in disgust, "...they ain't got no morality: no respect for nature or God. I should have killed them when I got the chance," he said, ashamed.

And then, the scene changed to another man, whom Xi did not know. A reporter was holding up pictures of the suspects' faces for the man.

"Yeah, I recognize those two," the man started, pointing to the woman and the little boy. "That little boy's my son," he said, suddenly breaking in to sobs. "That other one there [and he pointed towards the woman] kidnapped my son and forced him to do all these nasty things. I've been searching for my son for months now...a boy needs his father," he lamented, "especially in these hard times." At last, as the man stood weeping against a wall, there was a voice over saying:

"This is what happens when men are presumptuous enough to try to challenge the will of God. You have evil incarnate—men existing only to destroy that which God has made. We must be purged!"

Xi's mouth was dry; he felt *horrible*. Then, as the woman's picture reappeared on the screen, his knees almost buckled as he remembered something. About a year before the apocalypse, he had worked on a project for Shaka: actually, the primer for The Hand of Evolution. He had created a computer-generated spokesperson that when viewed would prepare men's minds for The Hand...but then something had happened that he had never accounted for: the appearance of a 10-year-old girl whose facial contours had matched those of the spokesperson. Instead of following the spokesperson, people had started following the little girl. A *cult* had grown; and just as was the case now with the PinkEyes, confused messages had made the people increasingly unstable….Shaka had tried to kill the little girl—but that had driven the little girl and her cult underground. Shaka had blown up the little girl's apartment, killing her mother….

Xi groaned. He felt faint—especially as it occurred to him that he really was responsible for all their gods! He was single-handedly responsible for the rise of Shaka, Mendez, The Horde…and now, the Goddess. This revelation was so brutal to his senses that he forgot that Shaka was by his side—and that Mendez could see him over the videophone. When he eventually came to his senses, he looked around nervously, wondering if the two men had noticed him! Shaka still had the serene look on his face as he stared at the screen. But there was something in Mendez's eyes that immediately told Xi that he was undone. It occurred to him that Mendez had perhaps put out this report to turn Shaka against him. The man had to know that he was with the woman. Maybe it was some form of bribery, with the implication being that Mendez would reveal the rest if Xi did not come over to his side. It also occurred to him that maybe Mendez and Shaka had already decided on an alliance. Maybe they wanted to make some kind of example out of him—parade him around like one of those wretches on *Throw the First Stone*! There were so many unwholesome possibilities that his mind felt polluted with sludge—congested with filth that would never allow cogent thought. The only thing that seemed clear was that he would die soon—and that that death would be at the hand of a man of power.

Mendez was talking now: "Yes," he said, with pride rising in his voice, "these saboteurs must be weeded out." He looked at Xi then: "Do you have any suggestions, Dr. Wang?" he asked, his dead smile returning. "You've always seemed to have a grasp of all the little conspiracies going on in the city."

"Is that so?" Shaka asked, smiling serenely.

There was something in his eyes—*in both of their eyes*! They knew: they *had* to know! Something in him died: shriveled away to nothing, so that he thought that he would collapse right there. He expected guards to come in then and take him away; he expected guns and knives. However, Mendez was inexplicably changing the subject of the conversation now. As quickly as he had broached the topic, he was dismissing it. Xi stood there silently— *ineptly*—while the other two men took their conversation to the social vagaries and then parted with their usual cabalistic mirth.

Xi was still standing there pathetically when Mendez's image flickered off. Did he dare hope that he could escape? The thought seemed like madness, and yet he was rushing towards it! "Shaka," he said in a hoarse voice, "...about that helicopter?"

"Oh, of course," Shaka said in an offhand manner. "I almost forgot. I'll have one waiting for you on the roof."

"I'll be back in a short while, sir," Xi lied.

Shaka nodded; Xi rushed out, fleeing upon legs that seemed weighed down by lead. When he glanced back, Shaka was staring at him intently.

Some people talk about civilization as though it were something that miraculously sprung into being, and which has to be protected at all costs from infidels and vagabonds. In speaking of the death of civilization, they talk of it as if it were a flame that can be extinguished by a passing breeze. Civilization isn't a flame: it's a weed, which grows without cultivation and even in the face of determined attempts at extermination.
VERSE 345:5 OF *The Teachings*

By now, time had become strange to the girl named Boy. She always seemed to be awakening from sleep—and was rarely able to remember what she did in those fleeting moments of consciousness. Indeed, she had begun to distrust consciousness. Consciousness was like a string that bridged a great chasm: not only was it impossible for the string to bear her weight—the other side of the chasm seemed just the same as this one. She had been sleeping her life away—and was becoming increasingly content to do so. Lately, she had been annoyed when her dreams were disrupted by her strange, robotic captors. She was no longer terrified of them. They became part of the tapestry of her ongoing dream: annoying characters that showed up from time to time to feed her or lead her to the showers. For feedings, huge canisters of a tasteless, viscous soup were usually wheeled into the chamber and distributed by row; for showers, they were all shepherded through some doors on the near side of the room—again by rows—and then made to shower 100 at a time in a huge room with shower nozzles against the wall. It was strange how she never really felt hungry, and how none of them menstruated or had to use the bathroom....

Sometimes, she awoke to find herself in an observation room, where one entire wall was a mirror. She would just sit there, strapped in a chair, while various gasses flooded into the room and various images (none of which she seemed able to recall in retrospect) flashed before her eyes; and then, she would become unconscious again. It was useless to try to keep track of time under such circumstances. Her only grip on reality was the African girl in the cot next to hers. They still could not speak to one another—which was to say that neither could speak the other's language—but over the weeks, months, years, *whatever it had been*, they had developed a kind of pantomime to communicate what they were feeling: their fears, their hopes...all the things that occupied their minds when they were dreaming.

Nothing separates man from the beasts, save for his need to
explain (away) his bestiality.
VERSE 985:3 OF *The Teachings*

E ven before Mendez's report was broadcast, the Goddess had been feeling trapped and restless. She had spent the entire day in her room—and had been up most of the previous night, unable to rest. In an effort to keep her occupied and entertained, Mansmann had brought her an old TV. It had been on this that she saw Mendez's report. She had been lying in bed with the little boy at her side, and her last three followers sitting on cushions on the floor. Even before the report, the three followers had been panicky about her leaving—or being taken from them. They had kept staring at her, like dogs desperate for their master to throw a stick or give some command that would acknowledge their existence and evince their worth.

...Earlier that day she had been thinking that the more she watched television, the more it seemed to hold clues about what was to come—and she had not just meant The Horde, but the inner workings of the men's souls. "News" broadcasts blared every few minutes, with the same panicky information on The Horde. The shows that interspersed these news broadcasts were all either so senselessly violent or gratuitously sexual that they seemed plot-less. People stripped and had sex in the middle of the most mundane conversations; when the screwing was over, they went back to talking as if nothing had happened. In fact, most of the time, they did not even strip: they would be suddenly naked. There was no logic to it—as though someone or something was just throwing scenes together: an explosion here, a sex scene there...and there did not even seem to be anything *sexual* about the sex scenes. The human element seemed gone somehow. The characters' lust only seemed to be a mechanical interpretation of lust...And the violence was not much more realistic. It seemed as if everyone had a sawed-off shotgun hidden in his shorts. Once, she had found herself chuckling when a gunslinger in a western pulled a laser-guided surface-to-air missile out of his holster. They played havoc with history and reality. Cavemen were armed with machine guns and tanks.

...After Mendez's report ended, no one moved. In fact, no one had moved during the report—except for the little boy, who had twitched nervously at the sight of his father. She could not believe what she had just seen—and how completely her recklessness had trapped and destroyed her....And now an entire city was after them. *An entire city!* It seemed like only a matter of time before she was discovered. There were no secrets—*could be* no secrets—in this place. Everything—if it *was* hidden—was hidden in the open. She had to get out of here—but where was she to go? All the men knew her face now. She was almost overcome by an impulse to hide under the bed—to sneak away to some dark place that only a desperate, puerile mind would consider. She looked to the window then, and the outside world, seeing it as a horror that was slowly walling her in. Her mind went back to the scene at the mall (where that wretched man had been stoned to death by that mob). They would take her like that. There would be no trial: no detention, no fact-finding. Death would be quick and violent: *mob* justice....

She got up from the bed abruptly and began pacing nervously. On the TV, they were repeating the report; more computer-enhanced representations of her face were shown. She had a wild impulse to hurl something at the television. Her followers were staring at her with new desperation—

"Get the doctor!" she spat at the three men, partly to get them to leave her and partly because the old doctor suddenly seemed like the only thing that could save her now: the only rational thing in the universe. Her three followers ran off, but their absence had the strange effect of making her feel vulnerable. Death was creeping up on them all: she could hear it shaking the bushes—like a huge predator getting ready to strike. For the first time since her nightmare flight from that place in the forest, she had that self-destructive wish to get it all over with: to call the beast to her so that she could dispense with the indignity of having to wait. Still, as the news report changed to images of Mendez's rampage through the city, she all at once realized that she was no different from the men on those streets. There was a strange, suicidal streak in everyone. It was in the air, like a virus. Everyone was waiting around for death, as though it were some kind of divine fulfillment. Somehow death (which was simply an inevitable byproduct of living), had been lifted to the sublime; and when the inevitable and trite became sublime, then Salvation (the spiritual payoff for living a righteous life) became only a continuance of their meaningless earthbound lives—

"What's happened!" Mansmann demanded, still panting as he ran into the room. She tried to explain, but when Mendez's report came on again, she merely pointed to the TV. Mansmann's jaw dropped. They were all staring at the screen in silence when the door suddenly opened. They were so mesmerized by the images on the screen that it did not immediately occur to them that everyone that should have been in the room was already in there. The Goddess was the first to look up and see the two strange, robed men standing in the doorway. Her last three followers, seeing the men (and more paranoid about the Goddess' safety now), rushed to place themselves between their master and the strange men. Mansmann froze when he recognized the Brotherhood men. In fact, in that strange moment, the only movement in the room was the chaos on the TV screen.

"Who are you people?" one of the robed men asked, looking at the woman oddly.

No one said a word. The three followers looked back at her for a sign; the robed men, seeing that she was the leader, again looked quizzically at her. There was something in their eyes that she could not quite gauge: they were not merely looking at her, they were dissecting her—cataloguing everything that she was—

Mansmann suddenly came to his senses. "Get out of there!" he yelled at the men.

The men looked at Mansmann, confused.

"Never come in here again!" Mansmann went on.

"We don't understand."

"Just don't come in here again!" Mansmann yelled, gesturing violently for them to leave. The men looked at one another with glances that were pregnant with meaning and intent, then they nodded to the doctor and walked off. When the men were gone, Mansmann looked at the Goddess in horror!

Sometimes, only selfishness can save us from sharing the fate of those who refuse to be saved.
VERSE 1984:1 OF *The Teachings*

What Mendez had started, the men took over. More mobs set out, hungry for justice. Collaborators and saboteurs were cornered and shot. All that it took was someone pointing a finger. Sometimes the leaders of the mobs were later pointed out and killed. None were spared: only the dead were beyond suspicion. As Xi had foreseen, the PinkEyes were making the men more unstable by the minute. The moment of no return was approaching. Around them was forming the ultimate stage of existence. The final death throes of the human race were being played out on the streets. Hundreds of men had already been killed for the misfortune of bearing a slight resemblance to the figures in Mendez's special report. After dispensing justice on one man, the mobs moved on, killing more men for a crime that had supposedly already been avenged. They remembered nothing; all they knew was that they had to kill: they had to purge the body of its cancers…And if they died along the way, so much the better. No one could stop it; gripped by the instability of the PinkEyes, few wanted to. Sometimes men would be sitting in groups—eating and laughing, perhaps—and a mob would come along and take one of those men away screaming and yelling. The others would just sit there, still talking amongst themselves: laughing perhaps. This was another of those strange new things: the ability to shut things out instantly—and do it so that the action was no longer affected. It was as if something were saying: you will die eventually, why not now? You will forget eventually, why not now…?

Hitler, Pol Pot and Idi Amin are three of the great martyrs of the 20th century. By embodying evil, they saved individual Germans, Cambodians and Ugandans, respectively, from any otherwise troubling considerations of their evil.

VERSE 2963:2 OF *The Teachings*

After a premonitory chuckle, the Jehovah pulled back on the throttle, and the helicopter shot into the heavens, like a startled bird. Xi stared straight ahead as the stomach-churning ride began. He grabbed onto his seat, but that had no effect on the forces wreaking havoc on his body. As the Jehovah darted through the smog banks, the sun seemed brighter than it had ever been before. When the Jehovah began his breakneck descent, Xi braced himself: both for the ride and for all that he would have to do when the vehicle landed. He went over what he would do in his mind: how he would see the woman and Mansmann, then activate The Hand. His mind could not think beyond those few steps. Besides, thinking long term was pointless as his window of opportunity—if not his entire existence—counted on what would take place in the next few minutes.

Over the PinkEyes, the mobs seemed to be getting more and more agitated by the second. Seeing them, he was again overcome by that old feeling that they were all going to die—and die horribly. Yet, now, as he watched the men, he was possessed by a potent kind of anger that grew within him, until he felt faint and disoriented. He hated the men, and hated them *totally*. This had never occurred to him before: he had feared them at times and been repulsed by what they had become, but never had he felt this kind of hatred. It *seethed* within him, so that he found himself thinking that they all deserved the horrible deaths that were coming. On top of that, his mind suddenly erupted with thoughts of killing Mendez and Shaka: of killing *all* the men in fact. With The Hand, it would be so very easy to do! These thoughts grew in him like a kind of cancer; he, himself, wanted to surrender to this all-encompassing hatred, but his soul's last few defense mechanisms struggled against the abyss....

The helicopter landed—actually, it landed on the same block where Xi had been picked up the previous night. The entire ride had again taken less than a minute. The Jehovah was basking in the proverbial afterglow of the trip. There was a look of wildness in the man's eyes—as seen in the eyes of thrill-seekers after riding a roller coaster. Xi looked away uneasily, focusing on the world outside the helicopter. In the light of day, the outside world seemed horrible. Maybe it was an illusion of rising pockets of hot air and water vapor on the bricks and concrete, but the world seemed to be melting. Xi focused his mind on Mansmann and the woman. Now that he was so close to his prize, he grew more anxious. He thanked the Jehovah for the ride and went to leave, but the man stared at him like a stray that had accosted him on the street and now refused to leave him.

"You want me to wait for you?" the man asked.

"No."

"You sure?" the man said, disappointedly.

"Yes!" Xi said, a little more angrily than he had intended. Then, to get away from the idiocy of it all, he got out of the helicopter and ran down the block. He did not look back: all he could think about was the woman—and the fantasy that once he had activated The Hand, they would all be safe. There was something about that thought that was like heroin. He felt suddenly revived; he ran on faster, forgetting about the Jehovah and Shaka and all the mundane things made irrelevant by the opiate in his veins.

Mansmann's clinic seemed quiet from the outside. Xi had been so consumed by his flight—and mesmerized by the fantasy of peace and safety—that he practically forgot about the imminent danger that the woman was in. Just then, digitized images of the Goddess and her cult were again broadcasted over the PinkEyes. Xi ran on faster, but then noticed the man lolling about the front entrance. With so much reason to be paranoid—especially this close to his prize—Xi was about to stop in his tracks, but then he recognized Kramer. The latter was wearing a fluffy blond wig and a big pair of glasses. The man also held a machine gun at the ready. Xi nodded to the man; before he could even say a word, Kramer took him by the arm and led him to the back of the building.

At the back of the building, behind a bush, there was a hole in the base of the wall. At Kramer's insistence, Xi squeezed through the hole and found himself in a dark, dank basement. There were no windows; only a dark recess in the wall showed where there might be a door. Dozens of thick, dusty pipes crisscrossed the ceiling, making him cringe at the thought of it all collapsing on his head. A lone lamp was burning in the corner, casting everything in a macabre light. Everything was so still that he did not initially realize that there were actually people in the room. Around the dim flame of the lamp were Mansmann, the woman, and the rest of the band. They were sitting on the floor, on old mattresses, their faces seeming horrible in the light. They got up and rushed towards him now. The sudden movement took him aback—

"Did you see the report!" Mansmann whispered.

Xi nodded; he told them that he had been in a meeting with Mendez and Shaka when it came on. He ended his statement with, "They know."

Just then, Kramer clambered to the floor. They all turned to look at him, then turned back to Xi.

Xi looked at the Goddess ominously then: "Mendez and Shaka probably have people watching this place now."

"*God!*" she whispered, "what are we going to do?"

For once, Xi felt reassured. In a matter of seconds, he would activate The Hand and they would all be safe. "Join hands," he told them now.

"What?"

"Join hands—I'll explain later," he said with more urgency. Then, once they had all joined hands in a circle, Xi closed his eyes to focus his mind. First, he established a link with the Image Broadcast Complex. He then accessed The Hand—and smiled as he did so—but to his horror, he found that he could not interface The Hand with the Complex! Shaka had put in a failsafe! To bring The Hand online, he would have to go back to the Image Broadcast Complex—he would have to do it *manually*! He searched the PinkEyes to see where the interface was, and received a jolt to his system when he realized that it was on those subterranean floors! Shaka had laid down the final gauntlet: if he brought The Hand online, he would have to do it as Shaka's slave, under Shaka's terms. He opened his eyes and looked into the confused, expectant faces of those around him. He felt as though he had betrayed them. Worse than that, he felt as though he had lost: that Shaka had mastered him as though he were a fool.

"What's wrong?" the woman demanded.

"...Shaka had an insurance card," he whispered vaguely as he detached himself from the circle of joined hands. He looked drained and devastated now. He needed to sit down, but he was too agitated to rest. He had to *think*...and then an all-encompassing impulse came over him. It told him that defiance was life, and that all else was death. He could give up and wait here for The Horde or Shaka to come and kill him or...He shook his head: going back to Shaka as a beaten man was not an option. As he searched his mind, logic (or perhaps uncompromising madness) pointed out only one other alternative: he would have to fight his way into The Company—kill Shaka's guards and *fight* his way down to the interface. In his current frame of mind, even death at the hands of Shaka's guards and soldiers would be a victory—because Shaka would ultimately not have The Hand. Also, as the strange logical madness grew in him, he realized that Shaka could not afford to kill him, because he was still the only one that could activate The Hand. He rushed ahead quickly, before the madness passed from his system and he had to accept that he was doomed. He looked up at Kramer then:

"You have more guns?"

"...Yes," he said, confused.

"Any bombs? Hand grenades?"

"Sure," he said, looking at the others to see if they were as clue-less as he.

"Where are they?"

"Right here," he said, pointing to a sack in the corner of the room.

Xi rushed over; after rummaging through the sack, he stood up and looked at the others with a new intensity shining in his eyes: "Okay, this is it," he began. "We have to act now. We have to go on the offensive. We have to go back to The Company. There is a device there that is our only chance for life." The others did not know what he was talking about, but something about his decisive tone kept them from speaking. Xi nodded, as though all had been settled. "Okay," he went on, "we have to get down onto those subterranean floors I mentioned before—or *I* do, at least…no use risking anyone else. We'll need some kind of diversion—a bomb or something."

The others nodded grimly.

"This is it," he said again. "There is no going back. Even if I survive, Shaka will surely have cameras or something, alerting him of what I've done. There'll probably be more guards waiting down there." His mind tried telling him that it was a suicide mission at best, but he did not care anymore—*could not* care.

"—And maybe I should be wired with a bomb," he rushed on, "—it might be my only leverage to get out if caught: they won't want to lose the device… or me."

The woman looked at him dubiously for once: "And what happens if there actually are women down there?"

He stared at her for a while; his newfound logic returned one answer: "Women are irrelevant for the time being."

"—And you don't care if you die anymore," Mansmann observed. "What *is* relevant to you now? The world is on the verge of life, Xi—*we found a cure*: men will be able to have daughters."

He thought about it for a while, but did not have the patience to unravel it—or to allow himself to become infatuated with the fantasy of it. "We have to do this *now!*" he said in frustration. "There's not only Mendez and Shaka to worry about: there's The Horde. We have to get down there before The Horde comes. If The Horde comes, it will take the women and kill us all. If we stay here, we die."

It was then that Xi looked to the doctor grimly: "We need a diversion."

"…What do you have in mind?"

"Shaka's men are probably waiting outside for us now," Xi said quickly.

"Blowing up this place might be our only chance of escape."

The Goddess gasped at the maddening escalation, but Xi went on in the same decisive tone: "We have to put them off our trail long enough to do what we have to do."

Mansmann stared at him, seeming horrified for a moment; but as he stared into Xi's fierce eyes, he soon nodded, agreeing with him—perhaps *relenting* to him. The woman nodded as well, bowing her head.

"Now," Xi continued, "we have to find a way to get out of here without getting caught in the explosion."

"…I know a way," Mansmann said. "There was a cave-in in the boiler room, leaving a hole that leads to the sewers. There are some crates in front of it to keep out the smell, but it won't be hard to get out. I guess we could set the explosives, sneak out, and then blow it up.

"Yes," Xi said. "They'll think that we were killed in the blast; at the very least, they won't know where we are."

"Okay," she said, taking a deep breath, "let's do it."

When politicians think that you are rich and powerful,
they are always eager to make you believe that you know them.
VERSE 3112:6 OF *The Teachings*

Mendez had his old computer console with him again. He sat behind it, typing rapidly; in an adjoining suite, all the technology he had requested was being assembled to his specifications. Everything seemed right: he had the power and the knowledge. Suddenly, there was a knock on the door.

"Come!" Mendez yelled, the way men in authority were known to yell. Into the room walked two men dressed in robes. "What is it?" Mendez asked, curtly.

"Our agents say that Xi Wang is up to something, sir. He has just arrived with the other saboteurs at the clinic: should we go in and find out what's happening?"

From behind his console, Mendez thought for a while; then, nodding his head, he said: "Yes, send them in." The time for secrets was over: he wanted to know everything Xi knew. "Take Wang alive," Mendez went on, "—kill everyone else." Having said that, he went back to typing.

Everyone desires happiness, and accepts its consequences blindly;
no one desires sadness, and watches its ramifications warily.
This is why pain is such a useful teaching device.
VERSE 2232:14 OF *The Teachings*

The boiler room had not been operational in years. The massive boiler stood in rusty disrepair in the middle of the room. The scores of pipes, which had taken the hot water throughout the building, created a corroded tangle along the walls and ceiling. Some of them dangled from the ceiling, needing just the slightest touch to be sent crashing to the ground. This was the domain of rats and roaches. Years of accumulated rat dung covered the floor, so that walking alternated between disgusting crunching and squishy noises. Every crevice seemed alive with vermin. The beasts hissed when Xi and the others entered the room. As there were no electric lights, the lamp had to suffice. They stayed close together, like scared children. Mansmann cautiously led the way.

"Where's the opening?" Xi asked as he carried the sack of ordnance.

"Over here," Mansmann said, raising the lamp up, so that its dim light fell on some crates against the wall.

After putting down the sack, Xi went to the wall and started moving the crates aside. The others stood watching him. There was something eerie about the way that noise carried in the chamber. They shivered as the crates grated and banged against the floor; they shivered at Xi's harsh breathing and his specter-like appearance in the darkness. He was sweating profusely. He had tossed his new jacket to the ground. His new shirt was already ripped and stained. In his haste, he seemed like a murderer trying to hide the evidence of the crime. They watched his back with a growing anxiety that they could not really put a finger on. They found themselves thinking that when he turned around, his face would be that of a nightmare creature. Thus, watching him like this, they hardly could have noticed the soft footsteps behind them—

"Nobody move!" a voice boomed in the darkness behind them. They all turned around at the sound of the voice, but a blinding light made them put up their hands to shield their eyes. One of Kramer's mates reached for his gun, but he soon lay on the ground with a bullet hole in his head. Kramer, who had been about to go and help Xi move the boxes, realized that he had rested his gun against the far wall!

The blinding lights of their assailants moved in closer—there were two of them.

"Get away from there!" one of the assailants ordered Xi. As he moved numbly over to where Mansmann and the others were standing, he became increasingly outraged by the realization that this was how he was going to die. He could not believe it would end like this. In that moment of darkness, he found himself thinking about Quibb—about how he had been forsaken. He shook his head in disgust at these idiotic thoughts. He felt inconceivably empty now—*cheated*!

When Xi was with the others, the lights were finally lowered, so that they could see the faces of their attackers. Before them, they saw the two Brotherhood doctors. Mansmann groaned, cursing himself.

"Xi Wang," one said, "stand aside."

"What!" Xi yelled, panicking.

"Stand aside!" the men said in unison.

"What are you going to do!"

"The body must be cleansed!"

Xi faltered; they all looked at him—

"Stand aside! Mendez wants you to be spared!"

But Xi did not want to live—not like this. An insane impulse to rush the men grew in him. It would be his last blaze of glory: *a kamikaze run*! He imagined his body riddled with bullets, squirming in the filth of the floor—

but at least he would die as a man. He steeled himself. His mouth opened to let out the death yell; his muscles tensed up—

But at the moment of no return, there were two more thundering shots. He froze; he was lost—*confused*. Had he run? Was he hit? He looked around confusedly. However, just then, the two flashlights fell to the ground—along with the two Brotherhood men of course. There was someone standing behind the two (now prone) Brotherhood men. Xi and the others stood frozen, squinting as the shadowy figure took shape before them. The man bent down and picked up one of the fallen flashlights.

"You!" Xi yelled. The man smiled back: it was the Jehovah!

"Shaka asked me to watch your back. I came looking for you—but I could not find you anywhere. And then I overheard these two here [and he gestured to the two corpses] whispering about following Mendez's plan. I followed them." At that, he smiled smugly.

The others all stared on in disbelief. The woman, for some strange reason, found herself considering what a perfect scene it was—how convenient it all was, with the savior coming just at the height of cinematic tension. She should have been relieved, but was not.

The Jehovah was still grinning. "Now that that's over with," he continued, as if gunning down the Brotherhood men had been a mere inconvenience, "we can return to The Company, Dr. Wang. We all have our roles to play," he said looking at Xi intently, "—our parts in the hand of evolution." There was now a strange kind of tension in the air. The man had ostensibly saved them, yet they all noticed that he was still pointing his gun at them; Xi glanced at Kramer then. An understanding was passed between them in that glance. Xi moved towards the Jehovah now, slowly.

"What happens now?" he asked.

"Shaka is in need of your services, sir," the man said with another smile; but then, as a single shot echoed in the chamber, that smile was replaced by a look of confusion. Nobody moved; everyone seemed undone by the escalating treachery. They seemed caught in a pocket of time, unable to escape. Only the horrible echo of the shot seemed alive anymore; it stalked them like a beast in the shadows…And then, the Jehovah dropped lifelessly to the ground. The sound of his body hitting the concrete saved them all. They all looked at him with a kind of gratitude. Xi looked at Kramer, who still had the smoking gun in his hand, and nodded. They could all move again—*breathe* again. Xi quickly returned to the one thing he knew to be true: "We have to get out of here!" he said.

They all went to the hole now and continued moving the crates away. The stench of the sewer beyond the hole made the miasma of the boiler room seem like mountain-fresh air. They moved quickly: they could not stop now. The three dead bodies behind them were a reminder of what they were fleeing. They all kept glancing back, partly to remind themselves that it had been real, and to reassure themselves that no one else had come in.

The stench beyond the gaping hole was impossible to describe. Their eyes watered; they felt dizzy and *sick*. Beyond the hole, they heard rats squeaking and scurrying about—at least, they hoped that they were rats.

Xi went back into the room and got the lamp, then he went to the sack of ordnance, took out a gun for himself and shoved some ammunition in his pockets. After that was completed, he walked up to the others with the sack. Mansmann and the woman took guns as well. Kramer took the sack then, extracted one of the bombs, and its remote detonator, then placed the bomb by the huge boiler. Xi held his gun in his right hand now. In his left hand, he had the lamp, which he shone into the hole. A fungi-coated tunnel stretched perpendicular to their position; within it, a thick, swamp-like stew stood. Millions of translucent worms, which had never been in the light, squirmed around aimlessly in the scum, seeming like hairs standing on a massive brownish-green scalp. Xi and the others faltered a little: they would have to crawl through that! God only knew how deep it was. However, the maddening feeling that there was no retreat soon seized him. Steeling himself once again, he stepped out into it. His foot went down, down… seeping into the enveloping filth! The sucking sensation against his foot was maddening enough as it was. His foot was still going down into the sewer sludge. Now the scum was past his calf…almost to his knees! He was about to panic and cry out, when his foot finally touched bottom. The filth came up to just above his knees. He looked back and nodded to the others. The little boy would probably have to be carried, but the others would probably be fine. Maybe in a few hundred meters there would be an exit leading to a manhole.

Xi set off as quickly as he could, with Mansmann second and the woman and what remained of her cult following. Their lungs burned. Xi kept the focal point of the lamp off in the distance: he did not want to see what he was walking through. The thought of those millions of worms made his innards quiver. And in the back of his mind was the horror of wandering out into a region of deep quicksand. *God*, to die in this filth: to *drown* in it, feeling that thick soup seeping into one's lungs…! The slurping sound of their movement only made him more anxious. He searched the tunnel ahead, but there seemed to be neither exits nor turns. It simply stretched out into infinity, retreating into darkness. The darkness was getting to him as well. He thought about getting lost down here…!

Time went on; playing in all of their minds, were their secret horrors. They stopped every few minutes to rest their legs. Walking in the soupy filth was like walking on a planet with gravity several times that of Earth. They were panting—both from exhaustion and the fact that there was little oxygen down here. Moreover, who knew when the toxic fumes would make them collapse for good? That thought steadily drove them towards the increasingly close brink of insanity. Xi, ready to crack, was exhorting them to move faster now. He could not stand it. He almost tripped and fell—his arm went into the soup. He shuddered at the horrific repugnance of it. He got up again, moving quicker yet. There was a corroded metal ladder ahead! He shone the light on it, his hand trembling. It led to a manhole! He was moving even quicker now! The others, seeing what he saw, rushed insanely behind him.

They had perhaps come 300 meters—it seemed a safe distance to explode the bomb. Even if it was not, none of them cared by now. Xi waited for the others to come up to him. They looked at him quizzically, wondering why he had stopped.

"The bomb," he said, panting for air, "—let's set it." He looked at Kramer: "give me the detonator."

Mansmann spoke up then. He nodded to the manhole: "What if it doesn't open?"

Xi gestured to Kramer, who handed him the detonator and scaled the slime-covered ladder. Pushing against the manhole, it seemed locked in place. Kramer put his shoulder to it, grunting as he applied all of his strength to it. At last, it gave. Kramer, overcome by the madness, went to rush out—

"No!" the Goddess called to him. "Not yet—someone might see you."

She looked at Xi then: "You sure we're far enough away?"

"No," he said, simply.

Xi went to activate the detonator, but Mansmann placed his hand on Xi's arm: "No, *I* have to do this," he said.

"*You?*"

"Yes." They all stared at him; Xi nodded at last and handed over the detonator. The old man's finger lingered a moment before pressing the button; but when it did, they were all rocked by the tremors of the blast. From way down the tunnel, the flames shot out of the hole in the basement. It seemed like a liquid, flowing towards them. They all realized, at the same time, that there were probably leaking and broken gas pipes down here. The blinding flames were still pouring out towards them! They could already feel the heat from the flames. Frozen, they all seemed to be resigned to death. But luckily for them, Kramer pushed gruffly against the manhole cover, calling for the Goddess to come out. His action brought them back to their senses. They were rushing up the ladder now. Mansmann was last, his mind on the "patients" he had just blown to bits. *I've killed them all*! he thought, first trembling in the wake of the act, and then reveling in the same feeling of freedom he had felt when fleeing from the hospital the night The Horde bombed. They were all dead, and now there could be no pretense of caring anymore. He stood down there, unable to move or think of anything else. There was a strange peacefulness about him as he watched the flames. Luckily for him, the flames began to dissipate about 35 meters away. When he came to his senses, he went up the ladder and joined the others.

*Once revolutionaries get a taste of power, righting injustice isn't
as important as getting revenge and maintaining power.*
VERSE 19:3 OF *The Teachings*

The report came from a guard post near 57th Street: Horde troops had been spotted! The troops, clad in their impenetrable battle suits, had appeared out of nowhere, as if leaping from another dimension. The ten or so soldiers at the post had first tried to fight; but after six of their number had fallen, the remaining men had run for their lives. None had made it out alive.

Logic demands this: if there is a God—an all-powerful being—
then the existence of a Devil becomes superfluous, if not
contradictory…unless that Devil is in fact God.
VERSE 6123:2 OF *The Teachings*

Xi and the others ran at first—ran for their lives it seemed. Over their shoulders had been the plumes of smoke coming from where the clinic had been. A few blocks away, panting and dazed, they stopped. Xi threw up, overcome by it all. Mansmann spotted a hydrant down the block and they all rushed towards it. Finding it closed, Kramer hit its rusting cap with a nearby pipe until it burst open. There was no circumspection left in them. They almost fought amongst themselves in their efforts to wash away the filth.

Luckily for them, passersby hardly noticed—or seemed incapable of noticing. To begin with, perhaps 60% of the PinkEyes had been drawn towards The Company by now. Some of them went as mindless slaves—others merely coaxed by the PinkEyes' unremitting suggestion to go down to Company Square to defend The Company. As for the other 40%, they were too unstable to know what was going on. This being so, as Xi and the others looked around, the streets were relatively bare. The few men that could be seen had never worn PinkEyes. There were still the video billboards however. There was one across the street from where Xi and the others were washing themselves off; and seeing that The Horde had arrived, they knew that there was no time to waste. Moreover, as images of The Horde's handiwork on 57th Street blared over the screens, the men who watched those images inevitably became seized by panic, so that the handful of men on the street ran about like chickens with their heads cut off.

Knowing that they had to get down to the dark pyramid as soon as possible, Xi and the others began running, still dripping wet. After a block or so, Xi realized that this was the way he had come after getting out of the helicopter. Looking ahead, he saw that the helicopter was on the next block! The Jehovah must have left it there when he came spying on Xi. Using his PinkEyes, Xi downloaded the schematics for the helicopter as he ran up to it, so that moments after he and the others had piled into the vehicle, they were airborne. He flew at the same breakneck pace as the Jehovah. There was no time to waste—they were in fact out of time: down to the final minutes, if that. The woman was in the passenger seat, with the little boy on her lap. Her face was contorted with horror and discomfort as the helicopter darted into the heavens then swooped down towards The Company. The little boy just stared ahead, as though in shock from all that had happened. Mansmann and the woman's remaining two minions groaned in the back, as Xi handled the controls brusquely. As for Xi, being at the controls somehow negated the nauseating effect of the ride—or maybe it was only his numbness.

When The Company's immense skyscraper came into view, Xi sensed more than saw how bad things had become—how unstable all those millions of PinkEyes had gotten. As Xi began his descent, he saw that the streets surrounding Company Square were all packed with men—with men wearing *PinkEyes*. From the air, they stuck him as ants rushing out to defend their hill, swarming over some hapless creature that had bungled into their midst. He was going to have to land in Company Square—it was the only place—but the Square was *packed*. Men were jostling with one another—some were firing guns and screaming out either in pain or madness. Xi steered the helicopter to land right outside the lobby of the main skyscraper. He crashed on top of about a dozen men—others were running wildly in all directions. It was again horrible to be in their midst. The Pink Eyes were telling them that there was danger and that they should fight, but the PinkEyes were now so unstable that the men could not follow directions anymore—just respond with panic. Some of them were gunning down their fellow PinkEyes; a few shots hit the side of the helicopter—

"Give me some bombs!" Xi demanded from Kramer, who still had the sack of ordnance. He shoved two of the orange-sized bombs into his pants pockets. "You have to take off again!" he told the others. They looked at him as though not understanding.

"You can't stay here—someone will shoot you!"

"What about you?" the woman asked.

"If I don't activate the device, I'm dead anyway." Then, to curtail further argument: "Just pull back on the throttle to get airborne—go and hover somewhere!" Before they could respond, he rushed out of the helicopter with his gun at the ready. He bumped into about five panicking men as he ran up to the lobby, then hit another in the face with the butt of his gun when the latter drew too close. He was not exactly fearless, but he discovered that he was at peace with death as long as it was on his own terms and he met it head-on.

With enough planning and indoctrination, people can be organized
to do anything: kill themselves, kill one another…anything…
and nobody will complain or feel qualms of doubt, as long
as he is well compensated for following orders.
VERSE 632:3 OF *The Teachings*

"Stein!" Shaka screamed. The rage gleamed in his eyes as he stared at the screens before him and saw his entire universe unraveling. His operatives had just called him about Xi. "*Stein!*" he bellowed again; half a second later, Stein burst into the chamber. The man's face was blanched from terror. Shaka stood gnashing his teeth as the man ran up. He had a sudden impulse to break something over the man's head. "Where the hell were you!"

"Sorry, sir," Stein peeped, stopping three meters away from Shaka for safety's sake. Then, glancing at the screens, he grimaced when he saw the men running around chaotically. He wanted to ask what was going on, but he was terrified. Shaka's face was sweaty and menacing; his eyes bulged—

"Xi is on his way back here!" Shaka went on. "We have to recapture him at *all* costs! You understand?"—Stein nodded—"He will come in through the lobby and try to enter the door to the underground chambers."

"I understand, sir—"

"*Then what are you still doing standing here!*" Shaka screamed.

Stein ran off.

A work of art is always a messy undertaking. There is an element of chaos being tamed and subdued—because art is, at its basis, an act of violence against the randomness of life, if not the naturalness of life. All art is, essentially, manmade. It was the first thing that man made when he began to become self-aware, and it will be the only thing left when he dies off the face of the earth.
VERSE 923:34 OF *The Teachings*

As Xi ran up to the front entrance, he saw that men were running about inside the lobby as well—*hundreds* of them. The guards stationed in front of the secret door were dead; others were being choked. One crazed man was biting the ankle of a corpse, gnawing at it like a dog contentedly enjoying a bone—

Xi looked up and noticed that Stein was running through the lobby with a drawn gun. They both froze when they saw one another. Xi brought the nozzle of his gun up, to defend himself; but then, inexplicably, something exploded outside, in Company Square, and he—*and everyone else in the lobby*—found himself being tossed in the air. A hot wave crested over them all; those closest to the glass wall of the lobby were shredded by the jagged shards of glass. The glass was like shrapnel in the air now. Xi lay cringing on the ground as the fire wave crested over his head. He felt it singeing his hair and clothes. As he lay dazed, there were cries of agony and terror the likes of which he had never heard before. Men fully engulfed in flames were running about him now. There was something mesmerizing about their crazed movements. Dead and burning bodies were dropping on top of him now. The sickening, charred smell of burning flesh was everywhere. At least five men had piled on top of him. A dying man twitched spasmodically beside him; as the man's eyelids had been melted off, his eyes seemed nightmarishly huge in their sockets. Xi cried out as the man's twitching hand grabbed him by the throat. He screamed like an animal. In his madness, all he could think was that he had to destroy the eyes: the eyes were the source of the man's power. He clawed at them savagely: the goo soon oozed down his fingertips...Yet, as the man had already breathed his last breath, his death grip on Xi's neck had only been an involuntary reaction. Pushed over his limit of his endurance, Xi burst up, heaving the dead and burning bodies from him. In the smoky air, pockets of flame danced over charred bodies in various stages of animation. His first impulse was to flee: to run towards the light of the sun and be done with this nightmare world, but then something very horrible occurred to him, and he froze—felt as though his last stores of life had been drained from him.

The only thing big enough to cause such an explosion was the helicopter! The bombs and all the other ordnance must have exploded! The woman and Mansmann and the others must all be dead now! He stared through the smoke in horror! All at once, there did not seem to be any point in going on. It had not occurred to him before, but without the woman and Mansmann, he had no reason to go on living. His plan to activate The Hand seemed pointless!

What now...? He had no idea. He almost *wanted* to die now, and this disturbed him on some level, because it was a resignation of power. Dying in the process of trying to live was one thing: rushing towards death blindly, and without hope, was pointless suicide. He felt weak. He coughed on the thick smoke; his body slumped and he fell down to his knees. Shards of glass tore into his knees and the soft tissue of his lower leg, but he did not notice. Almost by chance, his eyes went to the guard post in front of the secret door. He stared at the door for a while, blinking through the tears as his eyes watered from the smoke and the horrible realization that he had nothing to live for....He really did not have anything to lose now; and as thoughts of suicide palliated his soul, he found himself being enchanted by the idea of doing one last magnanimous thing before he died. It was too late for him, but he could be a kind of martyr of fate. He had to not only destroy The Hand, but destroy the interface *and* the Image Broadcast

Complex. He had to destroy it all so that in some distant future, when men could have daughters again (and the women were returned to the world), no scheming gods would be able to steal their souls.

Mesmerized by these thoughts, he got up from the ground then. An alarm was pealing in the air now—maybe it had been pealing for a while. Water from the sprinkler system was raining down as well. He moved towards the secret door, clambering over the dead, dying and unconscious. He saw Stein lying on the ground: there was a jagged shard of glass in the man's neck; on his face there remained the expression of someone screaming out in terror, but his voice had been hushed forever. As more of Xi's senses returned, he heard far-off voices, but they seemed only like his own hectic thoughts….The door to the subterranean floors was locked and he suddenly realized that he had not gotten the keys from the woman. He fired at the lock with his gun, but the door still would not open! He was about to give up when, looking down, he realized that there were two dead bodies jamming the door shut. Still numb, he pushed the bodies out of the way, like trash. When he pulled on the door again it opened. For a second or so, he stood there, staring down the dim stairwell. Part of him had expected to find the staircase gone: find that it had only been a delusion…but it was there.

The voices behind him—in the smoke and mist of the lobby—seemed to be getting closer. Once again coming to himself, Xi darted in and pulled the door shut behind him. It was done. He took a deep breath, made sure the gun was still in his hands, and the bombs in his pockets, then started running down the staircase.

He ran down wildly, almost toppling twice. In the place he remembered, there was the grating that blocked access to the floors below. However, instead of a lock, there was now a computerized keypad. He panicked at this, then shot at it: the universal locksmith. Another alarm went off; the orange lights in the staircase begin to flash. He pushed open the grating and ran down. There were no doors—that is, no doors leading onto floors—just this staircase leading down….He looked over the banister and down the crisscrossing network of staircases, seeing a light somewhere in the immense depths; he looked up, panicking as he saw nothing but darkness: there seemed to be no going back. The weird alarm, alternating between two off-tune screechy noises, was eroding whatever sanity he had left; the flashing lights were making him dizzy. He made sure his grip on the gun was still firm: he was now so numb that he could not be sure anymore. He had gone down at least 15 stories already, yet the light in the immense depths did not seem any closer. He wondered, while he hied down the staircase, if he was still actually running. Maybe his madness had become complete and this was all just a delusion. It was one of those bizarre thoughts that threatened to make him topple headlong into the darkness. Thoughts of running back up flashed in his mind: he had to get out of this endless hole somehow or another. However, he had run down at least 30 stories by now and it seemed too late to go back. In his mind, this was not a staircase: it was a bridge between worlds. He was trapped on a one-way road between realities. His only hope was that other reality down in the depths....

Finally, after another ten minutes of descending, he finally reached a floor with a door. It was imperative that he keep descending the stairs, but curiosity got the better of him. He opened the door cautiously, then stood there, surprised by the size of the room beyond it. It was a chamber reminiscent of a warehouse. It was huge and dark...and *cold*. He realized that he could see his breath. At first, it struck him as a kind of library, with uniform aisles of stacked items...but the aisles did not have books at all. The aisles were actually composed of monolithic, boxy devices that were about five meters wide and reached all the way to the ceiling. The aisle straight in front of him had to stretch at least 500 meters! Peering to his left and right, the wall stretched at least 250 meters in each direction. So many aisles! He took a tentative step in, but held the door open. There was the hum of power; he realized that every so often, a light would blink on each of the aisles. There seemed to be some kind of console on the front of each aisle. He had to know what it was. He checked the doorknob to make sure it was not locked, and then he went in tentatively. He felt dwarfed. He expected any moment for something to leap out of the darkness. His steps echoed horri-bly—the intensity of the siren was diminished in here. There was an inscrutable numerical notation on the console—nothing else. He walked to the next aisle, realizing that the number on the console was consecutive with the previous aisle. He was shivering from the cold now. Maybe this was some cryogenic system—and there were women inside! He felt the metallic device: it was certainly cold enough. And with this floor, and all the others, there was certainly enough space to hold *millions* of women. He looked to see if there was a way to open up the huge devices, but there did not appear to be any doors. Each device—each *aisle*—seemed to stretch the entire 500 meters without one opening. It got him so frustrated that he almost shot at it. He regained his senses. Could there really be women frozen in these things? His imagination faltered; and ultimately—like he had told the Goddess—women were irrelevant just now. He retreated back to the door; after opening it, he stepped back out into the flashing chaos of the stairway. According to the schematic he had accessed over his Pink Eyes, the interface for The Hand was down another 30 stories or so—*down in the light.* He was running down the staircases again, passing more doors. He kept reminding himself that the women were irrelevant for now. Images of The Horde—or at least panicky stories about them—were still being broadcasted over the PinkEyes. He had to rush: he had to do this before they took over The Company....

He had come at least 50 stories by now: he was definitely getting closer to the light. He instinctively started tiptoeing as he descended the last couple of floors. He was hearing voices now—and a rhythmic clanking sound! The staircase ended. There was a kind of mezzanine, and then, about 50 meters below him, on a floor, was a chaotic scene, with hundreds of men running about the dark, monolithic machinery that was their master. Of course, with the PinkEyes in disarray, none of them was doing his job anymore—just running around, panicking and fighting. Xi realized that this was another power chamber. All of the power that The Company generated had never been entirely for the billboards and the Image Broadcast Complex, but also for whatever was on the floors with the cryogenic equipment. It was the perfect cover. With the disorienting elevators, which never showed the floors, the workers had no idea where they were. These men were working their lives away, and yet they never suspected what was right over their heads—and below their feet.

These were Xi's thoughts when he heard a step behind him. He reeled and brought up his gun. The person had been about to hit him in the head with a pipe. They stared at one another in disbelief. *It was Quibb*! Xi stared in amazement. There was a cut on Quibb's lip, as if he had been in a fight. The man's anorexic body seemed somehow plumper—*softer*. Also, his stare was not as confident as it had been. His face seemed forlorn now, and he seemed harried and fatigued all at once—as if he had not slept in weeks. As Xi stared at the man's face, he realized that Quibb seemed to have aged—as though *years* had passed since their last meeting! On their first meeting, Quibb had seemed like a teenager. Now, he seemed endowed with a mature kind of beauty that Xi immediately found disturbing. He looked at the man uneasily.

Quibb only smiled. He put out a hand and helped Xi up. "I knew you'd come," he said, pleased. His voice was different, too. It was not as deep and reverberating as before. There was something soothing about it. Xi shook his head at the idiocy of his thoughts. Still, there was a strange softness about Quibb's face and his movements that left Xi undone. With Mansmann and the woman gone, all he had was Quibb now. The debilitating loneliness he had felt before returned again—with all its accompanying desperation. Quibb had been his god once; and on some sick level, the man still was—

"The moment of truth is here," Quibb mused, looking out on the men below.

"...What are you going to do, Quibb?" Xi said, suddenly remembering that Quibb was supposed to be a Horde spy. Yet, he did not know if that fact was relevant anymore. In a world of emptiness, a side of him did not care which side Quibb was on: he just did not want to be alone just now—

Quibb smiled, then tapped Xi's pants pockets, where the bombs protruded: "We still think alike," he said, smiling. "I was just about to plant enough explosives to cave this entire building in, when I heard you." He looked at Xi's bulging pockets again: "Give them to me—I guess I can use them, too."

"Did The Horde send you, Quibb?" he asked in bewilderment.

"The Horde?" the man said with a laugh. "Why would you think something so stupid?"

Xi opened his mouth to explain—

"There's no time," he said, the residue of his old calmness still there. "Give me the bombs—and then get out of here while you still can."

In defeat, Xi took out the bombs, but then he faltered: "What about the women…?"

"What women?" Quibb said, laughing again, as if the thing were ridiculous. "There are no women down here: just a few million liquid-nitrogen-cooled canisters of their DNA and eggs."

"Then why all this?" he said, gesturing to the machinery.

"If you have DNA, you don't need people," Quibb said with a sorrowful smirk. "Their bodies only take up unnecessary space." At last, he shook his head as to signify that it was all immaterial. "…It'll make sense in time," he said; then, more urgently: "You have to get out of there now."

Xi seemed suddenly pathetic, sounding like a child begging his mother for something. "Let me stay with you, Quibb," he pleaded. "I have nothing else….I'm *tired*, Quibb," he went on, referring not only to his current state of mind and being, but his entire life (and the *prospect* of life). "Let me stay: let's end it…*together*." While he stood there, pleading to die with his one-time god, Quibb suddenly laughed at him, but not in a condescending way, but in a way that showed that he was pleased:

"I'm glad that you got your memories back, Xi," Quibb began with a bitter-sweet smile. "You got a chance to choose what kind of person you would be, and you took advantage. I knew you were a good person inside—I always sensed it." Then, with a sigh, he continued, "But you have to get out of here now. Time's short: I'll give you 15 minutes to get away from The Company."

"*What*?" he said when he deciphered what Quibb was saying, "—I'll never make it all the way up in that time!"

"You will," Quibb said, smiling at him again. "If you go up three floors, there'll be an elevator."

Xi searched his mind, but he did not remember having passed an elevator.

"Trust me, Xi," Quibb said reassuringly. "I'll wait until you're out of the building before I set off the bombs....We're still connected, Xi—I'll know when you're safe."

"Quibb..." he did not know what to say—where to begin. He opened his mouth feebly to explain to Quibb that he had nowhere to go—and no real reason for continuing to live—but it was then that Quibb kissed him lightly on the lips. The entire thing lasted a few milliseconds at most, but at Quibb's touch he felt somehow as though he had been severed from time. He shivered, stepping away. "Quibb!" he whispered—just as he had whispered from the very beginning—

"Leave now," Quibb said, sternly. Xi opened his mouth to...he did not even know what. He stood there confusedly, but: "*Leave!*" Quibb said again. Xi stared, then looked away in defeat and shame. He took a few pathetic steps up the stairs, but then he stopped and looked back at Quibb. He expected to see the same stern face, but it was soft again. Somehow, that was even worse. He ran off then, hoping that the flashing chaos of the stairway's emergency lights would drag him into their madness and subdue him.

*Throughout the ages, men have shown themselves willing to die
and kill for their beliefs, but how many of those same men have
even conceptualized what it means to be alive?*
VERSE 1382:4 OF *The Teachings*

The last image that Shaka got from the surveillance camera in the lobby was Xi and Stein facing off. Everything had gone blank after the explosion. Shaka had felt the explosion up in the penthouse; and then, a few minutes later, a surveillance camera from the secret floors had shown Xi descending the staircase—

"Stein!" Shaka called, before he remembered that the man was gone now. He stood there uneasily for a moment, then rushed to his desk and got a machine gun. There was something strange in him: a sense of anxiety that he would not allow himself to acknowledge. There were no more minions to do his bidding; most of his guards were either dead or occupied with trying to fight off madmen. As such, for the first time in a long while, it was solely up to him to handle matters: to step out into that world of filth in order to bring his will to fruition. As he ran towards the chamber door, he felt unreal—as though he were running in a dream. In the ride down the elevator, he clutched his gun so tightly that his sweaty hands began to ache....

As soon as the elevator door opened, he rushed out. Burnt, gruesome forms were still lying on the ground. Actually, now, besides the hundreds of men killed and wounded in the explosion, some of the crazed soldiers from Company Square were rushing into the lobby and fighting with one another. The burnt men on the ground were being trampled and kicked (and even *shot* at) by the soldiers. Shaka looked at all this not in shock or awe, but with a rising sense of hatred. It was probably the case that the more powerful one became (and the more one relied on his power over men) the more one *hated* his fellow men. At base, the powerful were probably all misanthropes. Accordingly, now that Shaka was in their midst (and was forced to accept that he had lost all power over them) the hatred, freed of all barriers and restraints, seized him completely—

A crazed soldier was rushing up to him with a huge knife in hand: Shaka pulled the trigger of his gun and peppered the man's chest with bullet holes. When he looked up, other solders were rushing towards him. One fired his gun; Shaka ducked, pulling the trigger of his gun as he did so. He caught the man in the chest, but the man was so insane that he kept coming. Shaka kept firing; he shot at the man's head until it exploded. Even then, the man did not fall until about two meters from him, where he lay twitching on the ground. Shaka scrambled to his feet and ran against the wall. The secret door was on the other end of the lobby. However, the lobby was *packed* with crazed soldiers by now, and it was only a matter of time before some of them saw him as a likely target. Shaka fired his gun at the first one to run up, then he fired it at the next one, and then the next...He was about 15 meters from the door when he ran out of bullets. A pack of three men had fastened their attention on him. He had just shot down the first one when the bullets ran out. Acting on wild instinct, he knocked the second one in the jaw with the butt of his gun, and then the third. He was wild with the hatred by now. He threw down his gun and picked up another—guns were lying about like leaves in the forest. It felt good to hold the weapon in his hands; he pulled his trigger again, seeing more bodies dropping. It did not matter if the men were aiming at him or not. He shot many of them in the back as they turned to fight others. It did not make a difference—

But then, miraculously, Circe was there! Shaka's face had worn a malicious grin while shooting the soldiers, but that died away when he saw her. Circe was standing about 10 meters from him, in a simple flowing dress. Shaka suddenly remembered that he had been on his way to head off Xi; but as he watched Circe, and the handiwork of his shooting spree, he realized that that did not matter anymore. In fact, nothing mattered now, and Circe's being there was only a reminder of how empty and pointless his life had become. The hatred, which had been curtailed for a moment, seized him again. While he was standing there, one of the crazed men's bullets hit him in the thigh; but annealed by his newfound hatred, his only thought was of obliterating Circe. Before he was even conscious of pulling the trigger, Shaka fired his gun into her. As Circe stumbled backwards with the impact of the bullets, Shaka had a feeling of vindication—even as he felt hot lead entering his chest cavity and ripping apart vital organs. He fell to the ground, writhing in pain, but reveling in the knowledge that his love had somehow been avenged. It was only when he looked up and saw that Circe was still standing, that his feeling of triumph dissipated. At first, he thought that he had missed; when he looked, he saw that she was indeed wounded and that the bullets had found their mark…but there was no blood; and on Circe's face, there was none of the pain that he felt. She stared at him calmly— almost *sorrowfully*—in that strange moment. Still unable to understand it, he looked closer, seeing that instead of bloody guts, the gaping hole in her abdomen had revealed circuit boards—which sparked, as though short-circuiting. He stared at it in amazement…and then with a sense of horror when he realized what Circe was—and that the only person he had been able to give his love to, was a machine. As he looked on with a kind of crazed horror, Circe's wounds miraculously healed themselves. Circuits reforged connections; skin grew over wounds and sealed itself without leaving the slightest blemish. Shaka watched these things with bulging, quivering eyes. Circe stepped up and stood above him now, still looking at him sorrowfully.

"What strange creatures you men are," she—or rather *it*—lamented as Shaka breathed his last breaths, "—your love is so easily corrupted by your insecurities…."

More often than not, the moment of truth is filled with the greatest lies.
VERSE 3934:5 OF *The Teachings*

The Horde seemed to be very meticulously and carefully probing for something. They blew up army installations; they provoked soldiers cringing behind battlements, as if to test their strength. And then, when they were satisfied, they left—always as quickly and nonsensically as they had come. They took nothing. They seemed to want nothing. When Mendez's men told him this, he cursed them and called them fools. "Everyone wants something!" he screamed.

In the meantime, he stared at the screens and secretly trembled at the realization that they were nothing against The Horde. Seeing that Shaka's "army" had been reduced to madness, he realized that he was alone, and that his men had nothing to fight The Horde with but their own madness.

In a world where no one is innocent, justice and injustice are meaningless.
VERSE 1521:6 OF *The Teachings*

Xi locked himself away and ran up the three flights of stairs. Actually, he was so dazed that he ran up four flights before he remembered what Quibb had said. He descended one staircase and looked around anxiously. At first, he saw no elevator, but when he looked into a dark recess of the wall, he saw it. Xi could hardly believe it—and the thing had controls. As soon as he pressed the "up" button the doors opened. He entered it numbly. There was a keypad; he pressed the lobby button. The elevator took off so quickly that he groaned. Yet, his mind kept returning to Quibb. What had it all meant....It was when the elevator opened onto the ground floor lobby that Xi realized that this elevator was the "executive" elevator that the Jehovah had put him on a few hours before.

Men were still fighting one another in the lobby. He stared at them almost absentmindedly for a moment. The thought that he was doomed to be alone—and that Quibb would blow himself up any moment now—drained more of his strength and will to live. Accordingly, as he moved beyond the doorway and into the lobby, it was with a certain amount of carelessness. He expected to be shot at any moment, or attacked by some crazed soldiers....He made it out to Company Square and watched the old scenes of chaos. Hundreds of thousands of men were fighting one another—those that died were merely replaced from the throng of millions outside the Square. Xi shook his head: to hell with it—there was no point in going on. Even if he could find some way to get though those men without being killed, he had *nothing*. He was not going to play this game anymore. He was not going to pretend that he had a reason to live—or something to escape to. His only thought now was that he would die when Quibb died, and that his pointless existence would end at last.

It was then that he looked up and saw a helicopter descending from the heavens. Actually, it was *the* helicopter. As the craft drew closer, he looked through its windows and saw Mansmann and the woman—*all* of them were there and alive! How was it possible? He looked over his shoulder then—to the gaping hole that had been left in the lobby by the explosion. It must have only been a grenade or something! He could not believe it!

The sound of some of the crazed men firing their guns into the helicopter brought him back to his senses. When the helicopter was close enough, he leaped up and grabbed its runners, then clambered into the back, where Kramer, the other cult member and the little boy were. Unfortunately, the crazed men of Company Square were now trying to follow Xi's example; but as they reached up, Kramer fired at them. Xi was lying sideways, jammed between the men's laps and the front seats. He could feel the helicopter being riddled with gunfire—

"Take off!" he screamed.

The woman pulled back on the throttle and the vehicle shot up into the heavens. A few of the crazed men, who had been holding to the doors and windows, fell off in midair. Xi and the others seemed saved. Unfortunately, from the way the helicopter rocked, and the whining sound that its engines made, it was obvious that it was not going to stay airborne for long: it had been riddled with too many bullets. In the front, Mansmann and the woman were screaming as the vehicle alternated between breakneck dives and stomach churning leaps into the air; in the back, the little boy was digging his fingernails into Xi's shoulder. Xi was glad that he could not see what was going on. When the vehicle crashed and flipped over, Xi lay in a heap, wondering if he was dead or not. They all seemed to be in this state, because for the first minute or so, nobody said a word. The first sounds were groans; the first movements were by outstretched hands searching to make sense of the world.

Mansmann was the first one to clamber outside his window. He helped out the woman next; then, by banging on the back window, he got Xi and the others to come out as well. When they got their bearings, they saw that they were on top of an office building—or at least, what used to be an office building—about two kilometers from The Company. Crashing on top of the 50-story building had probably saved their lives, as the helicopter would not have made it to the ground. The helicopter was smoking and Mansmann coaxed them away from it, as a precaution against it blowing up.

It was then that the thing happened. There was a powerful explosion; when they turned towards it, and looked over the rooftops, they saw the 150-story skyscraper collapsing. They felt the earth buckling beneath them, as if they were in the midst of an earthquake. The once-majestic sky-scraper—that palace of crystal and light—was collapsing in on itself; and, along with it, were the Image Broadcast Complex and all of Company Square. Xi suddenly realized that the PinkEyes were not online anymore... but millions of men were dead now. The falling rubble had no doubt crushed all those desperate men, who had been compelled to come to Company Square. A cloud of dust and debris was now spreading through the air. It was upon them within seconds, and they all coughed and tried to shield their eyes and mouths.

It was Kramer who noticed the approaching figures first. His peripheral vision picked up something flashing in the cloud of debris. He turned to see some helmeted figures walking up calmly. The woman saw them next, screaming out, but she and the others were already surrounded. When they squinted through the debris, they saw that a kind of jump jet had appeared in the sky—out of nowhere, it seemed. There was no noise, no blowing or displacement of air from jet engines—nothing. It simply appeared....The last thing that any of them remembered was a blinding flash of light.

BOOK 4
DEATH BEFORE LIFE

XIII

To truly hate something, one must once have loved it and placed
absolute faith in it. There is no such thing as passive hate. Racism,
for instance, which is passed on through culture, is not hate and should
not be regarded as such. The bigotry spawned entirely by social attitudes
is impersonal—aimed at symbols of things that make us uncomfortable,
like foreigners, or individuals of another race. On the other hand,
the object of true hatred always has a definite face.
VERSE 4491:31 OF *The Teachings*

Mendez watched the buildings of The Company collapsing from his
window at the hotel. In particular, he watched the 150-story skyscraper. It was one of those awesome sights that chilled a man's
insides. He stood at the window in mute horror, staring out on the thing
that his mind kept telling him could not possibly be real. If The Horde
could bring down The Company, then what chance did he—or *any* of them—
have. It was perhaps only then that The Horde became real for him. Before,
it had merely been a theoretical construct—a far-away possibility that was
only a concern to people stupider than he. His hubris had insulated him,
but seeing the 150-story skyscraper collapsing into rubble, stripped him of
that arrogant stupidity and set off new reactions within him. Moreover,
when that skyscraper toppled onto the Image Broadcast Complex, many of
the men of the city—including Mendez—felt something strange go through
them. The dark pyramid, which had been broadcasting the contradictory
message of peace and jingoism to the men, seemed to send a wave of pure
madness through the city—and the *world*. It was like a tidal wave caused by
an undersea earthquake thousands of kilometers away. It appeared out of
nowhere, battering the coastline and dragging countless thousands back
into the depths of the sea. The few that managed to swim back to shore—
to make contact with reality again—were left cowed and devastated. Mendez
was one of these; and as soon as he realized what had happened, he bolted

from his suite and out into the hallway. He had to get out of the building before The Horde came. Three guards were waiting for him in the hallway—or at least they were in the hallway when he got there. They seemed dazed and unresponsive; he screamed for them to protect him, until his shrill cries brought them back to reality. They and Mendez ran on together—towards the staircase at the other end of the corridor. However, it was when they turned the corner that they saw the rampaging men. About a dozen men, all of whom were in the throes of the dark pyramid's parting madness, were running down the hallway. Some waved knives; one fired his gun into the wall—and then into the skull of the man next to him. Mendez's guards, still following his commandment, rushed ahead to protect him, while Mendez stopped and watched the outcome from the relative safety of a doorway. The first of his guards was butchered horribly. A man with a machete cleaved his head in one mighty blow. Even after the guard lay lifeless on the ground, the insane man continued to hack at his body, so that blood sprayed everywhere, painting the walls red in a masterpiece of abstract art. Simultaneously, about five of the rampaging men leaped at another of Mendez's guards. The man managed to shoot one of them, but the others were soon clawing and biting at his limbs. Mendez had an urge to look away as a crazed man bit off a chunk of the guard's shoulder, gulped the flesh down, and promptly went back for more. Nevertheless, Mendez was mesmerized by what he saw—and by what he *felt*. There was a strange kind of artistry about all that he saw before him. There was something magical about the movement of their bodies. It was a kind of dance, in which the rhythm of death was infectious. It suddenly reminded him of when he was a boy, watching the neighborhood kids playing football. He had not been athletic himself, but he had liked watching the other boys playing and fighting. Their brutal sports had excited him; their movements had mesmerized him and called to him in ways that he could not even begin to conceptualize.

It was only when the last of Mendez's guards was slaughtered by the mob that he came to his senses. He turned and bolted. When he got to his suite, he locked the door behind him and cowered behind the couch. Even while he listened to the approaching footsteps of the mob, all he could think about was the magical artistry of death.

Death is like any other wild beast—when you run from it,
it begins to think that you are prey.
VERSE 2112: 12 OF *The Teachings*

When one is surrounded by nothingness, seconds can seem like lifetimes; minutes can seem like millennia; and with the passage of time, consciousness can seem to evolve to encompass the breadth and majesty of the universe. After all that Xi had been through, he embraced this expansive consciousness and found that he was at peace. More than merely experiencing peace, he felt triumphant. He conceptualized his former existence only as a time of unpleasantness. He had been a man back then—*less* than a man in fact—but he was a god now. The foibles of men could not even register in his mind any more; and with this divine detachment, he further separated himself from all the things that had troubled him—and that *ever* could.

However, one day, after eons of floating peacefully in the abyss, a strange sensation came over him. He suddenly felt as though his head were in a huge vise, and that the monstrous machinery of the vise were incrementally tightening the grip. He could feel his skull cracking now—as though it were an eggshell; and as the shell cracked, he felt the yoke of his brains oozing out messily over the rest of his body. Also, by now, he felt as though his entire body were being squeezed and confined. With this confinement, he could not move a muscle; but as the universe contracted rhythmically, he felt himself moving though the void. With the squeezing and confinement, and the plates of his skull breaking apart, it suddenly dawned on him that this was how a baby must feel during labor. It made sense—as far as such a thing could make sense to a grown man. He was some fetus being aborted or miscarried. Some mortal error had happened in the genetic code of his soul, and now the entire malformed mess was being extruded....His journey through the birth canal continued. The squeezing became more violent— more *urgent*—and he moved along with the demands of this spastic rhythm. He did not feel as though he had bones anymore—but as though he were a slab of bloody flesh. He suddenly realized that he could not breathe, but his body's natural response to gag and gasp was neutralized by the confinement—

And then, *birth*: a final, brutal spasm pushed him out into the world of light and sound and chaos. He gasped at last, but all he could do was lie there, broken and fragile. After the peacefulness of the void, this new world of color and sound and movement was like a hell dimension. Like a baby, his first impulse was to cry, so that some mother (some protective entity) would come and clean him off, then supply nourishment and support for his broken body.

His brain did not seem to have the ability to make sense of what he saw and heard and felt. All shapes were blurred—and too bright; all noises were slurred, like a barbaric language that was being spoken backwards; and as his body flailed around, the things that he touched seemed at once painfully hot and numbingly cold.

Minutes seemed to pass before the vague outlines of the room made sense to him—or rather, it was minutes before it occurred to him that he was in a room. Even then, trying to make sense of what was in the room with him was like looking at something far off in the distance with an unfocused pair of binoculars. On top of that, the outside world was still too bright and noisy. He would have to ease himself back into consciousness before he could make sense of it all. Thoughts of himself as some miscarried fetus left him now; fantasies about himself as a god in a universe of nothingness disappeared back into the ether of his dreams, and he blinked deeply to clear his vision and fully emerge from the nothingness. Just as his mind deciphered the vague forms of other people in the room with him—and other *voices*—his mind suddenly flashed with images from the city: the huge skyscraper collapsing...men being blown to bits! These aftershocks of terror seemed to dislodge him from his consciousness. The vague forms of the people around him went further out of focus; noises became even more nonsensical....He tried to block all of that out; desperately, he tried to recollect what had happened to him—and how he had come to be in this place. He blinked deeply again, but this had no effect on his blurred vision. Taking stock of his body, he realized that his head still pulsed with pain, as though it actually were being squeezed by a vise. He gathered his strength then, and moved his hands to his head, checking for cracks—or some monstrous device...but his fingers were numb.

He still had no idea where he was. He was not sure if he *wanted* to know. He instinctively wanted to retrace his steps, but his mind seemed as though it had been stripped—*brutalized*. Even now, something gigantic seemed to be trying to force itself into his head. He felt it rewriting his soul in a haphazard manner that was more like mindless butchery than anything else. There was a tingly feeling in his extremities—like the type that came before the body was able to acknowledge horrible trauma....Once again, he clamped his eyes shut, then opened them slowly. However, the room around him was still so blindingly white that he began to suspect that a short circuit had happened in his brain. It was as though his irises, which should have responded to the bright light by shrinking to their smallest aperture, were stuck wide open....He realized that he was trembling—like a man freezing on the tundra. For a moment, this made perfect sense as well: maybe he was freezing in the middle of the arctic. However, as he stared out on the world, he saw that there were colors in the sea of whiteness, and that these colors seemed to bleed into one another, like a child's watercolor with too much water. Xi did not even try to make sense of it: he just stared ahead, like a junkie surrendering to a psychedelic trip....

He had no idea how long it was before his vision improved to the point where he could discern that there were seven other people in the room. Before he could see them clearly, he was able to make out their blurred forms against the whiteness. They were in a kind of semicircle around him. He counted them over and over again as the minutes—or *hours* or *days*—

passed by. His sense of smell returned by stages, and the odor now in the air was unmistakably that of fermented urine and feces. He realized that he had soiled himself and that his pants, and whatever he was lying on, were damp with urine. There were voices in the air: some high-pitched, some low and reverberating...but none were decipherable. He could not even tell if they were speaking English. He probably lay there for hours, trying to detect a single word, like a faithful dog that knew only its name and a few other commands, and which looked on hopefully as its masters conversed with one another....He counted again: still seven people; he counted yet again and grew frustrated with the madness of the game....

More hours passed, and his vision improved with these hours. However, the better his vision got, the worse his head ached—and the more disoriented he felt. When his vision reached the point where he could actually discern individual faces, the feeling of disorientation forced him to clamp his eyes shut and turn his head away. He lay helplessly for a while; but then, gnashing his teeth, he marshaled his strength and sat up, using his right forearm for support. He looked out on the world again: except for the seven people and their clothing, everything in the room was still blindingly white. To be specific, the walls, ceiling and the floor were covered in what seemed to be white tiles. As for the room's proportions, his best guess was that it was about 10 meters by 10 meters. However, with the fluorescent lights blazing overhead (and the white tiles acting as mirrors) the glare made it almost impossible to ascertain where one wall ended and another one began. He could not discern any windows or doors in the walls—*if there were even walls at all*! It was possible that they were floating on a plane—a white abyss without boundaries. He instinctively turned away from the seven and stretched his hand out behind him, until he touched the wall. It was not a far stretch. His fingertips seemed hypersensitive, but it was good to rub them against the tiles—to feel the rough grout and the smooth, regular shapes of the tiles. This somehow confirmed that he was in the real world—or at least in a world with dimensions. With this foundation, he now had the basis for making sense of the rest of the world, so he turned back towards the seven and looked at them critically. His head still ached, and his vision was still a little unfocused, but with his new sense of dimension, and the assumption that he was in a square room, he realized that he was the only one on his side of the room. The seven were spread out along the other three sides of the room—which explained why he had before thought that they were in a semicircle around him. They were all lying on discolored mattresses—himself included. As colors still had the tendency to bleed into one another, he *knew* that he was not seeing things correctly; still, his first assessment of the seven was that they looked like the kind of creatures one would expect to see in a medieval dungeon: lice-infested wretches with matted hair and faces crisscrossed with the peculiar kind of pain and lack of hope that robbed one of all connection to reality. Again summoning his strength, he managed to prop himself up against the wall; and from this vantage point, he looked at his neighbors one at a time. The first two struck him as autistic children locked away in an asylum, so that he began to wonder about his own sanity. The two were staring blankly into space and had long trains of saliva oozing from their mouths to their pillows. The next one had eyes that seemed to roam randomly—as though following an invisible fly about the room. As Xi looked closely (actually, he was practically mesmerized by the man) he noticed that the entire left side of the man's head was bald—and that the man had pulled out his own hair. It was when Xi transferred his gaze from the man's half-bald head to the rest of his body that he was confronted by one of those universe-changing realizations: the person had breasts—*and so did the previous two*! They were all exposed: barely covered by their rags. Xi's mind stumbled over the craggy surface of the realization—

Where those…*women*? He looked at them more closely, but knew that he had neither the mental nor physical wherewithal to make that kind of assessment right now. Besides, all that he could think was that the people before him were like islands of filth and darkness in a universe of light. They seemed almost *supernaturally* filthy—as though some vengeful god had stripped them of all connection to their humanity, and *consciousness*. He had no idea what to make of them. He was just about to turn away from them all, when his gaze happened to fall on the fourth person. At first, he only stared (and became caught in the old game of rechecking what his eyes saw). When he finally allowed his mind to admit that the fourth one was Mansmann, a horrible chill went over his body. Mansmann was staring ahead blankly, rocking like a lunatic and groaning a refrain that had an eerie, hollow quality in the room. Xi stared on in disbelief—and with the ever-diminishing hope that what he was seeing was a dream to be awakened from: a passing nightmare with no consequences.

It was not long before he realized that the fifth, sixth and seventh members of the room were Kramer, the little boy and the other man from the Goddess' cult. The latter were huddled together in the corner of the room like bats in a pit. Their lips seemed to be moving, and, as far as Xi could tell, a high-pitched screeching sound was coming out. The sight of them seemed to wreak havoc on reality—on the possibility that there was a rational universe.

It was as more images of the city, and his final moments of consciousness, flooded Xi's mind, that he gasped and looked about the room once again: *the Goddess was not there*! Xi sat up a little straighter. He checked the room for the Goddess several more times, becoming trapped in the same madness of rechecking. "...The Horde," he whispered at last...but he did not even know if those words made sense to him anymore. He had to reclaim all his memories—all the horror—before he could place everything in the proper light. He looked up at Mansmann again. He was just about to call to the man when a door suddenly opened to his right. A rectangle of blinding white light appeared about two meters from Xi's head. As he scurried away, two people entered. He looked up at them in amazement. The first was a Horde soldier arrayed in one of those battle suits—but without the helmet. The soldier was a man with closely cropped hair. The man seemed dazed—in a trance—so that Xi found himself thinking that he was in a dimension where everyone but himself had been stripped of his consciousness. The soldier placed a chair about three meters in front of Xi. Then, once that was done, the soldier moved to the side and waited for the second entrant. When Xi looked up, he gasped. *It was Quibb*!

Xi could only stare. Quibb was in a kind of tight-fitting pants suit—some remnant from corporate America. As Quibb sat on the chair that the soldier had brought, Xi's eyes roamed over the shapely contours of Quibb's body. His mouth gaped.

Quibb smiled at his reaction. "You never guessed what I was?"

"You're a woman...!" Xi was not sure whether he actually said the words or only thought them. He knew only that they reverberated in his mind like a new kind of madness. He was beyond disbelief now. Quibb was still smiling at him—however, in a way that conveyed not joy, but heartache and resignation to pain. As Xi's eyes scanned the smooth contours of Quibb's face, the realization that Quibb was a woman at the height of her beauty, triggered a painful spasm in his abdomen. Her lips were soft and red—not from lipstick, but a natural vivaciousness that seemed to go against all he had seen of this strange new universe. Her eyes were bright and direct, and her hair flowed gently to her shoulders. Xi looked at Quibb's supple breasts; as she crossed her long, shapely legs, another bout of disorientation came over him. The colors of Quibb's face began to bleed into one another then, so that her face took on the appearance of a patchwork quilt. He clamped his eyes shut, rubbing his temples to soothe the explosive headache. When he opened his eyes again, his vision had cleared up somewhat, but all that he could think was that the universe was mad. Quibb was a woman, Mansmann and the others were all demented, and he was locked away in a cell of madness. When he took a deep breath, he realized that Quibb smelled like a fragrant spring day: a field full of flowers after a shower. As he looked at her, he was acutely aware of his own filthiness—perhaps also the irreclaimable loss of his humanity. Seeing her beauty and cleanliness made him realize how he must smell and look—and what he had become. Moreover, in the way that we often hate that which reminds us of what we have lost or what we can never attain, Xi now found that the sight of Quibb was repulsive to him. His eyes timidly returned to Quibb's breasts and the graceful curves of her body, then he looked away, shaking his head....It did not matter if Quibb was a man or a woman. Quibb's femininity was not a license to do anything: it was not homophobia that had kept him from Quibb when she appeared to him in the city....Deep down, he had never wanted to touch

Quibb, nor had he wanted to be touched. He had never desired to derive pleasure from Quibb's body—either in reality or in his fantasies (*be it male or female*). Over the last seven years, he had fantasized of course; but in retrospect, in none of those fantasies had he wanted to derive pleasure from anyone's *body*. He had fantasized about the *idea* of a woman—about the *idea* of love and companionship and all the things supposedly central to human psychosexual contentment. Knowing this, he sensed (on some level) that something vital had been lost. For the first time, he understood the horror of the apocalypse—the *depth* of the horror. As he looked at Quibb—rather, as he looked at Quibb as a *woman*—he had never felt so distant from another human being in his life; and, accordingly, he had never felt so distant from his own humanity.

"...What's all this about, Quibb?" Xi whispered at last.

Quibb nodded to the soldier then, and the latter exited the room and closed the door. Xi kept his eyes on Quibb, who had dropped her eyes until the door was closed. When the lock clicked, she looked up and said: "You are all Horde prisoners now."

He gestured towards Mansmann and the others: "What did you do to them?"

She turned in the seat and looked at them sorrowfully. Her graceful movements were disturbing somehow. She stared at Mansmann and the others for a moment; when she turned back to Xi, she seemed even more drained. She sighed before continuing: "They are under mind control." Then, in a lower, more pained voice, "The only reason any of you is still alive is because our general wants to use you, Xi."

"Me?"

"Yes, she needs your technical expertise."

"*She?*"

Quibb could not help laughing at him again: "...Haven't you figured it out yet, Xi? The Horde *is* the women."

Nothing could really shock Xi anymore. Still, he stared at the floor so that what he had just heard could seep into his consciousness: become part of him, rather than just a gadfly on the periphery of his imagination. He looked past Quibb then, to the three figures with the exposed breasts: "Are they women, too?"

"Yes."

"They are under mind control, too?"

"Yes."

"But you said The Horde is the women."

"Most of the women are under mind control." As she said it, she gestured towards the door, referencing the soldier waiting outside. "However, sometimes the mind control doesn't *control*...it *incapacitates*...brings dementia..."

Quibb's voice had an eerie quality; at this point, Xi listened more to the sound of it than to what it was saying. Actually, while she talked, the events of the city flashed in his mind again. He saw the buildings of The Company coming down...The Horde troops approaching in the dust. His mind rebelled against it all—

"*Why?*" he said at last, cutting off Quibb in mid sentence. "Why all this?"

She looked at him helplessly: "...We thought it was the only way we could survive."

He looked at Quibb as though still not comprehending: "You were part of this?" He knew that Quibb was part of The Horde; he knew that she had been a spy, but that, combined with the fact that she was a woman—*and the fact that The Horde was the women*—was too much to grasp at once.

Quibb sighed: "...We got our power from this place."

Xi looked about the room, as though the source of power were within it. "What is this place?" he asked.

"Before the apocalypse, it was some kind of top secret military base. That's how The Horde got all its technology. Hundreds of thousands of women were taken here after the crisis," she continued. "Millions more were taken to other hidden fortresses, all over the world. A few of us managed to rebel. The men had drugged us and pumped these subliminal messages into our minds, telling us to be docile...when to eat, when to shit—*everything*—"

"My technology," Xi mumbled to himself. Quibb went on:

"The same messages are playing in the air now." She again shook her head, as if shaking away a bad thought; and as she did so, Xi suddenly realized that he could hear them himself. He had not been able to decipher it before, but there were several voices in the air telling him to be at peace—and several other things that did not exactly make sense to him, even though he could understand the words. He shook his head more forcefully, then returned to rubbing his temples. Quibb continued: "Anyway, some of us had, to some degree or another, a kind of natural immunity to it. Out of the hundreds of thousands of women, only about 60 of us had this immunity—but luckily there weren't too many guards: maybe about 100. I guess they didn't think they needed that many—especially with the mind control.

"…We managed to take them by surprise and kill them. That was about five years ago—"

"Wait," Xi interrupted her, "you mean that for *five* years you've been free? How come you only started attacking the cities recently?"

She thought about it for a while. "…After we rebelled, we were going to set the women free: to destroy the mind control apparatus—but then our… [she searched around for the right word] our *general* managed to convince us that what we needed were soldiers: grunts."

"You mean, like the one who brought in the chair?"

"Yes. There are millions like her. Our general told us that we had to defend ourselves, so we kept the mind control up, so that we could have troops. We started out by 'liberating' the other fortresses….The main thing was to acquire fortresses and garner power that way. Our general was patient," she went on. "She sent spies like me out to the major cities. With the technology we had, we could be halfway around the world in an hour and nobody would ever detect us. And we had access to satellite feeds: we saw what the men had done. It wasn't hard to hate them….We lost ourselves to the hate: the self-righteousness…Once you get a taste of power, injustice isn't as important as revenge; and so, after a while, we found that we didn't want to abolish the power structure that enslaved us: we only wanted to take it over— to control and *manipulate* it." She chuckled here again, shaking her head.

"…I believed that you were God," Xi said in the silence.

She chuckled sorrowfully to herself. "I did it all with technology from your lab."

"…I know," he mused; and as he said it, he suddenly found himself thinking that technology had reached the point where they could recreate all of Jesus' miracles; but he shook his head then: "Why did you do it, Quibb—The Voice of Consciousness…all of it?"

She smiled as though that would take a lifetime to explain. Then, after another sigh, "I was one of their spies, sent in to get some things from your lab at The Company"—Xi nodded uneasily—"...but we couldn't get access to what we really wanted," Quibb continued, staring off into the distance. By the tone of her voice, Xi knew that she was talking about The Hand of Evolution. He again rubbed his temples to soothe the biting headache; Quibb went on, "About a week before The Horde's first bombing I...I realized that I couldn't do it any longer. I just left them—went AWOL....The Horde had already figured out that the most likely place for holding the women was at The Company. I was supposed to leave the city and come back to them, but I saw things that made me have doubts. I was having doubts before: The Horde does things to the women that are probably worse than anything the men ever did—especially since we're women." She looked over her shoulder uneasily then, at the three women. "...The men of the city were sickening, but at least they were free—or, at least the ones that didn't use PinkEyes and weren't mad..." She shook her head then, as if to keep some horrible realization at bay, or to remind herself to get back on track. "...Anyway," she continued, "I became The Voice of Consciousness in an attempt to fight The Horde—to at least give the men a fighting chance...but then The Horde recaptured me after the Central Park rally—"

"That's why you disappeared," Xi whispered to himself without looking up; Quibb nodded before continuing:

"They brought me back, interrogated me...but I escaped and went back to bomb The Company before they got to it and its technology."

"Then you're not really with them?" he asked hopefully.

"No...not really...but that doesn't matter anymore."

"...How did you escape?" he asked.

"Circe helped me."

Xi frowned: he had forgotten about Circe. "Circe is against The Horde, too?"

Quibb smiled wistfully: "As far as I know. Nobody really knows anything about her. She just showed up here one day—like a stray cat. Either we liberated her from somewhere or...well, I'm not sure. She came and went as she pleased. You forgot all about her—like a cat that wanders alone all day, then sneaks into your bed in the middle of the night. One day, when I was spying in the city, I spotted her in Times Square performing—leading that Goddess cult thing....I got her to help me break into your lab at The Company...and she helped me escape from here after they captured me.

"—Anyway," she said with another deep sigh, "none of that really matters anymore." She looked at Xi ominously now: "The Horde needs you, Xi."

"...To reconstruct The Hand," he whispered.

She stared at him intently, as he bowed his head and sat there rubbing his temples. "...They didn't even know who you were," she went on, "—they only brought you guys here because they thought you were part of Carolyn's cult. Our general was going to use you guys to control Carolyn. Your being here is only a case of being in the wrong place at the wrong time."

Xi looked up as if doing so required effort—was *painful*. "How long have I been...unconscious?"

"A few hours."

"Is that all?" he mused. However, just then, his head pulsed with new pain; and as he looked around, the colors of the world began to bleed once more. The murmuring voices in his head seemed to scream out as well. He closed his eyes and rubbed his temples harder, but the headache was so severe and disorienting that for a moment he could not even tell which way was up—

"What did you do to me?" he gasped. He did not even try to look up: he just sat there rubbing his temples with his eyes closed.

"They tried to use the mind control on you," Quibb began, "—but I guess you're immune too—like me. They weren't able to control you, but they managed to get the schematics for The Hand from your mind....They want you to help them build it."

"Why do they need me?"

"Having a blueprint for a nuclear bomb doesn't mean you can build one—they need your *expertise*, Xi."

Xi went to laugh at what seemed like an old joke. He remembered that the expertise—the *knowledge* behind all his inventions—was still floating in the netherworld of his consciousness, and went to laugh at Quibb and The Horde, but then he suddenly realized that all the knowledge had returned to him. It had all come back—or at least all the knowledge about The Hand had! There were no more fragments and blind spots. The Horde's attempt to use mind control on him must have speeded up the process of linking all the disparate bits of data into a cohesive whole. This terrified him somehow. Moreover, from the first moment he woke up in this place, he had had the feeling that something was being imposed on him. While the mind control had made him whole again, it seemed somehow conflicted about how to deal with him…it was difficult to explain. He suddenly had the feeling of being close to something that he had long been in search of. However, that thing, whatever it was, seemed to be both calling to him and trying to keep him at bay. It was as though the mind control were somehow *schizophrenic*—

"Xi?" It was Quibb. She was looking at him anxiously.

"…Yes?"

"Are you all right?"

"…Does it matter?"

She sighed thoughtfully. "I guess not." Then, returning to the matter at hand, "What about The Horde? Will you help them?"

"…What about you?" he asked, looking up at her earnestly—through the pain and disorientation. "What do *you* want?"

"What?"

"Do you want me to help them?"

She sighed again. "What I want isn't important. It's about what you're willing to live with—or to die for."

Xi chuckled. All at once, he realized that it would never end. No matter what he did, he would continue to be a pawn in the schemes of the powerful. He felt so tired just now. Everything seemed so farcical that he laughed again—

"Don't laugh like that, Xi," Quibb pleaded. However, it was then that another jolt of disorienting pain went through him, cutting his laughter short. Maybe it was that pain that shaped his mindset now, because for once The Hand of Evolution—and the nothingness it would bring—did not seem like a horrible prospect. Human self-destruction seemed inevitable: holding it back with grandiose acts of heroism was pointless. He wanted only to be free: to have his consciousness forever separated from the demands and weaknesses of the flesh. He was so sick of life that it was not merely death that he craved, but the sterility that only a machine could guarantee. He wanted to be subject to The Hand and live out his existence in nothingness. Consciousness—the *soul*—was an inherently evil instrument: a gift not from God, but the Devil. The desires and demands of the soul never led to peace, but chaos. Only a soulless machine could give them peace—

"I'll do it," he said.

"…What?"

"I'll help them build The Hand," Xi clarified. Quibb stared at him in mute horror, before nodding her head and collecting herself.

"Come on," she said, getting up, "I'll take you to the lab."

Fear can sometimes lead to good choices—
even in the absence of sound judgment.
VERSE 304:2 OF *The Teachings*

Mendez cowered on the floor as the mob banged on his door. Luckily for him, as the mob had no focus, it quickly moved on. Now, as Mendez rose from the floor and looked around, he suddenly remembered what he had been working on before all this happened. He returned to the adjoining suite then, where he had all his technology. He had been working on a satellite link before he heard the loud explosion and went to the window to watch the 150-story skyscraper collapsing. Regaining his focus, he sat at his console and worked with an urgency he had never felt before. After a while, the reality that The Company was actually gone hit him hard again. Bewildered, he got up from the console and went to the window to check the skyline for the 150-story skyscraper. Shaka was gone... Mendez was hardly able to conceptualize it. There were men who were so deeply defined by what they fought against that they mourned the deaths of their enemies more deeply than the deaths of their loved ones. Mendez was one of them. Men worked for and *with* the ones they loved; as there was this cooperation and affinity, they often joined their motives with those of their loved ones, losing sight of the fact that their loved ones were separate, *real* human beings. However, with enemies, the mutual antagonism separated and *defined* them, so that they were always concrete figures. Men planned for their struggles with their enemies; indeed, they defined themselves with respect to those struggles. This was especially true in Mendez's case, because he had never loved another human being, and had at best loved the *things* around him only shallowly.

It was while he was finishing some modifications to the makeshift satellite broadcast system that one of his aides burst into the room. Mendez at first thought that it was another crazed man, and jumped up to defend himself. However, when the aide revealed that they had found a Horde jump jet, Mendez nodded his head with full awareness of what this meant.

"Take it to a safe place," he had said then, "—I have to finish this first."

Never accept perfection—it is only a delusion that arises when
a mind has reached the limits of its imagination.
VERSE 1712:16 OF *The Teachings*

The Goddess emerged back into consciousness, the way she had that first morning in the woods. She was lying supine, reveling in the peace of her dreams, when that easy bliss was suddenly invaded by the realization that she was not alone. She opened her eyes and burst upright, looking around like a caged animal. She had no idea where she was—and there was a strange face hovering over hers! She went to flee and immediately fell off the gurney that she had been lying on. She fell bluntly to the tiled floor; after the initial shock of the impact, she scurried into the corner of the room. The person hovering over her had been a woman! And there were two others standing guard against the door on the far end of the room. Her mind reeled! She seemed to be in a hospital of some kind, because everything was an immaculate white. The gurney was more like a dentist's chair, with many daunting attachments arrayed on a side tray. The chair was the only embellishment in the room, and it stood in the center of it. The room, itself, was brightly lit—almost to excess—but an even more blinding light shone above the chair in the center of the room. The attendant—the doctor, medic...whatever she was—was still standing by it. The woman seemed annoyed that her patient had moved. She gestured to the two other women, and as the latter came up, and the Goddess saw the emblems on their battle suits, she gasped. It was The Horde emblem—the purple sky…the green sun. The guards pulled her gruffly to her feet. It all happened so quickly that she did not have time to react. The Goddess could see the guards' blank, haggard faces for once. Their eyes were pale and soulless—as if they were walking mannequins. She stared at them in horror, wondering if they were human beings. She suddenly remembered her first moments of consciousness: walking down that endless corridor and seeing a column of women walking phlegmatically past her. Those women had worn the same expressions as these women. In fact, it was while her mind was sputtering closer to the realization that The Horde was the women that the attendant nodded to the guards (who still grasped the Goddess firmly) and they all exited the room together.

The same blank, wide corridors that she remembered from her first moments of consciousness, stretched out eerily before her. The realization that she was back in that place on the mountain was like a roof collapsing on her head. She suddenly remembered the last images from the city: the terrible sight of the skyscraper coming down…and then The Horde troops approaching through the debris…! By now, the two guards were practically dragging her. It was not that she was protesting, but that she was too terrified to use her legs properly. The corridor was the same immaculate white as the room; but unlike her recollections, it definitely was not unending: it turned to the left after about 50 meters. In a sense, she was like an adult visiting her childhood neighborhood, only to realize that all the imposing structures of childhood were now less imposing—less imbued with the magic of childhood memories. Still, as the guards dragged her along the corridor, the realization that she was again a prisoner in this place, wreaked havoc on her. She felt as though she had acid in her veins, and that her insides were being liquefied. When it occurred to her that her consciousness would again be taken away from her—and that she would forget all that had passed in the city—she went to cry out…but she was too weak. In desperation, she held onto her fleeting moments of consciousness dearly—even these. She savored all that her senses could analyze….The Horde placard was still on the walls. That, along with the fact that the guards were wearing Horde battle suits, should have told her that The Horde was the women…but this was a case where facts were too cumbersome—and *nonsensical*—to be of use in reaching conclusions—

A gaping entrance was on their left; within the huge barracks beyond it, there were *thousands* of women in fatigues. The guards pulled her past the entrance quickly; she turned her head and looked back at all the dazed women. Her mind gulped it all down hungrily—like a glutton too impatient to savor what she was eating. She felt like someone on the way to the gallows, sucking down her last gasps of air, smelling the last scents she would ever smell....She was shepherded down several long corridors, which turned at right angles. They passed five more huge barracks, where there were thousands upon thousands of more dazed women in fatigues. Then, she looked around in a panic as she began to hear the murmuring voices again. What was more disconcerting, was that she could actually understand the murmuring now. One droning voice was whispering, "Peace...peace," over and over again. Another voice was babbling some nonsense about duty and loyalty. There was something maddening about it; but as she was conscious of it, she was able to block it from her inner consciousness—her *soul*....

At the end of the next corridor, they entered a cavernous, dimly lit room. A map of the world was displayed on a huge screen against the far wall. On the map, multi-colored lights blinked continually; and all along the walls, there were scores of flashing computer consoles and things that looked like radar displays. As the Goddess' vision adjusted to the darkness, she saw that there were about 30 women in the chamber. Most of them were posted at the computer consoles along the walls. What piqued her interest was that none of the women in the chamber had that dazed expression on her face. They looked up at her when she entered; some of them turned to one another and whispered.

The attendant that had led the Goddess and the two guards into the room, detached herself from their group and went up to a woman—who was staring up at the huge map. The attendant approached the woman diffidently, as if mindful of disturbing her. When the woman turned to face the attendant, the Goddess gasped. Even though her mind was still in a daze from all that had happened, her heart skipped a beat as she recognized the woman that turned to talk to the attendant. It was the woman from her vision at the rally: the strong, resolute one—the ageless one that was beyond them all. The Goddess had gasped the way someone gasped when seeing a ghost. It was almost as though a current went through her. She was left so disoriented—so *undone*—that she feared that she was having another seizure. As her body slumped, the two guards held her up. She stared ahead, mesmerized by—and instinctively terrified of—the woman. More disturbingly, after listening to the attendant, the woman turned and followed the attendant back towards the Goddess. The woman was wearing a military uniform with gaudy epaulets and about seven chevrons on each arm. It seemed like a mockery of what a general was supposed to look like—

"Carolyn!" the general bellowed, beaming as if she had just recognized her, "you've returned!"

Being addressed by her name (or at least the name that was supposed to be hers) was still strange to the Goddess. Her mouth was dry; she swallowed before she began: "…You *know* me?"

"Of course I know you!" the woman said through a grin. "We all know one another here."

The Goddess looked around warily then. "…What is all this…? Who *are* you?"

"I'm a woman like you. That's the most important thing."

She looked at the insignias on their clothes again—this time with a heightened degree of awareness and clarity. She wanted to ask about The Horde—rather, about their relation to The Horde—but she did not entirely know how to phrase it. Instead, she approached it like a coward:

"What is that picture?" she said, gesturing to the insignia. The woman—the General—looked at her with a slight smile on her face, then said, simply:

"We are The Horde."

The Goddess looked around anxiously. It was not that she was struggling to digest new information, but she was reacquainting herself with something that had been buried in the huge garbage heap of her mind. She had to go through much trash before she could reach it; and even then, what she found was so filthy that she did not really want to grasp it. She frowned and looked at the General's gaudy uniform again: "But…*why*?"

"This is how we survived after the men shipped us off to prison camps," the General began, a kind of religious zeal gleaming in her eyes. "We fought for and won our freedom, then we built ourselves up. While the men became animals, we became this—"

Images of all the destruction from the bombings flashed in the Goddess' mind once more. "*Why?*" she said again, like a child asking an adult to explain the grand enigmas of the universe.

"*Why?*" the General said, before chuckling. "Have we done anything so horrible?" she asked, rhetorically, looking around at the other women, who nodded and smiled and laughed too enthusiastically. "We've simply responded to history."

"History?" the Goddess whispered, feeling suddenly weighed down—*exhausted*.

"All women have ever wanted," the General went on sententiously, talking to everyone in the room now, "was to have their rightful place—to be equal partners with the men. But they degraded and devalued us. [A few of the women moaned in solidarity, nodding their heads.] Even when the world found out that there would be no more women—a situation that made our value skyrocket—we were treated like cattle....*History*: it demands that we take our rightful place; it demands that we do so through *power*. Love and kindness can be reclaimed later from the ashes. This is the men's jungle: we can either be predators or prey! Later, when the beasts are subdued, we'll—"

But the Goddess was laughing to herself. It all seemed like some cheesy 1960s spy movie, with a melodramatic madman plotting world domination. She wanted to laugh it away; she wanted to laugh at all the improbable and senseless things that she had seen over the past few weeks; but looking around, she realized that no one else was laughing. They were staring at her. Some seemed horrified by her laughter—others seemed enraged. Remembering that the General knew her—that *all* these women supposedly knew her—was chilling. While their eyes seemed to reach every hidden place within her, she did not have the slightest inkling of who they were. Her only window into their souls was the nonsensical datum that they were The Horde—and had slaughtered *millions*.

Strangely enough, it was while she resumed her old struggle with her past that that old feeling, of drifting within her mind, came over her again. It was as if a tornado appeared out of nowhere and sucked her up into its funnel. She twirled in the chaos, along with all the debris of inanimate objects and people from her past. There was no use in fighting it. Indeed, she did not *want* to fight it, only to slow it down somehow, so that she could make sense of it. The outside world became irrelevant. The General and the staring Horde women became faint echoes in a world resounding with the roar of the tornado. Now, all around her, she saw the relics of her past, all of which had been uncovered and sucked up by the violent churning of the funnel cloud. She braced herself as her limbs flailed about in the chaos, knowing that if she was not wrenched apart, then she would finally have answers....Faces suddenly came out of the chaos, and she found that she could apply names and personalities to them. However, as there was no logical grouping to all the faces, the information she gleaned was like garbage taken from one pile and deposited in another. For a moment, her revelations threatened to be just more nonsensical data; but corralling her will, she scoured the tornado for information on her family; and for once, something concrete and *empowering* returned from the chaos....

Her strange existence in the South Bronx was like a kaleidoscope of contradictions. She remembered her morbidly obese mother, who had been somehow delineated by the ghetto: by poverty and the constant, self-destructive yearning to be somewhere and someone else. She, herself, had been on her way to escape: a ten-year-old already imagining life beyond her neighborhood—and away from the dearth of imagination that existed there. She had been flying high over all of their heads, grasping possibilities that none of them had been able to conceptualize....She had started up her little Website for fun, but then strange things had begun to happen. People had started looking at her peculiarly...calling her Goddess. When she walked down the street, people had stopped on the sidewalk and stared at her— sometimes entire blocks of people! Stranger still, people had seemed unable to think straight when they looked at her; they had followed her around as if mesmerized. Some had *stalked* her, following her home, or to school.... And then, the accidents had started happening—like the stove exploding in her apartment; twice, she had almost been run over by cars; and after a while, she had gone around with the feeling that it was not only the world of men that was after her, but something huge and powerful—some actual or metaphorical devil.

Yet, in the beginning, being God had been fun. In the beginning, she had wanted the attention—and the power. Her small site on the Internet had become one of the most popular in the *world*, and she had reveled in that. People from all over the world had flocked to her. Even while they babbled on about God, she had only laughed joyously at the power she had…but then the stove had blown up…and her mother had died…and she had finally begun to realize that people were not seeing her at all—but some mask that had nothing to do with her….Some anarchists had taken her into safety—or at least that's what they had called it. She had been so desperate by then that she had believed. They had taken her and hidden in a ware-house, talking about the Second Coming of God and all the other nonsense she had before laughed at. Her followers had risen up before her as a face-less mob—even now, she could remember no faces, no voices…nothing concrete…And the way they had looked at her—*and the things they had done in her name*—had told her that she was a conduit for every kind of madness and irrationality. Worse yet, as atrocities were carried out in her name, the police had not been the only ones after her: other sects had been searching for her as well. Soon, all the sects had been fighting one another over her. It had been during one of these gun battles that she snuck away. She had run for her life. Desperate to hide, she had disguised herself as a boy and worn sunglasses. The latter had seemed to help, as she realized that people mostly seemed to lose themselves when they stared into her eyes. Her eyes had been the trigger for something horrible within the human soul….She had lived in abandoned buildings, hiding her face from the world lest she trigger the madness. Once, a man had attacked her while she was skulking about an alley for some food. He had actually thought that she was a boy and had tried to sodomize her. She had stabbed him in the neck with an ice pick—a trick one of her followers had shown her. Then, she had scurried behind a garbage can and watched the man die, mesmerized by the horrible messiness of death….

When the apocalypse came, and the end of woman set humanity plummeting into further darkness, she had almost been relieved that there was something to take the attention away from her. From her hideout in the abandoned building, she had stood by and watched anxiously while most of the women were gathered up and taken away to so-called camps. She had seen through it right away, and had wanted to scream out to those desperate women... but that desperation had been their undoing. Their search for safety and reassurance in a world of pain and brutality had sealed their fate; and by then, she had had neither patience nor sympathy for people that refused to see the brutal nature of the world....

She had stayed in her hideout for months, looking at the savagery of the outside world. One day, she had donned her disguise and gone out to get something to eat. Troops of some kind had set up a checkpoint a few blocks away from her hideout. When she turned back from the checkpoint, the troops had followed her. She had run for her life, but they had cornered her in her hideout....After her capture, she remembered sitting in a bus with a few dozen frightened girls. And then, once within the massive underground complex, she had been confused at the insensate existence of everyone else. She had been immune from the mind control for some reason. She had kept quiet—for *months*—trying to pretend that she was soulless. Thus, when the attack led by the General had finally come, she had at first just looked on, unsure. Even when she stepped up and addressed herself to the General, she had never really been a true believer. She had been young and had followed the adults instinctively, especially as they were women, but she had been wary of all groups after what she had been through. All philosophies had seemed to have madness and treachery built into them. Accordingly, when she fell out of favor with the General and the others, it had merely been because she was not able to *pretend* to believe in their doctrines— rather than any true conflict of wills or philosophies. When Quibb and a few others began to question the General, the Goddess had found herself with them by default....The General had tried a new kind of mind control on these heretics (with the exception of Quibb of course). Most had died or been left in a kind of dementia. In the Goddess' case, she had lost all her memories...and then Respoli-Priestess' cult had rescued her and taken her to the city....

The Goddess gasped as she came back into consciousness. Somehow, she was lying on the ground. Something soft had been placed beneath her head, but her body felt deflated somehow—as though all of its energy had been exhausted, and she were now just a flabby bag of flesh. The others were standing above her, looking down. In the darkness, they seemed horrible— like vultures waiting for her to die. The General was asking her if she was all right; as the Goddess looked around confusedly, she suddenly remembered Xi and the others:

"—Some men!" she blurted out, "...I was with them...the last I remembered...."

If there is a Devil, it waits not for men's moments of weakness,
but for those moments when they manage to convince themselves
that they are the most powerful.
VERSE 4323:13 OF *The Teachings*

In the city, the hours following the collapse of The Company and the Image Broadcast Complex were hard ones. Perhaps two million men had perished when the buildings collapsed; hundreds of thousands more could still be heard groaning under piles of rubble. On top of that, dust clouds still hovered in the air, casting the city in a kind of perpetual twilight.

...Everyone had been in shock at first—especially with the PinkEyes and the billboards offline. After the initial madness wore off, they had again been forced to confront the real world—and to see themselves as they were. That had been a moment of possibility, when they might have taken a step towards their lost humanity, but it was then that Mendez finished rigging his satellite communications system, and broadcasted a message of his making over the screens. The dazed men looked up at the screens in disbelief; and then, when Mendez appeared over the screens to tell them how they had pushed back The Horde, they were desperate to believe.

"...They have run off to lick their wounds," Mendez screamed at them from the billboards. "Like any beast that knows that it cannot win, it is getting desperate. It will heave itself against us again, the way a trapped beast heaves itself against the bars of a cage in a foolish attempt to get at its captors. It does not yet know that it cannot reach us! It does not know that it will eventually kill itself in the effort! We will teach them! If they want war, it is war they will get!"

Yes, by now, they were desperate to believe; yet, it was difficult to say if they even had the wherewithal to actually believe anything anymore. In their desperation to cling onto something, it was not really important *what* they believed. In a sense, they were all playing a game—fulfilling roles not out of any conviction or stance, but because the game was the only thing that gave meaning to their lives. This might have been the moment when they tossed aside the entire farce. However, Mendez once again appeared over their heads. This time, he announced that they had not only captured a Horde jet, but that they were only moments away from cracking its codes and learning where The Horde was. Pictures of the jet appeared on the screens then. As the men saw it and allowed themselves to be swept up by Mendez's exhortations, some of them found that they genuinely believed.

*No nation has ever had (nor can ever have) the separation of church
and state. The national religion of every nation is nationalism.
All nations try to convince its citizens that its actions are inherently
good, and that those who go against it are inherently evil.
What are national anthems but prayers to the nation?
What are calls for patriotism but calls for faith in the nation state—
and in the particular demigods chosen to lead the state?*
VERSE 412:5 OF *The Teachings*

The Horde soldier that had brought Quibb's chair into the room,
now supported Xi's weight as he shuffled down the corridor. Quibb
walked ahead with very soft, precise steps—like a dancer. Despite
himself, Xi stared longingly at the movements of Quibb's body, even
though his vision was still distorted. As the soldier supported him, and he
stared at the increasingly ghost-like movements of Quibb's body, he could
not help thinking that he was trapped in an escalating delusion that would
eventually collapse under its own ridiculous weight. Moreover, the world
was still too bright; colors—even shadows—continued to bleed into one
another; and as the murmuring voices became more urgent, further wearing
away at his sanity and his resolve, he began to realize that there was something
about this place that exceeded the limitations—and *imperatives*—of mind control. Something was off. As he had thought before, the mind control seemed
somehow *conflicted*. It had helped to make him whole again: he could even
sense it directing him to more revelations. Yet, at the same time, he felt it
fighting to keep him in the dark—and to obliterate him before he reached
whatever revelations it was protecting. Something was very wrong with
this place. Now, it felt as though the mind control—*or something beyond it*—
were attempting to *crush* his will, not merely to guide it. It did not let up,
even while a side of him cried out for the oblivion it promised. In this context,
The Hand of Evolution took on the majesty of an oasis in a wasteland. He

moved towards it with rising joy, already forgetting the suffering he had endured in the wasteland—

He tripped and fell to the floor. When he looked up, he saw Quibb's face hovering over his. With his vision still distorted, the white walls of the corridor were blurred, so that Quibb seemed to be floating in a cloud—like an angel. Nevertheless, when she touched him, he shrank away. She stared at him with the same sorrowful expression, then ordered the soldier to help him up.

They continued walking. Rather, the soldier continued to pull him along as he shuffled down the corridor. Even though his body had wasted away to skin and bone, and he was not much of a burden, he was impressed by the strength of the soldier. It was while he was considering the effect that the mind control might be having on her strength and pain threshold that it occurred to him that he was still wearing the PinkEyes—and that they were probably the only reason he had not succumbed to the mind control! The PinkEyes were acting as a shield—albeit an imperfect one. The brutality of the mind control was probably in response to this supposed defense....

In time, they made it to the central command chamber. The General and her lieutenants were still bent over the Goddess when Quibb led Xi and the soldier into the chamber. All the women in the chamber turned and watched them approach. Xi looked at them anxiously—not only because they were women, but because there was something about them that made his skin crawl. In the dimly lit chamber, they seemed like a coven conjuring dark magic. He had thought before that only the women could save them, but it occurred to him now that all flesh was corrupt....

"Has he decided to comply?" the General demanded of Quibb.

"Yes," Quibb responded as she stepped up to the woman. Then, once she had reached the General, she stood to the side and allowed the soldier to bring Xi up to the General. As he looked around, he found that the darkness of the room made his disorientation worse somehow. The General was saying something to him, but he could not really hear her above the voices still murmuring in his head. It was actually as though the voices of the mind control were screaming now. He grimaced, and an unconscious groan escaped from his lips; as more of his strength ebbed away, the soldier bore more of his weight. His movements were feeble now—like those of an old man. As his eyes once again came to rest on the General, all that he knew was that he did not like the woman's smile. She was what would classically be referred to as a handsome woman. She was not young enough to be considered pretty, but she had not yet reached that age when men stopped considering a woman's beauty. Actually, there was something familiar about her face that mesmerized him—*disturbed* him. As he looked at her, he realized that she was a projection of how Quibb would look in 20 or 30 years. He grimaced again, then clamped his eyes shut and shook his head. He was beginning to see Quibb everywhere. In the few weeks that he had known Quibb, she had appeared as everything from a teenager to a woman on the verge of old age. She was either beyond time, or his obsession with her was beyond all limits....

"You're making the right decision," someone said; looking up, Xi realized that the elderly Quibb—the *General*—had spoken to him. As he tried to make sense of her through the distortion, he again realized that there was something disturbing about her smile—something *unwholesome*. He stared at her, again mesmerized by the effect: the ability of a smile to hold so much malice.

It was then that he looked down and noticed the Goddess lying on the floor. She was looking at him confusedly; however, when their eyes met, he looked away uneasily. He did not want to know why she was lying on the ground. He did not want to care about anybody anymore. Ultimately, they would all be better off succumbing to the nothingness of The Hand. As the General continued to smile, he nodded to himself, thinking that even she would be sucked into the nothingness. None would be spared—none *could* be spared—from the wonderful sterility of The Hand of Evolution.

"I'm ready to start now," he heard himself say. The General smiled even wider and nodded to Quibb—who again ordered the soldier to bring Xi. They walked through the entire command chamber. Xi's legs were practically dragging now. He closed his eyes as he was pulled along, because he found that this reduced the distortion somewhat.

The lab was in an adjoining room, on the far side of the command chamber. Actually, only a transparent glass wall separated the two rooms. Xi opened his eyes right before they entered the lab. Even before he entered the chamber, he saw that it was about 30 meters by 20 meters—and that it reminded him of his lab back at The Company. There were several consoles just beyond the entrance, and these consoles controlled a multitude of generators, diagnostic tools, holographic projectors and communications devices. All was in readiness for The Hand; and seeing this, he moved with more urgency—again like that man shuffling towards the oasis on the horizon.

However, when he crossed the threshold of the lab, something strange happened. The murmuring voices that had been blaring maddeningly in his mind suddenly fell silent. Xi stopped and looked around in amazement, realizing that his vision had miraculously cleared up, and that his strength had returned. He felt as though he were bursting with energy—but not necessarily good energy, but the energy of a drug: of lost control and altered consciousness. He looked around the lab anxiously then. His first impulse was that whatever was making him feel this way was man-made. Yet, he could not get over the feeling that he was in the presence of God—of something responsible for every molecule of his being. He felt both as though it were something he had always known, and something not only beyond his conceptual ability, but also the conceptual ability of all men. He had no idea what to make of it. He turned and looked back at the command chamber, remembering the disorientation and lethargy he had felt when within it. Just the contrast of that disorientation with his current feeling of energized clarity should have made him feel triumphant, but that was not the case. It was not that he believed that the command chamber (and the rest of this complex) was hell, and that this was heaven. On the contrary, it was as if this room were beyond the gravity of good and evil.

Quibb was looking at him closely: "You all right?"

"…Yeah," he said; and as he did so, he detached himself from the soldier—whose support he no longer needed.

"You feeling better?" Quibb asked then.

"…I don't know yet." He walked away from them and went to the consoles. In order to burn away some of his nervous energy, he began a preliminary inventory of the equipment in the lab. As he did the inventory, he kept looking up anxiously at objects in the room, still somehow expecting one of them to be God.

When Quibb saw him begin the work, the same sorrowful look came into her eyes. "Everything you need should be in here," she began, "—we managed to get copies of all the things in your lab." At the sound of her voice, he looked up from his work and they stared at one another oddly; she continued: "Do you need any help?"

"No," he said curtly. His energy—his *nervous* energy—seemed to be increasing, as though the drug were taking its toll. More and more, something within him trembled at this place; he still sensed the thing that seemed responsible for his existence: the thing that the mind control had both been leading him towards and trying to keep from him. That he no longer heard the murmuring voices told him that the thing was beyond mind control—was beyond the vulgar demands of power.

When he glanced over his shoulder, Quibb was still staring at him.

"I still have faith in you, Xi," she said then.

He stopped what he was doing and looked at her. Then, chuckling and shaking his head, he went back to his inventory. "…Meaning what?" he said.

"Meaning that I have faith in what I saw in you."

He chuckled softly—but this time without any true amusement. He looked at her earnestly: "You're only going along with the others because of me, right?"

"Yes."

Then, with a sarcastic air, "They promised to do terrible things to me if you didn't go along?" When her face remained grim, he pursed his lips and gestured back towards the command center: "That woman is your mother, isn't she?"

"Yes."

He opened his mouth to say something else, but as he happened to glance towards the ceiling, he saw some surveillance cameras and could not help smiling—it was just like old times at The Company. The powerful of the world were still keeping track of his movements. However, it was then that the feeling of boundless energy evolved into a prickly sensation—as though his skin were crawling with insects. He scanned the room uneasily again, searching for the thing that he *knew* was there.

"Something wrong?" Quibb asked when she saw his reaction.

He continued scanning the room. The feeling he had had in the corridor (that something was very wrong with this place)…that feeling seemed to have increased a thousandfold. He was still relieved that he could no longer hear the murmuring voices—and that his vision had cleared up—but there was something in this chamber with him that was more powerful than any mind control. There was something *tangible* in this room…he just could not figure out where it was—

He shook his head and took a deep breath. Quibb was looking at him intently: "You sure you're fine?"

He waved her away and rubbed his head uneasily.

"Are you ever going to talk to me again?" she asked at last.

He turned and looked at her, then he returned to work: "Doesn't this count?"

Quibb stared at him, then smiled faintly. Xi, despite his better judgment, turned and looked at her closely, again seeing her beauty…but then he shook his head.

"Why are you shaking your head?"

"It doesn't matter," he said, pressing buttons (somewhat arbitrarily) on the console; thoughts of working on The Hand kept him away from the eerie reality of the thing in the room—

"Tell me," Quibb pleaded, "…*please*."

He turned and watched her again. He stared at her for a while, as though trying to remember what she had asked him; then, coming to the conclusion that there was no use in keeping it to himself—and needing a respite from the thing in the room—he began, "I was thinking that you're beautiful. Men are supposed to like it when beautiful women laugh at their jokes."

"But you don't?"

He sighed again: "It's too late for laughter."

Quibb stared at him quizzically as he went back to work: "You're really going to build this thing?"

Xi did not look up.

"…Is this because I didn't tell you what I was? You know that I could not tell you. Would you even have *believed* me if I had told you?"

Xi looked at her almost sorrowfully; he sighed again, then shook his head: "There's no time for this either, Quibb. There's no more time."

"Then what is there time for?" she said, stepping up to him and pointedly holding his upper arm. He shook his head; he wanted to wrench away her hand, but he did not want to give her the satisfaction of seeing his discomfort. "—*Talk* to me, Xi," she demanded. "Tell me *something—anything*! Why are you suddenly willing to do this?"

"—*Because I'm tired*!" he said in frustration; he took a step back, so that Quibb's hand dislodged from his arm. "There will always be someone else to step into the void of evil—there's no point in fighting it. Get rid of Shaka and Mendez steps up. If we challenged your mother, there would only be someone else—*maybe even you!*"

"*Me?*"

Xi faced her then; The Horde soldier went to advance at this supposedly aggressive stance, but Quibb waved her away. Xi chuckled sardonically at it all. "Don't allow yourself to believe that you're not susceptible to evil, Quibb. Don't allow yourself to believe that you're not being guided by it even now."

She stared at him for a long while; he turned away from her and returned to work. She touched his arm again so that he would acknowledge her; then, when he looked at her in annoyance, she started, "The only truly evil thing in the world is believing that you can hide from evil—that you can take steps to *isolate* yourself from it." She went to walk off, but turned back to him: "I was inside you, Xi. I shared your soul for a while. Yes," she conceded, "that sharing was dishonest, but what I saw of you was honest. Even when you didn't know who you were, you were honest. Maybe you were honest *because* you did not know who you were….Either way, there was a fairness about you, Xi. I loved that about you….It may be too late for many things—love in particular [he looked at her uneasily]—but when it's too late for honesty…when that time comes, I'll be the first one to rush to death: to push the self-destruct button and end the human race—"

"*Damnit, Quibb!*" Xi yelled in frustration. Even after Quibb slunk away, he stood there trembling. He was *tired*, just as he had told her, and he wanted this all to end…but he still felt the powerful force calling to him from somewhere in the room.

The poor and wretched, in their hearts, never really want to abolish the
unjust privileges of the rich and powerful: they only want to be included.
This is why there will always be suffering.
VERSE 5433:4 OF *The Teachings*

As soon as Mendez broke the codes for the jet's computer system, he appeared on the screens again. Actually, he now appeared in a worldwide broadcast. He had an algorithm that translated his words into the language of the local country and/or region as the satellite broadcasted it around the world. Now, all the men of the world listened to Mendez's plea for unity. The Horde was an enemy to all of them, he told them. Now that they finally knew where The Horde's base was, they could *attack*. Instead of waiting for The Horde to bomb them into oblivion, they could fight The Horde on its grounds: stab the beast in its cave, before it came to their homes.

All over the world, the insane cheers rose in the air. The men would finally be able to *attack*, and the euphoria of being able to take the offensive filled them with a feeling of strength that they had not felt in years. Mendez's words had done that to them; and in return, they found that they were willing to do anything for Mendez. Indeed, after the speech, even Mendez felt revitalized. His greatness was now guaranteed; and with his greatness ensured, he felt himself entitled to explore possibilities he had before shied away from. With this in mind, he left his impromptu broadcast center and returned to his private suite, where an aide was waiting for him.

"Are they ready?" Mendez demanded.

"Yes, sir."

"They know what I want?"

"Yes, sir," the man responded. Then, gesturing to the room around them—which was the living room—he continued, "I had the furniture moved for you, sir."

Mendez looked around in surprise and nodded: he must have been more preoccupied than he thought for him not to have noticed the missing furniture. All that there was, was a chair in the corner of the room. He sat down in the chair then, and nodded for the aide to begin.

The aide left, then, a few moments later, two little boys came in—rare seven-year-olds, just as Mendez had requested. The little boys wore nothing but spandex briefs. Their skinny, prepubescent bodies had been greased, making their little muscles shimmer. They walked to the center of the room, then bowed to Mendez. When he nodded, they leapt at one another like animals. One got off a good shot and the other staggered back, his mouth bloody. Seeing his chance, the aggressor leaped at the staggering boy and they both fell to the ground. Mendez sat on the edge of his seat, staring with a strange gleam in his eyes. "Yes," he groaned breathlessly, as the aggressor straddled the other one's chest, "*choke* him...just like that..."

History teaches one lesson above all others: as advanced and civilized as we now consider ourselves, our descendants will look back on us and marvel at our crudeness.
VERSE 2921:6 OF *The Teachings*

When Quibb and the soldier returned to the command chamber, the others were all staring up at a giant screen, on which Mendez's broadcast to the men of the world was playing. When the broadcast was over, the General and her lieutenants turned and stared at Quibb with unveiled malice.

"Your sins are finally catching up with us," the General began, her voice low and menacing.

Quibb opened her mouth, but she found that she had nothing to say. In truth, she did feel as though she had betrayed them. It had been her jet that Mendez found. She had *created* Mendez; and now, all her former attempts to change the world—to play *God*—were rising up from the burial ground of her best intentions, like indestructible, unstoppable creatures from a bad horror movie.

The General smiled when she saw her daughter's resolve flagging: "Now are you willing to admit you were wrong?"

"Was I wrong? *Yes*...but nobody's right in this," she said defensively.

The General laughed—and some of her lieutenants joined her in chuckling at the pathetic tone in Quibb's voice. "I see you're not ready yet."

"...What are you going to do, Mother?" Quibb asked warily.

The woman's smile broadened; she leaned forward a little bit, so that her mordant smile came prominently into view in the darkness. "I'm going to do what I should have done in the first place." She nodded to some lieutenants then, who went quickly to some consoles to carry out her intentions, then she continued, "I'm going to make an example of Mendez—obliterate him and the city—so that no one will dare to challenge us again."

Quibb groaned. "…But you're already having The Hand of Evolution built."

She nodded: "We'll use The Hand in time, but we have to keep the men in line until that time." Then, again making a speech to her lieutenants, "The time of our hiding has come to an end. It is now time to go out into the world and *take* what is ours. This will be our final message to the world," the woman went on, theatrically. "We stood by before and watched the men tear the world apart. Look at the open sewers they call their cities! It is time for us to step forward and put the ship of humanity back on course!"

"—Stop this, Mother!" Quibb begged. "It's gone too far!"

"*Too* far?" her mother said, laughing. "We haven't even gotten started yet!"

The lieutenants cheered at this; and as the bellicose madness spread through them all, Quibb realized that the murmuring voices were mobilizing all the troops in the complex. Hundreds of thousands of soldiers were putting on their battle gear; thousands of missiles were being prepared; hundreds of planes and helicopters were being readied for the final assault on the city. The scale and scope of the mobilization left Quibb trembling inside. Yet, she had always known that this day was inevitable. They had all known it. For years, they had been accumulating power; bombing the cities of the world had whetted their appetites for brutality. They were now beyond the stage where mere bombing could satisfy them. They needed the pure violence of hand-to-hand warfare: of seeing men falling by their hands. Killing by dropping bombs was like a video game: they needed to *smell* death: to see it in the eyes of their victims. They needed to make it a more *visceral* experience. Quibb nodded gravely, seeing where it was all leading. It was a simple matter of economics: The Horde needed resources, and the only way to get them was through territorial expansion. The Nazis called it *Lebensraum*; Israelis called in "Buffer Zones"; but whatever it was called, it was all territorial expansion based on the excuse of self-defense. The Horde needed colonies to supply it with resources; and when The Hand came online, they would have droves of brainwashed men to build their factories and supply the raw products necessary to ensure their ascension...And it would not be so difficult to do. The Europeans had done it to the rest of the world. They had bent entire continents to their will by manufacturing need and dependence; with The Hand, these machinations would not even be needed. Even *without* The Hand, The Horde could do it easily. With their technology, they could easily conquer the men by brute force. Then, all they would have to do was interject some bogus, self-deprecating philosophy into the male population—*like the Goddess*—so that they would spend more time hating themselves than The Horde. To distract the men, maybe they would disseminate new but essentially trivial technologies, like more potent PinkEyes and pornos. They could perhaps lace the everyday drugs with mind control agents, or even cause chaos and disruption, just so that they could prop themselves up as the only force that could bring peace and order. They could put in puppet governments and spies in every country... And it would not be so hard to do: the men already hated themselves; they were already easily led and poised on the brink of self-annihilation. It would not be so difficult at all—

"Mother, *please*..." Quibb begged.

But the woman only smiled coyly, looking around to the others. "See?" she said with feigned exasperation. "Some say I am blocking thought— becoming a *dictator*—but see: I am taking this from my own daughter."

Quibb scoffed: "It's only that the others are too frightened, that's all. They fear the men—the *myth* of the men that we've been spreading all these years— and they fear you even more."

"My patience is wearing thin," the General warned.

Frustrated, Quibb screamed, "We still can't survive without the men!" There was a collective gasp from the others; her mother glared at her, then she chuckled with effort, trying to control the rage that made her voice come out guttural and hoarse:

"You little fool," she began, "you have no idea!" At that, she looked around cabalistically at her lieutenants, who nodded, knowingly. At last, she looked back at Quibb with cold eyes: "We have at last freed ourselves of the men."

"What…?"

Her mother was smiling menacingly again; she nodded to the Goddess, who had managed to regain her legs after her vision: "The men experimented on us when they brought us here—used us as guinea pigs."

"And?"

"And they developed a cure that will allow daughters to be born—we used it on Carolyn."

"You have no idea what those drugs will do to her! *You* used her as a *guinea pig*!"

The lieutenants bristled at the sacrilege of her implying (albeit correctly) that the General had used the same methods as their male captors. For a moment, the General stared at her daughter with cold, unmoving eyes, then she again laughed softly. The lieutenants instinctively laughed along with her before the General continued:

"Now that daughters can again be born, we'll start a new society." The woman's facial expression was serene now—as was her voice. "We already have women," she continued, "—more every day from our emancipation raids. We can have men's DNA anytime we want. In fact, in order to continue the human race, we don't even *need* the men anymore! The human race has advanced beyond them—and *in spite of* them!"

Quibb shook her head: "Is that what you are going to reduce us to: a world of brainwashed, artificially inseminated women! Is that your paradise!" she protested. "Do any of you even have an idea what death is—have you *seen* death!" One of the lieutenants went to quiet her—to slap her down—but the General stopped her. "—No, Mother," Quibb protested, "let her come. Let her prove my point—let's fight it out like animals. I'm no better than a man anyway, right? Isn't that what you've all been saying? I went to the city and pretended to be a man, and now I'm stuck in that role, right? We're all stuck in a bad game—a *stupid* game that nobody has the sense or courage to stop—"

"Enough, " the General groaned.

"How much longer are you going to let this go on!" Quibb continued.

"Enough!"

"Damnit, mother—"

But then a lieutenant lost patience and slapped Quibb across the face, so that she fell to the floor. The General froze. Her first impulse was to go to her daughter, but this passed quickly; and when this happened, she realized that she had no daughter: that Quibb was dead to her. Finally, she nodded to the others as if coming out of a trance:

"…We have a lot of work to do," she started. At that, some of her lieutenants returned to their consoles, but most of them followed the General out of the chamber. They left Quibb lying on the floor. Only the Goddess had not moved. She advanced and helped Quibb up.

"…Associating with me might be bad for your health," Quibb warned her sardonically.

The Goddess smiled wryly: "You're the only one that's making any sense."

It was then that a monstrous tramping sound came from beyond the exit. They turned to see an inexhaustible tide of soldiers marching past the open doorway. Mesmerized, they walked over to the doorway. The murmuring voices were telling the insensate women to make haste—to rush towards battle. The corridor was *packed* and they were all going one way. Thousands upon thousands of women were now marching past the Goddess and Quibb, their stomping boots creating a chaotic symphony. There was something awesome about the sight of all those soldiers who, even after their greatest victory, would feel nothing. The Goddess found herself dumbfounded at the efficiency of it all. Suddenly, efficiency seemed to be the root of all the evil in the world. The entire push to cut down on time— to cut down on human interaction and the need for *thought*, itself—was being harvested right before her eyes. What could be more efficient than the mindless human machine?

How foolish it is for men to trust their control over the human mind:
even the gods have failed in this.
VERSE 369:8 OF *The Teachings*

When Xi was alone in the lab, the prickly feeling came over him again. There was something *calling* to him—not verbally, or in any way that seemed verifiable—but with a strange magnetism. He left the console and started wandering the room, as though he were a dog following a scent. The prickly feeling seemed to intensify when he was on the right track; rather, he used the prickly feeling to gauge his closeness to God, and assumed that it would intensify with closeness. Strangely enough, as the feeling intensified, he felt like a drunkard—a fool experiencing the short-lived euphoria of drunkenness....

It was about after five minutes of this strange search through the lab that he reached the far corner. He stared at it in amazement. It was like a rift in reality. There was a huge machine there, with flashing lights and a daunting console; but the more he stared, the more he realized that the machine was not there at all. Instead of the machine, he saw what seemed to be a crack floating in space; and from that crack—*that rift in reality*—emanated the most brilliant light he had ever seen. The odd thing was that despite that brilliance, there was no distortion. His eyes did not burn: his senses did not retreat. On the contrary, he felt everything in him opening up. As the light pulsed, the prickly feeling seemed to undulate in concert with those pulses. He stumbled ahead with giddy euphoria, foolishly thinking that he had found God.

The ancient Greeks were right in having a god of war:
they understood the divine madness.
VERSE 181:3 OF *The Teachings*

After his dealings with the boys, Mendez retreated to his bed and lay unmovingly in the darkness. He felt as though he had eaten a meal that his body would never be able to digest. He was full—*stuffed*—but he was not satisfied…nor did he feel as though he would ever be satisfied again. He had taken a step into the darkness, foolishly thinking that he could dart back into the light. However, that step had been a step away from everything he had known and everything he had pretended to know. It was not even that he felt guilty: guilt was also something that was lost to him—like satiety. In fact, if his experiences with the boys had left him with the feeling of being full, it was because he was full of emptiness. He could feel the emptiness eating away at him from the inside, so that he kept thinking that he would soon be empty inside and out. When this happened, it would be as though he had never existed: he would merely disappear, like an ill-conceived thought that had fallen out of favor before being forgotten.

He forced himself to move—to get out of bed. He went to the window then, and opened the blinds to look out on the city; but with all the dust and smoke still in the air, there was nothing to be seen—besides the vague outlines of the buildings across the street. There were supposedly hundreds of thousands of men in front of his hotel—soldiers who had pledged their lives to protect him. He could hear them milling about outside….He went and turned on his television. After watching a recording of his plea to the men of the world (it had been playing continuously since he gave it an hour or so ago) he realized the extent of the farce that he had perpetrated—and that was being perpetrated on them all. They had no wherewithal to attack The Horde. They did not have trucks to transport the men; they did not have planes; they did not even have long-range missiles. All that they had were numbers: millions of men in the city (and billions worldwide) who were joined only by their desperation—if not madness. The men outside the hotel began chanting something then, and the sound wafted eerily up to Mendez's window. He cocked his head to listen, realizing that they were calling his name. His first impulse was a feeling of panic; but with the emptiness expanding within him, the feeling of panic left him almost instantaneously, and was replaced by a strange insouciance....He had no doubt that The Horde would come tonight and wipe them all out. He wondered how many of the men realized that. Even while the recording of his exhortations began to play again—and his TV self urged the men to be unified and courageous—he found that he did not really care what happened. Maybe he had never cared. In fact, now that Shaka was gone, and The Voice had faded from the ephemeral memories of the men, even power was a game without rewards. What was the point of leading men who were so obviously imbeciles? He had risen high in the world, but he realized that he was only standing tall because he was standing on a garbage heap. He was sick of the entire farce; and as he was eager to put an end to it all, he realized that the inevitable Horde attack would be an opportunity to exercise one last act of power and brutality. He would hurl all of his chess pieces against the enemy and end it all in a grand, cataclysmic burst of glory. He was like an artist planning his magnum opus. Indeed, his only real concern now was getting a suitable vantage point for when the end came. He found himself thinking of the war between the men and The Horde in terms of a cockfight: you get the creatures stirred up, then you toss them against one another; and even if you lose, you will at least have chicken soup that night. *Let them all die*! he rejoiced, as a cult leader rejoiced when the unavoidable realities of the world threatened to prove to everyone—and himself, foremost— that he was not God—

Someone knocked on the door. Mendez shuddered as he came out of his reverie. "Come," he called, but without the decisiveness of a few hours ago.

An aide ran up to him, still panting from his efforts—or the weight of the news that he brought. "We've detected Horde missiles on radar, sir!"

"...So be it," Mendez mused.

When Mendez did not do or say anything else, the aide looked at him oddly: "Aren't you coming to the bomb shelter, sir?"

"...No, tell the men that I'm not going to run and hide."

The aide ran off with a look of pride in his eyes, but Mendez knew the real reason why he was not running: he was full of emptiness; and again like a man after a huge meal, all he wanted to do was sleep.

History favors the vigilant—and the ruthless.
VERSE 232:4 OF *The Teachings*

When Quibb and the Goddess rushed into the lab to plead with Xi, he was nowhere to be found. They started to call to him; then, after they heard a groan, they ran to the far corner of the lab, where they found him writhing on the floor.

"Xi!" Quibb cried as she kneeled down to hold him, but he was semi-conscious at best. They sat him up, hoping that this would return him to consciousness. While the Goddess held him up from the back, Quibb shook him. She was getting so desperate that she was getting ready to slap him across the face—

"What's going on?" he mumbled.

Quibb's face brightened. "You must have passed out."

He felt as though something had siphoned off his soul. Somehow, he felt even worse than he had when he woke up in the white-tiled room. Every time he began to think that he had reached the bottom, there would always be some new abyss to fall through. He had felt high when he first entered this room; now, it was as though the drug had worn off and he was experiencing the grim aftereffects of his addiction—the *withdrawal*. As he looked around, he realized that he could hear the murmuring voices again. They blared almost threateningly in his mind then, and he groaned as he heard their commandments.

"They're attacking the city?" he said in bewilderment.

"Yes," Quibb said, still coaxing him into consciousness. "They're sending the entire fleet—they're going to wipe the city out, Xi," she entreated him. "We have to stop them now, while there is still a chance."

However, Xi was not even listening. He was staring into the corner again—the place where he had seen the rift in reality. He gestured with his head then: "What do you see when you stare into that corner?"

Quibb and the Goddess looked at the corner, where they saw the huge machine with the flashing lights and daunting console, then they glanced at one another confusedly: "An image processor?" Quibb said.

Xi rubbed his temples again. "I think I'm losing my mind," he whispered, then he grabbed Quibb's hand and stood up with her help and the Goddess'. "...You have to help me," he said then.

"Help you do what?" Quibb asked.

"Help me to the corner," he said, still staring at that place where he felt the presence of God.

Quibb looked at the Goddess hopelessly, then agreed, the way an overworked nurse relented to a mental patient's delusions, in the hope of eventually tricking him into taking a shower. Quibb and the Goddess each took one of his arms, and they all took a few steps towards the corner; then, before they were about to hit the putative image processor, Quibb stopped.

"*Come on*," Xi demanded. Then, lunging forward, and pulling Quibb and the Goddess along, they entered the rift in reality. It was like a waterfall of light: every possible color of the spectrum seemed to flow from the heavens. Rather, there was no up and down: everywhere was light and magic. For those few moments, they were acutely aware of infinity—of boundless possibilities. A tingly feeling went over them—as though every atom of their bodies were being taken apart, purified somehow, then reassembled...and then they were in another chamber beyond the waterfall of light. They all gasped when they reached the other side. After that place of light and boundless possibilities, the place before them seemed cramped and dour. For a moment, nobody moved: they were too terrified—perhaps too undone by their strange journey. Xi stood up straighter, realizing that he no longer had a headache—and that the disorientation had passed; but more than that, he finally understood. He turned and looked back the way they had come. There was a normal doorway there, which led simply to the other chamber. There was no waterfall—no grand vortex.

Xi nodded his head and turned back. The room before him was filled with more consoles and more equipment. He nodded again, finally understanding the feeling of being in the place that defined his existence....Once again, it was all his technology. He walked up to a nearby console; but even before he looked at the display, he knew everything. He chuckled suddenly; at the sound, Quibb and the Goddess, who had been standing in shock just beyond the doorway, began to look around anxiously.

Quibb rushed up to Xi's side; the Goddess followed, seeming like a child that stayed close to a parent when walking through a dark, creepy place. "What is this place?" Quibb whispered warily; Xi chuckled again. "What are you laughing at?" Quibb demanded, instinctively clinging onto his arm.

"It's all a joke!" Xi laughed, looking about the chamber again. Quibb and the Goddess glanced at one another as if to ask one another if he had gone mad, but Xi went on, "This entire building is some kind of research lab for holographic warfare."

"Holographic warfare?"

"Yes...It's all my technology," he said with another chuckle. "I remember everything now. I programmed all my mind control devices with a failsafe, so that they would always recognize me—even if I came under the mind control. When I returned to my lab at The Company, it recognized me and showed me who I was; when I woke up in this place, I sensed that something was wrong: I sensed my *technology*...and it sensed me. It was drawing me here—trying to show me what was really going on."

The Goddess and Quibb were still confused. The Goddess spoke up then: "You said this was a place for *holographic* warfare?"

"Yes, I helped the military develop it. I started them in the right direction.... If you can make your enemy think that you're stronger than you are—if you could *scare* him into surrender—then you'll have the ultimate weapon." When Quibb and the Goddess still seemed confused, he nodded his head as to acknowledge their confusion; then, thinking of the simplest way he could tell them, he continued, "There aren't hundreds of thousands of women in this complex—only a couple thousand at most." He returned to the console and checked some more things. "...And there are only about 10 planes." Then, looking at Quibb and the Goddess pointedly, "Don't you see," he said with a whimsical smile, "it's all a mass delusion. Satellite-mounted lasers destroyed a few buildings and set a few fires around the world, but there were never any missiles—no bombing. The Horde never inflicted as much damage at it thought—it could not even destroy the city if it wanted to—but it could make the men in the city believe that it did. The Horde is a projection of the machine in this room. The Horde is just as much a victim of the machine as the men in the city—in the *world*. It's nothing but a case of mass schizophrenia—"

Quibb shook her head: "But my mother and the others are all headed for the city now."

"No," Xi corrected her, "only about 100 of them are on their way—the others are lying in a chamber dreaming that they are." As he said that, he pressed a button, and the women appeared on a screen. They were all sitting in a huge hangar, sitting zombie-like on the ground. Quibb and the Goddess gasped. Xi continued, "Even if your mother had wanted to turn off the mind control, she would not have been able to: everything in the command center is an illusion, so that The Horde would think that it was powerful."

The Goddess shook her head: "This can't be...I've seen all the destruction in the city."

Once again, Xi could not help chuckling. He pointed at Quibb: "Look at what you're wearing."

She looked down, expecting to see the suit, but she was clothed in rags!

Xi looked at her intently: "Deep within you've always known it was a lie. Think about it: did you ever have the resources to feed millions of soldiers? Where did you get their uniforms? Who fixed the jump jets and other machinery? Where did you get *fuel* from...?"

Quibb looked up at him in shock as the true extent of it hit her.

"That's right," Xi coaxed her along. "Nothing ever got broken, did it? It was a little fantasy world: everything you ever wanted was provided for you. You wanted to be strong, so the machine created a fantasy where you were strong; through satellite projections and space-based weapons systems, it spread your delusions worldwide—"

"But all our bases!" Quibb protested again.

Xi checked the console again; he pursed his lips: "There are bases—other labs like this…all at former military facilities; but in all, there are only about 20,000 women."

"Where are all the other women?"

"They were never real."

"What about women outside the labs?" the Goddess asked then.

Xi shrugged his shoulders. "I suspect that most of them were butchered or enslaved…or are still living like slaves, like the rest of us." Then, standing up straight again, and looking out on the machine, he sighed and lowered his voice ominously, saying, "What do you want to do?"

"…What is there to do?" Quibb said, still in shock.

"I can turn it all off," Xi said.

"…But then the men will attack," Quibb protested. Now that everything had been turned upside down, she was lost—*unsure*.

Xi shook his head and smiled: "How are the men supposed to attack? You think Mendez has planes to launch attacks? You think he has trucks to drive troops up here? The world is full of fools pretending to be stronger than they are—who have no idea about the extent of their weakness!" Quibb went to speak, but Xi continued: "You're the first person who should want me to turn off the machine, Quibb. Remember what you told me about the only truly evil thing being the belief that you can hide from evil? This machine is clearly the most evil thing in the world. It feeds fears and delusions to everyone on earth—corrupts their souls…and it controls all the other Horde complexes. We have to turn it off—*destroy* it. We can't allow ourselves to believe that we can use it: it will only end up using us, just as it did with your mother. We have to end this for once and for all."

Quibb again went to speak, but Xi stopped her. "No more illusions, Quibb. No more *lies*."

The Goddess looked up at him warily: "What about me? Am I really the cure? Will we really be able to have daughters again—or was that just another delusion?"

"...I don't know," Xi said with a sigh, "...but if we have to die, then let's die as human beings—as *animals* even. If these are our last days, then let's live as real people in the *real* world—not as characters in a video game."

There was a moment of uneasy silence—a moment when they all contemplated the uncertainties and possibilities ahead, and came to the conclusion that there was no other way.

"Okay," Quibb whispered at last. "Let's turn it off." She held Xi's upper arm again, like a scared child; the Goddess did the same at his other side, and Xi reached down his hand and touched a button on the console.

Tuesday, September Ninth, 1997; 5:16PM;
Monday, May Twenty-fifth, 1998; 12:49PM;
Friday, June 11, 2004; 1:20PM
Brooklyn, New York
Grenada, West Indies
Eshowe, South Africa

ABOUT THE AUTHOR

D.V. Bernard emigrated from the Caribbean to New York City when he was nine years old. He is the author of *The Last Dream Before Dawn* and lives in Brooklyn, New York.
You may contact the author at dvbernard@hotmail.com

Intimate Relations with Strangers

BY D.V. BERNARD

COMING IN 2005

War had a way of making romantics out of desperate men—out of soldiers whose lives were the bargaining chips of governments and generals; out of those who had killed and *tasted* death, and who were now trying to resist its addictive flavor. War made men believe in love, so that any passing affair they had ever had became a grand love story; girlfriends and wives they had left dispassionately were now mystical goddesses, whose declarations of love would guarantee their safe return. And whatever slums, barrios and trailer parks these soldiers had left in favor of the Army, were now the paradises of the most whimsical daydreams. When reality was stark and depraved, the mind compensated with fantasy.

Accordingly, now that the killing was done, the soldier was left with nothing but the haunting image of the woman. Fifteen minutes ago, there had been gunshots and screams, and the sounds of men rushing over the sun-baked earth of the Sahara Desert. He had killed all five of the prison guards. Their bodies—*corpses*—lay on the ground before him, like the grotesque figurines of a child's play set. After the killing was done, he had freed 20 of his fellow prisoners of war from the hovels that had been their jail cells; like captured animals being released into the wild, the men had scampered into the craggy hills beyond the prison camp, reaching the summit just as the sun was about to set over it. He had stood there, watching them from the camp—mesmerized by the strange illusion of his countrymen escaping into the sun.

It was only when he lost all sight of them that he realized that he, himself had nowhere to go. He looked at his surroundings now, as if just waking up in a strange bed. The landscape seemed barren and *brutalized*. At the same time, the African desert had a way of opening one's eyes to what was essential. That was one of the lessons that the soldier had learned in the years he had been here. ...The prison camp consisted of seven earthen structures, which seemed as though they had been there since the dawn of time. They were composed of the same sun-baked earth that was everywhere; like everything else, the hovels had been sandblasted smooth by the inescapable punishment of the desert winds. The hot, arid air left his nasal passages desiccated, so that it was almost painful to breathe. It occurred to him, in an offhand manner, that he was dehydrated. The prisoners of war he had freed into the desert heat were no doubt dazed and dehydrated as well—and would succumb to the heat in due time.

Just as he was nodding his head absentmindedly, the cat came up behind him and brushed against his leg. It was the same spectacularly white cat that he had been seeing for years now. As he looked down, the last blinding rays of the setting sun seemed to refract off the cat's immaculately white fur, so that the soldier had to clamp his eyes shut. In a world of dust and death, where everything succumbed to the harshness of nature and man, the cat was an oasis of life and possibility. Its movements were lithe and carefree; as it rubbed against his leg, it purred, and he felt the sound washing over him, like a soothing breeze. He smiled as he stood there daydreaming. However, when he opened his eyes, the cat was gone, and he felt suddenly melancholy. He had spent the bygone months wondering if the cat was a figment of his imagination, or a protective spirit guiding him on his journey; but presently, as he began to tremble all over, he knew that the time for conjecture had come to an end. He lowered himself to the ground then, and leaned against the side of the hovel, realizing, for the first time, that he had been shot by the prison guards. Rather than being painful, the bullet holes that riddled his body were points of numbness. He had been shot at least once in each leg. A bullet was embedded in his left shoulder, and there were two in his abdomen. As the blood flowed, the points of numbness seemed to expand in diameter, so that he knew that soon there would be no sensation at all—no *life*. With these thoughts in mind, he looked towards the hills, where the sun had set; then, he lay down flat on the ground, closed his eyes, and sighed—as if anticipating the fitful sleep that always possessed him when he dreamed of the woman.

All those months ago, before the soldier became a prisoner of war, the war had not been going well. The enemy had won no great victories over them, but the era of grand victories was over. In its stead rose a stalemate between those who were clearly mad, and those who were dedicated to being more brutal than the madmen. When the American Military originally swept into the African desert, the war fever had been with all of them. All their minds had been gripped by the *idée fixe* of revenge. Seared into their souls had been the terrorist act that had precipitated this war: the smoldering remains of the White House, and the subsequent announcement that the president and half the cabinet had been murdered by a suicide bomber. The resulting war had been inevitable—like the impulse to scream once someone had stepped on one's foot. In the terrible war cry of America, there had been a kind of purity. The war had been a transcendental event; the military had been holy warriors in a new religion, no longer concerned with the finite resources that had defined all previous wars. Instead, these new holy warriors had set their sights on the infinite possibilities of the human soul.

Nevertheless, after two years of war, America found that while it could conquer, it could not rule. Military might had allowed it to overthrow a regime; missiles and bombs had decimated the conquered regime's army; its infrastructure of power had been systematically dismantled and replaced by a structure sympathetic to America. However, the battles and skirmishes continued—not against an army; not against anything with a structure that could be dismantled by military might or political will. This evolved foe, realizing that it could not fight America face-to-face, created a kind of shadow cult out of death. For most of human history, the warrior had equated victory with staying alive. But these new warriors saw victory *in* death—in mutual annihilation. They worshipped death and *craved* it. The only way to win against such a foe was to apotheosize death as well—to see meaningless deaths as a sign of courage and fealty to God. That was the state of the war before the soldier was captured.

By then, he had been a thirteen-month veteran of nighttime raids and roadside bombs. He had escaped from all those engagements with his life, but each one of them had taken a little of what he needed to *live*. More and more, he had been possessed by the feeling that he and everything in his pocket of time and space had been severed from the surrounding reality; and that out there, beyond the war zone, another world existed—a parallel universe, in which people still loved one another, and lived full lives, free of the kill-or-be-killed logic of war. At that time, he had not yet begun to dream of the woman, but he had dreamed nonetheless: of his mother and father, sister and brother; of the little house in Queens that his parents had scraped and sacrificed to buy; of the essential goodness of his parents and their values. In the back of his mind, he would always tell himself that he was fighting this war for his parents; when he rendered his terrible justice onto the people he came upon while out on patrol, he would tell himself that he was showing a son's love for his parents—and the American way of life. …But a few days before his capture, the Army, in an attempt to boost morale, had allowed all the men of his unit to call home. The soldier had naturally telephoned his parents. He had already been smiling as he listened to the phone ringing; but during the meandering conversation that followed, he had been devastated by the realization that the voices he heard over the static of the connection bore no relation to the fantasy that had been sustaining him. The voices had been those of decent, loving people, but whatever mystical ideal his parents had represented, had been shattered forever, like the easily corruptible faith of small children.

That was the day that the soldier went on his final nighttime raid. He and the rest of his ten-man unit were in an armored personnel carrier. It was deathly quiet on the sprawling outskirts of the city—except for the intermittent sounds of gunfire and sirens. Within the carrier, there was no conversation. Men stared into space, conjuring their intimate fantasies; some closed their eyes and said prayers—either to gods or men or chance, itself. Directly across from the soldier, a corporal was leafing through a miniature edition of the New Testament, the pages of which had become grimy from the Army-issue grease they used on their guns, and the musty sweat that their bodies futilely sent out to combat the desert heat. The soldier looked over the entire unit; but finding nothing to reassure him in the faces of his comrades, he grasped his gun closer to his chest. Soon, the unit would spring out and raid the home of someone presumed to be a terrorist. The soldier saw it all in his mind: knocking the door down then rushing in to find the man sleeping. Women and children would begin to scream and cry; the presumed terrorist, wrestled to the ground, would be yelling with the interpreter, explaining that he was innocent. In time, he would be handcuffed and hooded. …Then, there would be the search through his household, maybe uncovering a machine gun and a few hand grenades. The women would continue to cry, perhaps pleading their man's innocence; if there was an adolescent son, he would attempt some kind of bravado—for family honor— but he would be slapped to the side if he was too young to be bothered with, or hooded and handcuffed as well, if he, like a newly caught fish, seemed big enough to fry. The father would complain that he only had the weapons to protect his family; he would say whatever words of English he knew—trying to bypass the interpreter and address those with the true power—but the unit was not there to hear him: only to capture him. He would be led away, to be held somewhere until he could prove that he was innocent…and another night in a war without end would pass away into the nothingness, with frightened women and children crying in the aftermath, and men morosely following the roles dictated by power and might.

The door of the personnel carrier opened. The night seemed repulsive somehow— like something dead and rotting. A wave of intense heat seemed to ambush the unit as they exited. Some coughed inadvertently on the hot, dry air—and the stench of decay that it carried. A stray dog, which had been sleeping in front of the gate of the presumed terrorist's home, fled as they emerged from the vehicle. It ran down to the next compound, then crouched behind a pile of garbage, watching them timidly—but not barking. The unit moved quickly. They had done this so many times that they hardly had to think. Two of them kicked at the front gate, so that it collapsed onto the dusty ground. They ran up to the door of the house. It was quickly kicked down as well. They entered, screaming out "clear!" as they progressed through the empty rooms…and at last, after about a minute of searching and screaming, they realized that there was no one in the house. A quarter of the unit fanned out to the backyard, looking for bunkers—but there was nothing. Eventually, they all congregated in the living room. The lieutenant made a call to headquarters, reporting that there was nothing here, and that they had been given bad intelligence.

The unit began to relax. The adrenaline was beginning to ebb from their systems. They breathed deeply and made fun of the tacky knickknacks that the family of this house had accumulated. …The soldier was looking out of the living room window when he saw it. Initially, there was a white blur, and then he saw it clearly: the cat, sitting in the middle of the yard, staring at him. The last time he had seen the supernaturally white cat had been on a horrible day in his childhood, but those recollections were locked away so far in his past, that it was as if he were seeing the cat for the first time. In fact, it *mesmerized* him—the way that one was mesmerized by something new and amazing. Before he was conscious of having done so, he had exited the room and walked outside. He took a few steps towards the cat—which was still sitting there, staring at him—before it occurred to him that he should perhaps stay with the others. He looked back towards the building uncertainly; through the window, he could see his lieutenant arguing with whoever was on the other end of the radio; the others were joking amongst themselves, already reveling in the post-battle sense of relief and well-being that always possessed them. However, the cat was purring. The soldier looked back at it, again mesmerized. The purring was like nothing he had ever heard before. It soothed him—filled him with a sense of peace that seemed spiritual. Nothing else existed at that moment. He found himself transported away from war and death, to a place where there was not necessarily life, but at least the *possibility* of life. That was more than enough for a man who had seen what he had seen, and done what he had done.

When the cat began to walk away—through the broken gate of the backyard, and into an alleyway—the soldier found himself following. The fuzzy sense of peace and well being that the cat's purring had instilled in him was still soothing him. He had forgotten how it was to feel this way: to feel at *peace*. For the first time in months, he was more than a mindless killing machine. Accordingly, he followed the cat the way a hungry child pursued the scent of freshly baked pastry.

The cat walked about 30 meters away from the building; but as the soldier followed it, that journey seemed beyond all definitions of distance and time. What was in reality a walk of 40 seconds, seemed to take *hours*. At last, when the cat finally stopped and stared back at him, he approached it haltingly. It had stopped beneath a streetlamp; and for the first time, the soldier saw the color of its eyes. They were the most startling shade of blue he had ever seen: an almost phosphorescent aquamarine. He stumbled up to the cat, which was waiting there patiently for him; as he crouched down, and stretched out his trembling hand, he was already smiling—already giving praise and surrendering the last of his will…but just as his fingers were about to touch the cat, there was an explosion behind him, and he was knocked to the ground by the blast. For a moment, he lay semi-conscious on the ground—or maybe it was only that the blast had knocked the wind out of him. Either way, the first thing he did when he opened his eyes, was to look for the cat. It was gone; but then, as there was a secondary blast, he looked around, realizing that the explosions had come from the house his unit had raided! Huge plumes of red flames rose into the air. He could feel the heat from where he was on the ground. He got up groggily and took a few shambling steps towards the building, but another explosion made him turn his face away and shield his eyes. If his unit was still in there, then they were dead: there was no question about it. In a strange way, he was too numb to be panicked, but he was acutely aware of his position: of his isolation here in the middle of nowhere. He began running. He cut through a neighboring yard, then ran through another alleyway—so that he could get to the front of the building, where the personnel carrier was. However, no sooner did he reach the mouth of the alleyway, than he saw that the vehicle was also engulfed in flames. The entire thing had been an ambush: *he was the only one left*! No doubt rebels where hiding in the shadows at that moment. He turned and fled back into the darkness, wondering what he was going to do—and realizing, again, his utter isolation and vulnerability. Just as he was about to give in to the hopelessness, he saw the cat waiting at the other end of the alley. For the first time, it occurred to him that if the cat had *saved* him—*protected* him, in this world of insecurity and death. If it had not led him away, then he would be dead now as well. The cat was some kind of protective spirit—there was no other conclusion that could be drawn from the facts that tumbled through his mind. His legs trembled as he approached the newfound spirit guide. Understandably, by the time it began to lead him away, all he could think about was following it to his destiny.

ALSO AVAILABLE FROM
STREBOR BOOKS INTERNATIONAL
All titles are in stores now, unless otherwise noted.

Baptiste, Michael
Cracked Dreams (October 2004) 1-59309-035-8

Bernard, DV
The Last Dream Before Dawn 0-9711953-2-3
God in the Image of Woman 1-59309-019-6

Brown, Laurinda D.
Fire & Brimstone 1-59309-015-3
UnderCover (October 2004) 1-59309-030-7

Cheekes, Shonda
Another Man's Wife 1-59309-008-0
Blackgentlemen.com 0-9711953-8-2

Cooper, William Fredrick
Six Days in January 1-59309-017-X
Sistergirls.com 1-59309-004-8

Crockett, Mark
Turkeystuffer 0-9711953-3-1

Daniels, J and Bacon, Shonell
Luvalwayz: The Opposite Sex and Relationships 0-9711953-1-5
Draw Me With Your Love 1-59309-000-5

Darden, J. Marie
Enemy Fields 1-59309-023-4

De Leon, Michelle
Missed Conceptions 1-59309-010-2
Love to the Third 1-59309-016-1
Once Upon a Family Tree (October 2004) 1-59309-028-5

Faye, Cheryl
Be Careful What You Wish For (December 2004) 1-59309-034-X

Halima, Shelley
Azucar Moreno (December 2004) 1-59309-032-3

Handfield, Laurel
My Diet Starts Tomorrow 1-59309-005-6
Mirror Mirror 1-59309-014-5

Hayes, Lee
Passion Marks 1-59309-006-4

Hobbs, Allison
Pandora's Box 1-59309-011-0
Insatiable (November 2004) 1-59309-031-5

Johnson, Keith Lee
Sugar & Spice 1-59309-013-7
Pretenses 1-59309-018-8

Johnson, Rique
Love & Justice 1-59309-002-1
Whispers from a Troubled Heart 1-59309-020-X
Every Woman's Man (November 2004) 1-59309-036-6
Sistergirls.com 1-59309-004-8

Lee, Darrien
All That and a Bag of Chips 0-9711953-0-7
Been There, Done That 1-59309-001-3
What Goes Around Comes Around 1-59309-024-2

Luckett, Jonathan
Jasminium 1-59309-007-2
How Ya Livin' 1-59309-025-0

McKinney, Tina Brooks
All That Drama (December 2004) 1-59309-033-1

Quartay, Nane
Feenin 0-9711953-7-4

Rivers, V. Anthony
Daughter by Spirit 0-9674601-4-X
Everybody Got Issues 1-59309-003-X
Sistergirls.com 1-59309-004-8

Roberts, J. Deotis
Roots of a Black Future: Family and Church 0-9674601-6-6
Christian Beliefs 0-9674601-5-8

Stephens, Sylvester
Our Time Has Come (September 2004) 1-59309-026-9

Turley II, Harold L.
Love's Game (November 2004) 1-59309-029-3

Valentine, Michelle
Nyagra's Falls 0-9711953-4-X

White, A.J.
Ballad of a Ghetto Poet 1-59309-009-9

White, Franklin
Money for Good 1-59309-012-9
Potentially Yours 1-59309-027-7

Zane (Editor)
Breaking the Cycle (September 2004) 1-59309-021-8